IO691160

COLOURING BOOKS
GALLERY ONE

COLOURING BOOKS
GALLERY ONE

GREYGLASS, L'AMBER, TO INDIGO & WINTER WHITE

Tanith Lee

IMMANION PRESS
Stafford England

Colouring Books Gallery One: Greyglass, L'Amber, To Indigo & Winter White
By Tanith Lee
© 2019

Publishing history (in the English language) of the novels and story in this omnibus:
Greyglass, Immanion Press, 2011
L'Amber, Immanion Press, 2011
To Indigo, Immanion Press, 2011
Winter White, 'Women as Demons' collection, The Women's Press, 1989

Cover Art by John Kaiine
Cover Design by Danielle Lainton
Interior layout by Storm Constantine

Set in Garamond

ISBN 978-1-912815-09-8

IP0160

Author Site:
Daughter of the Night: An Annotated Tanith Lee Bibliography:
http://www.daughterofthenight.com/

Facebook Page for Tanith Lee's readers: Paradys Forum – Daughter of the Night – Tanith Lee

An Immanion Press Edition
www.immanion-press.com
info@immanion-press.com

CONTENTS

PUBLISHER'S NOTE

Tanith Lee began working with Immanion Press in 2010. She'd been looking for a publisher to release a series of short 'slipstream' novels that didn't fit easily into traditional genres. These books were Tanith's own brand of psychological thriller with a sprinkling of weirdness and surreality thrown in. The series was to be known as the *Colouring Books*, as each novel within it had a colour theme. We published seven of these novels before Tanith died in 2015. She planned to write two more and had the title 'Wintergreen' for one of them; it's a great loss to literature these never came to be written.

The first three books in the series, *Greyglass*, *L'Amber*, and *To Indigo*, were all released in 2011, since Tanith had already written them. These were followed by *Killing Violets* and *Ivoria* in 2012, *Cruel Pink* in 2013 and *Turquoiselle* in 2014. Immanion Press is now rereleasing the books in three omnibus editions, rather than keeping them in seven separate volumes, as we are committed to keeping Tanith's work available in print and to make this as affordable as possible.

In these three omnibuses, we also include an extra story with a 'colour theme'. These have been selected from Tanith's uncollected stories, which appeared in magazines and rare anthologies. 'Winter White' in this book is a story from *Women as Demons*, a collection that came out in 1989 from The Women's Press. The piece also appeared in foreign language versions of her short story collection *Cyrion* but has not been reprinted in any other publication.

EXHIBIT ONE
GREYGLASS

BOOK ONE

I

She lived in a vegetable house. As time passed, it grew about her. Rooms and passages added themselves, stairways, attics, cellars; windows formed. Outside, and all around, the gardens also extended into mossy terraces with pools, massive stands of huge trees, thickets of rhododendrons. Where visible through these, the house appeared like an orange pumpkin – the one in Cinderella perhaps, which became a coach to take her to the ball. However, the house was only volatile in an accretive, sedentary way, adding to itself, certainly determined not to move anywhere else.

"We're going up to see the old lady now. Put your coat on. Hurry up."

Susan glanced at her mother and laid down the nail scissors with which she had been cutting figures of thin paper.

"Are those my nail scissors?"

"– – –"

"I said, are those my nail scissors?"

Whose nail scissors, after all, could they be?

"Yes, Mum."

"Don't call me Mum."

"– – –"

"Say Mummy."

"Mummy."

"I've told you not to use the nail scissors for that. It spoils them."

Susan looked at the spoiled scissors. They appeared the same as when she had taken them from the bathroom cabinet half an hour ago, as her mother was peeling vegetables for – don't say dinner, say lunch – *lunch*.

"Go and put your coat on. Will you hurry, Susan!"

Susan ran out. She was twelve. For a year she had been menstruating regularly, using deodorant and mascara, and wearing tights. She felt twenty, then fifteen. Then eight. Even between one running step and another she might change.

Her mother was calling again. Susan had been supposed to put on her school blazer from the hall. But Susan ran into her bedroom and took up the jacket from her chair. In the mirror, as she passed, she glimpsed a plump ugly girl, with short fair hair, who, sometimes, by careful arrangements of light and shade, the mirror and herself, might be transformed into something else, someone of consequence, even perhaps attraction.

9

"Susan! What are you doing?"

"I don't want to go up *there*," said Susan, to the corner of the room. The corner did not reply.

It was spring outside. More spring than had yet got into the year, or the old building, or the flat on the second floor. The Georgian pillars and porch had burst into slices of sunlight and the steps were warm.

"Why have you put that jacket on, Susan?"

"You said..."

"I said a coat. Your blazer."

But now there was no turning back.

The sun dappled leopard spots through the chestnut trees by the wall. The buds were sticky, still red but not green.

Susan looked at her mother. A slim beautiful woman, a fully formed creature, at no disadvantage since adult. Her hair, which was black this month, gleamed with a reddish light like that on the chestnut buds.

"Why do we have to?"

"What? Why do we have to what?"

"Go up *there*."

"You know why. You know perfectly well why."

"But..."

"And we're late."

They walked quickly along Constance Street, where the tree roots had here and there upheaved the pavement, and into Dunkirk Street, where there were no trees and the sun fell hot, burning on their heads.

"You brushed your hair," said the adult woman.

"Mmm."

Susan had not, what a bit of luck.

Sundays would be all right, if it weren't for this – this, and the approaching shadow of school tomorrow, but that was almost a whole day away.

"Oh damn, we're so late. Come on."

In at the park gates. People were strolling about. There was a van selling ice-cream. Dogs rushed barking, and somewhere children screamed, and a big blast of exciting drum-thick bad music roared from a radio on the lawns.

"Bloody music," said Susan's mother. "People."

They were almost running now.

Straight through the park, with its possibilities of life, straight along the gravel path by the black, still-winter beds, a handful of crocuses and anaemic daffodils, and out of the other gate.

Here was ominous, curving Tower Road, with its enormous beech trees and oaks, its gardens behind ten-foot stone walls clung with ivy. Set far back, roofs of houses showed, like the upper turrets of the Sleeping Beauty's castle.

"Mum, I've got a stitch."

"Mummy. Damn, it's ten past twelve. Oh damn."

"Why do we have to *go*? You don't want to. She just goes on."

10

The road curving and coiling, like an ancient riverbed, slid in under the trees, cold now in the fragmented shade, heavy as smashed masonry, sky watery as broken blue eggs. And now, landmarks, plants lodged in a wall. A turn, a gap where grass grew, rather long for the time of year, and the two particular oaks, sentinels which marked the border of the witch's kingdom.

Her mother pushed the tall, old and rusty ironwork gate, and pushed herself and Susan through it.

"*Why*, Mummy…? She doesn't want us here – she doesn't like us."

"No," said Susan's mother, defeated after all, stopping dead, just over the border, there under the weight of cascading evergreens, the overgrown drive running away and away towards the orange pumpkin that was the witch's house.

"Why, then?"

"You know why."

"I don't."

"She's your grandmother."

The housekeeper, Mrs Danvers, opened the door. Danvers wasn't really her name. Susan's mother had coined it for her from the character in the book by Daphne du Maurier.

Mrs Danvers was very thin and hard of frame. She seemed made of iron, and then clothed to hide it, just her head and neck and hands, and sometimes her lower arms and calves, if visible, gone over with a flesh substituting material like sallow creased rayon. She was old, over forty. (Susan's mother, also over forty, seemed somehow not old, her few facial lines invisible, her skin and make-up flawless, her hair, now blonde, now black, her eyes large and grey.) But Mrs Danvers had got this all wrong and in reverse, black eyes and grey permed hair.

"She's been waiting," said Mrs Danvers.

"Yes," said Susan's mother, shortly.

The hall was very wide, much wider even than in the house where the flats were. A stained-glass panel in the door, once it shut, threw jade and crimson shapes along the old cracked lino which was, apparently, 'dangerous'.

Susan stepped on each of these shapes, to see the colour seep instantly up through her feet and appear instead on the top of her disappointing flat shoes.

But her mother had left Susan.

She had walked forward briskly, into one of the great rooms which opened to one side of the wide hall. This she crossed and went through another door and vanished into another room.

Mrs Danvers too had moved off. Susan left the shapes and ran after her mother, across two rooms or three, down a step at one or two of the doorways, into a sunken part of the house.

A green-rain light flooded the rooms here, from the bay trees and conifers pressed close to the sides of the house. The old furniture caught the green

11

reflections, shining in a watery way.

"I'm sorry we're late, Mother. I had to dash out to the shop before twelve, everything was hung up."

Susan was not really aware of the irony of this scene, so familiar, not only from repetition, but from similar scenes of her own: the daughter standing before the mother, making lame excuses.

Susan's mother had a mother, but this did not become apparent to Susan until years after. Susan's mother was simply performing an unavoidable ritual before Susan's grandmother – who must always be called Grandmother, not 'gran', 'nan' or any other degrading counterfeit.

The grandmother sat in a window, where a big pot contained a plant with strange scarlet leaves, which Susan had long ago christened Martian Rhubarb.

The grandmother did not turn her head. Her profile stood there against the greened glass like something stamped into a coin.

Mrs Danvers was old, but the grandmother had passed on into another country. She was no longer human. Which gave her, it seemed, inordinate powers.

"Well," said Susan's mother, "how have you been?"

"She steals from me," said the grandmother.

"No, she doesn't," said Susan's mother.

"How would you know? You're never here."

"I am here now."

"Once a fortnight."

"Once a week, Mother. Sometimes more often. But I have a job, Mother, and a child, and I can't always…" the words were bitten out, "do exactly as I want with any spare time I might have."

"Butter," said the grandmother.

"What do you mean, butter? She steals butter?"

"Food. All types of food. What can I do? I have to rely on the woman."

Susan's mother sighed, opened her bag and took out a packet of cigarettes.

"Yes, you may smoke."

"*Thank* you."

Mrs Danvers came back into the room. On a tray she bore two glasses of a pale, dry sherry, and one of fizzy lemonade, a dish of nuts and an ashtray. The ashtray she placed at once by the chair of Susan's mother.

"Thank you, Mrs Marks." Marks was Mrs Danvers' real name. But not really, no, never.

Susan took the lemonade and sat in a chair drinking it like a parched alcoholic. She knew better than to wander about the room. She must stay still, as must her mother, all attention fixed on the old woman.

If Mrs Marks-Danvers was made of iron and a partial covering of rayon, from what substance had the grandmother been created? Her thinness was so acute, every bone in her body had been accentuated, distorted. Her skin was folded and refolded, sewn down in tense appliquéd lines. Her skin was brown, like that of someone tanned, or from a foreign country. Her eyes – her eyes disturbed Susan – they were full of something but not colour. Perhaps they had been grey once, like her mother's.

Mrs Danvers had gone.

"She takes the sherry, too. And the wine. You'd notice, if you stayed for lunch or dinner, that she fills the bottles up with water. Tap water I may add. How is your sherry? No, don't say it's all right, Anne, I know quite well it's watered down."

"Mother, I'm sure it isn't."

"Yes, you're sure of everything, Anne."

"Have it your own way," said Susan's mother, Anne.

"Have it my own way? I have nothing my own way."

"That's ridiculous."

"Look at me. What do I have *my own way*?"

"You have this house, you're well looked after…"

The grandmother broke in here with her usual curt melodramatic laugh. "Oh yes. Oh yes. *Very* well."

"Mother, what am I supposed to do? What can I do?"

"Nothing, of course. You can do nothing. You couldn't possibly move into this house with me."

"I live as near as I am able."

"If you lived in this house, you could give up your job, as you're pleased to call it. The child could have proper clothes instead of the extraordinary things I see her wearing every time I do see her…"

Susan, feeling the terrible eyes turn to her at last, flinched her own away, finding some sudden fascination with the worn Persian carpet under her feet.

"Mother, I've explained all this to you. I simply can't throw everything up on a whim."

"A whim? A whim? To be with your own mother?" There was neither anger nor pleading in the tone, scarcely, now, even any sarcasm. The old, unwhole voice, with its well-educated accent, was devoid of anything but clipped abrasion.

"I like my work," said Susan's mother crisply. "And I like a little independence. God knows, it's a good thing I do."

"What is that supposed to mean?"

"You know perfectly well what it means."

"That you could not rely on me for help."

Susan's mother sat with lips of smooth coral stone.

The grandmother had twisted her lizard profile fully round into the room, her gaze fixed with a blind still ferocity on a row of china ornaments in the black hearth.

Susan put down her empty glass.

She got up and edged away from the arena's centre.

Absorbed now, they let her do it.

13

"Can I go and look at the books?" Susan whispered, too low to be heard. They heard her.

Not glancing at her, the grandmother rapped, "You have only been here five minutes. If you want the lavatory, say so."

"Then may I go to the lavatory?"

"Yes. Wash your hands afterwards."

Humiliated beyond blushing, Susan left the room by another exit.

Along the passage, where other curious plants luxuriated in narrow winding spaces, Susan heard the voices still. "I have never asked you for anything."

"I have never refused you anything."

"There were always terms. Impossible ones."

Susan heard this conversation, or dialogues of the same kind, on most Sundays.

She opened the lavatory door and went in.

The lavatory was quite big, for what it was. The suite, if so it could be called, a dingy white, both toilet and bowl and hand basin verdigris-stained, with long hairs of cracks. The hot tap did not run hot, nor even warm. In winter, Susan had sometimes marvelled to find its issue felt colder than that of the cold tap.

Before drying her hands, Susan scooped a handful of water up onto the runner of the towel, to make it very wet, proving she had used it. But the water also sploshed on the floor by the don't-say-toilet, making it look as if she had pee'd on the lino. So then she had to take some of the soft toilet paper and mop the floor, and then, to dispose of the paper, she had to flush the lavatory again. And if they heard all this, as they well might, or if the housekeeper heard it, her grandmother might later say to her that the lavatory was there for its 'purpose', and not to be played in. Or, worse, that Susan should have attended to her bowels before she left home.

Leaving the lavatory, Susan crept up a brief staircase and went along another corridor and sidled into what her mother called the book-room.

Susan did not really like these books. She was averse to them. They were fairly uniformly sheathed in uninviting dark skins, and some had gilt lettering, and many were anyway out of her reach. Long ago the old woman had said she might 'look at the books'. Susan had assumed this was exactly what she might do – look. She didn't touch them, except now and then to put her finger on their spines. The titles besides were unencouraging, even unintelligible, like gibberish, and some were in other languages her mother said were French or German, or Latin.

On the long table was a dish. It was of yellowish pale glass, the colour the sherry had been, and it was kept empty.

Susan looked into the dish.

She would have to go back in a moment or be accused of something, having a bowel movement, trespassing, something.

The sun went in beyond the window and sudden rain began to hiss over the thick wild trees which closed the view.

"Susan."

Her mother's voice.

Susan ran from the room, along the corridor, back downstairs, into the passage. Her mother was standing, smoking, in the doorway of the sunken room, and behind her the grandmother stood, not leaning on anything at all, not on a stick, not even the arm of a chair.

"Where have you been?"

"To look at the books."

As if rationally, the grandmother said, "Why don't you stay to lunch, Anne? There's plenty for three."

"No, thank you, Mother. I have to go out this afternoon. I told you. Besides, I left our lunch ready. I can't afford to waste it."

"Let the child stay, then," said the grandmother, hard as granite, demanding a hostage.

"Susan has homework to do."

This was a lie. The one they usually told, when this thing came up about lunch, as so often it did.

"And what," said the grandmother, "will Susan have for lunch in your flat? A sandwich, I suppose."

The mother did not answer. The grandmother stared now, right at the child, "You tell me, then, what is this so-splendid lunch you can't possibly miss?"

Susan looked at her mother, but Anne had turned away.

Hopelessly Susan said, "We're having omelette and chips, Grandmother."

"Ah."

"And tomatoes," apologised Susan.

"Indeed." The grandmother walked across the room. She moved very slowly, stiffly, but without apparent effort. Where was she going? The fireplace? She reached the fireplace, stretched her arm across the mantelpiece, and drew off a small ornament, an apple of rosy china. "Look, do you see? Chipped. That precious woman, who cares for me so well, wantonly chipped it. That's what I think of when I hear the word *chips*. I think of accidents to china, Anne. And so that is what you're giving my grandchild for her lunch. Bits of smashed china ruined by careless servants."

Then she gazed at Susan again. Her eyes were full of – what was it – milk, or venom?

"I shall be taking soup, homemade, of course. Cream of celery, I think. Then a casserole of lamb with dumplings. Roast potatoes and green peas. Then there is some Stilton, but naturally I have raspberry ice-cream, if anyone were to want it."

"Mother, I'm sorry. Perhaps next Sunday..."

"You haven't eaten a meal in this house for ten years."

15

"That isn't true."

"It is true. What is the point," said the old woman in the pumpkin house, "of my being alive? There you are, the two of you, flesh of my flesh, children of my body, there you are, and I am alone. Alone with a petty thief. This is what I have come to."

Or tears. Was that what it was in her eyes? Thick resinous and opaque as glasses fitted *under* the lids. But Susan's grandmother never wore glasses, not even to read. Her eyesight, like her hearing, was still phenomenal.

"Oh, for God's sake, Mother." Exasperated, Anne. "Then we must stay. We'll stay for lunch. Yes, very well. Only I wish you'd made this more clear before I'd peeled all those potatoes at home."

"No, no," said the old woman. "No, I can't ask you to stay, I'm afraid. If you'd said before. But there isn't enough for three. Oh, there might be, if that woman didn't squirrel so much of it away for herself. But as it is..."

Somewhere, in another room, a clock struck. One o'clock, or two, who knew, in this limbo of mind-fuck and exasperated despair.

Mrs Danvers, however, re-entered, punctilious as a robot.

"Yes?" asked the grandmother. "Lunch? Already?"

It seemed it was.

"Well, goodbye, Anne. Goodbye, Susan."

They shook themselves, outside, like dogs shaking off the fluids of the vegetable house. They walked for thirty minutes back to the flat in the rain.

"Can we play the card game this afternoon?"

"No. I've got to get ready and go out."

"Oh. Oh…"

"Don't start, Susan."

"You said you'd read through my essay with me."

"I will. Tonight."

"You'll be in late tonight."

"For Christ's sake, stop it."

"Where are you going?"

"Somewhere."

"To the pictures?"

"Perhaps."

"I wish I could go."

"You can. I'll give you the money tomorrow."

"Tomorrow's Monday. It's school."

"Don't talk as if it's spelled H E double L."

"It is."

"I mean, I will take you tomorrow night. If you promise not to make a fuss about getting up on Tuesday morning."

"Will you? Will you? Won't you mind if you've already seen it?"

"No, I won't mind. Eat your chips."

"China chips," said Susan.

"Poor old bitch," said Anne. "God, what can I do?"

"I said we shouldn't go."

"You were quite right."

"Why do we? She hates us. Doesn't want us there, even though she says all that stuff."

"She doesn't hate us. She's very fond of *you*."

"She *isn't*."

"Yes, she is. It's just difficult for her to understand. She's a very old lady."

"You said bitch."

"Yes. She is a bitch. So am I. I expect you will be too, when you're older."

Susan, cheered by this inspiring prospect, finished her lunch.

Later, she sat on the edge of the tub as her mother had a bath, admiring Anne's taut curved body, the shallow but beautifully rounded breasts, the fleece of pubic hair, not black or blonde or auburn, but a cool mouse brown.

Then Susan watched her mother paint her toenails, put on a new dress, redo her make-up and spruce up her hair.

"Just made it."

"When will you be back?"

"No later than eleven. Now remember, supper is in the fridge. Don't open the door to anyone, even if they insist they're your fairy-godmother. TV if you like, or that book I've just read was good. It's on my bed, I think. Bye for now."

No information was given, and no question asked about whom she might be going with. Who all the delicious scent and powder and scrupulous time-keeping were for.

A man, Susan did know that. Susan knew about men. Her father had been one, after all, even if she had never seen him. Her mother had only seen him, apparently, one more time than Susan.

When she was younger, Susan hadn't liked being alone so well. Even so, she had *been* alone a lot. Now she didn't mind. Sometimes it made her feel grown-up, the fifteen – or twenty-year-old phase.

She fetched the nail scissors and began cutting out more thin paper figures. At nine p.m. the phone went.

Susan answered and gave the number, as people still did then, something which, ten years later, she would never have done. A woman spoke.

"Is that Susan?"

"Yes."

"Can I speak to your mother, please, Susan."

"Mum's out." Should have said Mummy.

"Oh." A long pause. "When will she be back?"

Well drilled in this, as in so much, Susan said, "I'm not quite sure."

"Where is she, do you know?"

"Just at a neighbour's." Also part of the drilling.

The voice sounded relieved. "Oh then, would you mind going along to

17

fetch her for me?"

"I'm not supposed to go out."

"No, but this is urgent. I'm afraid you must. You won't have to go far if it's just one of the other flats…"

Susan did not know whose the voice was. Presented with the now insuperable dilemma of not revealing that her mother was out until eleven o'clock, (or after) at a location Susan could not be sure of, Susan hesitated.

The voice said, "This is Mrs Marks, Susan. I *need* to speak to your mother *at once.*"

Susan did not know what to do, and so she put the receiver down. She had seen her mother respond with this solution quite frequently. When the phone rang again, Susan ignored it, but when it kept on and on ringing it began to make her panicky. She went into the front room and turned up the TV. Finally, the phone stopped ringing.

Then it rang every quarter of an hour, rang twenty or thirty times. It began to seem alive, the phone, an enemy.

At five to midnight, when Susan's mother came in, looking tired and drained and lipstickless, the phone had just started to ring again.

"Who on earth is that at this bloody time of night?"

"It's Mrs Danvers."

"*What?*" Anne picked up the phone.

Standing, neurasthenic by now, ears still phone-ringing on and on in the silence, Susan watched her mother's drained face alter, become horribly alert with some invading life-force that had nothing whatever to do with her; heard her say, "When?" Heard her say, "Why?" Saw gradually *through* her, as if through a sheet of filmy paper, to some other place beyond that was unidentifiable and yet, peculiarly, also to be recognised.

It was the middle of the night, about two-thirty a.m., when a policeman arrived. After Mrs Danvers, they had gone to bed, and so had to get up again. Anne, confronting the youthful PC, snarled, "I suppose you have to be up all night, so sod us, so do we, is that it?"

"No, madam."

"I thought you always waited twenty-four hours for a disappearance."

"Not always, madam. I understand the lady is very old."

He sat in the front room, asked questions, took some notes. Susan sleepily wandered about making coffee for her mother.

When the policeman had gone, Anne did not return to bed. She paced up and down, smoking cigarettes, frowning.

"Mummy…"

"I'm all right. Go and get some sleep. Bloody woman. Bloody old woman."

They had learned, from Mrs Danvers, that the grandmother had vanished from her lunch table between one fabulous calorific course and the next.

Since this had once or twice happened before, Mrs Danvers hadn't been unduly put out. "She has a habit of coming back, you see, and eating the rest cold."

However, Susan's grandmother did not do that on this occasion. The rich food congealed in its tureens and on its dishes. The half carafe of red wine stood undrunk. "She always has the wine. Her doctor says it's good for her."

"I'm sure it is," Anne had said, "it's claret. Ten quid a bottle and that's supposed to be economising, isn't it?"

In the afternoon, after the uneaten lunch had been cleared and the service washed, Mrs Danvers put her feet up for a couple of hours, as she generally did, before preparing the five o'clock tea.

"That was when I still couldn't find her," said Mrs Danvers. "At five o'clock."

She then looked, she said, everywhere, and Susan conceived a perhaps-accurate picture of Mrs Danvers patrolling the length and breadth of the abnormal house, up and down all its twisting stairs, along all its tunnels and slopes, in and out of the endless and uncountable rooms. "I even looked up in the attics, Mrs Wilde, and she hasn't been up there for years. The stair is too steep for her, she says."

At nine o'clock Mrs Danvers, concerned and unsure what to do, had called the flat. "But there was a fault on the line, your daughter and I got cut off."

"Yes, quite."

"I kept trying. I couldn't get through."

"No."

"Did I say, I looked all over the garden? I even went through the garden again, in the dark, with a torch."

Standing there in her militant belted mac, like a spy for the Eastern Bloc, Mrs Danvers, who had summoned a taxi to bring her to their door, now announced she had also contacted the police.

"Why?" Anne, (Mrs Wilde) was aghast.

"Well, Mrs Wilde. She hasn't left the house for several years. I think – she's a bit fearful of the outside world. I do all the shopping. I do everything. She never has to go out."

"Obviously then, my mother is still indoors. Mischievously hiding from you. What else would you expect?"

"I hope so, Mrs Wilde."

"Was the cup of coffee all right?" Susan asked, as she was about to leave her mother pacing in the room where the policeman had sat and Mrs Danvers had stood, and where a kind of hollow still remained from their unwanted presences.

"The coffee was disgusting, thank you. Go to bed."

Obscurely frightened, still Susan slept, her body used to the habit of slumber – a handy, childish knack she didn't then suspect might ever desert her.

The next morning, anyway, her grandmother was found.

She had not after all been in the house, or the vast, accumulated garden.

19

She was sitting on a bench in the municipal shrubbery by the Long Pool in the park. There had been a late frost that night, which gathered on her edges, like white crochet. She was completely dead.

"I thought she'd live to be a hundred," said Anne, sombre, speaking softly. "There was nothing wrong with her. Her doctor checked her every three months. He saw her last in January. Her heart was sound. No diseases. She didn't even have rheumatism for Christ's sake. How can she be dead? Oh God, now we've got this death business, forms, mess, and the bloody funeral."

The bloody funeral was actually rather pathetic. She had left, the old woman, explicit instructions for a low-budget burial, at a local cemetery, the plot already purchased. (There was no adjacent grave belonging to anyone. Her husband, Anne's father, had been lost, body and soul, to a Second World War flying bomb in the City.) Anne and Susan attended, and Mrs Danvers in a black coat that was too large and too hot for the tepid rainy afternoon. No one else came.

They stood together over the oblong hole in the earth, and watched the coffin go down, and heard the elderly priest speak about a Christian resurrection that, Anne presently declared, not quite out of earshot, her mother had never believed in.

Afterwards they walked to the nearest pub.

"Of course my daughter is over sixteen," snapped Anne at the barmaid.

In her high heels and eye make-up and lipstick, Susan tried to look worldly and old.

The barmaid let it go; even at sixteen you couldn't supposedly drink alcohol in a pub in those days, and Susan was only having a pineapple juice.

Anne and Mrs Danvers talked desultorily. Susan ate crisps, wondering incoherently and too lightly what it meant, that hole, that box of darkness and its descent.

She had been aware of the fact of death since she was nine, sitting up one night from sleep, thinking, *One day I'll die*. She never knew what prompted the revelation. She didn't know really if it made her afraid or not. Sometimes, since, she had tried to imagine dying and stopping, or not dying and going on for ever. Both solutions seemed equally alarming and appalling. Gradually the problem faded back in her mind.

Now, she wondered where the old woman, her grandmother, was. If she was anywhere.

"I heard from the solicitors, yes," Mrs Danvers was saying, sipping her magenta vermouth. "She's been generous to me. I did my best, but that's my calling. I certainly didn't expect anything like that."

"The cats' charity will be pleased, too," said Anne, acidly, drinking her second double gin and tonic. "And the other one. What was it? Some medical research or other."

"I'm sure it was an oversight, Mrs Wilde."

"Are you?"

Mrs Danvers seemed uneasy. "It must have been."

"Well if it was, she made a damned good job of it, didn't she? What's the matter with you?" she added to Susan an hour later, as they rode home on the bus.

"I don't know."

"You're not upset, are you?"

"No. I didn't like her. She was awful."

"Yes, she was. I didn't like her, but I'm upset."

"Are you?" Susan stared.

"Because I'm not crying and tearing at my hair doesn't mean I don't feel anything."

Years, twenty years after, Susan would think, That was her mother – *was* she upset? *What* did she feel?

Susan was depressed, and when they got to the flat, the grey wet warm light trapped inside, depressed her further.

She understood, from what her mother had told her, that the grandmother had left all her money, except for the mediocre funeral expenses, and several thousands of pounds for Mrs Danvers-known-as-Marks, to various charities. Even the house had been left to a charity devoted to the succour of cats. "I didn't know she liked cats," Mrs Danvers had remarked, defensively bemused. "She never had a cat. A shame really. I'm quite fond of them myself. I'd have had one, if I'd known."

Anne had been left nothing. Not even a keepsake. Nor, as far as Susan knew, had Anne taken anything for herself from the house. But who would want any of those heavy and dismaying things, the non-edibly chipped pieces of china, the cumbersome Victorian furniture, none of it, even so, properly antique or of any beauty. Anything of value was itemised and to be sold. Had there been jewellery? Susan saw none.

"Did you ever live here when you were little?" Susan had once asked Anne, years before the disappearance, the park bench, and death.

"No. I lived with my aunt in Lincoln. I've told you."

"Oh, yes." Estranged, always separate. Strangers going by the misnomer of Relation.

"I don't want to go to school tomorrow," said Susan.

"You never want to."

Susan hung her head.

"All right, all right. It's Friday anyway. Have a long weekend."

A weight hung about Susan's neck through Friday, alone in the flat, while her mother worked. And also through Saturday. Like the Albatross, or one of the walnut mammoths of furniture from the vegetable house.

On Saturday night Anne went out with a man.

Susan mooched about the rooms, unable to sustain an interest in anything. She put all the lights on, too.

"Why are all the lights on?" said Anne when she came home at 1 a.m. "I've said, don't do that, Susan. I have to spend enough on bills as it is."

"A light bulb only costs a penny for three hours. I read it somewhere."

"Rubbish."

The next day was Sunday. Sunday, the day of visits to the old woman.

There had already been two Sundays after her death, of course. But they were taken up with seeing to things to do with the funeral, or the clearing of the house.

What had she died of, the grandmother?

"Old age."

"It says heart failure on the form."

"That's what everyone dies of. It was old age."

But Susan thought of the words *heart failure*. A lapse of the heart, not only unable anymore to beat, but to reason, to reply, to communicate... This heart was a failure.

Between Saturday night and Sunday, Susan dreamed of her grandmother, which surely she had never done before.

Somewhere she must have seen a photograph of her. Perhaps even somewhere in the vegetable house, though she couldn't recall this, before or while it was eviscerated and cleared. This certainly was how Susan's grandmother appeared in the dream, in a photographic sepia tone, and young.

What she was doing, under her light-coloured, piled-up hair, Susan never noticed. Maybe nothing. Maybe she just stood there, young and slender, half-smiling, wide-lambent-eyed.

"Who's that? It's Catherine."

In the dream all the name took on meaning for Susan, for she had seen it on a marriage certificate among dusty black boxes of things, as her mother swore and wrestled with the eldritch furniture.

"Was this her?"

"What? Yes, yes, that was her. And that was my father. Richard Arlen John Wilde. They were married in 1907."

"It says. But that's her own name."

"That was her maiden name. It's an odd name, isn't it? She used to be proud of it."

So the old woman's name was not Grandmother, or Susan's Grandmother, or even Anne's mother.

Catherine Greyglass, that had been her name. How strange indeed, for had that been what Susan had been seeing all the time in her eyes, only that, glass – grey glass?

II

The summer, four years later, was incredible. Glowing day followed day, under skies of thick stretched blue light. It felt like Italy, or, when the dusty-spicy sunsets came, the edge of Africa in a film.

In late August, one evening, walking home, and seeing the running honey sunshine reflected high up in the trees of the common, Susan felt that something, not just summer, was coming to an end. And it was.

"What's for dinner, Anne?" (Mum and Mummy – both were gone more than a year. "I want to call you Anne." And, to Anne's flawless, raised eyebrows, "You're a person, not just my mother." Irrefutable compliment. "Yes, all right," said Anne, and became Anne. Because you couldn't keep on saying Mummy, after you were fifteen.)

"Dinner? Hyena on toast."

But it was salad. Anne had, for about eighteen months, been leaving her book-keeping job in central London at three-thirty, to beat the rush hour. "I'm indispensable, I've got another raise, too. No one can add up nowadays. Not even you." This was true enough. Susan was sometimes impressively literate, but nearly innumerate, and had failed maths without a backward glance.

"You don't want to go back this new term, do you?" Anne had said.

"No."

"Do you want to try Silverguilds?"

They had looked at each other. When Susan didn't reply, Anne said, "Art college is fine, Susan. Your Miss Whatsit said Silverguilds would certainly take you, and you could get a grant."

Susan shrugged. She was secretly afraid, at sixteen, of the enormous adult world she had always, until recently, hankered after. Its seeming freedoms having gradually, by her own observation, been revealed to her as slavery, a condition of grim responsibility and personal onus childhood had not equipped her for. And she must Work, have a Job. But what? For Susan, she existed. That was the Job. But it wasn't enough. You had to earn money and take your Place. And surely she was fairly ungifted? You can speak French, they said. It could be got to a higher standard, and you could teach. (This thought was withering.) Susan began to stammer whenever she spoke French in class. Otherwise the art mistress, a long, pear-shaped woman with a wet nose, told Susan she might make a career in commercial art, and so the phantom of Silverguilds had swum into sight. "I won't get in," Susan said. Even if she did, art college was just another kind of school. The child's, if not the adult's slavery, would go on. Getting up at the crack of dawn in winter, told what to do, given homework, bored, frustrated. Not inarticulate, yet she did not say, could not sort it out to say, only look sullen. Would not enthuse. True to form, Anne ignored her. By August there had been a successful interview, the grant promised, everything settled.

When the salad was eaten, Susan made coffee. They went on to the balcony to drink it, for this was not the flat of four years previously. Six weeks after the old woman died, they had moved nearer to inner London, and a couple of years after that, moved again, here, an upmarket, three-roomed apartment, with clean white walls and a view.

It was Friday, and Susan knew Anne was going out again tonight. Then

Anne surprised her by saying, "What will you do this evening?"

"Oh, I'll play records."

"Or," Anne paused, "why don't you come with me?"

"But you're going out."

"Yes."

Susan looked at Anne. "But you're going out with a man."

"*Yes*. And the same one I've been seeing for quite a long time."

"Oh good." Embarrassed, accustomed to total exclusion in this quarter, and happy by now with that, Susan felt a prickly unease creep through her body. "So…"

"So, why not come and meet him."

This was unheard of. Unheard of for anyone. One's mother's boyfriend.

"Why?" said Susan. She felt frightened. She often did, now. The fright was never coherent, yet vaguely everywhere, lurking.

"Why not?"

"No thanks."

"All right." Anne gazed across at the trees of the common, divided from them only by the wide and noisy, fuming main road, the ashes of the day. "But you'll be meeting him anyway, Susan. He's coming to lunch tomorrow."

"Well, I can go out. Jo and I were going to look for some shoes…"

"No, I don't want you to go out. I want you to stay in. Doll yourself up and make yourself a pretty girl and meet Wizz."

Susan's mouth opened. A laugh leapt fluttering and cackling out like a demented hen.

"Yes, it's a funny name isn't it. A nickname. Glad you like it. He calls us Wizz and Wilde, the Unbeatable Duo. Alliteration, the thing you like such a lot."

Anne, at nearly forty-six, still kept her pure, scarcely-lined skin, was svelte and glamorous. Her hair was nowadays a shoulder-length, lustrous copper. On her good days, which were many, she looked forty or less. Only first thing in the morning, sometimes last thing at night, did she seem her age, or any real age at all.

But Susan had still not become herself, and intuitively knew it. She was not pretty. Heavy, and inclined to acne, she hid in her own long fair hair, like a pig in grass. She hated, of course, to be inspected. Preferred to forget her outer case, waiting, in the hope of miraculous change, some science fiction invention that might save her.

She had never, herself, essayed a boyfriend. No one had been 'interested'. She had had 'crushes' on unattainable beings glimpsed on buses and trains, in films and on TV.

Her mother was quite another animal and lived in another world.

"I can't make myself *pretty*."

"Yes you can. Wear your blue dress."

"I spilled something on it."

"Oh, for God's sake. I'm not asking you, I'm telling you, Susan. Listen to me. Things have become serious, between Wizz and me."

"Wizz…"

"Yes, Wizz. *Wizz*. His real name is Derek. He prefers Wizz. Wouldn't you?"

"No."

"You have to meet him."

"Why? He's yours not mine."

"You're jealous?"

"Of course I'm not…" Incestuously affronted, Susan felt her face go scarlet.

"Listen, Susan. No more arguments. You're going to meet him. It's important."

"*Why?*"

"I'm going to live with him, you stupid child. Are you really so dumb? And there is a chance – a wonderful chance – we may be going to America."

"Wh…?"

"Yes, the States. Now what do you say?"

Told to open the door, Susan stood behind it for as long as she could. Then of course he rang again. So she opened it wide and tried to smile confidently and in the correct hostess manner. But the smile stuck, keeping her face pulled open in a rictus, like the door. Wizz had amazed her.

"You must be Sue."

"Yes, I'm Susan."

"Hi, Sue."

He was not American. From the little Anne had said, Susan had half expected him to be. But he had a strong East London accent. That was a surprise too.

Over the years, very, very occasionally, Susan had caught odd glimpses of the men her mother was dating. They were seen from the front room window, for example, walking Anne home from the bus-stop, or pulling up in a car. Once even, one arrived at the flat when Anne was out with someone else. No one was 'serious', but they were all quite presentable, two had even been handsome.

But Wizz looked like a film star.

"Can I come in?" Wizz asked, with arch enquiry.

She let him through, and straggled after him, and saw him go straight into the living room and plaster himself straight up against Anne. The x-certificate kiss left both Anne and Susan speechless.

"What do you think?" said Anne, that night, when they were alone again. This too was arch – or nervous?

"He's very good-looking."

"Yes. He's nine years younger than me. Oh, he knows. What's nine years? And his clothes are so good. Even his casual wear is smart. He can afford a tailor."

25

"What does he do?"

"Oh, this and that. He's with a firm of importers."

As one would expect from a film star, Wizz's teeth blazed white in a mahogany tan. His dark hair had that thick combed lushness. His long narrow eyes were clear, and of a pale arctic blue. His manicured hands were horrible, vulgar, hairy, with thick sausage fingers, one looking lethally constricted by its gold ring.

His voice got louder during lunch, too, as they drank the wine he had brought. He smoked, and mashed out his fags, Chesterfields, on the plate.

He acted like a boy. "What's for pudding, Mummy?" he asked Anne. He said, innocently, of the flowers he had also brought, "Who gave you all those flowers?" Susan hated the stodgy expression 'pudding'. Where had he picked it up? Why did he need rethanking for the flowers? He spoke more or less grammatically, but his loud voice mangled the words. Sometimes he donned a fake American accent, like a DJ. He sprawled in the chair, spreading, his lunched waist bulging now he had undone his jacket. He smelled of expensive aftershave and something else.

He boasted.

"This guy, right, I'm telling you, we had nothing but trouble with this geezer. So I goes to him, Hey man, I said, Are you going to stop mucking us around or what? And this guy, you're not going to believe this – this guy says, It's the delivery boys. I said, And I've got fairies at the bottom of my arse."

Anne was tight from the wine. Wizz was either tight or drunk. Shut out from this camaraderie of the pissed, as she was from their sexual union, Susan felt older than either of them, impatient and annoyed. And petrified, scared of what they might do next.

When she sobered up, Anne would realise this man was awful. Evidently, he could never have behaved like this before.

But no, he must have. She thought he was all right.

"Okay, ma'am," said Wizz in a Texan accent. And Anne laughed.

He made little conversation with Susan. He flashed her white smiles, (toothpicked pristine at the table) and expected, with a touching self-confidence, that Susan must like him. But within half an hour even his extreme looks were turning like eggs. The teeth, so displayed, were too long. His eyes too small. He was too – *there*.

Wizz changed things. He never addressed Anne as Anne. When not calling her ma'am or Mummy, he called her Wilde. "Wizz and Wilde," he said to Susan. "the Unbeatable Duo." Susan he called, Sue, Suky, Sue-Ellen and once, Suey Fuey.

"Here, I've got to go over there next week. Might have a couple of spare tickets." He was speaking now of the U.S.A.

Susan felt sick with terror. She had only felt startled before.

He saw her face and said, "Never been up in a plane? Flying – nothing to it. Sometimes I do it four, five times a month."

"I'm supposed to start at college," said Susan.

"College'll keep."

Susan offered to wash up. They let her. As she was running the water, she heard Wizz murmuring and then Anne said, laughing, "No, not now, Wizz."

"We'll go in your room. She's not a kid. She knows the score, don't she?"

"Not here."

"Send her out. Send her to buy something. What haven't you got?"

Later, when Anne was in the bathroom, he came into the kitchen, which was small, and so he seemed to take up all the space. He looked into cupboards, picked things up and put them down.

"Well," he said, "what d'ya think?"

"Sorry?"

"About The Trip?" It had two capital T's.

Susan mumbled something, trying to placate him. She was afraid they would accidentally touch if he didn't soon leave the kitchen. His smell was overpowering, aftershave and booze and, somehow, some sort of bad smell she couldn't identify, for he was immaculate.

Afterwards, she could not, must not say to Anne, "He smelled funny." Anne was fastidious and choosy. And she liked him. She slept with him, even if she wouldn't do it in the flat when Susan was there. So… it must be Susan's imagination, the faint stench.

When she had finished the washing up, Susan had to go back to the balcony, where they were both now sitting in the sun.

"How about I take both my girls for a ride?"

Wizz was including Susan, trying to make her adult and important, attractive, valuable enough to be a possession: my girls. Susan smiled wanly. "You go. It's all right." As if tactfully giving up a treat so the lovers could let rip.

She thought Anne would argue, insist. But Anne only laughed. So they went. From the window, Susan saw Anne and Wizz (Wizz and Wilde) drive off the flat forecourt in his big, expensive, gleaming car. It was three o'clock. Anne came back at midnight, alone. "That car is so comfortable. That's the fifth car he's had since I've known him. He's always changing them."

"What does his firm import?" Susan asked in desperation; obviously they had to talk on and on about Wizz.

"I don't know. Everything, I think."

"How did you meet?" Trying to be interested, to please Anne.

"Oh, that." Anne, taking off with cold cream her cosmetics, what Wizz had left of them, paused. "He came into the office. There was some kind of palaver about something. I wasn't really listening. Mr V got in his usual flap. Then… *he* came and leaned over my desk."

In the stories Wizz had told, stories which never seemed to have a beginning or any real ending, the other characters were always making excuses, crawling – in a flap, like Mr V.

27

"What did he say? Did he just ask you out?"

"He just said, Are you free for dinner tonight? I said, No, I can't. He said, Tomorrow then. I said, Yes."

The flat had smelled on and on of Wizz after he left, despite the summer-wide windows. A stagnant odour, like old plant water.

They had had cocktails, apparently, at the Waldorf. And probably, Susan thought, gone up to a bedroom.

"I'll write to Silverguilds. You can start the course a week or so late. It won't hurt."

"No, I don't want to go."

"Don't be silly. Not *go* – to the States! I haven't been abroad since I was in my twenties. Never America. I can't wait. Of course we'll go. Thank God I got the passport situation sorted out last month. There, you see, you've even got a passport. That's a thrill isn't it?"

"I don't…"

"Air travel is nothing. It's easy. They won't expect us to fly the plane ourselves."

"It's just…"

"Susan, listen to me. Soon he may be going to live over there. Indefinitely. And he wants me to live with him, and I want to, Susan. Oh God, do I. I'd get shot of this flat. No rent to find. He'd see to visas, everything."

Susan felt her carefully knit expression cracking into sections, which slipped from her and lay along the floor.

"Don't pull that face. What's the matter with you? It's a glorious, wonderful chance. Christ, Susan, what's here that's so special? Silverguilds? You've never shown much enthusiasm."

Susan found to her own shock that she started to cry.

"Stop it. *Stop* it, Susan. I don't want to spend the rest of my bloody days in this dump, breathing in car fumes, working in some hole-in-the-corner job. I want to see some action." A phrase Wizz might have used? "New York… oh, Susan, you can't begin to see, can you, it will be so exciting. Any other girl, she'd be crazy to go."

"He's weird," Susan blurted. "I think he's a crook – a gangster…"

"Oh, don't be so ridiculously melodramatic and…"

"All those men he told us about, saying sorry, sorry, and blaming other people – and he smells."

Anne's face reached a crescendo of rage and burst, unexpectedly – to both of them, it seemed – in a torrent of helpless mirth.

"*Smells?* You're mad, child. Smells of money, yes. Of life. Go to bed for fuck's sake."

And so they parted for the night, Anne laughing, Susan crying.

In the morning, as usual in the holidays, Anne left for work before Susan woke. Anne had pinned a note on the corkboard in the kitchen, but all it said

28

was, *Please get another pint of milk and a large Hovis. Merci.*

Susan showered and dressed rebelliously. She made up rebelliously, painting out her spots by the accustomed method, using a paintbrush and disc of white eye make-up, then applying layers of powder and blusher. Jo had once told Susan she put shadow on her lids like a panda. Anne, though, her mother, never made a criticism like this.

"It won't happen," Susan said to the painted face in the mirror, (make it laugh at that.)

After she had gone out and bought the milk and bread, and a pound of plums, Susan checked her funds. There seemed quite a lot of money saved from her allowance.

When she thought of the Trip, which constantly she did, Susan felt sick. When she thought of Wizz she felt sick.

The flat throbbed with induced nausea.

All that summer break she had been roaming about with Jo, her half-friend from school, a looming, argumentative, ungainly girl who wore glasses. Susan was tired of Jo by now, and anyway, it would only take one long bus-ride to conduct her back in time, to the land before Wizz and America.

When she turned into Constance Street, the aura of its familiarity was sharp, almost surreal. Dazed, Susan gaped at the old houses and the tall dusty trees, so well remembered, the garish off-licence on the corner, the Chinese take-away, the post-office. Here it all was, still intact, the past. But then she came to the wall of the house where she had lived with Anne, and the wall was there but the house was not.

Susan stood in the open gateway, staring up a tarmac drive parked over with cars, to a five-storey modern block of flats. On either side, the other houses rose aloof, entire. Only her own building, hers and Anne's, had been eradicated. It was like a plot against them, to expunge their image, pretend they had never been, and if they said they had – they *lied.*

A woman flounced out of the flats. She wore a white suit and a lot of gold jewellery. She unlocked a bright red car, got in, and presently drove out right past Susan, still standing gawping in the widened gap in the wall, where once a gate had been.

Susan walked along the street. She stared up into the burnt green clusters of the chestnut trees. Everything was there, just the same, except for the house where she and Anne had lived.

Turning into Dunkirk Street though, Susan found some trees had been planted along the pavements in wire cages. Someone had white graffitoed over the Dun of Dunkirk and written in above, *Capt.*

Susan walked, not knowing whether to turn back, to see if her own building had reappeared. But that was silly. So she kept walking, and Capt. Kirk Street led, sooner than she recalled, into the park. Susan bought an ice-cream, from a van in the park, with a chocolate stick stuck in it. This was to compensate for the demolishment of her roots, and also for all the times she had been dragged through the park and not allowed to stop.

The park still looked big but swept bare. Had it always been so bleak, even in summer? Long blank vistas of lawn, the groups of trees standing well back to the sides, as if unwilling to ask each other to dance. Among the trees in the left hand areas were the public toilets, and beyond, the path which led to the shrubbery and the Long Pool.

Susan finished the ice-cream, even the less-appetising comet. Then she walked through the park and straight into Tower Road.

"I don't want to go up there," she had said. And Anne had always made her.

I don't want to go to America and live with Wizz.

Could Anne make her do that too?

Tower Road, the prehistoric riverbed, roped its way among the cliffs of mossy, tree-hung walls, the cascades of foliage. It was midday, the sun directly overhead and raw with fire. Grasshoppers scratched among the hot stones. There was the antique sound of water, hidden behind brickwork, trickling, and in the blue-black recurring shade, a visual silence.

Why go on? No one was making her, now. There was no reason. The reason had been found on a bench, in a crochet of white frost, four years ago, dead.

"Hello – are you Helen Colly?"

"No."

"No, I thought you weren't. I think she's older. And delayed, obviously. But it's okay anyway, if you want to come in. The more the merrier."

They walked up the drive.

The thing that struck Susan first, when the door was open, was the excruciating reek of cats' urine. It was like a blow, so she grunted involuntarily and put her hand over her mouth, then took it down, because that would be rude.

"Yes, sorry about the pong," said the woman, unconcerned. "We do our best, but we've got around two hundred on our hands now, and a lot of them aren't litter trained as yet, or neutered. It's the males spraying that's the worst."

She was about thirty-five, slim and boyish in her jeans and T-shirt, with spiky brunette hair, a clear sandy complexion and aquamarine eyes.

The stink, and the sight of several black and white cats among the bushes outside, now augmented by three tabbies cantering almost in tandem across the wide hall like a chariot team, provided recollection.

"Oh, the cats' charity."

"That's us. Cat Samaritans. I thought that was why you were here, to have a look and choose one – or preferably six or seven of the buggers. Aren't you?"

"Sorry."

They stood in the hall. Meows sang through the upper air.

Aside from the cats, it was not as she remembered, not really. It seemed more empty, lighter. Bars of sun fell dramatically across the floor, which had new lino of a cold beige. Some of the trees had been cut back, by the walls, that was it, allowing the sunshine to pass in. The drive, though, had been if anything more overgrown, all but a central strip where the wheels of jeeps had recently smashed through the weeds.

The house itself, seen from the outside, as Susan had stood there on the driveway – the house... Somehow she had kept looking and looking at it, trying to see it, for somehow it wasn't there, just like the flats in Constance Street. Somehow, the house had vanished.

And yet – they had just walked through the door. They were inside the house.

The woman, who had come around the non-house and advanced toward her, mistaking her for the delayed Helen Colly, now said, "Oh come and have a cup of tea anyway. If you can stand the smell."

"It's all right, really. I like cats."

"Yes," said the woman. "I like cats better than people, frankly. There's five of us here at the moment, on the team. But I'm the only real peoplephobe."

"I'm people... " said Susan inanely.

"Oh, you're all right. You're a cat really," said the woman, strangely. "I'm Jackie, by the way."

"Susan. My grandmother used to live here."

They were in the kitchen by then, the lower kitchen right at the back of all the sunken regions of the house. They had waded there through waves of cats, which came rushing, screaming, towards them. Every one had a name, by which Jackie greeted them. Some had only three legs, or one eye, but all looked spruce, well-fed and healthy. Snake-like, they rubbed their soft fur over the women's legs. And when Susan sat down at the long wooden table, two jumped as one into her lap.

"Just put them off if they bother you."

"No... they're great."

"Let me get this straight. Your grandmother was Mrs Wilde..."

"Mrs Catherine Wilde." Susan smoothed the cats, which slapped her under the chin with their tails, trampling her knees down to the proper consistency. Then she smoothed the kitchen table. It was the library table. That was where she had seen it last. In the book-room with the pale jaundiced dish on it, reflecting back her own round, half-formed, twelve-year-old face.

"She left us the house," said Jackie, "as you know. It was an absolute godsend, I can tell you. We were trying to do this out of two basement flats."

The lap-cats settled, edges and tails overlapping.

The rest of the tidal sea of fur ceaselessly moved back and forth through the kitchen, reminding Susan of the Countess Gertrude in *Gormenghast*. All the dim chambers of the house rang with meowing, purrs, snarls and screeches,

31

sudden skitterings and thumps.

"I remember that plant. I used to call it Martian Rhubarb. It's got much bigger."

"Yeah, there were a lot of plants left. We take cuttings and start new ones, sell them when we have a jumble sale for the cats."

Another woman stalked into the kitchen, older, with long grey hair and a cross face.

"Do you know where the tablets are for the Putney Six?"

"Try behind the rag-cupboard like last time."

"That window needs fixing again upstairs. And that knocking's started again."

She marched out. Susan drank some of the tea Jackie had put before her. She was becoming used to the urine-reek, noticing it less or not at all.

"Must seem strange to you. Us being here now."

"Yes."

"I gather she was quite a character, the old lady."

Susan didn't know what to say.

The strawberry-red leaves of the Martian Rhubarb, either the original, or a cutting, and now a massive three-foot high in a plastic tub, stirred suddenly, whispered to each other, rasped like dry old skin.

Jackie glanced at the plant.

"Did you want to look around the house?"

"Oh – maybe."

"Go ahead, if you want."

"Oh, but…"

"Frankly, Susan, I trust you. And even if you were a thief, we haven't got much to steal, apart from the cats. And providing you can prove you have a good home for them you can have as many of those as you want, free."

"Wish I could," said Susan, politely.

She didn't know if she wanted to go over the house. She had never, so far as she could recall, even come this distance, in her grandmother's day, never seen the lower kitchen or the scullery. But now she supposed she must, must look at the house. It was full of an ocean of cats. No longer as it had been. No longer – *here*.

As she flexed her legs, wondering how to remove the two sleepers without jolting them, both woke and instantly sprang from her, indifferent to the passage of humans and random fate.

Was this a bit like having to go round a stately home on a school visit, something she had to do, and pretend to be interested in? How many rooms *were* there? They had been added on decades before, the house – already large – extending in all directions. Some rooms even no longer had windows, being trapped between outer rooms which did, or so Anne had once said. Susan found none of these. But Anne hadn't seen much of the house, had never lived, *consciously* in the house. The grandmother, Catherine, had conceived Anne unexpectedly in her late forties. And then World War II had happened, and Anne, only about four or five, was sent to a well-to-do aunt, (her father's sister) on a farm outside Lincoln. She never came back.

But really, Susan knew nothing about all that, as Anne seemed not to. Susan knew nothing about her – about Catherine. Nothing.

Of the cats, with which the house was now mainly furnished, Susan met all kinds, even a pair of Persians on a landing, who stared at her with demented apricot eyes.

Once she saw another human, a thin hurrying girl in trousers, who simply muttered "Hi" and trotted past.

A few doors were shut, and Susan left them alone. In some open-doored rooms were large cages, with single cats in them, presumably segregated due to ailments or unsocial temperament.

But the house – room on room, corridor on corridor, steps, annexes, was, despite cats and absence, still a vegetable house, a pumpkin: the Labyrinth.

Then somehow, coming down a crooked back stair, Susan emerged into a wide room empty of all furniture. Trees pressed at the windows, fir, pines, bays, and beyond lay an unexpected growing wall of garden, turning back from a once-pruning into a jungle.

This was the room, still cased in its emerald light, where Susan and Anne had last seen the old woman alive.

Cats lay in patches of sun on bare boards. Marks of territorial cat sprayings decorated the plaster, to an impressively high point.

But it was still *that* room.

Susan stood there.

She had thought she was lost in the house, had even uneasily wondered if she could find her way down to the front again, and if not would she be unable ever to get out?

But here she was.

The room was full of an immense stillness. Nothing moved that made any sound, not even the cats. Before a window, standing on the floor, another Martian Rhubarb, darker and greener than the other, raised its heavy flags to the scattered sun.

One by one the cats lifted their eyes, some their heads, looking all one way, towards a vacant spot in the room where a shaft of light faded slowly, perhaps unaccountably. The cats watched. They looked steadily up into the air, where nothing was, and followed it with their gem stone eyes.

Fine hairs rose on the back of Susan's neck.

After a moment, the light changed again. A cloud must have crossed the sun. The cats resumed former occupations, mostly sleeping. Two began to fight. One bounded into the pot of the plant and urinated.

Jackie was standing talking in a room off the hall, with a big woman in a Laura Ashley dress. "Oh, yes, I'd like to adopt three, even four." Helen Colly?

That was all right then.

Near the front door, the grey-haired woman bent over a hamper with kittens in it.

"Thanks for calling," she said to Susan, harshly. "Thinking of joining the team? It's a tough life, you know. We'll be out again tonight, all night, I expect, trying to catch ferals and bring them in. And every cat needs to be thoroughly checked over, you know, neutered, some need drugs. Look at these, abandoned in Hawthorne Road."

"Poor things," said Susan. She gazed at their milky grey eyes.

"Oh, they'll be all right now. But it costs a lot. We do like a donation, where possible."

Flushing, feeling like a criminal, Susan rummaged for a pound note and gave it to the woman. She imagined over and over, as she walked back up the drive, the woman saying to her colleagues, "Flash little bitch, handing me a pound like some duchess." Or, alternatively saying, "Mean little cow. Only gave me a quid."

"Had an okay day?"

"Mr V had one of his famous attacks," said Anne, scathingly. "I get the feeling they're going to fold the business up."

Susan turned her head from the rescuing spectres of Wizz and America the Golden, glinting at the back of her mother's silver eyes.

"Anne – tell me about Grandmother."

"What? What am I supposed to tell you, after all these years?" Anne flopped gracefully back in her chair, drinking icy orange-juice from the fridge, shoes kicked off, her feet, with their perfectly enamelled nails, propped on the stool. Heat lay over the flat like damp washing. "I'm tired, Susan. I'm going to have another bath. The trains are bloody in this weather…"

"I'll run the bath for you."

"Thanks."

When Susan came back, she said, "Do you remember anything about the house, Anne?"

"Which house?"

"The house in Tower Road. When you were little and lived there with Grand – with Catherine."

"No."

"Not even…"

"I've said, You've asked me before and I've told you all I know. I remember being about four, and saying, Am I four? And someone said Yes. That may have been my father, or her. I don't recollect. And I don't remember anything about the house, it was just a sort of space around things. I don't even remember the garden, except a piece with roses growing up something. That's all. I'm not putting you off, Susan. I truly don't remember a thing."

"But you remember the farm. The drive with the lilacs. And Lincoln. How

34

it was so flat, except for the hill with the castle and the cathedral. And the Roman arch in that street. All that."

"Oh yes. But I was there until I was in my twenties."

"I went there today."

"Lincoln?" Anne looked quizzical, waiting.

"The house. Her house."

"My God. What sort of state was it in?"

Susan smiled. "It was full of cats."

"Yes, it would be."

"No, it was nice. They take care of them and find them proper homes and everything."

"How much did you give them?"

"Only a pound."

"That's quite a lot at your age, on our income."

"But they let me look round. I'd never seen so much of the house, and it's so peculiar, and I couldn't make any – sense of it..."

"No," said Anne. "They kept building on. It was a shambles. They were both mad, you know. Richard and Catherine. And then he got killed in London, when that bomb landed in the street. And that just left her to be mad on her own."

"Did she want you back then?"

"No, she never wanted me at all. They didn't want children, and she thought she'd never have any. And then, there I was. She was forty-seven, forty-eight. A horrible difficult birth. They had to sew her up. She told me once."

"Oh – ugh..."

"You asked. So listen. I think she'd have given me away whatever happened, the War just provided a decent excuse. Before my late twenties, I saw her only once, when I was twenty-one. She came to my party. I didn't know who she was. Aunt Margaret said, 'Here's your mother, Anne.' Can you picture it?"

"What did she look like?"

"Old. I was twenty-one, and she was – what would she have been? – about sixty-seven or eight – nearly seventy. She had on a cream costume, and her hair was still fair, or she'd had it dyed, and it was permed in the latest fashion. Blood-red nails and lips. This was in the Fifties. Women looked like that then. But not necessarily old ones. She gave me a present. Oh, I'd had things before. They came by post. She *handed* me this."

"What was it?"

"It was a cheque for a hundred pounds. That was real money then. Go and turn the bath off before it runs over."

Susan went, shut off the taps, darted back. But now Anne looked at her moodily. "Look, Susan. I don't really want to talk about this now. I didn't know her, and suddenly she expected to be my mother. Margaret wasn't exactly peerless, but she did her best. She was the closest I got. And then this dolled-up praying mantis appears before me."

"You said…"

"I've said enough. Shut up. I'm going to have that bath. Oh," pausing in the doorway, deliberate and cruel with her ace card, "thought any more about America?"

The phone rang when Anne was in the bathroom.

It was Jo.

"I tried you all afternoon," accusingly. "Where were you?"

"I went out."

"Can you come for a walk? I want to ask you something."

"Maybe. I'll see. What?"

"Tell you then. Meet you by Stratfords."

Jo was already waiting by the shop, looking carefully at an array of oil-heaters, kitchen implements, and crockery in the window. Her tall sausage-like body was clad in a longish skirt and loose blouse. Her short, naturally **blonde** hair, her only potential attraction, was greasy and pushed back behind big ears, as if she meant deliberately to be as charmless as she was able.

Susan could not be proud of Jo. Could not introduce her to anyone with a flood of pride – "My friend, Jo." She resented this in Jo and felt guilty for resenting it. It didn't matter what people looked like. (No?) On the other hand, Jo could also be tactless, critical, and sometimes something that Susan would later refer to, in her late twenties, as *spiritually obtuse*.

They walked along the public paths of the common, as the last russet light dripped through the trees.

Young men, bare bronze-armed and legged, strode or bicycled past them, casting neither of them a single glance.

Nor did Jo have a boyfriend. She appeared not to want one. She was going to secretarial school, and an uncle had already promised her a lucrative secure job in a big London office. This seemed to be her only goal. Jo had never been in love, not even with anyone on celluloid. "Oh him," she would say. "He's all right, I suppose." Even when Susan spoke admiringly of some glamorous woman: "Wish I could look like that," Jo would sniff, "They don't look like that in real life, you know." How did Jo know anyway? Jo was very good at maths.

"My dad says I can have a flat," said Jo abruptly. "I mean, when I start college. It would mean I was nearer to college and save time in the long run."

"Really? A flat?"

"Well, a room. But a good one in a respectable house. Clean. No people taking drugs, fixing."

"You *are* lucky." Susan did not know if she really thought this, but clearly congratulations and envy were expected. "Are you pleased?"

"Well, I will be. But the only thing is, Dad says I have to share with another girl. He says it's not safe, me being there on my own. And if I shared, the expenses would be halved, of course."

"Yes."

"So, what do you think?"

Susan stared at Jo. "Me?"

"Dad says you're steady. He likes your Mum – the Brave and Fair Anne, he calls her," she added, too thick to be ashamed of him. "He said I should ask you. It would be handy for Silverguilds, too, because that's near my secretarial college. We could travel on the same bus. And you'll have your grant, same as I will, and there'll be what Dad gives me, too."

Susan thought about sharing a room with Jo. The prospect was rather unappealing. Jo was a stickler for all sorts of things – she liked rules, (knowing where she stood, as Jo put it.) She liked lots of little ornaments, and dusting them...

"Only," Susan said, "my mother – we may be going to the USA."

"For a holiday?"

"Sort of. It's a bit more than that."

Jo's unemotive face settled. "All right, then. I'll have to ask someone else."

"Jo – I don't want to go to the States – I'd hate it – she's got this horrible man – he's foul..."

Jo stared at Susan with a deep latent intriguement striving behind the dough of her cheeks. "Why?"

"He just is. I want to stay here."

"Shall I speak to your mum," said the deadly grown-up Jo, "about my flat?"

"No. I'll talk to her. Tomorrow."

"All right. But I need to know soon. I'm already having to start college from home, and that's going to cost a lot and be a long journey."

America seemed familiar because of TV. There were the same terracotta and brown brownstones, baking in hot, late summer light, the same sidewalks, playgrounds and lots, and, at the centre of the city of New York, the same incredible surrounding image of a metropolis of the far future coexisting here and now.

Coming in over the highways and bridges, darkness already down on the September air, (which smelled of cinders and gasoline) the lighted skyscrapers rose from the void, pinned by a million diamonds to the night. And then later, other floodlit buildings lifted twenty miles above the ends of Manhattan's cobbles, like waterfalls of blue ice with ruby spires.

But wonder was prevented from spreading its wings. Because Wizz was there, in the car, and the aura of Wizz overlaid everything.

"What d'ya think?" he asked them, driving boldly on the 'wrong' side of the road in yet another vast flash car. As if he had invented the city, or *discovered* it, like a sort of belated Columbus. Did they have to thank him for building New York?

Downtown, Upstate, said the signs slung above the road.

They drove into Manhattan, to Wizz's loft.

After all, Anne and Susan hadn't flown to the States with Wizz, he had only picked them up at Kennedy International (JFK, said Wizz.)

At Heathrow, Anne took Susan straight into a bar. "Let's pretend you're eighteen, Susan. Then you can have a gin and tonic with me." This by now sometimes happened at home. And Susan was so nervous she had been more than glad of the dizzy quick glow the gin gave her. By the time they walked down the claustrophobic area, (screened as if from horrors), onto the plane, everything seemed feasible, and all right.

The flight was uneventful, enervating due to the cramped seats. Wizz's tickets had put them in Business Class, but Anne had seemed a little disappointed. At one time she had been speaking predictively of Concorde.

Sometimes, beyond the window, Susan saw clouds below her, wrapped over the blue surface of the world, as if she watched the earth from space. Coupled with the glass of wine she had had with the plane meal, this too seemed to put everything in perspective. The in-flight film was oddly dreamlike; she dozed. When she came to, they were nearly there. Susan now felt warm and sleepy and dirty. Apprehensive. Anne though was all alight, make-up redone, hair burnished, only the lines rather too deep at the sides of her eyes and mouth. "Wizz! Wizz darling!" she exclaimed, as they emerged from immigration – where arrest had seemed, to Susan, imminent.

"Baby!" sludged Wizz. He was more American, but also more East London. A confusing combination, if perhaps not for him. "Hi, Suey."

The loft had been organised for him by the firm, he said. A huge open space, with other rooms leading off it. Only five floors up, it was reached by a cranky elevator Susan was afraid would stall – or fall. She was generally afraid of the elevators in New York. Of travelling up and down hundreds of floors, with the legacy of all the cable-snapped crashing elevator cars she had seen in thrillers.

The floor of the expensively furnished loft was of naked polished wood, with rugs strewn over. "See those patterns – Native American Indian." Ranks of windows looked out over buildings which, in day's sunlight, would burn rose-red and cobalt. There was a domed jukebox on one wall, which flickered lime green and played scratchy, ancient numbers for a dime – or was it a quarter? "Art Deco, see. Brilliant," said Wizz.

Anne and Susan got ready in the big, brand-new, black and gold bathroom – there were two bathrooms – where there was a pair of black and gold washbasins, and also a pair of black and gold lavatories. "Anne – does that mean two people go to the loo – at the same *time*?"

"I guess so," glittered Anne, Americanly. If she was offended, nothing

38

showed. (It was only years after Susan learned that two-looed bathrooms were not the US norm.)

The bath in the big bathroom was also big. When full, you could put your head on an air pillow and float about in it.

Wizz drove them to a restaurant. "They call New York Pig's Paradise," said Wizz. "You can get any food here. Anything in the world – French, Italian, Thai, Hawaiian, Sudanese, Jewish, Japanese. And I gotta take you to Chinatown."

The restaurant was overwhelming. It seemed full of black light, with spotlit tables, tall white lilies, impeccable, automatic waiters. Susan propped her eyes open. They seared with tiredness. She felt fluey.

Wizz and Anne drank and drank.

"Don't give her any more wine, please, Wizz. She'll have a hangover."

Susan didn't want any more wine. Or any dinner. She already felt sick from the need to be asleep.

Everyone else in the restaurant was smart and beautiful, wide awake, and sometimes loud with confidence. Susan grew smaller, but not in the correct way. She knew she was too fat, her skin pebbled, her hair not right, her clothes all wrong – how had immigration let her in?

In the morning, she was still exhausted after eight hours sleep. But they had to be up and out by ten, because Wizz wanted to take them 'around'.

The days became a kaleidoscope crush of events, food, places, moving figures, information: of a terrifying elevator ascent of the Empire State Building, the zoo in Central Park, the Brooklyn Bridge strung with pearls of lamps, subway rides. Cops with their guns in their belts. And they seemed always to be eating, too. The coffee shops and restaurants Wizz chose were high-class, with menus like novels. Even the dim burrow under the red banners of a smoking Chinatown, was select.

They stood and gazed up and up, at Wizz's instruction, to the tapering reflecting heights of glass mountains, while below humanity rushed through the canyon, and the yellow taxis zipped like angry bees.

And there were the dress stores, Wizz waiting to pounce with his American Express Card, where the assistants said to Anne, "That is just gorgeous on you," and to Susan, "I guess the bigger size is in order." And the dresses sticking like toffee to her shame-and-heat tacky back, and never quite fitting, regardless.

Height on height, slight on slight, humiliation on humiliation.

She was overweight in the country of physical perfection, and sixteen. And – it went on and on.

"Come on, wake up. You got just half an hour to shower and get ready. Put on the white dress Wizz bought you."

"It doesn't fit. I'm tired."

"No. Come on, Susan. We're driving out to Penn today, have you forgotten?"

What did she afterwards remember of Pennsylvania? The hours-long drive. Fields. A bridge over a river. City night; skyscrapers, and a forgotten movie in an air-conditioned cinema so cold she shivered. They stayed in a hotel. Susan's room was pink. Across the hall, Wizz and Anne made love.

Susan dreamed of driving, or being driven, forward, onward, endlessly.

Back in New York they went to the Cloisters and the Met. Inexorably, Wizz escorted them. The Met had an exhibition, what was it? Great suits of Eastern armour, perfumes wafting on electric breezes. Girls slender as pencils.

"We could drive out to Washington DC, if you like. Take a look at the ol' White House."

The Statue of Liberty swirled in a greenish miasma of fog and jet lag.

"You can't have jet lag still. We've been here over a week. And I didn't have it at all. Buck up, Susan. You're being a drag."

"I didn't want to come," Susan said, humbly.

"Yes, I know that. And now you're intent on cutting off your nose to spite your face, aren't you?"

Then Wizz had to be at work, in something called the Anchor Building on Broadway, the New York branch of the firm. He took Anne with him, wanting to show her off. Susan was also meant to go. That morning her period started, early and painful.

She imagined Anne telling Wizz why Susan couldn't go with them.

Yes, she had told him. He winked at her as they went out. "You poor messed-up women," the wink said, "I can guess what you go through. Lucky me to be a man."

Susan thought how the male Jews thanked God every day for not making them female.

She thought of thanking God for not making her Wizz.

In the afternoon she felt much better. She felt she could breathe, even in Wizz's loft.

Alone, she played the jukebox, leaned from the window and watched the streets below She began to think about America, what she had seen of it, to acknowledge the excitement of it from a distance. If only she could have been here without Wizz being here. If only without the threat of Wizz, and, the future with Wizz, hanging over her – but with whom? With Anne? Alone? Yes, perhaps alone…

Sitting on the four-seater white couch, Susan thought about Anne saying, "How can you stay behind in England, Susan, if I go to live overseas? Tell me that. I don't care if you are sharing with this Jo. You're sixteen and a minor. I'm legally responsible for you."

"I could lie about my age," Susan had said. She did not add, Like I lied all the times you were out at night and I had to pretend you were next door.

Anne had concluded, "Don't be stupid."

The American afternoon went quickly.

Anne had declared she and Wizz would be back by four from the Anchor

Building. They were catching a show that night. However, when the elevator clanked to a halt by the doors at four fifteen, only Wizz walked in, in his sharp light suit.

"Where's Anne?"

"Oh, Wilde made a big hit. She and Eve Frenowsky just clicked. Gone off to Macy's. She'll be back in a while, calm down."

Wizz went to the Coca-Cola machine that stood by the water dispenser and got two ice-cold cans.

He drank both of these, walking slowly around the main room of the loft.

Susan grew frightened. She could always get frightened of things, but especially now she was frightened of Wizz, of being alone with Wizz. She didn't know why. It was like that other time in England, in the kitchen.

She was scared too in case he took off his jacket and shirt. That had happened already, one morning, seeing him roll from the bathroom in just pyjama bottoms. His body was good, muscular and brown, except at the waist, where it bulged a little... He was also very hairy; his back was hairy. His back scared her most of all.

But now Wizz only walked about. Then suddenly, he turned, and came towards her. He sat down opposite her on the blue couch, which faced the white one.

Susan felt her heart hammering in her dry throat.

She could smell the faint bad smell she always associated with Wizz and knew couldn't be there.

"Look, Sue, let's have a talk, shall we?"

She stared. He was waiting. She managed to say, "Oh, yes, if you like."

"Well, you know, Sue, it's not really what I like. I just think we oughta. Okay?"

Now Susan was the one to wait.

She could see him, studying the floor rug, thinking, mulling it over. Then he looked up, and his pale eyes settled on her face and she couldn't glance away from them.

"There ain't no nice way I can put this, Sue. You've been a right little fucking arse-wipe, ent ya?"

The elevator, which so far had never fallen, now plummeted through Susan's ribcage into her intestines.

Even if she had wanted to speak, it wouldn't have been an alternative.

He wasn't talking loudly. He was quiet and level. So she had missed a bit, too, from the shock.

"... you here and tried to give you a real good time, but you won't have it, will ya? You just can't handle it, can ya? But you see, Sue, your mother means a lot to me. And I want *her* to have a good time even if you fucking poker-arsed bloody won't. So let's make a deal, okay? Let's just say it was your time of the month..." (even in the abysm of terror she writhed with embarrassment) "and now you're gonna be like a normal fucking girl. Okay?

41

Like any other girl with a great mother and a guy like me trying to make it special for her. Not like some fucking little constipated tart. Is that it, eh Sue? You're constipated? That can turn a girl into a bitch. Take something for it. I've had enough of you. You were like a fucking wet weekend from the word go. Little bitch. Jealous maybe. Well, I can see that would happen. You're no oil painting, eh, Sue? With those big spots all over your face and that fat body like a bloody porpoise. Christ, I look at her and I think to myself, Where'd she get this kid? Your dad must've been – he must've been a real prince. But you can't help the way you look, I guess. They might even get you ironed out over here. They can do that, you know. Get girls like you looking halfway human."

All this venom, squeezed out, bit by bit. So level and controlled. Not raising his voice. This hatred. As if he held her there and vomited, slowly and methodically and over and over and over her.

She thought, in a giddy whirl of horror, *I must get away*. But her legs were leaden. She couldn't move. The ton weight of his vomiting malice held her there in place.

"…see what I want now, Sue, is you act like a proper girl. You act like you appreciate what I done. What *she* done for you. She deserves a life, Sue, don't you think, after mollycoddling you for the past sixteen fucking years. So pull yourself together, girl. I want to see a change in you, I really want that, Sue. No. I expect that. Okay?"

Then he stood up. She had thought he would never ever stop. But he moved off, and as he crossed the loft, through its strips of red westering sun, he began to whistle softly. And then he was gone along the corridor to the bedroom he used with Anne.

After a while, Susan too got up, very slowly. She found she could walk. So she walked into the bedroom he had said she could have. She shut the door and sat on the bed. Then she shut her eyes.

Susan visualised Anne coming home. Trying to get Anne alone. Telling Anne what Wizz had said. Susan knew she would not be able to. It could never happen. She knew she could never speak of it, to anyone.

And he too must know this. That she could and would never speak of it, that she would, from now on, try very hard to appear as he wished her to, and that she must fail. But still, she would try.

He had split her apart from Anne as even the act of birth had not done, and Susan understood that exactly, even if the thought did not enter her stunned, reeling mind.

Alone? She was. She thought anyway she might be afraid now of Anne, too. Since Anne belonged to Wizz, was a part of Wizz, like that thing in *Hamlet* about husband and wife being one flesh – *therefore my mother*.

By the time Anne got back, triumphant with Macy's bags, Susan was all ready for the show. She had put on the ghastly white dress, which rode up over her fat hips. She had painted out the large round stones of her spots, two more of which had come up since her talk with Wizz.

"All set?" cried Wizz. He was buoyant as a balloon, lightened of his load.

Whenever he was 'nice' to her through the evening, Susan thanked him. She tried to smile, and the smile cut her face like a knife.

In the interval of the show she went, (alone) to a cubicle of the ladies room, and retched and retched, embarrassed also by the noises she made, and by the kind woman who, when she came out, pale and sweating, said, "Are you okay, honey? Was it something you ate?"

Which was, in a way, quite apt, for if not precisely eaten, certainly swallowed.

"I *thought* you were going to be late," said Jo, "and you are."

"Sorry. The train didn't come for ages."

"Well, let's get cracking, then, it's just down this road."

English autumn, no longer fall, the yellow leaves hung out from the trees. It was raining, and cars splashed through an overflowing drain on crystal tidal waves.

"I thought your mother must've delayed you."

"Oh, no. No, that's all right."

"She didn't mind, then?"

"Oh no. No. She may not be going, anyway."

"Fallen through, has it?"

"Maybe."

"My dad says you can't ever trust a Yank. He learnt that in the War."

"He isn't a – I don't want to talk about him."

The houses were in a terrace, each one narrow, with pointed purplish roofs.

"We're number 17, Flat 3."

Their room was about the size of the main room in Anne's flat overlooking the common. Here the two girls must do their best, with the two mattresses, the gas rings, the light which would flicker like a gas lamp and was always going. With each other's contrary personalities. The bathroom one floor down. And with the wit of the jovial father of Jo, who sometimes called on them to bring them things they 'might need' and catch them out.

"Will your mother want to come over?" Jo asked, that first morning. "Will she want to look round?"

"No, I don't think so."

No, Susan didn't think so. Anne would soon be back in the States, but Jo wasn't going to know that.

Susan had lied to Jo, ably. Long practice. *Oh my mother's only at a neighbour's. She's only in the flat by the common.* But the flat by the common had already been given up. Next month someone else would live there, and Susan would only have to pretend, now and then, to visit.

"If you don't let me, I'll run away."

"Oh, Susan don't be so dramatic. And silly."

43

"I mean it."

"What is the matter with you?"

"I don't want to go. I've said. I want to stay here and go to art school."

"You could have fooled me."

But Susan did fool Anne. Even when Anne said, "Is it still this idiotic thing you've got about Wizz…?"

"I haven't. I got over that. We had a chat one night." Susan, her voice coming cool and steady from far off. "He's all right. He'll take care of you. It was him really. He said, if I wanted, I ought to start making my own life."

"He – said that?"

"Yes. And he said how he felt about you, how he thought so much of you. So, I feel I'd just be in the way."

"Susan, that isn't true…"

"Yes. Oh, come on, Anne. You've never had a life either, have you? Go on, go with Wizz. It'll be great. Everyone here can think I'm eighteen, except at the college, and they'll think you're still in England. It will be okay."

Anne phoned Wizz long distance.

Susan would not even listen to her voice, speaking to Wizz over the Atlantic wires.

But at length Anne came into her room. "He said let you."

Susan said, airily, "Told you."

"I said you'd said you liked the talk you'd both had. It made you more confident in yourself. He laughed. He sounded pleased. Well… you've never had a father, have you."

"Oh, look at that sparrow on the sill," said Susan. "Look, isn't it sweet."

"Susan, you *will* be all right?"

I always was, when you left me. And if you don't leave me now, if you make me go and live with him, I will never be all right. I will die.

"I'll be all right, Anne."

Anne's grey eyes, startled, evasive. "If anything doesn't work out – you must write – no, call me collect – reverse the charges. I'll show you what to do. And I'll be over, often, of course I will – we're bound to be. I'll send you some money. The grant isn't much."

She's glad.

I may never see her again. Is that possible? Oh yes. She isn't mine any more. She's his. What I'm seeing now, this woman with grey eyes and dyed red hair, it isn't my mother.

"Oh, don't cry," said Anne. "What am I to think now? *I* don't know. What should I do?"

But she did know, and she would do it. And the tears meant nothing, not grief really, a reflex, like that drain overflowing in the downpour.

III

Patrick was like an animal which changed its coat for the season. In summer he tanned quickly and easily, the long thick hair, that hung most of the way down his back, turned gold, his eyes a light brown. But in winter his eyes darkened like his hair, while his skin paled. Then he resembled, in his long black leather greatcoat, a straggler from some nineteenth century war. He was well-built and slim, but only about three inches taller than Susan was today, in her flat sandals.

She looked at him covertly. It still half surprised her, to see him there, to be with him, even though they had gone around together for over fifteen months and had sex regularly.

Fierce May sunlight hit the pavement. She was glad they had left the crowded, noisy pub – but was not quite so sure, however, about their intended destination.

"Patrick – you really do still want to go over there?"

"Yes."

"It'll be three buses from here."

"I thought you said the train, then the bus."

"Oh. Okay."

"What's up?" he said. He spoke kindly, but she knew he had made up his mind and would lose patience if she now tried to dissuade him. He would say, justifiably, she was making a fuss about nothing, and look, he'd brought his stuff, and the painting stuff too, and so had she, so what was the problem suddenly.

And what *was* the problem suddenly?

Last night, sitting over their glasses of beer and wine in the Silver Tavern, she had touched, without thinking, on the subject. Finding him interested in what she said, which always inordinately pleased, foolishly almost inebriated her, she had gone on and on.

"This place. Sounds visually fantastic. Especially with all those trees. Could it still be like that?" he had asked.

"Oh, I'd think so. More like it really. More overgrown and so on. They weren't into domestic stuff, just cats."

"Three years ago."

"About three years."

"So, for a *donation*... They'd let me paint there, wouldn't they?"

"What would you donate?" she had asked playfully, glancing into his summer-golden eyes.

"A fiver. Why not? And give them a painting maybe, for their jumble sales. Anyhow, they'll remember you."

"They might not," she said carefully. "I only met that woman once, and I've changed a lot. I was only sixteen."

45

By then they had walked back to Patrick's room in Belmont Court. Sitting on the floor with the coloured candles lit, they discussed their – Patrick's – plan. By midnight, when they lay down together on the bed, it was all decided. The next day was Thursday and life-drawing, but everyone already knew the regular model had bronchitis and might not come, which would mean improvised still life of something unappetising, like stacked books and chairs. They were into their third year, both worked generally with application; blind eyes were sometimes turned to absences.

After their lovemaking in the bed, with which the room was furnished, and as Patrick slept, Susan lay looking up at the two authentic plaster roses in the high ceiling. The electric wiring was tied off there, only the roses remained, like the ornate acanthuses at the big room's corners, and in the halls outside. Then the last candle flickered out. An odd thought came to Susan as she drifted asleep, that the plasterwork had actually physically vanished now it was no longer visible.

Belmont Court's old Victorian lift woke her, as it always did when she was there, clanking up and down from 6.30 a.m. onwards.

Susan got up, used the bathroom on Patrick's floor, and left. It was only twenty minutes through the early streets to her own room – space no longer shared with Jo, or with anyone.

Susan's room though was not so gracious as Patrick's, nor did she have Patrick's small fridge, and the milk, left under cold water, had gone off in the warmth of savage May.

She had arranged to meet him in the college pub at noon. They would have a sandwich and a drink and then set off for the house. For the house that was, which had once been her grandmother's.

Even in the bright morning, gulping back Nescafé and washing underclothes in the grubby bathroom downstairs, Susan did not feel any qualms about having elaborated to Patrick on the jungles of the vegetable house. Or about travelling over there with him later and asking the cat women if they could paint in the wild garden, or stay overnight a couple of nights in a sleeping bag, on one of the empty floors.

"After all, it's your rightful ancestral home," had said Patrick, jaunty. "From what you said, they're not going to object, unless we evilly molest their cats."

How had she got on to speaking about the house, the garden, her grandmother? By nine the next morning, she began to wonder, but couldn't recall. Of course, Susan had mentioned Catherine to Patrick before, just as she had told him rather a lot more about her elusive mother, Anne.

Patrick himself seldom commented on what Susan revealed, though he listened thoughtfully. But then he rarely made comments on anyone, apart from their looks. He was always more interested in appearances, objects, views, the things which were integral to his work as an artist. He was, she thought, a very good artist, an active artist. For herself she seemed only able to copy what she saw to a more or less adequate degree, but Patrick – reinvented.

He hoped to get to one of the top schools in London after his time at Silverguilds, to which he had anyway migrated, halfway through Susan's post-foundation first year, from Manchester. But they never discussed that at any length either. Just as they never discussed any protracted or developed union between them, or its cessation. Sometimes, when she caught herself surreptitiously watching him in shock, Susan considered if they, as a pair, were bound to go anywhere beyond their present condition. Really she did not think so, could not imagine it. The future was endless, but indefinite. Even now, she never made demands or suggested extensions, such as their living together. That was from a sort of lazy fear of his possible – probable – unwillingness. And from disbelief too, for Patrick never seemed entirely real. Though she admired him, was quite happy when with him, he also placed a definite sense of duress upon her – because he was another person. He was a stranger. Susan thought she didn't understand him, could never do so, beyond the most obvious elements. Perhaps she did not try. She was, in a way she did not fully know then, and only saw years after, afraid – not only of upsetting or offending him – but *of* him. Of his presence in her life.

So, to lose him simply inevitably through the course of time and events was a miserable idea she did not dwell on, but one which also brought her a feeling of relief.

As she pushed another T-shirt into the canvas bag, Susan realised she didn't want to go to Catherine's house.

Between one thrust into the bag and the next, her mood was altered. It had seemed all right, mildly adventurous, last night or earlier today. But now it seemed – wrong.

She knew it would be difficult to change Patrick's mind. That much she had learned about him. He was absolute in what he wanted to do where it concerned his work.

The first time he had come up to her had been to do with his work. She had already seen him here and there in the college building, next in the pub. Although she was casually friendly enough with members of her class, she had made no personal friends, no one to nudge about Patrick, "Look at *him*," as other girls did. Then Patrick was moved into Susan's class, and at the second coffee break, he came over to her table and stood next to her, only one inch taller since she was wearing her boots with heels. "Can I sit here?" She said he could. Other tables were quite full. She thought it was that. Then he said, "I want to talk to you. I've been looking at you. You've got this wonderful face. You're like a Mediaeval painting – do you know the ones I mean? Only you're prettier. I'm just so drawn to your face. I'd like to paint you. Could we do that?" The combination of politeness and calm effusion was arresting. And exhilarating. All the times after that when they met, had a drink, and then went to Patrick's flat where he sketched her, Susan thought the end of the painting would be the end of their connection. But by the time he had primed the canvas, he had also kissed her, standing barefoot on the earthing utility carpet of his room, holding her in a circle of his arms.

Presently, "I'm sorry, I'd better say now, I'm not on the Pill."

Patrick had been unfazed, indeed munificent and gentle. Susan had been nearly businesslike. Anne had seen to it her daughter knew exactly what she must do, and which, therefore undone, had resulted in Susan.

"I can wait," he said.

Susan visited the Family Planning centre the next day. She took no chances, and observed the full four weeks, while the Pill became effective, before allowing herself to make love with Patrick. Armed with knowledge, Susan was not shy or disillusioned by the pain of her first times, or the seeming unpreparedness of her body. She thought Patrick's body very beautiful, with its lightly muscled spare maleness.

She was also no longer ashamed of herself physically. The shame had gone with an alteration in her shape, both physique and face, that had somehow happened during her foundation year. Though her body was heavier than those of many of the girls she saw, her form had acquired contours, an indented waist and smooth belly, and breasts which, she had suspected, and which Patrick soon showed her, were lovely. The acne had also perished, due perhaps to her total avoidance of cheese, which she had one day read, in a dentist's waiting-room magazine, might trigger spots. Her clear skin was very white, luminous. Better even than Anne's.

Even so, sexually, Susan felt herself awkward, and eventually inadequate. As pleasure began regularly to overwhelm her on Patrick's bed, she noted a curious limitation in herself. She was so completely and utterly satisfied always. Surely there was more to the act of sex than this? What she was looking for she didn't know. Love? Perhaps. But then it would have to be the great hopeless yearning love of obsession or fantasy, which she had felt brush her in earliest youth when only unattainable beings off a screen were the fodder of her desires.

Sex, as she had it, was like eating. You were hungry, you ate, enjoyed the food very much, felt good, went on to do something else.

For Patrick it seemed to be the same.

They were not, perhaps, very experimental – but why did they need to be when fairly straightforward caresses and positions brought such exquisite paroxysms? Nor was it some sort of sexual acrobatics which Susan craved. As with everything to do with Patrick, she did not ultimately evolve a theory, or dwell on any of this very much.

At the station, as on the bus, they bought their own tickets. The train seemed exciting, as if they were going away together on holiday to some new place – instead of back into a disintegrated past.

Susan stared at the railway banks of grass, the purple and lemon weeds and white butterflies.

Patrick sat reading a set book from the college. He was conscientious, in an off-hand way.

Then the light became a blond strobe between rows of poplars, and Patrick burned golden, dark, golden, dark…

Why don't I want to go back? I don't want to have to explain to those women about us painting. Ask them if we can. But why does it matter? And they'll like Patrick. They won't mind.

Do I remember her, Catherine?

The image of an old woman, like a hard grey cobweb, superimposed upon the gold-dark-gold of sunlit Patrick.

Perhaps the house isn't there anymore. Like the flats when I lived with Anne.

Susan thought of Anne, doing something with Wizz in the USA. What time was it there? About 8 a.m. Probably having breakfast then, in a coffee shop, or at the bar in the loft. Coffee and bagels, or donuts or English muffins. Or Eggs Benedict.

The last letter had contained a postcard view of Central Park, some news, (like what they ate for breakfast this spring) and some money. Quite a lot of it, in the form of an International Money Order.

Susan thought of the first money order Anne had sent, and how she had decided to break away at once from Jo, though she had only been sharing the room at Number 17 with her for three months. How Jo's face had disapprovingly fallen. How Jo had said, doggedly, "You won't manage on your own, you know. You make a mess. The washing up will be up to the ceiling and you'll get mice." Whatever happened to Jo? She sent Susan a Christmas card, also doggedly, every year, a conservative card with a slightly religious theme, inside which Jo had always written, *Hope to see you in the New Year, Best Wishes, Josie D. Cartwright.*

The train stopped and shadow came, and it was their station.

In fact, the only way to go that Susan could remember was the old one, along Constance Street, into Dun-Captain-Kirk Street, the park and Tower Road.

She was bracing herself then, in Constance Street, for the place where the flats had been removed. Bracing herself more for not caring now, than for astonishment or affront. And then they were walking by the open lunch-time off-licence and Susan saw the two women she remembered from the cats, coming out of the shop, with a pack of Coke in cans and a bulging carrier bag. A man followed them onto the sunny pavement.

Both women seemed the same as before, they hadn't changed. Jackie was still slender and boyish in her sleeveless T-shirt that showed pinkly-tanned, rounded arms and neck. Her eyes were jewel-blue, bright. The grey-haired woman had put her long hair into a ponytail, but she looked bad tempered still, frowning over her change and a box of Kit-Kats. The man was about

49

thirty, balding and gangly, with an amused face.

"Excuse me," said Susan. She felt self-consciously and fakingly adult, something that had not happened much for two or three years. "It's Jackie, isn't it?"

"That's me," said Jackie.

"And who are you?" barked the other woman, frowning worse.

"Oh, you won't remember me – I was at the house once, and you let me go round, because my grandmother was the one who owned it before. Susan. I'm Susan Wilde."

"No, I don't remember you," said the woman.

But Jackie said, "Hi, Susan."

"This is Patrick," Susan said, feeling she must, at this point.

They looked at Patrick, and Jackie said, "Hi, Patrick."

Then the amused balding man said, "We ought to get a move on, Jackie. Or we'll miss our train."

"You make it sound like the royal train," said the bad-tempered woman.

"We're going to Devon," said Jackie. "Have to get into London first."

"Ten bloody hour journey by the look of things," said the other woman. "Bloody murder."

"It isn't ten hours," said the balding man.

"Yes, all right, Clive."

Susan said, "Is someone else looking after the cats?"

"Oh, the cats are already down there. That was quite a do, I can tell you, six vanloads of the beasts. But worth it. They love the new place." Jackie delved into the carrier bag, took out a chocolate orange and sniffed it like a connoisseur.

Susan said, "But what about...?"

The bad-tempered woman said, "We got a better offer than that house. The Devon deal is a bloody mansion, with seven acres attached. We'd hardly say no."

"Cat Sams in style," said Jackie, putting the orange back in the bag. "The old house here is up for sale. But we'll get most of the proceeds from that too, so we've done really well."

Something meowed stridently and Susan saw the man called Clive carried two huge wire-fronted cat-cages, which seemed to contain two or three cats a-piece. His arms were very long; years of transporting such burdens had no doubt lengthened them.

"These are ours," he said to Susan. "They travel with us."

Patrick spoke for the first time. "So, Susan's gran's house is standing empty?"

"Oh, yes. We were actually all cleared out by last week. Some couple seem to want it, the agents said. They're prepared to do it up, and it will take some doing, I can tell you, after our lot." Jackie laughed, proud of their legacy.

The bad-tempered woman glared at Susan. "And it's haunted you know. Did you know that?"

Susan stood there.

Jackie said, "Mill, why say that?"

Something had changed, nearly indefinable. It was like the first premonition of nausea, or flu. But – up in the air.

"I'm not superstitious, you know that, Jack. But I also know that house was full of something. And the cats knew it too."

"Mildred," said Jackie.

Bad-tempered Mildred said, "Those windows that always opened by themselves. And the noises. You and Bill didn't mind them, but you two sleep like logs. I don't. And things being moved – hidden..."

Patrick said, "You're saying there was a ghost?"

"There was and is psychic activity. We've left, but that has not."

Jackie looked at Susan. "There may have been some odd things sometimes. But none of it that couldn't have a normal explanation. Mildred isn't saying it was old Mrs Wilde."

"She didn't die in the house," Susan heard herself blurt. "They found her on a park bench. She had hypothermia, probably. She was covered in frost. Her heart failed."

Mildred's intolerant face softened as if a blow had spread it.

Susan wished Patrick would say something, but he didn't, merely stood there, looking at all their faces, Mildred's in particular, almost certainly because he thought hers the most drawable face, with all those cracks and fissures of inclement temper sculpted into it.

But Mildred looked at Susan and said, "I'm sorry. I shouldn't have said anything."

"It's nearly quarter to two," said Clive, who still appeared amused, but now with a type of smiley embarrassment.

"Come on," said Jackie.

"Good luck," Susan said.

"Thanks. You too." They turned, moved off, a single entity, garlanded by raucous meows.

"Where are you going?" Patrick asked Susan.

"I want a drink."

"Right. Sure. Then we can get on."

"No, we can't. The house will be shut up. We won't be able to see anything now, or get in or stay."

"There's always some way in. We can get over the wall or something. I'm not giving up now."

He stood in the shop and waited while Susan paid for her diet Coke. Then he selected a chocolate bar for himself and bought it.

Susan felt a stab of irritation. Why did they always have to pay for everything separately – okay, meals or alcohol perhaps, but a Coke – a

51

Marathon – bus fares?

"I don't want to go there now, Patrick."

"Because of what they said?"

"No. I'm not sure."

"She had a marvellously crazy face, that older woman. I suppose she was marvellously crazy. Anyway, it'd only be your gran."

"She had to be called Grandmother, and her name was Catherine Greyglass. It isn't that. I don't want to go scrambling over walls and getting tetanus and arrested."

Astounded, Patrick stared at her. Then they stood there on the street under the high afternoon sun. Neither of them made a move either forwards or back.

He ate the Marathon.

"Look," said Patrick, "why don't we just go and see? If it's ropey or they've got security, obviously we'll leave it. But the way you spoke about it – I've got a feeling it's just what I've needed for some outdoor studies – and no one else will have anything near it. It really would help me, Susan."

So, they went on.

Of course.

She had gone up to look at the books in the book-room. Despite having been sold once, they were all still there, all those sombre black or maroon volumes stretching up and up, like bricks in the cases. And the long table was there, and on the table the glass dish. In the moonlight, the glass wasn't yellowish but grey.

Something was knocking somewhere, or tapping. Tap-tap. A tree branch on a window in a wind that didn't blow. Or something in the turned-off water pipes.

Hearing it, Susan was not disturbed. Not afraid. Even when the book-room window slid up with a sharp hiss, not even then.

But she had to get back downstairs and return to the sunken room where Anne and Anne's mother, Catherine, were confronting each other.

Susan didn't hurry. She was grown up now. She went out and along and down the stairs, and when she reached the room, she stood in the doorway, glancing about.

Why had Anne brought her at night? They never came here then. That time before the funeral, even, when they had been each day, clearing up, they had always left the house before it got really dark.

The trees outside were huge, monolithic, and heavily furred as black bears. Through the crystal panes they cast their ink-black shadows.

There was no one in the room, no one and nothing. No furniture – not even any cats now, not a single plant.

Then something screamed in a terrifying way. Susan leapt out of her skin of sleep and crashed against Patrick in the depths of the double sleeping-bag.

"Hey – what? What is it?"

"Oh God…"

"*What?*" He rolled aside and switched on the torch, blinding her with a broad eye of light.

"Something…" she said. "There was a noise."

"It's those cats in the garden. Ssh. It's all right."

She lay down against him. "Patrick, I dreamed about her – only she wasn't in the dream. Only – I think she was. Patrick?" Patrick was silently asleep once more.

Susan looked up where the eye of the torch still flamed on the ceiling of the bare upper room. Cat's-eye.

Outside she could hear them now, the eerie wailing of the small tribe of cats, which still remained rampant in the eldritch garden. She and then Patrick had counted nine or ten of them in the undergrowth outside.

The smell of cats' urine was still strong in the house, too, but Patrick dismissed it, did not seem to care. He did not mind the several boarded-up ground floor windows, or the leak which had occurred in the drains to one side and added another foul odour.

They had got in without trouble. Others had already been before them at the gate, breaking boards, squeezing through. The *For Sale* sign had *Under Offer* pasted over. There were no notices about dogs or vigilance.

He had stood on the drive, among the vast architecture of trees and thickets, and the deep green sea of nettles, gazing at dim faded wedges of cut pumpkin walls.

"The colours are like you said – but even better than you described them. It's almost prehistoric-looking out here. The whole thing is worthy of Cézanne. Or – Klimt."

To have pleased him so much should have been enough, but now it was not. She had hoped the outer wall would be impassable, and then, when it wasn't, that he would hate the house, be repelled.

The garden, where, during the afternoon and evening, they had come to see the cats, was what involved Patrick most, the glimpses of the house slotted into boughs of cabbage green foliage.

He left Susan quickly and suddenly. Taking his sketchpad and a handful of crayons and pencils, he was off, dumping his rucksack beside her in the grass, so she felt she had to stay to guard it.

Then she saw him too in glimpses, climbing a terrace by a pool clotted with enormous fretted angelica leaves, between the bay trees and the holly and rhododendrons. He sketched, leaning at angles, matching the angles of the house, perhaps.

Finally, Susan dragged the bags to one of the side doors. Standing outside this door, she could not recall it. With all the boarded windows, only the colours of the house – as Patrick had partly said – were really as she had recollected them. Ivy was growing in festoons along brickwork and drainpipes.

53

She thought the door would be locked. But it gave. Very likely the others had already broken in.

Patrick was by then up an apple tree, among the last of April blossom.

She shoved the bags inside the door, then sat down on the path in the sunlight, her back to a wall.

Later, she began to see the cats, some black and white, and a tabby one, then three gingers, moving singly, or poised in groups behind ferns or high grass. They must be escapees from the flight to Devon. Had Jackie known?

Somehow – I don't remember that apple tree. Did they plant one – a mature one? Oh, he's climbing down now. Nor that monkey-puzzle up there. They always look man-made, monkey-puzzles, but by someone very artistic. Made out of papier mâché, then covered with prickly black velvet.

The sun shifted. The path sank violet with shade, and it became colder.

At last Patrick walked over. "Don't you want to make any drawings?"

"No. Thanks."

"Okay, let's take the bags in. See where we can sleep tonight."

"Do you still want to?"

"Sure. That's fine." As if to please her, since *she* wanted to, which she had (feebly?) tried to tell him she did not.

"This light," he said, "is so good. Look at the sunshafts. I'd like to set up for a quick study with paint – just gouache. Before the light goes."

It was after five-thirty. Beyond the doorway, the house gaped in cracks of shadow, split with long passages and the side of a staircase. It looked totally unfamiliar. Susan might never have been here before. Changed so many times by the on-building of Catherine and Richard Wilde, did the house still go on altering itself, adding parts, shifting rooms around?

"I'm hungry," Susan said.

"Yes, I am. Did you bring anything?"

"No. You do the bags. I'll go down to the high street. What do you want?"

They decided on fish and chips, and he said keep the bill, he would give her his share when she came back.

"It's all right," she said briskly. "Anne sent some money. I'll get it."

When she and Anne had lived in Constance Street, they took a different route to reach the high street. She almost thought of doing that now, to make the walk longer. But that would mean going back through the park, and they had crossed the park earlier and it had subtly depressed her again, it's barren openness, its increasing irrelevance.

Westering sun lay brazenly along the roads. The roar of homeward traffic rushed like the sea.

Homeward, she thought. All those people going home.

Susan thought of Anne, of going home to Anne in the various flats. Of nights when Anne stayed in and taught her card games, or they read books, curled in the armchairs, or watching TV, and sometimes ate toasted cheese sandwiches with grilled tomatoes before going to bed. Susan never ate cheese now. A small price to pay for good skin. But even so, one more fun delight forever lost.

Had she been happy then, as a child, with Anne? Yes, quite happy.

As she stood in line in Chiporama, Susan weakly regarded her nostalgia for a past only some three or four years away.

Wizz had stopped the past. Sliced it clean through. As she had known she wouldn't, she hadn't seen Anne since. Oh, seen photographs Anne sent, there had been a ton of those, usually with Wizz – on a beach in Florida, at a wine-tasting in New England... that sort of thing. And she and Anne had spoken now and then on the phone, but seldom, for Susan's phone was always a shared one in a hall, and unless a time was scrupulously pre-arranged – and stuck to by Anne – the phone was not often free.

She looked happy, Anne. Always slim and vivid, well-dressed, tanned, her hair still undergoing metamorphoses – *Do you like this short style? Wizz says he likes it for the summer.* And, *Don't you think this curly mane is neat? Eve fixed it for me. We had a ball.*

Wizz too was tanned and well-dressed and looked a bit fatter. But Susan tried not to see him in the photographs. Because of Wizz she pushed them all into a box at the bottom of the curtained-off rail that was her wardrobe. Because of Wizz, and not wanting to see him, even the ones of Anne on her own. (Husband and wife: one flesh.)

When Susan got back to the house with the fish and chips, a bottle of wine and a cheap corkscrew, Patrick had vanished deep into the garden.

She thought of eating her fish first, before locating him. The food was almost cold by now anyway.

But then she went to look for him.

The garden never struck her as anything but abnormal. There was something more than verdancy or undiscipline about it. Prehistoric was Patrick's word, but an apt one.

Briars clawed at her, rose bushes that had become tall hedges, all thorns. Paths tunnelled through the black green cavities between terrace-sides, clumps of giant docks, and trees whose roots had cracked up the paving as if a bomb had fallen.

"Here I am. You wandered right past me."

"I've been trying to find you for an hour."

She thrust the fish and chips at him. She didn't know where they were, in some insane wilderness or forest, staring out through a sort of hole in the trees, at a ruin with boarded-up windows, while the sun died and the sky turned khaki.

"You seem fed up," he said.

"I am."

Did he even hear her? Yes, he heard, and was sympathetic – but indifferent. They were two separate people. They were bound to have unlike

55

states of being. It didn't concern him. Painting did.

His painting of tonight was slapdash, watery, effective. They drank the wine.

The sky looked better now, a blue-grape dusk with some stars. Now and then, as the shadows meshed the garden into solid darkness, the whitish forms of two or three cats glimmed and faded.

"What a wonderful place," he said.

"Is it?"

"Don't you think so? We were lucky, getting in before they started pruning and cutting down and wrecking everything."

But the wine made her feel better. The wine said, Oh, it's all right.

"That house," he said, "is strange, isn't it? I just put the bags upstairs. There's a room there with some old curtains on the windows. People have got in. Someone had a fire in a fireplace, recent, could have burnt the house down. How many rooms are there, do you know?"

"No, not really. I told you, my grandparents built a lot on."

"Why didn't you get the house, Susan?"

She glanced at him. In the dusk, Patrick too was a shadow, with gleaming cat's eyes.

"I said. Anne and Catherine didn't get on."

"I wish you had," he had said. "I wish it was yours."

"So you could come here and paint it," she said.

"Yeah."

And the wine said, Oh, it doesn't matter.

Perhaps the wine, or the greasy fried fish, caused her to dream of the book-room. And of the sunken room below.

For a long while after she woke from it, Susan lay tensely, with the torch-splash above her like a parasol of useless hope, listening to Jackie's cats courting and fighting in Catherine's garden.

Then she must have slept again, because she woke up and bright light was coming in at the threadbare curtains.

Had she dreamt anything this time? No.

Patrick, though, had.

"I was following this old woman all through the house," he said to Susan.

"What old woman?"

"Well, I thought it was probably your grandmother."

"You don't know what she looked like. What did she look like in the dream?"

"Well," he said, "really more like that one we met in the street – Mildred."

"She wasn't like that."

They ate the now-stale buttered rolls Susan had also carted back from Chiporama and drank some Coke he had brought. Susan offered him the money for her Coke, and he accepted it, even though she had paid for the previous night's meal.

None of the taps worked in the upstairs bathrooms, but downstairs, he said, was an old cloakroom, where the cold tap was still on for some reason.

Susan did not use this cloakroom. She had squatted outside in the rhododendrons to pee and would attempt nothing else until they went to the nearest pub at lunchtime.

During the morning, Patrick worked again outside, somewhere in the garden, and Susan sat again on the path by the house wall, in the sun, reading a novel. She was bored and uncomfortable, unwashed and indigestive. She kept thinking about Anne, and her own childhood. Not Catherine, though. She did not think about Catherine.

Then there was a noise behind her, above her, up in the house. It sounded like someone easing up a window. Susan stayed where she was. Then she rose and walked out, and down as far as the apple tree, and stared back and up through the towering evergreens, to the upper storeys. But nothing seemed to have happened.

They took their bags to the pub; they had both said it would be unwise to leave them behind. Besides, Susan needed her spongebag.

Patrick put down his beer glass. "Do you want another?"

"Yes, please. No, not wine – here's the money. Could you get me a gin and tonic?"

When he came back, he said, "I think there's someone in the house, Susan. Apart from us, I mean. You know I saw there'd been a fire lit. I could hear someone walking about this morning, before you woke up. Very soft. And then when I was painting, I saw someone at one of the windows."

Susan drank her gin. "Who?"

"Couldn't see. Just someone looking out."

She thought of Anne, and the other flat, with the balcony and the ashes of the day and the first time the name *Wizz* had been spoken. What was *Wizz* meant to mean? A whiz-kid. A *Wizard*?

Patrick said, "I think I'll call it a day. And you don't want to paint anyway, do you. And maybe it's not that safe hanging about there."

"I thought you loved it," she said, "and didn't care."

"Why are you narrowing your eyes like that?"

"Am I?"

"I've just done enough," he said, dismissive. "It's all the same, isn't it? All the views are alike. Let's go back. We could go into college. Or just stay at my place."

Surprising herself, she felt rebellious. She wanted to say, No, now *I* want to go to the house. I want to make love in the garden, and rush indoors and scare the squatters and light a fire and dance on the bare floorboards.

"All right," she said.

He's boring me, she thought, as they sat in the train. *Is he? Not how he looks, he looks amazing. And his painting is great. But – this not talking about anything. Not doing anything.*

He isn't interested in me. I'm not, in him. I want to be, would be. But he never lets me see. I don't know...

Even so, they gravitated back to Belmont Court, and had a bath, and then had vibrant sex. That evening there was a party, and they went to it, Patrick incredibly handsome in his white shirt with the straps. And she thought, *This is all right. It doesn't matter. Yes.*

IIII

Next summer, about two months after Patrick had gone, Anne called Susan at five to midnight.

The moment she heard the phone rattling down in the house, Susan knew it was Anne. Perhaps because it was one of Anne's times – her times of return in the past.

"I'm sorry, did I wake you?"

"No. I think you woke a couple of people though."

"Too bad – or are they giving you grief? Tell them it's your mother."

"It's all right, really. How are you?"

"Wonderful. I'm wonderful. Or Wizz says so. It's evening, about 7 here, and ninety in the shade. We're going to dinner with the Sepplevines – I only have a moment. But I just wanted to let you know. I'm coming over next Monday."

"Over..."

"To London. What do you think?"

"That's – are you? Is Wizz coming too?"

"No, can't. We're having the apartment done up, he has to be around to monitor the builders, and anyhow he's up to his eyes at work. But he said I should have a break, come and see you. It's just a trip, about five days, I think. But we can meet and do things. English things. I bought you the most sensational dress this afternoon. I won't say what it cost. Wizz said you ought to have some New York clothes."

Susan's voice, which had sounded only mildly affable and concerned when she spoke of Wizz, now sounded mildly enthused. "I can't wait to see. But Anne – you do know I'm generally a size sixteen."

"Oh, these are fine, baby, don't fuss," said Anne. She had never lost her English accent – which was apparently very popular with and intriguing to all their US friends, even to taxi-drivers and waiters in bars. Only her syntax had sometimes altered. "Look, honey, I'll call you Sunday night – a bit earlier – when I confirm my flight. Okay?"

"Yes. I can't believe..." Susan heard herself saying, her voice now suddenly puzzled and unsure, "that I'll see you. You really are coming?"

"Still Susan," said Anne. "Why else am I phoning you up at the dead of night?" She seemed tickled, herself excited, in all her whirl of active and opulent life, that she was going to meet her daughter.

They met in London, at Anne's small, plush hotel by Regents Park. Susan was nervous. She had put on a loose black summer dress which made her look slim, and showed off her white skin that never browned, try as she sometimes had, and pale gold sandals, and earrings, to be festive.

Anne came straight down to the foyer. Once Wizz had looked like a film star. Now Anne did.

Her hair was very short and sleek and ice-blonde, shining and expensive. The cream linen dress was expensive too, entirely plain. On her left hand, but not on the wedding finger, was a square-cut and brilliantly faceted emerald, as big as a five pence piece. Her golden hands had pearl-white nails.

She was immensely, and seemingly totally, tanned. She looked as if she had been dipped in liquid amber and brought out evenly coated. But as they drew closer, Susan noticed the sun had also cracked Anne's surface here and there. They were couth, fine cracks, but they were cracks.

"Honey!"

Heads had turned already anyway. How Anne looked, walked, her clothes and ring, her costly scent. Though the hotel was a place for the moneyed, not many of them, for all their dollars, had managed to look like Anne.

Susan hugged Anne carefully, afraid to spoil her immaculate veneer. Anne had no such reservations it seemed. Her embrace was warm and strong – hard. Her body felt hard. Susan wondered why, for Anne had never carried any superfluous flesh.

"How are you? My God, you do look sweet. Look at you. Your face is so pretty, Susan. And your lovely eyes. Why didn't you ever send me a photograph like I asked you?"

"There were never any really nice ones. I kept waiting for a really nice one…" (Actually, waiting for Anne to stop asking. How could Susan send a photo of herself that Wizz might, even for a split second, look at?)

"But now here you are. Susan Wilde."

Anne's eyes were alight. Not moist, but vivacious and full of excitement.

She's more excited than I am.

"You're not feeling tired?"

"Oh, I never have this jet lag stuff. I sleep on the plane. I feel fantastic. Let's get some lunch, I *am* starving."

Anne drank a vodka tonic (no longer gin) and Susan a glass of cold white wine, as they leafed through the pink and fawn menus. It was nearly two o'clock, the restaurant half empty, but no one hurried them of course.

"I can't believe you. My God, Susan. Look at you. It's been almost four years. Why wouldn't you ever come over and see us?"

"I wanted – it's just – the college, and the holidays are so short to get anything arranged. And they give you holiday projects to do…"

"Yes, yes. Well you're nearly through with that. Come in the fall, yes? We'll

59

lay on the red carpet treatment."

"Mmm. Thank you. Only I may have to do an extra course then. One of the tutors, Rod Ayres, he wants me to do a specialist course on design, book jackets, that sort of thing. He knows some people in publishing." She added the mysterious proviso, the Masonic code everyone seemed to grasp but herself. "It could mean real work, a job."

But, "Rod Ayres?" said Anne. "What an English name."

"I think he's Irish."

"Well, but what happened to your Patrick?"

"Rod's a *tutor*. I still see Patrick," Susan lied.

"He sounded very fuckable," said Anne, jolting Susan. "Now I've embarrassed you. I get used to the States. Our crowd is pretty open in what we say."

"We – yes, we have sex together."

"And you're on the Pill. Good. Thank God for intelligence."

They ordered. Susan grapefruit and then grilled chicken, Anne smoked salmon and steak with mashed potato.

"So what is Patrick going to do after college?"

"He's already got into the Royal College of Art. He's actually there this year. They raved about him, so he started early."

"Impressive."

But Anne had lost interest in Patrick's prowess as an artist. Would she have been more inclined to hear details of his sexual abilities?

Susan thought, *I don't know what to say to her. All this is so stilted.*

Perhaps extra alcohol might have helped – but after her vodka Anne only drank water with the meal, so Susan did that too.

In any case, Anne then took over the conversation, effortlessly at last. She spoke about America, and about Wizz, about cities and landscapes, about going to Canada last fall, (the spectacular leaves), about their friends, and their friends' houses and apartments, that all seemed to be in areas named things like this or that Heights.

The last time Susan had been in London was with Patrick, after the Royal College had accepted him. They had gone out (splitting the bill) for a meal at a steak-house, and afterwards he hadn't invited her back to his new flat, they had just walked along the Embankment, and parted at Charing Cross, presumably for ever.

"Let's go shopping this afternoon," said Anne. "But first come up to my room. I want to give you all the things I've brought you."

Up in the room, drink became available again, a bottle of Smirnoff, ice, glasses, tonic and limes. A waiter conveyed this, and on his way out Anne tipped him two pounds.

"Try this on." Anne didn't work now. Like everything else, including the lunch, Wizz had in fact bought all this, everything.

The dress was red, with a halter neck, low in the back and very short. The vaunted price must be in the silk, not in the *amount* of silk.

Susan got into it, feeling uneasy, not taking off her bra, which then looked tacky and ridiculous. But the dress did anyway. It was too red, too showy. However, it did fit.

"It's great, Anne. I'll wear it to the next party."

"Wait till you see the blue one. Yes, now your eyes are blue. But I like it when they look grey. Mine have got greener. But yours are like mine used to be."

There was also a make-up kit, a miraculous object, like a child's paintbox, which seemed to have all the colours in the world, even turquoise mauve for the eyes.

Anne drank another couple of vodkas as Susan struggled to get through her single. Then Anne stopped drinking.

"I have to go down to Brighton tomorrow. Something Wizz asked me to drop off to a business colleague. Wizz wants me to meet this man, his wife – charm them, Wizz said. They have a big house, Tudor, I think Wizz said. I'd ask you to come, but they might think it was a bit much, two of us turning up."

"That's okay. I should go into college tomorrow."

"All right. But I'm only here six days. When I get back Wednesday, come up and stay. I'll book you into the hotel, yes?"

"Yes, yes great."

"It's so strange," Anne said, "seeing you. You know I'm hardly a possessive mother. But you're not mine now. You're your own person."

"Am I?"

"I'm impressed with you, Susan," Anne said. "The way you stuck to your guns. I mean, about staying here. Getting on, on your own."

A desolate wave rolled in through Susan, and retreated, leaving unidentifiable sticky flotsam behind on her inner skin.

"This house I have to get to is at some place called Rothsdean. No, it isn't Tudor. I can't remember what Wizz said it was."

Abruptly Anne's perfectly managed face changed. It seemed to loosen and sag a little on the firm bones. "I'll tell you. I wasn't going to. We had a bit of a fight, Wizz and I. One of the reasons he sent me over, to make up for what happened. I probably shouldn't tell you."

Susan didn't know what she was expected to say or feel. Did the idea of Anne and Wizz falling out aggravate or please her? Not please. It wouldn't have – it hadn't – lasted. Was anyway – too late.

"We're over it all now. That was in June. He had a little fling, shall I euphemise. You're *slow*, Susan. I mean he was screwing someone else."

"…oh."

"Yes. Oh yes. I found out because the damn girl wouldn't let it go. Kept calling him up at the loft. I said to him, 'Who is this bimbette called – would you believe it – Madison, who keeps calling you?' He said, 'She's from the office. She's dumb, forgets stuff all the time, calls me to ask me.' Then one afternoon I came back with Eve, and there was this Madison, standing downstairs, and she said to me, 'I have to see Wizz'. And Eve went scarlet. And, well, I figured it out finally. The little dope made a scene, then I told her what I thought of her. Then Eve took her outside and shooed her away. I don't know what Eve said, but it was effective. And when he came back that evening, I tackled him."

Susan sat gazing at Anne. Had she ever heard Anne so voluble?

Anne said, "He admitted it. Straight off. He said he was sick of her, couldn't get rid of her, had been trying. It just happened one time he was away alone, and she was a stand in for his regular assistant, Chloe. I guess Madison made all the running. Do you know, this Madison was the ugliest little bitch I've ever seen? She had bushy black coarse hair, all over the place, and little girl shoes. Skinny. I mean so thin you could snap her in half. And glasses, let's not forget those. She is blind without them, I gather. But she was kind of young, you know," said Anne heavily. "Only about twenty-five. I couldn't miss that. I said to him, 'If you want younger women, let's call it quits, Wizz.' And – he started to cry. Well, we made it up. It's okay now. Really, it's okay now. And we went to Bermuda for a while. And then he said, let's get the apartment done, fresh start, and he said, 'You go and see that girl of yours. Tell her to come over. And he bought me this ring. Did you notice the ring?'"

"It's beautiful."

"It's vulgar," said Anne. "Or it would be, if it weren't an emerald. He was talking about diamonds, but I said I am not Liz Taylor, Wizz. You note, the finger. I never wanted to marry. That wasn't the deal."

By the time they left the hotel it was late to shop. They wormed in and out of boutiques tucked in among white pillars, then ended up after all in the park, watching ducks and having cups of tea at a plastic table.

"I miss this," said Anne. "That exact wet green in the water. Just that shade. It isn't ever like that, there. I don't know why. I'm crazy. It's just me. Wizz says England is like a back garden, and the States is the real world."

This is my mother, Susan thought.

Really, this is Anne.

Then the ducks did something quaint and spontaneously they both laughed and for a second it was the past, on-going uninterrupted time that had never shifted, and then they stopped laughing, and it was gone again now, and different, not the old Susan and Anne, but the new Susan and Anne, with Wizz and the Atlantic still between them.

When Anne didn't ring on Wednesday, Susan thought she was undoubtedly at last tired, after the journey to and from Brighton performing Wizz's errand, on top of the flight. Thursday came and began to go. Susan phoned the hotel. "Ms Wilde? Yes, she's due back Saturday."

Saturday was the set day for Anne's departure.

Susan thought there must be some mistake and resumed waiting for Anne to ring her. Was she worried? She told herself she wasn't. But even so the little gnawing knot in her stomach that kept her from college, and haunting the downstairs hall for the phone, did not make her feel anything for Anne – but a little gnawing knot.

On Friday morning Anne called.

"Susan, I am so sorry. No, I'm still at Rothsdean. It's been an experience. Oh, I wish I'd brought you with me, Keith said it would have been fine – I should have risked it. This house, it's like a stately home. Genuine Georgian. The Prince Regent, it seems, used to visit. In acres of parkland. There's a boating lake. I've had the most fantastic time. But, God, Susan, I'm sorry, I'm not coming up to London again, there just isn't time. The hotel is sending my stuff down, Keith arranged it all. A powerful guy, I may say, and she is very nice. Susan, it's just too much hassle, you see, and I can get to Gatwick so easily from here – they've seen about changing the flight and everything – look, I have to go. I will write you as soon as I get back. And you'll come over and see us, Wizz and me, in the fall, won't you? That's a must."

Rod Ayres tired Susan, talking always about the 'technical side' of drawing, reducing art relentlessly to a kind of mathematics. He was thin and smelled too much of aftershave. Though over fifty, she thought, he had begun to seem interested in her in an amorous way. At first, she hoped it was just his manner, then she realised from things said to her by other students, that they were considered to have something 'going'.

Susan became increasingly frustrated, feeling she must keep in with Rod Ayres to ensure fulfilment of the Masonic code of the Job, but wanting to avoid him. He knew she was no longer unavailably involved with Patrick.

As Rod lit his fifteenth cigarette, his voice droning, Susan thought of Anne, re-installed by now in Manhattan with the straying Wizz. She thought of Anne's odd new garrulousness, her rhythm of talking which seemed to have altered so much, perhaps only inevitably mirroring the phonetics of the people she now spent all her time with. The mirror too, obviously, of Wizz.

"So, we'll go and see old Mike, see what he can suggest. Then maybe I'll take you for lunch, eh, Susan."

"Oh, I can't," she said. "Sorry."

Rod looked displeased. Affronted even, as if she had loudly burped or spat at him.

What was she supposed to do? If she simply said, 'I'd hate to have lunch with you, or anything else', he would cease to assist her up the ladder of Work.

"I have to see a relative."

"I thought your mother was now in the States again?"

"Yes. I have to visit my grandmother," Susan said.

"Your grandmother? Do you have such a being?"

"Oh yes."

Why did I say that? Never mind. His ruffled plumes were settling.

"Keep the old folk happy, eh," agreed Rod, refusing to see that to Susan, and the other students, he was one of the happy-needy old folks, too.

So, I'm coming to see you Catherine.

Sitting on the train, alone this time, Susan did not feel strange. She felt slightly amused.

Another day off college, but then, she'd have lost far more of them if Anne had returned and she had stayed with her at the hotel.

But what, really, was she doing?

After the bus and train, another bus, then Constance Street, which now meant absolutely nothing, and then the other street and the park, which was full of a schools' match of football, boys shrieking and jerseys. And Tower Road. But Tower Road was meaningless, too. The vast houses looked smaller and a lot of trees seemed to have been scythed down. Even the two great oaks on the grass as you approached the final wall, had been viciously pruned, and had produced hardly any summer leaves.

The witch's house. The vegetable house. The Labyrinth.

Susan loitered along the wall. It was stripped of most of its creepers, the stonework tidied up. The *For Sale – Under Offer* board was gone, and the old iron gate was gone, replaced by a new green-painted wooden door, with a name in iron letters on it: *Borders.*

Why had Susan come here? Why had she come here the other two times? Patrick had wanted it last time, yes, but it was more than that. She could have resisted. And she had come here before then, the first occasion, when Jackie and the cats had Catherine's house.

Was it the lure of the past, where things were safer since they had already happened?

Surely, the past hadn't been in itself that appealing, *not* safe, or really ideal in any form.

Did this always happen? Any previous time, however dull or bad, was going to seem better than the time you were stuck in now?

Susan opened the green door by its natty metal ring, thinking as she did so of the green door which led to the Afterlife or astral plane in H.G. Wells.

And the door did open. Not surprisingly, of course. Deliveries, postmen, Jehovah's Witnesses would need to get in.

The drive had been cleared substantially, the trees cut close, as if pushed back. Things had a glossy, well-kept garden look, and framed by their widened avenue, the house broke clear, shocking Susan. It too had been stripped and cleaned, and repainted a bold, dazzling primrose. There were shutters on some of the upper windows, polished blue, like the front door.

A vague rumble she had been aware of now solidified into a moving machine, some sort of small excavating digger, trundling out around the far side of the house. Earth sprayed about it. She could see anyway, as Patrick had predicted, dense vistas of growth had vanished. Open space was in Catherine's garden now, spatially marked by the poles of so-far surviving trees.

I'm trespassing.

What now? What now?

What did she want from this ever-metamorphosing place?

As she walked along the drive between the neatly manicured plants, the gaps of ground from which nettles and docks and briars had been wrenched, Susan formulated her plan. A silly plan, and why anyway do it? But why do anything – it was all a sort of game, with intractable yet deadly-inane rules.

There was a bell, as there had been in the days of Catherine and Mrs Danvers. It shrilled through the house in a horrible attempt at two melodic notes.

At the same moment the digger started to make enormous gulping sounds.

No one would hear.

Standing there, Susan realised the stained-glass panels of Catherine's door had been incorporated in this other one. She thought of wading through the pool of coloured lights inside, jade and crimson, the last okay part of Sunday before her grandmother.

The door opened.

"Ye-es?"

Susan felt herself blushing, but took no notice of it, carried on. (What point was there ever in taking too much notice of the constant betrayals of the body?)

"I'm sorry to bother you. I'm looking for Jackie – she used to live here, the cats' charity, Cat Samaritans…"

"Jackie. Oh yes," said the woman who had opened the door, her face in turn betraying her, too, hardening and seeming fixed and intent. "Yes, I've got her address somewhere, Devon, I think. Come in a minute. I'll have a look."

"So you knew Jackie?"

"Yes – I had a cat from her."

"Of course. Yes. We had to contact her about some of the cats that were left behind. They kept on sneaking in and fouling, which was a bit of a drag – the house was nearly a ruin, you know, not kept up at all – and we were trying so desperately to get everything fixed, and the decor sorted out."

The decor in the wide hall was now Pale Milk, (Olivia said) with one Coffee wall and some Chinese Red accents. In the side room where they now were, a large room Susan didn't recall – perhaps made out of two rooms knocked through – it was darker Coffee, with notes of Royal Blue, and kaftan upholstery.

Everything smelled immensely clean, slightly of paint still, and of induced aromas, *pot-pourri* and scented candles, and the vast cloud of roses and freesias in a black pot by the fireplace, (which had green marble inlay.)

Olivia rummaged vigorously through some old address books from a bureau. She seemed one of those effortlessly groomed, youngish women that Susan had always marvelled at on TV, or in London – they appeared to spring out of bed or the shower sparkling, and fully clothed, the make-up minimal on unblemished matt skins, and their hair washed and made delicious in the night by pixies.

Olivia's hair was long and densely blonde, as blonde as Anne's had been, but this looked natural. Unlike dyed hair, the roots were of a deeper, gleaming platinum colour, by the hairline and the casual, perfectly designed robot parting.

Susan watched Olivia with envy and some uneasy visual pleasure. Olivia was the Unattainable State, the patently *other* kind, as were her conditions, her persona, everything about her.

She had told Susan quite a lot, quite quickly and fluently, as if telling strangers who she was came quite naturally. Her husband, Jeremy, was in the City now in his twelfth-floor office above the Thames. A girl – an au pair, Susan deduced – that Olivia seemed to call Dosha, was due to come in and bring them coffee for which Olivia had shouted lightly along the hall.

"Here we are. Yes. Now – Jackie – I can't read the second name, Jem's awful handwriting – but I expect you know… look, see if you can make it out."

Susan took the book and carefully copied out Jackie and the cats' address in Devon, on a piece of paper from her bag.

While she was doing this, the girl who must be Dosha rushed into the room.

"Dosha – gently, gently –" said Olivia. But her voice oddly had an edge of something that did not, suddenly, belong to the flawless Olivia-Jeremy World.

"Olivia – it's there again – it's there on the stairs. I see it when I am coming to go out of the kitchen – and then the faucet spouts on in sink…"

"Dosha," said Olivia, "calm down, please."

But Dosha only poised, a dark-haired slender girl of about Susan's age, waving her hands and her eyes wide.

"Oh dear," said Olivia. She glanced at Susan. "It doesn't do anything, Dosha. You know that."

"It is *there*."

"Yes, it's there. Look, go back and get the coffee. It'll be gone by now. It always goes as soon as we see it, doesn't it?"

"I don't want to see it."

"No, but you have and now it'll be gone."

Dosha slunk out of the door.

Olivia turned round and looked at Susan. Her own eyes were big and frank. "We have a ghost, you see."

Susan said, "Do you? Really?" She sounded polite, quite interested, pragmatic but open-minded.

"Actually, Susan, I was hoping – as you knew Jackie a bit – that you might know something about this – oh this *bloody* house." Olivia flushed angrily. She stood up and flexed her well-shaped legs in their tailored jeans. "When I think of the K's we've poured into it, the mess it was in. And the garden, they're still working on that, and the landscape gardener – all these things we've had done. And then no sooner did we get in the bloody place than all this starts. I thought it was a poltergeist, but Jeremy says they're always caused by young children – and we don't have any kids."

Susan felt now as if she were not necessarily operating her own body. As if she were only sitting up inside her head, like Jeremy in his office gazing down like God on the city and the river.

"What happens?"

"Oh – just lots of unimportant *awful* things. All the time. I hoped it would stop. I had a friend in, she works with crystals and that sort of stuff, professionally. She exorcised the house for us, she got the energies going the right way – or so she said. But it actually made things worse. Look, did Jackie ever mention...?"

"Well, yes. She said there was a knocking sound and windows opened by themselves. And Mildred – one of the others – said that things went missing..."

"They *do*, Christ knows they do. I lost my first wedding ring – I mean the ring from my marriage before I married Jem. I don't wear it; I keep it in a box – and then it was gone. And I thought for a minute Dosha had – well it was terrible, because she's a darling girl, from Helsinki, and she would *never* – and when I got that sorted out, the ring reappeared – *under* the box, where I'd looked – but then my jogging shoes went missing – *jogging shoes*. And oh, lots of things. And yes, there are sounds. Not knocking, I haven't heard that, perhaps Dosha has – more – sort of *breathing – pacing...*"

Susan stared. She saw that Olivia was pale, Pale Milk, like the hall without the splash of stained-glass window light thrown there.

"But the worst thing is, we do see things."

Susan no longer felt removed. She felt as if she were trapped, one of the lesser stars, in a horror film. "What?" she fumbled out.

Dosha came in wobbling a tray of priceless coffeepot and cups, and some exotic biscuits. She seemed calmer now, as Olivia had told her to be. Putting her tray on a coffee table, Dosha said, suddenly, "It has gone."

"It always does," said Olivia. But she had by now frightened herself out of any pretence at organisational cool, and Dosha stood there, shaking her head bleakly.

"Mr Jeremy say," said Dosha, "he has never been the one of us to see this thing."

"No, he hasn't, the bastard. He never sees it. Or hears it. He says it's possible but won't believe *we* have it. He thinks I'm mad. Dosha's mad. That we're hysterical and affect each other and imagine it. Even about the ring, he said *I'd* lost it."

"What is it," said Susan, "that you see?" She didn't want to know.

Dosha spun round and stared at Susan wildly. "Up on the stair, out in passage. Or in rooms. Once in my room – is on the wall – like a *fly*…"

"Yes, she saw it in her room, didn't you, Dosha. And I have, in the bedrooms and even in Jem's study. Down here, everywhere."

Susan heard herself again: "Is it – a person?"

"No," said Olivia surprisingly, and with abrupt flatness, most of the energy seeming to leave her. "I can't describe it. It's – a sort of absence of anything else. Like – oh, if you look at something too bright and there's a dark patch on your vision a few moments. Only not like that. And then taps turn on, and sometimes lights, or they go out when they're on. They fuse all the time, too. At least Jeremy has to believe in *that*."

The coffee sat on the table. They all looked at the coffee, not making a move to try anything with it.

Susan said, "What will you do?"

"I hoped you might know something. I haven't had the courage to ring up Jackie. Honestly, I'm afraid of what she might say, after the thing with the cats."

Susan said, "I do know an old woman used to live here, once." As she said it, she felt the hair rising on her own scalp.

The digger outside had fallen quiet again. An enormous silence filled the house, a stillness as if time had come to a stop.

"An old woman. Oh God. And I suppose she died here."

"No, I don't think she did."

"Only that was it about the cats. Let me explain. Even though this will sound crazy. Crazier. Cats were in the garden, a lot of them, about fourteen. I saw them, Jeremy saw them. The *builders* saw them – some of them left bits of food, which Jeremy put a stop to. But the cats got in anyway and peed up the walls, apart from screaming the place down every night. So I called Jackie and said could she do anything about the cats she'd left here, and Jackie said they hadn't left any cats, they were all accounted for. So I said it must be a feral colony then, that had moved in when the house was standing empty for a few weeks, what a strange *coincidence*, sounding sarcastic because I didn't believe her. Then Jackie said, of course a few cats had died during the years they were here. Old ones or sick ones that didn't make it. Which got me thinking, because by then I'd heard the noises, and Dosha had seen something in her room – Oh, I don't know. I just know I'm bloody sick of it."

Dosha had by now sat down in a chair done in complex jazzy russet weave.

Olivia said, with fresh sharpness, "Coffee, Dosha."

Then Dosha got up and poured out coffees and handed them round with the biscuits.

"Could you get a priest?" Susan said, lamely.

"*Tried* that. They won't come. We're not Catholic, anyway. They're the only ones who pay attention to ghosts or demons. And what have we got? An old lady and some cats."

Susan said, "She really didn't die here, the old lady. She – I think she left the house and went into the park and they – she was found on a bench. It was cold."

"Christ."

Dosha said, "That's why she is here, then."

"Oh Dosha," said Olivia.

"She has to come back she thinks, though she should go elsewhere, for she's dead. So she goes the wrong way, and is stuck now."

"No, Dosha. Just shut up."

Dosha said in a low stubborn howl, "I have written to my uncle. I am to be going home."

"All right, Dosha. Let's talk about it later with Jem."

Out in the wide hall, the light had moved from the glass in the door.

Susan looked around. The entry into the other succession of rooms had surely been moved, it was further along. On the blank of new wall thus provided, hung a sepia photograph of a Roman aqueduct.

But she thought of how she dreamed once, of Catherine, in the sepia photograph she, Susan, had perhaps seen, or not.

"She was called Catherine," Susan said. She felt ashamed.

Olivia looked at her, evidently wanting her to go now, and to forget all this nastiness until the next thing happened.

"I mean the old woman. Catherine."

With no warning Olivia turned and shrieked violently, malevolently into the ringing body of the silent painted house: "Go to hell, Catherine! Clear out, Catherine! Fuck off! Fuck the fuck off!" Then turning back to Susan, no longer quite flawless, and hair ruffled, her eyes like those of a scared bacchante, Olivia murmured, "Great to meet you, Susan. Take care."

BOOK TWO

V

This isn't for me. It's for Flat 6C."

"I know. She's out again. Can you take it?"

Susan looked at the postman's pale, stare-eyed, harassed face. "All right."

He, or one of the many postmen who came and went, was always pushing letters for Flat 6C through her own door, which was marked, obviously confusingly, 6E. This however was a package, not very large, but too big to fit in either door.

6C was directly across the hall. Susan had never glimpsed the occupant, although she knew her name from all the wrongly-delivered-letters – Ms Crissie Fielding.

Crissie Fielding, the only truly adjacent neighbour, was very quiet. Which was also explainable if she was out a lot. The faint strains of popular music or TV that frequently strayed from the other flats, (6A, B and D) down the corridor, never emanated from 6C.

Susan took the package back into the kitchen.

Sitting at the small table, with her half-eaten croissant, she glanced over the package. Apart from the address, it bore a small label. G.D. Register.

Vaguely, Susan felt reluctant to confront Crissie-of-the-unusual-spelling Fielding with the package. (Before it had only been a matter of putting post through the letterbox.) Why on earth?

Perhaps meeting anyone, here, talking to anyone, here – which generally, so far, for a whole seven weeks, Susan had meticulously avoided – was going to feel peculiar.

She had after all met so many people here, and none of them the original person, which person she had met over and over until she was nearly thirteen, but never met, *never,* in any real sense of the word.

Susan was thirty when two quite major things happened in her life. First she won the Cameron Award for Book Cover Art and Design, a prize that made her dear to Paragon Books, and also enhanced her bank balance with an astonishing ten thousand pounds. The following month, at a party thrown by Paragon, she was introduced to R.J. He was the writer whose work had had her prize-winning jacket.

"I liked your cover," he said, rather stiffly, "thank you."

After all the fulsome praise, this sounded grudging and awkward. Susan assumed R.J. had not liked her cover for his book at all.

It had been a difficult novel to exemplify. Ornamental yet subtle and convoluted, but having to have Paragon's required bold, eye-catching image. In the end Susan had constructed the artwork from layers of cut and pasted paper, a method she hadn't employed for some years. The three main characters of the book, represented in this glowing, yet ghostly and fragmented way, seemed to catch the eye of everyone, the prize committee included.

Susan was never sure what she thought, but then she never was with her own handiwork. Sometimes, looking, months or years after, at covers she and other people had only thought adequate, she sensed genuine effectiveness. Conversely, jackets which had been enthused over repeatedly, seemed lacking in anything save the careful draughtsmanship she had learned.

She still thought of herself as a fraud who had somehow managed to fool them all, Paragon in particular, that she was a bona fide artist. In the beginning, when she had had to work full-time in Paragon's art department and was herself commissioned only to execute one or two covers a year, Susan had thought this was probably her proper station. When more cover work came her way she was always sure she would soon be found out. And since the award, she lived in a sort of ironic guilty alarm, waiting for the clock at midnight.

"I'm sorry, I did try to reflect something of the novel, but I felt I hadn't. It's a complex book. And mostly in – quartertones. The watercolours I did though, were hopeless."

R.J. gazed at Susan over his glass of red wine. He still looked preoccupied, but seeming to hear her now, if from a great way off. "But you won the Cameron," he said.

"Yes. That was wonderful."

She felt self-conscious at confessing to him what he must already know, her failure to do justice to his work.

She also felt frightened of him, had done so as soon as she saw him, a thing that hadn't happened for approximately a decade.

R.J. was forty-four, as his book jacket copy told anyone who cared to read it. He was tall, about six foot three, and heavily built, though it was bone and muscle, not excess flesh. He had an olive complexion, like a Spaniard or Greek, neither of which he was, dry dark curling hair beginning to lose its pigment, and bloodshot golden-yellow eyes like a bird of prey.

"Your glass is empty," he said next.

"Yes. I don't want any more wine."

"Let me get you an orange juice," he said, and turning round plucked one, she thought, fantastically, from thin air. This he handed to her. "No," he said, "I did like your cover. I didn't recognise it, that's all."

"No."

"But you get used to that, and at least it was attractive. It was elegant, in fact. It reminded me – not of art but music. Bach, totally precise yet cunningly split in overlapping sections."

"Your book reminded me of Chopin, the piano concertos," she returned boldly, because she felt timid and refused to be. And because he had said something that might have been pretentious, but it was not, and she wanted to aid and abet this, somehow.

"Really? Chopin. Why?"

"I can't explain. Its sadness... the under-orchestration – I don't understand music technically."

"And you *read* my book too," he said. "Few illustrators bother to do that now. They just want a note of what to draw. And my God, you've helped sell it for me, you know."

Then he half turned and said, "Oh, that's my wife signalling. I'll catch you later, Susan."

Rod Ayres had actually got her the job at Paragon. Or, his 'friend' Mike Hammond had done so. Mike had leafed through her folder as Rod perched

71

on a chair-arm, a fifty-year-old avuncular teenager. "There's some pretty good stuff here, Susan. And your qualifications are fine. Now, you've done this design course, you say?"

Susan, on Rod's suggestion, had done six months by then of the course, for which the council had refused her a grant, but Anne had sent her money.

Rod said, "She's a star pupil, Mike," and Mike had looked at him, and long after, when Susan was working for Paragon as a dogsbody in the art department, Mike had said, "Do you still see Rod?"

"Oh, no," Susan had said.

"That's probably as well. I think he was a bit serious about you."

And embarrassed by it all, and by Rod, she had said forcefully, "It wasn't ever anything like that. He was my college tutor, that's all." But Mike only shrugged.

Of course, there had been the inevitable scene, after she got the job, when Rod insisted – that was *insisted* – on taking her for a meal in an Italian restaurant.

He ordered a bottle of wine, (the first of three), at once, and before the food came downed three large glasses. He kept talking about the divorce he had had from his wife 'last August', stressing he was a free man, saying the things he would like now to do, such as going to France or Rome to paint in the summer, trying to entice her.

They ordered desert, which Susan didn't want, but, "Oh you must. Go on. Look, they've got Death-By-Chocolate..." disappointed when she only selected a fruit salad, and saying, "God, I hope you're not trying to lose weight, Susan. You're lush and lissom, you know, just right..." so she felt herself redden. Rod had the chocolate death, spooning it up like a famished child. Then he reached across and took her hand. "You'll come with me to France, won't you, Susan?"

"To France?" She looked blank, surprised. "Why?"

"Why. You know why. I thought you understood what I've been trying to say."

"No," she said dimly.

Rod still didn't give up. He leaned towards her in a wave of Mandate and said, "I really like you," in an eager young voice.

"Oh – I'm sorry. I didn't realise."

"Don't be sorry. Now you do."

"You see, I'm – *with* someone."

He looked at her. Then he drew back. "Oh yes?"

"Yes. We've been together for a year."

"You never mentioned it."

"Well... I didn't see how it was relevant."

"Come on."

Ashamed now of herself, (though why? It wasn't because she was lying), she looked away and said, "I'm sorry. But Joe and I are living together."

"Joe."

"I'm in love with him," she rushed out angrily. "I'm not going to want anyone else."

Rod looked both squashed and belligerent. "I think you might have said. I've been trying to help you."

Susan wanted to say, 'So you wouldn't have helped me if you thought there was nothing in it for you?' But she said, "Yes, I know. Thank you. You've been very kind." And then, fawningly, hollowly, "I'd never think someone like you would be interested in me."

"Why not?" he roared, making other people turn and stare, to add to the jollity of the occasion. "I'm too old, is that it?"

Then he pushed back his chair, which drunkenly fell over, threw some notes on the table, and walked right out of the restaurant. Leaving her to settle the bill, which after three bottles of wine and the deathly chocolate was considerable; the twenty pounds he had flung down did not remotely cover it. Luckily Susan had meant to go to Sainsbury's on the way home and brought extra cash.

About ten days after this, a letter arrived. *'Dearest Susan, can you forgive my irrational behaviour?'* It hadn't been, she thought, at all irrational, perfectly logical. *'I know the situation with your boyfriend, but I'd still like to see you. Nothing heavy. Do say you will…'*

She tore the letter up and put it in the bin.

Two weeks later, receiving a now regular monthly pay cheque, she had moved into another flat, where she would not have to share a bathroom. She did not send Rod Ayres her new address.

Following the Paragon party, where she had met R.J., Susan began work on a cover commission for a difficult manuscript she had been trying to read without much success. Something strange occurred. The book's anti-hero had dark curling hair and eyes described as hazel. Though in his late thirties, the anti-hero now assumed the lineaments of R.J. And suddenly, Susan could read the book. She tore up her provisional sketches and started inadvertently to draw R.J. She had been warned before never to use the appearance of any well-known actor, even where the author likened a protagonist to one. Houses had apparently been sued.

Susan did draw R.J. however, several times, on a sketchpad. The drawings dissatisfied her, naturally.

Four or five nights after the party, she dreamed she and R.J. were walking in London; somewhere, she thought, near to the British Museum.

The next morning, he called her.

"Hello, Susan."

She knew who it was, and her breathing stopped. She said, without a breath, and uncertainly, "Hello…?"

"I'd like to talk to you. Is that possible?"

"…yes."

"That's good. Shall we meet for a drink somewhere? Do you have a place you like?"

When she went to meet him that evening, the compendium of terror and joy she felt worried Susan almost in proportion to her exhilaration.

She kept saying to herself that undoubtedly he only meant to discuss something to do with business. Perhaps he had a contract with another publishing house and wanted her for another cover, there, which might cause bad feeling since she still worked part-time in Paragon's art department.

Now and then too she reminded herself he was married and had made no secret of it in front of her.

He was waiting for her outside the wine-bar, greeted her with a grave, absorbed face, and opened the glass door for her to go through.

They sat in a window, looking out over the river and its lights. It was spring, the dark still came early.

"That was nice, that you agreed to meet me. I like your dress very much."

"Thank you."

"But then, I like everything about you, Susan. Look, I'm not going to muck around. I'll just say it straight, and then if you're not interested, we'll finish our drinks and part friends. Okay?"

Stunned, mesmerised, Susan nodded.

"I'm married. I think you saw my wife. She's a lovely and intelligent woman. I won't say I've never had any relationships outside our marriage before. But it's only happened twice in twenty years. Frankly, they didn't mean that much, and both were some time ago. Then, I met you. I'd like to know you, Susan. And I'd like to make love with you more than I can say. I felt there was something between us – or was I just being presumptuous?"

"No."

"Good. Oh good, thank God." The smile broke through his face, relieved and flame-like, dazzling her. "But is the fact of my marriage a problem for you? I know it should be. It should be for me, and in a way it is, but – well. I realise this isn't a very salubrious offer."

"I don't care," Susan said.

She didn't, not then.

The wine-bar was lit by an intense bright lambency, which increased and increased, because she could plainly see it shone also for him, he felt it too.

And when he took her hand, her blood filled with a tingling sexuality that travelled through her whole body in an instant, waking every inch of her skin, outside and in, undeniable and irresistible, making age, marriage, even life, irrelevant.

It was one of those part-time days when she still put in at Paragon. When Susan got home, in the black December evening, there was the package for Crissie Fielding sitting where she had left it, on the table in the kitchen.

Susan looked at it. Then she poured herself a glass of white wine from the fridge. Taking the glass and the package through into the main room, she sat down there.

The main room of this flat was large and very beautiful from its proportions, its faultless ivory walls, and the high, high, ceiling, which was painted a translucent lavender. None of the floor-length windows were square, but Gothically arched at their tops. In here, one of these had an opaque, smooth white pane, set about with round jewels of purple and topaz stained glass. This window would have looked out on the entry and a wall, a dark space the architect obviously thought was better obscured. But Susan didn't mind the white window; she found its nacre opacity mysterious. The other windows in the room were on the opposite side, French ones stretching from floor almost to ceiling. These gave onto the gardens, her semi-private area. Three steps led down to where, against the evergreen mass of two flourishing firs, a small ivied stone Pan stood on goat legs, playing a syrinx. Beyond the curve of the trees, a green lawn, regularly mown, tumbled to a lily pond and stands of birch, after which bay trees filled the view. The gardens were magnificent, as the agent had proclaimed when showing her round. And though communal to all the flats, Susan had seldom met anyone in them, except the old man with the little dog from Flat 14G. Maybe moving in halfway through October accounted for this. On the other side of the trio of steps down to the garden, was an ironwork bench, coloured deep peacock blue. Sometimes, on an unseasonably sunny morning, Susan had sat there with her coffee. The master bedroom, which opened straight off the main room, also had French windows to the garden, these not needing steps.

Susan tapped her fingers on the package for 6C.

She had come to terms with this flat. In fact, she hadn't had to. Not really. Everything was so changed. And after the succession of rooms and poky 'self-containeds' she had had before, this was a palace. Too enjoyable not to enjoy.

So. The next step was simply to deliver a small light box to a neighbour. To ring her bell, and say, "This came for you."

It was nothing.

Nothing.

Susan put down her wine, got up and carried the package to her front door.

When she opened it, looking across the waxed wood floor of the well-maintained outer hall, she studied the exterior of 6C. Indeed, it was identical to her own door, and painted indigo, like all the doors in this section of Tower Gardens.

("There are, in all, thirty-five flats, of one, two, three or four bedrooms," the agent had announced, grandly. "They seldom come on the market.")

6C was silent, as ever. Was Ms Crissie Fielding even in? Perhaps she wasn't.

Susan took a step across the hall, and a sudden coldness enveloped her, despite the radiator which warmed the corridor.

6C was part of the sunken rooms. Yes, it was. Just as her own flat was, but you would never know, everything had been altered, partitioned, opened out, even the landscape of the garden.

Then she was at the door and she had rung the bell.

And again she thought, Perhaps she's not in.

The first time, they went to a hotel he had found, quite pleasant. They had lunch, which she couldn't eat, and then went up to a comfortable, clean room. The story was they had a plane to catch that evening, and needed to sleep, any luggage having gone on ahead. They acted up to this pretence, but whether anyone believed it, or cared, who knew.

Susan was frightened and nervous when she was alone in the room with R.J. But the moment he touched her, began to kiss her and hold her, and explore her with his hands, the most violent desire flooded her body. She had never felt anything exactly like this. It was like diving into a fiery sea. Her need gave her, too, a confidence she had never known during sex. She lost her politeness, diffidence. Any outer awareness. She wanted him to do all and everything to her, and to do the same to him, and when their untrammelled actions reached their heights, she felt herself let go of everything.

After Patrick, she had had a few brief affairs – they could not be called relationships. She had always liked sex very much, found it easy and rewarding – but beyond the obvious pleasure, unimportant.

It was not that, with R.J., her ultimate pleasure heightened – although she suspected orgasm had changed its aspect – but the act became earth-shatteringly significant. Afterwards she could not stop thinking about what had happened twice in the hotel bed. Just as, from the first, she had not been able to stop thinking about R.J.

They met a couple of times every month, usually Thursdays, sometimes Friday. He lived in Hampshire and travelling into London could only be managed like this. She wondered how he did manage even this. Presumably his wife, (who Susan knew from the party was called Maria), thought his trips were to do with his writing – jaunts to research, buy books, or visit necessary sites, publishers and agents. Or *did* she think that? Although never asking him, Susan sensed that perhaps R.J.'s Maria knew where he went, even with whom.

Some people had such arrangements. Didn't mind it. Did Maria also have somebody else?

The trouble was, R.J. was nothing to do with Maria, or anyone else. He was only to do with Susan.

She knew this was absurd. Incredibly they had their separate lives and did not only come into sentience in each other's proximity.

Sometimes R.J. could manage a night, even two, away. Then he came to stay with Susan in the latest of her self-contained Lilliputs, the one in Brashspeare Road.

These were holiday times, sometimes even extending through part of a weekend. They would cook meals in the tiny kitchen, eat out at pubs by the river, walk along the towpaths and over the local common. Their lovemaking grew slower and more sensual. They slept back to back. They told each other things about their lives, things about work and inspiration, and self-doubt, and necessary arrogance, their childhoods, people they had known. No one too recent, though. No one who had been a serious lover. Or a wife.

Sunday, if there had been Friday and Saturday, was always the day for parting from R.J., the day he went – home.

She began to dislike Sundays. There was something unwanted that must be done on them, and the next day was... school.

Susan did think about Maria, of course, inevitably, now and then. She didn't dislike Maria, was not even envious of her. She felt sorry for Maria, in case she was being deceived, and could be made horribly distressed by finding out. And, naturally, she feared Maria, for Maria could perhaps, at a stroke, end the flimsy yet imperishable bond which tied R.J. and Susan together.

Otherwise Susan did not believe their communion would end. It was only a matter of sticking to the rules. Of keeping it quiet, and keeping quiet about certain things to each other, and hoping, without ever voicing it to each other, but hoping for *what?* Maybe Maria would fall in love with someone else. Or she would die, (she was older than R.J. but not by very much.) Then again Susan steered well clear of the banal viciousness of wishing death to Maria. Besides, R.J. seemed, in his way, to love Maria. On the rare occasions when he mentioned her, (then never intimately), it was gently, fondly, and with respect. And, obviously, accustomedness.

The year passed.

Nothing altered.

They met in London – went to one of the two or three hotels which seemed welcoming, and where falsehoods were no longer offered or expected. Or R.J. came to Brashspeare Road and the kitchen, bathroom and 'studio' room woke up and grew bright.

One evening, near Christmas – a solitary strange time always for Susan, led up to by insane parties, socialising, drinking, unreal sentiment, ending in her own Christmas days alone – Susan was making R.J. a private pre-Christmas Christmas Dinner. The turkey was a chicken, but free-range, with stuffing, sprouts, roast potatoes – all tasty things she had learned to cook in the past eleven years, astonished at how easy it was to prepare food simply and well, if not inventively. There were even crackers, in shiny red jackets, and a bottle of Champagne in the fridge.

R.J. said, "I love this, with you."

Susan said, "Do you?"

"You make it fun," he said. "New. But you're young."

"I'll be thirty-one next year."

"As I said, young."

There in the candlelight, and the smoking scents of cookery, he looked, with his hawk's eyes, older, so she abruptly saw. His hair had more grey now than dark. His body seemed unchanged, tawny and muscular still from playing football and running in his youth. Yet, didn't he stoop now, a little?

A shadow of sorrow moved across Susan, as if the bright-lit light had dulled, or the candles, half of them, gone out. He was older than she was. He was the one who might die. One day, not now, but there, there ahead of them.

Susan said, "I wish we could be together. I mean I wish we could live together. Is it ever going to be possible?"

He shook his head. "No."

They had never had such an exchange before. And yet each of them slipped into it as if practiced – could it be he was?

Susan said, "I mean – wouldn't you rather be with me? I mean, would you rather? Or does Maria always come first?"

"No one comes first."

"Which means *I* don't."

"You can't, Susan. I'm sorry."

"Does she know about us?" said Susan, drinking the red wine they had already opened to give each other presents by. And by which they now gave each other this.

"Yes," he said. He was looking away from her. At the small tree she had dressed only last night, for tonight.

"She *knows*?"

"Yes."

"Does she know who I am?"

"Yes. She said you looked pretty and smart. She likes your book jackets."

"Oh, for Christ's sake…" Susan's voice had become high and loud, not pretty or smart, or artistic at all.

"You asked me," he said, flatly.

"Yes, all right. I asked you. Why does she put up with it?"

"She loves me," he said.

"And *I* love you, so *I* put up with it. That's very convenient, isn't it, for you."

He got up and walked round the small enclosure of the room restlessly.

She heard the chicken spitting in the oven. She ought to go and baste the bloody thing. Let it wait. Let it blacken.

"Susan, I've never made this a secret, to either of you."

"Very noble."

She thought, I sound like Anne.

She thought, was this how Anne went on to Wizz that time, over that girl – God what was her stupid name – Madison? Anne wouldn't have behaved like Maria. She'd have got hold of me and shaken me to bits…

"I explained. You knew the situation."

"That makes it all right."

78

"No. But I didn't lie. You could have told me to fuck off."

They stood in silence, R.J. looking at the tree, Susan looking away into the kitchen, hearing the chicken spitting and spitting like a deranged feral cat.

The bell sounded tinny, as if its battery was going.

Susan stood there, holding the package for Crissie Fielding.

Now the hall seemed too hot, though beyond the main front door, only about ten feet away, the December wind was rising, howling in the empty garden trees.

She was not at home.

Susan considered leaving the package by the door of 6C, because otherwise this might become a nuisance, trotting back and forth and never finding the woman in.

The door opened.

Her hallway, similar in size to Susan's, was illuminated by one soft rosy lamp on a side table. Its floor had stayed bare, the same waxed wood as in the outer hall. This, and the pale walls, totally unadorned, bloomed in the rose glow, floating, somehow unusual.

The girl too was limned by the light. It made her a veil around her fair, long hair. But her face, as she leaned closer, caught the low outer light in the main hall. She was beautiful, and like many beautiful things, even people, seemed familiar.

"Hello," she said. She smiled. Her smile was one of familiarity, as if they had already met several times, always happily.

"Hi. I'm from 6E. The postman brought this, this morning."

"How kind of you. Thanks." She was Susan's height. Her slim young hands slid out and took the package. She turned it over. She said lightly, "A gift from an admirer, I fear."

She must have lots of those. She was very slender, wound like a delicious pen in a silvery-white wrap. No rings, no jewellery. No make-up even on that white and unmarked skin. She seemed, from the sophisticated way she was, at least twenty-two or – three. The flat was hers, too. Susan knew very well, no one not well-off or in a lucrative job, could handle these mortgages.

It was an old-fashioned turn of phrase, and an odd thing to say: *An admirer, I fear.*

Susan moved, about to go.

"We've never met before," said the girl. "I'm Crissie."

"Yes, I know from the parcel. I'm Susan Wilde."

"Yes, *I* know too." How did she know? Oh, no doubt more wrong deliveries – which she must have refused to accept for Susan, since she, Crissie, was so often away. "It was kind of you to bring it across. Would you like to come in and have a coffee?"

An appetising coffee smell had come stealing out of Crissie Fielding's flat, along with another scent, equally appealing, fresh but faintly floral.

79

"I'd like to, but I have to take a call in a minute, from the States. My mother. Thanks anyway."

"Okay. Hope to see you," said Crissie.

Her smile was so carelessly inviting, it made Susan smile back.

She thought, *Maybe she is a lesbian, and I'm giving her the wrong impression.*

Then Crissie, stepping aside, shook the parcel and said, "I bet this is my Gerry. He will overdo the generosity."

Susan didn't know if she was expected to comment. Then Crissie said, "So long," and the door of 6C glided shut.

She was extremely familiar looking. *Who is she like?*

Someone in the movies, conceivably. But then, not really anyone *now*. More like Vivien Leigh, or the most youthful Jean Simmons – someone like that. A bit.

As she closed her own front door, Susan heard something fall brutally in her kitchen. Going to see, she found a plate had slipped from the rack into the stainless-steel sink. It was in three pieces.

The wind hit the arched windows.

Once there had come the first lesion, others followed. Soon it became a habit with them to row. To begin with he was reluctant, trying to stay calm, non-committal, decent even. He tried to make it up to her, in all the wrong ways – through sex, excursions, even buying her a new TV and video she didn't want. Vulgar and useless things.

They tried too, to be as they were. But that was now too difficult.

Susan became petulant. She whined and could not stop herself. R.J. grew taciturn. Then he stopped meeting her.

Their meetings had always depended on his phoning. He simply did not.

She thought of getting his and Maria's ex-directory number from someone at Paragon, for whom he was again writing a novel.

But what would she do with it? For all her ghastly whining, she did not have the crassness to call up their home in Hampshire. This was partly her fear of Maria and partly her pity, her sympathy, for Maria.

Susan felt sick, from the moment she woke to the moment she managed to fall asleep each night about 3 or 4 a.m. She couldn't really eat, lost half a stone in a month, which weight loss by now had no attributes of anything.

Only when she worked on a cover did she lose track of the rift with R.J. – but then only momentarily. And her work was not very good. Like a disobedient child, she was sent back by the editor to re-work the canvas massively, made a hash of it, and had to start again.

"Is something wrong, Susan?"

"No – I'm just a bit upset. My – grandmother's not well."

"Oh, lord. I'm sorry. Yes, you look worn out. Is she dangerously ill?"

"Oh no, no, she'll be all right. She's very strong. But – well. She's the only family I've got in England."

Why such a ridiculous *lying* lie? Never mind, it got her off the hook, though someone else took over the cover job. Too many more of those and Paragon wouldn't want her. Her fame from the Cameron was fading fast. As had the ten thousand pounds.

One night he called her. She thought it was Anne, who promised in a letter to call at 10 o'clock. But Anne seldom now kept any promises to Susan, including the ones of sending her more money orders, coming to England again, or of making it financially possible for Susan to visit New Jersey, where Anne and Wizz now lived. The last, of course, was a relief.

Instead of the by now slightly Americanised, at last slightly aging, voice of her mother, Susan heard R.J.

"Are you free to talk a moment?"

"Yes," she said, and fell back into the chair.

"I've missed you."

She started to cry.

Standing above herself, she thought, *Shut up, for Christ's sake*, just as she had when they rowed and she sniped and whinged.

He said gently, "Don't cry, Susan. Let's – look, I have to come up to meet Hammond next Tuesday. Shall we have dinner? Maybe we could. I'd like to see you."

They met on Tuesday. She wore a new black dress, and earrings he said were like stars. He was supposed to get back to Hampshire, but in the end he rang Maria from a callbox. Susan stood there and heard him say he had missed the train and would stay over at a hotel.

She wondered, even as they travelled to Brashspeare Road, if later he would tell Maria the truth.

This time their lovemaking was hesitant, and in the end, for Susan, disappointing. There was no longer an electric current between them. It was only sex. Had she stopped loving him, being obsessed by him? Or was she only afraid to be?

She didn't care. She had to see him, have him, even if only now and then, if only for the most methodical sex.

He looked older. But so did she, she thought.

That night, lying in bed with him while he slept, she wished Maria would die, couldn't hold the wish away, like a cruel and unavoidable sneeze. The next day it haunted her.

Sorry, Maria, she thought, after he was gone, at 8 a.m. But she cried again.

She cried off and on all through the next months. So that by the night they stopped seeing each other once more, this time for good, she was practice perfect in the abysm of tears.

Susan had made a second bedroom, which opened independently from the corridor of her flat, into her workroom. It too had a large window which looked out over the lawns, to a winter-bare apple tree and the edge of the pond. Some days after she had delivered the package, from this window Susan saw the girl walking across the grass.

Viewed in cold morning sunlight, she was arresting. The long skeins of fair hair incandescent in the sun, her slender equilibrium, and the choice look of her pale clothes. Later, Susan left her flat to go to the supermarket, and saw a white cat running along the corridor towards Flats A, B and D.

She had never seen this cat before, but now and then a few cats appeared in the gardens, pets of other residents, or even visitors from over the walls.

The cat reminded her oddly of Crissie Fielding. She didn't know why. Perhaps it belonged to her?

Susan had asked the estate agent about cats the first time, when he brought her to see the flat last spring.

"A feral colony in the gardens? Not anymore. I've never heard of it, I must say. Probably some cat place caught and re-homed them."

He had vouchsafed nothing about Olivia and Jeremy, either, let alone about Catherine. But he was very keen on the virtues of the flat, showing it off to Susan like an impresario with shares.

"Oh. There's no window in the bathroom."

"No, 'fraid not, but there *is* the latest in extractor fans. And look at *this*..." He pressed a switch, and a false window lit up, with a stained glass picture of Rousseau-esque leaves and flowers, reflecting in the midnight blue suite, with its gold sea-shell taps.

When he showed her round the gardens, which were now like a well-stocked park, with pools, roses, terraces, trimmed hedges and trees, statues and vistas, Susan had been perplexed by the exterior of the house. Naturally it had undergone endless internal rearrangements and additions and had gained about seven main entrances to give access to all the flats, plus all the arched windows, French doors, and balconies. But certain parts of the masonry had also been, she thought, cut into and excised, other portions extended outwards. But she had never been sure of its contours. Even the house had not, constantly changing its shape. Now it had been made also strong and youthful, with a succulent, painted skin. "Mediterranean Gold," described the agent. "But they repaint, when they do the other major maintenance, every five years."

With all the cover charges for the upkeep of garden and house, the general price, and the vagaries of her semi-self-employed status, getting her mortgage had been quite an endurance test.

Soon after Susan returned from the shop and was unpacking her groceries, her doorbell sounded.

She knew before she opened it – knew also the next scene would contain the white cat.

Sure enough, Crissie Fielding stood there, holding the cat in her arms. Both of them were so relaxed. Not a care in the world or a hair out of place.

"Is he yours?" said Crissie.

"No, no he's not."

The cat purred and looked at Susan from half-closed bluish eyes. She reached out and stroked his forehead with one finger, but quickly.

"He's gorgeous," said Crissie. "Is he a stray? He looks too sleek. I'd have him, but I'm out half the time. It wouldn't be fair.

"He belongs to 6A or B, I think," hazarded Susan. "I saw him going that way earlier."

"Oh, what a con-artist. And I gave him a piece of ham."

Crissie leaned fluidly down, with a dancer's grace, and set the white cat on the wooden floor.

Instantly he shot past Susan into her flat.

"Oh," said Crissie, "I'm sorry."

"It isn't your fault."

The cat flew along the flat corridor and bolted straight into the main room.

"Well, it is my fault, really. Shall I catch him?" asked Crissie.

That was all. It seemed quite uncomplicated. She too entered Susan's flat, and as she went by, looked into Susan's face with a quiet, "May I?" They were the same height.

They walked into the main room together.

"Ah, I do like your ceiling," said Crissie, "mine's a sort of puce. I keep meaning to repaint it, but I just haven't got round to it."

The cat stood in the middle of the floor, looking at them idly. He chirped a comment and leapt on to the round table, knocking two books off to the carpet.

"They say," said Crissie, "a cat never knocks anything over unless it means to. Come here, Catty. You must return to your rightful owners."

Susan was taken with the undeniable beauty of these two creatures. It occurred to her Crissie had precisely the cat's quality, an animal quality, the good looks of an animal, which even clothing, and today's cosmetics, did not lessen.

The cat let Crissie reach him, then sprang away and trotted to the floor-length window, which he stared at meaningfully. His meow was now very loud, masculine. "Is that what he wants?"

Susan crossed over and undid the French door.

The white cat flipped himself out and down the three stairs like spilled milk, then vanished through a gap in the fir trees.

"Not even a good-bye. That's a cat for you. By the way, thanks again for bringing the parcel across the other night. It wasn't from Gerry, it was poor old Ed. I'll have to ring the agency."

Unenlightened, shopping not unpacked, Susan wondered whether she wanted the girl to go, or to stay.

By daylight she looked even younger. Her skin had no markers, not the faintest frown-line, or infinitesimal lapse.

She was moving, leisurely, back towards the corridor and the front door.

"Would you like some tea?" said Susan. "I've just made some.

"I'd love some."

"It's not normal tea – I mean, it's mint tea-bags."

"Even better."

In the kitchen, Crissie picked up a lemon, and then a lettuce, from the kitchen counter, and examined them reflectively. "The shape of fruit and vegetables is so intriguing. Everything is, really, when you look at it."

They went back to the main room and Crissie sat on the couch, kicking off her shoes so her clean, exquisite feet could burrow in the carpet. There was black nail-varnish on her toenails.

"How long have you been in this flat, Susan?"

"Not long. A month or so."

"I've only been in mine a few months too. Do you want to change a lot? Because you're an artist, aren't you? I noticed the easel and canvases in the other room."

"Sort of an artist. I do book-jackets, sometimes."

"That must be fascinating, to be able to do that."

Susan said, politely, "What kind of work do you do?" She was curious as well, she half expected Crissie to say she didn't have to work.

Crissie smiled her sweet and amiable smile. "I'm a prostitute."

The months had gone by after R.J. Foolishly, believing the propaganda, Susan anticipated constantly that the hurt and sense of desolation would ease. They did not do so.

"Susan, you seem to need a break."

"I'm sorry about not getting this done on time."

"It's okay. I understand. But well. Why not take some leave?"

Near Christmas, Susan saw his book in the display at Paragon. Then in the shops. The jacket illustration was very ordinary. She ordered a copy, but then, having got it home to Brashspeare Road, found she couldn't read it.

She put it in the bookcase with his other eleven novels, the ones he had given her, and the one with her cover. And then in the New Year, she pulled them all out and took the books to a charity shop.

But it didn't help. Of course not. Nothing could.

It was not that she thought of him, longed for him, every minute of every day and night. It was that a kind of sludgy darkness hung over her. She couldn't be happy, even in little ways. And if ever she managed to be, for a moment or so, the darkness shifted and made a strange sound in her brain, resettling itself, reminding her.

She went through stages of misery and anger, sarcasm and self-dislike. She drank too much. Stopped drinking alcohol altogether. None of this led anywhere, except back to R.J.

In February there was a party Paragon gave, and she was asked and expected to go, but he might be there, so she didn't.

However, she finished two covers on time that were all right.

Anne called and said she might come over in the summer, (alone, Wizz was always busy) but Anne had said this before at least ten times.

Anne now and then sounded old. Certainly sometimes elderly. Her voice would suddenly croak on random words. She was over sixty. Her laughter, too, was finally very American. She said, "Oh, boy, is Wizzy fat. He has to diet. What a blimp."

Susan found she was oddly shocked. Never before had Anne said anything so derogatory about Wizz.

Anne said, "So, you're still in that dump you told me about in Shakespeare Street?"

"Brashspeare. Yes."

"Look, honey, I'm going to send you some money." This too had often been said, but recently nothing much had evolved from it. "I mean, this fat guy of mine is making millions. You should see this place. Wall to wall everything. He's in Hollywood right now, would you believe it. He wouldn't take me, he says I complain. It's only for three nights, and I admit I hate L.A. I'll send you something, okay?"

This was incoherent, seemingly, but then the money came, a dollar cheque now, which Susan's bank would not baulk at, since she had for years been receiving US dollars for some of her work. The bank did baulk slightly, however, because the cheque was substantial. It was for thirty thousand dollars, about eighteen thousand pounds.

What was she supposed to do with it?

Find a new flat? Eighteen thousand wouldn't be anywhere near enough, obviously. Visit her mother and Wizz? No.

Susan had been working an extra day a week at Paragon, to make up the money for her slippage over covers. Coming back from London in March on the train, she picked up a local paper discarded on the seat beside her. She had decided to look for a new flat after all, the eighteen thousand providing some sort of down-payment. The flat in Brashspeare Road was where she had been in love with R.J.

The local paper covered an area she knew. She had lived there once, with Anne.

The carriage was fairly full. A man with a penetrating voice kept talking on a mobile phone, arch insults bounced off his (presumably) girlfriend, but it was more a display apparently intended for the uninterested and resentful other passengers.

Rain smashed into the windows, trying to get at him, but failing.

In the colour photograph, it looked a sort of salmon shade, the house, the deep green trees grouped selectively and graciously, as in a theatre set. Where the drive had been widened was an ornamental thing, perhaps a fountain.

("Yeah, Donna, I ain't saying you ain't a sharp dresser. I mean I ain't *saying* it, Donna.")

Tower Gardens. 'A fine and large house, of great character, parts of which were built prior to 1900, but all extensively modernised in its conversion to self-contained flats, with gas-fired central heating and double-glazing throughout.' Two of the sought-after flats were now on offer.

One of these was spacious, the lounge twenty-seven feet by thirty-six, and having two bathrooms and four bedrooms. The other flat was two-bedroomed, with bathroom and cloakroom, and modern fitted kitchen. Both flats had 'beautiful views of secluded communal gardens.'

She could afford neither, even with Anne's (Wizz's) money.

I'm thirty-two, she thought.

She felt old and dry. How long before her voice began to crack?

("Donna, just don't push it, girl. No," he was stern now, "just watch your mouth.")

Old enough to saddle herself with a mortgage.

Perhaps strangest of all, when told, Anne had never queried the new address, which might, surely, have rung some sort of bell with her – Tower Gardens etc: coupled with the known area. Could Anne have *forgotten*? But then, Susan had never said just which house she was thinking of living in.

Susan waited. She said, "Yes?"

I didn't mishear. I know what she said. She said she is a prostitute.

"Funny, isn't it," said Crissie, drinking her mint tea. "Actually, it's quite a good job. I mean, if you like it."

"Do you... like it? No, sorry..."

"Why? I wouldn't have told you if I was upset about it. I don't tell everyone, obviously. But we're – neighbours." Still carefree, lovely, smiling. "I'd better reassure you, though, I work through an agency, and I never bring my work home."

VI

Summer came and went. Autumn arrived, turning much of the rich green of the garden to ochre and sallow red. In the autumn, they repainted Crissie's ceiling, perched up on a couple of high ladders, dust sheets everywhere, rollers, and pale peach emulsion. It was the second repainting. She had wanted to try coral before.

Crissie's flat was, Susan supposed, what might be called minimalist, but without that spindly starkness she, Susan, associated with the term.

Crissie had kept the ivory walls, hanging in the main room only two faded prints, one seeming to be Pre-Raphaelite, and one of a drawing by Mervyn Peake, representing a curious elongated child. There was also a big mirror in a black lacquer frame. The floor was the bare polished wood, which someone came in to 'do' at regular intervals, with a couple of rather tattered but glorious gold and maroon rugs with gold fringes. There were also two armchairs, narrow, old-fashioned wingbacks, in a dark coppery velvet. No couch. The French window had rough blanched muslin curtains, which at night, when the four side lamps were switched on, would hide nothing. There was also, despite the lack of noise, an involved music centre with four speakers, and a smallish TV.

This was really all.

Sometimes two tall blue willow pattern vases manifested, holding up flaming gladioli or vermilion lilies. There were hardly any ornaments – a misted-glass apple, the slim figure of a Greek god, perhaps Apollo, nearly three and a half feet tall and done in white marble. On the polished table, of which there was only one, stood a fruit bowl that changed colour with the fruit.

It was not obviously a moneyed room. It was full of air and space and reflections, and sometimes the soft uncanny music of Debussy or Scriabin.

The bedroom, where sometimes they went to fetch something or compare some new garment, or try out new make-up, was undersea and blue, with a low single wooden bed, a Chinese chest and carved yellow wood armoire to hold clothes.

Susan admired these rooms. Their oblique colour-combinations and shapes, which worked together, and the lack of clutter. There were no awkward hung-on-to objects. No plants, even. The few books were in a case against the corner.

"I always want to change my flat after I've been in yours."

"Yes, I do sometimes after yours. But," said Crissie, "we don't, do we?"

She didn't play at assertiveness or indecision, or at anything, it seemed. Not Crissie. Even her sexual ventures with men were unfazed and unfaked. "I just *like* sex so much."

"But – even if your clients – if they're…"

"Nasty, you mean? No, I avoid nasty ones, or unhygienic ones. But anyone else is fine. I don't mind how he looks. Or if he's old. Or what he wants. Or if he's too fast. I can come…" she said, airy as her rooms, neither boasting nor apologising, "*like that*." Her turn of phrase, still somehow old-fashioned. Charming. Unfazed

Susan also helplessly admired Crissie. For her work not the least. Though it must also be unwise and risky – and every day the media carried more horror stories of HIV and AIDS. But Crissie had even spoken about that. "The agency, G.D. – is very *good*. They try to screen everyone. We use protection. And I have a check every couple of months. Oh, it's not foolproof. I could get it, I know that."

"You're only nineteen…" That was another astonishing fact that had been established early.

"Well, I am nineteen. But even children die, Susie-Woo."

"You mean, if it happened, you would be dead-pan and philosophical

87

about dying."

"No, not *dead*-pan. But, well, we all die sometime. I mean, you can die at seven or seventy, nine or a hundred and nine."

"You're not afraid of dying."

"Maybe. It would depend how, perhaps."

"No, I mean, you're not afraid of being *dead*."

"No such thing," said Crissie. In the lamplight, like a creature of clear glass; easy to believe she meant what she said.

"I see. You know."

"Oh, we all know."

"*I* don't, Crissie."

"You do. You've just forgotten. Look, Susie," (Susan never minded it when Crissie did things with her name) "think of it this way. You're born and you're alive. What's your earliest memory?"

"I'm not sure..."

"Well, but how old were you when you started to be aware of things that you still remember now?"

"About three, I think. I know my mother said her first memory was when she was four."

"There you are."

"Where?"

"You were alive and in the world, from nought upwards, but you don't remember it. Nothing for three or four years. So it's just possible there was something even before *nought* that you don't remember."

Later Susan had said, "Under hypnosis people can sometimes be regressed to earliest childhood. To birth, even. Then they seem to remember everything."

"They sometimes remember other things, too."

Susan's first visit to Crissie's flat, soon after the New Year, had been for a meal. As in all else, Crissie was open and pulled no punches.

"I like female company, too. I don't mean I'm gay. I enjoy sex with men. But women – they're fun. And here you are. I was alone at Christmas. I don't see my parents now. And I love cooking things for people. I'm greedy and very clever. Come on, I dare you not to like my risotto with baked lamb."

Susan, drawn in during the cooking by Crissie for a glass of buttery claret, sat on a stool in the identical fitted kitchen to her own, but looking-glass effect, everything the opposite way round. She watched Crissie moving about in a huge black apron, effortlessly cutting and chopping and mixing, speaking of a hundred different things, while the wonderful scent of the food intensified.

"Taste this."

"Oh – it's..."

"You like it. Guess the vegetables? Well, guess the herbs."

"I can't – it's like everything in the world..."

"It *is* everything in the world."

88

They drank all the large bottle of wine with the meal, and afterwards Crissie brought brandy, and Algerian coffee in little blue cups. They had moved to the main room by then, having eaten in the kitchen at a table with an apricot cloth, with one tall church candle.

Presently Crissie put on a single short piece of music to be listened to. It was winding and serpentine. Then they talked again, then grew sleepy. It was only 10 but, "Time for bed," said Crissie softly, rising without subterfuge or excuse. "See you tomorrow." They had been all evening in perfect agreement, or rather, perfect counterpoise. And it was the first time since R.J. Susan had slept really well. Afterwards, she could never remember the name of the music, or its composer, or remember to ask Crissie what they had been. Like the life before life?

They were divided by thirteen years, but like the hallway and the two front doors, this partition seemed to mean nothing. If anything, Crissie was far more mature, Susan thought, than she herself. Perhaps her extraordinary job had contributed to this, but there were other things.

Contrary to the first evening, when they had parted after only three and three-quarter hours, there came to be nights when they sat, in one or other of the flats, talking until 2 or 3 in the morning. Or later. Once they had even both fallen asleep over a late night TV horror film, running on Susan's larger TV, and woken up at eight in the morning. Then they had breakfast, (Crissie insisting on making porridge, with oatmeal brought from 6C) like lovers.

But they were not lovers. They were – what were they? Friends? More than that.

There was a closeness, a *knowing* between them, almost from the first. No, *from* the first. Though they liked many different things, were separated by an age gap, their backgrounds, and by how they earned a living, they somehow tied up with each other, as Crissie one day, unembarrassedly said, like two gloves.

"Which is right and which is left?" Susan asked.

"Oh, I'm the sinister one."

But Crissie was not sinister. She was mild and transparent as the muslin of her sitting-room curtains, which by night showed every glowing lamp and movement in the room beyond: nothing to hide.

Susan thought, I *do* love her. And briefly felt uncomfortable, wondering if this were somehow wrong, to love a woman if one weren't gay. But why would it be? And Crissie seemed to like, to be fond of – to love Susan.

It was not that they were always exchanging touches, or hugging, though now and then, as on Crissie's birthday in November, this had spontaneously happened. They simply co-existed. Yes, that was the word. With most people you got by, you evaded or pretended, or as in the case of a man you loved, became absorbed – and the bits of you that were left outside ached in the cold. But with Crissie, with Crissie and Susan, they lived their lives together and apart, with no sense of chafing, no desire to break away or – more terribly, push closer, thrust inside.

Crissie did not even look so much the younger, nor Susan much the elder. Susan looked young for her age and had often been taken for someone in her late twenties. Crissie of course looked older, a woman in her *early* twenties.

Though they dressed for differing tastes, they did not, as Anne might have put it, *clash* in their appearances.

Their light brown hair and pale skin were similar. And their eyes. Their height if not figure.

Nothing demanding was said by either about a filial resemblance. Sisters – no, this was not it at all. They were *not* alike in that way. Two gloves of nearly matching colours, but of uncorresponding materials, and patterned quite differently. But still, two gloves.

When they went out, usually in the middle of the week, or the odd weekend when Crissie was not working, Susan felt unavoidably proud of Crissie – "This is my friend." Sometimes men would be interested in them, and gravitate their way, sitting at the next table in the restaurant, perhaps, or picking them up in the bar or on the train after a film. They were nice to them, these men, liked their fleeting company, but never wished to develop the liaisons. Susan actively did not want another man after R.J. It had become almost cosy, this state, since Crissie. Whereas Crissie had said privately, during one of the long night talks, those talks when the afterlife and AIDS and so on had been mooted, "It wouldn't be fair on a man. Maybe one day. I can't see it, somehow."

Crissie, (at nineteen) did not look into the future, although sometimes into the past.

"Dad was a builder. My mother – well, she was into being a Gold-Medal Mother. We were quite well-off. I went to a fee-paying school, you know the sort of thing. But – there was some trouble. I told you, I don't ever see them now. I haven't since I was fifteen."

Susan imagined Crissie meant she had discovered, under-age, the lure of sex, perhaps become pregnant, and so incurred the wrath of her parents, whose characters Crissie had not really filled in.

Crissie said, as if Susan had asked, "It was something that happened when I was a child. As Dad said, after I was nine, I was fine. He said it a lot. And it rhymed, so we couldn't forget it. Mother's contribution was that bloody name she gave me." Crissie didn't sound angry, only momentarily exasperated. "Crystal. Oh what a thing to saddle a kid with. As soon as I ran off – which you won't be surprised to learn was with my boyfriend of twenty-two – I changed it to Crissie. I suppose I could have changed it totally. I think, then, I meant to keep in touch. But I had to realise in the end I never wanted to."

"Did they try to find you?"

"I expect so."

"You don't know?"

"I don't know what they did. Or do. They could even be dead. Dad worked too hard and he was a big drinker, and Mother was scared of every disease under the sun."

Susan wondered what Crissie had done that was so awful, when she was a child. She wondered if Crissie would say, but that time Crissie didn't, and soon they were speaking of something else.

One night Susan told Crissie at length about her own past. Her own mother, and Wizz, and then about R.J. Crissie sat listening, sympathetic and involved, tender, gentle and cool as rain. She let Susan recount it all, all she wanted. Sometimes Crissie said things, unjarring and so apt that afterwards Susan forgot what they were – they were the same things Susan might have said to console and reassure herself, perhaps. There was nothing judgmental or self-expanding about Crissie. She never told Susan she had been foolish, or badly-used, or that Wizz was a monster or R.J. a bastard, or what she, Crissie, would have done, or what Susan *should* have done. She seemed to have said, Susan thought afterwards, only that life could hurt you, yet here they were. But there was also the kindness of Crissie, her eyes and how they looked at Susan, and the way she brought her the glass of wine, and then touched the tip of Susan's nose for half a second with her warm, smooth finger.

Like a mother? No. Not like that. Not like any of that. Like Crissie.

There came a gloaming afternoon in late November, when Susan, walking along the Strand, saw Crissie near the Savoy with one of her clients.

Crissie, working, was not very altered from the everyday Crissie, in appearance. Glamorously and expensively dressed, faultlessly made-up, and this time with blood-red lipstick, that on her young mouth looked only edibly correct. She was standing with an oldish, overweight man in a Savile Row suit. He was holding her hand, and she was looking into his eyes, smiling, sweet and affectionate, playful and calm. Then he said something, and she laughed and he laughed.

Susan turned away and walked on. The crowd was thick and surging, it was nearly 4 – she had left Paragon early to pick up a book at Zwemmers.

Then Crissie was there.

"Hello, Susie. I saw you go by. That was my lovely Heinrich. We were just bidding adieu. Thanks for not saying anything. He'd be shy."

Susan knew that the deal with the clients was often to lunch or dine first, the mask of the agency being that it provided social escorts. There was one young man, Crissie said, Todd, who seldom wanted sex, only that Crissie go with him to various functions, and act "as if I can't keep my hands off him."

"Isn't that...?"

"No," cried Crissie, "it's fun, like acting in drama. I love it. He's brilliant too. We scream afterwards."

She spoke of them all undamningly. She never told Susan anything much, either, carefully not betraying them, and sometimes stressed that *this* was not the man's real name, she didn't know what that was.

"Shall we go for tea? This is a rotten time, the trains will be getting packed," said Crissie.

So they went to Zwemmers, then had tea and scones, and then Crissie got them both a black cab all the way back to Tower Gardens.

Anne rang that night, at a quarter past midnight.

"Anne…? Are you all right?"

"Sure, I'm fine. Just bored as hell. So I thought I'd call you. What time is it there? Oh. Well it's just around 7 p.m. here."

Wizz was away on one of his, by now, perennial excursions. This time it was to Hawaii.

"I didn't want to go," said Anne. "I mean, take-off in winter, with ice on the wings when you land?"

They talked for a while, Susan holding the receiver away to shut off her yawns from her mother – she had been in bed, drifting, when the phone went.

Finally Anne said, "You know, I think the rat is playing around again. No, I am sure he is. He's been doing it, on and off, for years. What a skunk. Christ, I've long thought he even had the Hispanic maid that time."

"I'm sorry," said Susan.

"Not as sorry as he is when I start on about it. But God, Sue, I'm old. I'm so old. That's what it is. It never matters if you're a man. But for a woman – past fifty is shitsville."

Anne had never called her Sue. Anne perhaps, would never have said *I am old*. So who *was* this on the line?

VII

Outside the vegetable house, the vegetable trees of the maintained garden were putting on again their sticky, chestnut-red buds. A man came and gave the bench below Susan's French doors a new coat of glaucous peacock paint. Later there was a solitary blue paw mark on her steps – the autograph of one of the pet cats. Probably not the white one, though. She hadn't seen it, nor had Crissie, ever again. That cold day of the bench painting, too, a letter came from Anne, the first for some time. The airmail envelope had come undone, which had happened once or twice with registered mail in the past, but the sheet of paper was not lost. Susan took it out with a definite feeling of unease.

But, to begin with, there was no fresh update on adultery or arguments.

I'm coming over, across the Pond, to your neck of the woods, in a week, maybe two. I mean to London. It will be great to see you. This visit, let's really have a good time. Wizz says stay ten days. And cash isn't a problem. But of course I have to *earn* it. Even when he gave me those trips I took to Paris and Germany – did I ever mention those? I sent you postcards, I'm sure I did – even then I always had to go meet someone for him. Unpaid courier for the business. Although to be fair to him, I guess I do get paid, don't I. And the couple in Germany were great. Anyhow, this time is the worst. It isn't some packet to deliver this time. I have to bring this darn girl over to her father. Eve spoke to me about it, too. Eve is her aunt, or something, God knows and who cares. Obviously they don't want this brat travelling alone, so I have to be the chaperone for the trip, and I am dreading it but dreading it. Can you picture me? Stuck with a twelve-year-old for eight hours in a plane. My favourite thing. And then an hour or whatever into London. Oh well. Why don't you meet me – us – at the airport? I've enclosed details of a good cab firm Wizz knows, near London. I'll pick up the check. All you need do is call them your end. Okay? Did I ever say Eve and I had a falling out, too? The bitch took his side, I mean Wizz's side. Over this fooling around stuff. She said, men do it, I'd better put up or shut up. I'd suspect Eve of being part of the stuff *done*, only she's two years older than me, and now she looks like a crow that's been through a car-wash.'

"I'm not looking forward to seeing her. I can't help it. She says she may be here ten days. I don't know if she'll want to stay in a hotel or come out here. God – I really – I don't want to see her."

Crissie nodded. "It's difficult. Perhaps she won't stay as long as she says. Or she'll go off on her own like last time."

"I don't think she will, now. She sounded so fed up on the phone. She must be very unhappy. I feel sorry – but I still hate the idea. And I hate saying I hate it, too."

"Whyever? Why lie to yourself?"

"Don't you?"

"Not often, Susie-Woo."

"Well, who do you lie to, then?" Susan said, unexpectedly.

She answered thoughtfully. "Men, sometimes. I have to, or they don't have the best sort of time with me. Let's see, who else? Oh, you. About your birthday present. But that's all I'm saying on that score."

Susan smiled a little. Then she said, "How is it I didn't break all contact with Anne, as you did with your parents? I mean, I only had one to get rid of, and you managed both."

"True. But then I think they really wanted the break too."

"*They* wanted it –"

"They were scared of me, Susan. I mean really scared. And even when everything was all right, and stayed all right, they kept expecting it all to happen again, despite what the psychiatrist, or whatever he was, said. Hence my dad's awful little mantra, fine after nine. It was meant to keep the devilish bane at bay. To frighten *me* into suppressing – oh anything that might bring it on."

Susan sat, watching Crissie, the twilight deepening in the unlit room.

Crissie looked down at the waxed floor, at her reflection in it. She said, "I know my mother was petrified when I began to have periods. She thought that would trigger everything again. But it didn't."

Susan undid her mouth. Then closed it.

Crissie said, "I've never told you this. It isn't that I'm afraid of myself, I'm not, although I don't understand it. Or ashamed, either, as I think I was meant to be. But not everyone wants to hear about things like this."

A swift nausea wriggled through Susan's stomach and mind.

What had Crissie *done*?

"This was the thing you said happened when you were small."

"Yes. The daft thing is, I don't remember any of it. Well, not much. Do you remember when I asked you what your earliest memory was, and you said around three, or four."

"Yes."

"Well I don't have – how shall I say – *proper* memories, not until I was nine."

There was silence.

Susan held the coffee cup, which had ceased to mean anything, though half-full. Crissie sat quietly, looking down into the lake of her waxed floor. She seemed as ever serene, perhaps just a little melancholy. And all around the grey-blue shadow bloomed like fog.

"Had there been an accident?" said Susan at last.

"Amnesia? No, it wasn't that. Nothing happened. My mother had a perfectly ordinary pregnancy, gave birth, according to Dad at least, without much bother. It was a quick birth, he said, only a couple of hours from start to finish, they barely got to the hospital in time. And I was a healthy six pound baby, just a week early."

The silence began again. It was like a noise, a recollected noise, but of what?

Beyond the arched French door, so reminiscent of Susan's, the blue-grey garden sank into the space and oblivion of night.

"You see, I say I don't have real memories, but I do have a type of memory. From the beginning, I think. I'm not sure, I never have been."

And silence again.

This time it went on and on.

"Crissie, if you don't want to talk about this, please don't."

Crissie looked up. Across the silent blurring of all things, her eyes shone, clear and feral as a cat's, but colourless as a cat's never were.

"I'm concerned that you might rather not hear."

It was true. The hair moved slightly on Susan's scalp. Suddenly, though she had never thought of it, or no more than once, before this hour, she recalled that they sat in what remained of the sunken rooms of the insane metamorphic house of her grandmother.

"Maybe you're right, I don't want to – but – look, can I put a light on?"

"You know you can."

Susan got up. As she crossed the room, she blundered against the table

94

with the fruit bowl. The tangerines leapt and rolled away. "Sorry." Then the light came on to her touch. The room moved from nothingness to a golden magical normalcy. Even Crissie's books gleamed in the bookcase, the beautifully illustrated fairytales, and books of photographs of India and Egypt, the Shakespeare in red and the Chaucer in black.

Crissie had also got up. She switched on the three other lights.

She turned back in her dancing, dancer's way. "It's still me, Susie." It was not a plea, not a challenge. Only an absolute.

"Yes, sorry. That was just sitting here in the 'tween-light, greeking of auld ghoosties, or whatever."

"It wasn't a ghost," said Crissie. "It was a poltergeist." She stood on the floor, on her reflection. "Look, here it is. No sooner did they get the baby – me – home to their posho house in Kent, than things started to happen. At first not every day. But then, every day. The things that happen with poltergeists. Psychokinetic activity. Lights blew out, furniture moved dramatically, pictures flew off the walls, even some of the windows broke, apparently. My parents would hear banging noises, knocks and thumps. My mother said on one occasion something had mowed through the dining-room carpet – as if a lawnmower had gone over it, she said. My mother was the one, you'll gather, who made sure I had all the details as soon as I was 'old enough'. At first, when it started, they tried to *ignore* it. They got panicky. They attempted one or two solutions, which achieved nothing. Then they found this man near Harley Street. He explained about the phenomena. He said this happened sometimes round young children, even adolescents. He said it would stop. But they still had six and a half more years of it. And then – then it did stop. By then they'd got well used to it. Which meant Dad drank and went out a lot, and my mother was on tranks. The au pairs regularly left, too. Well, they would, wouldn't they?"

"Yes," said Susan woodenly. She said, "This was in Kent?"

"Marion Hill, Kent. Yes."

"And you don't remember…"

"What I remember is this. A kind of blaze without colour or light. Being furious and frustrated. I remember walking and walking through a sort of – well, I thought, when I was older, it was a kind of train tunnel. The light there was very faint, but I could see, and I wanted to get somewhere. Only I didn't get there. And of course, how could I be walking in a tunnel like that, it must have been a recurring dream. I remember striking at things too – what things? I don't know – but it made them shake, only I don't think I did it with my hands. I remember being lonely in a way I never have since. I remember being in the dark."

Again silence. The light flickered in the lamps, but sometimes that happened here and elsewhere. The lamps might flicker as the electric grid was overloaded, or the power source changed over.

"My first distinct, logical memory," said Crissie, "is of my father saying to

95

me, 'You've been a good girl.' And I didn't know what he meant, but my mother nodded, I can see her now, nodding. And I felt pleased with myself for being this Good Girl. The poltergeist activity hadn't happened, apparently, for a month, which till then was unheard of. My father said, 'Now you can have that bike I promised.' And I didn't know what he was talking about. But you see, I understood language. I'd learnt how to talk and walk. I could even read and write, rather well actually. I just couldn't recall how I'd learnt any of it. Like I didn't recall the paranormal stuff that seemingly I'd caused until it stopped, and I was a Good Girl, and earned the bike."

Susan said, "There was a poltergeist here, in this building, before it was converted into flats. So I've heard."

Crissie glanced at her. She looked intrigued not dismayed. "Really? I know they crop up here and there. Mine wasn't the only case."

"Why did you take the flat here, Crissie?"

Susan heard the churlish, Inquisitional note in her voice. Perhaps Crissie didn't.

"The agency found it for me. They're really helpful that way. I was living in Highgate, but I wanted a bigger place. They sorted it all out. I just moved in. That was the first time I saw the flat."

What is it?

Look at her. She's twenty years old now. She looks it tonight. No make-up, her old sweater that cost perhaps only a hundred pounds. Barefoot.

No it isn't anything.

A coincidence.

It could all be rubbish, lies, anyway. She could be a total fucking romancer. Even all this about her job – whore – how do I know? All I know is what she's told me. And that one man I saw her with – some rich old sugar-daddy – even, for God's sake, *her* daddy, the builder. Her money comes from somewhere, but why from working at anything? She's out a lot, so she goes out a lot.

I don't know a thing about her. Have taken her on trust, like I take everyone. Ghastly useless selfish Patrick and conniving oh-so-genuine R.J., and my bloody slapper of a mother, who is the real hooker, if anyone is, lapping up Wizz's dollars, first in exchange for sex, then in exchange for keeping quiet about his sex with all the little Madisons.

Christ, this *sound*s like my mother, like Anne, as she is now.

I feel like her.

I am not Anne.

I am me.

And Crissie?

I don't know what the fuck Crissie is.

"Crissie, look, I'd better go. Thanks for telling me. But I shouldn't have stayed so long – I've got to organise a few things, if Anne's coming."

Crissie smiled. Nothing to it. Unfazed. Knowing.

"Yes, Crissie, it did sound a bit weird. Sorry. But."

"It's okay, Susan. I've got some washing to do anyhow. I'll see you tomorrow."

She has conned me.

She is the con artist.

Lulled me and listened, and been lovely, and then told me her ghost story and made my skin crawl…

In her own flat, Susan switched on all the lights. Then she pulled the wire out at the telephone point, afraid the phone would start to ring and ring.

The driver wanted to chat all the way to Heathrow. He began by asking Susan where she was flying to, though she had no luggage. Then, when she said she wasn't going anywhere, he commenced asking in-depth questions about who she was going to meet, where they had come from, why they were here – it was, Susan thought (inaccurately) like an interrogation.

She had felt already tired and depressed when she got into the cab. Walking into the terminal, where the crowds swirled over endless floors, she felt drained – by the crowd, the space and its synthetic smell, the dull morning light, the cabdriver, her mother, everything.

Is she going to recognise me? Perhaps I should hold up a card printed with my name or hers.

Then another thought, worse. Will I recognise *her*?

It was a long wait.

Sourly, the thoughts pressed home. What are we going to say to each other? *Do* together? (I could have introduced her to Crissie – the gush of pride – "This is Crissie, my friend –" But that was out of the question, now. Susan had been avoiding Crissie, and Crissie made no overtures. Susan… didn't know about Crissie.)

(Or anything.)

When Anne finally came through, Susan started almost in alarm. For Anne looked just as she had always done. She wore a well cut navy suit, not even seeming at all crumpled. She was tanned, eyes and lips painted, her shortish hair a sheer bold white. Her nails were pale gold and on her hand flared the emerald. She carried one small suitcase, a piece of hand luggage and her American purse.

"Anne – you look wonderful!" Susan cried in a shambles of shame. And even as she said it, having now come near enough, she saw that the suit *was* crumpled, a very little, that the white hair was too dry, the brown skin creased, the mouth too bright. And with this too-bright mouth Anne leaned forward and kissed her, hugging her in the bony embrace, leaving a lipstick mark Susan could feel on her cheek, and had to wipe away surreptitiously. Anne would never have done that, not even last time – but ten, twelve years had passed. Had it really been so long?

"God, I am exhausted," said Anne. Her eyes were not very clear, she looked half-cornered with irritation. "What a goddam bloody flight.

97

Turbulence – delays – how late am I?"

"About two hours."

"Christ. That was the other thing. My watch stopped. Wouldn't you know it? One year old from Tiffany's, and it stops. This is Delores."

Susan looked where her mother off-handedly indicated. Susan had forgotten the annoyingly foisted twelve-year-old child who had had to fly in with Anne.

Delores had a honey skin with large black eyes. Her soft dark springing hair was tied in two long plaits. She wore a jumper, ski-jacket and jeans. She did not, Susan thought, look like a child, at least not really like an English child – or not like any child from Susan's childhood. Not like Susan, of course, not at all. Susan, at twelve, would have envied Delores her spotless complexion and slight figure, possibly her pierced ears and the little gold studs.

Delores did not smile. She seemed bored and evasive, her eyes shifting off from Susan. She didn't bother to return Susan's greeting.

"Is the cab waiting?" said Anne. "Good. Let's get the bathroom, then I need a drink."

Anne had been drinking already. She smelled of alcohol, again something Susan didn't remember from before. Even after her nights out, Anne had never smelled of anything other than cleanness and scent, or perhaps a partner's cigarettes.

In the bar, Anne had a double vodka tonic. Susan had a white wine spritzer. The child, when asked what she wanted, said, "Coke," untainted either by please or thank you.

"Is she all right?" Susan said to her mother, when Delores suddenly got up and walked away. She didn't go far, only to a fruit machine, at which she stared.

"Depends on how you class all right," said Anne. The drink had freshened her. She sounded less husky. Face to face her US. accent was hardly noticeable, except on certain words – class, God, and so on.

Delores meandered back. She looked at Anne, looked away. "I wanna dollar change."

"Dollars don't work over here, Delores," said Anne, briskly. "Eve gave you some English money at Kennedy, didn't she?"

Delores blinked. She didn't open her own small purse, a buckled denim creation.

Anne said, "She forgot, then. What is it you want?"

"I wanna play that."

Susan said, "Here, have this."

When Delores had gone back to the machine, Susan said, "She seems a bit..."

"She *is* a bit. Oh boy, is she. A brat, I said."

It was a relief to be able to have the child to talk about.

"Maybe she's just nervous. She's Eve Frenowsky's niece?"

"Something like that. Look, she's got the darn thing working. But it won't cough up, so she's hitting it…" Anne called across the bar, nearly stridently, "Delores, lay off!"

To Susan's surprise, Delores turned a fixed, somehow bleached face to Anne. She nodded swiftly. She looked terrified.

"Funny kid," said Anne. "I can't make her out. I tried to talk to her, asked her if she was excited, coming to see her father. She shook her little head. Well, I guess she's been over before. Eve says they're separated, the parents. Rich as hell." Anne shrugged. "But she is a bloody graceless child. But then kids are."

"Are they?"

"Wait till you have one."

Susan said, "I have waited. I don't want children."

Anne said, "Sensible."

Susan thought, Is she going to say, *I wish I never had?*

But Anne only said, "I asked him to come, you know."

"Wizz."

"Yep. I knew he'd say no, and he said no. I have a feeling he is all set for a mad fling while I am over here. Some nubile eighteen-year-old. Or why stop at only one?"

"Do you think we ought to go and find the cab – he's been waiting so long."

"Yeah, I guess. This vodka is crap. That is one of the many benefits of the US, decent food, decent booze. And the vitamins, what you can get there. And the treatments."

Susan went over to fetch Delores from the fruit machine. She hadn't won anything. She was the sort of demanding ungiving child you expected to win.

"We're going out to the car now, Delores."

Delores glanced at her, away. Any fright at a raised voice was gone. But she left the machine without demur.

The driver didn't chat now; he seemed to expect them to converse with each other, and so perhaps entertain him and feed him information.

They all squashed in the back, the child wedged uncomfortably in the middle like a thin bolster.

"Eve said she has to sit there, and the window seat on the plane. She doesn't like other seats."

This seemed strange, for if Delores wanted to be by the window in the plane, why not the window in the car?

Susan felt uneasy, as they breathed wine and vodka over her, talking across her inert dark head. But then, Anne had already baptised her in this, no doubt, during the flight.

"I can't wait to see London," said Anne. "It looks so small and old."

Then she leaned back. She shut her eyes which were overlaid by shadow and a mascara too black for the aging tan and the white hair. The knuckles of her hands had enlarged. Probably now she could never take off Wizz's emerald ring, even if she wanted to.

Susan gazed from the cab window, watched miles of concrete streaming past, houses and trees and a succession of disturbingly big, low planes.

When she turned to her mother again, she saw Anne had fallen asleep, her mouth slightly open.

Susan's heart sank lower. She felt wounded, *defiled*, by Anne's decay. She felt – embarrassed by her.

Then she remembered her childhood – Anne, in the bath, or varnishing her toenails. Susan wanted to cry. But she was too old herself for that.

And then Susan thought of pouring all this out to Crissie, and how Crissie would be, kind and tender, encouraging and interested, philosophical, never saying the wrong thing. Helping, wonderful Crissie.

But there could be no more indulgence in Crissie, who might after all be a dangerously crazy liar-lunatic.

I never told Crissie about Catherine, Susan thought. Everyone else, but not my grandmother. I nearly did, when she was going on about her poltergeist nonsense. Nearly then. But I didn't.

The suburbs trailed by. Susan thought of being hurried, always late, to the house on Sundays. She thought of Catherine standing there, that last time, straight and hard and ruined.

She could see Catherine now again, in the face of Anne.

The journey didn't seem to take long. There was a lot of traffic rumbling the same way, to London, but no significant hold-ups.

"Look, there's Big Ben," said Susan, stupidly, to Delores. Who took no notice.

But Anne gave a little snort and woke up.

"God. Was I asleep?"

"I think so," said Susan. "You must be tired."

"I don't get that jet lag stuff," said Anne stubbornly. "But I guess I'm tired." Then she seemed to shake herself together, sitting up, moving her hand over her hair, redoing her lipstick in a car-jolted compact mirror.

"Okay, Delores, we'll be there in a minute."

Delores moved vaguely on the seat. Her mouth looked sulky, her eyes almost moronic.

"Where does Delores have to go – I mean where is her father meeting her?"

"It's an address I have here, off Whitehall. I told the taxi."

A few minutes later, they turned into a street of large, flat-faced terraced buildings. Broad stone steps, guarded by stone lions with heraldic shields, led to glass doors whose handles glinted cold gold in the muddy sun.

"Impressive, your daddy's office," said Anne.

"What number was it, madam?"

The taxi crawled to a halt.

At that instant the child glanced again at Susan. Delores' face was a total blank. Perhaps there really was something wrong with her mentally. The great black eyes seemed to have no one in behind them, not a child, not a person, no one at all.

Unnervingly, before Susan could get out of the cab to give her access, Delores scrambled unheedingly over her. Anne was already on the pavement and took the child's hand firmly. Susan could picture Eve saying, "You have to hold her hand on the street."

"It's okay, Sue. I'll see to this. There's the doorman."

A porter had appeared. Anne conducted the child up the stone steps and spoke to him. A snatch of Anne's voice, over the traffic noise, said a foreign name, (not Frenowsky, Susan thought) something she didn't quite catch, or afterwards recall.

Anne and the child went through into a plush, black-carpeted lacuna beyond the glass doors.

Unexpectedly, the driver didn't start to chat now, either. Susan had assumed he would break loose again, if he and she were alone. Instead they both sat there, dumbly waiting, he with his back to her. Minutes went by.

Susan said, "Perhaps I ought to –" But exactly then Anne came out of the swing doors alone.

"Thank Christ that's seen to. Someone came down in the elevator. *Not* the father, mind you. A big guy in a suit. Well, he looked like a bouncer to me. But he knew about Delores. He was very pleasant to me. She just took his hand like a lamb. You know, little bitch, she was all goofy smiles for *him*, flirting away."

"Where to, madam?" said the driver.

"Oh, take me to a decent pub," sighed Anne.

Susan was unsure, but the driver said, "What about the Royal Lion, just around the corner there. Nice enough place, and quiet."

So they drove round to the Royal Lion.

Anne paid the driver in cash, (he did not offer to assist with Anne's luggage) and the cab moved slowly off, ahead of two big cars that had also pulled into the street.

The pub looked shabby to Susan. It was not very clean, but there was picturesque sawdust on the floor and old, dark green pots with deadish plants in them – perhaps things the driver thought an American might find quaint. A few people drank at tottery tables. Through a doorway there came a rap of balls in a pool game.

"Shall I get some sandwiches?" Susan asked. "If they do them."

"If you like," said Anne. "I'm not hungry."

But the Royal Lion did not do sandwiches, only bags of crisps and peanuts. Susan thought Anne would be able to get something to eat when they reached her hotel, something to soak up some of the alcohol.

As Susan brought the drinks back to their own rickety table, a tall man in a leather jacket came in from the street. She noticed him for a second because,

101

though younger, he reminded her faintly of R.J.

"Cheers," said Anne. "That's English enough, isn't it?"

Susan laughed falsely. "Oh, yes."

Anne swallowed some of her drink. "I've had enough," she said.

"Well maybe if we eat soon…"

"No, Susan, I don't mean the booze. I mean I have had it with him. I have had it."

Susan cleared her throat. She wished she were not so conscious of the man like R.J., somewhere behind her. R.J. was not what she needed to be reminded of. And not now.

"You mean Wizz."

"Yes. Who else? I am going to leave Wizz. Oh, I haven't told him yet. He thinks I'm all set to go on clinging tooth and claw to our non-existent relationship. But I am not. No way."

"What will you do?"

Don't, please *don't* say you will move back to England and live with me.

Anne parted her enamelled lips to tell Susan what she would do, and instead of elaborating, looked up in surprise. The shadow lay over their table. It was the man like R.J. He wasn't like R.J. There were three other men, casually dressed, well-built, and a woman in fawn slacks and a cashmere sweater.

The man who was not R.J. had something which he was showing them, some sort of I.D., like a plain-clothes policeman.

"Get up, madam."

Anne's face was furious. "What the hell is this? What the fuck do you want?"

The man leaned over and pulled her to her feet, and Susan found she too stood up at the same time, as if some cord connected them. And Anne seemed to struggle, and the woman in the sweater was there. She spoke softly. "You and the young woman come with us now, and quietly. Or we can cuff you and drag you out. Which?"

Outside the sun had gone in. The two large dark cars waited with open doors. This was a dream.

As Anne was 'helped' into one car, and Susan into the one behind, Susan tried to speak. "Save it," said the man who wasn't like R.J. Then she was sitting crushed between two of the other men, just as Delores had had to sit between herself and Anne.

During the hours when she stayed in the steel-white room, she thought it through, and saw the shape of it. *Having* seen, Susan saw that it was obvious. She should have known. Anne should have known. Or had Anne known? *They* thought so. Or – did they?

A uniformed woman sat at a small table in the corner. First, she ate a bar of chocolate. Then she took another one out of a drawer in the table and ate that. Later, much later, she took out another, and ate that too. Each bar was of a different make.

The light was too bright. There were no windows, and they probably locked the door, although Susan wasn't sure; she never attempted to open it. Once she asked for the lavatory. They made her wait nearly half an hour, then another woman came and took her to a toilet of three cubicles just along the passage. "Leave the door open." So Susan left the cubicle door open, and sitting pissing in front of this other woman, who did, actually, turn her head slightly away, Susan remembered the awful bathroom in Wizz's loft, with its two pally lavatories done in matching black and gold.

At other times, a man and a woman questioned her. She supposed that was what they were doing. They were not any of the men, or the one woman, who had taken Anne and Susan into custody at the pub. The man had gingery hair and a freckled scowl. The woman looked French, a delicate and sharply made brunette. But she spoke with a slight trace of a Scottish accent.

"Where's my mother?"

"Don't worry about your mother."

"Of course I am. What have you done with her?"

"The same as we're doing with you, Miss Wilde."

"Why am I – why are we here?"

It turned out they were there because of Delores, that brain-dead, rude and graceless child, who, with the man from her father's office, had become melting and friendly.

It turned out too that Delores' attitude and manner were undoubtedly the product of her intense conditioning, over a period of time, to know who must be made up to, and who must not. Also, of course, to a fear and horror and misery beyond anything such a child should ever know.

As it came clear to Susan, she was racked not only by her own leaden fear and panic, and her appalled concerns about Anne, but by remorse. The very young girl Anne had brought from JFK to London was no relative of Eve's, no daughter of a rich friend of Wizz's. She was one of those lost children, there to be taken by stealth or connivance from the sinks of most cities, warped and worked into the appropriate consistency, then flown out like refrigerated flowers to any destination that could pay.

She wasn't the first *commodity* that Anne had 'delivered' for Wizz, and therefore for the firm. Anne, the paid or unpaid courier. What had those things been in the past, the thing she had had to take to the Georgian manor house near Brighton, the *packets* for Paris, and Germany. Illegal smuggled jewels or art treasures? Hard drugs?

They imported everything, the firm. Anne had said that once. A joke? Imported and exported.

Susan, as she put the pieces together, began trying to explain them to the people who talked to her on and on in the steel-white room. They were already aware of them, naturally.

"My mother didn't know – she's been duped. He's used her."

Basic psychology. Wizz wanted to get rid of Anne. He hadn't known she'd planned to leave him. So if she were caught – too bad?

Susan grasped *he* would be safe away. Already she could tell this operation would have been far reaching. There would be others working on the other side of the Atlantic, to trap Wizz's firm. But most would escape. Wizz always would.

He's a gangster.

She had sensed it at sixteen, and Anne had not. But then, Anne was in love with him. What could Susan say she had known about R.J., really known? Love was blind, or blinded itself.

Had Anne, *had* she known? No. Anne, for all her crash into age and unbeauty and vodka, was not that kind of woman who could consentingly bring a kid of twelve to England to become the sexual toy of some wealthy group or outfit of paedophiles. Was she? Was she?

"Do you think *I* was in on this?"

"Well, Miss Wilde, were you?"

They must have tapped Anne and Wizz's phones. They would have heard conversations between Anne and Susan. Did these people suppose it was all done in code, in case?

After they had photographed Susan, searched her – so shocked by then, numbed, she barely noticed this search, carried out by an expressionless woman, but wondering if there would be an internal search – there was not – then later wondering if Anne, the courier, had been – a woman of almost sixty-two – subjected to one – after they had done these, and other matter-of-fact, intrusive things, some of which Susan only recollected hours later, Susan thought, *They do think I'm guilty of this. And Anne is guilty.*

But she kept trying to persuade the gingery man and the svelte Scottish woman that neither she nor Anne was guilty at all.

Susan told them about Wizz, and what she knew about Eve. It was so little.

She supposed they would not catch Eve, either. Perhaps not anyone from the firm.

And so Anne and she might have to do.

"What time is it?"

She thought the chocolate woman might not answer, but she glanced at her watch and said, "9.35." They had taken Susan's watch away, along with some of the things in her bag. If this was expediency, or another form of coercion, she did not know.

Some unmoist cheese sandwiches had been brought, and some tea. They had let her have a glass of water, too.

"I don't know what I can ask you," said Susan, "what am I allowed to ask?"

The chocolate woman looked at her.

"When can I see my mother?"

The chocolate woman said, "I wouldn't hold your breath."

"She isn't young," said Susan. Even in this extremity, saying that, she felt disloyal. "I don't think she's very well."

The woman nodded. The nod meant nothing.

At 1a.m. Susan asked the time again. And at seventeen minutes past one, when she asked again, the ginger man, the Scottish woman, and another man – fat, with glasses – came in.

Susan got up. "Let me see my mother, please."

"I'm sorry," said the fat man. He sounded sorry, apologetic, not unkind, which seemed unbearably threatening now, or had Susan only watched too many shows on TV?

"At least tell me if she's all right."

"Quite all right. Rather distressed, of course."

Susan suddenly found she was crying. She sat down. The tears ran across her face and stopped. She wondered, removed and bleak, were tears a show of innocence to these people or only of culpable fear?

The fat man came over and pulled out a chair and sat sidelong to her. The ginger man stood. The woman perched on the larger table, across which all dialogue had previously been lobbed.

"This hasn't been pleasant for you, Miss Wilde. I know that. And I'm sorry to tell you there will be charges brought against Anne Wilde, your mother. Personally, I'm of the opinion she's merely been incredibly naïve, but at the moment not everyone is happy with that. I suppose rank stupidity could be counted as an offence in a case like this."

Susan felt void. It was like the last stages of a virus. She didn't care anymore. She said, mechanically, "Will the child be all right?" Because in the distant future she might sometime want to know.

"Perhaps."

"I thought…"

"Oh, we've got the child away from them. There won't be any more of that for her. But I'm sure you're aware, in these situations, certain things will already have happened. She'll be damaged. They always are. But, she's young. As you are, Miss Wilde. We heal better when we're young."

Beyond the room, a bell rang, once, twice. It sounded almost like a fire drill, but no one took any notice.

"There's just one other matter I need to mention, Miss Wilde." He waited, as if for her to say brightly, *Oh, what?* Then he said, "Your friend at the flats, Crissie Fielding…"

Susan thought, *Who is Crissie Fielding?* She thought, But they will have watched me, too, they know everything. They probably know what I have for breakfast. They probably know my whole life story. They know I have a neighbour who is unhinged and called Crissie.

"What about her?"

"It seems she has some influential admirers, Miss Wilde. We wondered a little, you see. But she isn't someone who would need to be involved in this sort of dirty little game."

"You thought Crissie…"

"No, we didn't think anything, Miss Wilde. Nor do we think it about you, you'll be relieved to learn. And now that's sorted out," (what had been?) "maybe we should get you home."

Susan started to say, in her viral voice of halting cotton wool, "You must let me see Anne first…"

But nobody took any notice.

The fat man went out, smiling and affable, his work, whatever it was, well done. Susan had to sign a couple of papers. They took her down to another room and gave her back her watch and the things from her handbag.

Then she had to sit and wait, and now she didn't know why. Unless it was all a ruse, and they weren't going to let her go.

In this room, which was bigger, with pale, grey-washed walls and more-padded chairs, and an unoccupied desk, there was also a clock.

The clock and Susan's watch showed almost an hour's difference. Obviously, it would be her watch which had gone wrong, slowing down in captivity as she had.

And she thought of Anne somewhere in the building, (as if she had only just realised this), her own watch useless, and should Susan have made more fuss? But no, it would accomplish nothing.

She thought, *What do I have to do? Do I have to get her a lawyer?* Maybe Mike Hammond, or Laurel, could advise her. She would have to talk to someone. It was all such a business. She remembered Anne saying, soft and sombre, "Oh, God, now we've got all this death business, forms, mess, and the bloody funeral." After the police found Catherine sitting dead on a park bench, twenty years ago.

It was 5 a.m., or 4.10. Someone came in, a man. "Come along, Miss Wilde."

She followed him, and they went through a lot of fiercely lit corridors, and at the windows, which any new room they passed had, the black sky seemed never likely to give way.

She fell asleep in the car, as Anne had, during the drive back into London. The driver woke her in a side street. Here she had to leave the big car and get into a cab. She was cold. She thought confusedly the cab driver would start to talk: Where have you been? Where are you going this time of the morning? He never spoke.

She wondered if she had enough money on her to pay him. This grew frighteningly important. She started to elaborate mental plans of how she must explain, leave him what cash she had, rush into her flat and bring the rest out. In the end, he pulled up in Dunkirk Street, where now the trees were large and fine and covered with the spearheads of buds. It was so cold. Something like white sugar coated the gutters, the roofs, the limbs of boughs. She got out, but the cab drove off before she could begin the rigmarole about money.

In the early morning, with the milk-floats going by, under the thinning sky, where light had broken through the blackness after all, in the smell of the cold. Walking.

Why hadn't the cab brought her to Tower Road? They would have had to come by another route. Was this to cause more disorientation? Or a mix up?

Over fences, creepers had shawls of ice. Would the park gates be closed? No, they were open. Someone was collecting litter. A bird sang shrilly from the direction of the public toilets.

But the grass was all slathered in brittle white. It crunched under her shoes. And then people hurried past her, off to catch the early trains, and she thought of Anne, left behind. And she thought of Anne.

As she let herself into her flat (6E) Susan recalled she had gone by Crissie's flat across the hall, (6C) and hadn't seen it, as if it were not there.

Had she gone by the statement about Crissie like this, too?

What had the fat man said? What had he implied? Crissie had influential admirers. Presumably men she had slept with, in her trade as a prostitute. So, what she had told Susan about that was a fact after all, not a fabrication.

But also – also had the fat man been saying that they had investigated Crissie, and to protect Crissie, or her 'admirers' – they had left Susan herself ultimately alone? Or did he mean that Crissie had somehow learned what had happened, and asked someone, some admirer, (Heinrich maybe, Ed, or Todd) to intervene at a high level and save Susan's skin?

Why? Why would Crissie – why would she care so much?

The curtains stood open at the arched windows, undrawn last night.

Beyond the French doors of the main room, as on the drive leading to the house, lawn and trees were frosted white.

Susan found she had switched on the central heating. It made a knocking, tapping sound. She walked up and down across the room, trying to be warm again. Should she make tea? Pour a measure of brandy? The decision was beyond her. It was like the time after R.J.

In the end, she went to the French door, unlocked it, let the icy air come slicing in. She didn't know why she did. She didn't understand at all. None of it.

On the recently painted bench to the left of the steps something was.

Susan turned to see.

Someone was sitting on the bench.

Susan looked.

It was the figure of a woman. Slender and straight, with loose fair hair – or hair that had been loose and fair.

"Crissie…?" said Susan.

The woman sat there, on the bench. Her skin appeared monochrome, nearly colourless. Nearly sepia... her clothes, her hair, these were covered with the white lace of the frost, which at the edges of her garments, hair, had turned to a crochet of white. In profile, one eye of dark grey crystal – that seemed daintily fractured as if by a flung stone.

But it was Susan's eyes that had fragmented, one pane sliding across another.

She was back in the past of this living, metamorphosing house. The face she saw was not dead, but only mummified with its bitterness.

"What is the point," said the old woman in the pumpkin house of Susan's memory, "of my being alive? There you are, the two of you," (She means me, and Anne, my mother) "flesh of my flesh, the children of my body, there you are, and I am alone. This is what I have come to." It had been her fault, and perhaps she had realised that. Was it tears in her eyes? All that poison and tactless cruelty – made of regret and tears. We hated her, were allergic to her, Susan thought. As now I dislike and dread my mother.

Catherine. She had died. There in that cold park. And after that she had haunted this house. Not as a ghost, but as a poltergeist expressed from the body of a baby that became a child, miles off. In Kent. (I knew in her flat that evening, in the twilight when we put the lights on – and that's why I've avoided her. Not because I thought she was insane. Because I saw what she'd told me – was true.)

As someone had said, Catherine hadn't known she must go away. Rather, she had thought she must return to her house. And return she did in the only way she then could. Years of fascinating the cats in Jackie's rescue centre, terrorising grumpy Mildred with knockings, opened windows, hidden things, distressing Olivia and Jeremy's trendy existence. Only finally settling into her reborn physical self at the age of nine: Crystal, the daughter of a wealthy builder and his gold-medal wife. And Crystal's life was to be as different from the life of Catherine as Crystal could make it. Until fate, or her burning inner will, manipulated the world, and brought her again to the vegetable house. After which, Susan knocked on the door of her flat.

Catherine had wanted love from those two who never loved her. Only this second time, one of them had.

Catherine sat on the blue bench, covered in the frost of her previous death, living now, but demonstrating how it had been.

Catherine. Who had become Crissie.

Crissie turned. She turned her head. The frost came with her lightly, like a veil. It was in her fringe, on her eyebrows, lashes. It was over every inch of her. But the grey crystal eyes were not fractured, only webbed, and they saw. She looked at Susan and smiled her ice-rimed, frozen, triumphant smile of grey glass.

EXHIBIT TWO
L'AMBER

PART ONE

I

Two years later, I saw the book.

It was with a collection of good condition second-hand novels on a table, in the shop in Frayle Street. Of course, I saw her name first.

At the start, her name used to irritate me a little. I thought she must have made it up, and it was a silly name, contrived. Jilaine. But it's a real name, simply a phonetic spelling of Ghislaine – and it was on Jilaine's birth certificate. And now, there it was on the book – *You and I: Jilaine Best*. And that too, the direct address of the title – *You – You and I*. I felt physically sick for a moment, and hot with excitement and a sort of embarrassment – the whole world could see and hear her speaking out at me from the good-condition cover of this novel. And I was frightened. What had she said?

The point is, she'd written only three books – four now – and they were all autobiographical to a large extent. She didn't even alter the characters' names very much. For example, in the third novel there was a man she called Dan Blake, who she once confessed had been a real man called Don Black. Oh, and Françoise, in the first one, was called Frances.

By then, sick and excited and embarrassed and scared, I'd picked up the book. I stared at the blurb on the inside flap. The cover was nearly pristine. No one could have read this copy yet. But then, when I found I'd scanned the blurb and not understood a word of it – it might have been in Chinese – I looked behind the title page and saw it had been published the year before. That is, one year after. One year after she knew me, and I knew her. And even if it hadn't sold all that well, some people must have read it. A lot of people by now.

I flicked through the pages, as you might, if trying to get the feel of a stranger's writing, to see if you liked it. I always did like her writing. It was pale and undressed. I'd admired its nudity and almost-innocence, the way she seemed to try to tell the truth – naked. And pretty soon I saw a name I definitely knew. She hadn't even changed this one. 'A tallish man' she wrote, 'dark-eyed, with unusually thick hair.' Yes, he had been.

So, it was that very time, then. That summer time. Those months.

I paid for the book and took it out with me into the November street. All this while I hadn't ever thought she would write about any of it. After all, she was a painter. (Although even that aspect I'd tried to avoid. The small gallery where she sometimes had a show, she had said. And *The Painted Box*. I'd avoided them with care. Not because I thought I'd *see* anything in her paintings – she didn't often paint people. Merely... not to get hurt, I suppose.)

111

But now here was the book, *You and I*. *You and I* was (were?) going home with me to my nasty room, in the rain. And all the way I was thinking, what trap had she laid down for me, to facilitate my punishment and humiliation? What dagger of the mind?

She had laid one down. My God. The worst she could have, that's the thing. The very worst of all.

II

Jilaine first appeared before me like the Angel in an Annunciation. There was nothing religious, or announced, just the wonderful golden light that sometimes fell across the café at that time of morning, about eleven o'clock.

The coffee-and-tea ladies had come in and sat down at the tables for their caffeine. I had just taken table 5 a tray of steam-plumed pot and cream jug, (the café tried to observe such niceties) sugar packets at least in a little bowl, and hot toast with butter. (Do people still eat like that in little cafés tucked up in the wombs of bigger shops? This was only a few years ago. But they don't seem to.)

Straightening from the tray, I turned towards the next waiting table, and saw Jilaine walking up the stair, right through the gilt-crystal light, shining.

Someone once told me, Oh, you're a woman. Of course, you fall in love so easily.

A bad thing, obviously. To be easy.

But it was new summer. The year was young yet legally of age. And *she –* *You, oh you,* as the young man says in *The Tempest.* (Or is it Miranda?)

The light was gold crystal and so was Jilaine, just for one burning moment. Her ashy blonde hair, curving over the shoulders of her white short-sleeved top. Her white, untanned glowing flesh – was ever skin so white? And great eyes, blue I suppose, although for me, who studied them after, so intently, every blue possible under the sun or the moon.

She was slim, but not thin. Not slight. She had breasts and hips. All curves, the body, the white arms, the curving shield-bright hair. Red mouth. About twenty-eight, thirty.

When I look back I feel strange, because I was younger than she was then, and now, obviously, I'm older than both of us then. And why is this odd? Just because it is, somehow.

She crossed out of the light and became almost human. Not ordinary however. Only her shortness lessened her drama. But it was lovely, her shortness. Lovely.

She sat down at table number 6, which wasn't mine. And Doll, whose table it was, came ambling up to her with her pen and pad, and I could have struck Doll down then and there, with one of the knives all ready for lunches from twelve o'clock.

They didn't know here, I liked women. It hadn't ever seemed wise to let slip the facts. Where I'd had to, I'd spoken of my *boyfriend*, (we still had boyfriends then.) As I'd lied, too, about having another part-time job, because I had learned the hard way these people don't like you to be free, I mean at liberty, when they are not. And who do I mean by *these people?* Come on, you know.

I took the order from table 4, for tea and a macaroon, and went to get them, and in the kitchen the evil old cook turned to cast at me her sandy-haired evil eye. "Wash up soon, Jay," she said to me. "Your turn, I think." Then bent back over her cauldrons.

Doll was waiting for a coffee pot.

"Don't she go on," Doll said. Doll added, "This bloody change. It's driving me mad. I'm going that hot all night I feel I'm on fire. I get out of bed and he says, 'Keep still, can't you.' He should put up with what I have to."

"You don't look well," I said. Unlike some, Doll preferred to be accorded the medals of sickness of the menopause. She had once paraded before me a surprisingly elegant foot minus its little toe.

"I keep getting dizzy, too."

"Why don't you sit down for a minute? Have a drink of water. I'll take your tray. What was it? 5?"

"Yes..." said Doll, suspicious. She was thinking of the tip.

But I took her tray, and left mine standing there, the tea and macaroon, and walked out of the infernal door, back into heaven where the angel sat, reading a book, at the table.

I didn't think she'd bother to look up. She would thank me, yes, she seemed gentle, polite. But why look up? She'd think I was Doll, and anyway, I was nothing. Only myself in the café's regulation black skirt and top, which they didn't even supply.

But as I set the coffee pot down, her eyes did come up with a flash like blue fireworks.

And then. Something so bizarre.

Surely there are still gods of some kind. They play tricks, to watch us go mad.

"Oh, hallo. I didn't know you were here. Really, I didn't."

"Yes, I am," I said. I smiled, shrugged.

Jilaine, whose name I didn't then know, said, "But what happened? You're all right? Are you just helping out?"

"Mm. That's it. Helping out."

I was dazzled by the craziness of it. She had mistaken me for some other, one of her own tribe, too noble and fair to work in the café.

She had a lovely voice. With the slightest lisp, of all things. In her, it was – it melted the mind.

And she was beautiful. Flawless skin, teeth, smooth mouth in its honey of lipstick.

113

"Then you're still working – but not with Chris?"

"Oh – you know," I feebly replied.

She seemed gravely serious. "You should have gone back. Stayed. The other stuff shouldn't have interfered. I agree he can be a bit of a bully sometimes, but he's very expert. And you are good. That last one – I'm sorry, I can't think of the title..." She seemed very restrained, choosing her words slowly, careful of my feelings.

This was so insane, I took the risk. "The Galloping Magi," I said firmly.

"Was it called that? That's clever."

What had I named? A book – a *ship?*

Just then Rita approached. She snarled in my ear. "Your table 4 is kicking up a stink. Where's her hot drink and cake?"

"It's my fault," said Jilaine quietly. "We're old friends."

We were old friends.

My feet were numb, and when I brought out the cold tea and abandoned macaroon, I might have been walking without every toe, Doll magnified.

Then there were thousands of customers, a 'rush'. We rushed.

I saw her in glimpses. Once she smiled again, sympathetically. Poor me, helping out and treated like a skivvy. Poor me, who had made the Magi, whatever the fuck they were, gallop.

And then – she was gone. I turned, and she wasn't there. She had spread her angel wings of ashy hair and flown away. She *did* leave a tip. I handed it to Doll.

"You have half," she grudgingly said.

So I took one of the coins. And I thought, I'm going to be like one of those songs, and keep this coin.

But, things being what they were, *tight,* (as they *always* were) I'd spent it a day or so later.

I lived at that date in a room of number 12, Compton Road. It was a mangy old house, four storeys and a basement. The drive was all potholes that unified with rain into a lake, where dustbins and any stranded car reflected like liners. Tall trees loomed, moaning in fear either at the scent of drought or winter.

Needless to say, my room was at the top. Only an attic rose above me, and below all the other tenants regaled me with their noises, then came to complain about mine. Bathing in the communal tub one flight down was unpopular after 9 p.m. because of the racket the plumbing made, along with post-midnight visits to either of the two lavatories. ("I heard you go to the toilet. Gone 11 it was. Kept me awake an hour.")

What else can I say? I don't want to over-emphasise the Room, but in a way I have to put you in the picture. At number 12 no one was allowed to decorate, and besides I couldn't afford to. So I had peeling walls with patches of damp. The inside window sills rotted quietly, holes stuffed with newspaper, the free ones. No central heating, of course. A two-bar electric fire, which was undoubtedly dangerous as well as anaemic. I had once put some new curtains up, and laid rugs on the floorboards, and blankets on the mattress which also lay on the floor. In the beginning I had even tried to make the verdigris sink grow white again, scrubbing with Ajax until my whole body took its perfume. I did replace the cracked window at my own expense. (*'All breakages and etc must be attended to by tenant.'*)

I *had* bought a coffee maker and a small fridge with an icebox. I'd cleaned the cupboards of the kitchenette and lined them with nice clean paper, and put in tins of baked beans and soup, packets of pasta, rice – I even installed a bread bin, but it made the bread go stale. How was that possible? Such is life. Or, my life.

There was a plant too, and this was the one great success. It had cost a handful of loose change outside an old-fashioned 'oil'-shop. Now, after three and a half years it towered at the window, the dark, deep green of a sacred grove.

They say women writers tend to do this. Give too much detail. But she – I mean Jilaine – she *never* wrote like this. What would she have said? 'The room was small and mean; impoverished. It had one success, a green plant.'

And I must stop addressing you – she would never have done so. Probably you find it impertinent. And I don't know who you are, anyway. My priest, really, since this is my confession.

But perhaps I must mention how I came to be living in the squalor of the Room, working part-time as a waitress just three or four days a week, when everyone else slaved the full five or six, and brought back enough to cement mortgage repayments on their home like guano.

There is little to say, luckily. In childhood I was dragged about from place to place in the wake of my mother, a dancer. Fatherless. I beheld a number of men come and go – which was, actually, exactly what they did. I had some schooldays. And there I wrote well enough and somehow gained eventually the illusion I could Write. However, the unvarnished cause of my adult life and Room was not failed idealism. Simply put, I'm lazy. Yes, not a struggling genius in lagging health, unfortunate and doomed. Work-shy.

Sometimes I do apply myself to things – like the new curtains, the lining paper on shelves. Then I always lose interest.

Naturally, being lazy, too, I didn't ever want to work honestly for my living. Yet, also from pure laziness, I refused to fall in with the benefits system, which just might have supported me, if I had not been too lethargic to be persistent, too mute with ennui to lie.

I opted for the easiest route, which was, then, to wait upon tables of persons sufficiently unlazy to have earned their toasted scones and cappuccino.

There it is. The sum of my parts.

But of course, I *wanted* more. Lazily wanted it maybe, and without ever thinking I could get it.

Did I ever resent the ones who had it by right? I mean, obviously, the rich.

Not the rich, no. But the affluent – oh, yes. Riches look like hard work to me after all, but affluence is undemanding. Just a bit more than you need. Er, quite a bit more.

And I saw these creatures who were like that, through a kind of scorching lens. So that reveals I covetously hated them. They didn't deserve their wealth, most of them. So why should I, who didn't deserve it either, have it?

You see how unlikeable I am. Not a charming or an appealing woman, would you say. But there I go, addressing you again.

III

A week later, Jilaine reappeared – manifested. This was not inside the café, but down in the store foyer below, at closing time. I'd managed to get away a few minutes early, I forget how on that occasion, I often did, it was one of the reasons they finally sacked me.

She was standing under the clock, by the pillar with the store's directions. She was looking coolly up the stair to the café. There was no dissembling. The moment she saw me, she raised one of her light hands in a graceful static wave. She smiled. As if we had arranged to meet and here I was.

"Hi," I said, wondering why I hadn't fallen down the steps.

"Hallo. I wondered if I'd see you."

"And you have," I wittily rejoined.

She opened her perfect mouth, (the lips of Jilaine were – are – like those of a classical statue) to say something. And then the store voice sang out its syrupy farewells, the polite method of shooing customers outside.

"Oh," she said. "Shall we go for a coffee?"

"Ah, all right."

"Or you've probably been drinking that all day. We can go to a pub."

She walked ahead of me. She seemed used to taking the lead. To leadership. Though about five inches shorter than me, she led the way out of the store, and I followed.

On the pavement, the roasted 6 o'clock young summer evening was turning to copper. It was a time I always find amorphously exciting – late afternoon, sunset, dusk, I don't know why, exciting things have seldom happened to me then.

We walked up to *The Knight's Arms* – the old gag, of course – I'm stepping into the knight's arms – ha! She went in first and I followed her. I'd have followed her off a cliff possibly. Or maybe not.

She was wearing a lavender-coloured dress, rather long, with cap sleeves, that belonged in some glamorous 1940s movie. She had high-heeled sandals, (and was still inches shorter than I was), her toenails were painted plum, but the nails on her hands were oval and clean and bare, so you wanted to nibble at them.

The pub was only just getting its evening vigour on. A fruit machine quacked. Glasses clinked discretely.

"What can I...?"

"No, let me. I asked you, after all."

I said I'd like some white wine. I would have preferred a double vodka, but even I can sometimes rise to a falsehood. Oh God, yes, as you will see.

We sat in a corner under a stained glass panel showing some Arthurian maiden clenched among roses. Outside, a little walled yard with flower-tubs was filling up, with men and girls and thick sunny shadow.

"I saw Chris," she said. "I did mention I'd seen you."

Who? What? Oh right, this man I'd been supposed to stay with, or whatever it was... a lover? Husband? I studied my wine. "Of course, he can be very obtuse."

"Yes, he can," I agreed. Always agree, where remotely feasible.

"But Ron was there."

Wonderful. Ron! I tried to seem cautiously pleased. Jilaine that-I-didn't-even-know-was-called-Jilaine took out a pack of low tar cigarettes. Smoking was, every day faster, losing favour, but she opened the packet with neither qualm nor shame. "May I smoke?"

"Yes. Please."

"Do you still – would you like one?"

"Thanks."

I took her cigarette and she lit it for me from a long streaming match. Everything, everything, the fags, the match, the pub, the world, was fascinating.

"There's a party tonight. Ron's going. I thought I might go. Why don't you come?"

"Well. I..."

"Make it up with Ron. Then talk to Chris." Suddenly the madness of all this, or the wine on a stomach empty of toast, scones, lunch, made me laugh. She laughed at once, with me.

"I'm sorry. I don't mean to be bossy. I was wrong before. But this seems such a pity. Your paintings are good, and Chris is a clever artist. I'm sure no one wanted to upset you. It was a misunderstanding. Truly, Philippa."

"I'm not Philippa."

There, it was out, escaped like a frog from the ugly princess's lips, where the beautiful princess could only speak gems and fragrant cigarette smoke.

"You're not Philippa." She looked blank. Or – hidden.

"No, I apologise. You mistook me for this woman – and I, well I..."

"I didn't give you much chance to explain." But she was far cooler now. A kind of transparent visor stood before her face. Her eyes appraised me.

I'm seldom lazy when first engaged.

I lied neatly, quickly. "The thing is, *I* thought I recognised *you*. A girl I used to know at school – Liz..."

"My name is Jilaine," she said.

"Jill Ames..."

"No." She was patient, used to this. "Jilaine." She spelled the name out.

I thought, Christ, pretentious. She's made it up. One flaw at last.

"Shall we have another drink?" I said.

I thought, *Now she'll get up and stalk away*. But she smiled. "Why not? It's all rather funny, this, isn't it?"

Hilarious. I'm rolling on the floor.

I went to the bar and got two new drinks – hers was the vodka, with just ice and lemon. The way I prefer mine. But I was reckless by now. Sod the expense: I had one as well.

We sat under the glass roses. Outside, some red-brown men were pulling a squealing girl about – her string of beads burst and showered everywhere like bullets, one hitting the half-shut window.

Jilaine told me quickly about Chris, an artist-tutor, and Philippa, who had left his studio in a huff. Fed up, I surmised, at making tea, fetching beer, and/or being mauled.

Jilaine glanced at the now angry, de-beaded girl in the yard, the men jeering and mocking her.

"Why do men treat women so badly over such little things?"

It might have been one of those crude jokes. But she only sounded mystified, genuinely, as if she came of another race entirely from men and women both.

"You sound like a sightseer from Venus," I risked saying, or the vodka did.

"Do I? Well I suppose I've just been lucky, with some of the people I've known."

And now your luck has changed, Jilaine.

She had only smoked one cigarette, and we'd been here an hour now. Only drunk half her second drink. No laxity there, or not much. *No* dependence.

I said, "Anyway, it was nice to be asked to the party." I am cunning too, you see. A chancer always.

"Come along anyway," she said. "It won't get going until nine or ten. Look, here's the address." She wrote it for me on a piece of paper torn from a little notebook.

I said, "But you *will* be there?" Her eyes then somehow paler, and new-aquarium clear. "I mean, I don't know any of the others, despite our – mistake."

"Yes, I'll be there. But they won't mind. They love a crowd. Just tell them you know me."

Then she got up, fluid as a wave upon a shore. And left me.

And I thought, I don't know where she lives, and she's gone now and won't bother with the party. She thinks she's sussed me out. A slaggy girl who wants a 'good' time, free booze and lots of men around.

But then I thought, *They know her. They'll know where I can find her.*

So I bolted to the street, managed to catch a bus, and got back inside half an hour to Compton Road – in time to grab the sequestered bath.

I'm always seeing it with envy. This Friday night thing. All caution flung away, drinking and jollity, because tomorrow is Saturday, and no one has to get up. But almost every job I've had, I have to work on Saturdays. They are the busiest, most 'demanding' days.

This Friday night party, anyway, was at a house in Heathways – the area locals once called Little Highgate.

The cab I'd had to take went through the quaint cobbled Village, there in the heart of the seamy suburbs. Fake gas lampies, and little antique shops with real antiques, dress shops with two-hundred pound belts and three-hundred pound jumpers in the windows, a wine bar with Cecil B DeMille Egyptian pillars. Then up the hill, under gardens of drooping luxuriant trees set with faintly glimmering windows, so for a moment Victoria still reigned.

When we found the house on Jilaine's piece of paper, and I'd got out, the taxi driver got out too. As I stood looking up at the flight of white stairs to the dim-lit door framed among the oak trees, he stood beside me. Was he going to harangue me about the mean tip I had given him?

"Sure that's the place?"

"I think so."

"Doesn't look much like a party to me."

I glanced at him. Was it any of his business?

Until then I hadn't noticed him really. A bit of obligatory mundane chat I'd forgotten – during which I'd obviously mentioned the word 'party'. He was just another man, driving a cab. The cap-thing on top of the car read *Surefire*.

I took a step away and he said, "I'll hang around if you like. Until you're certain."

"I am, thanks."

"Only, you see, I had something like this *last* Friday. Same area, down behind the Village. Couple of girls, all done up. And when they got there, wrong address. There's some guy makes a habit of it, maybe. Stringing girls along."

"Oh, don't you all do that?" I flirtatiously asked.

He laughed. "Not me, baby."

I saw him, by the wan greenish gleer of a posh (pretending to be gas) streetlamp. He was young, about my age, and taller than me, which, if I'm wearing heels, older men are sometimes not. Good-looking. Knew it. Ah, he was trying to pick me up. I must look as good as I'd hoped to, in my short black dress and eye make-up.

I've had to get used to being OK with men. It isn't always safe to be otherwise.

I smiled at him. "Look, it's really nice of you. Not everyone would bother.

But I know these people. It's fine."

"You know *them*, but not the house."

"That's right."

He folded his arms. He would be my bodyguard. I was nervous anyway. Eager – but not for him. I could have shot him and stuffed him down a drain. It's a very good thing, oh yes, such people as I have no power. Although I think, actually, some of them must do.

"I know," I said brightly. "Why don't you let me have your firm's number again? Then I can call them from the Village if anything goes wrong. Not that it will."

He grinned now. He had white teeth. Any other woman would probably have been pleased with him. He even had a London accent, as opposed to gutturals.

While he wrote on the card, I heard some music start in the house. Nothing very interesting, party music of a sort. Look, you see, it *is* a party.

The driver of course was writing his own personal phone number on the back of the card. He gave it to me. "Call any time. Ask for Jud."

"OK. Thanks. Bye for now."

He watched me up the stairs. The door, when I reached it, was after all on the latch, and I went straight in. I forgot him.

If you're rich, I imagine it's all right to have a bit of damp. I could smell it here and there, and in the old Edwardian bathroom. But the bath was enormous – even the lavatory was – a thin drunk guest could easily slip right in and drown.

I sat on the closed seat, disdaining the cute wicker chair in the corner. I studied the mock Cretan wall tiles. There were plenty of other conveniences in the house. I had counted at least two apart from this one. And I was in retreat.

She wasn't here. It was after 11 o'clock now, and she wasn't. Nowhere in the tall, wide-roomed house, not even in the vast white kitchen of steel gadgets, with which Angus and Ginny doubtless tortured their staff, not even in the au pair's room with the en suite everything.

Angus and Ginny dealt in art. What more can I say?

We'd 'met' in the through dining-living-chattering room, already among about a hundred people, as I feebly tried to say Jilaine had invited me, was it all right? He asked my name with hearty laughs and assumed I was another artist. I baulked, I don't know why.

"No, I'm a writer."

"Wonderful. Would I have seen anything?"

I thought of lying. Before I did or didn't, Angus added, "But I have to be truthful now. I don't read. Quite dreadful, isn't it? I've lost the knack, really. Unless it's in pictorial form of some kind, I can't make it out."

He was a large middle-aged russet man, hair and face. He wore a tartan bow tie, but his accent was Chelsea. Ginny, I saw her across the crowded room, was around thirty-five. She was a slender garden rake with tines of black hair, and an accent of glottal stops.

Jilaine knew these people. But you could know people quite well and not be of their herd. I, presumably, belonged with Doll and Rita and the cook. Or with the outcasts of Compton Road.

There was lots of quite serious food. Smoked salmon, and fresh pâté and cheeses. Turkish bread. Every sort of wine, including Retsina, and other booze – a Russian liqueur spelled something like XCΔP.

Some people had talked to me, then lost interest. Men were attracted perhaps by the beacon of an unattached girl. But I wasn't for them. I should have made more effort. Would I be asked to leave? I wasn't sociably getting pissed or even tipsy. I wasn't making small talk or big talk, bedroom eyes, money... useless.

I did see who Chris and Ron were. A gay couple who began by kissing a lot, then later sniped at each other. Could it be the phantom Philippa had also made an appearance, this someone who looked like me? But no one else had mistaken me for her, thank God.

There was Art on the walls, inevitably. I don't like those sorts of abstracts, drawn mathematically around packing boxes or sprayed on through cogwheels. But in the upper halls there were some gorgeous drawings, slightly pornographic, washy ink and charcoal, one of which might have been an original Degas – if he ever did such things. But they were unsigned mostly.

However, Jilaine.

Was she pinned up on some wall somewhere? Or out in the small priceless garden, naked, posed among the bay trees in pots?

I ought to leave. Even I could tell it would be sticky getting her address or telephone number from anyone here. Less their guardedness, although that might be a factor, more their incompetence.

Someone rapped like a schoolmistress on the bathroom door. "Are you ever coming out?" it was the voice of Chris, bitchy with grenadine and California dry white.

I flushed the lavatory, ran some water, exited.

"Sorry." I am placatory only through cowardice. Chris looked feverish and dodgy.

About to brush past me into the bathroom, he paused. "Oh shit, you're that girl she thought was Philip, aren't you?"

My heart fell down, splashing in the one glass of wine I'd had.

"Er – do you mean...?"

"Philippa. That bloody girl."

Supposedly I am gay – a Lesbian. This seems to establish that I should be loving and caring of my brother gay men. But I've met a lot like Chris.

I looked at him. He was less dangerous than bats.

"Jilaine thought I was Philippa."

"But you're not."

121

"No, of course not."

"Well, I'd hardly know any more. That was all over a year ago. She couldn't paint her arse for fucking toffee."

"Is Jilaine...?" I had got it out. To the wrong one. To no avail.

"Oh, Jilaine. She's not here, is she?"

"Excuse me."

"Yes, I excuse you," he snapped, and locked himself into the bathroom. The whoosh of his urine was so loud, I heard it all the way down the stairs. I hoped I would be gone before he started to barf.

Off the wide hall, across from the through-room, was a kind of sitting room that led into a conservatory. And there were a few people there, sitting talking. The music was less loud and had anyway switched to a nostalgic CD, songs from long ago. I had stepped into the doorway to avoid a chuffing train of people from the kitchen. Then I saw on the wall of the sitting-room one painting, not very large, beautiful. I knew the moment I saw it. I knew Jilaine had painted it.

Why? I didn't even know then that she painted. She hadn't said so, no one had. But it was like *her*.

I walked across and stood looking up at it. A watercolour, it was behind glass, but that glass which doesn't reflect. In the low light, it might have been – naked.

A scene. Low hills in a floating distance. A nearer view of fields with three strange spreading trees. It was dusk – just one mauve scarf of colour left behind – no, lilac is the adjective. And the time that was – still is, I don't know how – magical for me.

"That's one of mine."

I didn't even turn round. "I know," I said.

Then the shock hit me. I managed not to drop my glass.

Better turn now. I did.

She had just appeared behind me, from nowhere. Off a wall, out of the floor. She had the same dress on she'd worn earlier, with the cap sleeves.

"I didn't think I'd see you."

She shrugged. She was so composed. That was her quality, more than all others.

I don't mean control of self, or even serenity. Just resting lightly there, soft yet held all in one piece, herself. Composure. Stillness.

Of course, I've seen her lose both. The scene of that is burnt in on my mind. A hospital brain scan would probably show it quite markedly.

"Are you having a good time?" she asked. She had a glass of red wine. She looked herself like a toned picture – the single glimpse of plum red to match her toenails. But white wine would have been all right. It would have matched her hair.

"Oh, yes."

"You don't look as if you are."

"Well... I don't know anyone."

"Surely somebody's tried to rectify that?"

"One or two."

"Oh dear." It wasn't a jibe. But nor was she concerned. She had thought I was out hunting for a man?

"They're not my sort of people," I said. "It's like being at the court of the Czar or something. Another language, another world."

I hadn't meant to be so honest. Or, I had.

She nodded anyway.

"Yes, I know what you mean."

"Do you?"

"Yes."

"Why did you come then – and why so late?" It was by now past midnight; I'd just seen a clock. But I sounded challenging, as if I had rights to feel – my God – stood up.

She said, "I got sad this evening. I do sometimes. Then I thought I should just drop by. Angus is my oldest friend. Since childhood nearly. He lets me exhibit sometimes at his place in London. But he always says I only ever paint one picture. And that one on the wall, he says, is the best I've ever done it. So I gave him the picture."

A lot of information.

I said, randomly, "I met Chris."

"I see he was rude."

"Sloshed."

"But you're not Philippa, so it won't matter. Who are you? May I ask? I didn't think to, before."

"Jayne. Only I prefer Jay."

"Darling," she said, with no affectation – it rocked me, though evidently it meant not one thing, "I just have to go and have a word with Ron. He looks so wretched. If Chris is being awful, I can see why. Why don't you get us another drink? I'll come and find you."

You could find me in the Sahara Desert, I thought.

Ridiculous.

Anyway, I thought, this is an excuse. She's done her duty by me. She won't come back.

But I went to get the drinks. There was a very good claret I located for her, and a new cold Pinot Grigio.

Actually I took the bottles, which were both two-thirds full. I went and sat in the little garden on a hand-carved bench behind the bay trees. My incredible arrogance.

"*Darling...*"

Someone else found me instead. Another of the roaming males.

"Hi. I'm Charles. How are you?"

"Waiting for someone."

"Aren't we all? Who is the lucky one?"

123

"Just a friend."

"It's Jilly, isn't it? I mean Jilaine Best?" I shuddered at the abbreviation of her name. "Ronny's got her. Crying buckets on her shoulder. You'll have to make do with me for now."

Some of those words seemed to imply something. My ranging mind worried at them – make do – knowing at once who I'd meant – was there something to this, some clue?

"How did you meet Jilly?" wondered Charles.

"What? Oh, in a café."

"*Really.*"

I drank the pinot, offering nothing, but he had a full glass.

Above, the stars, temporarily free of the Lucozade globes of common streets, glittered languidly, expensive white and blue.

His full glass was empty.

"I used to have a crush on Jilaine once," he said, to the stars. "But she's a funny little thing. She never had to graft. Rich mother – Lesley Spender – maybe you've heard of her?" A long wait, then his demanding stare.

"No."

"You haven't? But I thought you were a painter?"

"And decorator, actually."

"Good God, *are* you? I could do with some help there – do you have a card?"

"Not on me." But oddly I thought of the cab man's card and considered for a moment giving him that, see what he made of *that*, in the cold light of morning. "Tell me about Lesley Spender."

"Oh, she painted. Wonderfully. Tiny little portraits and domestic scenes – exquisite. Then she got cancer and died. Jilaine was eighteen. Left her everything."

"Including the grief," I heard myself say.

"Yes." Insensitive, he only mulled the idea of grief around. "Yes, she did like her mother. You girls do, don't you?"

"I didn't like mine."

Careful, I thought. *Just be careful.*

But Charles was all interested, naturally. "You didn't get on."

"Well, she was a whore, you see." And she had been. But one too stupid to charge for it.

"How fascinating."

"No."

"No, but what about you?"

"I'm not on the game."

"I didn't mean..."

He lapsed.

Then he slid his arm around me. My bare shoulders spasmed at his touch.

"I've got off on the wrong foot. How about we go on somewhere. There's

124

a club I know."

"Sorry. That would be lovely, some other time. Not tonight." Placatory enough? He seemed moodily to accept it.

"Some other time, then. Are you in the book?"

"Under Painting and Decorating. Look for *Surefire*."

"What a fabulous name. Shan't forget that."

He had gone, and the noise in the house was louder again, but perhaps no one cared. There seemed to be a park the other side of the house, and a distant high wall with a gateway etched in starlight.

She was rich, then. Her mother had been a famous painter. And he had said – *You'll have to make do with me.* But that wasn't a clue to Jilaine's sexual tastes, just the male tendency to amusedly belittle their own grandeur, which everyone knew was supreme: A mere man, etc. etc.

She didn't come back.

I had known she wouldn't. It was 1.30, a quarter to two.

I left the bottles on the paving, on about three thousand pounds' worth of it.

Back in the hall, the CD was playing *September Song*. A couple were on the front steps, not snogging, as in the days of my teenagedness they would have been, but secretively comparing dreamed personal power numbers. He in his Armani suit and she in hers.

IV

As I was walking down the Village cobbles, glad of the coolness of early morning, Jud drove up in his cab. "Want a lift?"

I had meant to walk to the all-night taxi place behind the pub I'd seen on the way up. But *Surefire* would do, provided the guy wasn't too off his head.

I didn't get in. I said, "Maybe. What a coincidence though, your being here."

"I been hanging around," he said frankly. "I got off at midnight, come back."

"So you're not working."

"No. I won't charge you for the ride."

"Then I don't think I can accept."

"Oh, come on," he said, rueful and boyish, the way they go, even the young men. "I was a bit concerned. I'm not after anything."

I've been raped. So what.

Into the cab I got, into the back seat, and he let me.

He drove me back across Heathways, across benighted suburbs, garish shut high streets, and down into the slums, to Compton Road. He talked a bit, more as if to put me at my ease. He told me things about him, his credentials. I wasn't listening properly, but I tried to be sweet and polite and a worthwhile person who should be driven home but not attacked. He didn't attack me. And when I insisted I must pay, he let me, but half price.

He stood on the pavement with me outside number 12.

125

"This you?"

"I'm afraid so."

"Yeah. Looks like the dump I was in till last year." He had some sort of house now, I'd gathered, shared with a friend – though he'd left his girlfriend. He would probably want a kiss and a feel. I'd let him have it. We were out of the car, probably safe. What did it matter?

"You know," he said, "you need looking after."

"Do you think so?"

"Well, I wouldn't mind doing it." He didn't lean forward to slobber. He just put one hand very gently, warmly, on my shoulder.

"I'd better go in."

"Yeah, it's getting chilly now. Be some rain in the morning, I reckon." And a weather forecaster too. "Go for a drink with me tomorrow night?"

"I have to work."

"Well, after work."

"No, I work late."

"So do I. Up till eight. Meet you then."

"No, I can't. Sorry."

"Sunday."

"Sorry."

"Monday, Tuesday, Wednesday?"

"I'm really sorry."

He smiled. Bold in defeat or just undefeated. He must meet so many girls, women, females. Few would say no. He even smelled nice, of cleanness and health and some masculine cologne. Film star hair, better cut. I didn't mind him. Should I say yes, should I try? Why try, I knew, I knew.

"Well," he said. "Great meeting you. Take care, then."

They're not usually like that. They sulk, even get angry. One lectured then hit me, once, just for saying no. That was when I learned to be careful in my speech.

Only I'm not always careful enough.

He waited until I was up the drive and on the top step and letting myself in before he drove smoothly away in trusty *Surefire*.

PART TWO

I

Sometimes I think I do remember my father, but he doesn't have a face. That is, I seem to remember his figure, even some of his clothes, thick short hair, even his well-shaped ears. But his face is smudged out. He left her when I was three. I never knew who he had been until long after he had gone, and then from things she said.

I've told you she was a dancer, my mother, and called her a whore. But she wasn't practical enough to be a stripper. She used to be in chorus lines, and once, in Plymouth, she was second lead in a production called *The Mutineers*. And then she got pregnant. Me.

"I thought about having you out." She often said that. As if I was a bad tooth.

On the other hand, I never felt any recrimination, and she invariably added, "But you were alive, weren't you, Jayney? So I couldn't."

She never said *You ruined my budding career*. And that was her damned truthfulness. Because I hadn't. She never had one, never would have done. I don't know if she was talented. The times I saw her dancing, usually when I was a child, ill-sick with tiredness late at night, stuck in some corner of a rehearsal room, hated by all for being there as if it were an undeserved treat for me – those times she looked all right. Once I saw her on stage in a weird production, a sort of precursor of *Cats*. She played a tabby. She was amazing in that, fluid and dreamy. It didn't make me love her, but I admired her.

What did she look like? She was, for then, tall, five foot eight – that hadn't helped her career either – the shorter men didn't like it. Slim and strong, with satiny bubbly fair hair she sometimes bleached. She had long, long legs. Her legs were her greatest assets, and the mini skirt had been her one true friend.

The funny thing is, she died when I was eighteen. Like Jilaine's famous successful mother.

I was at the seaside, (Bournemouth) with a boyfriend – a genuine one, because in those days I was still attempting to be traditional. The police arrived at nine o'clock, when we were still in bed, and I remember how uncomfortable the man looked, and the WPC retributive, God's judgement on me for my sins of the flesh, this death of my mother.

It wasn't illness. She fell off a train – a train that was stationary – and hit her head. When people stopped stepping round her and started to fuss and pick her up – she was dead. Blissfully quick, as the boarding-house woman said to me, crying the tears I wouldn't or couldn't.

I suppose it was. She was on her way to another audition, and she would never have got the bloody job, she was over forty by then. Death gave her a job instead, the job we all get, of being dead.

Weeks passed, nearly a month.

Did I forget about Jilaine? No. In the café, I kept expecting her to walk in suddenly, in a shaft of angelic light, not remembering me at all. Some days I felt sick with thinking she would come in. And one day when a young blonde woman was at a table, for a second I thought it was Jilaine, and it wasn't.

"I've cut my hand. I need to go for a plaster."

"Can't you wrap a cloth round it?" The evil cook spun like a spider among her poisonous brews, which I would never eat, though for me a café lunch would have been free.

"I'd better not. Look, the blood's going in the salad."

She gave her insane sneering laugh. I'd do anything to skive off, even sever a main artery.

I was shaking, not like a leaf, but like a woman who thought she just saw her beloved, found it wasn't, went to cut a normal tomato and instead sliced herself, tomato red, all over the coleslaw.

Jilaine would avoid the café. Avoid *me*. Then again, why ever had she, daughter of the famous, rich and upper crust of Heathways, *ever* been in this *place*?

I was being very silly, thinking about her so much. They came and went. Even if this one hadn't *come*.

The idea was that on my three days off, Sunday, Monday and Tuesday, I would write, or just please myself. Now and then, to supplement my income, I worked a five-day week, or they 'asked' me to work extra days if one of the others was off. Then I only had one or two days left. This had recently happened a lot. So, I decided I too would now fall ill, and take the whole week, except Saturday. If I didn't work, they didn't pay me, but if I missed a Saturday, that day of 'demands', I might be sacked.

It was a glory of a week. Summer was spilling over. The ancient trees in Compton Road, briefly brave, lifted their viridian crowns to a tinderbox day. Everything smelled of car exhaust and geraniums and the scented bodies of women.

On Wednesday – were you ahead of me? – I took the bus to North Heath Station and walked up through Heathways Village.

I walked right up the hill to the house by the park, or whatever open space that was. Obviously, there was no information to be gained from standing on the street, so I crossed over, climbed the steps and rang the bell.

No one came for about ten minutes. Then the au pair answered the door, as all good au pairs should.

She was young and bored and dark, from Italy, I think.

"Yes?"

"Is Angus in?"

The cheek of me. I never afterwards grasp how I can do such things. I do them sober, even. I do them without a quiver. The shakes and cut blood arrive later.

"Mr McIndoe out. In London at *Painted Box*."

"Oh, I see. Ginny then?"

"Mrs Ginny at hair-makers. Baby in crèche. Who I say called?"

(There had been no sign of a baby, either in the house or about Ginny. Perhaps it had also been in a crèche during the party or locked and gagged in a cupboard.)

"It doesn't matter. Oh..." an afterthought , "I'm trying to get hold of Jilaine Best – about a painting – Do you have...?"

Impatient with my time-consumption, she flicked me through into the hall with imperious narrow hands. She was a pretty girl, rotten as they come. An idiot too. I could have been anyone. I *was* anyone.

On the polished table by the fern and the white telephone, a book.

"Mr McIndoe keep all 'is people in here."

Prisoners. The baby too, perhaps, when at home, slammed shut inside.

"Thanks." I tried under J, but he had filed her, as he seemed to have done them all, under surname. *Best: Jilaine.* Best Jilaine she was, better than all Jilaines, a paragon among Jilainians.

Not a Heathways address. Too far south, towards the river.

"Great."

"Who I say called?"

"Oh – Clytemnestra," I airily exclaimed, descending with Her address, Her phone number, inebriated with mad joy, down the steps. "Clytemnestra Fitz-Havard."

"Fizz Hover?" she wailed behind me.

Poor bitch.

I walked round the street and up a leafy lane, to help confuse the Italian girl in Algiers as to my destination. An old ride went in through the hedges, and then I found the park or gardens, wild in sunlight, and the towered arch rising behind in a stone wall.

There were poppies and cornflowers growing wild in the savage grass. What a curious and blessed place. Like something in an imaginative children's book, an alternate land found unexpectedly. Even *Narnia,* that delight of the middle classes, which I had also loved, though failed to understand until too old to see any more as a child, *clearly* through the dark glasses.

Beyond the arch, a circuitous way ran down to the Village and this world.

I went into a tea shoppe and had tea and scones I couldn't afford. I was waited on by a smart woman in high heels. She treated me like the wandering rubbish I was. I didn't leave a tip, since rubbish doesn't have to.

Jilaine is in London, said her lovely, slightly lisping, recorded voice. *Try The Painted Box or Wendovers. Or leave me a message, please, after the tone.*

How unwise to tell us all, the burglars who reportedly call numbers to learn who is from home, the wicked who will deposit untrue communications.

I left no message

What could I say?

I think of you? I think of you in all possible ways, sacred and profane.

I cut my finger off thinking of you. A sacrifice.

It hadn't even needed stitching anyway, the finger. Although the scar might be interesting, if it lasted.

Would I now go into town and seek this thing called *The Painted Box* – or Wendovers, whatever they were?

I lay on my mattress, considering it, and the dusk came, alight with its spurious anticipations.

Feet on the stairs turned and moved to my door. Light footfalls, but not a woman's. And the knock was male.

When I opened the door, there he was. Surefire Jud.

"Hi," he said, "don't get scared. The girl with green hair let me in."

"Olivine."

"That her name?"

"Olivine Pratt."

He grinned. He was handing me something. It was yellow flames, three sunflowers on sword stems like angelica.

"Now no – I can't..."

"Go on. They're what you ought to have."

I liked them, the sunflowers. I *like* sunflowers. How odd, how bizarre, there had been sunflowers, little ones growing wild, in the park at Heathways. But these were wrapped in gold tissue paper.

"It's very generous of you."

"I hoped you'd change your mind."

The landing was hot, and ammoniac from cats that sprayed there and everywhere so the rest of us knew our place.

"You'd better come in."

He walked into the Room. Jud was tanned, and glamorous. His hair had grown even longer and thicker, to his shoulders. So seethed in his powers he was, how could I say no? I can't always cope, you see. The Will of others. I don't know why I can't.

As I put the flowers in water, he stood in the Room's centre.

"That's a great plant."

"Yes. Would you like some tea?"

"Yeah. Or, why don't you come for a drink. Just down to your local. It looked all right."

He wore jeans, tight as skin. He was only bones and lean muscle and tan. The shirt was white as snow. Dark eyes.

Any girl would have to say yes, yes please. "All right. Let me buy *you* a drink then. To say thanks for the ride the other night. And the flowers."

"You're on."

But I'm not. I'm saying I'm buying you – off.

How long since I had done this, walked into a pub with a handsome man, my own age and taller. A Boyfriend.

"No, it's OK. You can get the next lot."

He had pre-empted me. He'd bought the vodka, and his Budweiser.

We sat down.

I didn't think of Jilaine, a month ago in the Knight's Arms. The local was called *The Cock*, with obvious results.

Now what? What would we say?

"Bet you think I'm pushy," he said.

"Yes. But of course, I'm flattered."

"No, you're not. Thanks for coming out."

"Well – that's OK. But you see, I..."

"You're involved with someone else."

"Yes."

"Some seven-foot guy with a proper bank balance who works reasonable hours."

"No, but..."

"It's all right. It's just nice to see you. I like looking at you." He smiled. "You're special, I'd say."

We all think we are. It was a line, but psychologically a clever one.

"What can I say to that?"

"Say, yes. Say, Jud, you're right, I am special."

I smilingly lowered my eyes. The vodka was strong and cold, delicious, and suddenly I was heavy with hope. I knew her address. I could find her. I would try again. Always try again. Like Jud.

He started to talk, about his terraced house, his dad – family – I think he did. My mind didn't stay with him. They usually think you're listening. I looked gravely at him, nodding. When he asked me questions, I could always dodge them in various ways.

I got the next round, mine an orange juice to save money, and I was going to say, "I'm sorry but I have to call someone at 10."

"Do you like Indian food?" he asked.

"No, not much."

"Italian then?"

"You see..."

"Jud. Say my name."

"Jud..."

"And you are what? Go on, you can tell me."

"Jay."

"Jay. I like that. Like the bird. Blue-jay. Do blue jays like Italian food, or do they prefer Thai...?"

"Jud, you've been so nice, really, and I do like you, and if things were different. But I am involved..."

"And he lets you live in that room," he said, flatly. No condemnation. A statement.

"Shall we say, I value my independence."

"Yeah. I should keep my trap shut. Sorry."

"It's perfectly all right. But now I have to get back."

"And you don't want me calling round again."

"It's just so difficult – you are very nice, and I feel wrong seeing you, when he..."

"Yeah. No, you're right. Yeah. Come on, I'll walk you back."

He looked sad. Not sulky or embarrassed or bad-tempered. Sad.

Sad because he had failed to woo me. Not knowing the ghastly frigid cow he had been spared the vileness of.

"What happened to your finger?" he asked, when we were almost there.

"Salad knife at work." Better be truthful. Or he might think my Male Involvement had done it and want to bash him.

But Jud only said, "Weird. Looks like a wedding ring."

Outside number 12 he kissed me on the cheek. A car went by, explosive with bad, pointless beat music. In the mind-shelling noise of it he was somehow gone.

Sorry.

Oh shit, sorry, sorry, Jud.

II

I got the number of *The Painted Box* from directory enquiries. Then phoned them, as it were, *blind*. But their identity was at once revealed.

"*Gallery Painted Box*. How may I help you?"

Before this cold, ultra-courteous voice spoke to me, I'd had half an idea I would simply ask to speak to Jilaine. Somehow I couldn't, now, ask that of this voice. But a deduction was easy enough to make.

"Jilaine Best has an exhibition with you?"

"We will be showing examples of Best and Appleby from the 16th. The Gaunt prints are already showing upstairs."

The 16th was tomorrow. Friday.

I didn't want to wait. I got an address from the voice and caught the 12.08 for Charing Cross.

The gallery was just off Covent Garden, a yellow toy block decorated in rose, wedged among the pubs and office buildings.

You had to ring at the door, and then they let you in. It cost ten pounds – no nonsense of free admissions.

I did what they expected and went straight up the winding stair and idled about in the cramped upper gallery, looking at the strange Gaunt prints of nude men and women like balloons, balloon rats making tea and balloon dogs waltzing.

No one else was there in this crowd but me. Only light streamed in, intermittently fractured by external flying pigeons.

Below, in the ground floor gallery, I could hear a rumble of sounds, things being moved, voices.

Presently I walked downstairs. I edged around the rack of postcards and troughs of prints. There were two long spaces, each through an arch. In the farthest of them great activity went on, the hoisting of huge canvases onto whitewashed walls. I glimpsed, among the overalled men, and men with untamed hair and jeans, red Angus McIndoe. Suddenly he gave a cry. "No, no, that can't be right!" And I heard a miraculous note of Edinburgh.

The other space seemed to have all its pictures hung. And these, I saw at once, were hers. Were Jilaine's.

The woman who guarded the door and the ten-pound-eating till had gone. So I walked through into the white room.

There were about thirty pictures, watercolours, gouache and oils, some quite small, a few much larger and a couple very large, almost too big for her – a foolish thing to say, but that was how it seemed to me. As if she would have had to struggle with them physically, and maybe she had.

She had said to me that Angus said she only ever painted one picture. Perhaps this was so. Although the subjects were different – landscapes, of hills, of water, of woods, and some groups of objects, flowers or fruit –yet they had a similar mood, a similar ambience – and almost all of them were caught in that web of 'tween light, that mysterious time of day (mine) between the westering of the sun and the close of darkness.

"Dear, dear, young lady. Now you shouldn't be in here."

Drifting in the sunfall, I nearly jumped out of my body.

Angus stood beside me, playfully wagging his finger.

Then he too seemed surprised. "Why – Philippa, is that you?"

I collected myself. (So I did resemble phantasmal Philippa. Whoever she might be.) "No, I'm afraid not. We met the other night. Your party, I was with Jilaine." Raised red brows. "Jay," I elaborated.

"Oh, really." Properly bemused now he shook his head. "Well even so, dear girl, you shouldn't be in here. We're not finished yet and Jilaine has yet to approve our toil."

"I'm sorry."

"Well, no harm done. I expect you've seen some of these before."

I smiled.

Angus said, "Tell me now, what do you think of that one?"

I looked where he pointed with the versatile finger. It was one of the biggest canvases, an oil painting. I had half been avoiding it, because it seemed to try to overpower all the rest.

"After the example I possess, this is her finest to date, I hazard," he said, knowing and contented. Then, "Would you say so?"

"I don't know enough to judge."

"Very modest and most sensible," he approved. In a moment I sensed he would place an avuncular arm about me. As if considering, I moved away and nearer the canvas.

Oh, it was beautiful enough. Very nearly an abstract, yet you could find images within it – yet perhaps too, they were only imagined or random – some collusion of the individual brain with chance. Like the Rorschach test,

I thought I could see a lake gleaming at the bottom of a bowl of mountains or hills. A sky of vast clouds, in dying sun. The colours were transparent oranges and tawny embered browns. But at the outer edges, and in one thin interior rift, I sensed some other colour, which seemed to have been drowned

133

or burned away, leaving nothing but a shape – a ghost – *colourless*.

"You know the name of this?" he sternly queried.

"I'm not sure. I don't think I do."

"Lomm Bay," he announced.

Then I had been right visualising water – only it must be the sea, not a lake.

"It's to do with the child, of course," said Angus abruptly. "But most of them – I may say all of them – are. That was when she started to paint. She wrote books before that. She makes no secret of it, so I expect you know."

I hadn't turned, and before I could, I heard the till woman clip-clop to the arch.

"Mr McIndoe. Casper Reynolds is here."

"Oh, Peggy, yes. Tell him I'll be with him straight. Well... Jayde – it was nice to see you again."

I thought, after he had gone, I could stay in the room with her painting, and with Lomm Bay in its flambeau glory, puzzling. But no. Cloppy Peggy was back.

"Can I help you? I'm afraid this part of the gallery isn't open for public viewing yet."

I'd spent much of my unearned non-existent week's wages, I now spent some more to placate her, buying postcards from the rack, of Cotman and Gwen John.

As I emerged on the street, I saw Jilaine getting out of a black taxi.

We always think we are the centre of Everything. Why not, for ourselves we inescapably are, what else. But when these things occur, their fatalness is all in their seeming aptitude.

My natural sense of treachery made me draw away at once from the door of *The Painted Box,* which had closed behind me. I stood anonymous outside a pub named *The Globe* – one more girl waiting for one more man who was late.

And she didn't notice me. Didn't remember me.

I watched her, walking across to the yellow toy cube. She too wore jeans, and a loose silky top, cream.

Then, just before the door of the gallery, she stopped. A few people were going by. Most were in the pub or outside at tables. If I was aware I was at the universe's centre, Jilaine knew she was way outside.

I never saw anyone cry like that. Her face didn't move, was uninvolved. Only her eyes, so large they let the tears so easily fall.

The wetness sparkled in the sunlight. Pigeons flew by. Somewhere there were cheers, cars roaring, a plane rupturing the sky.

Should I go to her? I wanted to. I wanted to take her in my arms. Don't cry, don't cry, darling don't – what is it? Let me help you – anything you want...

But for God's sake, who was I, to *her*?

So I just stood there under a flower basket, in a shadow, watching her. Cry.

And then she turned, and walked quickly away, and in my head I heard his cultured Chelsea-Scottish voice. "It's to do with the child, of course."

She had gone. London had swallowed her up as the orange inferno had swallowed up that other colour from her painting.

III

When I got back, I saw at once the sunflowers had drunk all their water in the heat and were dying. I filled their jug from the tap. I was sorry. This is always the way with me. I miss all danger until it's far too late.

Then I paced about, looking from the window, looking inside at the rotting walls, the stained sink and filthy cooker I never cleaned, and also hardly ever cooked on, so how did it need cleaning anyway?

Christ, Jilaine. Why were you crying like that?

The child. Of course?

What child? Which child?

Hers, I supposed, must be hers. She was young, but old enough. She could have had a child – even when she was as young as thirteen, perhaps, like that friend of my childhood, Mary, a disgraced Catholic. I could still recollect the tale she told me, over coffee and fags three years later, when, unknown to my mother, Mary and I met at a Wimpy Bar.

She gave me a long sermon, Mary, about how the nuns, in the place they sent her to have it, were so kind, and explained what a wonderful experience it was for a woman to *bear* a child – she didn't have to keep it. And they didn't let Mary keep it. And Mary didn't want to, but at sixteen she was still sobbing away into the coffee because she hadn't.

So, that was it?

This child.

Then I went down again to the payphone in the lower hall and called Jilaine's number. Olivine was on the stairs playing with one of the cats. With food colouring (she said), she had turned its fur in patches green, like her own hair. The cat didn't seem to mind.

The phone rang. No message. Then I heard her speak. "Hallo?"

It was as if my heart stopped. Everything stopped. And I threw the receiver down. In those days, you couldn't trace an unspeaking call.

Olivine did not comment. The cat shrank against her as I ran back upstairs. When I came down again, they were both gone.

Using buses, and then walking the last bit, with the map I'd concocted from the Geographia, it took me an hour and thirty-two minutes to reach Jilaine's address.

It was that time. Sun westering, sunset beginning. The sky was bronze.

A long wide road leads towards the river, with trees. Then there is the building, hers. Cobham Court. If I say flats, that doesn't quite convey the picture.

135

The shell was old, but marvellously renovated. There were gardens around it, manicured trees standing black on the metal sky, like a detail from some Renaissance painting of lords or saints. The piece they reproduce to demonstrate something, and which I always prefer to the whole.

I walked all around the wall and the building. I looked at the sculptured conifers against the sunset. To the front, the land shelved down. There were mudflats above the river, and gold-washed ducks were mucking about in the tidal shallows. A green island grew in the middle of the water, drenched with falling sun.

I had no excuse for coming here. The moth has none, flinging itself into the flame. How dare it burn its wings and die like that? The cheek of it.

Back at the entrance, which lay to the side on the street, I took a paved walk, went by discreet garages screened in cedars, and up to the big glass-fronted doorway.

There would be a porter, this sort of place. What would I say?

The facts. I've come to see Jilaine Best. Apartment 4.

"I've come to see Miss Best. Flat 4."

"Good evening. Just one moment while I buzz."

Was he a wasp?

Who? she will say. Throw this impostor out, throw her in the river.

"That's fine. Take the lift, if you like to."

He didn't even ask my name, *she* didn't.

She must be expecting someone.

I did use the lift. My body felt insecure, and there were three flights of marble stairs otherwise.

When the lift halted there was a wide vestibule, with two broad, sunlit windows. Just one door, facing me – number 4.

I didn't touch the bell. I stood there, frightened. Too late, as ever. And the smart flat 4 door was opened.

"The bell doesn't always work," she said.

In a place like this? "Yes..."

"It's you. That's a relief. I was afraid it was – someone else."

"You're expecting someone?"

"No, but I messed them about at the gallery. I was supposed to go over. Please do come in."

Did she know who I was? I had stood not much farther from her this afternoon, and she hadn't seen me. But she had been crying then.

Not now. She was still wearing jeans, another loose top, this time pale grey. It made her look so slender and almost not there.

"I brought you these."

"They're gorgeous. Thank you."

She drew from my arms the flowers I'd spent a third of my rent money on. Not sunflowers, but a kind of blue convolvulus, a twilight shade, and some giant marigold things.

Jud had shown me what you had to do, in situations like this. But even Jud hadn't been successful.

She did this effortless thing, gliding across the long luminous floor, taking up a bulb of clear glass, pouring in water – not from the tap, but from a bottle – letting the flowers down into it gently, gently, so they fell at once into a flooding alignment, which she placed on a round table that seemed only to have been waiting for them. All in about five seconds.

"Would you like a drink?"

"Yes, thank you."

"You drink vodka, don't you, like me?"

This was much too easy. I would have the drink, and then I would be expected to go. Did she even know, really, who I was?"

She said, "When I called Angus, he said you'd dropped by the show. Of course, it's not officially open until tomorrow."

"He thought I was Philippa."

"You are very like her. It was odd, the way you named her painting." Her eyes, just for a moment, crystal clear on me.

"*The Galloping Magi.* I shouldn't have."

"Well, you see, it was a picture of running horses – under a star. Curiously apt."

"Life being stranger than fiction," I said.

"Yes. Often."

The room was very, very big. The floor, with a pool of light in it, was sunset marble. I don't exaggerate. It *was* marble, I know that for a fact, pinkish white marmoreal, with a faint patterning of dilute red. There was a tall fireplace for actual fire, but empty now, nothing standing there to screen or apologise for it, but a smooth stone cat lying in front. Some pieces of furniture stood about. Mirrors, one convex, this one showing up all the room again coiled in little, in a frame of gilded leaves and acorns. Not any pictures that I registered.

Outside two tapering open glass doors was an octagonally paved terrace, with greenery on it and a statue of some modern classical kind. And beyond that the river curved there in the air, and then all the rest of London went ebbing away into the sinking sun.

I didn't absorb much of it, that first time. It was so like what you hear of and don't believe in because you will never be among such things, let alone possess them.

The Magic Castle. Beautiful anyway. Like her.

We went out past some filmy curtains looped back, and sat at a dark turquoise iron table in two dark turquoise iron chairs, to drink the vodka out of, not glasses, but black lacquer beakers. She had brought the bottle, some ice, lemons and a knife. No cigarettes.

"Thank God it still gets cool in the evenings. That isn't going to last, I don't think. There may be a storm."

And a weather forecaster too.

I drank the vodka. Something moved in me. I can be such a guarded one, I can hold away from all of them so long. And then, then this.

"I saw you this afternoon, when I came out of the gallery."

"You saw me?" She looked only mildly, politely, interested.

"You were upset."

"Was I?"

Compared to her sheer impervious sweetness, not a ripple on her surface, my connivance was and is laughable and almost obscene.

"I must have been mistaken," I said.

"Oh well." She shrugged. "It's been one of those days."

Just then a tiny shining high-up plane murmured over. It sewed a distinctive pathway through the glowing sky, turning eventually, with a fiery flash, as if it had just seen the sun, and knew it must not dive into it.

This was a route all the planes took, going over Jilaine's terrace, each turning at exactly the same spot, which must have a distinctive signpost in the sky, invisible from below.

She hadn't even asked me how I knew where she lived. I'd had my lie all ready... *Oh, someone at the party mentioned these flats, this road.*

"I'm glad you dropped by," she said. "I love being alone, but sometimes – sometimes a little company is very welcome."

"You get sad sometimes."

"You remember my saying that? Yes, I do. We all do, no doubt."

"Yes."

"My mother was like that," she said. "She had her melancholy times. In fact black depressions, possibly."

I thought of the amiable Charles telling me about Jilaine's mother, the famous artist, who had left Jilaine all her wealth.

"Lesley Spender," I said.

Jilaine glanced at me. "Oh, that again," she said. Her eyes, only for a split second, were hard. "No. They always get it wrong. My mother wasn't Lesley Spender. My mother was Françoise Corrizonde. They were very close friends. Oh, they were lovers, actually."

An electric spear passed through my stomach.

"Yes?" I asked.

"Yes. Are you very shocked? It's worse. I lived with both of them from childhood, they brought me up. Hence the confusion. Then Lesley died, and my mother..." Jilaine hesitated. She said firmly, "My mother ran away. I don't to this day know where she went. If she's alive or dead. It was all right then. I was eighteen, old enough and brash enough to know what to do with myself. And Lesley had left us – and so me – financially well off. There were complications, but that's what lawyers are for. And friends."

"Your mother was an artist?"

"She painted, but mostly she was Lesley's model. Lesley did some beautiful studies of her. There's one in the Tate, if you care to know." She didn't sound arch or irritated, only used to recounting all this.

"Did she paint you?"

"Yes. They both did. But those weren't so good. I used to get bored, wouldn't stay still. And anyway, she loved my mother, not me. And Françoise was – well she was absolutely stupidly beautiful. Her looks – they could be terrifying. I remember once, when they were going to some dinner, I was eleven, I think. And my mother came in to say goodnight. She had coal-black hair, masses of it, like a thunder cloud all around her head and shoulders, and this dress, gold on silver lamé – she looked like the goddess of lightning. She was one of those people who don't have any fat at all under the surface, their skins just flow like pelt."

I was staring at her. The sun was drawing in with gilt her profile, nose, lips, lashes.

"I wrote my first book about them, Lesley and Françoise. It was called *You and She*. I was only twenty. That's my excuse anyway."

She was telling me so much, like that other time. It's interesting perhaps to note how much sparser her writing is than her speech. Just as I rarely say very much, yet when writing incline to floridity.

And they had been lovers. Two female – Lesbian lovers had brought up Jilaine.

This exotic forbidden beginning, and all wrapped up safe among the banknotes and the silver and the gold.

I was jealous of her. Of it all.

And I knew she wasn't of their persuasion. She had grown away from their lesbianism as children do grow away from the *familiar* thing. As I had.

I wanted to say, harshly, *Tell me about this child you had – did that die or run away, too?*

My mouth stayed shut on the rim of the beaker of vodka and then I heard her telephone ring, back across the marble room.

The sun was down. The pool of light was sinking into her floor. I watched her standing there talking on the phone. Laughing. Why should I care if she were sad, or desperate? She deserved to suffer like the rest of us.

"Yes, I promise, I promise I will. I'll be in tomorrow at 8. Yes, Ginny, 8 a.m. I know, Ginny. Yes. Well, I did oversee a lot. I'm certain whatever Angus has done is perfect. Yes. Goodbye."

I got up.

"I'd better go."

Did I hope she would say *Please don't* or even *Must you, so soon*? But I'd been there an hour or more. And she didn't say that.

The ringing phone had rinsed the madness off me. I was sour and scared. I *wanted* to be gone, feeling now the crisping of my wings.

She found an invitation in a drawer.

"Come to the opening tomorrow. About 12 –there'll be drinks and a buffet, that sort of thing. It'll be nice to see a friendly face."

139

The foyer was grey. The sun was down, the trees shadowed the river and the street.

Dusk. *And one by one the stars come out, like girls in silver gowns, with lamps lit for the feast...*

"Oh yes. Thanks," I said. "If I can, I'd like to."

I wouldn't.

She must know I'm nothing. What could I be? I didn't paint. I wrote but hadn't published a thing except half a dozen short stories more or less by accident. And I hadn't any money. I didn't belong in Jilaine's polished marble world. She even had to assure me of free food and drink at the opening.

At the door, she leaned forward, upward. Kissed my cheek.

Just as Jud had done.

She smelled fragrantly blonde, of subtle powder and shampoo, and her own physical delights. Yum. Let me bite you, Jilaine, *eat* you Jilaine.

But the wolf turned from her door and went down in the lift.

"Goodnight, miss," said the porter.

IV

Where does wickedness begin? Do we achieve it or is it thrust upon us? Undoubtedly, some of us are born that way.

I didn't say. Before I left her flat, I'd asked to use her cloakroom. The journey was a long one, and I'd had a couple of drinks, but it wasn't that. I wanted to see a little more of the exclusive palace, the castle in the clouds.

Three corridors led from the main room. She showed me into one of them. There were five doors along it, all standing open.

I glimpsed massive vistas, shimmering partial colours and forms in flat fading light. The cloakroom was second along. Basically, it comprised a lavatory and washbasin. It was the size of a small but not so small bedroom. This thing for details...

The lavatory was almost not there, encased in what seemed to be mahogany, and with a mahogany lid – standing up, of course, not to pretend to be a euphemism. Its inner skin was icy white. The basin was an ice-white scallop shell with brass taps, not in any trendy shape, but gleamingly old-fashioned. (The handle of the flush mechanism was the same.) There were soaps that looked and smelled like honey. The walls were this colour too, and there was a carpet like fallen beech leaves – that colour, that thick. There were three towels on three brass hands, white, burnt sienna and chocolate. The ceiling had a lily lamp arrangement, but was also a pale blue sky, with cirrus.

Above the basin was a print of a green apple on a ruby plate. (Not hers.) Facing the basin, but set just right not to reflect the bog, was a kind of mahogany dresser with a tear-shaped mirror clasped in gold. Tissues stood on the dresser, and a soapstone dish, palest ephemeral yellow. In the window was what looked like Art Nouveau glass from 1901, blazing crimson, peacock green and indigo, even though it lost the light.

That then, the cloakroom.

I didn't try to scan the other rooms, or go in. After all, I'd seen enough. No lights were on. In the dimming evening dark, this sense of so much empty space. Her flat-apartment was the size of a great treeless field, divided by walls of opaque air.

But I won't say my wickedness started through any of that. It was already in me, naturally. I'm not a good or serviceable person. I'm a scavenger. A hyena – without a hyena's fondness for familial ties.

I waited nearly an hour for a bus. Then half an hour for another bus. Then I walked the last part to save waiting for *another*. I got home past 11 and used the communal lavatory in number 12 Compton Road, so my neighbours would curse me for it.

Up in the Room, the sunflowers were growing limp and languid, throwing down their petals. Why do things die? Why is it necessary? Oh yes, new things want to take their place, but are the new things always more valuable, *better* than the things which have been obliterated to give them scope.

I had toast and Marmite, four slices. I was ravenously hungry. And I made coffee, which never keeps me awake. I slept like the dead, generously making room for others who were awake.

Next day I set out, not to Jilaine's artshow opening, but to work. I needed some cash.

"Marge Gate wants to see you."

I went up in the store lift, and into the dingy managerial area. Marge Gate, the fat tarty woman who had first interviewed me, sat waiting in her greasy chair.

When I came for the job, she had said to me, outright, "We don't pay a great deal, because you can make it up in your tips." The first statement was true, the second false. Little elderly ladies who want one coffee, and leave (sometimes), one small grey coin, do not make up that kind of differential.

Now Marge Gate was going to be both less true and less false. I could see it in her bulging face, her mouth distempered with dead red.

"Yes, Jay, I'm afraid we're not very happy. You've taken a lot of time off recently." She waited for me to speak of my ailments, show off my scars and amputations. "We try to be understanding, but this puts everyone out. The others need to be able to rely on you." Ah, we were an ace team of warriors, forging through the frontiers of an alien land; Marge Gate tightened her Gorgon's lips. "You're often late, as well."

"Buses," I said.

"Then you must leave home earlier."

"At 5 a.m.?" I asked.

"You do leave far too early in the evenings. Besides, you are allowed five

141

minutes, morning and afternoon, for a smoke break, but you're often away much longer. And you appear to visit the toilet a great deal."

I wanted to say, *Would you rather I peed on the lunches*? I didn't, but I might as well have done.

"This isn't good enough, Jay. You seem to have lost all interest."

Of course the job was crucially interesting.

"You need," said Marge Gate, "to pull your socks up."

"I don't wear socks."

A quarter of an hour later I was out on the pavement. Free, but with only half a day's pay to collect, and that forbidden me until Saturday.

V

My emergency fund is in a bank. Strange old habit.

I drew out one hundred pounds. Which left seventy-three pounds.

I wasn't much afraid. I could soon find some other awful job. This kind of thing had happened before – which was why I tried to maintain the emergency fund.

I dressed in something casual, jeans, a loose top which looked more costly than it had been, courtesy of Oxfam.

I was late again. It was after 2 and all the buffet food had been consumed, and the bottles had been drained down to their last dregs.

The door of *The Painted Box* stood open. Hot or begging entrants?

When I presented my invite, the girl with blue lipstick laughed, as if I were mad to bother.

There were people standing about under the paintings, in both the rooms downstairs. They looked the way people do at the end of these functions, dulled, losing interest, talking about their own concerns with their backs to the exhibits.

I took a drink of flattish fizzy water. I couldn't see Jilaine. Couldn't see Angus or anyone recognisable. As for getting close to any of the paintings, that was out.

Ron found me as I was leafing through the programme by my old friend the postcard rack.

"Look here, I want to know, what do you think you're playing at?"

Always guilty, I flinched.

He was a big ageing man, he had about twenty years on the barbed Chris. The face was setting in miserable lines, but now laced with anger. His breath smelled of brandy.

"Yes, I do mean you. I can see you're not Philippa Wise, but you're too much like her for my taste."

"I'm *very* sorry," I said.

"And perhaps you should be. What are you up to?"

"I don't know what you're..."

"Talking about? That won't wash. You've latched on to Jilly just like Philippa did. She's had enough to put up with, Jilly has. She's just too gullible for people like you."

His voice was becoming quite loud against my adamance. People were looking round, leering a little, amused.

If we had been alone in a back alley, I'd have tried to defuse him. Here, safe among the throng, I couldn't be bothered.

I stared at him and for a moment thought he might still take a swipe at me.

"You bloody little bitch!"

"Softly does it," someone said, some other man.

"No. I want the truth. What is she, Philippa's sister or what? She could be, she's enough like her."

"No, a passing resemblance..."

"Shut up. I saw far more of that little whore than you did. Always crawling round Jilaine. Trying to get Jilaine to look after her, trying to get Chris interested in her – *Chris*, for Christ's sake..."

"Ronald, just calm down. This is a public place. *My* public place. For me, Ronald, I entreat you."

It was Angus McIndoe, in a fabulous linen suit, his hand on Ron's arm.

Ron shook him off. "Am I the only one can see this?"

Angus glanced at me. "The likeness is there. Jilaine agrees on this. But Jilaine should know, this young lady is nothing to do with..."

"Jilaine is off her head," said Ron furiously. "Of course she is. First all that stuff in France when she's a girl. Then losing a baby before she was even twenty-three. Jilly's a divine porcelain, but rational she is not."

"Thank you, Ron," said a crisp cold voice that I didn't identify.

But Ron went puce.

"Jilaine, er..."

"Hallo, Jay," said Jilaine, her small figure cutting through them like a chill pale knife. Her winter voice had already withered them.

"Jilaine, my dear, I was thinking of you, only that..."

"How kind of you, Ron. Angus, I'm off now. I've given Casper Reynolds his several pounds of flesh. I have to meet a woman at *The Waldorf* at 4. So I'd better get going. Jay, coming?"

She was holding out her hand to me. She was wearing a pale tapering dress. Her face was stiffer and whiter.

I went with her, even after she let go my hand, in a trance, under a spell. And we walked out through the noisy soundless enchanted gallery, where she had turned all the rest of them to stone.

They'd both been wrong, she and Jud. There hadn't been rain or a storm. But now, as we walked the brassy streets, thick spaced drops began to come down.

I had thought she might just burst out with her held-in rage. She hadn't said anything at all, and I, of course, kept silent. Then, with the crying of the rain, she sighed.

"Have you had any lunch? No. I haven't either, talking to that bloody Reynolds man. One must always be lovely to critics, but he doesn't return the favour, never writes anything very flattering or even encouraging. We'll go in here."

'Here' was a narrow bar slotted in a side street. The room, aqueous in summer-rain light, ran back and back.

There was a mosaic table cold to the touch, a wall-long fish tank with pebbles and skeins of tiny glinting fish.

"I'm sorry you had to put up with all that."

"He was drunk. Like his catty boyfriend the other time."

My own scathing tone shocked me – I didn't want her to see my nasty side. I realised I'd been rather shaken up, not least by her rescue of me.

She said, "I have this idea you are intolerant of homosexuality, Jay."

"No. But I didn't like *that*."

"Of course not."

"What about your interview at *The Waldorf*?" I asked in a while, to break the new silence.

"There isn't one."

She ordered a salad and so did I, and a bottle of white wine. When the food came neither of us could eat it. We drank the wine, and I offered her one of my cheap cigarettes. Without demur at my poverty or the quality of the cigarette, she took it and smoked it to its stub.

"I feel I should explain something to you. A few things. Maybe."

"You don't have to," I lied, thinking, *Tell me, tell me everything and all. I want to know less than I want you to talk to me. So Best Jilaine, let me hear your age and star sign and shoe size and bra size, your blood group, the weight of your heart.*

"There used to be an infantile joke Ron and Chris coined about Lesley," said Jilaine after a moment. "They used to call her, in front of me, 'The Les in Suspenders'."

"That sounds like them."

"Françoise was my mother, not Lesley. But Lesley was my mother too, a second, more distant mother – a father perhaps, but that's too like divisive jargon, the *male side* of the partnership. She wasn't a male."

Then Jilaine didn't say anything. The wine was gone. When they took our full plates away, she ordered another bottle. But we didn't drink much of it. We sat there.

There was a high porthole in the ceiling, on which the rain softly drummed. That, and the fish tank – we were under the sea.

"It's like being under the sea," I said.

"Don't say that," she said. "Don't ever say that."

"I'm – sorry..."

144

"No, *I'm* sorry. You're in a minefield. You couldn't know. My mother – may have drowned herself."

I said slowly, "You said she ran away."

"Yes, she may have. Or she ran away into the sea. After Lesley died. Lesley had a horrible, horrible death. It took so long. I thought she was getting over Lesley. One morning she just went out of the house and down to the beach. I saw her from the balcony. I thought she was just going for a swim and that it would be good for her." Jilaine's eyes were dry and empty. Somehow I thought of her flat – exquisite, dry, empty.

She said, "Her body was never found. But that could happen there. The tides, funny sudden tides, variable. Then again, perhaps she only walked away. Some of her things were gone. Some jewellery, her passport."

I sat there, rubbing the condensation off and off my glass, as the cold wine warmed.

"Oh, I probably am a bit mad. I wrote my book about them, and then – then I was an adult. I may as well tell you the rest. The man wasn't important, really, but he was older than I was. When I found out I was pregnant, he was already gone. But I was just – so happy." She looked directly at me. For an instant I saw the ghost of joy dancing in her face. "So many girls get pregnant, and they don't want to, do they? It's a terrible thing for them, frightening, awful – they hate what's happened. But I was – I was so *glad*. They said afterwards I'd been trying to make my family come back. By becoming a mother – getting my *own* mother again. How trite and futile. It didn't feel like that at all."

There was a droning noise in my head, more than the patter of rain, cancelling all sound but Jilaine's voice, and now my mouth was so parched I had to gulp some of the wine.

She said, "I was in love with her – Françoise – my mother. They said I was, these counselling people. Well, perhaps I was in love with her, with Françoise. I used to tremble as a child, just seeing her. At fifteen I used to. My mother. It wasn't sexual love; I don't think it was. Not like Lesley's way of loving her. Have I had times with women? Oh, yes. Yes, of course. Inevitably. But – that isn't really ever what I want. There was a girl in France, one of Lesley's other models – about my age – no; I don't want to talk about that. I prefer men. That's all there is to it. With women, I have to think what I'm doing."

My heart galloped in my throat. *The Galloping Magi*. Wild horses of lust and fear. Under a single star.

"I lost my baby. I'd had her eight months inside me. It was just something that can happen, they said. Unfortunately, it damaged me so that now I can't have a child. Very simple. Do you know, Jay, how difficult it is, even with considerable funds, to *adopt* a child – I mean to do it openly and legally and fairly? No, why should you. How can you know how much – oh how much – I wanted – wanted..." She stopped. She said, "This is the bit about Philippa we're coming to now."

The bar was dark. Its lamps made no impression. Waves broke against my eyes. Trembling, just seeing her and guessing what was to come. What had been done.

"Philippa was going to have a baby *for* me. She offered. I'd look after her, she'd produce the baby. Then I would keep the baby and she would be suitably recompensed. She strung me along for a while. But in the end, she didn't do it. She just threw a big scene and told me I was crazy and walked off. Vanished. She was a good artist. All those rows with Ron, those two – they'd taken her in before I did, how we met, you see. A mistake. Theirs, mine. It doesn't matter. I've told you enough to have bored you. Curious, though. When I saw you in the café, I did think you were like her. Then despite what you said, I wasn't sure. A year can change someone, how they look and act. You're not anything to do with her, are you? Some sister, cousin... Please, will you tell me now?"

How controlled she had been that day, after all. But I – I thought I wouldn't be able to say anything, but I said, "I don't know her. I was just being stupid and playing along. I'd never heard of Philippa Wise. But everyone's supposed to have a double." And then I heard myself say, quite normally, in a brisk little voice, "Only why were you there, I mean in the high street and the store – that's not your sort of place. It's always surprised me."

She smiled. She looked tired, relaxed and helpfully kind. "I just like wandering about. I'm always doing it. Anyone will tell you. I get on a bus – I don't drive, never have – and I just get off somewhere or other and walk around looking at things. And I wanted some coffee, so I went into your café. Chance. Kismet."

My throat closed suddenly. I couldn't even swallow. I sat like a waxwork.

I heard her say, bright, mild, reassuring me, "Angus said you liked that big painting of mine."

Lock-jawed, I nodded. Then my voice came out. "Lomm Bay."

"Oh, he *will* get that wrong. They always get it wrong – it's wrong in the catalogue. Angus should know better. Even Ginny has it right by now. Look, it's spelled like this." In the gleam of her sweet normalcy, as perhaps she had with Casper Reynolds, she took off another leaf from her notepad and wrote on it. I looked at the letters she had written. *L'Amber*.

"Angus insists on thinking it's some French conundrum, as he puts it. Hence the pronunciation and someone putting it as *l'Ambé* in the catalogue. That's not it. It's *amber*. Like the colour. With an l apostrophe – pronounced lam-burr."

I thought if I didn't speak to her at once, say what I must, I might pass out. Everything came and went, pressing in and going away. Tidal. Irresistible.

But I said, "Why?"

"Yes, why? I'll tell you one day, Jay."

"One day. Will you know me so long?"

"Why not. Let's try to, shall we?"

"You won't want to," I now heard myself say. "Not when I tell you what I have to do next week." And the great seething sea-cave steadied with a jolt. I could see and hear, and to my amazement, tears were running from my eyes, as they had from hers. And through the tears I saw her stare at me.

"What's the matter?"

"This is like a bad joke. I shouldn't have said. You'll hate and despise me."

"Will I?" Her own eyes were dry mirrors. But in them I could see no reflection of myself.

"You wanted a child."

"Yes, Jay, very much."

In her dry mirror eyes the dry mirror of her apartment, walled in air, a field barren of flowers, a place of stones.

"I shouldn't have said anything. Let's forget it." She stared at me but didn't speak. I said, "I – I have to go to a clinic."

Just her eyes. No expression.

My false tears ended. I was able to say, with the triumph of duplicity that had been working inside me, aware before I was, planning without my even knowing it, my evil genius: "I was careless. Only once. That's all it takes. I have to – to *have it out*, as my mother used to say."

PART THREE

I

He didn't make me wait; he was waiting for me. And when he saw me – his face lit up. Was I immune to that? No. But mostly, thankful. After all, time had passed. He might have lost interest, found someone else. I was surprised really that he hadn't. Perhaps he had, and would now dump her. One more crime on my slate.

"You look good – great," he amended, unshyly generous.

"Thank you. You too."

We walked into the shade out of the evening sun.

It was one of those wine bars where they didn't serve spirits. But I'd probably do better sticking to wine.

I looked into my drink. "Well. As you can see. I'm here."

"Yeah. I liked you calling me."

"I hope it wasn't a bad time – I woke your father..."

"Oh that. He often goes for a sleep about 9. Then he gets up at 9 a.m. and has a read, or sits in the garden, this weather. His sleep patterns went weird since the op. But he says that's fine, he goes up again later. He liked your voice a lot. He's a good bloke, my dad."

"Yes, he was nice."

"He likes the ladies. Always did. Runs in our family."

"Yes."

He refilled my glass although I hadn't quite finished it. The wine was clear and very cold. "You don't have to tell me, Jay, if you don't want to, but..."

"Does my calling you mean I'm no longer involved with someone else."

"Right."

"I'm no longer involved."

He sighed, grinned. "Christ, that's a relief, then."

I had my speech all planned. I sometimes do, although I'm effective extempore too, as you've seen. People like me, the chancers, we have to acquire these skills. That's why the villains always have the best lines, (and the Devil the best tunes).

"You see, when I met you, he and I were already pretty rocky."

"That's why you were going to that party on your own."

"Exactly." (How helpful Jud was being.) "I don't want to say a lot about him. It isn't fair on him, because you won't hear his side of things." Please note, Jud, how honest and noble I am. "I'll just say I think we were going on together because of a sort of loyalty. And then – well. That isn't enough, is it?"

"Thanks, Jay. Thanks for telling me."

"I didn't think you'd still want to see me," I modestly added. But I *had* thought he would, and I'd frantically gambled on it. Perhaps I'd even sounded flatteringly frantic on the phone.

"Course I do."

"Yes."

"I'll get another bottle. Or – I booked the table for 8, but we can have another drink there if they ain't ready."

Interesting, his grammatical usage. Sometimes correct and sometimes not. He seemed careless of either. Like such a lot about him. Take it or leave it, in the quietest, least confrontational way.

We went on to the restaurant, walking up the hot evening streets. He didn't try to take my hand, only put his palm, gentlemanly, under my elbow as we crossed the road. He *was* a gentleman. Gentlemen book tables. They hold your chair as you sit. They ask you things and listen.

Outside, the dusty trees and ochre streetlamps. In here the white tablecloths and real red carnations. An evening out.

The food was sort of French Italian. Very good food. We switched to red wine – he asked me to choose it.

I didn't eat very much. I never do. But this had become almost a problem, right now, like a lot of things. But there, help was at hand.

When I didn't say much about myself, Jud talked about himself. But mostly he talked about his father quite a bit, with my encouragement. It seemed reasonable neutral territory, where he could shine by being proud and I could by approving. Also, I was intrigued. I'd never known anyone who enthused about a parent, even really saw them as a fellow personality. Now there were two. Jud and his father. Jilaine and Françoise.

It seemed Jud had bought the house, with his father's financial assistance, and they'd moved in together. Before that, the father had been living somewhere in Putney, and Jud had been living with the last girlfriend, Carol. He didn't say anything bad about her, either, as I honourably hadn't about my non-existent ex. But somehow, she sounded a bitchy cow.

Obviously, Jud had a thing for bitches.

When the meal ran out, and the last coffees and liqueurs, a new – or old – unease settled on us.

I went to the Ladies. Standing there in the tiny cubicle by the pink-tinted mirror, I stared at myself.

There was no way out. For this had to be.

Why make a fuss?

He was young and handsome and fit. Not even the spectre of AIDS had yet laid sufficient hold on London and its environs to deter us. And I was hardly untried. My virginity had gone by the time I was fifteen. How many men had I had? Enough. I knew how it went, even how it went when things got kinky, or rough, or in the corner of the park, at 1 a.m. where the merry rapist dragged me. I knew how it went, and *that* it went, that it *came* and went, and then was over.

I powdered my face, and combed out my hair and sprayed my perfume, like any normal woman, and walked out with a light step to meet him.

We idled under the dusty ochre trees.

"I can find a cab," he said. "Or we can walk. Your place isn't far.

I felt terror for a second. Did he or didn't he want me after all?

He must have seen my face, read it for once.

He laughed. "Or there's my place."

"What about your father?" I should have sounded more hesitant, less pre-planned strategic.

"Oh, he's out tonight. He has a lady friend, you know."

So, I was not the only strategist.

We walked anyway. The night was dense yet high as space. Between the blots of light pollution, the stars jaundiced tinkling crystal.

He did take my hand. I didn't mind it, his firm dry hand holding mine. I didn't mind, by the wall of a garden, where a willow tree hung over, his soft, "Can I kiss you?" Nor the kiss, discrete, well-mannered, the lips closed until mine parted. I didn't mind the internal second kiss, it was soothing, almost. I rested in his arms and gave myself up to it. This would be all right. All of it would be, all the things I was about to let happen to me.

But then, as he drew away, I remembered her, as if I could ever have forgotten. Like a white spark, she flashed and lit my brain.

We walked on, and the streets flowed down to the thin tributary of some piece of a river. The terrace of houses curved above, up over a hump of land,

and somehow the suburbs and the city were far off, across a playing field beyond the river's bank, yet seeming shut away behind some Mediaeval wall that perhaps had been there when the trickle of river was young and wide and thick with fish, and all the stars burned white.

"That's mine."

A narrow house among narrow houses, all two storeys. All new double-glazed windows in regency sockets. No front gardens, just another strip of grass before the road and the river and the field. "That bothered me at first," he said. He checked. "But there's a garden at the back."

A few lights showed up and down along the row. Only one streetlamp, not close.

He reached out to hold me again.

In a moment we would be in the house, in the bed, in each other the closest and most innermost.

"Jud?"

"Yes?"

"I –I don't think..."

"It's OK. Look, it's OK, really."

"I'm sorry. What bloody manners I have."

"It's fine."

"It isn't. I want to – but it's a bit, just a bit..."

"Too soon. Yeah. I know. After Carol I was the same."

His sweet playful good-humour undented, his hard, longing erection fading back into his body unappeased.

Sorry. I'm sorry.

You fool, what's the matter with you? You did it with all the rest. You did it with the fat Asian man who gave you twenty pounds in Birmingham. You did it with the rapist so he wouldn't cut off your earlobe. And now you really have to do it – you won't. You fool.

Standing there on the grass, Martian brown from the lamp, under a Mediaeval black sky.

"I don't want you to think I'm messing you about."

"Come on, Jay. I don't."

"It's been a lovely evening..."

"First of many. What we'll do, there's a pub still open down there. We'll go in the pub and I'll call you a cab. From *Surefire*, so he'll know to behave himself. OK?"

"Yes. Thank you."

"And I'll call you tomorrow."

"No – let me call you. I'm not actually – I'm staying with a girlfriend. She doesn't like people calling me. I know it sounds odd, but the situation..."

"It's all right, Jay. I understand. You'll call me." He was serious now. Afraid, as I was, he'd blown it? Why wasn't he fed up? Why did he still want me?

"Jud, I'll call you at five. Is that all right?"

"Yes. I'll be around till just on six, then I'm working."

"Five, then."

We stood there a while longer, not touching, looking at each other, into each other's eyes. In his, the night river moved. For God's sake, what did he see in mine?

II

With her, I had been far cleverer.

She had had to persuade me. *Bully* me into it.

Of course, she was conniving too, by then. A trickster and deceiver. I was aware it must have made her feel rotten and unclean. Something those of us who are truly rotten surely never feel, since it's indigenous.

The funny thing is, I don't remember much more of the conversation we had, she and I, in that bar in London. I suppose she must have paid for the uneaten salads and wine – I didn't. Then we were walking, and it was getting dark. But that may have been the leftovers of the storm, not nightfall. (This was about three weeks before I first rang Jud.)

"Jay, listen to me carefully. I know you're very upset. Of course you are. But you must listen."

I suppose I said I would.

Jilaine said, "Please, *please* don't get rid of your baby. Not for my sake, because I'm sensitive about losing my own child – that was six, seven years ago. Not for the baby, either. I don't know what they can feel, and you say it's only a few weeks. Not for you. Although I think you *will* feel it. Oh, not for any of that. Oh God, Jay, what can I say to you? Just don't."

"It's six weeks," I stupidly, brashly, said. And in my head, I made a mental note. I added, "To the day."

"Are you absolutely sure then?" she suddenly asked me. "Have you seen a doctor?"

Seen a doctor? Naturally I had seen a doctor, hadn't I? If you thought you were pregnant, once the initial disbelief had passed, perhaps after a few feeble half attempts to trigger the dilatory period – drink, exercise, baths – these things don't necessarily go out of fashion – the doctor it is. "Yes."

"But six weeks – usually they say..."

I said quickly, "He said he was ninety-nine percent certain. Something about my pelvis. I can't recall. The clinic is to make sure. Then they'll go ahead. At once."

"How did you manage that?" She starkly asked me. "They generally want grounds. You're young – what are you – twenty-four?"

"Twenty-six," I said.

"Young enough. And you're healthy, aren't you?"

"Yes."

151

"And what else?"

"Nothing else. He was understanding."

"But there's no physical reason why."

"No. There are a hundred other reasons."

"What?" she said. "Name some."

Because I knew I had her in my hand, not cruel, but sensing my power, I lingered. I had the margin to evade. "Jilaine, you're very kind, but I don't want to argue about this anymore. I shouldn't have said anything."

"But you did."

"Too much wine."

"You shouldn't drink too much wine. Not now."

"It doesn't matter, does it? If I'm not going to *have* it."

She turned her face, as if at a blow. And looking beyond her, I saw we had reached a place of high walls. Storm or dusk hung heavy on the choppy streets. People were hurrying as if on wheels. And lights were on in the tall black buildings.

"There must be more to this," she said.

Her exquisite face. The walls beyond. Then the dark.

"Jilaine, I don't have any money and I live in a filthy damp room that's falling apart. I try to write, so I don't have a proper job, and I'd lose that anyway. And anyway, anyway, I was sacked. They sacked me – I'd actually forgotten. It was only this morning." Inspiration slinked through me like a snake. "I'd had to go several times and be sick. They said, and I quote, 'You have been going to the toilet a great deal'."

"They should be shot," she said.

I glanced at her again. She looked as if she meant that, and you could believe it of her, that she would shoot them. I saw the sandy viper of a cook felled by Jilaine's gold bullets. I laughed before I could keep it back.

"Jay," she said, "this is all wrong. I haven't been fair to you."

"No." She hadn't, if what I'd said were true. "Come back with me, to the flat."

"No, Jilaine, thanks." I'm so professional. It sounded quite genuine.

"I understand. Let's meet tomorrow, then."

"I don't…"

"Please, Jay. This isn't the time, you're right. But we must talk."

"I don't want to. I spent hours talking to that doctor, convincing him I needed an abortion."

"There's a taxi," she said. Her arm rose like the neck of a swan. The taxi sailed to an appropriate point and stopped. Magic.

"Jilaine," I said, firm as rock at last, "I can't afford a taxi."

"*I* can. Take this. Just tell him where you want to go."

That Asian guy, he'd thrust the wad of money on me. He was almost crying with shame. What he'd done, soiling himself and his God with me. She did it with grace. It was as if the money meant nothing. To her, maybe.

152

I took the taxi to Charing Cross, although she had meant me to go home in it. I kept the surplus notes. Thirty pounds. You see, I'm not lying to you. I apologise for that.

Next morning about 11.30, very civilised, she called me. I didn't know she had my number – the communal number of number 12. But obviously she had got it from me in that lacuna of unmemory at the wine and salad bar.

Olivine seemed to be about twenty, and she had a son about eighteen. I'd never worked out how this could be. But it was he who banged on my door, and his shaved scalp and savage eyes I saw. "Some posh bird wants you. Sounds like a fucking frog porn star."

As I went downstairs, half asleep still, I gained my first real curious clue to Jilaine's voice. That lisp, that soft delicious hesitation. An accent – French? She had never lost her own beginnings, it seemed.

"Hallo. Jilaine?"

I'd had something to drink myself last night. Jilaine had inadvertently bought it for me. A half bottle of Smirnov and two lemons, plus a slab of Brie and a loaf of plaited Greek bread.

I listened again as she told me we should meet. I was reluctant, cautious. She was charming and not to be resisted. So, I gave in.

How was I? Do you picture my disgusting glee as I got ready, my Machiavellian-Borgian schemer's mindset? I was scared. And – happy. I was happy.

This began a second phase, the week of Jilaine's courtship of me. That is, of me as a candidate mother carrying a potential child.

Philippa she had tried to persuade. But in my case, I was already up the duff. That saved so much time.

And I played my part. With her, I tried to eat more – I was already too small – I drank juice and only one coffee. I even went off abruptly to the lavatory. She followed me after ten minutes. Was I all right? Had I been sick? No, a false alarm.

She said, that day, "I was never sick. I felt so well. Somehow, I sometimes think that it's a good sign, to be ill at first."

"Not for me."

"No, of course. I'm sorry."

We were working in the dark. She because I was lying to her, and I because I knew next to nothing about what I was lying about. I should have attended more carefully to Doll and Rita's lurid accounts of their difficult, never ending pregnancies. But I'd taken in more than I thought. Even my mother had possibly told me things my brain now produced from its backroom filing system.

There were long silences between us. And long assaults of talk, when she tried to win me to her cause. Not once did she say, have this child for me. As she must have done with Philippa.

And yet I began, superficially, to dislike her. This is true. Just as if I *were* pregnant and all this was real. As if she were trying to make me have a child I didn't want, and then presumably hand it over to her.

Not until Day Six did she say, "Jay, perhaps I haven't made it clear. You know you can come and stay with me, don't you? You're in an awful position. Let me help. I've got a lot of space. You can have the guest flat – it's quite private, has a bath and shower and a little kitchen, even a terrace so you can get some sun."

"I can't pay any rent."

"I wouldn't want any rent. You're a friend."

And that day, Day Six (we were in St James's Park, the water full of ducks and herons and geese and wading birds with red legs everyone kept remarking on, saying something about how they were meant to be still in Egypt), that day, I heard myself lash out at her. "Look. What do you *want?* I'm not Philippa."

It had to be done. I had to clear Philippa off my path.

Jilaine sat outwardly composed, feeding some bread to ducks with emerald heads like the stoppers in bottles.

She said, "Yes, I see. I won't deny it – if I could lift the baby out of you and put it inside me, I would."

"I wish you *could*, Jilaine."

"But we can't do that, can we?"

And in those days, only a few years back, we couldn't.

She said, "But there is an alternative, which I'm offering you."

"If I go through with it, what then?"

The bread was gone. The ducks, faithless chancers, waddled away. She looked at me.

"Whatever you like, Jay. So let me be frank with you. If you don't want the child when it's born – yes, I *will* want the child. But that isn't what I'm after."

"What are you after, Jilaine?"

Did it stir me, electrify me, duelling like this, along the edges of her sanity – and mine? Oh yes. More than any kiss. But it also made me feel very sick.

"I don't know, Jay. I just don't want you to lose the child, and to go through what I had to."

"You *wanted* it."

"Don't you? You shake your head, but are you so sure? Is that because of the father?"

"I told you, it wasn't anything special. The classic One Night Stand. It was more of a one-minute stand, actually."

She laughed. As if I hadn't been crude and crass, but witty. And when that happens, I wonder, *have* I been witty? Or generous and ordinary – by mistake, without knowing? And does that mean that in fact, under cover of the dark, I could pass as human?

But these notions don't last.

I never went back with her to her flat that day. As if, once she got me there, she would imprison me. Instead we went on with the walks and orange juice wine-bars, and interesting restaurants she knew, and once a shop for, My God, maternity wear, but it was stuff a film actress would buy. And she made me look at things, and to me the woman said, "Oh, this would suit you. When you're a bit bigger."

She tried so hard, Jilaine. And I let her. Had to let her.

Come on. If I'd said at once, yes, yes, here I am, I'm yours – wouldn't she have been a little suspicious?

It was uncanny enough, wasn't it, already? I resembled her elusive Philippa Wise, who had promised to conceive and bring to term and give the fruit of her labour to Jilaine – and then vanished. Just as Françoise had, into the seas of France. It had occurred to me, maybe Jilaine's life was so beset by such coincidences, another was only too likely.

Myself, six weeks, now seven weeks, fecund.

At that time, she never lost her dignity, or her ethereal calm. Even when she got angry with me.

"The clinic appointment is tomorrow, am I correct?"

"Yes. I *don't* want you to go with me."

"All right. But will you call me as soon as you know?"

"As soon as I know, I'm going to have it *done*. Removed. Taken *out*."

"They won't do that, you know, Jay. It doesn't work like that."

"In this case it does."

She shrugged, a little French shrug.

How much like Françoise did she look, I caught myself thinking, Françoise with her black thundercloud of hair?

"Please, just take a moment and call me."

"You've been so kind," I said, hanging my degenerate head. "Yes, I will call you. I promise I will."

And I did.

But I made her wait until 7 o'clock, when the sun would be bleeding on her river like the blood of loss.

"Jay – don't cry. Try to tell me. Have they...?"

"No – no, I didn't let them."

Her breathing, then. I heard her, how she tried to breathe. But her voice was silk.

"Let me get this straight. You are pregnant. But you haven't had the termination."

I cried. I can almost cry at will. Another knack I learnt long ago, although peculiarly, sometimes it comes on its own, like an over-used tap, leaking.

"I am. I'm pregnant. No. I – couldn't..."

"Tell me where you are," she said, brisk, efficient, (greedy?), "I'll come and fetch you."

"I walked down to the Law Courts. I've been wandering about. I'm there, somewhere."

She managed to find out from my carefully dislocated sentences where. I had to take a taxi again, to get there before she did.

Why did I opt for the law courts? Justice – no, I don't think so.

The battle, after this point, started to be all with her. Because it was so exhausting after that, to be with her. The very thing I'd striven for and won. Not from remorse, obviously. But the constant act of my pregnancy.

I was driven quite quickly to respond, "No, I want to stay with my own doctor. I'm sure you know a better one – but I don't want to see anyone else, Jilaine, however good. Please leave me alone." I was *driven* to marching out of her flat, (she had given me keys) walking along the riverbank below. (So much water now, these rivers everywhere.) "Don't hedge me in, Jilaine."

Does it go without saying that I at least subconsciously knew I would have to do more than simply fake this business? I would have to *be* the business. Perhaps it had crossed my mind. Oh, of course it had. I think. I was meant to be pregnant. Wouldn't I need to *become* pregnant?

But not yet, oh Lord, not yet.

Evidently, at seven weeks, I *was* too small. *When you're bigger*, the saleswoman had said, as if *I* were the child, growing up. Like some very slim people, even men, I have a little round belly, as if the non-present fat, drawn off at my making, left it behind. Trying to eat more, I worked on my belly, coaxing it, sticking it out. I wore tighter clothes, to try to emphasise it, then saw it was pathetic and wore looser things to pretend I had something to drape.

Perhaps Jilaine, in her pregnancy, hadn't shown much herself. Some women don't. She'd never said to me, in some subtle roundabout way, Is there really something in there, Jay? And only once or twice did she look at me with that intent manner of hers, (now I was her property), and murmur, "I wish you could eat a little more." But then she'd laugh it off, "My God, I sound like some magazine from the Fifties, eating for two. No, you're much healthier as you are."

And I would say, reluctantly, since talking about the physical aspects of my state apparently embarrassed me, "The doctor says that. He says I'll probably show it suddenly. But the weight will be all the baby." (Another dredged up item from the box-files, some oldish woman in the fabric shop where I once worked, thin as a pole, who proudly told this tale of her pregnancy when she was All Baby. That was all you could see, she said, when she turned sideways, the Baby, sticking out. And, I would think, her large nose.)

The other major problem – a poor joke – I was, of course, still going to be menstruating.

Thank God for the private guest bathroom. And when I went out thank God for the handy chemists. I laid in the packet of tampons, thrusting them to the back of a drawer. Would she look for such evidence, when I was away? I couldn't imagine Jilaine doing such a thing. She wasn't duplicitous. Not even now. She had spoken the truth, (almost all the truth) hadn't she? She trusted me.

She let me come and go as I wanted. She could see, naturally, that I felt cooped up, virtually guarded.

The stupid part was, I had until the last moment thought I'd want to be with her all the time I could. Just to look at her, hear her voice. Maybe move forward a little, to proximity, in case there was the slightest chance I might friendlily caress or fondle her, lay my head upon her breast. She had been with women, at least. She wouldn't recoil in astonished nausea. Or would she, from me?

Anyway, that was out of the question. As soon as I entered her world and became hers, the phantom foetus between us made me her adversary.

I said, I disliked her. I nearly hated her. How perverse of me – well, yes. Did I say that I was sane, or to be liked, or even to be thought an object of compassion?

But her tentacles were round me. Before I blurted out my lies by the fish tank, improvising on her own words, just as I had the first time in the café, making out I was someone she knew, before that, I'd have killed to be with her. While to live in the luxury of her apartments, to come and go with airy ease and the money she now gave me, such gifts sometimes sly and sometimes tactful – this wonderful new life – to sit with her in the evenings on her terrace, and watch the glittering planes turning always at that one spot in the sky – to sleep only a few miles of yards from her bed... A fantasy daydream. But no, now I had it, a nightmare.

Oh yes, yes, obviously because it was built on a falsehood, one which must be constantly sustained. One which must, sooner or later, be brought to its climax.

My choices: I could go out one morning, fail to return, send her mad with alarm. Then appear wan and shaking, having miscarried. Or I could simply say I had reconsidered, had an abortion. She might even give me the cash for it, seeing that she'd spoiled my earlier chance. My other choice was impossible. To become pregnant.

If only the female term were longer – nine months, nine and a half if the baby was slow. Even ten at an absolute stretch. Sometimes doctors made mistakes, too. Perhaps I'd had a later, unmentioned sex romp. But if only it were eighteen months. Or two years. Then I'd have more time. More time to be with her, and not have to waste it all and all my feeling for her on plots and lies and covering up, hiding Tampax. I'd have time to decide.

But nine or ten months didn't allow for that.

Jilaine was out quite often. Looking smart and ravishing, she used to go and see people – vague business affairs, (an accountant, a bank) or to do with her painting. Even socially. And sometimes on the non-business jaunts, she would invite me to go with her. And I refused. I disliked the people she knew, but then I dislike most people anyone knows. Mostly it was that I couldn't play our game, too, in front of them. I'd already said, "Don't – please *don't* – tell anyone about this." When she assured me she wouldn't, I believed her. But then, why was I with her? Wouldn't they get inquisitive? An affair? She might let them think that. But I didn't want to play that game along with the other game. You see, I don't like games much, though I'm so brilliant at them.

When Jilaine was there, and sometimes when she wasn't, her domestic help would come in. They came about once a week though their timetable seemed erratic. They were well dressed, educated, youngish women, one black, the sort you'd expect to meet in a high-class office. So far as I was concerned, they were A and B. Sometimes A, (the black woman) didn't come, only B, usually it was both of them. I'd retire to my suite to avoid the wandering brushes and droning Hoover. When the suite needed doing, I'd go out. After their visits, the laundry would be done, ready-prepared plates of cold goodies would be left stacked in the fridges, and now and then something would be cooking in the automatic oven.

Deliveries of food arrived downstairs at intervals. The porters or their assistants would bring them up to the door.

When Jilaine was out, and no one else in, *I* stayed in.

I explored her flat quite thoroughly.

Oh, I don't mean I went through her private things, her letters, diaries – if she had kept any – anything like that. You'll agree, I'm not above that. I'm capable of that. But there was no need. I get bored quickly with paper – which is why, I suppose, I've seldom written anything very long.

And I didn't want to know about Jilaine. Which may sound odd, since I had been, and still was, obsessed by Jilaine. But there. It was *her* I wanted, not her life. Lives weigh too much. My own is enough.

To return to the flat. Shall I describe it in typically 'female' detail. At the prospect at once I feel tired and can't face it. Even so, I should give you some idea, shouldn't I? Just as I told you of my Room, because both the Room and Jilaine's castle-in-clouds are relevant.

A voice – yours? – says to me, Was it then not Jilaine that I wanted at all, but Jilaine's standard of living?

Candidly I reply, *Both.* I wanted it, and her.

There were eleven, twelve large rooms. Not counting the utility room and kitchen and the little kitchen in the guest suite, not counting the three bathrooms, two en suite, or the cloakroom I evoked at such (gratuitous?) length earlier. Or various halls, annexes, twists and turnings. There were bedrooms, a library, a breakfast room off the kitchen, a *pantry*. There was her study, with a desk and – quite technological then – a word processor, and smooth white walls of extra books. The guest suite lay at the end of one of the three corridors leading from the main room. At the end of the third corridor, four shallow steps led up into her studio, a room where half the roof was glass, a chamber of light.

So many pale clear cool luminous colours, dove greys and pastel lavenders and creamed sunshine yellows. Dark polished wood. Jade green things, some of which were pieces of jade. But generally few ornaments. Some plants, well cared for. And hardly any pictures.

In her studio, between working sessions it seemed she put everything away. Or she *concealed* it. I said it was a chamber of light, and that was all it was when I saw it. Two easels were there, dismantled. There were slate-blue cupboards, shut, stocked with blocks of paper, boxes of things. A worktable had been cleared but for a few tall old brushes and knives standing in a wild green and yellow jug, and a box of rags with its lid closed. No hint of sketches, remnants. Not even canvases turned coyly to walls – go on, turn me round, look at me. Vacant.

Jilaine hung mirrors, mostly, on her flat walls, or put up bookshelves. The occasional painting you saw was never one of her own, and otherwise not evidently famous, and, when I began to search for it, never one either of Lesley Spender's. However, in Jilaine's bedroom, where of course I went, along with all the rest, my padding footsteps leaving no track in the soft, reseda snow of her carpet, I found a single small sketch. It was simply framed in white wood, and tucked in by the door to the dressing room, an original, on brownish art paper, a drawing of a cat lying stretched out and asleep against what seemed to be the foot of a pillar. It was a wonderful drawing, lush and heavy, full of fur and sleep and afternoon, and the dim drizzle of cicadas. A French picture. In the lower right-hand corner, a tiny scrawl: *Frse*. Françoise? Presumably. Her mother.

Which brings me to Jilaine's books.

In one of our new, in-the-flat conversations, I had asked her if I could read her novel about her mother and Lesley Spender.

Why did I do this? To flatter and propitiate? Authors like people to read their writing... or do they? I don't, not much.

She said, "How nice of you. You don't have to."

"I would like to. I tried to find them after we met – but I didn't know the titles." In fact, I hadn't tried.

Later that day she brought me a book. It was slender, with a mauve jacket. The title was *The Skaters*. That night I read it, all of it. A slight volume, not even a hundred and twenty pages. And it had nothing to do, I'd realised quickly, with Lesley and Françoise. It was a readable uncluttered quite funny heterosexual story, about nothing.

I told her I'd liked it but reminded her the one I'd asked for was the one she had mentioned, about her mother.

"I don't want to give you that now, Jay. I'm sorry, that must sound very organising. But this book is harrowing. It was to write. Because Lesley's death is described. I – I found it fairly horrible writing, myself, but I had to. And now – I never read it. And I don't think you should, right now."

"Because of the baby."

"Yes, Jay."

159

Instead, she gave me the third book in her opus, explaining there were only three. This novel – *One Day*– was a little longer and held me less than *The Skaters*. I skimmed it, admiring the pared prose, fretful.

That brought on my first serious during-her-absence foray through the flat – the day after. I found the forbidden fruit in her study. It too was short, two hundred pages of large print, and I can read fast. So I read it, sitting on her study floor, on the deep carpet by the sunny window, which, like her terrace, looked away over London under half the sky.

By the time she got back around nine, the book, despoiled of any secrets, had been returned to its shelf.

You and She. Had it told me anything? At the time, I didn't think so. Escaping to France, as Jilaine put it, when she was only ten, they had bought a sun-browned house among the olive trees. Cliffs fell to a blue sometimes tideless sea. Poppy fields, and cypresses, and peaches ripening on a wall. The French heaven-on-earth. Thereafter they led, the three of them, a reclusive, opulent, carefree and creative amalgamated life, ending in abject horror.

Obviously, the homosexual element interested me. Looking back to my teenage years, I would say my own sexual awareness broke free at last through reading the ventures of others. What was possible if not condoned.

Jilaine wrote about these lovers with a tender and controlled remoteness, yet first person, as a character plainly Françoise's daughter, herself. This girl – bizarrely to me – Jilaine had called Jane. My name without the wary Y my mother had added.

Lesley, Jilaine called Lindsey Spencer, and Françoise was Frances Blest, clearly enough from Best, the name of Jilaine's father.

There was also a younger girl, a sort of waif and stray, Gisla, who was presently idly adopted into the household in France, as Lesley's (Lindsey's) other model. I recalled Jilaine had spoken of knowing a girl in her youth, biblically presumably. In the book, somehow without any real comment, Jilaine was merciless to this Gisla. She didn't mention any relationship. Gisla was simply there, a useless, parasitic hanger-on. Probably resented by Françoise/Frances and her daughter. During the death scenes of Lesley-Lindsey – and harrowing they were, details sparsely clothed but nothing spared, set out like a medical dictionary – Gisla fled the house, leaving Jane alone with her distraught mother, amid the tumult of faeces and shrieking.

And did I compare myself to Gisla? Naturally. I too would have been off at a rate of knots. But then, how could I know? I'd avoided all that.

You and She ended in the other sequence Jilaine had already confided to me.

A week after Lesley's burial in some nearby provincial graveyard, for which special permission had been required, Jane saw her mother walking down on the beach below the house. She thought Frances was going for a swim, which she hadn't done for a long time, not daring to leave her dying lover alone. When Frances failed to return, Jane went down to the beach to find her. But she was gone without trace. 'Later, I found her passport was missing from among her things,' Jane writes, emotionless, desolate. 'And also a ruby necklace had been taken, and a ring; but I was not aware of that until later again. Others had searched by then, quite thoroughly. None of us found her.' The book ends after this flash-forward with the adolescent Jane standing alone on the open beach, hearing the sea, watching the darkness come.

One strange thing, perhaps. After Jilaine got back that evening, she made an omelette and we sat eating it in the wide kitchen under the Tiffany lamp. And I kept wondering if she would somehow know I had read the hidden book, eaten of the apple. This nervous guilt never affected me on any other of my excursions through her apartment and belongings.

But Jilaine didn't question me or seem suspicious. She seemed only worn out. We both retired early. I seldom have trouble sleeping. But sometimes I knew she did. Once that night I woke, and heard her moving lightly in the flat, out in the main room. I thought, *She knows I have read the book*. That was all.

III

I grasped I'd have to do something, after Jilaine told me about her dream. This was in the third week (phase three?)

Because I was pretending to her that I went regularly to see my doctor and to some sort of antenatal class, I'd been out, combing the long streets around the river. Then I got on a bus, and then I came back. At first, I didn't think she was home. Then I half sensed her. She had gone up to her studio, among the shards of empty light.

Self-effacing, I withdrew to the guest rooms, where I sometimes pretended to do virtuous pre-birth exercises. I was into the third month now, wasn't I? And if not flat as a pancake, I had less filling than one.

The guest suite comprised a bedroom and bathroom and kitchen, and a sitting room with a little high-walled terrace. Unlike the main terrace it didn't look towards the river, but the distant view was, even so, arresting, miles of architecture and trees which, being tall, I could see easily. (The main terrace had a wall topped by a balustrade. This was rather lower, and Jilaine seemed always uneasy when I went near it, as if I might, pregnantly unbalanced, topple over to decorate the drive below.)

While I stood here looking out, Jilaine knocked on the door.

The perfect hostess.

Perfect, certainly.

She was wearing a white filmy skirt and top. Ice-cream mist. Unlike most people when they wear white, her white skin didn't darken. It was the clothing which warmed. The sun on her hair made me want to tear it from her head, crush it to me.

She looked kind. Beautiful and kind and good. This, her mightiest defence

161

against me. I had tried not one errant touch or word.

"You're frowning, Jay. Have I disturbed you?"

"Just the exercises. They're a pain."

"You don't mean they hurt? No... Yes, I know about the boring aspect. But I'm glad you're doing them."

She walked forward. The snowbell of skirt swung, the gilded platinum bell of hair.

Her eyes. Indigo now. That happened when she was tense, I had begun to think. What was wrong? She had gone to see Angus, hadn't she? Someone wanted to buy the picture, the large one she had named to me, *L'Amber*. I'd heard her talking about this sale on the phone.

"What is it?" In such a situation, better to ask.

"I need to talk to you."

Bad? "Of course. Is it the painting – you don't want to sell?"

"Oh that. No. No, I have to – when you're OK, come out and we'll have a drink."

"The divine apple juice."

"I've made some iced coffee."

"You don't allow me coffee."

She laughed. The tension scattered sparkling from her and she gave me one of those *loving* looks for which I had begun to want to slap her. But surely, now, a reassuring sign?

"Am I so dreadful?"

"Worse."

"Come and have three or four coffees then, to pay me out."

I followed her after a couple of minutes.

She was magnetic to me. Even by then. As you see: still.

"This is going to sound very fey to you, I'm afraid. But whether you credit it or not, I'd rather tell you. You see, I lied to you."

"...Yes?"

"You asked me about the day I met you, at the café – you asked why I was there."

"You said you like wandering – it was Fate."

"I know. Fate perhaps."

She looked away, the looking-far-away look.

"Let me say first, sometimes I've had what I must call precognitive dreams. Before Lesley died – the morning before – I dreamed I saw her. She was well and strong and young, sitting on the wall by the house. She said to me, 'Look, they had to take away my right hand. But I'm fine now. And I can draw quite well with my left.' But when I stared at her in the dream, she had both hands. When I woke up, I knew this meant she would die that day. It's an ancient symbol. The right hand means the life. She died that afternoon."

Inside myself I, the arch liar, thought, *She didn't mention this dream in her novel.*

Jilaine sipped her coffee.

"There have been a few other times. Meeting someone I hadn't seen for years unexpectedly, but I'd dreamed I should. Silly things really. After the child died – my child – I..." A Pause. She said, "I dreamed of her, only she was a cat. A cat with wings. I expect that sounds twee."

"No."

"Well. The night before I met you in the café, I dreamed of Françoise."

"Your mother."

"Yes, my mother. This is the strange part, perhaps. She was very old. Bent and withered, grey – yet I knew it was her. It was – it frightened me. But she said, 'Take the bus, you'll find her.' And then I saw the bus, the number that runs by the store where you worked. I didn't say things to her I should perhaps have said. I said, 'Who will I find, Françoise?' She said, 'The one you want.' And when I woke up, it considerably upset me. But I thought, what the hell. So I found the bus route and got on the bus."

I was trying to collect my thoughts. As a rule I don't go along with things like this. Not that I disbelieve them. Anything's possible. They just don't mean that much to me. (Even that thing I sometimes sense which *plays* with all of us. Even that – doesn't mean much.)

But the words: *The one you want – You'll find her.*

Jilaine said, "I got off outside the store because I was hot, and I needed some coffee. And there, outside the store, was the board with the coffee-shop sign. Banal enough. But then I met you. And you're carrying a baby. Do you see?"

I didn't say anything.

She said, "I'm not trying to load you down with my own angst, or with hippyish mumbo-jumbo. I just wanted to confess, Jay. Otherwise, it didn't seem fair. We'll forget it now. Would you like a salad, or something more filling?"

I'd like you.

"Who did she – I mean Françoise... Did you think she meant me?"

"She meant the child I lost, Jay, or another child, like my child. She was a daughter, Jay. Perhaps your child is a girl."

I wanted to shout at her loudly. I wanted to hit her.

I said, "Maybe my child isn't a girl."

"We'll have to see." Then she crossed the room. She came and put her cool hands on my shoulders like the white paws of a cat, and she said, "Jay, when she's born, if you *want* her – I won't try to take her. You do know that? I lost mine. I *couldn't* do that to any other woman. Only if you feel then as you said you did and do. Meanwhile, let me just look after you both."

You don't want me and never will. You want this thing inside me, which isn't even there.

But I knew all that before we started.

Here I am, empty as your gaping mansion of a flat, flat as your flat. And soon, soon, you must begin to doubt me. You'll want to go with me to the doctor and the invented classes, you'll insist.

I can leave or I can facilitate you, madam. I can breed and swell, as if you were my demanding seventeenth century husband.

That was how I'd have had to live, then. By bearing the unbearable, over and over. And she only wants it once, poor cow.

And then I can say, I can't after all leave this child – but you *must* have her. Look what you can give her that I can't. And she will say, We'll share the child. The way Lesley and Françoise shared me.

So next day, when I was out, I called Jud from a telephone kiosk along the river, under the shining summer trees whose feet were deep in the rich mud, so they had no fear of the heat of the sun.

IV

"Hallo?"

"This is Jay again."

"Hallo. Thought I knew your voice. I'm afraid he's out."

It was five, to the minute. A lift fell through my body, crashing to rest on my womb.

Jud's father, the accent tangled more, a voice crumbling slightly at its edges, still centrally strong, holding itself quiet and gentlemanly against my ear. "He's off working. They called him back in this afternoon. Couple of the fellers gone off sick. He said, now I've got his note here – he says can you meet him at 8.30 at The Tower. Make sense?"

"Yes."

"That's the pub he means."

"Yes, thank you."

"He said sorry. He was fed up; I can tell you. He just come in and they was onto him. He can't give you a bell where you are, can he?"

"No, I'm afraid not."

"And he said don't ring him, he's up west and the office ain't very reliable. But 8.30 at The Tower. Is that all right?"

"Yes, I'll meet him there then, Mr – I'm sorry, he's never said your name."

"Davey. Just call me Davey."

"All right. Thank you."

"Bye-bye," he said, kindly. A gentleman, like his son. Who for a moment I thought had chucked me over.

Thanks to Jilaine's money, I could afford a cab all the way. It would have meant a lot of mucking about otherwise.

The Tower was up a hill, towards the better streets, about equidistant maybe between Jud's place and Compton Road. Perhaps he'd assumed I was still in this area. I arrived at eight 8.35, in the dusk, and he wasn't there.

I went into the bigger bar, and got a drink, then took it outside to the tables along the pavement.

People were laughing and prancing in their seats, for the drinker's night was well advanced. And I, the late arrival, just one more bird stood up or carelessly treated.

I sat on a low wall by a bush in a tub.

OK. I'd give Jud until 9. I had to do that. He must have been held up. This kind of mind-fuck wasn't in his repertoire, surely.

9 o'clock came, and I rose, put down my glass on the wall and began to walk away downhill towards the bus stop.

"Jay – hang on!"

He was there, running like a hot wind against me, taking my shoulders firmly yet lightly, lightly, for all his urgent speed, as if to hold me and also hold me safe from his own onslaught.

"I thought you'd decided not to bother."

"No. I got a drunk eighty-year-old lady in the cab, had to see her up to her flat."

Relief, the absurdity, something, made me laugh.

But his face was strained, showing its excellent bones. He drew me against him and held me closely, and I felt his strong heart hammering through his chest, from running, and from fear. I was safe, then?

"Let me get you a drink." The drink-drive ethos wasn't so strict then, but he still added, "I've left the cab round the side, I'd better stick to *Perrier*."

"That doesn't sound like fun."

"Fuck that," he said, smilingly. "Looking at you is like a double Scotch."

We stopped again. Full-lit by the lit-up pub, we kissed. Someone congratulated us with pissed approval.

"I don't really want another drink," I said. "I suppose... I mean..."

He stood back, examining me, searching my face and eyes for signals.

"Yeah," he said. "Look, why not come back to the house? Look, no strings. Just pay me a visit."

"Only, your father's there tonight. Will that be a problem?"

"No, I wouldn't be sharing a house with him if we had that kind of problem."

In the cab it took ten minutes. I sat in the front, of course, beside him. We didn't say much, nervous, both of us...? Yet, looking back I know he had foreseen this possibility, prepared for it, on the off chance I might have changed my mind.

Of course, he was irresistible. Before he had gone out again to work, he had obviously showered and made himself gorgeous. His clothes were fresh and immaculate. He had the aroma of cologne and toothpaste. And sex. Indisputably that.

But I was trembling slightly by the time I got out of the car. I should have had that other drink.

The daylight was all gone. The sky was hung with blue-green afterglow, turning violet then cobra-red on the blooming streetlamps of Mediaeval

London, over the playing field.

We crossed the grass, and he let me into the hall of the house.

The overhead light was on, too bright after the street. The house smelled cleaned but a bit musty. Then came a gust of mouse smell. Great, they had rats? Through a half-open door, an old man was looking round. He smiled at me and announced, "Just saying goodnight to the hamsters."

Lamely I smiled back.

I caught a glimpse of lamplight, a huge pen and a darting calico shape. The light was turned out and the door closed. The old man stood there.

Jud was frowning. "Dad..."

"I thought you'd be a bit longer up the pub." Then the old man bowed to me, graceful as an old actor. He had a wise folded face, which in youth was probably as good or even better than Jud's. But he wore an old grey shirt, perfectly clean but tatty, and there were slippers on his feet.

"This Jay? Pleased to meet you. You found him, then?"

"Hallo, Davey."

"I was late," said Jud. "I nearly lost her."

Oh no you didn't, Jud. You didn't.

"Would you like a beer, Dad? Or a glass of wine?"

"Wouldn't mind. I'll take it up." Davey smiled at me again, reassuring me his exit from our stage was all planned out and imminent. "Hamster bedtime, then mine."

Jud said to me, "There's a bottle of white wine. Dry, from Alsace. All right with you?"

"Yes, that's lovely."

The door had shut on the hamsters. Jud showed me ceremoniously into the small front room. His father and he went along to the kitchen and I heard the clink of a bottle and glasses. Their voices were soft. I didn't listen, there seemed no reason. Jud had wanted, despite what he said, the old man to be up in bed. But he was an unusual old man. He kept hamsters. He bowed.

The room – the lounge to an estate agent, a parlour in its day – had a retained fireplace with an electric fire, a TV of sane dimensions, a music centre and speakers. The decor was what I'd have expected, a mix-match of colours and patterns, but nothing loud, and the sofa, when I sat on it, was comfortable. The curtains, not yet drawn, were of some beautiful oldish green satiny stuff – so for a second you saw how, with a minimum of effort, everything could be improved. But it wasn't my business. How they lived.

Jud's father, Davey, walked in and handed me a glass of refrigerated wine. "I'm off up now. Nice to meet you." And he raised my hand and kissed it, a sparrow touch of dry old lips. Then he was gone.

Jud came in with the bottle in an ice bucket, and his glass. He sat down facing me, in a chair.

"You're right, I can do with this."

"It's good wine."

"That's a relief. I don't know much about wine."

"Nor do I."

"You know enough."

We fell silent.

Outside the lights grew harder over the field. A plane passed through the black vortex of night, stabbing with its red eye then the white one.

"Sorry about the hamsters," he said.

"They looked pretty."

"Oh they are, they're great, but they stink a bit."

"Your father – has he always kept hamsters?"

Jud burst out laughing. The laugh was too big for the room, the situation, us, all of it. He got up and drew the curtains and switched off the overhead light in favour of a sidelight and a standard lamp.

Uneasily he settled back on the chair. It was as if we were in a waiting room.

There was a bookcase, with books. I couldn't see what they were. Some videos were stacked on the bottom shelf – my eyes couldn't take in any titles. Did I need hints, anyway? No, I needed to lure him closer, through this room of waiting.

Perhaps he saw my eyes on the videos. "We could try that new cinema tomorrow," he said. "The one off Frayle Street. Late show. Has to be the late one for me – if you can..."

"What film is it?"

"Ah, I forget what. I thought it was one you'd like."

"Do you know what I like?" I heard myself say.

"Yeah, I reckon so. Something strong, brainy."

"Like you."

He glanced at me, sitting now on the arm of his chair.

"Why don't you sit next to me?" I asked. The wine was helping. This shouldn't be so difficult. It was easy. Easy. Difficult.

He stayed where he was.

I thought, *For Christ's sake don't get cold feet now. Do as I tell you. Hurry. For God's sake. Or I won't be able to.*

"Look, Jay, this was a bit of a mess tonight."

"It's all right. I deserve it anyway, for the way I behaved yesterday."

"No, you – it was OK."

"I thought about you," I said. "I wished I'd stayed."

"I wish you had."

"Can we pretend," I said, looking away from him, dazzled by the dull sixty-watt bulbs of the lamps, "that tonight is last night?"

"Are you sure?"

"I'm sure."

Not looking, I felt him move across the room to me, atoms and molecules swept up by his passage. A slow, dense, swirling, silent storm.

167

He sat beside me. Nothing to do now. Just give in. Make occasional sounds of assent. Nothing too noisy, luckily, with the dad in the house.

After a while, he said, "We don't have to go on, if you don't want."

"Please let's go on."

"Then – come up to the bedroom, yes?"

I thought he was afraid his father, wandering insomniac at 2 a.m., wouldn't want to stumble on us down here. Or was he a conformist, who preferred under-the-covers in a proper English bed? Or, as we climbed the narrow twisting stairs to the second floor, I thought, *In his suburban bedroom he has instruments of torture and depravity.* It can happen. I know.

But the bedroom was just a box-room, incredibly small and packed by a wardrobe and chest of drawers, the bed the smallest double it could ever be feasible to have. He must have given over the master bedroom to Davey. Or more hamsters, possibly.

The wine was warm now, but I swallowed it. Through thin curtains, the streetlamp along the way cast a sultry light upon our darkness.

I like your kisses. However gentle, even hesitant, no man's mouth is ever like the mouth of a woman to me. And your hands are sure on me now, finding their way over my body as if to remodel or to burnish me. And now you're fierce. Your breathing rasps in my ear, burning on my neck, my breast. Now I find your nakedness, its startling utter maleness, this dancing weapon sheathed in the firm flesh of a nectarine, so smooth, wholesome, and bursting full of its juice.

If it had been Jilaine.

If she hadn't wanted a child. If she had wanted me. If she had come into the room she gave me, and slid her cat's paws over my breasts, my thighs, as Jud is doing. If she had lain over me now, so much lighter, and placed *her* lips upon the core of me, the nub of pleasure, and lit the flame that the clitoris really is with the wet matches of her fiery tongue, like yours – but not – like yours...

"Jay, look, I've got these."

"No, we don't need those."

No, we don't, we *don't* need *those* at all.

"Thank God. Hate the bloody things..."

And the sensible and aware condom packet under the rug, and his smiling delirious body, heavily muscled as a puma's, and one final external touch...

It was easy. My hips tilted at that long ardent flawless thrust inside me. There is, in this filling up, despite everything apart, a sense of rightness.

He isn't kissing me now. He's watching me. Watching as he makes me come. For his pleasure, and for mine.

I would have made believe. Good manners, or at least insurance against abuse. I remember one long-ago crack, "If a gentleman always finishes last, a lady always comes."

Sitting up high in the back of my brain I hear the breath catching in my throat. I hear the tiny quiver of sound, I feel my pelvis arching and every wall inside tumbling over, like the domino effect.

No need to pretend, then. Orgasm really has happened.

I can still hear the low cruel sound he made against the pillow. As if I'd hurt him. As if I'd stabbed him through the liver or the guts, there in the dark.

It's done now.

Oh, we'll probably make love again, once more at least. No stress now. Our bodies are introduced, and on terms of friendly acquaintance.

And I am full of the young potent juice of him. I have everything I need.

In the past I had been scrupulous about contraception. The Pill, efficiently – pedantically – taken – so even the rapist had caught me coincidentally fully protected. Or else a sheath, and its complimentary cautious gallons of spermicide. Never any slightest chance taken.

I need do nothing else. Nature can take its course, or its revenge, however Nature sees it.

PART FOUR

I

My first lover – I mean a woman lover, the ones that counted – was called Christy. I met her on the tube. Maybe that is Freudian, or not. We just started talking. She was experienced, and doubtless had some idea what she was about. It was late at night, the mechanical worm empty but for us and a few drunks. It was going to be a long-haul home for me. So when she looked sympathetic and offered me a futon on her floor, I accepted. Don't go with strange women, Jay. But Jay did. I didn't spend the night on the futon either, though some of it was spent on the floor. Its boards, as well as her arms and teeth, bruised me. Just seeing the bruises later made me want her again. I was nineteen. Just one year after my mother fell six feet to her death.

After Christy and I 'broke up', there were many more. I got to know the signs. Or, maybe not. I did make mistakes. Usually a mistake was greeted by ribald laughter. Sometimes you could even pass it off as a game, a joke. Surprising how many 'straight' women like to fool around with each other after a few drinks, when the men are away. I once spent an hour at a busy night bus-stop French-kissing with a woman of thirty-three from the Co-op, after chucking-out time. But next day, when I saw her at lunch, she only went on about her husband's bad temper, and that the cat had been sick on her library book – the sort of events which normally beset her life. With her I knew better than to push it. With Sharon from the shadowy little insurance office where I clerked for six months, I had made a very big mistake, and got a slap in the face. Later, her husband sought me out, all violence and threats.

"Oh, come on," I whined, "you know how it is when a woman can't have a man." So then I had to have him and be thankful. I was of course very thankful, very noisy. After that Sharon wouldn't come near me. I found instead a note in my drawer which read *Shitty bitch get your own husband or I'll dig your eyes out.* At which I retired from the insurance office.

Was I ever in love? Endlessly in love. Sometimes with the most elusive. I remember a late train, (another one, but above ground) and a woman with dark red hair. The carriage was packed, and the cold night whistled in through the half-open windows no one had been able to close. She wore sheer stockings – I could tell – and fur – unwise. She looked like a Russian aristocrat inadequately disguised. She got out at Waterloo. I didn't follow her. She had on a wedding ring of heavy gold, and in her ears, diamonds. Why was she on a *train?*

Had it been different with Jilaine, seven years into my infamous career, because she carried some phantasmal aura, unseen yet omnipresent, of those other lovers, Lesley and Françoise – *Lindsey, Frances, Jane and Gisla?*

Four days after sleeping with Jud, my period was due. I am very regular – years on the Pill. And regular as always, I came on.

When I saw the blood, I couldn't believe it.

I was as shocked – frightened – I think, as when I first started at twelve years of age, in the lavatory at school. My mother had told me – warned me. And anyway there had been plenty of 'sex education'. If I'd missed all that, Mary, who soon fell by the way, had seen to it I knew. Even so – my God. I stared at the scarlet fall and thought, *I don't want this.*

And now I looked, and I thought, I don't want this.

How was it happening?

I've tediously explained all about my diligent adherence to contraception. And why so diligent – because I'd always been sure than one slip would mean pregnancy. But Jud had had me three times that night, before I murmured I had to get back, (later spinning some tale of an ill friend to an exasperated, pale Jilaine, who said only five chill words: "Next time call me, please.")

Three unexpurgated spasms of seed. And nothing. Nothing.

Or was the blood only some show, which would taper off? No. It was the usual monthly event. After another day, with no indication of an unusual lessening, I had to acknowledge that I was not, even now, in the family way.

I hadn't called him. Of course not. Our dealings were done. He'd had what he wished of me, and I, I'd thought, got what I had to have from him.

Except he had let me down.

The ghostly vision of all those women who desire conception and are unable to conceive, went rioting along the mind-screen. Rubbish. I was able to be pregnant and Jud was able to make me pregnant. And I had to be pregnant. Didn't I?

"You don't look very well," she said to me. My supernal gaoler.

"No. I don't feel that great."

"I'm sorry. Your friend was ill and all I did was to snap."

"My fault. I *should* have called. The thing is, also, I *should* go and see her again."

"Please do, Jay. I was acting like a fussy old aunt. Do whatever you have to. You mustn't get upset. And please, take a cab. I will see to the money."

II

She was going out a lot. To give me some room, I half thought. This ridiculous situation, every energy and thought spent on everything but Jilaine – so I could *stay* with Jilaine.

And the way she trusted me. It made me – sick.

I called Jud from the flat that Tuesday, when my period had stopped.

"Jud, I'm so sorry – there's been a lot going on. I can't say much. It's been – awkward."

"But you're OK?" he asked. He sounded grim and stony, as I'd expected.

"I'm all right. I'd like to see you."

"I don't like," he said, "this not being able to call you. You went off that night and it's like you've gone down some hole in the ground."

"Yes."

"What am I supposed to fucking think?"

"Yes..."

"You fucking hurt me, Jay. You done that. I didn't need it."

Men didn't often say that, did they? Do they more, now? *You hurt me.* Honestly, demandingly, as a woman might.

"Jud..."

"OK. All right. What do you want to do?"

"Can we meet – maybe in London...?"

"No, I can't. I've got – there are things going on here, too. And I'm working every night till midnight Friday."

"Saturday?" I asked.

"I've got stuff to see to most weekends. I'm working anyhow, in the day."

I braced myself and said, colder than he, "Are you telling me to piss off?"

"What, like you done that first time?"

"I explained about that."

"Yes. OK. Sorry." A silence. I waited. He said, "Thursday night. Come over here. About ten-thirty. I can get off, wangle it somehow. That's if you want to."

Two days. *"Yes,* Jud, I do."

Oh yes Jud. I do.

When I'd put the phone down, I was shaking, shaking. I went to her kitchen. I made a pot of some of the expensive Assam tea. Put in a teaspoon of ginger, as I'd seen her do.

Ten-thirty on Thursday. That wouldn't be straight forward.

"She's not so ill now, Jilaine. More depressed."

"But can you cope with that? It can be very draining. Jay, you really are too thin. And you don't eat or exercise enough, or rest enough."

"How confusing."

What would it be, to take that sweet face in my hands, and kiss that strawberry mouth? What's worth having, Jay, is worth waiting for, and fiddling for. And if I slap her the way Sharon slapped me behind the filing cabinets, I won't get any of it.

"She's an old friend?"

Is she jealous? Too much to hope for.

I said, "Mary. I've known her since school. She's had a rough time. Look – I might have to stay over."

"Then please call me."

"I'll try."

"Jay, please. I think I'm going to insist."

"Then I will call. If – I'm going to be later than midnight." And of course, I hope I am.

My mother was never like this. It was, "Oh are you going out? Bring me back some cigarettes, will you?" Or it was, "You'll be gone all night? Good. Then Mac/Tony/Craig can stay without you looking daggers at him."

Even so, Jilaine was reminding me of my mother now. She seemed vulnerable, as my mother was. Death found *her* an easy target. Was Jilaine like that, a heart of glass, a skull of eggshell under blonde hair?

I took a larger bag, stuffed with the normal things, toothbrush, knickers. Jilaine was in the main room, reading a novel by a French writer, in French. Somehow, I never believe it when people do this. I think they are pretending they can do it.

"Jay, is there any chance I could have the number of the place you're going to?"

"I'm sorry. Basically – she doesn't have a phone. There's the local call box – but that's a bit random. The area is a little – rough."

"Be careful, Jay. And remember to call me if you'll be later than midnight." Cinderella.

As I went down in the lift of Cobham Court, I felt deadly sad. I'd felt like that, when my mother left me at the school gates, and I was five years old. Abandoned to bullies and the slappy teachers and the concrete playground where I endlessly fell and cut my knees. I can remember lying there, knees and nose pouring blood, crying, "I want my mummy!" While the kids mocked. And I knew anyway 'mummy' was far off, kicking her legs up in some sweaty rehearsal room.

Don't think I'm trying to make you sorry for me. Poor skinny snotty kid, crying. We all go through it, you and I. Some of us just turn out better, that's all, amid which last I do not number myself.

I was slightly early. I got out of the cab on the road above the terrace of houses and walked down. A man was walking two big dogs over the playing field.

One kept rushing off in the darkness and bounding back, but the other faithfully kept pace with its owner.

All the lights seemed to be on behind drawn curtains. I knocked. Somehow, the house felt vibrant, and full of people, yet it was totally silent.

Then, a woman opened the door.

I hadn't expected that, a woman.

She was older than Jud. About thirty-five, nice-looking in a slight, loose, untidy way, her yellow hair scraped back in a tail.

"Yes?"

As I stood there, a child came out around her jeaned legs, and stared up at me from great still eyes.

I thought, I've come to the wrong house. But it wasn't. It was Jud's house – Jud and Davey's house – or it had been, a dozen nights ago.

"I'm..." I stared and stopped.

I could smell the hamsters. Their dainty rodent stink blew delicately along the hall, where I saw the wallpaper I remembered, and glimpsed the lighted kitchen where Jud had kept wine, and made tea for me at 4 a.m.

For some reason I looked down again at the child. She was a girl, with silky dark hair, dark eyes. About three years old, or four, because what do I know of children or their ages, now I'm no longer one of them?

And the child said to me, "Granddad's died."

Something dropped through me, like the fall of the lift that other time. Not quite like that. More like an alligator sliding from a bank into the river.

I said, idiotically, as I do with children anyway, "Has he?"

"Real shame," intervened the young woman. "It's all right, Annie. Look, luv, go and see if Hammy and Pammy are all right. I can hear them going bananas in there."

"OK," said Annie, agreeably. She turned at once and retreated into the hamster room, still leaving its door open.

"Her grandfather..."

"Yes. It was this morning. Or last night. Well, he was found, like, this morning. Died in his sleep, the doctor thinks. Bit of a performance too. They have to do an autopsy for some reason, 'cos he ain't been to his GP for a couple of months. I ask you. Didn't need to see no one. Bloody weird if you ask me. And they know he had the op and all."

"Do you mean Davey?" I asked.

"Yeah, that's it. Poor old Davey. Thought he'd go on now till he got a telegram. Lovely old boy. Not that old, nowadays. You knew him?"

"We met."

"Wait – you're Jud's friend, ent you?"

"Yes."

"That's it. He left me a note – where is it? I forgot. There's so much to do, ain't there, when someone dies sudden."

"Yes."

"And *Miss* is a little handful. Though I'm used to her. She often stays over with me."

She began to hunt along a table in the hall, but there were papers and keys all over it tonight. She didn't find the note.

"Will Jud...?"

"I don't know when he'll be back, luv. He's had a lot to do. But he said, you stay if you want."

"But maybe…"

"It's all right. His bed's all made. It's just the other room what's a bit of a mess, the police and all, traipsing in and out. Like a bloody thriller on the telly. Anyone'd think we done him in."

As if mesmerised, I went after her to the kitchen, I must have shut the front door.

When I passed the hamster room, I saw their cage was open, and they and the child were delicately playing in a sort of pen on the floor.

Who was she?

Not this woman's child. *Granddad died.* Davey was her grandfather. Jud then... her father. The woman was making tea.

"I'm Glory – Gloria Pretty." She spoke this name without dismay, used to it. She reached out and shook my hand with her cold and pointed feminine fingers.

As last time, a thick blind down at the window. The kettle on, as I had seen it last.

He had died, the gentle old man. Gone in a night, snuffed out. "Blissfully quick," I heard the landlady say in Bournemouth.

I sat on a hard chair at one corner of the kitchen table. Like his bed, the table, too big for the room.

Obviously, I would have to get out and go back. I didn't want to *be* here.

I could recall all the rigmarole with my mother. The death certificates and copies, and claims and refunds to be applied for, and bills to be settled, and the undertakers and burial, and the not having any money. And the utter silence, which this house now had upon it, under all its ordinary sounds, cars on the road, like the grave.

"Here you are."

Tea. The answer to our ills.

I sipped it, too weak and milky, but the taste of being alive.

The front door opened and shut. Not loudly, but angry. The child gave a squeak. "Dad – Daddy..."

"Hi, baby. Hang on. I'll just put this down. What's that?"

"Hammy bit me." She didn't sound upset, by the bite, or the death.

"Bastard. We'll have to shave him."

She laughed her child's laugh, high and rippling, and he walked into the kitchen, holding her in his arms.

When he saw me, his face never changed. Didn't light up. His face was

174

lead and couldn't move. "Hi. You OK?"

"I'm so sorry."

"Yeah. It's shit. He was only sixty-eight. The coroner's guy reckons he wouldn't have felt a thing. I'll never forget, he was singing when he went to bed. *Carousel* – one of those old shows." Jud sat down at the table, with the child still in his arms. We crouched round the piece of furniture, crowded to the tea mugs, and Gloria Pretty brought him another mug and crouched with us.

"He always got up a few times, now, at night," she told me. "I used to see his light sometimes across from us – we're on the curve, like. This morning I thought, that's funny, I ain't seen no light. I give Annie her supper," she said to Jud.

"Thanks, Glory. I just got some stuff from the service station. Milk, beans, bread. I'll get Annie to bed."

"I could've done that. I'll do it."

I rose. "Jud – I'd better go, hadn't I?"

"Yes, if you want."

Glory shook her tail. "I'll just nip up to the toilet a minute. I'll start Annie's bath, shall I?"

"Thanks."

Redundant, unwanted, an idiot spectre of past joys at the feast of death, I stood there on the lino. Only convention made me say, "Is there anything I can do?"

Jud didn't look at me.

Annie said, "Daddy, don't cry, Daddy."

And then I went across to him and put my arms around him. I held him and he held the child. I don't know why. Not for any purpose. Some reflex. I just did.

After a minute, he stood up and glanced at me, fearful to me as a man who weeps always is.

"Can you stay a bit, Jay? I'll just take her up. Glory'll cope. Glory's been wonderful."

"Glory hallelujah," said the child, some household joke.

And then they went out and left me in the desert of their kitchen.

He had a child. His father had died, and he had a child he had hidden before, perhaps at Glory Pretty's house 'on the curve', or somewhere else (in a cupboard?). He hadn't wanted me to see the child; the way Angus and Ginny sensitively hadn't let Jilaine see the upsetting baby in their house at Heathways. Jud's reasons were different. He hadn't wanted to put me off.

But now, the scythe of death had cut through everything, and nothing mattered, and it was all on display, the child's hamsters, the child, the memory of the old man bowing and kissing my hand, in his slippers and tatty shirt. Naked truth.

And he had said stay, but he had also said go on then, go.

Which delectable prospect should I choose?

III

Not much of importance has been said about the time Jilaine and I spent in each other's company, while I first lived at her apartment. I've gone into her absences and how I explored the terrain when she wasn't there. I've detailed her admonishments and vetoes. And I've told you about her recounting of her dream, which made me chase after Jud at once, to fill myself with a baby – literally under the spurs of fate. *Her* fate.

Of course, as I've said, I was wary and uncomfortable by then, with having to pretend. And when I came back from my night with Jud, when I might have felt able to begin to relax, she was stiff and armoured, angry at me for my unexplained nocturnal stop-out. Philippa, I reasoned, must have behaved like that. And then Philippa had disappeared completely. No wonder Jilaine wasn't going to like being left in the dark.

Strange really that she had trusted me at all to come and go. Yet she had given me on my first day, a set of the keys to her flat. "Otherwise," she'd said, smiling at me, "you won't be able to go out." And this was a fact, because there were two locks, one of which was operated from outside. What I mean is, without the keys, she could have locked me in.

At the time, I hadn't really thought about that so much, the locking in part. I had thought she was foolish to give me keys I might in turn give friends to copy, friends who were on the lookout for a rich place to loot or vandalise. I mean, she didn't know who the hell I was, did she?

And that stayed consistent. She didn't seem to try to find out about me. When we were together, she never asked me much about myself, just as I didn't ask very much about her. We talked about other things. About books and food and paintings and plays, about life generally, other cities, and, in her case, other countries. But even there, even when she talked about France, (and I knew she must be speaking of things from her childhood and adolescence, with her mother and Lesley Spender), Jilaine didn't include herself, and rarely the two women, in her list of characters. It would be "You'd see the old women sitting outside their doors in the sunlight, sewing," or "They pick the olives then," or "The wind would bring the storms down. And in the summer the smell of thyme and lavender down from the hills. And honey, a smell of honey."

Sometimes she did speak of named people. "Oh, Angus tries to look after me. He does manage to, sometimes. He's very reliable. I owe him a lot."

Why am I digressing? There is one afternoon I want to make a note of, here. For several reasons. Perhaps I should have written about it earlier. But structure isn't my strong concern, not as it is in Jilaine's material. She always wrote her books three times, she once told me. First as a sort of long synopsis – almost a short story. Then a second draft, working the flesh up over the bones. Then a third – not *draft* – more cosmetic surgery – paring off anything superfluous.

But I – well, as you see, that isn't what I do.

The afternoon in question: I'd been there about two days. I wasn't yet too desperate, and she had poured me a large glass of white wine at lunch. "Alcohol is good for you, in moderation. But I'd rather you drank wine than vodka."

Afternoon over the terrace and London. The little jewellery planes like dragonflies humming along the blue, turning always at the same invisible detour in the sky.

"Darling, please don't stand too near the edge."

"It isn't an edge, Jilaine. There is the wall, and the balustrade."

"I know. It just makes me uneasy. You're tall. The rail stops at your waist."

This was an exaggeration, but perhaps, seated over there in the reclining chair, in her mint-green shirt, this was how it looked to her.

I glanced over and down. We were about forty, forty-five feet up, far flung across the building's side, screened from other windows, the entry doors, by tall blue firs. Below was a short formal lawn and pruned shrubs, a strip of drive no one used, or I'd never seen anyone there. And more trees to the outer wall. Beyond, the shining river.

She didn't repeat her request. But I knew she would. Or she might come over and quietly lead me away, like the nurse of one hopelessly insane.

She was infuriating. But right then I thought, *If she comes over, she may touch me. Perhaps put her arm around me.* In the end, though, she didn't, and I came back to the table and took a peach.

She had put on her sunglasses again and was lying back. She looked so beautiful, her whiteness rising from the green like Venus from the sea. Her tilted face, her ringless hands. Her throat. I could make out the shape of her breasts lying nestled under the silk of the shirt. And the long neat swordlike Y of her crotch and thighs, firm in the sheath of the jeans. And the jeans had cost probably, even then, about two hundred pounds. From their ends, pale clean feet, with silver discs for nails.

Sitting down, I ate the peach. Looking at her. Thinking, *the peach I am eating is your body, Jilaine. Oh, Jilaine.*

I've said, I assiduously guard myself, and then suddenly, I don't. Like the clever crocodile tears I can cry more or less to order, but which, now and then, merely *escape.* Sometimes, all the subterfuge, the juggling – you think, *Christ, why bother?*

"You look beautiful."

She could have been asleep. Wasn't, had heard me. "Do I? That's kind."

"No, not kind. Just a fact."

Go over – risk it and go over – softly place one finger on one nipple's bud, feel it rise, questing, against the slight pressure. Undo the button, just one, and put my mouth inside against the warm, jasmine-scented skin.

"But me," I said, heard myself say, "apart from the baby," caution cast to the planes above, nearly laughing at the lies, "apart from that obvious reason –why are you so kind to *me?*"

177

She smiled. That was all.

Was she inviting me? It could be that – no, it wasn't that. I pinned myself down to the chair. She had *told* me. She preferred men. I said, "I mean frankly, Jilaine, I know you're not a snob, but compared to your life, I'm an impecunious nobody. I'm crap."

Her eyes didn't open behind the dark lenses.

She said, "No, Jay. You're one of the elite, just like me. Just like millions of others."

I digested this.

"Which *elite*?"

I hadn't yet read her books. When I did, I found the passage in *The Skaters*. It was one of her few self-indulgences. She rarely told the reader what she thought or what she thought to be Unassailable Truth. (Unlike some.) I can quote the passage, almost word for word, so I will.

"This world does have an elite. It manifests, this Upper Caste, in all races, all walks of life; among all physical types, throughout all social hierarchies, in every age group and across both genders.'

Now, she said, "I call us The Creative Classes."

"You mean artists – writers..."

"I mean anyone who can make and do something of value. A cook, an actor, a composer, a great teacher – the boy in the underpass who sings like an angel with a guitar. All those. All the rest."

"If there is an elite, then there's an opposite – a sub-class. Is there?"

"Oh yes," she said.

"And who are they? The ones who can't – make anything?"

"The ones who *un*make. The destroyers and jeerers."

I sat in silence thinking. Ah Jilaine. I write, so I must be a doer and maker – one of the elite. And you, of course. And the singer in the subway.

But no, Jilaine. *I* am one of the *un*makers.

Presently I spoke to her again, about something else. But she had fallen asleep, soundless and ingenuous.

I looked at her, so flawless, helpless, unaware. And thought, I could kill you so easily. Press the pillow over your face (I'm so much stronger.) Slice that alabaster vein in your neck with the knife from the fruit. Or scar you.

Unmake you.

Destroy you.

But I too lay back and went to sleep in the sun. Lazy. Didn't I say?

IV

Upstairs, I heard the bath running for the child. After a bit, Jud came down.

"Do you want some tea?" I, pretending to domestic nicety in tragic circumstances.

"Something stronger. There's some whiskey in the front room."

I don't like whiskey. But I didn't refuse it.

We sat as we had the other night, before things changed, I on the couch and he in the chair. But the harsh overhead light was left on. And we both hid from it, ducking our eyes down and faces.

"Sixty-eight – I said, didn't I. Christ. I thought he'd be OK after the surgery. That was the dangerous time. And he got right over it. He's been great – really better. They had me late, him and my mum. He was in his forties. God. I've got to call Ireland. Kieran, my brother. God. I haven't been able to face it. I'll have this and call him. Or is it too late? I don't know. Maybe tomorrow. No, I should have done it. Maybe the police did it. I can't remember."

He seemed to be waiting – for a lifeline?

"Why not wait now until the morning."

"Yes – I don't know. It's not that late."

"It's nearly midnight."

"Christ – and Annie – I told Glory, get her to bed. Fuck. I told her. No, wait, I said, let her stay up, she isn't tired. She doesn't understand. Annie. It was like that when Carol went off. And then when Carol came back and I took Annie and walked out. Annie just said a few times when's Mum coming home? And I lied to her, Jay. I said, soon, Baby. In a month or so. That sounds like forever to a kid. Never wanted her. Fucking bitch. She never even tried to take her back."

He started to cry. Stopped.

He stood up.

"Thanks for hanging on. I'll ring up the office, get you a cab. Listen, let me pay for it. You come all this way."

"It's OK."

He shouted. "No, it fucking isn't, isn't OK. Christ, it fucking isn't." Then he went white. "I can't seem to – I don't want Annie to hear – when Carol and I – she used to hear the rows – I don't want – any of this bloody shit."

My instinct, you will guess, was to run. But I went to him, and we put our arms around each other. Then he wept on my shoulder, only for a moment or so, but his tears were scalding hot as if they came from an inferno.

So, this is how one is meant to be. To feel and act. This is genuine. Take notes, Jay. A unique opportunity.

I only held him.

"Will you stay?"

"Yes, if you want me to."

"I do want you to. I'm sorry – I can't – I'm not..."

"That's fine." (He is so like a woman – apologising because he can't face having sex.)

And oh yes, fine. No copulation. No conception. But well – well.

"My mother went. I mean she died. I was eleven. He used to go for walks with us, Keir and me. Long walks. He really thought there was somewhere

179

else. Even when he was going in for the operation, he said, 'I'm not scared. If I go, I'll be there.' Crazy guy. Crazy bloody old man. He's there now. I hope there's a there for him to be."

We went up, creeping, like naughty children, and Glory was on the tiny landing. "She's gone right off asleep."

"Thanks, girl."

"I'll drop by about 8."

"Thanks, Glory."

"Night, Jud. Night, Jay."

She knows me. I am become one among them.

In his room, he was shaking, shivering. We got into the narrow bed and clung together, and soon a burning heat, infused from the inner inferno, enveloped us. He slept.

About 1, I woke from a doze. He stirred, murmuring.

"Jud – can I make a very quick telephone call?"

"What? – what called?"

"Just to my girlfriend. She gets in a state."

"I love you," he said, and slept.

Creeping down again. All the house black, but for the faint luridescence of the sidelong streetlamp. The child slept, and Jud slept, and in the empty bedroom, the ghost of the old man who bowed.

Jilaine worked late quite often. Besides, I'd had her ultimatum.

There was a phone in her main room and in the annexe off the library, and another in her study. Even so, would she hear? The machine came on. A second's relief – I could leave her a message – was severed when she cut off the recording.

"Yes?"

"Jilaine – I'm sorry to wake you."

Tight and frosted. "I wasn't asleep. Are you all right?"

"Jilaine, I'm OK. I haven't been able to get to a phone until now. I can't stay on long. Basically, someone has died here."

Her voice, altered, tender and sweet. "Jay, I'm sorry. Not your friend?

"No, not Mary. It's – her father. Look, I daren't talk now. I'm at a neighbour's. I have to go back to her. I'll explain – as soon as I can."

"How do you feel?"

"I'm – oh. That. I'm perfectly all right."

"Please take care."

Of course, she has a vested interest. I must not miscarry her child, for which she has already shelled out so much.

"Jilaine, really, I'm fit and well. Only I can't leave her now."

"I understand. Call me tomorrow, if you can. Let me know what's happening."

"If I can. No, I will. I promise."

"Oh, Jay," she said. She sighed.

I love you. He said that, in his sleep. Who did he mean? His child? Davey? Me...?

"Jilaine," I said, "you've been so good to me..."

"Nonsense. Just take care."

I love you, Jilaine.

But no, I didn't say it, until I heard the receiver go down.

In the kitchen I made a cup of instant coffee. I didn't want to go back to him, and yet the thought of him, alone in that restricted bed, made me drink the coffee quickly and return.

He was fast asleep but feeling me infiltrate into the space he made room for me, as if accustomed.

Sleepless now, I lay there.

He wouldn't want sex. Or might he? The rabid consolation of grief.

I would wait until morning. Then I'd go back. This was nothing to do with me. I had done all this, long ago.

He had a child. If I needed proof of his potency, there she was. But time was running out. Had run out. I was in my third month, with nothing.

This would be, however, a legitimate excuse. I could lose the baby the very way Jilaine feared, through the stress of all this.

Jilaine, I'm sorry. I was afraid to tell you. It just – happened.

And I could try again, couldn't I? If she wanted. All open and above board. *There's this guy I know. He's good-looking and decent. I think I could ask him.*

Not the Creative Class, of course. He doesn't *make* anything. But never mind.

But if I 'lost' the 'baby', after all, I couldn't just go bouncing back to her. Better delay then a couple of days, to consolidate loss and recovery. And I didn't have enough money, frankly, to stay anywhere else but with Jud.

All round then, the safest thing, whatever I decided – stay here. A couple of days.

When I woke again, a churlish natural light was making the curtain threadbare.

I slipped out of the bed. Easy enough, as I was right at the limit of the mattress. On the previous visit I used the lavatory and washbasin, not the bathroom next door. This time, I went into both. What pains he must have gone to, then, hiding all the child's things in case – the rubber ducks along the bath, the minute toothbrush and rabbit patterned towels and little-girl hair kit. I tried to be quiet. But outside milk floats were jangling along the street and jolly dogs barking and motorbikes being zealously revved. It was 5.30.

The kitchen led into a utility room – rather as Jilaine's did, except this pair would have fitted into her kitchen several times over. There was a bolt on the utility room door here, and a key in the lock. I undid them. A curious wide, fragrant air, unlike the inner suburbs, washed around me.

The sun was colouring the sky at last. Summer now was older and mature, less

181

clean and more cunning. Somewhere, someone was frying bacon. Nearer, roses bloomed.

After a minute I went out.

Where had I come to? I was in a forest, the glade of a deep wood.

Some rounded stones ran into a meadow of wild grass, thick with poppies blue and red, cornflowers, purple spires I haven't a name for, great white dish-plate daisies. The trees stood tall to either side. Against their tawny or inky-green, a lower spreading tree with hyacinth blue flowers, through which coiled garlands of pink roses, hanging heavy as festoons of grapes. Beneath the tree opened an irregularly shaped pool, where a strange shrub, with sheaves of what looked like green snakes, seemed to be drinking. Lilies rose from the water, and a giant tarnished frog squatted on a rock in the reeds.

I walked out, through the grass, selecting the occasional flat stones to tread on. A green-saffron willow trailed before a tower of clipped box. A deep red rose had married a mauve clematis, and they climbed a broken pillar of stone... I went up some mossy steps – a rivulet burst from a dragon's mouth, and so I found the sooty brick wall, clambered by ivy and golden hop, which was the garden's end.

"Hi," he said, when I turned and saw him, gazing down into the pool. "It's netted, see, to make it safe for her, Annie, I mean. So we've got fish. Look, there's the one she calls Toffee." A gold fin winked, just like in Tennyson.

"It's amazing."

"Yes. It's coming on. It was the first thing I started on. Out here, just rubble and junk. Two good trees they left. The ones I planted got growing fast. See that vine? I used the frame of the bed they'd dumped for a support. And that pillar thing, that come from the old gasworks."

"You mean you did this?"

"Sure. I used to work as a gardener. Landscaping. That stuff. Want to get back to it someday. But you can't get no work in winter. So the cabs are safer.

He shook back his hair, wet from the shower and still so thick. He had on a shirt tucked into jeans. For a moment, speaking of the garden, he was young again, careless again. Then he changed.

"Dad used to like to sit out here at night, when he couldn't sleep. It was warm. The honeysuckle smells. We even get a bat go over. He liked all that." He kicked a little stone across the netted pool. "I'd bury him here, if they'd let me. But you can't. Got to be the boneyard. Know your place."

The garden, as the sun slanted, revealed to me it was actually quite narrow. Its walls held it, though cloaked in ivy and curtained by oaks and elders, and conifers bought, he said, in packs of ten, like fags. In winter, when the leaves fell, it would lose its illusion of an enchanted wood. The pond would freeze. The flowers die.

"I should've told you about Annie. I would've done. I didn't want to frighten you. It's a bit much, some guy and his little kid and his – dad. Well. One hurdle that's gone."

"Jud, is it all right if I stay?"

"Oh God. Jay, yes. I wish you would."

"Just a day or so. Then I'll have to go back. Report in, as it were."

"She's strict, your girlfriend." He grinned.

"She just wants me to be all right."

"They're going to call me. The coroner. When I can have his funeral."

A bird sang in the blue-flower tree. The brass frog sat on the rock as a snail crawled slowly over it, and away into the leylandii hedge.

V

It was a hot high summer day, the afternoon of the funeral. There was quite a crowd. A 'respectable turnout', as one of the attending neighbours said.

I didn't know any of them, obviously, apart from Glory Pretty, who came swathed in black with long earrings. There were a number of oldish men and some elderly women. And a buxom sixty-year-old barmaid, straight out of H.E. Bates at his most voluptuous. She, apparently, had been Davey's 'lady-friend'. She was crying, copiously, but she knew her stuff, and had applied tear-proof mascara.

Jud's brother had 'come over' and stood there in a dark suit, like Jud. The brother's wife was also there in a dark suit. Too pallid distant people, to me like cut-outs. There was nothing new in that.

Annie had not been brought. She was staying with yet another neighbour. All the neighbours, the female ones, helped out with Annie, it seemed. I'd been glad of that. Children – and you will not be astonished, only further disgusted to learn – have little appeal for me. I don't like them. They're not even ready yet to be with the rest of us. This opinion they infallibly sense in me. She and I, when thrown together, at the odd meal or moment in his house, maintained between us a polite uninterest.

But she was a lovely-looking child. She had Jud's looks. They say girls take after their fathers, (so I suppose, too, I must look like that faceless man who sired me.)

The service wasn't religious. A couple of people spoke, in the sunbright chapel. They said he had been a marvel, Davey. Jud didn't speak, or his brother. They were both dry-eyed and – dry. As if all the moisture had been leached from them. Only Kieran's wife dabbed her eyes. The lady-friend wept, openly and bravely, undabbed. (You will perhaps see, only fools, tricksters, the desperate or the very brave, cry in public.)

In the sunshine we watched the coffin go down into a slot of black earth. But Jud and Kieran and the lady-friend had seen Davey at the undertakers, in his embalmed state. It was him all right, this box.

My dead mother I never saw. Someone else – the identification. Who? I wouldn't go. She was cremated. I don't really remember. Not really. I don't.

Blissfully quick.

The wake, or reception, or whatever it was, was in the private room of a pub. The air slowly turned blue then brown from cigarettes and the fumes of alcohol.

I wasn't often with Jud. Sometimes he would come over to me. "Are you OK, girl? Have you had anything to eat?"

"Yes, thanks. Are you coping?"

"No. But it's all right. Do you want another drink?"

"I'm fine, Jud."

Once he introduced me to Kieran and his cut-out of wife.

"Hallo," they both said.

All those flowers dying on the grave.

"I hate that, the flowers, they should be growing," he said. "But people like to. Annie wanted to. I had to give her a pound and make out that bought some flowers."

I had seen them – chrysanthemums – and the card. *From Annie, Hammy and Pammy.*

I thought, in fifteen years, she'll ask. He'll have to be able to say, "Yes, I did. There were flowers from you. And the hamsters." And she'd say, "What hamsters?"

Kieran and his wife were staying in some hotel. A cab arrived for them, not from *Surefire*. Everyone else ebbed away back into the pub.

Finally, just Jud and me, standing on a baked pavement tanned by sinking sun.

"Thanks for this, Jay."

Why had I stayed?

You know why. Or you can guess. That second morning after I saw the garden. We took the coffee upstairs. His sex was full of rage, but he never hurt me. It wasn't in him, to hurt me.

"...Are you all right?"

"Yes, Jud."

"But you – *are* you?"

"I don't always come. I don't care. I just – like making love with you."

"So long as you are. Or I can..."

"No. Rest. It was good. I like it, with you."

And I did. I did like it, with him. But that wasn't why. Whether I came or not, I was *full* of him. *Filled.*

I'd phoned Jilaine a couple of days later.

"I'm not going to be able to get back for a bit."

"I understand."

"There's the funeral. She wants me to be here. She keeps crying."

"Yes. Are you well?"

"I'm thriving, Jilaine. Death must agree with me."

A silence. She said, "Please let me know, when you can. "

She sounded far off at the end of a tunnel. A bad line.

"It won't," I said, "be more than a day or so. And I promise you, I'm very well. Everything is great." And this vow was now five days ago. But he and I had had sex at least twice every day. If she had known, she couldn't say I wasn't looking after her interests.

Back on the sunset pavement, he said, "Annie's going to go into London with Kier and Rosalie." (The wife's name, it seemed.) "They want to make a fuss of her. Buy her stuff – spoil her daft. Rosalie – she hasn't been able to have any of her own." Ah, Jilaine. So you're not unique. "That's for the next three days. So do you want to go somewhere? Let me take you somewhere, make all this shit up to you."

I looked at him through the opaque spun-sherry light. It was *that* time of day. The 'tween time. "Where?"

"Well – London, too. A hotel – I know a couple of good ones."

"Like Kieran's?"

"No. Theirs is rotten."

"But..."

He kissed me. I loved his kisses. A surprise? They made me feel I could let go, that I could lose consciousness and fall, and he would hold me up. That's the only way I can describe it, with him. As if all my identity were gone, and I had nothing to do or be any more. A sort of death, but quite safe – since I was still alive.

We booked into a hotel called *The Park*. Perhaps, evidently, with all his cab runs, he could find these places. It really was in the middle of a little park, with a lake and vast willows, swans and so on. The room was small, with a smaller en-suite bath, but everything so clean and all tended to by others. Like Jilaine's, without the onus.

We walked in the park, and through old city lanes beyond, some of which had rough cobbles (a film-set London) and one a piece of a Roman bath, about a mile down under the street. Otherwise we ate in the restaurant, or at a coffee shop nearby. We showered and lay in the big bed. We made love, we screwed, we played.

Oh, I'd done it all before. But not enjoyed it. I did enjoy it, now, with Jud. And I came. Every damn time, with him, in that bed among the willows, under the snow-white sheet. Or against the wall of the snow-white shower, the water running loud as applause.

Wow, you are a great lay, Jay.

No, he never said anything so bloody mindless.

He was – what can I say he was? He was the loveliest and best of men. But now I've put it down, should I just cross it through? What will you think of me?

No, I didn't love him.

You will see I couldn't have loved him, very soon. Is that, anyway, all you love them for? Because they are handsome, and they can give you an orgasm? One other reason, sometimes. They can make children in you. And he

185

couldn't. With Carol – but not me.

I knew. Even though I wasn't due as yet. I felt – somehow, I'd come to *know* the feeling – *vacant*. And I would be right.

So, there was no reason for it, all that conjoining. All that staying with him. Using up his money, which he didn't even *have* because Davey hadn't left more than enough to cover his funeral, and Jud wasn't working.

"Let me buy lunch, Jud."

He let me, but then came champagne with dinner.

And of course he was afraid to return to the house, but we had three days, and that was that. Annie would be brought back. And he wanted to see Annie.

"What do you think of her?" he said, on the third morning, as we dressed.

"She's great." I was careful not to sound too enthusiastic. Beyond a demarcation line, I wasn't going to lie about this.

But he took the cue all wrong. He got happy and praised her. He told me all about her, and I stopped listening, only murmuring now and then the right sounds, as I do.

He loved his daughter. That was as it was supposed to be. There is no law which says *I* had to. Except, obviously, one. But that wouldn't come into it.

I saw the man that morning. He was walking along, across the road from us. He paused to buy a paper. He was middle-aged but slim and strong, in a suit, with slicked-back iron hair.

"I saw him before."

"What – that guy there? Yeah. He was in the carvery last night."

"Was he? I didn't notice him then."

"Champagne," he said. He kissed me lightly.

"But wasn't he at the funeral?"

"What? No. Course he wasn't, Jay. Come on."

But he *had* been at the funeral, standing at the back among the trees, as Davey's box went into the earth. I had thought he was one of the so-many people there I didn't know.

You'd think, wouldn't you, with my twisted and devious mind, I might have reached some conclusion. But my mind is too clever to be bright. I miss a lot.

That afternoon, after lunch, we went back on the train to the terrace house. Jud began to be too lively, then he grew still.

I kept thinking, His child will be there – so I shan't, for long. And I have to call *her*. She'll be furious. And anyway. Anyway. Where is the use now, in any of this? I had made a half decision. A cowardly one, naturally. I would forestall her until the next period. Then, if I bled, as I was sure I would, I must own up, or at least get free.

We were both subdued by the time we reached the station.

He carried the bag. It was mostly full of the extra clothes he'd bought me during my stay – nothing much, a couple of cheap T-shirts, a filmy sleeveless dress, under-things, tights. More than either of us could afford.

I would have to pay him back. If anything did come of this, I must, just to set the weighted balance straighter.

The day was more cool, the sky a blue mixed with milk.

We walked.

As we went up the hill, he said, "What happened with that plant you had?"

"What?"

"You know, that huge plant at Compton Road – it was beautiful. In your room. If you moved out, what did you do with it?"

The plant. My one great success.

"I left it there, with some of my stuff. Olivine said she'd water it. She probably hasn't. The cats will have peed in it."

"God, you're heartless," he said.

He sounded weary and angry. And I felt a slam of rage. I had done the best I could. But no, I hadn't. Jilaine would have let me bring a plant into her flat. The plant, of everything of mine, (including myself) was the one thing that could have suited her or her world.

"Well, I can go and fetch it," I heard myself defensively say.

"Yes. Why don't you?"

"Only – I probably have to go back tonight, or tomorrow. I mean to Jill's." I had started to call her *Jill* to him. The simplest way, as so often, being the wisest.

"All right," he said. But he was stern. We turned down, and there was the terrace, the little river, the playing field, where now two amateur football teams were booting a ball with thuds and yowls.

As he opened the door, I heard her break from her quiescence. She rushed upward like a whirlwind.

"Dad – daddy – daddy – dad..."

"Hallo, baby." Up into his arms he swung her, and her hair blew like a black flame.

Now, there is love. Let this be a lesson to you, Jay.

Glory was in the kitchen making her weak tea.

"Break done you good I 'spect," she said. I wanted to correct her grammar with a sharp movement, like that of an osteopath manipulating wayward vertebrae. He got worse when he was with these people. Christ, I thought, listen to yourself. That doesn't matter. And besides, you know now, you've seen the garden. Jud too, is one of the inner *Elite*.

Someone knocked on the street door. A neighbour. They'd all be in soon, wanting to view him, and me, remind him – *us* – of duties and sorrows. But the child was all alight, giggling round a pink sugar biscuit shaped like an elephant...

And Glory went to the door. I heard her voice. "Yes?" Abruptly ruffled and unsure.

And then.

Then I heard Jilaine's voice. I was imagining it.

187

The imagined voice said. "May I speak to Jay?"

"Oh – uh – yes. Come on in. Full house." And then, incredibly primly, like a maid from 1915, "Who shall I say?"

The imaginary Jilaine replied, "Just say Jilaine."

Always breathtaking – even in the morning without make-up – even exhausted or in tears – she looked now positively supernatural as she advanced into that ordinary space.

She wore a sleeveless sea-blue dress with a scoop neck. The tops of her breasts were just visible, and her skin was like white velvet. There was a bracelet on her left wrist, a silver serpent coiling round three times. The sapphires in its eyes were real.

Glory and the child reacted in the only possible, the *primitive* way. Their eyes were round, their lips parted. Time had stopped.

And Jud. He raised his gaze. He looked at her and slowly got up, a gentleman for a lady. He towered above her. And she looked up the length of his lean graceful body, into his face. She looked full at him, as if to take a photographic shot of him on the camera of the mind. And then her eyes, which now were the colour of the dress, and of the snake's, moved past him, nearly *through* him. They came to rest where they must.

On Annie.

I've seen films where a vision, or the Catholic Virgin herself, is manifested to some girl amid the hills. It was that, now. The child's face – how to describe it – it became *transparent*, as if in X-ray light. But instead of seeing every bone of the skull within, instead, you saw the soul of her. The bones of *that*.

She held the pink biscuit in mid-air. And then Jilaine reached out, a gesture like the flicking paw of a cat, and touched the tip of the child's nose with a finger so light, so swift, it might never have been. But the child broke into laughter. And so, so did Jilaine. The same laughter, both of them.

And it was in that moment as if the rest of us had ceased to be. And everything else with us.

There was only Jilaine and Annie. Annie and Jilaine.

It was, as the French say, the *coup de foudre*. The lightning stroke.

PART FIVE

I

Although I didn't ask her, and she never explained, almost immediately I realised what she must have done. Fed-up with my absences and non-communication, she had learned my whereabouts from the cab company she herself had that night contacted for me and paid. And then she had sent a detective to seek and to confirm the address, my attendance there, and, decidedly, the company I kept.

So she soon discovered I was not with any ailing wailing school-friend, but a tall young charming man, with whom I finally spent three days, two nights, in an up-market London hotel. For all I know, he bugged our room, that professional, iron-haired man in a suit.

Glory spoke first. "Would you like a cup of tea, Jilay?"

Jilaine didn't amend that. "No, thank you. I'd just like to see Jay for a moment. I hope that's all right?" And she looked up at him again. Not a hint of irony or scorn. Instead, she held out her mint-cool hand, courteous and sane. "I hope you'll accept my sympathies on the death of your father. I'm Jilaine Best. Jay may have mentioned me to you."

"Thanks. Yes, she did."

"You're Jud? May I call you Jud?" (To the professional, mere names would have been easy.)

"Why not."

The kitchen, never big enough, was bursting, writhing under the pressure we were putting on it. In a paroxysm of instinctive panic, Glory suddenly trotted into the utility room and flung open the back door.

The child jumped from her chair. "Show you my fish!"

And Jilaine's eyes, which for an instant had seemed filled by Jud, now flew away from him and came again to Annie. "You've got fish, darling?"

"Yes – all fish – in the water..."

"That's good. They'll be more comfortable like that."

Annie was there beside her. She nodded at Jilaine's serious affirmation.

Jud said, "Maybe Miss Best wants to speak to Jay, Annie luv."

Jilaine said, her eyes on the child, "No, I'd really like to see the fish, if I may." Just like a well-mannered child herself.

And how could you deny this child, a blue Chinese-willow child, and golden-haired?

Hand in hand with Annie, Jilaine walked through and out of the back door.

And we heard her, we, the voiceless ones left behind, her soft clear exclamation, "Oh. What a beautiful garden..."

"My daddy done it."

"Did he? Did he, my love?"

No one moved now except me. I crossed to the window over the sink. I looked out. Annie kneeled and Jilaine crouched by the pool, under the blue-flowered tree. A pretty picture. All these blues. Perhaps too sentimental. The lovely young woman and her lovely child.

"Jud, I'm..."

"'S'OK. She was worried about you."

He wasn't going to cross-examine her, or me, on how she had found me. He wasn't going to race out and drag Annie from her grip. He had no reason to be uneasy. Women he knew liked children. And Jilaine was no exception.

"Jay, I've got to make calls. Better call up the office for one thing."

189

What did he think of her, though? Himself.

Glory had gone upstairs. The toilet again – her previous tactical tactful withdrawal from the field.

"What do you think of her, Jud? My friend?"

"She's all right. Good-looking."

"Yes, isn't she."

"Speaks nicely, like you. Jay, I'd better get on. Do what you have to. You won't be here, later, will you? Not now."

"No... Jud, I didn't think she'd ever come here."

"It's all right. She's OK."

"Do you think, Jud, we're more than friends, she and I?"

That did cut through this wooden shambling of his. He turned and looked at me. But I couldn't read his face. He shrugged.

Why had I said it? Panic. Like Glory flinging open the back door and doing more harm than good.

They were laughing. Annie was leading Jilaine through the green ways of the secret garden. They held hands. Lovers.

"She loves children," I said.

"Yeah. Well. Some women do."

"I'm afraid I..."

"I'll see you," he said. "Call me." Her line. His line, and her line.

"I will. Tomorrow night. Once I sort it out with her."

His eyes, all I could see somehow, in the tan of his face, the rest gone – like the face of my father. Like Davey's face, all too soon, down there in the devouring ground. "It was a mega coupla days," he said. "It done me – *did* me – good."

Never before had I heard him correct his own grammar when it slipped. It hadn't mattered. Now it did?

He turned and went out. He went out of the house. In the garden, *they* had vanished around some wend of the path, behind some flower-roped hedge.

I was alone again in the kitchen.

People disappeared. For a moment, the primal fear overcame me. And then, like two butterflies, there they were again, the young mother and her child. They were playing some game, moving their hands, lost in one another.

Glory walked back into the kitchen. "He looked a bit upset."

"Yes."

"He was all right till then." Animosity stirred behind her face. "He don't need no more rubbish. Not right now."

I walked past her, and out into the garden, and stood watching the lovers playing like butterflies. But Glory came out with me, and stood there too, her arms folded.

Ignoring me, and for that matter, Jilaine, she shrilly shrieked, "Annie – come on in! Time to go up Mrs Shaw's."

The child looked back over her shoulder, from her wonderland. Then she looked back at Jilaine.

"*Annie*! I said, *now*! Come on!" Bossy and harsh, Glory had lost her Prettyness.

But Jilaine bent down and kissed the child, the sealing enchantress's embrace to hold her forever in the spell, then turned her lightly back towards the house.

And Annie came running, light as down.

Without a glance at me, she put her hand in Glory's. They went in, and only Jilaine was there across the wildflowers.

"What a beautiful place. Did he really create all this from a dump, as she said?"

"Yes. He's a gardener."

"It's marvellous. He could make a fortune."

"Apparently not."

"Well perhaps..." She stopped.

Perhaps you could assist him, Jilaine? Tip off your rich friends, let them adopt him, help him up the treacherous ladder of employment?

There was no point in saying anything about where I had been or what I'd done. She knew.

Now she said, not looking at me, but away and away, "You've been less than honest, am I right?"

"Yes, Jilaine. Can we not do this here?"

"No. Then I have a car waiting up the street."

I scribbled a note and left it on the kitchen table under the salt.

Thanks for a wonderful time. I'll be in touch as soon as I can. But this may take a day or so to sort out. Please. Jud, take good care.

But I couldn't sign it with Love, could I. I just put my name, my half name, and then left the salt on it. And going out I thought, *It's all finished now.* The feeling in my guts was one I was long familiar with, sour and flat. All empty, not least, of course, my unfilled womb.

II

We didn't talk in the car, although it was a black cab, the driver shut away behind his partition. She could have brought a limousine, of course. Her inevitably flawless manners must have precluded that.

All over the approach to London, the evening crowds were milling about. Almost the place I'd just left, and here I was again. Dusty, stale air and light.

Then south, to the river.

The taxi dropped us at the door of the apartment building. No payment, not even a tip. The driver opened the doors for us, half saluted. Funny, really.

Oh, the clichés of wealth, one on another.

"Hallo, Harry," she said, smiling like heaven at the porter.

"Box of stuff from Fortnum's, Ms Best."

"There shouldn't be anything that won't keep. Can it wait till morning, Harry, please?"

Naturally it could.

As we got out of the lift and crossed to her door, and she unlocked it, I

191

thought, *The last time*. I didn't feel anything, beyond the blank dreariness inside.

I only ever plead for my life, usually. Begging for forgiveness or love – that's superfluous, isn't it?

"Well, Jay. Would you like a drink?"

I might as well go right ahead.

"Yes, please. A large vodka, if possible."

"And since you're not pregnant," she said, "why not?"

"Am I not pregnant?"

"You tell me," she said, looking at me. This limpid girl was now a sword of bluest steel. Her eyes were black. Was that fury? Or revulsion? Both, perhaps.

"No, I'm not pregnant."

"Were you ever?"

"No."

"That's clear, then," she said. She walked through the room, and made the drinks, not bothering with ice, or lemons. I didn't deserve them, did I? Did she?

Only then, while she attended to that in silence, and I in silence stood on the marble, did I see the picture. There it was on the sidelong wall across from me, like one more fiery patch of the dying sun. Too big for her and for the whole vast room. *L'Amber.*

I'd thought she was going to sell it. It seemed finally she hadn't wanted to, which I'd already suspected, hearing her haggling with Angus on the phone.

But it overpowered everything, the picture. Those bleedings of amber and pale tangerine and smolten brown. All seething in that outer ghost rift of something which had vanished... leaving only one long cicatrice to the heart.

If she saw me looking, at this point she made no comment.

"Here's your drink. Large, as requested."

"Thank you. I'll have it, then I'll pack and get out. "

She said nothing. We drank our drinks.

The evening light was going fast now down its drain. Only the painting obdurately held it prisoner on the wall.

Then she sighed and turned from me.

"You don't want to explain anything to me, Jay?"

"What's the use?"

"Perhaps I am owed an explanation."

But I wasn't going to give her that. It was far too dangerous for me.

"I was just being stupid. Like the first time, when you thought I was Philippa. Then I couldn't pull out. I didn't know how to."

"And this man you've been with – Jud."

"Just a man."

"But Jay, look at it from my side for a moment. I have to think, don't I, that you and he are united in some plan to defraud me."

"No, he didn't know anything about you. He's just someone – my boyfriend, if you like."

"I see. "

"He truly wasn't in on any of it. Didn't know. You saw how he reacted. He had nothing to do with it."

"Unless he could make you pregnant."

Ah. She had perceived the drift.

"I tried," I said then. "I wanted to please you. I would have done it, Jilaine. Had a baby for you. Only – I didn't take."

"That's so kind. *Thank* you. Jay." Her sarcasm stung. You didn't anticipate it from her. I should have done. I do from most of you.

"But you and he are involved with each other."

"No."

"No?"

"It's just for fun, Jud and me."

"I see. No commitment."

Should I have said something other? How could I? I was not involved. I had no commitment. Therefore, there was none.

"All along," she said, quietly, "I've doubted you. And sometimes I felt guilty for that. But I was right to doubt you. That makes me feel much better. Your glass is empty."

"Yes. Then I'll go and pack."

"Oh, come on," she said. Her lisp was more noticeable. The drink had gone to her head. "Have another," she said. "Since you're not pregnant." She moved towards me, smiling, soft, black-eyed. "Everything is now on the level. Why don't we get bloody drunk?"

Ah, Jilaine. With such an enemy, who needs a friend?

I'd better explain about me and alcohol. I can't get drunk. I get to a pitch, which isn't all that high, on one or two drinks. Then, after that, drinking more sobers me. God knows why that is, but sometimes it has been useful. You be the judge, my priest-of-the-confessional, if that night it was or not.

As for her, she didn't get drunk. But, for her, she drank a lot.

She smoked too, about ten cigarettes – as a rule I'd seen her smoke two or three times a week. When she offered me the expensive packet, I refused. I too can take smoking or leave it.

At first we went out on the terrace. She sat at the table of dark turquoise, and I stood over by the tall left side wall of her flat, where the pseudo-classical statue rose from the ferns and little trees in pots. (It was a male, the statue, some slim hero or god, standing there in the elegance of his nude slate body.)

We didn't speak, except when she said again, "Your glass is empty."

I began to get bored with the taste of the vodka and lagged behind.

Then she said, "My God, what are you plotting now? Drink up, Jay, knock it back."

So I kept up with her. We got through the bottle, and she went to her kitchen and soon returned with another, icy cold, and this time some foreign tonic water and a sliced lime.

"So why," she said then, "did you do all this?"

"I told you. I was stupid."

"Innocently stupid. Not out for any money."

"Obviously, that was attractive. But I tried to keep my side of the bargain."

"And if you had – what did you say? – taken?"

"I'd have had the baby for you."

"You really have no idea, have you, Jay? Having a baby isn't that simple. Things happen to you."

"I'm sure they do."

"And then after all that, the nine months, the labour, when you saw it – you wouldn't want it, wouldn't give a damn. After all your toil and trouble?"

"Children don't interest me much."

"You couldn't even imagine it, could you?"

"Not really."

"No."

I said, "But you, of course."

"I, of course."

"Annie," I said. The drink had done that much to me.

Then Jilaine looked up, smiling, nearly flirtatious.

She said something extraordinary. "Annie is lovely, but a bit old for me. I wanted to start at the *start*. A newborn infant."

And I knew she lied. As she put the fizzing drink in my hand, I knew she had tried to divert me. Because she and Annie had fallen in love at sight, mother and child.

Oh, I couldn't be so idiotic, could I, as not to grasp that had also been part of Jud's calculations with me? He fancied me. He *liked* me. But also, I was a woman. And he *needed* a permanent woman. Not only for his personal consolation and pleasure, as a female parent for his child.

Jilaine spoke softly through the dusk.

"You might recall, I said once I'd tell you about the painting. *L'Amber*. Let's go in. It's getting dull out here."

We went in. She didn't tell me to close the terrace doors, but I did. It felt colder, and all the lights of London were staring up at me.

Jilaine walked across and stood looking up at the picture. She had switched on a lamp. Its ray fell into the painting, waking the wild colour, showing up the psychic rift that ran across the canvas, and along the edges of it, from which something had been pulled away.

She didn't look at me, even when she turned her back on it.

"L'Amber," she said. "L apostrophe, then amber. That's because, fairly plainly, the picture is in tones of amber. The L stands for the other colour, which was there to begin with, but which I wiped away. I sometimes do that. But never so definitively as in this one. Also, in other paintings, I replace the colour I've removed with some other colour. Here, as you can see, perhaps, I've left what's missing."

194

"Yes."

"Angus said that was what made the picture fascinating. The missing element. It seems to have shaped what's left, and so it has, but then, like a mould and cast, it's gone. Leaving only the object – which couldn't have been formed if the mould first hadn't allowed it to. Do you see?"

"Yes."

"What do you really think of the painting? No need to flatter me now. Just say."

"I think it's beautiful."

"What was the colour that I wiped away, do you suppose?"

I said, "Some colour that begins with the letter L."

"Yes, Jay. That's right. My marking of the significance of what can no longer be seen. It was a strong rich lilac colour. L for lilac."

"Yes."

"I only realised long after, that's also a sort of unconscious pun. Because what do you have left if you take the first L away from lilac?"

I saw the letters in my mind – I, L,A,C. It meant nothing. I shook my head.

"Say lilac," she said, not looking at me, "without the first L."

I heard myself say, "I*lac* – I lack..."

She walked to a table, took up her cigarettes and lit number nine or ten.

"So you see, Jay, that picture is me, and my lack. It's me after I lost my child. It's me because I deserved to lose it. It was a punishment. And I'm damned by it."

I didn't say anything. She glanced at me. Her eyes had given up their darkness to the sky, they were very pale now.

Something made me say, although I didn't want to especially, didn't want to ask questions or play word games, "Why did you deserve to be punished?"

"Oh, don't we all deserve to be?"

"I expect so."

"Don't you *know* we do, Jay? You're just the sort of creature put here, I would think, by God or some other fucking mad entity, to pay us *all* out."

I put down my drink. She sounded calm but her choice of words was sharper. She had drunk a lot and might become hysterical or violent. A month ago I'd never have believed such a thing was possible, of Jilaine.

"Where are you going?" she asked.

"I thought you'd rather I left now."

"No. I want you to stay."

"All right."

"You don't sound keen. Wouldn't you rather stay? Don't you like it here?"

"Yes. But now..."

"Now I know your scam. Now I know you lied. So what? We all lie. No doctor and no pre-natal classes." (Her detective must have checked that out too.) "So, no need for you to go anywhere now. You can stay here all the time with me."

"Why would you want me?"

195

"Partners in crime?"

"What crime?" I thought, Shut up. Don't ask her. It's all a rigmarole. She's pissed. Let her say what she wants. Just say, Yes. Play along.

But she said, "Do you remember that girl in the book?"

"Which girl – Sarah?"

"Not *The Skaters*. I mean in *You and She*. The book you weren't meant to read, about Lesley and Françoise, and which you did read. Didn't you? How do I know? Oh, I sensed it. Of course you read it."

"Yes."

"That's right. I mean, then, the girl at Lesley's house in France, the girl I called Gisla. Her real name was Jeanne. A little fly. She was like that. She *settled* on things and spoiled them. A sweet face, though. Marvellous body, skin, and so young. Fifteen she said, when she arrived. Lesley liked her. Françoise was quite jealous. Until the cancer also joined us and intervened. Then – no time to be jealous. Then, nothing to be jealous of. I can tell you, she, that fly, she stole Françoise's jewellery. Her passport – well, who knows?"

Despite the lamp and the glare of the picture, (looking more red now than amber) the room was monochrome, and a forest of shadows.

As Jilaine moved about, going here and there, her eyes and the snake on her wrist caught the lamp and flashed. And the glass, sloshing with vodka.

Suddenly she turned and flung the glass against the wall, too low for the picture, but with a fearful mad pent-up wrath. The explosion of wet diamonds shattering was – terrifying.

And when she turned back once more to me, I thought I'd see a tiger, but she had softened again instantly.

"I get these moods," she said, reasonably. "It's all right. It's like the tears. It's over now. How lucky you are, not wanting a baby. Why don't you stay, and teach me how to do that?"

She was in front of me, very close. I could smell her perfume and her hair, and the smoke on her breath. She looked up into my face.

"Will you do that?"

"Whatever you want, Jilaine."

"My name. Did I say? It's a phonetic spelling of another name – Ghislaine..." She spelled this for me, as she had L'Amber. "Françoise was responsible for that. She used to get what she wanted. So now, yes: whatever *I* want. And your friend-for-fun. Why don't we invite him for a meal? So I can get to know you both?"

She had put her fingers on my cheek. She stroked my face, down to the jaw, next ran the side of her hand lightly along the vein in my neck. The hair rose on my scalp. But nothing more. It didn't excite me. Not now.

"Why not," I agreed.

"And why don't you kiss me?" she said. "I like women's mouths. I told you, didn't I?"

So I leaned forward and kissed her. It was the briefest least lingering touch of flesh on flesh. I didn't put my hands on her. She tasted as I did, vodka and lime. Even the tobacco was gone, the scented lip-gloss already rubbed away by her glass. I felt nothing and I wanted nothing. Except to be alone.

She slid aside from me. She laughed. Horrible, that laugh. I can't describe it, or why.

"You and I," she said. "We'll get to know each other. Yes?"

I thought, *Has she known all this while I've wanted her? Maybe she's even been seducing me, to see what I would do, if I could hold out.* Those days she lay there on the terrace, after a bath, in the belted robe, or the loose silks that fell back to describe her breasts, the sleeper's pose of trust and abandon before me. But I never made a move. I wouldn't now.

"You're very kind," I said, humbly. Placatory enough?

"I'm *very* kind," she said.

I recalled Philippa Wise. Had all this happened before? No wonder Philippa Wise ran away, *vanished* away.

People did vanish from around Jilaine.

Only after I heard her go out did a delayed frisson of desire sweep over me. I wondered if she had gone to her room, lay naked on her bed, her pale legs parted and her arms upflung, an X of lust.

What did I have to *fear* anyway? She wanted Jud – or she wanted his daughter. I had no obligation to protect them. And in any case, from what? She was drunk. She had lost her self-control and her composure. As mild people always do, to me, if ever they grow truly angry, she had seemed terrible and strange as a beast from a jungle.

I did consider leaving, though, that night. But I was dog-tired. It was late enough a cab would be unreliable or delayed, and the buses and trains murder.

We overemphasise emotion. Then we see this and misjudge the other way. So I went to bed in the guest room.

There was no disturbance. Not even any dreams I remember.

In the morning when I emerged about ten, she had gone out. Despite her debauch, she must have been fresh as the morning. The Fortnum's delivery had even been brought up and put away. She had left a note for me.

Off to Angus's box. See you tonight. Do ring Jud and ask him over some evening soon. Sorry for histrionics, I hope I didn't upset you. Don't worry about anything. We're friends. I baked you a cake.

She had. It was in the pantry cooling on a white plate, in a scent of cinnamon and fruit. A marvellous cake, for a cake-eating friend. I cut a large slice, took it to the terrace, and threw it over for the pigeons. It went down well with them. None of them dropped dead. No little feathery bodies. So I cut them another slice.

What did I want? What do I ever want?

The easy option, naturally.

197

III

The sea always seems familiar to me. I don't know why. I was seldom taken to the seaside as a kid.

It lay below, stretching to the horizon's mystical curve, soupy with dusk, as the stars pinned themselves up.

She had said the pub was well known. It was called *The Fair Fish-Maid*. On a sign of wrought iron, a smiling mermaid girl watched the ships go by, deciding which and whom to drown. The building dated from the fifteenth century, Jilaine said. Under its carapace of timbering, the low sloping rooms gave one on another.

We ate dinner in a long dining room, decorated with Mediaeval tapestry and Tudor portraits which, for all I knew, might be genuine. He had had to duck under the doorway coming in, I hadn't, quite. Jilaine, of course, sailed through, too short, even in her high-heeled shoes, to brush the rafters with her exquisite head.

Outside the open doors, a garden courtyard with soft lamps looked towards the ocean.

"The palms need feeding," he said. Not critical, just depressed.

The drinks in the bar had been good, and the starters in here, flawless wafer sliced avocadoes or grilled mushrooms and tendrils of Parma ham, on plates dark blue as the sky was now going.

No music. Nothing loud – not even the large jolly American gentleman seated under the picture of a knight whom he curiously resembled. We were all models of decorum.

Jud said, "This wine..."

"Do you like it?" she said. "I hope you do."

"Yeah, it's great."

"Please, just enjoy it. You've been having a rough time, I know. I think we need another bottle."

We sat. Well behaved-or-trained children. Just as we had on the way down.

A bright gold shooting star showed across the sea, and the American woman murmured, "Oh, look!"

Didn't they have them in the States? Or were English ones different?

But the man gazed at her lovingly. And she smiled. They were in their sixties, slightly overweight, rich, happy – comfortably in love. How dared they have all that?

Yet tonight we must pretend that we did, too. Though which of us, the lovers? Jud with me or Jud with Jilaine?

She was, like one and all, decorous. She was caring, generous, fastidiously reserved. *Her* smiles too were warm, but *not* amorous. Our hostess. How would it look? Of course. Tall Jud and I, the brother and sister. And she – the beloved. The object of desire. Whose?

When she came in, about 4 p.m., after she had congratulated me on eating the cake I'd fed the birds, Jilaine said, "I called Jud. He is so nice, isn't he? How would you like to go down to the coast for dinner? I thought we would. It would cheer all three of us up."

Fait accompli.

I didn't say anything, and she said, "Jay, why don't you wear that dress we bought you, the one with the beads? You'll look wonderful. And this is rather a special place. An old, old pub in East Sussex. The original structure dates from 1460, I think. The food is glorious. And the wine. I said we'd pick him up en route and take him down in our car. He must be sick of driving – and then he can drink exactly what he wants. They have a two-hundred-year-old brandy."

I said, "I thought I was meant to phone Jud."

"Oh, it just seemed easier. And why wait?"

How did she get his number? The same way she found out where I was and with whom. Or else, she had looked in my wallet?

I got ready and put on the beaded dress, which came from Harrods. She reappeared in a dress of plain, almost colourless muslin, that had only two straps, looking thin as silver wires, to hold it close on her body.

This time, it *was* a chauffeur-driven limousine, enormous, big enough to go to bed in. But there was no partition, to screen us away.

Jilaine said a few things to me, now and then, light as butterfly wings. The evening weather. The shape of the early moon. That it would only take one and a half hours to get there, at this time of evening.

The car smelled faintly of Fabergé, and leather.

We picked Jud up near the motorway. He was standing there on the agreed corner, waiting solemnly. It was – unreal. Apparently, the special pub didn't demand a tuxedo, but he had put on his suit. The one from the funeral. No doubt, he only had this one.

He glanced in at me as we pulled up, then away. At her he smiled, quick and tight. I hadn't expected him to be comfortable. What had I expected? Probably I'd expected him not to be *there*.

The car stopped, and Jilaine and the driver got out together. Jilaine and Jud shook hands. Her greeting smile was guileless and lovely.

"I'll sit up front," she said, with the carefree lilt of a child. "There's more room that way."

And she got in beside the chauffeur.

Off we swam again, and I thought, *God now what must we say?* But at once Jud said to me, "Are you OK?"

"Yes. Are you?"

"I'm fine."

These lying, overheard platitudes.

Brightly I said, "Jilaine didn't tell me about any of this until she'd fixed it. A surprise."

Of course she could hear me. But she didn't comment.

Jud said, dry and flat, "It's great. Nice to see you."

"Yes, me too."

We sat there in the luxury of the whale, and now we looked out of the windows and watched London change to motorway, and then to Kent and Sussex, and fields streamed by with sunset sheep, and overflowing fountains of trees that caught and tried to trap the falling sun. There were oast-houses, stables, six-hundred thousand-pound landed cottages up on hills, and villages with horse troughs and chip-shops, and between, several *Little Chefs*. The usual into-the-country drive. Jilaine said a few more butterfly wing things. Jud said something about traffic. The driver – and I – were silent.

We reached the rural town around 7, left the car dismissively, paused to admire the sea, (the air was salty) walked up cobbled streets between timbered houses only some of-which were older than I was, and into the bar of *The Fair Fish-Maid*.

She hadn't said to him: *But tell me about yourself*. She was more subtle and discreet, yet, with this curious appealing youthful spontaneity. In just the same way, she got on buses and went into random cafés, wandering, taking life as it came – as only the penniless or the rich ever do, surely.

And sure enough, unasked, he did speak a little about himself. He mentioned Davey, briefly. He talked about Annie rather more.

I looked to see if she now grew avid and watched to see if she would ply him with questions.

But no. As I was, with her, she had less interest in Annie's life than in – *Annie*.

After the starters there was pork with a berry sauce – they both had that, she chose it after he had, to demonstrate what a wise decision he had made... "Yes, I'd like that too." I had the local sole, I think. No one had dessert. No, she had an apple. She asked and they brought it, with a silver knife and a little vinaigrette thing of clear honey.

He was so uptight my own muscles had clamped into a vice. Drinking didn't loosen him. Yet he ate all the food, quickly and neatly. A good little boy who must clear his plate, or the adults will remark on it.

Once or twice he blurted something that was inappropriate – like the unfinished thing about the wine – which was some vintage from France that undoubtedly cost more than all the food. Then he would catch himself up, and seem angry.

It wasn't the place or the expense though, not really. Jud was one of the most couth men I'd known. No, she unsettled him. How not? Her beauty was like a wound. Nothing could be so beautiful and *breathe*. But there she was. When she came in, perhaps purely unaware of it, heads had turned, as they normally do only in fiction. And the faultless headwaiter, who came to wait upon her, inhaled her life like oxygen.

Did she say anything? She must have done. But she was a mistress of the art of social chat, when she had to be. Had she done that with me? Again, surely she had.

I don't remember a thing she said, not then.

Wait though. I do. She said, "I must just go to the Ladies." And she looked smiling at me and said, "The moon will be there on the sea, in a moment." In other words, watch the moon. No females going to the lav in pairs, now. And she'd said *Ladies*. Was that for our benefit? In case we didn't know what loo or lavatory meant?

"She's granted us a minute to talk," I said.

"Yeah," he said.

"Jud, I'm sorry. I didn't know she was going to do this."

"OK."

"You could have refused."

"She said you were asking me to come."

"I see. Well I wasn't."

"Thanks."

"I mean, she announced it at 4 o'clock. All arranged."

"It's a great place," he said. "Old."

"Yes."

He drained his glass, reached for the bottle, filled my glass and his again. I think this was bottle number three.

"We can just go," he said. "I can just call *Surefire*. Mates. They'll get someone down to pick us up."

"I can't."

"Right."

I thought, Why can't I? What have I left behind at her flat? Only clutter. I thought, If I go off with you now, I'll have given over myself. I'm in your pocket. I might like it there. But it's crowded. Your little girl is in there, and your life. And you, excellent you, are there. No room, no room.

"It's a difficult situation," I said. "There's no time to explain. She – she probably likes you."

"All right."

"How about you? What do you think of her?"

"I told you before. She's OK."

"Oh, come on."

"What do you want me to say? She looks like a flower. She's – I've never seen anyone like her."

"And she's generous," I said.

"You and I'll talk when we get back to London. Right?"

"I have a feeling... she may," I said, "want to stay over tonight. Take rooms here. They have them, here. She told me sometime."

"No thanks."

"She would pay for them, not us."

201

"No. I get the idea – even if we had a room, she might end up in there, with us. In the bed."

I laughed. He looked at me, laughing, and drained his glass again.

"Great wine. What's it supposed to be – *flinty* taste with apricot afterglow?"

"Would it be so horrible if she did?" I said.

"Not for you, maybe. Look, Jay. That don't bother me. You and her. But you and her and me – no. That's it. No."

"You said she's like a flower."

"I'm not interested in her."

My mouth opened on a hinge.

He said, "She's coming back."

Jilaine sat down. She said, "You see, the moon's just there, above the sea."

We looked at the moon, having badly misbehaved when she wasn't with us, and not watched for it at all.

After dinner we had a walk. She took my arm. Jud moved on my other side. Hemmed in.

I longed to take to my heels.

"We could go back and have a brandy," she said. "They've got a smoking-room, huge armchairs. And later, well, we *could* just stay the night."

"Can't," he said.

She said, "Oh, your little girl. Of course. I'd forgotten."

And I reeled at her technique.

Jud said, "No, she's with the neighbours. I just have to get home."

We were on a promenade. A low railing overlooked an immensely wide nocturnal beach, first of round, tabby pebbles, then of fine grey sand, and moonlight and sea and sky.

"I think I will go back," she said. "I need some coffee." Ah, recollected phrase. "Please do come and have some, when you're ready. No rush."

He turned to watch her as she walked away.

"She's foreign," he said, "what is it, German?"

"French. Partly."

"Doesn't sound French," he said.

"Well," I said, "she's stupendously rich and fabulously beautiful, and disgustingly talented. So who cares about anything else?"

He turned then and looked at me. Then he took hold of my arms. He held me, not hard or roughly but – inexorably.

"Let go, please."

"Yeah. But I just need to tell you something."

"All right. But let go."

He released me.

He said, "I'm in love with you. I want to have you, Jay."

"I thought you had."

"You know what I mean."

I said nothing.

The moon in our eyes, my right eye, his left eye, the moon, the sea and space and the curve of the world which moves. But we forget that nothing stays still.

"Jay, look. I haven't got much, right now. But I'm solvent. And I can make a go of it. Jay, I want to marry you."

"No," I said, before I'd even properly heard his words.

"Marry me."

"No. Thank you. I – No."

"Why? You don't like me? You like me. We're good. Why?"

"It isn't – I don't. I don't love you."

"Are you sure?" he asked, calmly. There was nothing frenetic in his face. It was an exam question I should reconsider, for my own sake. He looked intelligent, nearly omnipotent, and I was the scrabbling ignoramus. "Ask yourself, Jay? Are you sure?"

"Love doesn't mean anything to me."

"That's original."

"You're – I like you. And the sex. And everything. But I don't want to marry you, Jud. And I can't be a convenient mother to your child." I said, "*She* is a much better bet. "

"Oh, for Christ's sake. What are you – her ponce? Or mine?"

I looked away. I looked at the moon. Faintly mottled with blue, it hung tilted from an invisible chain, like one of Jilaine's shoulder straps.

I heard him walk off. Then he came back.

"That's final, then," he said.

"I'm sorry."

"You do change your mind," he said. "You have before."

"Not about marriage."

"OK. Well something else, then. I went too fast."

"No. Nothing else. That's what you want, and I can't give it to you."

"You won't," he said. Nothing in his voice.

Out at sea, a sort of rumbling. Perhaps only the tide on rocks. Or Leviathan, stirring in the depths.

But in his voice, nothing.

"I can't, Jud. I'm sorry."

"Tuesday, Wednesday, Thursday. Next year, sometime, ever?"

"No. You're too good for me, Jud. You deserve something – human."

No lies now. Not placation. Truth.

Why does truth always have to stink?

And why do we always have to tell it, or *face* it, in the end?

"OK," he said. "Is there any point if I call you?"

Yes, I thought. Yes.

"No, Jud."

"OK."

And then he folded me in his arms. Not expecting it, unresisting. I could only let him do it. He held me close, close, close, as if to shelter me and shield me from the madness of the spinning world. He held me like my father, and kissed my hair, and let me go, and walked away.

I thought he'd gone back to *The Fair Fish-Maid*. So I lingered by the rail, to give him time, before I too turned and walked slowly back to her.

On the way up the cobbled street, something. To this hour, I don't know who or what I saw.

The streetlamps were the muted upper-class kind. Ahead of me, by the wall, I noticed a man and woman kissing. Passionate. It was Jud, in his suit, but with the jacket off. And it was Jilaine in her ivory muslin dress, her blonde head tipped right back, giving way, surrendering.

It was sexy. But artistic.

I didn't even think. I assumed, I suppose, she had after all walked down again to the sea, and met him, and they had very quickly moved on to what, presumably, was going to be the only solution to our mutual mess.

And I slowed down, so I shouldn't embarrass him, or walk straight into it. I was planning what to say, some comradely thing with absolutely no tinge of malice or resentment.

But then the couple separated and moved away up the street and round a house there, and I thought they either hadn't seen me, or meant to avoid me. And I thought, *Will she get me a room here now? Or will I have to sit on a bench until the first morning train to London.*

When I came around the top of the street, no one was there. One street went off to my left, the other climbed on to the pub. Nobody was on either of them. But there were alleyways between the houses, dim and overhung by trees. Perhaps they'd wandered away along one of those, like dedicated lovers should.

My best course would be to go straight into the pub. Wait, and when they came back, be neutral and self-effacing.

But when I went back into *The Fair Fish-Maid*, across the lobby I saw into the smoking-room where they served the coffee, and Jilaine was sitting there in one of the big cherry leather chairs, cool, unhurried and composed – alone.

I'd seen two other people, then. A passing resemblance – mistaken in the half-light. Perhaps the keynote and signature to this whole sequence.

Even so, rather cautiously, I went in.

She was sitting there, and then I just knew she hadn't been the woman I'd glimpsed outside. This other room was as far as she'd come.

Her pale smooth arm lay along the arm of the chair, her legs were elegantly resting sidelong, the skirt dipped softly along her slim calves, and the palely-golden shoes catching two blurred shooting-stars of light. Her head rested back; her eyes dreamy, meditative. On the low table before, her, the tray of coffee-pot and cups, and three brandies in cut-glass, and a china dish of chocolates and marzipan.

And there was something – so fucking pathetic about it. The way she was sitting there, on her own, with all the treats prepared and proffered, the things we hadn't wanted, hadn't appreciated, hadn't enjoyed. These pleasures of gracious living that were above or beneath us. Or that we couldn't stomach, with her.

"Jilaine...?"

"Hallo, Jay. I was half asleep. Is Jud with you?"

No, it hadn't been her. Unless, of course, she lied. We all lie, as she had told me. "I think – he had to get back."

"But we would have taken him back."

We.

You, Jilaine. Your car and dosh. You.

"I think," I said, "he's gone anyway."

"Oh well," she said. She smiled at me.

There never was a face I ever saw, so – what word is there? A *Jilaine* face. The Best.

She said. "Shall we stay tonight, or should we go back?"

"Whatever you like, Jilaine."

"Oh, then. We'll go back to the flat, shall we?"

I sat down and took one of the brandies and swallowed it, (just Calvados, I think) down in a gulp.

"What happened?" she said, still in her soft, caressive voice.

I shouldn't tell her. Let her find out for herself.

But I said, "We have finished up."

"I'm sorry."

Yes, Jilaine. I'm sure you are. Nothing at all in the way now. Full steam ahead.

We drank some coffee.

"Would you like another brandy, Jay?"

"No thanks."

"I think I'll have it."

She paid the bill. It must have been spectacular. She tipped the man a fifty-pound note. "I hope you will accept this." Vulgar, stylish.

When we walked down to the place where the limousine had been stored, I kept feeling compelled to speak to her. But I stayed silent. What was there to say?

I wondered, when we were in, and the car started gliding off – it would only take an hour to get back, apparently, due to the low night traffic – if Jud had got a train, or phoned *Surefire* and they had come.

Come and go.

Come and go.

And was I shocked or sad or regretful? Oh, yes. As much as I can be. People like me. If there are any others.

205

It was after midnight.

"Tomorrow, sleep in, darling," she said. "I shall. Noon at least. Sea air. The perfect soporific."

She kissed my cheek, as I leaned towards her, wondering, What now?

I didn't realise – as how could I? – after that night I would never see her again.

IV

I was very tired – laden with sleep. I think I'd fallen asleep in the car, and when I got into the bed, that was it. All the wine, maybe. The coffee. But now, recently, I do wonder. She could have put something into my brandy glass or coffee cup, something mild but effective, herbal even.

When I came to, I had a headache, which even 'too much' alcohol doesn't normally give me. The room was blinding with sun as I'd forgotten the curtains. The (guest) clock said 11.17.

I did the usual stuff. After I'd dressed, I went along to the main kitchen, and made tea. Then I sat with it in the main room, looking out of the open terrace doors at the sky, which began to look choppy and changeable.

Probably I dozed again. When I looked next, it was nearly 2.

Jilaine was still in her room, asleep, it seemed, because even in this ultra well-maintained palace, the faintest ghost-mutter of water pipes would be audible when she ran her morning bath or shower.

I went back to the kitchen and made some toast – ignoring all the other choices, croissants and brioche and muffins and so on. And more tea.

Then it was 3 in the afternoon.

I'd never known her sleep so late. I decided she wasn't in the flat. It was all too quiet. Other times I had sensed her, somewhere. Now there was – a gap. That emptiness the flat always had, when she was gone. No friendly note had been left for me either, no fresh-baked cake.

Somehow, I didn't like this, and I don't know why, specifically, but we all have a basic instinct somewhere, of course.

In any event, why was I hanging around here? I should now do what I'd meant to, discarded, reconsidered, shelved. I was redundant in every way. So, pack up and get out. It would be easy, like this.

While I was putting my oddments together, I had the idea of ringing Compton Road, to see if I could locate anyone about my Room. Probably it had been let again – but then again, people often didn't stay put – or they ran before their next rent came due. I might get it back, the Room, though in what extra-worse state God knew.

When I lifted the receiver, the line was dead. That had happened to me so many times it meant little. Although I should have reacted. Jilaine's cloud-castle was surely exempt from such failures.

Bag packed, I took a can of Perrier from the drinks fridge.

Should I write to her? What was there to say?

The money she'd given me, here and there, I would keep, and the gifts of clothes. Including the Harrods dress for which I should get forty quid, in the Frayle Street Market. Though they'd sell it for eighty.

My exit would be simple, just close the door, lock it again once outside, and put the keys back through – in itself, a farewell, if a sparse one. I didn't look for the keys until I was all set to go. And then, I didn't find the keys.

They had been inside the top drawer of the desk in the guest sitting room. Or else, in my bag if I'd used them then forgotten them. But the keys were in neither of those places.

I'm not methodical – yet, in a funny way, I am. I've never had enough, accumulated enough, to lose things very often. And despite Jilaine and her gifts, I hadn't here.

So it was a matter of ten minutes to turn the whole of the guest suite inside out in case the keys had autonomously taken off and fallen somewhere in the vicinity. But keys don't walk. People are the ones who move keys.

My first thought – is this strange? – was that one of the cleaners, B, probably, she had a suspiciously polite air – had nicked them. Absurd. Why would they, after all this while, suddenly nick keys? And if they had, they'd have done what I'd visualised before, had them copied, and replaced the originals. Wouldn't they?

I must have dropped the keys. They were somewhere in the flat. I was a hundred percent sure I hadn't lost them outside. After all, I had had them when I went to Jud's that last time, and when I returned with Jilaine. Now I thought about it, I had left them in the other bag, the one that didn't go down to the coast. And since I'd already just turned this bag inside out, they must presumably have fallen somewhere in the flat.

Unless some stranger had stolen them. But why steal keys, and not money? And who, anyway...?

I went and picked up the phone again, and again the line was blank. So I tried the one in the annexe – the same. Then I went to the phone that connected down to the porters' desk, and by which Jilaine had so often stood, saying adorably, "Could someone bring the box up now, please, Harry?" Or, "Please tell the car I'll be there in ten minutes."

Now I would call down, and Harry, or Mervyn, or the other man, whose name I'd forgotten, would have to come up and let me out with some master key. I could warn them about the missing keys, too. Rev up security, make things safe for her.

So I tried the phone, and this also was dead.

A light would go on and a little buzzer, when the internal phone activated up here, and that happened too down in the foyer. But if no one used the phone, it didn't do a thing. So, unless they wanted her, or someone came for her, no one would try to signal up and see the fault.

I went through the flat, corridors, the annexes, (as the sky clouded) and tried her bedroom door.

It gave at once, almost naively.

There it was, Jilaine's serene room, with its pale water-green carpet, its books and mirrors, and the dressing-room door with the picture of the cat by Françoise in the white wood frame. The dressing-room was neat and tidy. As ever the bathroom was pristine. Everything looked newly cleaned, polished, hoovered. The bed was made and level as if never even slept in.

The last sun winked through, shone like brass and faded. The shadow of the storm closed down.

I knew.

Of course I knew.

I thought, *She will be back sometime today. Or tonight.*

And I thought, *Perhaps not, not today or tonight.*

I thought, *If she doesn't come back until tomorrow, there may be a delivery to come up. And besides, A and B will come, won't they, to clean. Only when?*

But I knew.

No one was coming. No one was going out.

The flat was stocked, as always, as if for a siege. Food, canned, dried, refrigerated, frozen, and drink both hydrating and alcoholic. Water in bottles and in the taps. Lavatory paper, tissues, towels – even an array of everyday pharmaceuticals, Elastoplast and TCP, codeine, valerian sleeping pills, sunburn cream. Vitamins.

Rain crackled and crashed at the windows, and lightning screeched over London. From up here, it looked lethal, that storm. The thunderclaps shook the marble floors. So, not even any use banging on the outer door, or opening the windows to shriek. Who would hear anyway? The whole charm of such apartments is their reclusive sound-proof privacy. Below either terrace I had never seen a soul. Throw something down? Some suitable note requesting rescue – I even did that, two days later. It lay there, large red-lettered, in its protecting plastic bottle, under the rain. And lay there. Unmolested.

A and B also did not arrive, although I'd never known their erratic schedule keep them away for more than six days – and the day of the seaside jaunt had been day six, I presently arithmetically worked out.

Did I try to pick the lock of the main door? Yes. To no avail. But that isn't my forté, really, picking locks. I also tried to smash the door with various implements, but it was stronger far than I. Escape for me has usually been a matter of talking my way out, not *fighting* my way.

I settled down. I ate some of the food, used the shower and lavatories. Read books, or bits of them.

I kept thinking I didn't believe this, because someone was bound to come, or she would come back. There was too that weird restriction which has to do with not making too much of a fuss. In my case this is never the so-called English reticence. More another sort of horror. Even when I tried yelling from the terrace down at the deserted drive, and even when I chucked the bottle there with its message – *Keys lost. Locked in Flat 4. All phones out. Please ask porter to call up.* Even then my fear, (and fear it was) was tempered by the other unease of the rescuers and their threatening mockery. (For example, even the phrasing of the message in the bottle – courteous, not hysterical, nearly fawning.)

But then again, I knew I wasn't a fool to be afraid. I've been in lots of seemingly normal situations where utter peril was only three or four inches away, round a corner, up a path, under a tree – and sometimes with a scalpel blade in its hand. So I'd been right to be scared. And now I was, the same. Oh. I knew. I knew.

I haven't said yet, the three TV's didn't work either. Nor the couple of radios. A sort of classic suspense scenario. The music centre functioned, but seemed – disturbed. The cooker was all right, but I became cautious of it. There was lots of cold food, and enough water and juice.

A dramatic background, the rain went on and on. The dark skies, mantled in cloud. The noise, that helped to hide away any cries of mine which, even in the lulls, probably weren't heard. Which definitely were ignored.

Heaven too was on the side of my adversary. And obviously I understood by then, by day three, certainly, my adversary was Jilaine.

Yet I wasn't sure why. That was the only puzzle – I had *meant* to leave, and she'd stopped me. I couldn't do a thing to her – could I? So why this? Take my keys, disconnect the phones or cut the wires – leave me here... a punishment, then? She credited punishments, didn't she? And, let's face it, she was insane. Just that, then, maybe. Her dementia.

Would she come back one night, one day, and stick a knife between my ribs, or throw the contents of a bottle of bleach in my face?

She'd had lots of opportunity before.

I slept however, when I did, with the chest pushed hard against the guest room door. But not, I admit, until after the fourth day.

You look at this perhaps and think I was myself crazy not to find some way out. You, perhaps, would have thought of a means. But then. I haven't finished yet, telling you what I did.

On day five, I became methodical. I went first to the small guest terrace, stood on a chair and peered right over. Directly below was a thicket of evergreen and pine. Lodged in the roots, two or three ancient Coke cans. As I'd thought, no one came there at all.

Next, I went to the main terrace, to the balustrade she had always been warning me against approaching. Peering over here, I saw nothing had happened. My message in an Evian bottle still lay there.

The TV's didn't work anyway. I lugged the smaller one through from the library, dragged it bumping and wrenching through the rain, and got it up on to the balustrade. Just before I pushed it off, I thought, *She'll demand I pay for this.* But then, she had to come back to do that.

Then I shoved it over.

209

It landed with a nerve-splintering bang and crash. Glass and various bits flew up and around and a magpie I couldn't see began to scold in the fir trees.

I waited quite a while. Until I was drenched, and the magpie had shut up. But no one *came*.

Never mind, someone *would* come. They would. Someone would have heard the crash. Reported it.

No one.

I went in.

Late that day, day five, the weather cleared.

A blue and rosy sunset flooded the sky, but no one had gone to investigate the broken TV on the drive below. It glittered, blue shards and rose.

That evening I went through her things. All, that is, she had left behind. And she had left virtually everything. My impulse was to think she must be coming back, because otherwise why leave so much? But then reason reminded me she had money. Anything was replaceable. The fabulous clothes, the scent and cosmetics, the books and music – her painting materials – anything. As for the appurtenances of the flat, they could be reconstructed or approximated elsewhere. The rich, like the poor, can travel very light. The Eye of the Needle threatens only those in between.

In her study, I found an ordinary unlocked box-file, with some personal documents – copies, I think. (There was no safe, or none I located. I didn't try hard, for how could I open it?) This was how I came to see Jilaine's Birth Certificate, saw her name clearly and carefully spelled out by the registrar. And her mother's name, and her father's – Neil Hanson Ford Best – a British name, so far as I knew. And a British occupation – at that era as at others – unemployed.

Failing the safe, there was no jewellery. No money beyond a porphyry dish of loose coins and change – if quite a lot, amounting to over twenty pounds. And no passport.

And no diary. I did find an art book among many I pulled out in my searches on to the floor. An entry had been marked. *Françoise Marie Corrizonde: Minor painter who enjoyed a brief prominence in the late 1960s and early 1970s, mostly due to the patronage and encouragement of her lover, the artist Lesley Spender. After the death of her husband, Corrizonde moved to France, where she lived with Spender at Signon, until Spender's death from cancer. Corrizonde is usually supposed to have drowned herself soon after, although her body was never found, and some air of mystery still surrounds events. Corrizonde's work shows the influence of many of the French schools, but most notably of Lesley Spender herself. It is pleasant, if derivative, all on a small scale – something which Spender also made her trademark, if with far less restrictive results.'*

I sat on the floor of the study under the window, where I had sat that other day to read, against Jilaine's wishes, *You and She*. There had been jewellery missing in France, I recalled, and a passport, hadn't there?

Finally, about 7 p.m., I got up and walked into her bathroom. I put the plugs in the long white bath and in both the hand-basins and ran all the taps.

Back in the main room, losing the light, the picture of her loss, *L'Amber*, glowed like hell on the wall. Why had I ever thought it was beautiful?

At 7.35, I could hear the water trickling out through the banked up towels beyond the door, into her bedroom, and along the passage.

The pipes though began to make a row. Then they roared and there was a steady vibration. This made me nervous. So it was only cowardice that sent me sloshing back at 7.45.

Everything was awash, the corridor was up a step, and had less, and that soaking away. But the bedroom carpet was a lake. The bathroom door had stuck but I forced it partly open. More water rushed out, and I saw the bathroom gradually emerge, floating in its own limpid reflections. I squeezed my way in and turned the taps off. Leaving them running might also be dangerous – I was still stuck in the flat. I couldn't risk flooding all of it. (For a similar reason I had not attempted the potential signal of fire.)

How long would it take the water to run through and down? In any other place, not long. In the sort of places *I* inhabit – about fifteen minutes.

But the floors – the floors of the flat were marble, and everything tightly sealed and properly maintained. Besides, how did I even know there was anyone living in the spaces below, to see the slow thick drip of water through their ornate plaster ceilings?

I was so sure my plan must work, even with the water curtailed, I didn't go to bed.

I sat in the main room, waiting either for pounding on the door or use of the master-key that spelled my freedom. Then, about 3 a.m. I fell asleep. And when I woke, it was morning, but no one had come.

I went to inspect my failed disaster.

Everything was still inches deep in water. An inky stain had spread along the corridor to the other annexe, and into another of the guest bedrooms.

Give it time, the soaking, dripping water. Just give it time.

I gave it time, having by now nothing else to give.

Perhaps no one would ever come here. Winter *would* come and the central heating – the source of which I hadn't come across or been shown, would prove inaccessible. The food would at last run out. I'd starve, or die of hypothermia, up here in the frigid marble tower.

What utter madness. It wasn't possible.

But what else, now, was?

Perhaps a visitor might come, or a supplicant. How did she pay for all this – would they want rent or bills seen to? No, obviously not. Some bank account always automatically full, automatically debited. And as for callers – she would have told them all she wasn't here right now.

Cut and dried.

On day seven, about 11 in the morning, I heard a lawnmower.

When I went out on the main terrace, it was a fine day, and there was a man down there, forty-five feet down, mowing the little side lawn by the unfrequented drive.

The mower made a lot of noise, but I shouted. I saw he wore mufflers over his ears to protect them from the volume of the mower, damn him.

Every time he turned the machine towards the building, I jumped and waved. But he took no notice.

To my amazement, I then registered the broken TV had now been cleared from the drive. The Evian bottle too, presumably *unread*, since it wasn't there.

All at once, I saw the mower was heading away again through the trees.

Then I ran, picked up one of her heavy painted iron chairs, and somehow got it up over the balustrade.

When it fell, the clang and shock seemed to shake the roots of the walls. And the man – glanced back. He glanced back, then up, right at me waving and yelling across the balustrade. And then he turned again, and went on, and the trees hid him.

He would return in minutes. Or he would tell the porters' station. Or he would call the police.

But he did none of those things.

He did nothing.

I suppose even I fondly believed that rational behaviour was the norm, and deviations – usually subject to reprimand – *noticed*. But not here, apparently. Of course, here was the country of palaces in clouds. We could do as we wished. Cause floods. Cast TV's and iron furniture from our terraces. That was our privilege. And no one would bat an eyelash or speak a discouraging word.

I don't really know how to describe what happened to me. Many prisoners must experience it. And even in that luxurious gaol, I was a prisoner, and I did.

I have no spine, of course. I am quite negative, preying on others, or preyed on. Whoever gets in first.

So perhaps I simply gave up.

Really, it seems unnecessary to tell you anything about it. And in a way, I can't. *I* – as they *say* – let myself go. I read a lot – and now can't recall any of what I read. I even sometimes played her music – frighteningly loudly, hoping for complaints. Then desisted. Besides, the music centre burnt itself out, and failed, like the other gadgets (and the flood).

I could list everything. How my digestion began to be affected, and my bones began to ache. How I couldn't sleep, but then slept for fourteen hours at a stretch.

And I talked to myself. But not much. Even with me, I was fairly guarded.

That's enough. You have the picture, I'm sure.

I didn't wantonly vandalise anything. I didn't even eat much from the vast stores – not to make them last – I just had no interest. That was it, really. I ceased being at all interested.

So that when I finally heard the lift, then the front door being opened, the two locks, one after another, I barely raised my head.

"Well, well, my lass. You *are* in a sorry way." He sounded pleased.

Always placate. Such sensible lessons stick, and I smiled at him, if rather vaguely.

"Can you stand up? That's a good girl."

The other one 'helped'. I was at the table in the main kitchen, and he was making tea for us, him and me. The other went to a fridge and came back with a bottle of her vodka and took a swig.

And then *he* said. "Careful, Boggie. Just a glass. You don't drink *that* stuff like lemonade. You don't even drink it like vodka."

It was the slight curl in his voice, more than the red face and hands or the navy bow tie, that made me begin to remember.

"Angus," I said, "McIndoe. How's Ginny? And the baby?"

"Oh, they're bonny," he merrily replied.

Then there was the tea.

"She's made a fucking mess everywhere," said the other one, youngish, tall and stocky, with long greasy hair and an expensive jacket. "Fucking mucky bitch." (This was me.)

"Shush, Boggie. That's neither here nor there. Go and sit in the other room. I'll call you if I need you."

One of the gallery painting-hangers, I thought, Boggie. One of Angus's men.

I sat there.

"Drink your tea," he said.

So I drank the tea, which oddly, since I hadn't had a cup now for about two weeks, went straight to my head.

"Feeling better?"

"No."

"Tough titty," said Angus, rather coy. He smoothed his rust red hair with one pork hand and was suddenly Chelsea again. "You know, dear girl, you *do* have a look of Philippa. I mean, like this, you do. All unwashed and uncombed. But then, it's probably just the situation."

I stared at him. Still uninterested.

He seemed to be enjoying it all. Not sadistic or gloating, just happy.

"Philippa, you see, was shut up here in very much the same way by Jilaine, in one of Jilaine's – moods. Philippa was causing such a lot of bother. Jilaine just locked her in and left her here. A whole week. It's been longer for you, hasn't it? I thought so. I'm so glad you didn't try Philippa's trick. That day, oh my dear lord. Jilaine rushing in to me all frantic, and driving back, and finding Philippa, the daft besom, there, down on the drive. What she'd done, you see," he confided, leaning over the table, having thrust the Tiffany lamp up on its chain, "was the thing they do in films. Knotted sheets together and tied them on the railing, and then started to climb down. They broke. Luckily for Philippa only when she was nearly there. Knocked her out however and smashed her ankle. And that's how we found her, Jilaine and I. Lying on the secluded drive. She'd been there an hour or so."

"Did you leave her there?"

"My good God, girl. No. We took her to a hospital, and she was duly repaired. Then she got on her crutches and hopped off. Never to be seen again. Ever noticed Jilaine studying your legs? Or me, for that matter? No? Quite nice legs, but not for that. We were looking for the scar where they put Philippa's plate in. Plastic surgery is so costly. After Jilaine saw you, she sent you round to me, so we could all be sure you *weren't* Philippa, or someone of Philippa's ilk, coming back to us, like the smell of a dead rat. But you're not Philippa, and you're nothing to do with Philippa. No. You're just yourself."

I drank the rest of my tea, and he refilled my cup attentively, from the glazed white pot.

"Where is Jilaine?" I said. God knew why. I didn't.

"Far, far away," he said. "She had things to do. All done now. So now you are free to go on your way. But here you are. She hopes you'll accept this, for your trouble."

He put something in front of me.

It was a greyish-green strip of paper, with some figures and a scrawl on it.

"It's quite generous," he said. "I told her you'd be content with half that amount. But she has her sense of honour, Jilaine."

I still didn't know what it was.

But I said. "And what are *you* getting?"

"What I always get now. A painting. Oh, it used to be money. But now I don't need hand-outs like that, so it is *L'Amber*. That's what I want and what I shall have. *L'Amber*" – he was still pronouncing it wrongly – Lomm Bay. "Perhaps one of the finest canvases modern minor genius will produce, before the Millennium."

"It's next door," I said.

"I know it is. I have seen."

"I might have thrown something at it," I remarked idly.

Then I saw his face. That is, the true face behind the other one. It was an awful and fearsome face, as often our inner faces are. "So glad you didn't, lassie. For your sake."

They smartened me up slightly, not much, gave me my ready-packed bag, and took me down to a car outside the main entrance.

I couldn't believe the outer air, the whirling size of the spinning world, and I nearly threw up. But Angus clapped his red, sweet-smelling hand over my mouth. "Don't, dear. Just don't." And I didn't. "We'll let you out at Charing Cross with your fare. OK?"

The porter, the one whose name I never recollected, didn't bat an eyelash or speak a discouraging word, busy with some paperwork at his desk.

And the grey-green cheque? It didn't have her signature, but that of some lawyer or other agent. And it was for ten thousand pounds.

PART SIX

I

Back at number 12, Compton Road...

"It's died," said Olivine. "I put it out for the bin men, but they din took it."

Her hair was no longer green but returned to its own weary darkness. She meant my one success, the plant.

"You don't look great," she said. "Bin ill, have you?"

Why did I say it? Had to, somehow.

"I lost a baby."

She took me into her flat then. I'd never thought she would be kind, didn't want her to be, and would have said nothing if I'd realised. Her flat – half a room, the rest blocked off with old curtains and boxes: her son's kip. I sat on a sofa with the springs out and cat torn as if by vengeful ghouls.

She brought me a lager. It was 10 in the morning, and I don't like beer. I drank it.

Olivine told me, my old room was occupied. "Pair of black guys. They're brilliant. See that window? Fixed it for me. Terry never bothered." Who was Terry? Not her son. Her new Man? Who cared?

Olivine said, "And the one before them, he run off with your fridge. Got it out at 3 in the morning, woke everyone up. I said, That's a fixture, that is, and he said, Up yours."

She said she had kept my other stuff faithfully, there look, in that cardboard box. Sorry yes, she thought one of the cats might have sprayed on it. And sorry, she didn't know where the case had gone I'd put the things in to start with. Terry, probably. Terry had also broken my coffeemaker. Mixed paint in it, or something. "But you was gone so long. Never thought you'd be back. That's good – have a bit of a laugh. Feeling a bit better?"

I found another room quite quickly. It was nicer than the Room, much bigger, and without any damp. Recently redecorated, even, in the most garish bloody awful way, with white and pink walls, a kind of lumpy paper, and large coloured borders everywhere – *dardoes*, the landlady called them. She lived-in downstairs, and was prepared to see to any repairs, providing tenants in turn were careful not to cause wilful damage.

She did give me an odd look, but I'd had a bath by then at Compton Road and washed my hair, cut my nails and put on some other clothes from my bag. Besides, I'd paid two months up front. How could she refuse?

"What kind of work do you do?" she asked.

"Oh, I've been working in Scotland," I said. "I have to find something."

"Well I do insist on rent being regular." I wondered, if it wasn't, what she would use as a laxative. But that was miles ahead, because I had paid Jilaine's cheque into the bank. I never thought it might bounce – and it didn't. And though I knew Winter was still coming, that the leaves of twenty- and fifty-pound notes would finally all have fallen, leaving me alone once more in the cold bare tree, that was still to be.

I made some coffee in the new coffeemaker from Argos and made the quite comfortable bed with sheets straight from their cellophane. Then I got in and pulled the covers up over me. I lay there in a coffin of warmth. I was rigid as a stone. I wouldn't move, even to turn over. I was aware that the hardest thing was going to be ever getting up out of this bed again.

After I'd tried the house all day, I rang the firm instead.

"*Surefire* Cabs. Who? No, luv. No, he don't work here no more. Don't know where he is now. Hey, Trace, you know where Jud went? You know, that young guy with the dad and the kid... No, she don't know either. Sorry."

The plant had been lying on its side in its plastic pot among the dustbins. Disdained by the dustmen, even the late summer rain hadn't got to it much. Why did I? I stuffed it in a plastic bag and brought it with me, no doubt causing my new landlady extra tremors... "Well, she had *no* bags to speak of, just something bulging in this black bin-liner."

When I got moving again, I set the plant up in its newly washed pot full of fresh earth from the local garden centre. The roots hadn't looked too bad and I'd broken off all the brown and grey ruin of its upper parts. That done, I saw the pale green sap still there in the lower stems. So there was still life in it. Jud had taught me that, about plants. (I can't remember when. I never really listened to what he said most of the time.) Then I fed the plant and watered it and placed it in the window in a large external pot of black ceramic, not to clash with all the salmons, reds and yellows of the walls and curtains.

It was Saturday when I went over. I took the bus, then walked. That wasn't my concession to the coming, far-off winter of poverty, only old habit. Those interim weeks of cars might never have been.

It was still hot. That dulled tired heat of a late too-long summer. The playing field was bleached out and gouged by the kicks of football players.

No one answered my knocks. I hadn't thought they would. *Known* they wouldn't. So then I went next door.

"Mrs Pretty? She's number 15, just up the curve."

Glory Pretty had her hair in the usual tail, wore black jeans and a white T-shirt like a man's vest. Her face flashed into vivacity when she saw me, but not necessarily welcome. "Well – *you're* a stranger."

"I just wondered if you knew anything about Jud."

"He's gone," she said. She grimaced at me. It was evidently all my fault. True enough.

I said, "I had some family trouble."

"Oh?"

"I've been away."

"Yeah. You upset him, you did," she said. She stood there, barring the way into her home. And just then a car drew up outside Jud's house, and as I stared, a man and a woman and two children and a lot of shopping got out.

"That's the Kennedys," said Glory Pretty loftily. "They took that house like a shot. Went mad on the garden and the fish. Even wanted the hamsters for the kids. Mind you, I never seen a house move so quick. Nothing with any agent. No chain nor nothing. That was her. She could get things done, he said."

"Jud said?"

"Come in," Glory decided, "you don't look good."

Her house seemed narrow and dark, though essentially it had the same structure that his had done. Then her windows seared from the dark, too bright.

"I'll make some tea."

She made the tea, and I thought of Angus McIndoe and the tea and the white pot. And then Glory Pretty said, "Are you all right?"

"Yes, I'm fine."

"I thought you was going to be sick."

"No. I'm just tired."

"Only if you are – I can tell that look, from the kids.'

She had children?

There was no evidence.

Evidence...

"You see," she said, sitting opposite, across the weak, un-Angus tea in cheery mugs, "maybe it weren't your fault, I mean, she cut you out good and proper."

"Jilaine, do you mean?"

"Jilaine," she repeated with such utter scorn she did me, for a moment, immense empowering good. "*Chilblain's* what I used to call her, to myself, like."

She had arrived, Glory said, just walked down as if out of nowhere, in this *dress*, and she just knocked on his door, and then she went in.

"Later on," said Glory, "I saw them." (She must have gone over to get a good second nose.) "She was ever so nice to me. Too nice. And somehow, I wasn't in there long."

After this, Jilaine came and went. And now and then a big car, always a different make, and Jilaine and Jud would go out. And then they would go out with Annie too. "I thought he'd park her with Mrs Shaw, or me, like he done when he took up with you. But no. Once it started, Annie always went with him and her, then. And once I seen Annie come back and she had this toy – well, I never seen nothing like it. It was a bloody great lion cub – I mean, I thought it was real for a minute – and Annie, she runs up to me, all excited, to

217

show me – but she, *Chilblain*, she comes over all smiling and says, "Show Mrs Pretty later, darling. It's *tea-time* now!"

It hadn't taken long. Just the short endless weeks of my incarceration.

"First I hear of it, Sally Walder tells me. They're off abroad. That place in France you hear all the talk about – *Provawns*. Somewhere like that. He never said goodbye to me, not properly. And Sally, she was that upset. All she'd been to his dad, to Davey, and just this card. I don't know what he wrote and told his brother – or that cow Carol. They was just off and gone. And that's *another* thing she done – like the house. Fixed Annie up with a passport quick as you like. Annie never had one, though Jud did. But *she* said to him, Annie could use someone or other's, some other child's. But that ain't legal, far as I know. But there you go. I s'pose they're *there* now."

"Provence."

"Somewhere like that. He said she said she grew up in France and it was lovely there for a kid. Be nice for Annie. But he was daft on her, that Chilaine. You could see it. He kept looking round for her when she weren't in the room. Well. I thought it was you he fancied. But you dumped him, didn't you?"

I stood up. "I have to go. Thank you."

"I never liked her," said Glory staunchly. She added, "Nor you. He deserves better than the pair of you."

"Yes," I said. "Yes, he does." But maybe I didn't say it aloud.

I must have gone back to the new room after that. Must have done.

The plant recovered slowly. As winter ripped Europe apart, the plant put on slow green. By spring it was doing well, and by the end of the following summer, it was almost itself again. Even when I had to move down a grade or two, it travelled like a more amenable wine. And here it still stands now, nearly four feet tall, in this most current, unwholesome room, the only splendour. My one success. A stunning proof that some things do return from death.

II

Her fourth book, (which I discovered those two years after I saw her last), begins not with her loss of the child she was carrying, but with the dream. The dream she had subsequently described to me that evening in her apartment. How Françoise, old and grey, came before her and told Jilaine she'd find 'her', the one she wanted.

Quite a brave start, to a novel. A reader might discard it, for this airy-fairy beginning.

But, with her pared, concise prose, the story moves fast. Soon things happen. And the dream comes true.

You and I. The title refers, plainly, to Jilaine and her found daughter, Annie. In the book she calls her Anna. Again, this inadequate, transparent 'changing' of names. The book is even dedicated to Anne. It is her testament to her child, lost and refound and never to be lost again.

And a lying testament it is.

But I would say that, wouldn't I?

Also the book rings with her couthly restrained but total adoration of and devotion to the child. The joy she has in the child is moving. Heart-breaking. All the more so for the writer's self control.

But you think, what will happen, when this child is fifteen or sixteen, or twenty-five? Jilaine will be about in her forties then, a little less or more. What happens when the time comes to let her go?

Or perhaps only I thought that. Think it – for in fact that time must by now be fast approaching. This controlled and self-aware woman will handle everything superlatively, though, won't she? And without a wasted word.

At first, then, when I got the novel back into my room, I wouldn't go near it. But then obviously I did.

She had *not* changed his name at all. She called him Jud. Initially I saw this as her accolade also to him, and as I sensed so strongly she would give the book to the child at some suitable age ("Not now, darling. I'd rather you didn't read it just now. When you're eighteen, say"). I imagined the picture of Jud would be all golden. Jud was, after all, Annie's actual biological father.

One thing did confuse me – how she described him that first time in the book. *A tallish man, dark-eyed, with unusually thick hair.*

Yes, his hair and eyes. But tall-ish? He was tall, even by today's standards, six foot three. And Jilaine – well she was only about five six, even in her highest heels. To her, he *must* have seemed tall. So why *tallish*? She saw him as less than he was? Or more, and so had to diminish him?

Looking back, he seemed to want to resist her, didn't he? (Did he?) Yet according to *You and I*, he didn't put up any fight. But then again. I wasn't there – she had made sure of that. I only have her account of how he gave in to her. Her picture is of a charming, attractive and weak man, handsome and honourable, and easily led, even into his own good. What is *my* picture of him? Better? Worse...?

The strangest and most jolting thing I felt, however, when once I began to read, selfish and self-absorbed as I am, is that, although she tells the entire story of their meeting and their coming together and their going away and their life thereafter, starting with the mystic directing dream which took her to the high street and the café where then I worked – *she never mentions me.* No. I am not there, or anywhere in her book. I have ceased to exist.

So that, after her dream when she goes wandering, she has her coffee in the café, (and she is fairly merciless about the café, but the only waitress she speaks of is seemingly ninety, and bears no resemblance to anyone there), Jilaine walks out, and calls a cab. And who comes in the cab, but Jud. And *so* she meets him. And from there her story with him progresses – as perhaps, afterwards, after she *had* met him because of me, it did.

Jilaine makes no secret of her pursuit of Jud. First as a lover. But then – when she has met his child – which she describes in her usual half-removed, stylish yet *truthful* way – as the father of the daughter she now desperately wants.

And the story does then become, still tersely told and crafted as it is, the love story of herself and the child. With Jud a beautiful bonus, a pleasure and a cherished minor addition. This reads, stripped and put in other prose, like the diary of some nineteenth century male, whose dear little wife, of whom he is quite fond, has 'given' him a healthy son.

The last third of the book is set in France, the poppy-lit France of novel one, *You and She*. The house, though, is different. In the book she explains that an earlier house, once her mother's, has been sold. The new house does not look over at the sea, but up through the olive trees at the mountains, where a forest dark as bears clusters round the white slashes of a plummeting road.

The last words of Jilaine's book detail, without too *much* detail, her utter delight, and the delight of Anna, her child. The one she was sent to find, and found.

A writer of a sort, I respect books. I threw *You and I* into a skip. Probably it's out of print by now. Because, having read it, many more years have gone by before I tried to write this.

Nevertheless, perhaps even before I did read *You and I*, some part of my mind had begun to work on Jilaine. The more I'd thrust her from my mental stage, the more something dissected her in the back rooms. What are these books of hers anyway? Aren't they all *confessions*, like this one of mine?

What I'll say now can be put down to pure venom. Or insanity. Or, I might have stumbled on a fact.

If I have, no one will believe me. Or if they do, so what.

So what?

It's the thing with names, partly. Her names in her books, always transparent, like her clutterless prose. Don who is Dan, Françoise who is Frances, Lindsey who is Lesley.

But when she wrote about herself that first time, in the first novel she ever produced, Jilaine called herself Jane. Very well, it's rather similar. But then she had told me the real name of Lesley's other model, the 'parasite' who came to live with them at the house in France. She had been called Gisla, in the book. But her real name was Jeanne.

In English parlance, Jeanne could be Jean or Joan or Jane. While Jilaine, she had told me, comes from Ghislaine, which in turn, I've found, has its derivation in the Frankish Giselle.

Do you see what I'm approaching? I bet you do.

After all, we've seen she lies. She removes things. People. Changes things about.

And think of this. It would ironically explain why Jilaine, for all her stupendous wealth, dared only adopt legally – and perhaps not even that – not wanting her personal history investigated.

It was, too, Glory's mention of the passport, I think, that finally made the creatures in my mind's back rooms begin to go to work.

Jilaine, anxious to be off with Jud and Annie, had been able to arrange for Annie to travel on the passport of another child. I don't begin to know how, or why she would risk this and not other things, but money can do an awful lot. And Angus was always there in the wings, Angus who had been such a help to her and gained so much cash from her he now only wanted her paintings in exchange. And Angus too who knew her so well, he even prudently hid his baby from her potentially crazy maternal lusts.

I picture her, that curvaceous young girl, with her lovely skin and hair, her 'sweet' face – about fifteen, or even less. No wonder Lesley noticed her, liked her. And Jilaine and Françoise – were they jealous, or did they like her a lot too?

In the end, when Lesley became terminally ill, the house full of screaming and the black wings of cancerous death – the parasite, as the book calls Gisla, fled. Taking with her, I deduce, some jewellery, to sell and so keep herself from starving. She was a 'waif and stray' – she was a chancer and a taker.

And then that dream. That other dream, of Lesley cured, and saying her right hand had been cut off. Which meant she would die.

It was *Gisla* who had that dream, by which I mean Jeanne. And Gisla-Jeanne slunk back to the house then and found all as the dream had foretold. Lesley dead. Françoise lamenting. And Françoise's daughter. So then Gisla – Jeanne – lingered there. And the other two, driven witless or uncaring by horror, allowed it. And then – then – what happened then?

Perhaps it was only what she said. She saw Françoise down on the beach. Perhaps she even saw Françoise walk into the sea and thought she meant to swim. ("I used to tremble as a child, just seeing her," Jilaine had said to me, of Françoise.)

Of course, it wasn't just Françoise she saw on the beach. It was Françoise and her daughter: the girl called Jilaine. She saw *them* walk into the sea – maybe hand in hand. It was *they* who didn't come back.

"My mother," she would add, Jilaine, when she spoke of Françoise. Remembering she'd better. Because all those scenes of Françoise could have been seen too by the young Jeanne (Gisla).

My mother – but Françoise wasn't her mother, because Jilaine, *my* Jilaine, wasn't Françoise's daughter. She hadn't been Jilaine. She had been *Jeanne*.

Adopted by that unusual household, she had learned so much from them. How to talk, even how to speak English. How to behave, perhaps more importantly how to misbehave. How to look, how to *live* and be rich. So when they were all dead – she couldn't give it up if she didn't have to. Could she?

Maybe she resembled the original Jilaine closely. Or maybe only just enough. It was around ten years, after all, since the true Jilaine had been in

England. And Jilaine, then, had been a child. And then again there was always helpful Angus, who even at that time must have been somewhere there, ready to hand. It has a feel of Angus, somehow, Françoise's missing passport. The little touch that said maybe she hadn't died at all. As for Jeanne, she travelled to England on Jilaine's passport. What else? She had by then become Jilaine.

Lesley and Françoise and the first Jilaine – all gone, all swept away. Vanished.

People do vanish from her life. She discards them. Like her exquisite and unvalued possessions, houses, apartments. Without a backward glance.

L'Amber. What actually forms and *makes* the picture, but which the artist then fastidiously rubs away. It wasn't just her unborn child. We were *all* that L apostrophe. Françoise and Lesley, the first girl called Jilaine. Philippa –whether alive or dead. Even Jilaine's own original persona – Jeanne – erased. And I, of course. Rubbed out. Gone. And Jud.

Why did I wait so long to write my own version of events? She wrote and published her account so very fast.

I can't answer. I had to wait. That's all.

Just before the triumphant ending of her fourth book, *You and I*, she tells, on half a page, how he left her. She is regretful and sympathetic. Scrupulously fair. And sorrowful. But since he leaves in her care Annie, (her child,) her pain is less, and she frankly admits to that. Naked and veritable Jilaine.

I remember her dream she told me about. Françoise appearing to her and telling and guiding her to find her lost child, who turned out to be Annie. If Françoise was ever Jilaine's enemy, or even her unfriend – isn't this odd? Or is it that Jilaine – that is, the woman I knew as Jilaine – truly believed that in the end, no matter what she did to us, we were there to be her helpers. Her servants.

There is a naivety to Jilaine, as, perhaps, with all of us who are so conniving, trustless and damned.

She was too strong for Jud. Her wealth, too, had no benign effect. He began to drink heavily. A bottle or two bottles of whiskey per day, local rough wine, absinthe, all that was to be had. And he argued about the little girl, he argued with everything Jilaine wanted. Until his own child seemed afraid of him. And then he stormed from Jilaine's house (I seem to recall she used a less clichéd word) and drove off up the mountain in the slick white car she had given him. He was blind drunk, and halfway along the slashes of the road, he met another car more ably driven, whose driver survived the crash, as Jud did not.

222

EXHIBIT THREE
TO INDIGO

As when a prowling Wolf,
Whom hunger drives to seek new haunt for prey,
Watching where Shepherds pen their Flocks at Eve
In hurdl'd Cotes amid the field secure,
Leaps ore the fence with ease into the Fold:
Or as a Thief bent to unhoard the cash
Of som rich Burgher, whose substantial dores,
Cross-barred and bolted fast, fear no assault,
In at the window climbs, or ore the tiles;
So clomb this first grand Thief...

Thence up he flew, and on the Tree of Life,
The middle Tree and highest there that grew,
Sat like a Cormorant...

Paradise Lost, Book IV
Milton

1

Breaking in was easy. Although of course, I had been thinking about it, and how to do it, for some time. Really the arrangement was very slipshod. I mean with the flat. And from what I had been told recently by him, it seemed to me anyone could have done something similar, someone with a grudge – or a fear – against or of him. I laid my plans such as they were over the weekend and made my 'move' on Monday. Which is far too alliterative a phrase, but there, it's a fact. Basically, in my own little way, I went in for the kill.

My own little way. And that sounds like Lynda. "You do like to have your own little way," she used to tell me. Not, you notice, my own *way*. My own *little* way. "Go on, then," Lynda used to say. "You just do what you want. It's no good me arguing..." ("*My* arguing" I used mentally to correct her with a sort of dry shiver), "you'll just have to have your own little way."

Did I have my own little way with Lynda? Now and then, I suppose. But that is another story.

When I got to Saracen Road, I stopped a moment and looked over at the park. It was summer. It still is. I wasn't really looking at anything over there, just taking my bearings. He had spoken about the park and the trees. It was as if I had to be quite sure they were all really there. And they were.

So then I checked the parcel.

This was my masterstroke. At least so I thought then.

It comprised a sturdy manila envelope measuring approximately ten inches by twelve and a half – and was far too stout to go through any ordinary letter-box, especially after I'd packed it full with old newspaper cut to size. I had stuck on the anonymous printed label. I had also placed a quantity of stamps on the thing, then lightly rubbed them with an ink-pad – as if they had been smudgily franked. I've had enough such mail in my time.

I didn't think anyone could trace this to me. But then no one, hopefully, would need to see it beyond a cursory glance, if that. After which I intended to remove it, along with myself, from the scene of the crime. On the other hand, if someone insisted on accepting the parcel, no crime could occur. It wouldn't matter. Perhaps not much would.

As for myself, there was my disguise. I'd finally done what he had often told me to do, which was to shave off all my thinning hair. Instead I had grown quite a thick moustache in the space of three days. I'd bought a T-shirt too, black, and put on my tired old jeans that look like every other ageing man's tired old jeans. Oddly, shaven and moustached, I thought I looked two or three years younger than my allotted fifty-fifty-one. There were the smart sunglasses too, somebody else's forgotten pair I'd swiped from the unmanned counter at Smiths those months before. A crime already, we perceive.

Did I look like a thug? No. Five foot ten, skinny, with my hunched shoulders, narrow hands and feet and nose – I wasn't bruiser material.

I crossed the street. It was a quarter to 12, noon.

Nearly time for *You and Yours*.

That was not what was thumping from the terrace of houses. A selection of rock or pop CDs were mutilating the still just morning air. Which was as he'd told me as well. He had said his particular terrace-house of flats, 66, Saracen Road, was a noisy place that got on his nerves, or on his 'tits', depending on his mood when remarking.

Not only was it 66, Saracen Road, either. His flat was at the very top. Flat 6 – the Number of the Beast indeed.

I had labelled my parcel carefully. Here was a mistake any flustered, overworked post-person might create.

I looked at the list of names above the bells. Then I pressed his bell. What does that say? My pedantry? My caution? He was not there. I had every reason to *know* he wasn't. Or even if amazingly he was, it might be one more lie, his not answering.

But for whatever reason he *didn't* answer. And I tried the bell annoyingly quite a few times.

About four minutes passed. Now I hesitated and clicked my tongue, perplexed, irritated. After which I started on the next five bells, one after another.

No 5 was in, it was some of their tasteless 'music' I heard hammering on above. They took no notice, perhaps couldn't hear their bell, which augured well. (A *rhyming* phrase now. Normally I would vet and remove it).

It was No 3A which spoke to me. "Yeah?" The voice was male and – shall I say – bored.

"I'm sorry to bother you..."

"*Yeah?*"

"I have a package here..."

"Put it through the door, man."

"I'm afraid it won't fit through the letter-box."

"Shit. I gotta come down?"

"No, no. Excuse me, the package isn't for you."

"Then why the fuck are you...?"

"It's for a Mr Traz..." – carefully I laboured over his name – "*kull?* Flat 6." Silence.

I said, "It was delivered to me wrongly in Sarandene Road – No 16..." (Such a road did not, obviously, exist).

And "So?" said the other.

"I've come out of my way," I replied sternly. "Mr Trazcool doesn't answer. This is a nuisance. Maybe you could let me in, and I'll leave the thing for him in the hall. I'm not coming back with it."

No response save the sudden wasp-like rage of a buzzer as the front door opened.

226

"Tha..." I tried. Old habits, like war-torn Celtic warriors, die hard.

I doubt the moron in flat 3A heard me.

Then I was inside the hallway, shabby, airy and patchily white from big and grimy opaque windows. A mountain of stairs rose ahead. Evidently, I wasn't going to deposit my spurious packet on the dusty table down here. Conscientious citizen as I must be, I was going up the whole bare stairway right to the top, all the way to N.O.T.B. 666. Where, please God, the door was as once he had described it, and the bloody awful racket from unmusical No 5 would continue, so no one would hear me as I smashed the glass panel, slipped my hand across and released the single Yale lock from inside.

ONE

Joseph. This, his name.

He liked to be known as *Sej*. He'd later told me he was dyslectic (normally erroneously spelled 'dyslexic') and possibly that was why he had taken the initial J of his forename and fixed it on the end of the 'se' from the middle.

Joseph Traskul: Sej.

It has a sort of Germanic, certainly European ring to it, his full name. It is like that of some mentally tortured poet, probably from a well-to-do mercantile family, dead before forty, circa 1800.

I wondered from the very first if his name was a lie.

I have wondered if all of him was, and is, a lie.

The strangest thing.

But it was all very strange. Or only – very stupid.

I had gone up to London to meet Harris Wybrother. He used to be my agent but had retired a couple of years before. Despite this he still sometimes put publishers my way, or me their way depending on how one looked at it. Harris was only two or three years my senior, but I had always found him much *older*.

Maybe he was a sort of authority figure to me. I always remember the first time we met, when I was mid-twenty-ish and he twenty-two-ish going on forty-ish, looming over me from his desk. "This isn't bad, Roy. It has potential shall I say? But you need to do quite a bit of work on it. Don't worry, old boy. We'll knock you into shape. And then – who knows?" Harris had been at Oxbridge. He had connections. I of course had been to the local grammar and then straight into the library service.

I stayed with Harris a handful of times, in the late '80s and '90s, at his father's 'place' in Hampshire. I think the first occasion I expected to step right back into a sort of between-the-wars Wodehouse scenario. It *was* a little like that. But not Wybrother Père. He was a piratical type who acted, and looked if it came to it, very much younger than his son. There was no longer any Mrs Wybrother. Normally a different woman, or once three women, were staying

227

in the house and sharing the pirate's bed, appearing at breakfast in silk dressing-gowns or sporty cotton undies. Harris, though unmarried, had a regular fiancée he seemed always and only to retain in London.

The 'place' itself was big. It was an old vicarage, worth apparently a 'bomb', though the drains and general plumbing were on the sleepy side.

It was surrounded by woods and fields and had gardens. These were maintained by a sort of ghostly ever-grumbling gardener. He would appear suddenly at the windows of the dining-room on summer evenings and stand silent, motionless and glaring horribly in on us all, rather like Peter Quint in *The Turn of the Screw*.

There were a couple of tennis courts as well, and Harris once or twice insisted I play some sets with him. But I'm no good at tennis, or any games, and dislike them all, perhaps only for that reason. That I always went along with his suggestions was less proof of an obedient guest than the fact Harris always somewhat reminded me of one of the more amiable bullies at school.

The house stayed Wodehousian even as late as 1997, by which time the fields had become town, and a new estate had been built practically on the front lawn. But Harris's father had sprung by then what I took for his final surprise. In his sixties he'd been expected hourly to die of drink, or other over-indulgence, but instead he had cut and run to Spain with a girl of twenty-four. She was rich apparently, too. The last I'd heard he was still there, seventy-one by now and going strong, his child-bride of thirty-something firmly at his side and "Serenely putting up with," Harris had said, "Dad's endless stream of bimboritas from the bars."

No doubt Wybrother Senior's youthful tendencies had moulded Harris's aura of age. (How I dislike the Americanised apostrophe 's *following* an s. But I've given up on that one. Hardly any publisher in the English language would now countenance the old tradition of Harris'. Not that this, as will become obvious, is ever intended for publication).

When I received the most recent summons to lunch with Harris in London, I went. The possible chances of a book contract were usually illusory. So one took what one could get.

Harris came 'down from the country', from the Wodehouse house. We met at a restaurant called *Le Grill* in Holborn, one of those small quirky venues that can sometimes supply *haute cuisine* and are a kind of Masonic secret among any that know. Harris had previously ordered me: "Don't tell anyone about this, eh, Roy? Keep it for us. The good and the slightly great."

We ate steak, Scottish, or so it purported to be. There had been starters of something to do with Scandinavian prawns, 'seasonal' asparagus. We drank the appropriate wines, which were very drinkable. Naturally Harris knows exactly what to choose. Frankly I can never be that bothered. If something is palatable, and in my case, affordable, I'll drink it. After the main course there was cheese – actually *very* good. We took coffee.

And now, I thought, having as always been careful and restrained, as my own father would have instructed, Harris might offer a titbit, some man – or more often now, a woman – who might be interested in a book from me. At this point I'd better add; my *forte* is usually the minor thriller or detective novel. But such basic works may, if wanted, be constructed to incorporate certain preoccupations. Or should I say *themes*.

This time, however, my lunch *impresario* did not suggest a single thing. Over the brandy and coffee his eyes grew suddenly like an infant's. And by that I mean through changing colour – to a sort of milky blue; by nature they're grey.

"Fuck it, Roy," he said, gazing out into the vistas of Holborn Viaduct, "Dad's dead."

Such a phrase, *bathetically*, heaven forgive me, alliterative. *Dad's dead.*

But I was shocked too, in my own (little) way. Both at the news and Harris being abruptly so unlike himself.

Stupidly I said, "Your father..." I certainly didn't mean to seem to correct him.

But he snapped, "Dad, yes. My bloody father."

"I'm so sorry, Harris."

"So am I. No, let me be painfully honest, Roy, I don't give a flying – I don't *care*, Roy. Which has to be wrong, yes?"

His milky eyes said something other. Poor bastard, he seemed not to know. Had some hidden unnoted weeping turned his eyes blue?

"When did it happen?"

"Two days ago. Two *days*. Can you believe that bitch Veronica..." he meant the thirty-something child wife, "only called me last night. And do I mean night? It was two minutes to 2 in the morning."

"Well, from Spain perhaps... And she must have been upset."

"Must she? How would one know? Perhaps. Oh, perhaps. I'll give the cow the benefit of the doubt. I have to go over for the funeral and to sort things out. And there has to be an inquest. Oh *not*," he startlingly nearly bellowed, so our fellow lunchers raised their brows, "like one of *your* bloody yarns. They just do it. Oh God, Roy."

I forbore to ask if Janette, his *glacé fiancée*, was going with him to give support. I'd only met her once.

Possibly she wasn't really as she had seemed to be, not when he and she were alone.

Just then anyhow his mobile phone went off. His ringtone was a special piece of Brahms.

At once, like Pavlov's dogs, trained to the right response, he was chatting into it in his ordinary Harris manner. His eyes unfilmed, went grey again.

"Sorry, Roy," he said as the call ended. "Emergency over at The Elms." *The Elms* was his name for a well-known publishing house near the Euston Road. "Get me a cab, will you?" he added to the waiter, "and the bill. Really sorry to run out on you. You must email and tell me all your news, what

229

projects you're working on..." Projects meaning books. Projects. "Don't rush off because I have to, stay and have another brandy."

We shook hands and he went away.

I didn't want another brandy, hadn't really wanted the first one. It was quite hot although only April, too hot for excess alcohol.

I walked down from Holborn to the Strand feeling rather flat, although Harris's lunches seldom led to much work nowadays. And I was slightly unnerved. Probably at the touch of what my father had been used to call the Grim Reaper. Harris's father had been just over seventy, but I was fifty. Well over the boundary on the downward path to old age and death.

After all I went into a pub and ordered half a pint of Wincott's Bitter, a funny old brew you see less and less.

Sitting in the dark corner, staring into the beer's murky depths, I had a bleak look at my life. What was I doing, where heading for? Why? What aims did I have, hopes cherish? It was a sorry and banal *resumé*. I was a plodder, and I did what I was told where I could find anyone – parent, employer, publisher – to tell me. I kept the 'wolf from the door' by hard graft in the softest of professions. I lived slowly and prudently, with little occasional and mundane treats, like the very glass-full on the table in front of me, Wincott's. My life was a glass of bitter.

There was only one thing I *could* cite – even if that too involved my trade. It was the sole manuscript I had never even submitted to an agent or editor. The untitled, unfinished book had begun life in paper form, but had currently lain in the files of my computer for six years. *Untitled* was not a work of suspense or detective fiction. It was a strange thing, perhaps even a sort of fantasy, set in an (also untitled) European country during the eighteenth century. The literary style of the book was also fairly unlike the normally carefully-clipped and controlled prose of everything else I typed in there. And it had a structure that was, perhaps, experimental. It involved no plotting whatsoever, dissimilar to every other novel I'd penned, typed, or ultimately tapped out on the keyboard. And of course, like anything never planned, unplotted, unresolved, meandering and 'free', it frequently stuck. I had begun *Untitled* in 1975, when I was in my twenties. Thereafter, section by section it flowed and stuck, and unglued and went on, until the next inevitable block. Printed up so far, it ran to 318 close pages, but aside from the revisions I sometimes visited on it, it had by now been stalled fairly conclusively since the turn of the century.

Now it came floating up as it were out of the beer glass. *Untitled* was, for all its failings and inertia, the one *interesting* book I had ever attempted. In fact the only book that flew in the face of everything else of any kind I had had to do and done.

Did I say what it was about? If only loosely, it concerned a crazed and murderous young poet, son of a once-wealthy mercantile family, a drug-taker and visionary with black curling hair and wide wild eyes. Aside from his genius, he took anything he wanted, but generally it was given him, and the silver salver his *far* from mundane treats were served on, was often also awash with blood.

Just as I glanced up from the beer, the pub door opened in a sudden sun flash. Two silhouetted figures walked in, two men. One was a suited business type with expensive shoes. The other was the black-haired poet from *Untitled*.

Obviously, he wasn't anything of the sort, the young man now leaning against the bar. Actual characters do not, as in one or two peculiar romances they may, leap from the page to take on sentient life.

The resemblance, however, especially as I had just then been thinking of it, was remarkable.

Realistically I've sometimes wondered since, if I *hadn't* been thinking of *Untitled*, would I even have noticed him particularly? Maybe on the train going back I might have thought of it: *Oh, that fellow in the pub. He was rather like Vilmos... wasn't he?*

Under *these* circumstances I was inevitably intrigued.

I stared a moment, checked myself, and started to scrutinise him more cautiously.

He was definitely quite a handsome specimen. As, naturally, was *Untitled*'s Vilmos. Lynda, with her prissy taste, wouldn't have liked him, I don't think she would. After all she made do with me and my little way for two whole years. Maureen though, I'm fairly sure, *would* have appreciated the man in the pub. She too spent time with me, but I had been a lot younger then, and her husband was also very good-looking in his youth.

This young man was himself about thirty-six or seven. *Not* so young really. And Vilmos – about thirty-five where I'd left him last, wallowing in a brothel on some shadowy cobbled side street of an arched and aching city. Here then, Vilmos abruptly aged by the next unwritten chapter.

He took no notice of anything around him that I could see. He spoke to the Suit-and-Shoes in a muted angry monologue, pausing only to listen to the Suit's own brief comments, here and there inserted, during which Vilmos – I might as well call him that for the moment – seemed both strung-up and contemptuous. The Suit drank a glass of red wine. It was a nice colour, like the bottle Harris had got with the steak. Vilmos drank a double vodka or gin without mixer, knocked it back and stood waiting for a refill. Which was duly purchased.

Already this, his demeanour, seemed aptly reminiscent of what Vilmos's *might* have been in some comparable situation. But what situation was it? Suit-and-Shoes looked composed, almost non-committal. There were a lot of early evening drinkers already in the pub, and more streaming in. I couldn't make out even a single word. Probably twenty years ago I would have. Then other barflies grouped between me and the two men, and I couldn't see them well either. Vilmos wore a black shirt and black jeans. They were neither expensive nor tat. He was wearing brown boots that looked as if they had helped him scale the sides of rough chalky buildings.

I took a few more gulps of beer.

It was nearly 5.30, the middle of what we used to call the Rush Hour. As a rule I avoided travelling this late, or caught the 7.30 train, which missed the worst of it. I'd dawdled. As if – I was meant to see this man, to be inspired, *Untitled* rejuvenated.

I'd use this scene in the next chapter. Find a good if bizarre explanation for it, the Suit man a creditor or lover, even a sibling. To work on the book tonight could ease the dull feeling of threat that had somehow fastened on me with Harris's words *Dad's dead.*

All at once the crowd round the bar was parting, like clothes in a big wardrobe, as some Narnian-like beast came shouldering forth. It wasn't Aslan.

"Yes?" he said, standing over my table.

My scrutiny, as I've noted here, had been intended to be discreet. Besides he and his companion had been hemmed in. How had he seen the slight low glances I shot at him?

"I beg your pardon?" I asked mildly.

"Well maybe you should."

I kept a blank face. I don't like confrontations, and don't often either invite or get snared in one.

"Well," he said, "you could buy me a drink, then."

His voice was not as I had imagined Vilmos' voice to be. I suppose I heard Vilmos, in my inner ear, speaking a sort of cod Franco-Russian-Hungarian. Something like that.

I thought, *Christ, he thinks I'm after him. Want to shag him. Now what do I do, for God's sake?*

"I'm sorry," I said, "I don't quite..."

He sat down across from me. There was an empty chair there somehow left unfilled. He sprawled out his long legs. "I know you, don't I?" he asked me.

For a queasy second I did think perhaps, despite all common sense, he truly was Vilmos. But I seized the one apparent saving chance.

"I thought I knew *you* a minute too. You're very like my sister's son." I have no sister, and this non-existent She has no son. But would that sweep the problem up?

He said, "Oh really?"

He levelled his black brows. He had good teeth, and a slightly crooked nose. Vilmos? Why not. Perhaps in some fight... I tried to keep my wits.

"I haven't seen him for a year," I elaborated. A writer, or my kind of writer, can do such things *extempore*. "They're in India, he and his girlfriend. So I was a bit surprised..."

"To see me here. Only I'm not, or he's not."

"No. I'm sorry if I stared. That was why."

"It isn't usually," he said.

"Well," I said, "have a good evening." I rose. Thank Christ he stayed in the seat. From the bar, I noticed, his former associate had melted away.

"Cheers," said Vilmos.

He had an actor's accent. His voice seemed trained, expressive, but more lazy now.

He still didn't get up and I wove through the pub crowd and got out on the scorched pavement. I was sweating. God, that had been – never mind. Forward march – my father again. Rise and shine, forward march, the touch of the Grim Reaper, easy come, easy go...

I was walking quickly towards Charing Cross. The best course however would be to go by and on to Haymarket. I could look at the theatres, I could simply...

"I just thought," said his unmistakable voice behind me. It came from higher in the air. I'm five ten, you may remember, and Vilmos about six three, "you might like to take this."

Trepidatious to the point of agony I turned. He held before me a business card. The very last item I would guess my nerves expected.

I gazed at it. *Joseph Traskul* said the card in plain black Roman on plain dull white. Then an email address and telephone number.

"Er – why would I...?"

"Be a sport," he answered with a menacing old-fashioned playfulness.

"Look, I'm really sorry..."

"I'll bet you are, now."

All around the crowd eddied. I knew that if he drew a knife and sliced off my ear, or kicked me in the groin, everybody else would merely fastidiously move round us, not to interrupt.

"All right. Thank you."

"You think," he said, "I'm a gay whore. Or maybe a bi-functional one. Look on the back of the card."

I did so. *Piano Tuner to the Bars* it said.

He laughed then, now not like Vilmos, more gentle, and almost shy. "Had you going there. I thought you looked the type of guy might have a piano, or know someone. Work is scarce this spring. I'll travel, just minimum expenses. The main rates are printed there, too. See you." And he swung himself about, the mane of hair springing up and flopping down on his collar. He strode carelessly away through the splintered westering sun.

TWO

My father used to keep a piano, (I put the word 'keep' advisedly) in the sitting-room. He could play quite well, if rather stiffly, a little Chopin or Schubert, and sometimes Victorian songs. I had piano lessons at the grammar school, which was one of the few still surviving locally in the 60s. Then I too could play a little, if like him without much magic and with less ability. I remember hot summer, cold dark winter evenings, practising, and my mother putting her head round the door. "That's nice, Roy."

Maureen had a piano too, and she could play very well. She played the kind of thing I liked, unless I only really started to like it because she played it. Rachmaninov and Debussy were a couple of her choices, and Scott Joplin. She'd found him long before his return to the public ear.

Now of course my home premises were pianoless. I had sold it four years after I inherited the house.

It was nothing like Harris's 'place', No 74, Old Church Lane. A long, sloping, winding street with some occasional careering oak trees, and semi-detached villas planted behind short front lawns. I'd grown up there, and later gone away, although only about an hour by train, to a succession of not very salubrious rooms. Gradually the street and the villas changed over the years, the former getting less cloistered and the pavement more worn, the trees being cut down or regularly pruned to stumps. The houses though perked up. They acquired bright red or blue front doors and new roofs, garages where side access had been, and ponds with waterlilies. "People value a house now," my father had remarked. "Because it costs more, it means more." I never really followed that. Houses had often cost a lot more than was affordable. I was more inclined to put the renovations down to the increasing frequency with which everyone else seemed to move out or in, tarting everything up for a quick sale or to please a mortgage company.

I assayed little improvement when I went back. My father had died, having a heart attack at the local, where he'd gone for an unusual drink with some friends. My mother had been dead for years. Breast cancer. There wasn't much they could do for it then. But the house was useful. It was paid for, and once all the legal business was solved, I was installed, only half an hour out of London's Charing Cross. I managed to find a gardener too. He was young, quite efficient. He scalped the lawn and hauled the worst of the weeds from the flowerbeds, where a scatter of flowers then bloomed by themselves for several seasons before, finally, untended and never watered except by God, they gave up. In the end the gardener too simply vanished without a word. Perhaps someone had killed him, as happened to gardeners and many others in quite a lot of my books. I got the back and front lawns paved over then and left the rest to itself. I sold the piano about the same time. I had never been tempted to play it.

That evening I got home around 8. I had just missed a train, then travelled standing on another, amid herds of commuters in the same case, reading papers, chatting on their mobiles, swaying there like bats the wrong way up.

Indoors I made some tea and took a biscuit from the jar, my mother's biscuit barrel that had a fat bear on it. As a child I had loved it, the bear.

I really had altered the house very little. Only neglected it. The agency cleaning girl came once a fortnight.

She was currently a German student, who seemingly spoke only five words of English: *Hello. Yes. No. Done.* And *Ifbee.* (Perhaps six words?) That last meant *If I can against all odds,* i.e.: Could you clean the cooker? *Ifbee.*

The sun was at last going down in the fir tree at the end of the garden, not mine, but that of an adjoining plot. Beyond my back fence ran the alleyway, but the fir tree mostly hid it from me. I'd used this tree in swift descriptions here and there, a handy example of nature, its needles against this sky or that. Now a fractured golden sunset sky that had been prefigured in London's radiance.

Mug in hand, I stared into the last light.

Sunset and dusk have a mystic significance in the East, I forget quite what. In France of course, with dusk comes *l'heure bleue,* when phantoms and hallucinations are seen.

The sun went. The fir grew darker and the sky like bronze. Then the twilight blueness. A bright star stood out over the roof of the Catholic church.

Vaguely heard around me the ordinary noise of a radio, some male clearing nasal passages careless of open window or listening ears, a Hoover; a night flight starting off for Europe.

And then, the phantom.

It emerged palely from the umbra of the fir tree and the gathering dark and gazed in over the fence. Bisected by the fence at the approximate level of his jaw, Joseph Traskul's disembodied head. Vilmos would have liked that.

I didn't drop the mug. Maybe I clutched it far too tightly.

And he? He watched me. He was smiling.

We said nothing, either of us.

And then the owl – there was an owl, it sometimes flew across the gardens in the spring and summer, although where it came from I'd never been sure – the owl sailed by overhead.

And both he and I looked up.

Both he and I – Vilmos – Joseph – and I, looked up at the passing of the owl.

When I looked down again, the phantom was gone.

2

On the third flight I met one of the neighbours. He came out of a door above and clattered down the stair towards me.

I got ready to show him the forged packet, with its address of Saracen Road and the apparently franked postage. But, thickset and indifferent, he shouldered past me, brushing me over with a leather jacket very unsuitable for the summer weather, not saying a word.

No doubt few of them took any notice of each other in this block. Inner London is like that, even more so than the suburbs where I exist.

I went up the further three flights and reached flat No 6. *His* flat.

It was as he had described it. A door painted a dull white like all the others I had already seen, but this one with a panel of crinkled glass. The door had only one Yale lock. Yet it did not have a number on it, unlike those below. Nevertheless it had to be 6. The stair ended here. There was nowhere else to go.

One flight down, flat 5 was still crashing out its horrible music, tuneless, with only the deadly beat and mostly indecipherable Neanderthal lyrics, to class it as any kind of 'song'. When I had walked by on my way up, not only was I deafened, I felt the racket through the soles of my feet, base of my spine, and punching me in the gut.

Up here, no one else was about. Through a narrow, unwashed window I could see the rear of the other buildings, and not a flicker of life. Beyond those, the London skyline.

I was scarcely furtive. I took the heavy-duty gardening glove out of my back pocket, put it on and made a fist. I smashed the glass with one smack, as if I'd been doing things of this sort all my life. Watching TV I suppose teaches one the worst skills; the morality brigade are right.

Most of the panel fell in. It must have been very inferior stuff.

I reached through and undid the door.

As it swung inward, I thought he would spring at me, out of nowhere, out of thin air.

But he didn't. The narrow hallway was empty. In fact very empty, no carpet down, the paper even scoured from the unpainted walls. There were two internal doors, each closed.

THREE

I went back into the house, through the kitchen door, which I shut, locked and bolted behind me. Then I switched on the external light. Its beam cut hard into the gathering dark, revealing nothing beyond what was normally present, the paved lawn and dead flowerbeds, the fir tree over the fence, the top of the Catholic church. The light dimmed the diamond star that had appeared there.

What had happened? Had I *imagined* him, Joseph Traskul the piano tuner, his floating head swimming by the fence and smiling at me, before the owl somehow diverted both our attentions to the sky?

I didn't think it had been imagination.

Well then, was I going mad?

Putting down the mug I went through into the front room and poured myself a finger of whisky.

Standing motionless, I peered out at the street. The curtains were still undrawn. My mother used to have nets up, to stop anyone looking in at our nondescript activities. But I had taken them down in the end. I had nothing fascinating to hide, did nothing in that room, nor in any of the living-rooms, to merit such strict concealment.

Out in the street a couple of surviving oaks caught the ugly glare of the streetlamps. The fifteen-year-old from three doors up was bicycling by, and the man who always walked his Alsatian dog was doing just that. Nor was anyone on the garden path that ran beside the house. The side gate was securely shut.

The clock on the church chimed. 9 p.m.

Nothing else was evident.

Soon I drew the curtains. I put on the hall light and went upstairs and put on the light in my study, which had once been my parents' bedroom.

Turning on the computer I checked for emails. There was only one, from Peakes about some stationery.

All this time I was thinking, *What did I see? Was it real?*

I didn't feel deranged. Nor did I think I had *not* seen what I had.

The frivolous idea that after all, and truly, the man from the pub in The Strand might be my character come to life failed to resurface. I don't believe such things can happen. And if perhaps they ever could, I would never reckon they could happen to a man like myself.

So it was a mystery. Or perhaps something in the prawns had not been quite right, or the cheese; something as silly as that. I'd heard of such incidents, a mild hallucinatory food-poisoning. But I felt cool and quite steady, not sick, and not sweating now.

Better let the episode go. Perhaps it would prove useful, if not in revitalising *Untitled*, then in my next commercial work. For honestly, now, I had no desire at all to uncork my unpublished novel from the files.

I did some small chores round the house, had a slice of supermarket cheddar on toast, and watched the news. The world as always was in unremitting chaos, and apparently the temperature in Britain had been an unseasonal 20 – roughly 70 degrees, we would have said in my youth.

I ran a bath, and afterwards went to bed.

Like many of my age, I don't sleep as well as I did.

What an unappreciated pleasure, the sleepful nights of my teens and twenties had been, the odd sleepless one an occasion for fretful wonder. Now they're a matter of course, and on a 'good' night I average five or six non-consecutive hours if I'm lucky.

But I lay back and watched the darkness and the faint municipal lamplight through the curtains. I put on my bedside radio, Radio 3. They were playing Handel, I thought.

I considered my next commission, which was a small thriller, one in a series devised by someone else and something for which I had no enthusiasm, but it would help pay bills. I often do a bit of work in my insomniac hours, even get up sometimes at 3 or 4 in the morning to push some notes into the computer.

My brain however kept going back to the pub, and, nastier, the fence.

At midnight I switched to the news, as I habitually do, and listened once more to the rehash of hell on earth.

What was it all for? What was to be done?

I used to get angry and have *opinions*. Now I take it in like a sort of slop. The bloody awful thing is, this rehearsal of horrors usually helps me drift asleep.

Which was what happened. We were on to the World Service by then, a report on some far off disaster beyond human belief, and I was asleep.

I dreamed he and I were sitting on a torn-out palm tree drifting on a salt-dark sea, and he said to me, "The thing is, Phippsy, it was written, us meeting as we did."

To this hour, this piece of dream-dialogue frightens me. Because he speaks in the dream as he *would* speak. Not as I would have him speak, at least partly grammatically. Us meeting, not our. And his use of my name, like the bullies at Chaults Grammar School. My father's, therefore my name is Phipps. Although my professional name is R.P. Phillips. Harris suggested that, while he was dismantling my first book and sending me home to reinvent it. "Phipps – no, old son. Doesn't have a ring to it. *Phelps*, I wonder...? No. No – *Phillips*."

In the dream Joseph Traskul was not in his black clothes and bashed boots from the pub. He wore Vilmos's garments, Vilmos's loose shirt and broken coat.

The radio must have said it, three hundred people were dead. Both the dream-Joseph and the dream – I heard this.

Joseph said to me, "And I only am escaped alone to tell thee," quoting the *Book of Job*, and also, naturally, Melville's *Moby Dick*.

One gets used to rising early. My almost ten years in the library service had marked this indelibly on my mental clock. Even when I sleep especially badly, I rarely get up later than 8.

I used to have a paper delivered, my father's habit. I stopped that too a couple of years back. I seem to listen to enough news. The post, which used to arrive at 8 or before, seldom now appears much before 11 a.m.

But today there was an envelope on the mat.

In the brilliant light of too-early-summer morning I bent to see.

No 74, said the hand printing on its surface. The writing was erratic, but I still took it for some circular, a charity appeal, Jehovah's Witness threat, or one of those *Householder* issues that suggest to us we can sell our house and then rent it back, must be aware of this or that road-widening, pipe-renewing or other potentially destructive plan, or that our government loves us, and we should be *en garde*.

I didn't bother to open it, only carried it through to the kitchen and put on the kettle for coffee.

Outside sparrows, blue tits and pigeons were flying over in squadrons to the bird-tables and baths of No 72, my attached neighbour, and unattached 76 the other side of the wall.

I have nothing against birds, or any creature come to that. My mother used to have a birdbath also, but I never remembered to fill it. It was drily down there somewhere by the end fence, among the weeds and ivy. And beyond, stood the fir.

Gradually I glanced out at the fir.

Which was how I saw the thing sitting there on the paving.

It was a large black plastic dustbin. Not, I hasten to add, a *dirty* one. This was spic and span. It looked brand new. There was even a red and white sticker left on the lid.

I switched off the kettle.

Nothing else out there was disturbed. Certainly the air force of birds wasn't nervous.

Perhaps ridiculously I picked up the bread knife. I undid the kitchen door and emerged.

The air was lit, and peaceable with noisy morning sounds.

I walked over the paving and inspected the dustbin.

It was definitely new, pristine in fact. I don't know why, possibly force of habit for this is what one does with dustbins, I reached out and pulled off the lid.

As I did this, complete terror gripped me. I had an instant mental picture of Joseph Traskul, like some handsome, hideous jack-in-the-box, leaping out of the interior – *Surprise! Surprise!*

But there was nothing like that. There was *something* in the vault of the bin. I could see at once what it was, but its incongruity made it incomprehensible to me. I stood there staring. In the end I dropped the lid on, walked back into the kitchen, shut and locked the door. And saw again the letter that had been on the mat.

Now I grabbed hold of it. Dropping the knife, I ripped the envelope open.

A leaf of plain white paper was inside with strong, erratic writing in black biro, not astonishingly the very same writing as was on the outside.

I removed it. It could be read clearly enough: *Back garden. See bin. Open to find* 1 *x bottle of Wincott's Special.*

Which was of course exactly what I had done, and found.

"Hello. I wonder if I could speak to Harris?"

"Arriz," said an unfamiliar and not very kindly female voice. "Mr Why Bother do you men?"

"That's right. I..."

"He's off."

"He's not there?"

"Noah. He's gone to Spine."

"Already."

"Yez. Abuts dad."

"I see. Do you know when he'll..."

"No I don't. I'm hellip for Miss Lornce."

"Oh, I see. I suppose Miss Lawrence isn't..."

"Mss Lornces owd."

"Could you tell her Roy called."

"Ray."

"Roy. Roy Phipps."

"Roy Fibs. Yez, I'll tell."

The phone went down quite forcefully before I could ask if Janette Lawrence, Harris's *fiancée*, would call me back, or when I could call again.

Once more a dead end, then. I'd already tried a couple of other publishing semi-friends, ostensibly to check on business matters, a contract, a payment. I had wanted to try them out, see what they thought it was best for me to do. There is a strange chap who seems to have followed me from central London. No, I haven't a clue why. He latched on to me in a pub, and now he's left a dustbin in my garden.

A difficult speech. No doubt they'd only assume I was trying out on them a new plotline for some sinister tale.

Actually, I could imagine Lewis Rybourne at Gates saying, "Oh come on, Roy. That's drivel. Why would someone do something so – well frankly *soppy*. Is there a *body* in the fucking bin or what?"

Should I therefore call the police? I could imagine *that* too. All the world reeling with terror threats, rapes, murders and burglary with violence, and myself phoning them about *my* problem. "Well, some people, sir, might be very grateful for a nice clean bin. Not to mention a free jar."

It got to noon, and I couldn't settle to anything, or decide what to do. I'd placed the note and envelope in a plastic sandwich bag and put them in a drawer, to protect DNA. The bin and beer I left where they were. A pair of pigeons subsequently flew over and landed there momentarily, and one had relieved itself on the purity of the lid. I went upstairs and belatedly shaved and dressed. I shut and locked every window, even the narrow one in the lavatory. Downstairs, all bolted and barred, I poured the cold coffee I had made and not drunk into the sink. Outside the bin was still there, undisturbed except by me and the pigeon.

The house has a burglar alarm. I didn't very often activate it, as it had a handy knack of going off for no apparent reason. Now I did. Next both sides had people in all day, 72 an elderly but spry couple, 76 a househusband with a child that went to school and came back for lunch.

I walked out of the house and double-locked the door.

Despite the sun it was cooler today. I scanned carefully up and down the street as I had already done with the path and the back alley from my upper rooms, my bedroom, the lavatory and adjacent bathroom.

All this was very silly. But I write such stories. I *know* how appallingly worrying these tiny incidents may seem. Anything that doesn't fit the everyday, even an everyday established menace – like a thug with a gun or a warning from a gang.

At the end of Old Church Lane, I turned into Bulivante Crescent. Round the curve of detached houses, meshed in their hedges and trees, lay the roaring high street. But even as I took in the vista, I saw him, seated on a low wall, drinking from a can of cola.

He wore white today, a white shirt and whitish jeans. Over his shoulder was that kind of male handbag that is so useful, and this too was in a sort of bleached denim. He had already seen me. He got up, smiling, and raised his friendly hand in greeting. No recrimination was obvious at his having had to wait for me so long.

FOUR

No one ever told me anything about the sexual act. As for love, it was something you saw in films. By the time I was seventeen, you could see quite a bit of the sexual act in them, too, particularly in foreign cinemas in the West End. I had also been handed certain educational books by my father when I was about fourteen. He suggested I read them; I was now 'old enough' to 'understand'. Needless to say I *already* understood. One's body tends to inform one. Despite all this however, I wasn't a quick learner, I wasn't ready to equate what I felt with any chance of sharing it. It was a solitary pleasure, as they were wont to say. I needn't, I think, go into details. My own writing is scanty in this respect. I will open the bedroom door and let my protagonists through. But what goes on thereafter the reader may deduce for himself.

Repressed? Of course I was, and am, and very wisely. I was an unattractive thin spotty youth, who grew into a short, thin and nondescript male adult. My hair was already going at twenty, despite all the preparations I tried on it. My height had never materialised. I wasn't a 'Tich', like Mark Brighton, the poor sucker in my last year at school, who was still under five foot. Men go on growing, they say, until they are twenty-one. Maybe he suddenly dashed a final thirteen inches and put them all to shame. But there are short men with plenty of charisma. Not me.

By seventeen I had liked girls, *fancied* girls. (*Fantasised* girls). But I'd never been to bed with one. Naturally I lied about this. Did anyone believe me? Doubtful.

Then I left Chaults Grammar and started to work in the central library. One night when I was eighteen, I went to the *Feathers* for a drink with some partial friends, and there in a corner I saw Maureen Parner.

Truthfully, I barely gave her a second glance.

She was well over thirty, and this was in the early 1970s. She was just a woman with done-up blondish hair, sipping spirits with a fat man who kept laughing. There were girls elsewhere in the bar with swinging hair and off-the-shoulder tops and blue nails. My three male companions ogled them, as did I.

"Look at her. What ya think?"

"I like her friend best."

"Her skirt's too short."

"Well, that's OK."

"Yeah but the legs aren't good enough."

The evening rambled on, getting smokier and darker. It was just October, and outside the then-white streetlamps lit a scene of rainy murk. In the *Feathers* rings formed about the yellow lamps, and over there Maureen Parner, barely seen by me, sat on with her fat escort, crossing and uncrossing her plump, shapely, stockinged legs.

Everyone smoked then. About 10.30, only half an hour from closing time, the air was tindery stale and brown. Mick and Steve had got off with a 'couple of birds'. Danny, who was a non-starter, as was I, decided he needed to get home. "Promised I'd mow the lawn tomorrow. My dad always wants it done, right up till November. Mad. It's my last Saturday off and all."

Left alone in the Bacchanalia, I had another half, I'd already swallowed five or six – abruptly it felt like a whole barrel.

And that was when I *did* see her. Maureen.

A lot of people did.

She got up, slung the contents of a full glass of gin and lime in the fat man's face and said, quite loudly and in a very beautiful voice that had a cockney accent, "You rotten bleeder! Well damn you, then. Get lost."

(Maureen's voice was lovely. When I heard her sing to her piano, the songs of Ivor Novello, Cole Porter, The Beatles, she had no trace of any accent. Hers was a clear rich soprano, silvery on the higher notes and plum-lush in the lower register. She'd sung professionally in her early youth. There'd been talk of light opera, the stage. But her husband happened instead. Back then, the late fifties, women's careers often finished at the altar.)

The fat man rose. He wiped his face, swore, and left her. He stalked past my table.

Even then I used to be careful who I stared at, or at whom I stared, mitigating my glances into something more clandestine, so I hoped.

But Maureen Parner merely got to her feet and went into the Ladies.

As for me, my head was now ringing like a bell. I too hoisted my thin frame upright, left most of my drink, and wavered out into the misty night.

I was sitting on the bench by the bus-stop in the main road when she emerged from the *Feathers*. She wasn't drunk. She had spruced up her pale pink lipstick and relacquered her hair – not that I could have worked that out then, she just looked fresh, almost new. She came straight along the pavement and sat down beside me, about a foot away.

"Has it gone?"

"I beg your..."

"The bus. The 176."

"Er, no."

That was my bus, too.

"Thank God," she said. "My watch's stopped. Thought I'd missed it. Then it's only the other one and all round the houses. Get home at midnight."

"Yes."

She faced front. After a minute she opened her bag and took out a packet of cigarettes. She lit one then turned to me. "Sorry, do you smoke?"

"Not – yes."

"Like one?"

I didn't often smoke, it had never got a hold on me, try to let it as I had. And I didn't want one now, I felt saddled enough by booze. But I said, "Thank you."

She let me choose the cigarette, then let me light it from hers. This was very thrilling, strange, disturbing. I could smell her powder and scent. She said, "Don't you speak nicely."

"Er..."

"I suppose everybody bloody saw all that in there."

I said nothing.

She said, "He's an absolute bastard. Don't know why I put up with him so long. And now he's seen someone he likes more than me. Some twenty-one-year-old bloody tart no doubt, miniskirt up her arse and thinks *he's* got some money. Which he hasn't, I could tell her. Worse than my Graham," she added. She had turned again and looked on out into the damp smoke of the night. Across the road cars, the odd last bus, sparkled by; vehicles were scarce now because it was well after 11, and on such roads, in those days, much of the traffic had eased by then.

She had a face that made me look. It wasn't pretty particularly, not beautiful or even very original. But it was a real face, flesh and blood, and with make-up tastefully applied, and she had such a nice smell. And her mouth was... I kept looking at her mouth.

Finally she said in a brisk sensible tone, "This damned bus isn't coming, is it? Cancelled it, the buggers." I had never, then, heard a woman of Maureen's age, (which was actually about thirty-three) swear such a lot. It had a kind of daring to it, a *finesse*. She said, "D'you fancy some fish and chips? There's a place down College Road. Just make it. Come on, you look like you could do with a good meal."

I scrambled up and went after her, frantically going over in my mind how much money I had left in my brand-new wallet. Her high heels clipped along the pavement, and when I got level, she reached across with a weightless gesture and took my arm, as though we had been doing this for months. Only then was I quite sure that I, though so short and she in her heels, was still a good four inches the taller. And that was the moment I felt the rush of desire, the enchantment of relief.

243

There were a few students from the art college outside the chippy, eating. They were just closing up. But when the man saw Maureen he grinned and said, "Got a bit of rock left, darling. Will that do?"

"What about my friend here?" she said. "He's starved."

"I can see he is. What would you like, sir?"

I said, stammering slightly, "Just chips are fine."

"Oh, go on, have a bit of fish, Charlie," said she, inventing a name for me. She leaned across then and kissed me on the cheek, taking my breath away, and in that second she whispered, "I'll pay, darling. Go on. Spoil yourself."

If I had been sober, I'd have lighted the shop with my embarrassed blush. But I wasn't sober, although my head had cleared out on the street. I felt ready for much, of which fish was only a minor challenge.

On my cheekbone, her kiss seemed to have been marked in hot and cold.

She and I both had rock salmon, huss as it's now identified, and bags of chips, all this in newspaper, as then it was, thickly dusted with salt and sloshed with vinegar.

Outside, as we ambled along eating, she said, "Didn't mind me calling you Charlie, did you?"

"No. But my name's Roy."

"Hello, Roy. I'm Maureen. Pleased to meet you."

"Thank you for the fish."

"Don't mention it. Well, I expect we'd better walk. If we hadn't missed the blasted bus, we have now. I cut down by the cemetery. Know the one?"

"Yes."

"Not that that's my place of residence. I leave that to the vampires. I've got a flat over the Co-op."

Knowing approximately where she meant I knew this overshot my own turn-off by about a mile. It didn't trouble me.

"I'll see you home," I said.

"What a gallant feller you are."

It was only when we reached the cemetery, running grey, dim, silent and ominous by the road, that doubt began to creep in on me. What would she expect? Despite all the fantasies and those unencouraging books – did I know – *understand* – enough to be capable?

I needn't have worried.

We reached the side street and the glass-fronted shops, bleak and dark, and an alley and a stone stair that led up to the flats, an L-shaped block two storeys high.

"It's been nice meeting you, Roy."

Was she putting me off?

In terror I leant forward and went to kiss her mouth. And she, adept as a dancer, met me with a peerless grace. We leaned there quite some while, kissing in the shadow of the alley. Then she murmured, "D'you want to come up for a coffee?"

Naturally I did want to. Up we went.

About ten minutes later we were through the bedroom door.

"Where shall we go?" he asked.

It reminded me of a politely eager child, not *too* interested, but *rather* interested. There might, on this boring grown-up excursion, be inclusions of toys and other treats.

I stood and – less confronted – then waited before him. I didn't have any idea what I should do. This in a man of nearly fifty-one is perhaps reprehensible, or contemptible.

Eventually I said, "I think you've made a mistake, Mr Traskul."

"Do you?" He sounded surprised, innocent.

"I don't have a piano," I said.

"No," he replied instantly with his smile, "but you do have a new dustbin."

Beyond the Crescent, traffic whooshed. It would be better to get to the high street. People were more involved with each other round here, not like the milling herds of inner London. Witnesses, even help, might be forthcoming.

I started to walk on and, as I'd anticipated, he fell at once into step with me.

"I had a fascinating journey down," he said.

I said nothing.

He went on airily, striding, the bag swinging on his shoulder full of God knew what. "The train broke down near Lewisham. We sat there for about half an hour. Then crawled. Or I'd have been here much sooner."

I couldn't contain it. I said, "But you were here last night."

"Was I?" He turned the charming smile on me again, I felt it beamed against the side of my face. "Are you sure?" I hadn't been. Now I was. "Of course, despite the slow train, I was here quite early. *Did* you like the dustbin, by the way?"

"I have a dustbin." I thought, *Shut up, don't respond.*

"Well I reckoned you did. But I needed something to put the beer in."

No, I had to speak. I sounded flat and level. "How did you know where I lived?"

He laughed. It was a spontaneous, melodious laugh. "How'd you think?"

And how *did* I think?

For a moment I considered the Web. After all I had a website, Harris had arranged it. And you can find the address of almost anyone now, seemingly, by a strategic search in hyperspace. But he didn't know my name. Or *did* he?

"I haven't any idea."

"Well, try to guess. I shouldn't make it *too* easy for you. I don't think I should."

We passed the last house in the Crescent. Here was the wide road with its cars and bikes, and people on the pavements by the frontages of shops. The crossing twenty feet further on was making its fretful hurry-up beeping, and women with children and shopping crossed both ways at once, in an unwieldy dance.

I halted again. "Mr Traskul..."

Predictably: "Joseph. Not Joe, if possible. We'll come to nicknames later, maybe."

"Mr Traskul, why have you followed me here? Why are you here? What do you want?"

Making my stand in the busy street reminded me immediately of my father meeting me unexpectedly from Chaults, of suddenly extricating myself from the attentions of the bullies with a "Leave me alone!" and hurrying to the shelter of a parent. Later when I explained to him the bullying, he said, regarding me with kindly seriousness, "Now, Roy, I can't always be there. You must learn to stand up for yourself. If they think you're afraid, it won't stop." I was twelve.

He faced me, seeming slightly puzzled.

"I followed you because I got on the train. I'm here to see you. What do I want? Same as former answer: To see you. "

"*Why?*"

"It's a surprise when someone wants to see you, then?"

"A complete stranger. Yes."

"Haven't you *ever* met a complete stranger who wanted to see you again? That's a shame. But there's always a first time."

A police car drove by. I wondered if I should hail it. I didn't. It was gone. No doubt they'd have ignored me in any case.

"I'm not gay," I said. I detest this label, although not the fact of homosexuality.

"Well nor am I, if you're asking. At least I don't think so. You can always get a surprise," he said, (that word *surprise* again). "Mate of mine, couple of years ago, plenty of women, and then one day he finds himself going mad about a guy in the Stock Exchange. I think they're in the South of France, now."

I tried to keep my bearings.

I said quietly and firmly, "I think you should go back to town, Mr Traskul. Thank you for the dustbin and the beer. If I owe you any money for them..."

Now he burst out laughing. "*That'll* look good. You slipping me twenty pound notes."

"I'm not rich. This really won't be worth your efforts to..."

"Well I didn't think you were rich. I'm sorry but you don't *look* rich. I'm not rich either. So, right. Where are we going?"

A woman barging past with a pushchair jarred into me. Joseph Traskul looked at her mildly.

I said, "I can give you the contents of my wallet. And my mobile phone. But it isn't new and probably not your kind of thing."

"But I like all *kinds* of things," he reassuringly told me. I therefore reached into my jacket and he said, "No, I *don't* want your phone. I *have* a phone – *regardez-la!*" And he flipped out of his shoulder bag a steel-blue mobile that might have come on the market that morning. "Tell you what, let's go into that cafe over there. I'm bloody starving. I'll buy you a coffee. We can discuss this. Will that do?"

Something in me gave way. He must have seen it. I said, "If that means we get this sorted out."

"Course we will."

Together we crossed at the shrilly belligerent crossing.

The cafe, which is situated in the bakers and serves fresh-baked bread and every type of English breakfast, welcomed me with the normal cheery "Good morning!" They seemed pleased I was with this nice young man, be he nephew, long-lost son, or rent boy.

We sat down at the far end beyond the coffeemaker.

The girl came over at once.

"Two coffees," he said. He smiled one of his endless variety of smiles, charming her, or playing he charmed her while she, perhaps used to it all, played at being charmed. "And can I have the full English, with wholemeal toast, no butter, and extra fries."

I thought sullenly, *I'll be paying for that, whatever he has said.*

Through my mind, influenced by so many of my plots, flitted the idea I might poison, or at least drug him. But I had nothing suitable on me, the aspirin were at home.

We sat in silence, his companionable, until she put the coffees before us.

"Well," he said then, "what do I call you? If you're nervous just make up a name. But you do know mine."

Is it only that I had been in some ways so rigorously brought up? I remember Lynda once telling me she had often given invented names to unwanted men who pursued her, though how many *had* pursued her was debatable. But my given name is common, and anyway he might know it. How else had he located the house?

"Roy."

"Roy." He rolled it round his tongue. "That means King, doesn't it?"

Did it? Maybe. *Roi*, Roy...

I tried the coffee. It tasted like nothing; usually the coffee was good here. Even so I hoped it could steady me. "Mr..."

"Joseph."

"If you prefer. No one does anything for no reason at all."

"Perhaps they should."

"Are you saying you've come after me like this simply because you thought you *should?*"

He smiled.

I thought, *He is mad. Possibly he's escaped from some lunatic establishment.*

247

Given that premise, I could only humour him.

But what was I to *do* with him?

If he refused to leave me alone, I would have to give him the slip somehow, and then run to the nearest police station. I wracked my brains. Harris might have helped but Janette wouldn't. There was nobody else. I heard again the voice of my helpful father, *If they think you're afraid.*

"All right, then," I said, and smiled at him in turn. "The breakfast here is good. You'll enjoy it."

"Will I?" At once, that ironic edge of danger, of challenge in his voice.

"Well, I hope you will. Why don't you tell me something about you?"

"You first."

A knot of sheer anger was forming in my gut. I ignored it. "Very little to tell, I'm afraid. My wife and I..."

"You're not married," he interjected instantly. It was not a question but a statement.

Jovially I answered, "I'm sorry, Joseph, if you somehow didn't discover that one important item about me. I *am* married."

"Then where is she?"

"She's out this morning. She'll be back for lunch."

"And what's her name?"

"Lynda."

"Right. But she wasn't there last night, was she?"

"How can you possibly know she wasn't, if you weren't here yourself last night? I believe you said you arrived only this morning."

"Actually, I don't think I did say that. Sorry, Roy. I haven't lied. But *you* have, haven't you, saying you have a Lynda."

"Lynda was away last night, staying with her elderly mother. She will be back home later this morning."

"Well I look forward to meeting her."

"No, Joseph, that isn't a good idea. Lynda's mother hasn't been well, and anyway..." inspiration – "my son and his girlfriend will be coming back with her."

Joseph Traskul widened his black glowing eyes and said, "If I didn't know you better, I might *just* believe you."

"But, Joseph, you *don't* know me better."

"Want a bet?"

The girl came up then with the large oval plate piled with breakfast. She laid it all out in front of him, and with the extra chips and toast the table became crowded. I moved my coffee back to make room.

This time he didn't thank her. He had eyes only for the food.

He did seem genuinely extremely hungry. I wondered if he was.

He plunged in knife and fork and began to eat, quite couthly but fast.

"I'll just go and pay. Get it out of the way."

The rhyme now was lost on me.

He murmured, an assent.

I took my chance. I got up, went to the counter and paid the bill, and all the while he never once looked up that I saw.

That done, I turned smartly and went straight out of the door.

Outside a boiling panic filled me. I didn't even look back to see if he was already up too and on my track. Pure luck – the crossing was already working. I ran across. I ran back along the road and into the Crescent.

I am not especially fit, certainly not athletic, but being thin gives me some advantage. I made it all the way through into Old Church Lane and, gasping, along to my gate. Only there did I look behind me. No one now was on my track.

Through the front door I rushed, locked and bolted it.

I checked every window, and the back door. The day was warm again but nothing could be unsealed.

I stood in the hall and picked up the phone. This time I did call 999.

IX
('Untitled': Page 124)

The clock on the ancient tower above the Artisans' Quarter was striking leadenly for midnight, and not a creature, asleep or waking in the great City, did not hear it. Its deadly voice entered dreams, entered reveries and fevers, and bats circling the ruined cathedral on the Hill of Kolosian, combered in a cheeping wave away into the dark. The moon had set. The end of its light had a sombre finality.

Vilmos had left the bed of the whore Shosa. She was quite dead; he had taken care to see to it. Despite the fact he knew she had had little choice, he permitted no woman to betray him.

Her blood had dripped down upon the floor, but by now, an hour after the act of murder, its movement had ceased.

Vilmos washed his hands and face in the basin. The night was very hot and now, as the clanging of the clock came to an end, its ominous weight seemed to increase, heavy as a stone lid upon the City.

No one met him as he descended the stair. From the door the old toothless portress had gone off about some affair of her own.

Outside in the alley no lamps were visible, only the thinnest starlight. Beyond opened the Street of the Silver Workers, and even there only occasionally the narrowest of illuminations was revealed between ill-closed shutters.

Vilmos bent and drew up an empty bottle from the cobbles. With a sudden unpredicted motion, he flung it violently against the darkened window of the tailor, Mirk, who had cheated him.

Thereafter Vilmos did not break into a run. He sauntered on along the thoroughfare, and indeed no one appeared to detain or upbraid him.

It was not until he had got on to the Flavel Bridge that Vilmos once again paused. Here he stayed some while, staring over at the blackness of the wide river, which poured on the northern side down to the City from the far mountains, and westerly swam away towards the port and the sea. There was little traffic on the water at this hour. A solitary boat had anchored about a quarter mile downstream, and a man's shape could be detected standing up in it, perhaps fishing, or at some more sinister task. The nearer bank was thick with houses and hovels of the meaner sort. Directly across the bridge lay some open land, and there Vilmos thought he glimpsed some things moving skittishly. They reminded him of large pale hunting hounds at play.

Then another came from the alleys and walked out on to the bridge towards him. It was Reiner, with his book under his arm.

"What are you doing here, Vilmos? Go home, for God's love."

"And why are *you* here, eh? To read your book?"

"I'm wanted at the Master's house."

"You are, and *I* am not?" Vilmos was astonished and in his arrogance slapped Reiner across the chest.

Reiner jumped back and the book fell to the bridge with a thud. "There's blood on your shirt, Vilmos! What have you done?"

"Amended something."

"You are *mad* – you are *mad...*"

"No, I am very sane tonight. Come, let's go to the Master's house, and ask him if I am not. Do you see those pale things running about over there? What are they, do you think? I believe they are the ghosts of dogs."

FIVE

The policeman I spoke to was the desk sergeant, and as I had predicted he would be, he was. After a brief recital of my fear that I was being pursued for reasons beyond my knowledge, he asked what exactly the young man had done. He listened. He said, "So this stalker..." his term not mine, although at once the word gained a resonance for me, "has followed you from a pub, come to your house, bought you, you say, a *dustbin*," an emphasis there, "and some beer. And you have bought him breakfast."

A short interval ensued.

I was about to speak when the sergeant went on. "Has he actually threatened you in any way, sir?"

I answered truthfully, "Not as such. But he won't leave me alone."

"Is he there now, sir?"

"No."

"Then perhaps he's got bored, sir. Or he's decided the breakfast was enough. It was a big full English, you said. Sounds very nice."

"But what am I to do if he comes back?"

The policeman sighed. His voice altered and became unpleasantly convivial, demonstrating he had absolutely nothing against my sort. "Well, if I was you, sir, I'd pay him off and tell him to get lost before the wife catches him."

I stood, nonplussed by the inevitable inference he had taken.

He ended, "Thank you, sir. Have a nice day."

After the police I tried Harris's number again. This time a perky P.A. answered. She belonged to Janette, of course. Janette was staying at the house in Hampshire while Harris sorted out his father's affairs in Spain. However, right now, Janette wasn't available, could the P.A. assist me? Obviously she could not.

After *this*, I went through an inventory of any person who *might* be able to assist, but as I had decided earlier, there was no one. The few non-business friends I now possess are of the acquaintance variety, and the males among them are my age or older, either skeletal or overweight, with diabetes and heart problems, or simply doddery.

I was on my own. The place I have been most often.

Every ten minutes or so I was going round the house, glancing from windows, out at the street, down at the side path and across the garden (where the dustbin still maintained its sentry post) to the alley to the back. I even scanned the frontal oak trees and the fir at the rear. Joseph Traskul, like Vilmos, seemed quite capable of physical feats, such as climbing up into trees. He must have scaled the back fence after all, toting the bin.

Belatedly I wished I had modernised my security. The locks and bolts and the temperamental burglar alarm were all I had. And I had noticed the alarm hadn't gone off when I let myself back in this morning, though I had fumbled in my haste.

At lunch time I checked the fridge and freezer. I don't eat vast amounts, and I had reasonable provender for a short siege.

I made myself a quick omelette and drank some tap water. I checked my potential armament, which is quite impressive, as in most homes it is, if ever analysed. Years of penning my usual kind of book had taught me quite a lot about what can be utilised, and even to some extent how. But I'm not a violent man. To describe a killing and a death neither excites nor upsets me. But the idea of doing it myself is still as alien to me as the thought of landing in person on the moon. Even so, we recall, men have landed there.

I put a couple of meat knives, a screwdriver, hammer, and a small drill and some other stuff, on the kitchen table, which by now I'd pushed up against the back door. I'd let the blind down over the side window of the kitchen, and stacked up pans in the sink, both to impede an entry and to make a noise. He would have to break the windows anyway. That would be enough.

On the credit side, if I ever felt able to sleep again, I never sleep for long unbrokenly, nor very deeply.

At the other windows on the ground floor I drew other curtains. The lower storey grew dark and menacing.

How long would this go on?

The telephone still worked. I kept testing it. Even if it failed – tampered with in some way – I had topped up the mobile and recharged it only yesterday morning. On the other hand, if I called them again the police might not bother. My sergeant had plainly concluded I was an ageing queer who had had a tiff with his young lover or not properly recompensed a male prostitute. They had more important things to see to.

I made some coffee and having parked the hall table against the front door and laid various bits and pieces by the curtained windows to announce entry, I took myself upstairs.

The computer switched on, I checked for emails. There were none.

I turned to the notes for the new dry little novel. Sat there staring at them. Was I being a complete fool about all this?

The phone in the hall rang at 3.07 p.m. It's handheld, and when I work upstairs I bring it with me. I wondered if the police had decided to contact me and quiz me about wasting police time.

"Hello."

"Hello, Roy." he said.

Christ, his voice, so soon, was entirely unmistakable.

What to say? *Who is this?* Or break the connection. Break it, and unplug the phone?

How had he got the number? He could *not* have got the number unless he had found out my second name. And there was no way on earth he could have. Or maybe there was, that thing about searching the Web – every house shown on some sort of map, every name, even the most obscure, locatable somehow...

I hadn't spoken. So he said, gently, "You're asking yourself how I got this number?"

I swallowed. "Yes. I was."

"Shall I tell you? You really ought to work it out for yourself, Roy, shouldn't you? But then, you still don't grasp how I found your house – or have you deduced that?"

Deduce. He knows me. He knows I write detective stories. Is *that* it? But I write as R.P. Phillips...

"I have," I said stolidly, "been in touch with the police."

"Really?" I could hear his smile, all the way along the wire.

"They suggest..."

"If only you knew, Roy, how pointless all this is, on your part. I have become *interested* in you."

Apparently he too understood the police would think this situation irrelevant. But how could he be sure? Perhaps – had he done this sort of thing before?

"Interested in what way?"

"Well, human interest, you know, Roy. No such thing as a dull person. What is that quote from the German – '*scheinst... And how the dull shine!*' Bernhardt, isn't it? Actually a Jewish philosopher, living in Germany. I'm sure you've heard of him."

"No. "

"There, you see, I could introduce you to his work."

"Tell me how you got the number."

"I'm just round the corner. It's taken me until now to digest that amazing breakfast. I'll be with you in..."

"No. You won't be with me in anything. Stop this now. I've told you about the police."

"Oh. That."

I cut the connection.

I sat there. I was imagining him scrambling ably over the fence, tapping out the window with a hammer and brown paper so it made no appreciable sound. I had never had the windows properly double-glazed. A cat could get in if it really wanted.

I went downstairs, carrying the phone, and with the sharpest of the knives I had previously selected.

From the front window I peered out, between my mother's heavy Dralon curtains.

The day had clouded over, adding to the indoor murk. The blonde woman from across the street, No 73, was standing on her front lawn, staring despairingly at her poodle, which was performing the first syllable of its breed name in the grass.

Could I signal to her? It would be useless. She and I anyway had never exchanged more than a polite grunt.

I waited rigidly for the phone to go again, but it didn't. Nor did he appear.

At this juncture I made a resolution. I pulled the phone plug out.

Instead I tried my mobile. Thank God, no sign of unknown calls, no *private numbers*.

I thought of Harris up to his eyes in Dad's Death, and considered he had, in all the thirty odd years we had known each other, never given me the number of his personal telephone or mobile. Harris too was not a friend. He could, would, do nothing.

I was very angry by now. I was frustrated, jittery, at the end of the proverbial tether.

Probably, I thought, he will get tired of this. And also, if he *has* done this before, perhaps he does have a criminal record. For example, if he had done this to a *woman*, the police would have been far readier to intervene. The name Joseph Traskul – it was much too dramatic. It could well be an invention, and each victim would be offered a different one. I hadn't described him to the police – I don't, in my ordinary fiction, go in for a lot of description, it slows the action down... But I had his letter – handwriting and DNA. I went straight to the kitchen and got that and in that moment the doorbell went.

Naturally I'm not brave. I nearly jumped out of my skin. Which has to be one of the truest analogies ever coined.

The bell went once, then twice, then again and again. And then the letter box flapped up; I could see the slot of light between the table legs of my barricade.

A voice called briskly through to me. "Roy. Are you all right in there? Can you hear me, Roy? Can you answer?"

It wasn't *his* voice.

In the shock of relief I couldn't think for a second *who* the hell it was. Then sense returned and I knew.

"George – yes, hang on." It was my attached neighbour from 72.

"Oh, that's good. You're all right, are you? Only..."

"Hang on, George. *Don't* go away." I got to the door. I was numb with the release of tension.

"But all your front and side windows are blacked out..." George insisted, anxiously harking back to the war years I so wisely missed, "and..."

"I'm fine." I dragged the table away.

George is old, about seventy-nine, eighty maybe. We'd exchanged a few pleasantries, the odd pint of milk or piece of advice on electrics or plumbing. His wife, Vita, once brought me a slice of the delicious cake she'd baked for his seventy-seventh birthday, after I politely cried off the party. But now George, perhaps, was an ally, a character witness. Too old to involve with a stalker, he might still make an impression on the Bill.

As I undid the door, I heard him reassuringly murmur something outside to Vita, saying it was all right, no need to be upset.

And I felt very sorry to have worried them both, these sprightly fragile pensioners. Then I opened the door and there they stood. George, and behind him Vita, with both her hands clasped round the right hand of the man beside her, who was a strained, almost tearful Joseph Traskul.

"Oh, thank God, Dad," he exclaimed. "I really thought this time you were dead!"

SIX

Having raised the blind, he stood in the kitchen, looking at the pans and bottles erected in the sink to bar his entry.

He seemed to take my precautions quite seriously. He appeared to be considering their value, giving them marks out of ten. As if I'd asked his opinion.

Naturally too he had seen the knives. Not the smallest one, however. I'd slipped this some while ago in my trouser pocket. It had a leather cover on it. God knows what it was for or if my parents had ever used it.

Finally he said, "Should I be flattered?"

"You should be somewhere else."

He smiled. He was, is, always smiling. Yet these smiles do not seem to be gratuitous ever. If I were writing this as an invented manuscript, stylistically I would need to edit some of them out. But then I'm not, this isn't a book.

At the front door he had leapt forward and grabbed my shoulders in a sort of abortive hug.

I tried to say to George round the lean, tall back of him, "Call the police, please, George. This man is insane." But George and Vita were beaming and George now had his arm about his wife. Relief, actual joy at our refinding of each other, his and mine, son and father, had made them both take on that look of sheer youth of which only the ageing or the old are ever capable.

They also looked incredibly and alarmingly frail. One swipe from Joseph's arm might snap all their brittle bones in two.

Besides he was already pushing me, friendly and determined, back into my hall, coming in after me. He called over one shoulder as he went, "Thanks so much. *Thank* you both. It's OK now. Don't worry, I've known about these moods of Dad's since I was fifteen. We'll be fine now."

And George gave me a little kind, rather cautious wave, and Joseph shut the door.

I wanted to punch out his lights, as used to be said.

But I'm no fighter in any area, let alone a physical one. He'd only floor me, and any puny blow of mine might make him worse.

He wasn't holding on to me now. I turned and walked briskly on into the kitchen.

He walked behind me, amiably saying, "It's dark down here."

And then there we were, him letting up the blind, calculating the barricade of the kitchen table and my mother's stainless-steel pans in the sink.

"I don't think that would keep anyone out for long."

The verdict. He sounded quite regretful.

"No."

"But then why would they break in?"

I just looked at him.

He turned and sat on the kitchen table. "You haven't got a drink, have you?"

My mind raced. I thought, Yes, ply him with beer from the fridge and then some whisky, get him pissed. It might work. I could powder some aspirin or paracetamol, the ones with codeine, in his later drinks. This might be an answer.

"All right." I said, careful not to seem too eager. "What did you have in mind?"

"Cup of tea?" he winningly asked me.

255

I saw, or thought I did, he was well aware of any other plans I might have. If he had done all this before, presumably things had been attempted.

I filled the kettle from the tap and switched it on. As I was setting out a mug and so on, he said, "You ought to use a filter."

Try to be normal, if reserved. Treat him like a minor annoyance, nothing too much.

"The water here is all right. They replaced the pipes last year."

"Well, I wouldn't trust it, but there."

I wondered if he would have some problem with the tea bags or milk – but he didn't. He didn't want sugar.

When I handed him the mug, he gazed at it, examining it scrupulously. I didn't think he was already checking for attempted drugging. He seemed curious, as one is sometimes about another person's things. This was confirmed.

"I thought you might still use a cup and saucer."

"How do you know I don't?"

"Well I don't know. Maybe you keep mugs for visitors only." He tried the tea. "That's good."

My mother had always stuck to the cup-and-saucer method. After her death my father did too. One of my last most tragic memories of them, before she died, was of her lying in her hospital bed and saying to him sadly, "I do miss my china. Isn't that silly?" A nurse had brought them both a cup of hospital tea. Me too, only I couldn't swallow it.

I wanted only to escape. But I could do nothing to help her except remain at my post, with him. We used to go to the pub when visiting hours ended, or later in an interval when they had extended the visiting hours indefinitely. This is a strange and awful thing. He was with her when she died. Not me. I had had to go to the lavatory. When I came back, he said, "Look, she's sleeping really peacefully now," and I thought he knew, but he believed she *was* asleep. I went and got a nurse, let her tell him. She held his hand while he cried, but he was very quiet, didn't want to distress this kind nurse holding his hand when she was so busy.

That came back to me with a terrible immediacy as I stood there, and Joseph Traskul sat on the table and drank the undrugged tea.

I wanted to kill him in that moment.

The first moment I ever truly wanted that.

I averted my eyes, in case he could read them.

Outside a pigeon had perched again on the black dustbin. It seemed to be inspecting the earlier pigeon dropping. Was it the same pigeon, come back to evaluate its own previous artistry?

I felt tired. I sat in the chair.

He'd finished the tea. He put the mug down on the table and said, "Did you figure it out?"

"What?"

"Any of it. What you were asking me over the phone."

"No."

"But you realise what happened next door?"

"You said you were my son and I was your father, and I had moods during which I drew the curtains in the daytime and – I assume – might be likely to attempt suicide."

"Close enough. I thought a son-father relationship would be more compelling than the uncle-nephew scenario you foisted on me in the pub."

"That was true. You do look a bit like him. Less and less the more I see of you. He wouldn't behave as you have, either." I had decided to keep my army of invented relatives about me.

But he only said, "You don't have a nephew, or if you have you never see him. You don't have a wife."

"I have a wife."

"But she's still away."

"Her mother has been taken to hospital. I'm supposed to go over too."

"But you won't be, will you."

"Won't I? I'm your prisoner, am I?"

I thought he would laugh this off in his inappropriately urbane way, but to my dismay he didn't. As with the pans, he seemed to be considering what I had said. "Are you?" he asked me eventually. "My prisoner? I wonder if you are."

I found I held my breath. I was irrationally relieved when he seemed to gloss it over.

"But we still haven't established how I found you. Shall I let you in on it, Roy?"

"Yes."

"Tell you what. I will spill all the beans in exchange for another mug of tea. By the way, can I use your toilet?"

"It's upstairs, to the right."

Did he glimpse the spurt of possibility in my face?

If he had, it had died even as it arrived. I had nothing to hand. Though I had carried the smallest and sharpest knife upstairs and placed it in my pocket, I had not thought on my return *down*stairs to bring any tablets. Demonstrably, in spite, of my planning, I could never really have reacted to the notion of his being here in the house with me.

He swung gracefully off the table and almost *loped* from the room. I heard him go up.

One frantic moment I rummaged in my mind for anything in drawers or cupboards. But there was nothing. A mostly dried-up bottle of Pepto-Bismol, the remains of some Cabman's Cough Mixture from January, the cod liver oil tablets I occasionally took – I did think of the bleach under the sink. But I shrank from that. It wasn't only cowardice, but the memory of the disbelieving policeman. I could picture the scene, having described it in various books, the body, the mess and bloody vomit. The police would see the evidence of an unfriendly tea party, and conclude I had now poisoned my former lover, malice aforethought.

I therefore simply made him another tea and left it on the table.

Upstairs the cistern sounded.

He came back into the room.

"Impressive," he said. "A bathroom with a loo and a separate loo with a washbasin. Very sensible, if you have more than two people living together. Which you do, of course, Roy. You and Lynda."

"You were going to explain about finding this house."

"I was, wasn't I. Thanks for the tea. Odd," he hesitated a second, looking down into the mug, "has a bit of a funny taste."

He looked right at me, into my eyes. Although I had done nothing, been *able* to do nothing, my gaze quivered. I said firmly, "The milk's probably going off."

"Or you added something to it. *Did* you, Roy?"

"No. "

"Well, I'll soon find out, shan't I?" He drained the mug and slapped it down again.

It seemed to me this too could only be play. He *knew* I had done nothing at all. He would never have drunk it all if he thought otherwise.

He sat again on the table, swung one leg.

"I followed you from the pub in The Strand. Then I gave you my piano tuner card. Then I walked off. Did you look back to make sure I kept going?"

"Yes."

"How many times?"

I couldn't recall. I began to see and saw also, obviously, I hadn't looked back a sufficient number. "Not enough it seems."

"*Not* enough. There were lots of people about to hide me. I just retraced my steps and then went after you again, only more slowly than you, lost in the crowd. You were perfectly followable. When you turned round, we actually passed each other, you never saw it. Then I turned round too. You got to Charing Cross and went in, and soon after onto a platform. Still lots of crowds. The train wasn't in, but the time and destination were on the board. I dutifully purchased a ticket from a very pretty Asian woman, then hung about until the train appeared and you got on. Then I went through the barrier and got on the train too. I had a real fight to do it, I can tell you. The carriage was jam-packed."

"What would you have done if the train had been due to leave and I'd run for it? You couldn't get through the barrier without a ticket."

"Well, I might still have found a way to do that. But it's immaterial. I didn't have to. It was meant to be."

"Then what? You weren't in my carriage."

He looked faintly offended. "Of course not, Roy. I just simply pushed my

258

way to the door and checked you weren't yet getting out. I'm tall, six three, I can see over people. And it became easier as the crowd thinned. I don't lie when I say I guessed the kind of station where you would alight. Not the *exact* station, just the type. And when you did, I got out too. Nothing was further from your thoughts at that time than our encounter. Rather wounding really. You didn't look round once and I, once again, merely took my time. You went out over the forecourt and I fell into step about thirty-five, forty yards behind. If you speeded up, so did I a bit. If you went slowly, I went more slowly still. You didn't look round even when you got out of the high street. Lost in your own little world, eh, Roy? The trees were useful in this street. Just coming into leaf. Shade, sinking light. Camouflage. I watched you open your door and in you went. And then I saw the passage running down a few doors up, the one that leads to the alley."

"Supposing I *had* seen you on the platform when I got off the train?"

"I'd have gone up and said hello."

I thought this was doubtless a fact.

I said, "You were in the alley behind the house. I saw you there."

"That's right. And then that fantastic owl soared over. I thought I'd leave us at that, for then."

"You were here all night. Where did you sleep?"

"There's a pub in the high street does B and B. Not bad actually. Though breakfast wasn't up to much, cereal and cold toast. I hate cold toast. How about you?"

"What about the dustbin?"

"I just bought it in the evening, a whim. There was a sort of bargain place still open, some sort of sale. They sell the beer you drink at the pub, so I got you a bottle of that too. Did you enjoy it?"

"When did you put the bin in the garden?"

"About ten to midnight. The pub goes on after it closes, regular den of vice, booze, weed, other stuff."

I thought, *I was awake at ten to midnight. But I didn't hear you. I had the radio on. I often do. Christ. I lay there and you were outside.* But I'd known that already, hadn't I?

As for the pub, I knew its reputation. It did not exactly provide B and B, even though it would, for cash, put certain people up overnight, no questions asked. I wondered if Joseph were into 'weed' or 'stuff', or both. I didn't ask.

I said, "Very well. And how did you get the phone number?"

"B.T."

"You knew my surname?"

"Not then. But I knew you were called Roy, or you said you were, and your address."

"You can't be given a number without the proper surname."

"I thought that too. So first I tried your other neighbour, Ian, the man with a tea-towel over his arm." He meant the househusband at No 76. "I said,

259

I'm looking for an old friend, short, thin, calls himself Roy Johnston, No 74 Old Church Lane. *Is* this Church Lane? And helpful Ian of the towel said, 'Oh yes, this is the Lane. Only that's Roy Phipps at 74.' And I looked knowing and said, 'Oh, it's *Phipps* he calls himself now?' 'Sure,' said Towelly, looking a bit fazed. I added, slightly uneasy myself, 'But he *does* still call himself Roy, does he?' 'Sure, 'said Ian. I could see he was dying to ask me why you used different names, but I thanked him, and then I said, 'It's really great, I haven't seen him for years. Used to be almost like an uncle when I was a kid. I'll just go and get the beer out of the car.' And off I went to phone you, leaving Mr Towel to marvel as he scrubbed his Cinderellarine dishes."

Had it been so basic? It could have been. At any point the scheme could have come unstuck, but it had not.

One had an impression of the fortuitous. That this Fate had been *written*. As in my dream he had said. But I ceased to believe in God or destiny when I was a teenager. No momentous event dissuaded me. A pity in its way. When subsequent horrors did truly befall me, as most of us they do, I had nothing left to curse or turn my back on.

His use of words had struck me. Was that inevitable for a writer? He was generally grammatical, and where not only with a sort of ironic colloquial concession. And *Cinderella*rine. There was a term to conjure with. But all this was a victim's cotton wool, in which I wrapped my awareness in order to accept the unacceptable. I must be wary, not only of the amiable fiend who sat on my table, but also of myself.

Presently we went into the front room.

That was his suggestion.

He pulled open the curtains and dull evening light revealed the room. I found myself examining it, seeing it through fresh eyes. His? The faded rose-pattern sofa and the two chairs, one of which had been recovered for my parents in a plain rose-colour fabric. The blocked-in fireplace with the electric fire. The wall-to-wall carpet, quite good in its day, but that day was long past. Most of the ornaments were gone. I'd given a lot of things to Oxfam. I'm not keen on clutter, and I hadn't been sentimental over any of them. All except the red glass dog my mother had liked so much. I'd kept that on the shelf above the fireplace, with the clock that still worked, although now on a battery.

Joseph went straight over to the dog. And something in me reared up, surprising me with its feral watchfulness, as my moment of wanting to kill him had not surprised me at all.

"That's unusual. It's quite beautiful, isn't it?" He didn't touch. I was ready to shout, perhaps jump at him. But he gave me no cause. He said, "I like things like that. It's old, is it? Victorian, maybe." Then he sat down in the old-new-covered chair. "Everything's very clean and tidy," he said. "I noticed especially upstairs. You don't strike me as domestic, Roy. Not like Mr Towel."

"I have a cleaner."

"Oh, not your wife, then?"

I swore inwardly. Damn him. *Damn* him, after all that he had tripped me.

I said, "My wife does some of it, but she broke her leg last year. I prefer her not to do too much."

"Oh dear. And now she's at the hospital, waiting for you."

"Yes."

"You think I won't let you go?"

"Will you, Joseph?" I used his name deliberately. But to use it was demoralising to me, as if I were an extreme arachnophobe forced to say *Spider. Spider.*

"Well not just yet perhaps. I want to get to know you a bit more, first. But why don't you call her? Surely she has a mobile? Explain you may be late."

"Use of mobiles is not allowed inside a hospital."

"True. But couldn't you leave a message? She'll check for messages, won't she? No? Well, it's difficult." He seemed concerned. "I wonder what we can do."

It occurred to me it was fruitless to permit more play to him on this. "Forget it," I said. "She'll think I couldn't make it. She'll probably call."

"Probably. And then you can tell her."

"And what do I say, Joseph?"

"An old friend has turned up and detained you. Or I suppose we could both go to the hospital. Would you prefer that?"

"I don't think either Lynda, or her sick mother..."

"I could always wait outside the ward."

"Joseph," I said, "I don't want you to go to the hospital. I don't actually want you in this house, but here you are. Let's keep to that limit, shall we?"

"What if Lynda comes back?"

"She will of course come back, and my son will be with her."

"And your son's girlfriend," Joseph reminded me helpfully.

"Veronica..." the first name I could now lay mental hands on, "may *not* be coming back. Just my wife and son."

"Your son," said Joseph. "What's his name?"

My mind went blank. Then it cleared.

"I called him after my father," I said with warped truth. "William."

"But it's rather strange isn't it, I think so, that your neighbours never mentioned your wife to me?"

"Why should they? You were talking to them about *me.*"

"Well next door, for example. The old couple. I implied you weren't – quite yourself, shall I say. Wouldn't they recommend we try to get hold of her, your nearest and dearest? They might assume, quite reasonably, if I was your son, I was Lynda's son too."

I didn't reply. What could I say?

Joseph smiled.

Abruptly he said, "Why don't you stop calling me Joseph and use my preferred nickname? I made it up myself when I was a child. Sej. Call me Sej."

Something in me pressed me to ask, "Why Sej?"

For a moment he seemed enigmatic, in possession of a secret, the way children are, when they think they know something important you have no idea of. But he answered at once. "Third and fourth letters of my name, with the capital J placed at the end."

To a psychologist this might be revealing. I am not one.

On the shelf by the dog the clock now showed as twenty past 5. He glanced at it. Engaging as a child – again – if not the cunning, demonic child he might – must – have been when a true child he was – Joseph-Sej asked me, "What's for supper?"

I'd forgotten them.

In a way not quite absurd, since I had taken only one, and not gone back for more. *They* were sleeping tablets prescribed by my GP for a particularly bad spell of insomnia three years ago. But that one I took, although I had forgone my nightly single whisky or glass of wine, and I had slept nine hours, made me feel nauseous and rotten for twenty-four hours after. One should flush unwanted medications down the lavatory. Had I meant to? Or had I *known*, on some ridiculous 'magical reality' inner level that, three years after, I might need to have kept hold of them?

They were in the bathroom cabinet, pushed behind the Elastoplast and spare flask of shaving foam. Three years out of date, but they would still have a kick in them. They'd better have. They were all I'd got.

Of course, it occurred to me he might have seen them. Opening up a personal cabinet would be nothing to one like Joseph Sej Traskul. Conceivably he'd taken the Grande Tour of the upper storey and looked in every closed-off place. Then again, these tablets were fairly anonymous, and stuffed behind other items. It seemed to me nothing had been moved.

Preparation was another matter. But as I keep repeating, I write that kind of book. (Which also a police investigation would swiftly dig up. Culpable through prior plotting. At this point I did not care).

Capsules that could be broken would have been easier, but I removed six tablets, and put them in the bath. Then I got in and ground them to powder under the heel of my shoe. Lack of hygiene after all was not a consideration. I kept rubber gloves for my cleaner in a box by the basin. I took one out, scooped up and put the dust of the tablets into the thumb of the glove, tied it off and cut it free with the nail scissors. Into my pocket it went. The rest of the glove I shredded and hid in the heap of socks in the laundry basket. He might investigate there, but perhaps he already had and decidedly it wouldn't be somewhere to search from choice. The last trace of powder I wiped from the bath with toilet paper and then flushed.

Having washed my hands, I left the bathroom and went down.

He hadn't made any objection to my going upstairs. Maybe he kept an eye on the front door. Now he was standing in the doorway of the other downstairs room, reading a book. This used to be a dining-room but for years it's been my library. The book he was reading, or pretending to read, was *Treasure Island*. But he glanced up and said, casually, "You have a lot of novels by R.P. Phillips, don't you? A favourite, is he?"

"Not really. People used to give me copies." Both these sentences were factual.

"Detective novels," said Joseph whom I was to call Sej

I said nothing but walked on into the kitchen.

Opening the freezer, I removed a couple of steaks. I employ the microwave seldom. It had been a present from Harris one Christmas, the only time he had ever given me a present actually. I'd always been slightly perplexed by it, but it had its uses. As now.

The kitchen clock told me it was five to 6. Normally I don't eat until 7, or later.

In my pocket the knife shifted, and the soporific thumb.

He had followed me in and put the book on the table. He watched me, leaning on the units. "Have you read that?"

"What? *Treasure Island*? Yes, two or three times."

"Boys' adventure yarn," he said.

"It's a bit more than that. You ought to try it sometime."

"I have. I couldn't get through it. Perhaps I should try R.P. Phillips instead."

He knew. How the hell – Ah. I recalled the dreary little photo of me, reproduced on one or two editions ten years ago. I hadn't changed that much, only got older.

He said, "You know, you ought to shave your head."

"Really."

"It'd look better. Make you look stronger."

"Oh, I doubt that."

"What are we eating, Daddy?" he asked.

This phrase, his playful tone, made my blood run cold. I thought, *You're having my best Sainsbury's steak and M and S salad and red wine, if I can get you to drink it, with five or six sleeping pills.*

"What you see," I said. "I usually have some wine with dinner. Do you drink wine?"

A smile. "Yes."

"Red OK? It's over there in the cupboard. Glasses next shelf up. Get a couple of bottles. We'll have a glass now. "

"Two bottles. That's lavish."

"I don't often have guests."

If he was wary of this first crack in my armour I wasn't sure, but he lifted two of the three bottles of decentish plonk from the cupboard, and when I handed him the corkscrew he opened one, driving the spike straight in through the cork and the foil wrapper, which is what I usually do myself.

"Just a minute," I said, "before you pour." I got the kitchen scissors and used the serrated part between the handles and blades to slice off the neck of the remaining foil. Lynda had done things like that.

Joseph looked amused.

I said, "Yes, pedantic I know, but sometimes bits of foil go in the wine otherwise."

He poured us a glass each and I let him. I wondered, as I raised mine to my mouth, if he had dropped something in it. But I didn't think so. I had to presume he preferred me awake and on tenterhooks.

The steaks cooked and the salad was on two plates. I put knives and forks and mustard on the table, and some kitchen towel for napkins. Oh, gracious living.

We sat down either side, with the table still pushed up against the kitchen door. He hadn't suggested we move it, nor had I. It would, of course, make any escape that way harder to achieve.

The second bottle of wine stood at the end of the table, with the corkscrew beside it; I'd placed the scissors there too.

He had already consumed glass one of the untainted wine. That was excellent. I remembered how he had been in the pub, downing a double gin or vodka, setting the glass ready for more. I refilled his glass.

"Cheers," I said. I made out my swallows of wine had relaxed me a little. It doesn't take great acting, that sort of thing.

"Well, here's to your books," he said. I knew he didn't mean the library.

"You spotted the photo," I said.

"Couldn't miss it. You haven't changed much. A bit less hair that's all."

I learnt early, about twenty-five, to ride the comments on my galloping baldness.

I said, "I'm not especially proud of them, those books."

"Why's that?"

"Oh – I write them like a kind of machine, to pay the bills. I find them quite interesting when I'm writing them. But afterwards – they're hardly profound literature."

"You set your standards too high," he said. "Don't people buy them?"

"A few. Enough I make a modest living."

He ate eagerly and quickly, but in a mannerly way, just as I'd seen him do with the breakfast.

It had been borne in on me by now he wasn't starved through impoverishment, merely had a healthy appetite. He could afford after all to stay at the dodgy pub, which I had heard wasn't cheap. He could pick up on a mad whim, and follow a man, even buy him a dustbin.

This time he refilled my glass, only half empty, as well as fully topping up his vacant own. I'd have to watch that, when we came to the next bottle.

"Funny your wife hasn't called," he said.

It was time to wax a little mellow. I hoped I had calculated properly, but a move must be made.

"I'd better own up, hadn't I, Sej?"

When I used his purported nickname, I glanced at him to see how he took it, both the name and my 'owning up'.

He looked smug. He might not be a fool, the mad cannot be relied on to be stupid, often the reverse. But he was solipsistic, over-confident – perhaps with good reason.

"So what's the dark secret, Roy?"

"Lynda left me, oh, about seven months ago. That's why my neighbours didn't mention her. As for George and Vita, if they believed you were my son they'd assume you knew, and that perhaps you had some real cause to worry about me, my state of mind. It was after she broke her leg. She met some man at the physiotherapy sessions. I also met him once. A fat chap with a long moustache and mop of hair. He was older than me, too. Nearly sixty. She told me the night she left. I hadn't guessed a thing, but no doubt it wouldn't have mattered. As for my son..." I sighed. I picked up my glass and drained it, and helped myself to more so we could finish the first bottle. "He and I haven't spoken or communicated in any way for years. The last I heard he was in New York."

Startling me, life intruding on fiction, Joseph said, "What about 9/11?"

I stared at my plate, mind racing. Then raised my eyes to him bleakly. "I don't bloody know. We did try to find out, but it was too vague. There were enough unanswered questions for parents who knew their sons were in one of the Twin Towers. I don't think, frankly, William would have been anywhere near. He didn't work, he bummed his way around, in the American sense that is. A waste. My son is a talented artist. He..."

My glass was full, I put it down.

Joseph drained his.

Perfect host, even in sorrow, I looked up and said, "Let's have the other bottle."

Before he could make a move, I reached for and secured it. I sat there holding it on my lap as if I had forgotten what one did to open a bottle.

Joseph said, "Fine by me."

"Yes," I said, "yes."

And I put the bottle down and gripped it between my thighs, pulling the corkscrew and scissors towards me.

The top of the bottle was just below the edge of the table. I sat there again, looking down at it, getting the plastic glove-thumb, unseen, from my pocket. Then I took the scissors and put them to the neck of the bottle, then took them off again and lowered them against the thumb on my knee.

"Sorry, Sej. Just give me a minute. The trouble is," I looked up piteously, "you do remind me of him – not any nephew, my son. He took after Lynda. Dark, good-looking..." How flattered she should have been, the real Lynda, dowdy little thing with her flat brown hair.

265

But he waited. Although he looked quizzical, I had bought just enough time. I snipped the top from the thumb, a tiny slice, meaningless to the uneducated eye.

Then I worked the serration of the scissors on around the bottleneck, got off the foil, replaced the scissors on the table and drove in the screw.

I did this efficiently, only blinking as if tears were in my eyes.

My hands were rock steady. They amazed me. My legs, gripping the bottle, were starting to shake.

The cork came out. Then, the final pass. I let the bottle seem to come loose, let it go down as if falling, gripping tighter with my legs while I grabbed for it with my right hand, now well below the table top. And crushed the contents of the thumb into its open mouth.

'Rescuing' the bottle I was able to give it a mixing shake. I plumped it back on the table with a grimace of triumphant misery. Fumbling for a non-existent handkerchief in my pocket, I restored the now-voided thumb.

Then I reached for my paper-towel napkin and wiped my face.

"Sorry. Didn't mean to get emotional."

"You need another drink."

"I don't normally drink much." I leaned over and sloshed the drugged red into his glass. Then I drank some of my own, left from the first pure bottle. I held the glass in my hand, keeping tabs on it now. I stared into it, and watched, distorted in its side, Joseph Traskul aka Sej gulp down half his new wine.

I played with the last of my steak, pushed it around with my fork.

"No. I can't eat any more."

He smiled. "I'll have it."

"Yes, if you don't mind. I hate wasting food."

"You look very pale," he said to me as he picked up the remains of the steak and neatly ate it with his fingers, dipping it in the mustard.

"Yes."

"Well don't worry, Roy. I'm not your son."

"I know that very well, Sej."

"For one thing," he said, wiping his hands, "I don't intend to leave you."

The shock of that, even in these circumstances, thrilled me with horror, as Poe might have said.

But I drank some of my wine and answered, "I don't see how you can have any interest in me at all."

"You'd be surprised."

He drained the glass once more.

How much of the powder had been in it? Had it dissolved properly? Had it all sunk to the bottom? So far, he seemed unaffected.

I tried to recollect how long that one tablet I'd taken had needed to become effective. About ten minutes, I thought. And that had been without the addition of four or five glasses of wine, besides anything else he might have had during the day. But he must drink more. I had to be certain.

Wonderful. He took the bottle and refilled his glass. Less wonderful, he leaned towards me to top up mine.

I snatched it back.

"No thanks, Sej. I don't like mixing two different bottles in one glass. It can spoil the taste, even with cheap booze."

"What an old fusspot you are," he said, as my father might have said it, if not about this. "No wonder Lynda got fed up and took off with that walrus."

His tactless cruelty, if the tale I'd told him had been true, was predictable. But I smiled and agreed. "He was like a bloody walrus. You're right."

He was drinking the wine.

He said, "You're right too. This bottle isn't as good as the first. Bit chalky." Did he guess?

I didn't react except to say, "Perhaps it's off. Shall I open the other one? That's all I've got." Say No, say No, this one is fine.

"You try it, see what you think," he said. And he held out his glass straight across the table to me.

He knew. He knew or he suspected.

I reached over and took the glass and held it to my face and sniffed the wine. There was no suspect smell.

"It smells all right." I would have to taste it now, my God it had enough in it surely potentially to stupefy me, just one sip. But sip it I would have to. I put it to my lips and exactly then his head dropped forward, sudden, without any intent or control. He was asleep, unconscious. The lacuna lasted two seconds and then he raised his head and I observed, licking my lips, "It tastes all right to me. Not the best bottle I've ever drunk, but few of them are."

Did he realise what had happened? He seemed not to. His eyes were heavy but he thought himself apparently only a little pissed.

"Give it here," he said. And he took the glass back, now unsteadily, and once again he swallowed the lot. Refilled it, drank.

I said, "Let's have some cheese, shall we? Only cheddar, but I've got some biscuits..." I stood up slowly. I said, joking, "I'm afraid I'm a bit drunk. I don't usually have that much at one go."

I watched as his head dropped again, then again sluggishly rose. "Me too," he said distantly. "I keep falling asleep."

"I just did," I said. "Maybe we should skip the cheese. There's a camp-bed upstairs. I'm told it's not uncomfortable. Will that do? Maybe we should both get some..."

His head surged down again. Stayed down. His hair curtained his face.

I could hear his breathing, heavy and slow, loud and solid as thick wet steam hissing through a vent.

How much had he drunk? I took the bottle and inspected it. About three large glasses were gone. Just a couple of mouthfuls left in his glass. That should be enough, shouldn't it? Enough to knock him out for several hours, and not enough to kill him.

XI
('UNTITLED': PAGE 163)

Black worms slide through
A needle's eye.
Slick with shattered gold

The crooked stair led up to a lofty attic of the house. As they climbed it a rat scratched enviously in the wall, and water dripped; the Master's house stood close to the river.

The general assembly had already gathered.

In the uncertain candlelight, Vilmos saw many faces he knew and besides, as sometimes happened, a couple of persons quite unknown to him. All would be sworn to the secrecy of the Order. Some would still gossip. There had been the occasional tale of events befalling one or two of these traitors. Whatever else, they never returned to the Master's house.

Reiner pushed through the throng.

"What will happen, Makary?"

"Who knows?" Makary shrugged. "There has been a summons. Here we are."

"How did his summons find you?"

"At the *Tavern of the Golden Grapes*. A boy brought it." Makary said to Vilmos, "Look at you, you disgrace. Your shirt's dirty. Is it wine or blood?"

"Blood. I fell down and cut myself."

None of the men in the room had donned the ritual robes brought out for particular meetings. None of the rare incenses burned. This anyway was not the Chamber of Revelation. That lay behind a hidden door far down in the creaking, river-damp timber warren of the house.

Vilmos said, "No summons was sent to me. Why do you think that was?"

Makary said, "The Master's messenger failed to find you. You're elusive."

"Or have I been excluded from our fine fraternity?"

"That's not for me to say."

Makary turned his back on the poet, went to a long wooden table and took up one of the greenish glass goblets, ready-brimmed with an oil yellow wine.

Vilmos also took one of these. He raised it to his lips, while his mind went on with its inner task.

And she lies red among the lilies
Of her sullen sheets,
Her sapphire soul hung wry-necked from a beam.

A dark curtain shifted. The Master had entered the attic, and deep silence filled the air like river fog.

Slowly raising his right hand as if at first, priestlike, to bless the company, the Master pointed directly at Vilmos.

"Step forward."

"I?"

"None other."

Vilmos smiled and swung, seemingly carelessly, through the crowd of men, which drew back from him, staring with all its eyes.

"I present myself, Master."

"Take this," said the Master. He extended his left hand, and now held before the poet a broken shard of stannum tin – whose original source or purpose was no longer apparent.

Vilmos accepted the object.

He found it very cold to the touch. The contact reminded him instantly of some memory he believed he had never accrued, concerning a garden by night, with vines crossing an arbour and white stars far beyond.

"Lean closer," said the Master.

Vilmos obeyed.

The old man's bearded mouth approached his ear and the Master whispered solemnly, without emotion or any energy, "You are accursed. The Arch Beast, Satan himself, has singled you out. Take yourself away now. In one hour, return. Come to the little side door above the river. You will be granted admittance. Ask nothing. Go. Return."

SEVEN

Her flat was the smallest I've ever seen in my life. It was the flat of a doll.

One entered and was in a narrow hall, that angled left in front of a red and white kitchen about twelve feet by six, and on to a sitting-room about twelve by nine. To the left at the start of the corridor was first a bathroom and then a bedroom, also both very small. The bedroom window, since her flat lay at the end of the block, ran ceiling to floor and looked out on the concrete hind roof of the Co-op, and the iron stairway from the flats above. She too had nets.

The oddest thing in the flat was the wallpaper. It had been there, Maureen assumed, for about twenty years, and was autographed with various blotches and scrapes, but in the hall, sitting-room and bedroom, it was all virtually the same: a tiny pattern of French *fleur-de-lys*, orange in the hall, dove-grey in the front room, pale blue in the bedroom.

Maureen didn't work for the Co-op. A friend had found her the flat; a male friend, I believe. She worked in Woolwich at Fernes, on the lingerie counter. My mother had been used to shop at Fernes. I think I'd been in the shop too, although perhaps obviously not in Maureen's section.

Aside from the bedroom I came to know the flat quite well. Sometimes on my day off in the week, she would have her half day. We would eat lunch in her kitchen and spend the afternoon in bed, eat supper, or make toast off the gas fire in the front room, watch TV, kiss and cuddle and drink gin. Have an early night.

The piano was in the front room too. That is where I heard her play and sing. I will admit, the first occasion she announced she'd play to me, I had been rather concerned.

As I've said, my father was an all right if not inspiring pianist. As for any singing, I had had at least one grim experience of the impromptu turns of friends in pubs, when a piano was present. It was pretty awful, if not much worse than the fiascos perpetrated by modern karaoke.

So when Maureen sat down and skimmed off a piece of Debussy, flawlessly, beautifully, my already engaged heart lifted like a kite.

She didn't sing to me until I'd known her nearly two months. When I heard her voice I wished I had been able to marry her, was worthy of marrying her. This is a fact. But then, I was young.

I was never in love with Maureen. But did I love her? I believe so.

And sex with her was what sex should be.

She enjoyed sex for its own sake. She made no secret of that. She'd picked me up that night because the fat man, to whom she referred only as that bugger Reg, had let her down. She said I had 'Something' she liked, something she 'took to'. But if I am scrupulously honest, I must suppose 'anything in trousers', i.e. reasonably OK and equipped with male genitals plus a will to use them, would have done. But she was kind, too. She once said to me she had never had a kid and I cheered her up, not that I, she hastened to add, was in any way like a kid to her, but my youth she valued. "Keeps me young," she said, "being with you young ones."

She had a lovely body. Not anything like any model girls, heaven forbid, all tightness and bones. Maureen was – voluptuous, I think is the best expression. She was like a day of full summer.

On the mantelpiece over the gas fire in the twelve by nine front room were a few photographs in frames. One of these was of a fair-haired, good-looking man in his twenties, with an unmistakable Maureen, then about twenty too, on his arm.

"That's Graham," she said. "My ex."

They had married when she was eighteen. He was a steelworker and brought home a good pay packet. She hadn't had to work and had devoted herself to tending the home. But they had wanted children, or had thought they did, and none came along. In the end Graham started on a succession of affairs. She put up with this, she said, because he still brought the pay packet in and slept regularly with her. This was during the miraculous sixties, when sexually transmittable diseases were both less known or, if they occurred, no longer lethal, and well before the universal phantom of AIDS. But it made her unhappy, of course, and in the end the last straw floated on to the camel's back. "Carol," Maureen said. Carol was the last straw. They lived in Charlton by then. Carol had lived six doors down, husbandless, childless, mindless, and red-haired. Carol had a russet aura that she displayed regularly to randy Graham, along with endless faulty lights and fridges he could repair, and a lot of flesh. "She just," said Maureen, "kept on smouldering at him till in the end he caught fire."

Maureen was capable of interesting phrases like this one. I confess to storing many of them in a corner of my mind and using them years later in my work. I'm not sure I could have invented word choices of such significance.

Anyway, inevitably Graham left with Carol, while Maureen was left with all the bills and the unpaid rent. Somehow she picked up her life and reassembled it. I once asked her why she kept his photograph. "Same reason I keep my wedding ring, Charlie," (she still sometimes called me that), "part of my life. My life. Don't throw the baby out with the water, eh?"

Now she lived over the Co-op and I came to call on her once or twice a week.

She had other callers. I didn't and don't deceive myself. Again, in that era, there wasn't much physical danger that any of us knew of. If danger for the heart, we risked it, one and all.

Maureen encouraged me too with my writing. My parents had never taken any interest: I 'scribbled'. They didn't mind so long as I had a proper job. Actually I am unfair to my mother here. Left to herself I think she might have been not unapproving, in a careful sort of way. If it was my hobby, she would perhaps have congratulated me as she had my piano efforts earlier. "That's nice, Roy." But naturally my mother followed my father's example. People at work I could never have spoken to. There were enough books on the groaning library shelves, no one needed any more written by such as Roy Phipps.

But Maureen was keen to know. She used to get me to read her what I'd done. She would sit spellbound – to this moment I really believe she was – gazing at me, devouring every word with her ears, eyes, and her forthright intelligence.

"Roy – I was on the edge of my seat. Send it – look, I found this magazine advertised in the paper – try them. That really gave me the shivers."

And I would duly send, and duly get back the soulless rejection slip, and Maureen would say, "What do they know? You're brilliant. You'll be another Ellery Queen one day, you'll see. Then they can eat their Y-fronts."

Love. Yes, I loved Maureen. In memory I still do. She was my good angel perhaps. Just as he, Sej, must be the bad one.

The first thing I did was haul him off the chair and away from the table. I laid him out on the floor in the recovery position elaborated in so many diary-backs. He was snoring thickly by then.

I had had a set ideal of what must be done and how I must operate afterwards. I hadn't had space to plan beyond it. I couldn't now.

For one thing I had no real notion of how long he might be out.

My success in overcoming him still... disturbed me. He had been omnipotent one minute, and now there he lay, at my mercy. I could kill him easily. I saw that. Perhaps I had anyway, but I didn't really think so. He was young and fit, big and strong. He would get over it.

I keep all my important personal documents in a folder in the study, another 'fussy' habit of my father's, rather a good one. (He it was, on the rare celebrations when he drank it, who never liked to mix two bottles of wine in one glass, even the same wine. To me, although I never bothered to adhere to the practice before tonight, this seems to demonstrate a certain common sense. Bottles vary.)

My overnight bag came down from the top of the wardrobe.

I put in what I might need for three or four nights, the ordinary paraphernalia – pants, socks, shirts, toothbrush, shaving kit and so on. Any spare cash I drew from the box. There was only seventy pounds, but I had my cards. My passport and birth-certificate I took, and bank and building society details, including the deeds to the house. Cheque books and other financial extras were added, even the used stubs of cheques and payments to me. I wanted nothing left that he could find.

I don't keep personal letters, the very few I receive. Business emails were mundane enough but too I always delete those. Like several of my species, that is the well over forty-fives, I avoid buying or paying on the net.

From the desk top drawer, I took up any discs I'd burned relevant to my work. Among these naturally was the great lumbering tome *Untitled,* plus the notes for the latest 'project'. Despite abandoning my house to God knew what, I selected none of my published books. There was only one I had ever been at all fond of, in retrospect, *Last Orders*, and that was still in print.

Then I set the computer to wipe all remaining data.

I employ passwords for every file, but nevertheless I was taking no chances.

As I've said, I'd had no plan beyond my plan. It might all have gone wrong anyway and never reached this stage, since he might have caught me out putting the sedatives in the wine and beaten me up, or worse.

Last prudent thought, I went next door to the bedroom again and took a sweater and a jacket. After that I went out and locked the bedroom door. It had had a key ever since I was thirteen, a perceptive unique act of politesse on the part of my parents. But anyone could break down a door, and anyway there was nothing there of any import. The study, with the buzz of complete deletion going on, I left open. I had everything from there either valuable or pertinent to my life. I turned all the lights off and pulled every plug, except that of the machine. Downstairs the same.

In the kitchen my guest snored on. He was quieter now. In sleep he didn't look distressed. He looked very young, softer. Perhaps I'd misjudged his age from his streetwise bolshiness, his very insanity. He could be under thirty even.

Scrupulously I emptied the last wine in the sink and rinsed out the glasses and both bottles and then slung the latter in the bin. I'd previously swilled the remaining sleeping pills down the lavatory; they were well on their way to pollute the sea by now. ("No, officer. He just collapsed, quite suddenly. Perhaps he'd had something before he came here. He did drink a lot of wine. At least six glasses.")

I disconnected the fridge and freezer next. The food, what there was of it, would doubtless go off quite quickly.

I took the sandwich bag from the drawer that contained his note and added to it the fork he'd used at dinner.

Once I had turned out the kitchen light and the outside light, I picked up my holdall and checked my mobile was in my jacket pocket, which it was. Then, in the hall, I ripped the cord out of the telephone and smashed the receiver on the wall twice.

Going from the house on to the front path I paused a moment, looking up and down. The curtains of 73 were drawn, a rosy pink. Elsewhere I could see the steely flicker of TV screens and, in upper rooms, computers. Outside No 80 the man with the paunch who smoked cigars was indulging in one, and animatedly discussing something with the man with the paunch from No 82, whose wife had made him dig and line the lily pond.

They paid no attention to me. I could hear traffic along the high street, and further off a distant train.

I shut the door but did not double-lock it.

In one of the budding oak trees something stirred, or seemed to. Nothing was visible, even in the denuding glare of the streetlamps.

Turning away, I walked towards the Crescent, and the station.

The Belmont is one of those smaller hotels and lies in the back-doubles behind Langham Place. It had quite a bit of gilt, and mirrors in the lifts, and jazzy carpets that to tired eyes resemble a dropped jigsaw, but it was very comfortable. I had stayed there quite a few times after various obligatory publishing do's. Now and then a particularly flush publisher had even covered my expenses there, although never, it had always been stressed, my bar bill. But my bar bills normally amount only to a glass or two of wine and perhaps a whisky; I'm so far able to pay them myself.

They remembered me at reception. I'd been lucky, for at this time of year usually they're full up.

"Two nights, Mr Phipps?"

"It may be three. I'm not sure at present."

The smiling girl said she'd make a note, but regretfully cautioned me she might have to move me to another room for the third night.

It was about 9.45 by the foyer clock. My watch said ten to ten.

When I got upstairs to the small alien luxury of the en suite room, smelling of floral cleaning fluids and regularly hoovered dust, I sat down on the bed and let everything hit me like a collapsing wall.

To my appalled distaste I even cried for a moment. But that passed. Then I took out the whisky I had also put in my bag and had a couple of swigs. I'd done what I must. I'd escaped. Now there was time to think. And think I would bloody have to.

EIGHT

"Janette. I apologise for calling so early."

"Eight o'clock? That's nothing for me, Roy, I can assure you. I'm up with the lark. What is it you want?"

Though rather a good-looking woman, she has an ugly, unmusical voice, Janette, which its university-trained accent only emphasised.

"Would it be possible to put me in touch with Harris?"

"'Fraid not, Roy. Didn't you know, his father died? He's had to go over there, and I gather there are some complications."

"Yes, he did tell me something about it."

"Veronica," said Janette. "The widow."

"Yes, so I..."

"I really cannot comprehend," expatiated Janette, "how a young woman with so much money of her own can behave in such a peculiar way."

"It must be difficult. But I'm afraid – I have a bit of an emergency on my hands. Or I wouldn't be troubling you."

"Oh, yes." The ugly over-polished voice was now noncommittal. It said quite plainly without words, 'It's no use at all your telling me or asking me anything. I am not going to respond.'

I took a deep breath and said, "My life may be in danger."

"Good Lord!" She actually laughed. But I had heard and seen her erupt into this type of laughter once before. On that occasion someone at a dinner party had just spoken of finding her dog dead behind a hedge. But while I had, that time, stared at Janette, the friend with the deceased dog had also loudly laughed. "Poor old hound," had laughed Janette. Would she now say something similar to me? No, it transpired not. "Are you ill?" she snapped with what seemed a kind of anger.

"No. It's nothing like that. I'm being – stalked."

"Stalked!" She almost hooted now. "You? Roy? Seriously? Who by for heaven's sake?"

Before I had called this time, I had known any chance of help was slender. Even Harris would probably prove useless. But I had made a mental list of avenues to try and this was the first.

"Please listen, Janette."

"You sound like a schoolteacher, Roy. Do rein it in."

"I'm sorry. But when you speak to Harris – I assume you do speak to him now and then in Spain? – would you please ask him if he could call me, if at all possible? I'm staying at *The Belmont* in Prince Henry Court."

"You want him to call you in London? From Spain? Oh really, Roy."

"I stress I wouldn't bother him unless..."

"All right. There. I've noted it down." She read back to me the alleged note in a tone that managed to be both scornfully amused and irritatedly impatient: "Roy – serious emergency – call at *Belmont Hotel*. There you are."

I thanked her wanting to throttle her and put down the phone.

Tish Ackrington, my most recent editor with the White Knife Imprint, took my call immediately.

"Hello there, Roy. Your book's doing awfully well! Really great reviews. Did we send you any? Oh dear, that's too bad. I'll get someone to. What are you up to now? Anything on your little screen we might be interested in?"

Tish was always like this. She seemed to want to cheer you up, promising things, exaggerating. I had been fooled at first, but after the initial contract nothing else ever materialised. I had once tested her with the name of an invented novel White Knife had supposedly already published, which of course they couldn't have. And she had acquiesced gleefully, "Super book! Stayed up all night with that one, couldn't put it down." However. At one of those aforementioned parties, this one organised by WKI, I had heard something about her which might now prove useful.

"The thing is, Tish, I'm doing some research in a certain area and I can't get hold of what I need."

"Oh, that's so tiresome for a writer, isn't it?"

"It's holding the book up rather. It's for quite a big house..." I named the firm, who were only less likely ever to publish anything of mine than to jump collectively from the top windows of their tall chrome building overlooking Hyde Park.

"Wow," said Tish, suitably impressed. "But can't they help you with this research, Roy?"

"Wouldn't you know it, my editor there is on holiday in Egypt for six weeks."

"Oh God. Well, Roy, if there's anything..."

"It's just that I do once recall your mentioning you had a friend, who knew someone who was a little bit on the shady side of the law."

A shocked silence. Naturally Tish had never confided this to me of all people. But she had confided it to someone, as it had been discussed as a fact by two or three fairly sober employees at the party. I could hear her now running a scanner over her memory, trying to find out how or why she had ever let slip such a matter to me.

Finally she said, in rather a different way, "Well actually, Roy, my friend – she doesn't see him now. He was rather – well, rather kinky, if you know what I mean." I didn't and was glad I didn't. She said, "Not the sort of person anyway you'd ever want..."

"It was just for some background. Obviously, I'd be happy to pay him a fee."

"Well I don't think – I mean, I really can't help you. Sorry. Oh Merlin!" she screamed, nearly deafening me. Either her Arthurianly named male PA had come in, or she was pretending that he had. "Roy – forgive me – Merlin's in a panic. I have to deal with something – big flap. Super to chat. We must do drinks sometime. By-ee."

I tried a few others. Before I could even get on to the act of confession, that was only about three sentences into a conversation, they put me off. Only Lewis Rybourne, my most recent editor at Gates, astonished me by saying, "Don't have a second now, but I'll give you a call next couple of days, Roy. You're at *The Belmont*, right? Talk soon." He might even do this. But also even one more day might be too late. I ordered room service breakfast, tried to eat it, and started in on my gallery of ageing friends, hoping at least for advice, some ideas.

Stanley had had another heart attack. He was 'all right, doing really well', but still in the general hospital. Matthew was divorcing Sylvia after thirty years of marriage. He was terribly distressed, and we had a longish conversation, while the hotel phone bill mounted to frightening proportions, "She's had a lover," he kept saying, "a lover, Roy." And I thought of the fictitious affair of my fictitious version of Lynda. Ed Erskine was drinking again. He told me candidly he never started until 12 noon on the dot. "What else've I bloody got, Roy, eh?"

The immortal, if unvocalised line, I have troubles of my own, drove me slowly back towards my starting point.

I went out for lunch. I walked round by Lang Gardens and into Langham Place, passed the Art Deco facade of Broadcasting House, and negotiated busy Oxford Street.

What a change there had been in London over the years. Elegant places had become squalid, abominations had been done up like *The Ritz*. By night liquid bars of coloured light washed everything to a succulent epic panoply, and from Westminster Bridge the city resembled, at least to me, the cover of a 1950s Science Fiction magazine.

I ate at the *Pasta Post*. Or I tried to.

Years ago, someone ritually would have asked, "Everything all right, sir?" But now they merely scooped up the nearly full plate, bore it off, and offered me the ice-cream menu.

It was as I was leaving the restaurant that I stopped, petrified, and so abruptly a young man banged into me and with the scathing aristocratic stare of Black Africa, drew aside and stalked on.

I had recalled something after all that I had forgotten and left behind in my house in Old Church Lane, to the debatable mercies of Joseph Traskul Sej. The red glass dog my mother had loved.

Needless to say, that second night I couldn't sleep. Nor had I, the night before.

Coming in again I told reception I did indeed want the room for three nights, and they told me, as if I must rejoice, there would be no requirement that I move to another one.

So I rejoiced that I was not required to move. At least sufficiently that they seemed gratified. For even the most superficial overlay sometimes means far more than we know.

Through the hours of the night I absorbed, through my portable radio, the turmoil of the world. I fell asleep near dawn and dreamed I was standing on a London bridge, I'm unsure which – perhaps a compendium of them all. No one was with me. The bridge was totally empty, and the river below, the roads beyond, devoid of all traffic. The lights of London glittered all about and there were many eccentric new buildings; one I recall looked like an apple made of windows, with a tall stalk lit palest gold.

During the time I stood there in my dream I anticipated the arrival of someone – something – I refused to look over my shoulder to see if it had yet come.

Waking fuddled about 5.50, the thin light struggling to penetrate the protective *Belmont* drapes, I thought instantly of Coleridge's Ancient Mariner, quoted in M.R. James's Casting the Runes;

'Like one, that on a lonesome road, Doth walk in fear and dread, And having once turned round walks on, and turns no more his head; Because he knows a frightful fiend Doth close behind him tread.'

NINE

Showered, shaved and dressed I went down to breakfast the next day. I had decided this would do me good. I forced eggs, bacon and mushrooms down my throat and drank several cups of coffee.

I had made another decision. I was going to the nearest London police station. I was going to tell them everything and make them listen. I would not mention the drugs I had given him, even so. Hopefully he wasn't dead, and so no post-mortem would reveal their presence or their type.

But was he dead?

Was it just conceivable he was? What, then?

He would be lying on the kitchen floor of my house, gradually decomposing, as so many had in so many abodes during my lurid tales. Who would believe I'd had nothing to do with it?

I went back upstairs to my room, leaving the Do Not Disturb light on. I thought through all of it carefully. It was very incriminating, but there would have to be some get-out. I was nearly an old man. And I had no record of violence. I wasn't gay, had no record of that either. I paid my bloody rates and taxes... A model citizen, Roy Phipps. Never trust the quiet ones.

At 12 noon on the dot, as Ed would have exclaimed, I got up and went down to the hotel bar.

It was another sunny day. Some Americans without apparently a care on earth, were sitting laughing in a corner booth, drinking colas and what I took to be screwdrivers.

A smart woman and man, who looked what one used to call European, were consulting a street map in the corner of a maroon velvet banquette.

"What can I get you, sir?"

I asked for a whisky and soda and hastily added, "No ice, thanks."

The man came back with the whisky as specified and set it on a small white mat.

I looked at that, then into my drink. I was going the same way as Ed. What else had I got?

Raising my glass, I drank a healthy swallow, and then gazed through the green and brown bottles along the bar into the shadowy mirror on the wall. You could see the foyer reflected there, a surge of incoming people, luggage on trolleys, a giggling blonde in her fifties, and Joseph Traskul, seated idly and relaxed, in a chair beside a potted palm.

3

It hid a cupboard, the door to the right.

Opened, that revealed an electricity meter, a plastic bucket and a tattered broom leaning sidelong in space. On a wooden shelf were two large boxes of matches, an empty milk bottle from the past, with a candle stuck in it, a London telephone directory with its cover off, a broken terracotta flowerpot.

These things looked to me like the accumulated and forgotten detritus of many occupancies. Even the matchboxes were void when I inspected them.

I had put on plastic gloves by then. The rest of my DNA would have to take its chance. I have never been fingerprinted. I have no form. And today anyway, I wasn't really myself.

The other door, to the left, gave on a not unspacious room, probably about fifteen feet square. To the left side a single step went up into an open plan kitchenette.

There was a lot of light in the room, from two front windows, and from the kitchen itself, which had two side windows plus a closed, locked and keyless clear glass door, that led on to a balcony above the street.

A door to the right of the main room showed a narrow corridor, off which lay a bathroom with a suite of an intense murky brown, a bedroom, and a further, narrower enclosure that must be intended as a spare room. These three rooms had back windows only.

Outside the bedroom was a fire-escape, and below the brief back gardens of the terrace, some beautified with small trees and plants in pots, others, like this one, left to weeds and ragged grass.

After I had gone through the whole flat, I returned to the main area, and stared about again.

The walls throughout had been painted white. That must have been at least five years ago. Nothing shows dirt, as my mother had been used to say, like pale things.

The radiators, also painted white, had streaks of metal striped through.

Nowhere was there any carpet. The floors were bare boards. The kitchen space had been tiled but the tiles were cracked, and some loose, coming up as one trod on them. On the electric cooker something had spilled long ago and, over years perhaps, been regularly baked into a sort of laminate. The once trendy units were without pans or tableware.

I found one overhead bulb with a shade. This was in the bedroom. I assumed it *was* the bedroom because there was a bed in it, a meagre double, with a pillow having no pillowcase. There were no sheets or covers. The mattress was nude as the floors.

Each of the windows however had a single flimsy curtain, wrapped over the quaint, old-fashioned, now intermittently fashionable rails above. These unhemmed strips of material, could – supposedly – be dragged partly across to offer some privacy.

In the bathroom there was a water glass, the kind one can pick up anywhere. Nothing rested in the glass, or anywhere else. A wall cabinet, a fixture maybe, was vacant but for a dead moth.

Here and there about the flat I found other small corpses, a beetle, a couple of flies, some spiders in sagging webs that had died most likely of starvation. On the windowsill of the spare room a dead leaf. My knowledge of flora is limited, but it seemed to have fallen from a tree that had once been a flaming red. But it had curled together and lost almost all its tint.

By the lavatory in the bathroom lay the single page of a book.

I picked it up at once, put on the glasses I need now for small print, and tried to read the words. But not only was it in a language I failed to recognise, but the Cyrillic alphabet. Russian?

There was a doughy odour everywhere of neglect and inanition – a word I use only because no editor will ever demand that I excise it.

Throughout the whole of the flat, at least during my first investigation, this was the sum of all I found. There was absolutely nothing concrete that indicated anyone still lived there, came from there, might go back there. Nothing of any sort.

XII
('UNTITLED': PAGE 191)

Vilmos was aware that the headache, to which he was often subject, was returning. Since the age of ten he had been its victim, and with the years it had increased its attendance on him. Now it arrived so frequently it seemed in fact it was his constant condition, the days without it being the curiosities. But too, strangely, when he *was* without the headache he quickly forgot it, being always filled by a ghastly shock on its reviving, and a sickened dread.

The pain invariably commenced with a stiffening of his neck muscles to the left side. Soon a burning tension began to fill his skull. Next there was the sensation of a shrill white violin string, tightening and tightening on an unseen peg, between the base of his skull and his left temple. Central to these two junctures, about the region of the parietal lobe, a large and fiery black nail began to be hammered through into his brain.

In youth he had wrenched clumps of his hair out of his head to mitigate this agony with another. Older, he had recourse to alcohol and opiates, which dulled the anguish but could not dispel it. It never lasted less than five hours nor more than sixty. In the latter, long form, it would in any case lessen from about the thirty-sixth hour. He could then feel the white string slowly slackening, melting away, while the hammered nail turned to a dying coal and went out.

This time the headache was Shosa's fault. His anger at her, the effort of slaughtering her. Perhaps even the sight of her beauty sodden with blood.

Vilmos, having once more left the stultifying venue of his father's house, had gone back via a circuitous route to the house by the river. Only in one place did he pause, rubbing his forehead violently against the angled corner of a building, momentarily to obliterate the claw of the headache in his temple.

But by the time he reached the Master's house, he was dizzy and the string of the demoniac violin had already wound tight.

The river here ran in a wide canal, and the house perched directly above. There was no invented light at all, and only the vaguest hint of starlight. Nevertheless something white was just now floating by under the brink of the house. It might have been a bundle of washing, or someone drowned.

Vilmos turned from it and scratched on the side door.

After a moment a slot appeared. The bloodshot eye of a servant peered out at him. Then the door was opened, and Vilmos entered the house, for the second time that night.

The premises had been emptied of any crowd. Only the three speechless servants remained; two of these were already concealed, and the porter too now slipped off down a narrow dank stair. Vilmos, unbidden but knowing the way, climbed the other stair upward, towards the Chamber of Revelation.

"Enter. No, you need put on no robe. You come to me in a robe of the Devil's, and veiled in the mask of Hell. What is that blood on your head?"

"I rubbed it on a wall. I have the hemicrania that plagues me."

"And your shirt."

"Ah, that."

"Yes, you have murdered again. No, say nothing of it. The act too clothes you. You are clad in the wreckage of the Sixth Commandment. Have you brought with you the stannum you were given? Then stand here. Now we shall see."

The chamber was lit solely by a half score of glims set high up in cups of oil. There were otherwise no windows.

The Master read words aloud from a large book on a stand, then made a single pass in the air with a wand of ivory.

Gradually something began to glow in the centre of the floor, about equidistant from the Master and Vilmos.

Vilmos had been witness to apparitions in this room before. Most of the Order, which was that of the Indian Mystery, had done so. The society was loosely alchemical in its nature but deviated strongly in many directions. Although it claimed, as did most such sects, the primary goal of knowledge, to be demonstrated by unlocking the secrets of firstly, the Making of Gold from inferior metals, or indeed filth, secondly finding the Source of Eternal Youth, and thirdly, Attainment of the Power of the Inner Self, these god-like gifts were construed through the spectrum of an Eastern philosophy by the group, at least, called Indian.

On the floor had been engraved the Wheel of life and Death, having to do in Sanskrit with the *Seven Cakras*.

The thing which now manifested evolved within the circle.

Unlike the ethos of the *Cakras* this was a hideous image.

Vilmos stared at it through the agony in his head, and saw it was the figure of a skeletal king, crowned with a diadem of bones that dripped blood. At its back shadowy wings stirred restlessly. Its garments were ragged, grave clothes perhaps. Through a hole both in the cerements and the being's chest, there suddenly peeked out the head of a lean, black, rat-like creature, whose eyes were like sulphur.

Colours began to burn up in the torso of the apparition. Yellow showed like the rat's eyes in the bones of the lower chest, and a surging muddy amber in its bowels. At the region of the male member a scarlet flower appeared, but a snake's head writhed in it, the jaws ejaculating sparks of poison.

Vilmos raised the cold piece of tin and pushed it against his forehead. For a second the pain sank, then flared to greater pitch. He had perceived that the ruinous and rotted king was none other than himself. It had his face. It too seemed in anguish.

A flash of nothingness filled the chamber.

Dropping the stannum, Vilmos fell forward and knew no more of anything.

TEN

I had thought, or would have done if I had ever compared it to anything at all, that the greatest and most telling shock of my life happened when I entered the hospital room where my mother lay, and my father said to me, in a kind of dreadful hope, "Look, she's sleeping really peacefully now."

In fact, it was not. Inevitably I had expected her death, and therefore perhaps that something poignantly terrible would accompany it.

And now too, doubtless, I had in some form expected *this*.

I replaced the glass of whisky, unfinished, on the round white mat.

Through the top of the bar counter I gazed down and down into the abyss.

All about me rational everyday life went on. I remember, someone laughed.

But it wasn't as if they laughed at me, at my predicament. That laughter of theirs was so far removed it came from another dimension.

When I looked up again, he was still there, sitting by the palm. He was reading a magazine. He wore black again today, the black jeans, and a light black sweater with a little green dart of something high on the left side of his chest, some logo.

Nobody out there took any notice of him. No, actually one of the women did, a young one with long hair. She looked round and gazed at him a moment, evidently liking the look of him, but not intruding, passing on and away.

What should I do?

There were a lot of people here. Should I grip the waiter and mutter, *Get the police!* This seemed unreal and useless. Again, who would believe me?

Besides, I had drugged him. I might have *killed* him. Was this phantom definitely there, or only an illusion...? But the girl had seen him too. There he *was*.

Exactly then he glanced up and met my eyes in the bar mirror. (How long had he watched me before I glimpsed him?) He raised his right hand, as he had in the Crescent, a friendly, almost non-committal wave of hello. He didn't get up.

I took the whisky, put it down again. I turned and came smartly out into the foyer.

Should I now walk past? Surely he would follow. The same if I got into a lift. Did he know my room number? Christ, he'd found me here, why wouldn't he?

There was another chair facing his, I think he had drawn it over into that position. I went directly to the chair and sat down.

I heard my voice come out cool and flat.

"Well, Sej."

"Well, Roy," he said. And smiled.

"I'd better explain at once, hadn't I? We both got tired of that last guessing game."

"How you found me here."

"Exactly. I looked in your books, the most recent publication. This very year. Then I contacted the publisher – Gates. I said I was trying to trace a Mr Roy Phipps. I didn't use the landline for this, of course. It didn't seem to work, perhaps because the wire had been ripped out and the receiver smashed. Whoever did that, Roy? You should have got it fixed."

I said nothing.

He said: "I kept insisting that it was vital I speak to someone about you. I gave your *nom de plume* – R.P. Phillips. In the end, I reached some guy – Lewis something. Lewis Ryburn, that's it."

He had the wrong name. Would that count? I guessed it would not.

"Ryburn said graciously Who is this? I said, Actually I'm Roy's son. I've been trying all night to locate him. I hadn't been, obviously, I'd been asleep. I do apologise for that, Roy, by the way. Falling asleep so boorishly. I woke up on the floor. I'm afraid I also threw up in your sink. That wine – it must have been off." Smiling ruefully now he looked at me. "Were *you* OK?"

I said nothing.

Joseph Traskul Sej went on. "Mr Ryburn was diffident at first. But I explained I'd been expecting you at Old Church Lane and was already there myself, but you hadn't turned up. I gave the address of course so he would see I knew this important personal detail, was an intimate of yours. Then he became quite concerned. He said he had had a call from you, and you'd seemed rather – what was the word he used? – *flummoxed*. That was it. I said I knew there'd been some family trouble. *He* said he'd never known you had a family, let alone a son. I said neither had I known I was *yours* until comparatively recently. But we'd been due to meet, and I was worried sick. After a bit more of my ham acting, he told me you were here. People do let one down, don't they, Roy? My God. You ought to tell the bastards to be more careful of their authors, lucky he only told *me*. It could have been anyone."

I could just picture Lewis Rybourne, intrigued by the story, (old Roy with a son!) and also delighted to shove me off his plate on to this handy other one.

And a son again. I could hear, mentally, how plausible and winning the demon had made himself sound. Even after his sedated coma and resultant nausea.

And he knew he had been drugged. By me. What else? *Who* else?

"How are you feeling?" I asked blankly.

Smilingly he said, "I'm fine. You seem surprised."

"No, I'm not." This was in fact true. Shocked but not surprised.

He said, "Oh, by the way, I brought your mail," and lifting his tote-bag off the jazzy carpet he presented me with two business letters and an electricity bill.

I'd forgotten all about post and what it might reveal to him, but he hadn't slit open any of the envelopes, not even cleverly undone them with steam from a kettle, thereafter resealing them, I knew the tell-tale signs, having experimented with the method for my work in the 1980's.

Without saying anything I put the letters in my jacket pocket.

"Where shall we go for lunch?" he said.

More or less just like the first time.

"I can't afford," I said, "to treat you."

"Don't worry. My turn. What's it like here?"

"Expensive."

He laughed. "I get the feeling you think I'm penniless."

Recently I hadn't. I said, "Are you?"

"No, Roy."

"Then why try to move into my house?"

"*Did* I? I thought it was just a visit."

"You mean you'd have eaten the food, finished the wine, and left?"

"I might have. I do have a place of my own. Up here, London. Not bad though not very cheap. Worse thing is the fucking awful music the rest of them in the building play." (I didn't think I'd heard him use a four letter word before.) "I prefer a bit of tuneful jazz – the old kind, Dixie, New Orleans, or Bach or Handel. Do you like Handel, Roy?"

It occurred to me he had somehow heard Handel playing on my radio that night he unloaded the dustbin, noiselessly, in the back garden.

"Sometimes."

"But in the flats they play rubbish. It gets on my nerves."

Across the foyer, through the glass doors, the slender-pillared dining-room was revving up for custom. The Americans had already gone across.

"What do you think?" he said.

"I don't want to eat with you."

Benignly he looked at me. He said, "Get over the guilt, Roy. I forgive you. It doesn't matter."

I knew. I said, "What?"

"Drugging me," he sweetly said. "Don't be concerned. I'm tough and strong. It takes more than that. I knew you had, anyway."

An insane curiosity took hold of me. I found I leant forward. "Then why..."

"Why did I go on drinking your plonk? Well, I didn't think there'd be enough to kill me."

"There could have been. It could have done."

"No. You know how to judge such things, or Mr R.P. Phillips does. I read one of your books, by the way. *Last Orders*. Really liked it. Well written and no fuss. I guessed who done it, but only three quarters through – and the twist at the end was a stunner. You had me fooled on that. I'm impressed. Why aren't you much better known?"

I thought, as once or twice in my youth I bitterly had, *Because I am not part of the Oxbridge fraternity and have no influence*. But such carping bores me by now, and anyway I've come to see it's more likely I am simply not original enough, don't have enough of the slightly deranged *zeitgeist* of the modern day. Presumably too I never did. I recall one review from a well-known and influential critic, which greeted my twelfth book: "Phillips is dependable, nearly always a pretty good read if never a magnificent one."

This was when something very odd happened.

Perhaps I was already disturbed enough, but the fact he had selected the only published book of mine I personally still rated quite highly, seemed to affect me in a way I could neither express nor explain to myself. I looked at him hard and seemed to see his face for the first time, handsome and quite ordinary, intelligent even, and couth, nothing in it to display madness or ferocity. I understood even as the feeling washed through me that this assessment was unwise. Everything he had done so far demonstrated ably enough that he was, as my father had once liked to say, off his rocker.

It was then that the woman rushed into the lobby from the street.

She was about forty, quite smart in a dry sort of way, with short thick well-cut hair. But she flew in and then halted, and like one entering in a Greek tragedy, she wore a mask of tears.

We all stared at her a second. Then most of us looked away. The English are famed for their insularity, and constipation of the emotions. Even those Brits of mixed blood and origin seem now to end up in this frame of mind, or heart. One sees displays of violence more often, of sexual passion more often too. But frank human kindness – that thing called empathy – is rare.

He'd turned his head.

In a fleeting gesture he touched my arm with his hand. "Just a sec, Roy." And he rose and went straight to her and stood there, and I heard him ask in a low, gentle voice, "What is it? Can I help?"

She started crying violently and noisily at once.

He put his arm around her and drew her over to another group of empty chairs, the whole distance of the lobby from everyone, including me.

Now was my chance to split and run. I couldn't take it. I was riveted. I sat there, reticence gone, and gaped at them.

She sobbed, he held her in his arm, bending forward to hear her muffled words, listening intently.

Then he let go, touched her arm rather as he had touched mine, and came back over to where I sat.

"Roy, be a gent. Can you get her a brandy?"

"What's the matter?"

"Tell you soon. Brandy first. *Thanks*, Roy."

Like the slave of chance which that moment I was, up I got, walked back in the bar and ordered it. Everyone in there was by now looking round too, and much less cautiously, the smoked glass screens giving them cover.

The waiter said to me, "What's up, sir?"

"I don't know."

"Your friend, he's helping her?"

"Yes, apparently." No point in stressing he wasn't any friend of mine.

I paid for the brandy rather than put it on the tab.

Going out I started to walk across and Sej came up to me and took it from me with a grateful nod and bore it to the weeping woman.

She tipped back her head and swallowed the brandy whole.

Her eyes were inflamed, and if her mascara hadn't run, she had somehow smeared it even so.

She spoke to him. He nodded.

Then he came over to me again and undid his bag, and pulled out a shirt.

285

It was dark blue in colour. "That should be OK," he said. Holding it he went directly out of the hotel doors and vanished along the street.

I sat back and watched the woman surreptitiously. In fact she was even a little older than I'd first thought, and her clothes were good, but not quite as good as in my initial impression. She sat motionless, head up. She stared through us all, through walls, through time and space. I have seen the look before with certain people. The look of sudden vital loss.

When Sej came back in he carried his shirt carefully now, wrapped around something. There was blood seeping through.

For a somersaulting instant I thought of a dead baby. But no, it wasn't that. From one end a pathetic white tail hung out. A dog.

He too noticed the tail in that moment and deftly obscured it in a fold of the shirt.

Standing by her, he spoke. Now I heard the words.

"The taxi's outside. He's OK. Shouldn't you call your husband?"

I heard her say drearily, "He won't care."

"There must be someone," he said.

"Oh." She gazed up at him with the sadness of the only half-alive. "*Must* there?"

"Then can I...?"

"No. No, you've been much too kind. And – please thank your friend for the drink. I should – I have to pay..."

"Hush, dear," he said.

Something caught inside me. My father had sometimes said that to my mother, gently in that way, if she was distressed. *Hush, dear. It'll be all right.* Lies, of course. But the human tenderness. Hush, dear. Hush.

Sej guided her out and both of them now disappeared. Beyond my line of sight he must have handed her the butcher's bundle, and put her in the cab.

When he came back in, he was chalk white.

Unlike the old, who can look so young, almost childlike, in certain situations of stress, the young have a way of looking abruptly aged. You see it in the faces of children from famine zones or bombed out villages on the TV news. I don't know why this is. Sixty looks six, and six – a hundred.

"Sorry, Roy," he said, and slumped into his former chair. "Some shit ran over her dog. Just out there. At least it must have been quick. He didn't stop, naturally. Poor little cow."

"You'd better drink something."

"No, actually. I feel a bit sick again. I had to – pick it up."

"I'll fetch some water."

I marched back into the bar and got him one of those small bottles of still water that are now so popular. When I came out, he had gone, his bag too. He was nowhere to be seen.

I stood in the foyer, staring round for him. Searching anxiously, confused and made uneasy by the absence of my enemy.

ELEVEN

One can make small excuse for some things one does. And yet perhaps all such things are in some way recognisable by the rest of us. And if not, then they may come to be. And if never, possibly they should.

When Joseph returned from the lavatories, which lie off the foyer of *The Belmont* and are, like the entire hotel, mirrored and gilded, urinals white as the brand-new false teeth of my parents' era, he was still gaunt and pale.

He sat down once more opposite to me.

"Really sorry, Roy. I had to throw up again."

My fault? Apparently not.

"I've always been squeamish," he said.

"You didn't seem to be."

"Well, you kind of put that on hold, don't you, when you have to."

I struggled not to say it, but *I* had to. "You dealt with all that very well."

"I tried. I was lucky with the cabdriver. Good man. He said he'd lost his own dog. He said drunks get in the cab and puke everywhere, so he had plastic bags... I saw to that. She couldn't. Poor little thing," he said, as if she were his younger sister. "Her husband must be a twat. But she got herself together. They went off with the dog on her lap. She said she'd bury him in a big pot, grow a plant. They don't have a garden, just this rich apartment in Hampstead. I think she said Hampstead."

He looked drained. He let his head sink back on the chair.

"Roy, I'm really sorry, now I *do* need a drink and then I need some food. Crazy I know if I was sick, but that's gone, and I feel hollow. As I said, I'm glad to pay, but it has to be in the next ten minutes or I'm going to drop. I could do with your company too."

Stiffly I said, "All right. Take this water. What drink do you want?"

"Tea, please," he said. "Black, *no* milk, no sugar, no lemon."

That would have to be the restaurant. The bar ran to coffee only.

On his left hand there was a little bright smear of blood. It was on the palm, which must have been pressed to the body of the dog – washing his hands must have cleared the rest. I hoped he wouldn't see it.

I wondered what I was doing. I should have made myself scarce long before. But I hadn't, had I?

We went into the restaurant and ordered tea for Joseph who was Sej, and a glass of red for me. Then we had lunch.

He perked up bit by bit.

He thanked me several times.

What did we talk about? Not much. The food, London, nothing. We ate, I a little, all the while watching him. He ate a lot. And at the end he paid, and left them a lavish tip, thanking the waiter with an odd, sophisticated joy, as if he had consumed a slice of heaven on a plate.

287

At *The Belmont*, just before you reach the lifts on the ground floor, there is a big blue function room, which that day stood wide open.

A few chairs and long tables were left about, the latter decorated with water glasses. But the dais from which, I suppose, the officers of various businesses address their captive, pre-empted staff, stood vacant, and the mikes turned off. To the left was positioned a piano, a baby *grande*, black and polished, its lid for some reason upraised.

I saw it because he had gone back that way when he went to the Gents again, and returning, told me.

Why this time had I waited for him? But then, why had I stayed and waited earlier?

Without ducking all responsibility, partly I blame my father. He had so often told me I must try to see the 'Other person's side'. Plus I had been heavily indoctrinated in ideas of polite behaviour. Of course this is absurd, for many of us, especially from my own and prior generations, have been and were so instructed, and often with physical beatings to augment the process. My father was not a brutal man, but he had his standards and his eye could turn very cold. "I'm a bit disappointed in you, Roy." The whole structure rested on a quasi-Christian ethic, despite the fact my father was strictly agnostic. It was not to be what one wanted oneself, but what would be 'fair' to others. As a kid I had absorbed this and sometimes sobbed in combined frustration and shame – at not being understood, at the fear that I had been understood too well and found unpleasantly wanting. Countless other people, as I began to say before, in the rambling way by which I'm allowing this narrative to proceed, were lessoned similarly. But later they rebelled, emerging radiantly assured and unappeasing. Not apparently Roy Phipps.

Only in my novels have I played with the matches and the fire of injustice and utter barefaced self-obsession. And there too, in the end, a penalty is normally exacted.

All this divertissement has been solely to say that, confronted by Joseph's continued urbanity, he had bought lunch, assisted a distraught woman even though it had made him ill, I couldn't bring myself simply to run away.

I would, of course. But first civilities, the acknowledgement of his rights, must be attended to.

And therefore I'd waited once more in the foyer, and then hearing of the open room with the piano, I rose from the chair and followed him to see.

Once I was at the doorway, Joseph went straight to the piano. He dragged out a chair and sat down. "Too high," he remarked, perhaps to me, or to the hotel in general. And then he put his hands on the keys.

"I'll play you a tune," he said, like my Maureen, all those years ago. And beauty had spread like butterfly wings from her fingers.

And with him?

He launched at once into a piece of Scott Joplin, the by now most well-known one. It came out perfect, yet – flighty. Flighty. It had wings.

Once or twice, as he played, he glanced up and back at me. He didn't smile now, he grinned. He looked happy. He looked – at home.

After this prelude he shot immediately into one of the etudes of Chopin. My father had played this. Joseph Traskul clearly demonstrated that 'play' was not what one did with it. Filigreed streams dashed sparkling and hopeless to a bottomless sea. A few dark chords barred their way, but died.

Behind me a woman murmured, "My."

The Americans had come, drawn by the sounds, which obviously were not the everyday musak of the hotel.

They stood, seemingly awestruck, then – passing me without a look – went into the room and sat down on some of the chairs.

Joseph played.

From Chopin he passed to Beethoven, and the character of the music changed – gorgeous despair to thundering rage. I believe it was the Appassionata. The room rang with the notes but more than that, with the power of the composition.

Maureen had played so very well.

But Joseph played as if each note sped new-born from his brain.

Now and then I've been to concerts. I had heard this kind of quality, ability and fire before.

Never like this.

Other people kept arriving. They passed by me as if I were some doorman, some of them even smiling or nodding at me as if I held the way for them.

In the end there must have been over fifty people sitting in the room, either on the chairs or tables, or the blue carpet.

If there was a pause, they applauded. But by now his face had set in a kind of visor of intention. He played on and on, one astonishing rendering leaping at once into another, Scott Joplin to Chopin to Beethoven to Rachmaninov to Prokofiev to Gershwin.

Certainly, some of the staff of the hotel had come in. The manager had apparently come down, or so I was informed, to the doors. He had meant to put a stop to this, the piano was valuable, not there for idle tinkerings. But he too had stayed a while to listen and gone away uncomplaining.

Joseph finished with a sudden little syncopated piece of jazz, the kind he'd spoken of. I didn't know it, but I hardly know everything and that type of music, while I like it, I don't know very well. Yet I had a feeling this one was really his own.

Lightly tapping in the last note, he sat back.

He sat there with his back to us, hands down at his sides.

The room erupted, naturally. They cheered.

At first, he seemed to take no notice. He seemed nearly in a trance. Then he lifted his head, stood up and, walking round the chair, bowed to them theatrically, but grinning again.

When some of them approached, crowding round, asking him who he was, where he played, he was all graceful good humour. He just, he told them, tuned pianos. And now he was handing out those cards of his. He got plenty of potential customers. The air bubbled with praise.

Finally, he extricated himself and came across to me at the door.

"Well, Dad. Made you proud of me for a minute, didn't I?"

"You're a wonderful and versatile pianist. But I'm not your father."

The grin was gone. The smile was there instead.

He lifted his eyebrows. "Sure about that, are you?"

Lynda had had a 'scare', what she called a scare, which was her supposing herself pregnant by me. After we'd married, for indeed we did marry and are still married, since neither of us so far has found the need to apply for a divorce, she had another scare. This will indicate, accurately enough, that neither of us wanted children, or at least I did not. Perhaps she only wished not to have any by me. Both scares anyway came to nothing, or so she informed me. After all, I'd always gathered she was on the Pill.

We were together approximately two years. When she left, which was not because of her having fallen for anyone else, only because she had the chance of living with an aunt of hers near Manchester who had some money, which – as Lynda pointed out – we did not – it could just have been possible she was, unbeknownst to either of us – pregnant. Or should I say, really scared. Her leaving me occurred in 1977. I'd been more relieved than regretful. The washing-machine went on washing my shirts, and I could cook in fact rather better than Lynda. As for sex, now and then there had been someone after she went. Not very often. I'm not attractive to the opposite sex, and I don't expect to be.

However. If Joseph were about the age I'd eventually thought him, lying there on my kitchen floor, twenty-eight-seven – he could maybe have been mine, mine and Lynda's.

Except surely she would have let me know. Not from any sense of my fatherly rights, but to get some extra financial support. At the very least, to blame me. Or did the aunt take care of everything? There was less stigma by then in having a baby without an adjacent man. Besides, we were still married. In the aunt's eyes, it would be respectable. And if the old woman liked children, perhaps this seemed a good arrangement, leaving me out of it, all the better.

But then again, could this – creature, this demon, who was physically so unlike either Lynda or myself, this pianistic genius – be the product of our midnight fumblings?

"Are you saying," I said, "you're my son?"

"Am I? Do you think I am, Roy?"

We had gone out of the hotel and were walking together along Lang Passage, up to the Gardens. When he saw them, he said, "There's a park near my place. Huge trees and rhododendrons."

"I didn't ask you about the park, Sej. I asked if you genuinely believe you're my son."

We stood by the low railing and looked into the Gardens. The trees were leafing early, the sun out and shining on them. A small bird was drinking from the drinking fountain drips.

"You tell me," he said presently. "Could I be?"

"I doubt it."

"But you doubt everything, don't you, Roy?"

I said levelly, "It's often the best way to doubt."

"Innocent until proven guilty. Guilty until proven innocent. Stupid until proven clever. Purple till proven blue."

"What are you saying?"

"Nothing much. Just passing the time. That bird on the fountain is a wren. You don't often catch sight of them in inner London. Or I don't. Did you know, they have pelicans in Hyde Park. That took me by surprise. Great big bills and red legs. What's the time, by the way?"

What to do? I glanced at my watch. "Getting on for 4.30."

"Shit," he said. "I have to be somewhere."

"Tuning a piano?"

"Not this time. Sorry, Roy, I have to get going."

"Really."

He turned and laughed at me, then he put his arms round me and hugged me, giving me also the obligatory masculine clap-on-the-back.

"I'll see you, Roy..." he said. "Daddy," he added, like a mischievous child that knows you love it and, though disapproving, won't really mind you just heard it use the F word.

Then he turned, vaulted the railing, his bag bouncing on his shoulder, and broke into a run, vanishing though the Gardens in the direction of Langham Place and Oxford Street. And I stood there, mind depleted of all coherent thought, staring after him, staring after everything.

4

My first search of 6, 66, Saracen Road had been fruitless. I went to a grimy window in the main room and looked out and down. Below, the street, and then Joseph's park of "Huge trees and rhododendrons". A few people were sunbathing there, I now saw. The June sun had brought them out like certain flowers. From up here they had a flowery quality too, already tanned and in bright colours. How easy it looked, to sample life.

As luck would have it, I peeled off the rubber gloves I had donned, because of their sticky hotness, and stuffed them in a pocket.

It was when I turned back into the room, wondering if all I could do now was go away, I heard the flat door, (already smashed and undone by me) pushed briskly open.

I thought instantly it would be him. Joseph. Sej.

Therefore, when the burly middle-aged man in shorts and T-shirt came into the room, I felt a most inappropriate near relief.

He stopped and gawped at me. He had a newspaper in one hand, and a six-pack of beer in the other.

I said, "Christ, can you believe it? Someone broke in."

"Er – yeah," he said.

I recognised, hypersensitive as perhaps I was in that moment, the voice of No 3A, he who had let me in via the main entrance.

"I came up here," I blustered on, "to deliver this bloody packet..." I pointed at my fake delivery, which now lay on the floor. "I meant to leave it by the door. You never know, do you? I mean, the table downstairs, anyone might have had it."

"You're fucking not wrong there," he rewarded me.

"And someone's smashed the glass window. Been in and taken – well – everything from the look. Even the carpets."

Roy was on form again, indeed he was. But I've said, I write this sort of drivel for a living. Improv comes with the job.

3A gazed round. He looked both disgusted and sullen. I sensed immediately he was not astonished, had been up here before and knew the flat was always basically exactly as now.

He said, "Like, I don't think they took nothing much. Tina don't have much to start with."

Touché, monsieur. Now he really had floored me.

I said, "Tina? But the name on the packet is for a Mr Trazcool. But I suppose she's his partner?"

"How should I know?"

How should he?

"But surely he lives here. Look..." I'd put a lot into the fake package and confidently picked it up and held it out to him.

He shambled over and scrutinised it. "Tra - skull, that his name?" he asked. (He could read).

"Presumably. The address is right, is it?"

"Yeah, man. That's right."

"So Tina...?"

"She's the only one lives here I know of. She gets people up here sometimes. I thought you was one of 'em."

Below us, the noise of No 5's bad music abruptly ceased.

Both 3A and I stared down at the floor.

"He's going out," said 3A. "Thank fuck for that."

3A, it seemed, didn't like 5's music either. But whether that was due to its volume or its type, remained obscure.

My mind turned back to what he had said just before.

People coming up... he'd thought I was one of them.

Was she, this Tina, on the game? A prostitute. I didn't want to ask. He too had come up here, had he not, with his paper and beer.

"Oh well," I said, with generated slight annoyance, "do you think we should call the police?"

"What the fuck for? They won't fucking come, man. If they did, what they gonna do? This place... 's always like this. Sometimes there're some chairs. Once there was a music centre – a fridge. That lasted about two weeks. I don't know how she pays her rent, but I gotta idea."

He had confirmed my own. Tina, whoever Tina was, was a whore.

"Well," I said, "I can't waste any more time. I've got things to do."

And that was when he emerged from his inertia. He squared up to me and said, quite pleasantly, "Yeah, but hang on a bit. How'd I know what you gotta do with all this?"

"All what?"

"The fucking door wrecked. Like what the fuck are you up to?"

"I've said, I brought his post up – or her post."

"Nobody fucking bothers to do that. These fucking stairs, no way. It's like climbing up Mount fucking Everlast, or whatever the fuck it's called. So if you wasn't after Tina what was you after?"

I hung my head.

"You've got me there. Obviously it is Tina."

"Then why," unfortunately astutely he inquired, "all this bollox with that letter thing?"

"Well it was for her flat – I found it on the table downstairs when I was here last time. Took it. Wanted an excuse to come back. Then when I tried the bell she didn't answer."

"Nah, she didn't. 'Cos she was 'sposed to be seeing me, man. Me. OK?"

"OK. Fine."

"I don't like all this," he said, sniffing at the air as if to detect, like a bloodhound, the clues of treachery. Perhaps he could. I was certainly sweating.

I said, "Look, I'm sorry if I'm in your way. I really don't want anyone to know I was here to see Tina. I don't want my wife to know."

"I bet you don't, man."

"In the past I've met her – other places. I didn't know it was your – time."

"No. OK. Right. Well, she ain't fucking here anyway, is she? She's fucking off her head. You'll know." He leered abruptly. "S'OK, man. Just wanted to be sure."

We were comrades-in-arms, love or war.

He added, "Reckon I know who done this anyhow. The door, I mean. That fucker from No 2. He's a headcase. She wouldn't touch him neither. Nasty cunt." Did he mean her? Presumably No 2. He looked at me for confirmation, so whoever it was dutifully I nodded. 3A went on, "Might pay him a little visit later. As for Tee, well, she's off somewhere. Both you and me had better make other arrangements, eh?"

"Yes."

293

"Give your old woman some Cream di Month or something. You never know. Might see another side of her."

"Yes..." He had moved out of sight, back into the outer hall of the flat. I didn't dare take the package with me I when I left. It was now officially Tina's. I dropped it again, and for a second stood regarding it, not wanting to leave such evidence. But in the hall 3A swore loudly. Sounding aggrieved he said, "You walked up them fucking stairs barefoot? Trying to scare me, eh? Eh?"

On the unpapered wall I saw two vague shadows thrown, mingling and unsure, 3A's and another's.

TWELVE

Outside the BBC I watched a well-known politician sweep through into the building, with his entourage. I've seen a few well-known persons going in there over the past twenty odd years.

I did some nondescript shopping in Oxford Street. I didn't see Joseph.

Before I walked back to the hotel, I went into Lang Gardens and called Lewis Rybourne on my mobile.

They told me he was in a meeting.

"Please get him to phone me. I'm at the *Belmont Hotel* until tomorrow afternoon."

I was just getting up from the bench when the phone made its noise. I don't have a piece of music. It simply imitates the old-fashioned sound of a phone ringing.

The call was from Rybourne.

"Roy – oh, good, good. Sorry about that. She didn't know I was back. Did your boy catch up to you?"

I said, carefully, "Which boy?"

"Ah. Joseph, I think he said."

"Joseph? I don't know a Joseph."

"Oh, lord, Roy, I think maybe you do. He said he was – a relative."

"No. I don't have any relatives left."

"Oh, come on, Roy. Your..." There was a long, dramatic pause. His voice had dropped and become intense, "...son."

I now left the interval.

"Hello?" he said. "Are you there?"

"Yes, Lewis. I thought you said son. Obviously you didn't."

"Of course, I shan't tell anyone. Strictly confidential."

"What are you talking about, Lewis?"

I could hear him breathing. Then he said, "A young man called us, said it was an emergency, insisted on speaking to your editor. Me. He told me he was your son, Joseph, and he was concerned as there'd been a family problem and he wanted..."

"I don't have a son. Who was this man?"

"I told you, Roy. He gave his name as Joseph – Joseph something or other. It sounded foreign. She has a note of it I think, but she's not in the office..."

"I have no son."

"All right. OK, Roy. The thing is, you'd already called me and you sounded – upset."

"I was."

"And then I spoke to this Joseph, and he wanted to know how he could trace you. He was already at your home. I made sure of the address. He knew you, and your house. Well."

"Really? That's news to me. What did you say to him?"

He breathed now like an obscene caller.

"I – er – I told him the hotel you were at."

I left a space. Then I shouted, "You did what?"

"Roy, Roy, listen..."

"You told a complete stranger, who claims to be my son, and over the phone, which hotel I'm staying in?"

He said, with an awful meaningless contrition, "Have I done the wrong thing, Roy? I'm so sorry. I was just..."

"I'm being stalked, Lewis. Yes, I know, it's crazy. I don't know who he is, but he turned up at my house and gave the neighbours the same yarn – that he is my son. I threw him out. And yes, he has been at my hotel. Now I know who to thank for that."

"Christ. Roy – have you told the police?"

"Yes. They don't believe me, or they think something else. And you have informed this lunatic of my hotel."

"God – Roy..."

"Think of something, Lewis. He may be dangerous. I need your help. This is your fault."

"Christ. Oh, Roy. What shall I do?"

"I don't know," I said. "But I suggest you come up with something."

I broke the connection.

To be truthful I wasn't sure how much, if any, use this would be. But the fact of Sej's pursuit of me had been established at last, with an independent and non-vulnerable source. Potential?

Having attended to that, however, I sat down once more on the bench.

The phone went again.

I looked at it.

I let it ring. I'd check any message later. Let Lewis Rybourne stew, if he was capable of it.

Meanwhile the images of the afternoon revolved slowly in my mind. I kept thinking of the women he'd helped, and the dog, its sad tail hanging out of his shirt – now ruined by blood and lost. And the piano. How he played. And how he had gone so suddenly away.

Bells were ringing from various places, including the nearby church. It was 6 o'clock.

I got up and walked to *The Belmont*. In the foyer a young woman came straight up to me, all smiles.

"Excuse me, but that guy who played the piano – you know him?"

"Didn't he give you a card?"

"Well, yes. Only I called the number and there was no answer."

I would have to bear in mind, Joseph was not only brilliant, but good-looking. This young woman was clearly smitten. I said, with a stiff smile, 'I don't know him well. Just keep trying the number. I think he's out until later." And walked to the lift leaving her there, crestfallen. Another stalker. This time of Joseph?

Tonight was my last night here. I couldn't afford any others. The entire excursion would already make quite a hole in what I call my Emergency Fund, that is my building society savings.

Would he come back to *The Belmont*? If he did, what then would happen?

I ordered dinner in my room and watched TV. Now I thought more solidly of my house and the possible damage that could have been done to it. Strangely, I didn't think he had caused damage. Partly too I wished not to go back. But I hadn't anywhere else to go. Perhaps, now Rybourne had some idea that Joseph was a danger, if the police confronted him at Gates he would have to tell them what had gone on. And any DNA test would show Joseph was nothing at all to do with me.

Unless...

Had he been Lynda's child? Hers and mine. That would make him only twenty-eight. Less? He didn't look quite that young, did he, or only when unconscious.

He wasn't Lynda's. He was neither like her, nor me.

The TV, even with its multiple channels, seemed all one chaos of unreal inanity, or desperate, unassuageable realness.

I turned in about 11. Check-out tomorrow was noon.

I would go back, see to the house, pack a few extra things, then maybe myself head up north. I'd said I had nowhere to go, but it's cheaper there, out of the main northern cities. And Matthew lived there, all on his own without adulterous Sylvia. I could go and commiserate with him.

Before leaving, however, I would get some extra security added to the house. Duran, the electrician who fixed my kitchen lights and the thermostat last November, had a side-line in villain-proofing. I'd gathered, from various hints, he'd been a competent burglar once, and now put former knowledge to good use for the other side. I hadn't taken him up on any of that, last time. Now I'd better. He was a tough guy too, Duran. He might have some brainwaves.

I slept well. Seven straight hours, waking at a quarter to 8, feeling drugged and out of kilter.

At reception, while paying, I heard of the manager's coming to see who played the piano yesterday. I had a last drink at the bar.

All the time I kept looking up at the mirror, looking for Sej to walk in. But he didn't. And I thought, Is it over? And a tide of relief swirled through me. And after the tide, a sort of pause. I can't describe it. It was still and quiet, without shadows, quite empty.

5

Less than a minute after, No 3A came back into the main room, accompanied by a skinny man with long greasy yellow hair, also in shorts, and barefoot as 3A had just accused him of being.

3A looked at me and jabbed his thumb back at the other one. "S'im. The one I told you about. No 2."

No 2 smiled at me with crinkled grey teeth. He was about twenty-six, and his uncovered arms unashamedly revealed the tracks of needles. He stank of sweat and – sugar. A chemical smell you pick up by some chocolate counters.

"Hi," he winningly said.

I nodded.

We all stood there.

"Where's Tee?" asked No 2, smilingly bemused. "I got some lovely stuff for 'er. I get it off of..."

"Shut up," decided 3A. "This geezer don't want to know, right?"

No 2 looked deeply at me from mad huge eyes the colour of a stagnant pond. "I seen this booful car down the road. That yours?"

"No," I said.

No 2 giggled. "Tha's good. I pissed up it las' night. I bin a bad boy. 'Ere," he added, "you want any stuff? I got this wicked stuff off of..."

"Shut up," said 3A again. "Look, you nosed-up prick-head, Tina ain't here. She's gone off. And we're just going. OK?"

"Who bruk the door?" innocently asked No 2.

"The postman," said 3A impatiently, "he couldn't get no fucking answer so he broke the fucking door in. All right? Now fuck off."

"That's awful that is – the postman – we ough-a get the pigs..."

"Fuck off."

No 2 seemed sad. "OK, Billy," he said. "Look, here I go."

And he left us.

"My fucking name ain't Bill, neither," said 3A to me with obvious emphasis.

I nodded again.

We left the flat and went down the stairs, leaving plenty of space for the ambling barefoot No 2 to get to his lair before us.

Reaching his own flat 3A lumbered aside, went in and slammed the door. In the absence of the noisy music of No 5, the sound reverberated throughout the building.

I hurried the rest of the way to the street.

After I'd crossed the road and reached the far side of the park I glanced back. At each of two of the windows facing front, presumably those of No 2 and No 3A, a solitary form stood looking out. 3A simply stood guard there. No 2, lower down and perhaps made far-sighted by his 'stuff', raised his bony arm in a wave.

THIRTEEN

The train left soon after two o'clock. I sat in the long carriage, with its ultra narrow aisles and seats, and tried to read the Radio Times. There were only a handful of people in the carriage. The whole train was sparsely filled. Beyond the polarised windows the suburbs unwound under a dismal sky. I took out my notebook and made a couple of notes for the commissioned novel.

As each station materialised, I wondered if Joseph Traskul Sej were peering out of another carriage, to see if I had alighted at an earlier stop to my usual one.

Once a young man got off the train who bore a fleeting resemblance to him. I stared, and saw it wasn't he.

The train was slow. It took nearly forty minutes. When I came to my station, I felt an edgy excitement, and reaching the platform, turned and looked round. A bald man from my carriage, in a brown shirt, had got off also. He was about forty. He looked straight ahead and went past me, down the steps.

Sometimes I get a taxi, though it's only a twenty-minute walk to Old Church Lane. Today I didn't. I'd spent enough, and if I went north soon, there'd be more to fork out.

Then, walking up the high street, busy with afternoon shopping and kids on bicycles careering along the pavement, I considered that a taxi-driver might have been handy if any surprises were waiting. Although in fact, he wouldn't want to be involved. Non-involvement is the key signature for most of us now, myself included.

Just before I turned into Bulivante Crescent I noticed the man in brown again. He was about thirty yards behind me, looking in a shop window.

Immediately I was tense. Was he following me?

Mentally I shook myself.

No. Not every person I saw was likely to follow me.

Only one person. And he, for now, was not in evidence.

All the way up the Crescent I anticipated him. He might step from behind a tree. Out of a house even, with a friendly farewell gesture to some now-collusive occupant, whom he had conned with one more inventive tale.

When I reached 72, I hesitated. George and Vita weren't to be seen. No doubt they were at the back, in the kitchen, making afternoon tea and chatting. I envied them sometimes. Their blossoming, undemanding dual companionship.

On the path I looked round again.

The man from 88 was watering his lawn with a sprinkler. So many men are at home now during the day, even the young ones; I used to be the exception. A cat was washing itself on the wall of 73, oblivious of the yapping poodle at the front room window.

Nothing out of place.

I reached the door.

Here I had the strangest moment of déjà vu. It was as if, not Joseph Traskul, but my parents had recently been on the premises. As if it had become their house again, I only their son, lodging there, coming and going, as many sons do.

But I braced myself and put the key in the lock. The door had been firmly shut, and now it opened. The hall lay before me, with four letters scattered on the mat. To my alert gaze nothing seemed amiss. Nothing was wrong.

The house had an air of silence and immobility, as if the owner had been away a few days. He had.

No residue of Joseph seemed to linger.

I was certain now he had not returned here.

Nevertheless, I considered leaving the door ajar. Then thought better of it. I went into the hall. I looked up the stairs. I meant to go to the kitchen first. That was where I'd left him, where he had recovered, thrown up in the sink. Something however made me go instead directly into the front room. As I did so of course I recalled again the vulnerable dog of red glass.

Maybe this is the most peculiar thing to try to convey at this point. Standing in the door of the room I felt no shock, none at all.

I suppose it could have been because the piano, which was now installed there against the left-hand wall, where the print of Monet's Sunday at Argenteuil had once been and was no longer, rested in virtually the same place as the previous piano during my parents' occupancy.

Unlike my mother, Joseph had set the red glass dog on the piano's top.

That night in 1974, Maureen invited me round, and she'd made me what my mother would have called a 'proper dinner'. It was roast lamb and roast potatoes with all the 'trimmings', and cheesecake from Mercers to follow, plus a bottle of decent red wine and some brandy for later.

Maureen was a good cook. She did it without any fuss either, whipping off her apron and appearing in a sexy dress. In the beginning her attire had sometimes even put me off the food I was so earnest to get her through the bedroom door.

"This is all really lovely, Maur," I said. "Thanks."

"I want tonight to be special, Roy," she said. And winked at me. "You wait till you see what I've not got on under this."

She was fun. Her lust was Chaucerian in its dedication, honesty and humour.

It was a special night.

After we'd settled down a little in bed, around 2 a.m. she sat up and lit a cigarette. I seldom wanted one. It was always, "Just take a fag if you want, darling."

"I've got something to say, sweetheart," said Maureen Parner in her pretty, Cockney voice.

"Yes, Maur..." I was half asleep. She hadn't lied about the new lingerie, and we'd done it justice.

"Sorry, luv, but you'd better listen. I really am sorry, luv. But tonight – this has to be our last time."

"What...?" I too sat up. I was wide awake, and the brandy suddenly sour in my throat. "Last – last what?"

"Our last smashing time, darling. Oh, Charlie, don't look so sad." Her eyes were full of tears.

Mine were dry and burned like acid. "I don't understand what you're saying."

"You know there've been – one or two others."

"Yes, Maur. It's OK."

"You are such a lovely bloke. Trouble is, I've met someone. And he – well he is... he's different, Roy. Roy, look, I'll be straight. I like him a lot and he wants to marry me. He's not rich but he's OK moneywise. I can stop work. We can have a bit of a good time. He's a bit older than me. Not that much. I'm pretty ancient, you know."

"You're not old."

"No. But you're young, Roy. You've got your whole..."

"Life ahead of me. Christ. You're dumping me because I'm a kid."

Then she started to cry.

And even in my total hurt and rage and shock, I put my arms round her. I held her, and soon we started to kiss again. We made love again.

But after that, when she held me, I had the sense to know this would be, as even the song had it, the last time. I wasn't yet twenty. I'd known her just over one year. She'd put a magic spell on me, I'd changed, growing one inch taller, sloughing acne and sexual insecurity in one bound. Even selling a story to a magazine. I didn't love her, but she was my love. She was mine. My Maureen. And now, not anymore. Never again.

It hit me. I stood there, stricken, the piano shining, over thirty years too late.

Not Lynda's – of course not hers. Joseph was Maureen's child. Hers and mine.

Mine. Mine and Maureen's.

She had had to marry the other older man. She hadn't wanted, being as she was, to pile that responsibility on a callow boy of nineteen with an assistant's job in a library.

Joseph was my son. He was about thirty – thirty-one...?

He was my son. Almost exactly as he had claimed to be.

When I walked dazedly out of the room, I saw the letters again, on the mat.

There had been four. I'd absently counted them.

Now there were five.

XIII
('UNTITLED': PAGE 213)

To dine in his father's house was always a custom of anathema to him. Yet here he was, seated at the long table of dark wood, the dishes set about, and his family set around them, conversing in their usual dull manner. Vilmos studied them. As sometimes happened after the talons of the 'micrania' had let go of him, he seemed both to hear and to see more clearly. Like a painting on glass, his stout anaemic mother and two pale, weed-like sisters. His older brothers, big, and tonight red-faced by contrast, jested and drank, observant only of the stern patriarch. Should he frown they would lower their voices. But otherwise they were always similarly obedient to him, worked at the offices he had demanded, wed when he told them they must. At or because of Vilmos he did not frown.

Vilmos was his curse, the devil somehow borne of the consanguineous line of his house. Vilmos he paid no attention at all. That he even suffered Vilmos, his youngest son, to live, albeit intermittently, in the family home, even to sit at table with him, was due only to a horrible and parsimonious religious ethic.

Meanwhile he did not know what Vilmos had truly done. He was not aware Vilmos had killed three women in the city, and at least eight men – perhaps nine – the fate of Reiner, of course, would never be fully ascertained by any.

Had he known all this, and of other matters to do with Vilmos, how would the patriarch have responded?

Vilmos himself sometimes pondered on this.

At certain times he believed his father would, himself, have summoned an assassin, and had the troublesome offspring excised from the pages of family life. But then again, his religious ethic might restrain him. Rather than murder his son, the father might only confine him in some cellar, feeding him and sustaining him 'mercifully', but never allowing him out again into the light.

Thus not only were dinners at his father's house irksome and angering, they were potentially dangerous. For that reason too maybe, Vilmos still occasionally attended them. His whole existence fled along a razor's edge, pursued by his own demons, and in pursuit of God knew what. Threat was the sea in which habitually he swam.

But now the father spoke.

At once utter stillness fell, respectful, or more properly fearful, as the Biblical canon decreed.

The three wan women, their lips parted, waited as if to receive his words not only through ears and eyes, but by mouth.

The brothers squared their shoulders, intelligent oxen ready to serve.

"This goose is dry, Saveta," said the patriarch to his wife.

"I am so sorry, Vladis. I will speak to the cook..."

"Do it. I expect my table, though now impoverished, to serve palatable food at least."

Vilmos, before he could prevent it, laughed. The patriarch did not even look at him.

When one of the brothers glared in Vilmos's direction, the patriarch spoke directly to this brother, diverting him. "I wish to discuss with you the cloth revenues. We are in arrears, it seems. Follow me to my study."

Once these two men had left the room, the women quickly got up. They went into a corner by the fire and took up their tatting.

The other brothers sat drinking. They had taken out a draughts board and now played a ponderous game.

Vilmos stayed where he was. He watched the candlelight creep on the ceiling, now and then faltering or flaring up. Two servants came in and cleared the table. The mother called them sharply. In a malicious undertone she berated then both over the goose.

Vilmos thought, with deep, comfortable melancholy, of Reiner, struggling and sinking in the river where he, Vilmos, had flung him. Reiner could swim a little. Besides debris was everywhere that he might reach and cling to. It was interesting to Vilmos inwardly to debate if his former companion had survived.

But then the image of the king, crowned with bones and with a rat in his breast, returned, slicing through memory like a knife.

In his chair, Vilmos sat upright. Something strange in the candlelight seemed to show him the king again upon the ceiling.

The colours in his torso, yellow, orange and crimson, were those of the three lower illuminated Cakras. They indicated appetite, greed, carnal desire. The added symbols, such as the rat and the snake, indicated blockages and perversions.

The higher colours, such as the green of the emotive heart, had not been contained in his vision. The piece of tin, when he revived and was shown it, had been burnt, apparently by some dreadful aspect of Vilmos himself. The Master was gone and had explained nothing. The servant, of course, had no tongue.

Vilmos now brooded on all this.

Few had ever attained the greater goals of the Order of the Indian Mystery. Few had seen as high as the sky-blue of the Cakra of communication, speech and song. And none, Vilmos thought, had viewed any higher. Unless the Master himself had done so.

Self-enlightenment, the dominion over self – and so over all other things – was reached only by unleashing the Gem of the Brow. It was the last stage of utter power. Beyond it no man could rise, save to reach up from the physical self into the Infinite, which was both Bliss and Annihilation: Death, Eternity. The Gem was therefore the ultimate state possible while yet living.

They said, not the Master but his Master, he who had ruled the Order before him, had done this. Armed then with the abilities of a god, he had vanished from the City.

"I want it," Vilmos murmured. He clenched both his hands on the table's edge, gripping it so hard a vibration seemed to pass through the wood.

When he went out, one of the servant girls, beaten by the cook because of the goose, wept against the panelling. She was about fourteen. Vilmos stared at her with a kind of revulsion. She smelled of grease, and her own unwashed body and hair. What wretched things humans were.

"Cheer up, my pigeon," he said to her in passing. "We're all damned. We'll all roast in the Scalds of Hell."

Her sobs choked to silence. She was afraid of him. He was the Chosen of the Devil. This notion filled him with great joy, and also with trepidation and a leaden disappointment. Why could God not have chosen him? Now he would never rise up beyond the genitals, the bowels and belly, the heart, the voice, into the dark blue sphere of the Elect. Unless, obviously, the Master was mistaken. Vilmos left the house thinking this. He walked through the darkness of the City to the lodging of the harlot Klavdisa. She knew better than to take other custom without his permission. He could practice with her his dominion over others, in case the Master were wrong.

FOURTEEN

Two of the letters were printed with my name and address. Two were handwritten.

The fifth, the last one lying on top of them, was different.

It was a clean, white ordinary envelope, the kind anyone could buy somewhere like Smiths, neither opulent nor cheap, empty of either name or address.

I picked it up and found it was sealed in the usual way. I ripped it open so roughly bits of it fluttered off back to the floor.

One sheet of typing or computer paper was inside, again medium quality. Unlike the envelope, the sheet was printed, a font widely used with nothing special about it.

One word, and three numerals:

Compasses. 7.30

I use the name *The Compasses* for the pub. This isn't correct. It was the dodgy place Joseph had stayed at in the high street. I've changed the name.

After a while I carried all the letters into the kitchen.

The table had been pulled back from the door, which had been relocked and re-bolted. Out on the paving his black dustbin-present was now stationed neatly to one side. When presently I opened the fridge, I found he had put the bottle of Wincott's into the chiller. The fridge had been reconnected too. It was as cold as it should be, and the freezer as well.

He had washed up the dinner plates and put them to drain, and the cutlery, (all but the missing fork), was standing in its proper section. I'd rinsed the glasses. These he had put away, in the right place.

There was no mess. In fact the kitchen looked as clean as when Franziska tended to it. There was a faint smell of bleach too, as then.

I felt a type of nervous curiosity. I went into the library. That copy of my book, *Last Orders*, lay on the little table. A piece of paper lay on top of it with an erratically written splash of words, (his writing, already recognisable to me). Really brilliant, Mr Phillips. Should have won a prize – or did it?

Nothing else seemed changed. At least he had not dusted the table.

Upstairs, the computer had completed its deletions but was still on. I switched it off. Nothing was disturbed that I could see. My bedroom door remained locked and had not been broken in.

The bathroom and lavatory were virtually as I'd left them, too. It seemed he must have used the lavatory and he had used the bath. One longish black curled hair lay on the edge. I stared at it, impelled. I picked it off. It had fallen from his head and he had not noticed it or did not care. In some crude past of banes and witchcraft I might have thought I could employ it against him. Now I truly might, if I put it into the sandwich bag with the new note added to the old one from the dustbin, and the fork he had used during our dinner, both of which I'd carried up to London and now brought back. DNA.

I had to find some access to the police that would make them listen. If he had done this sort of thing before, and they would take me seriously, they might discover him among their records, his DNA already lying in wait to catch him out. Or was it only me, only me as his target?

And then I sat down on the stair, the top stair where I'd sometimes sat as a child.

I held the cellophane bag in one hand, and the piece of paper that said Compasses: 7.30 in the other.

Suppose he really was my son? Mine and Maureen's?

Downstairs I'd been certain for all of sixty seconds.

But now?

He could play the piano even better than she had. Perhaps, like her, he had a singer's voice. His speaking voice was attractive, musical. It had that element trainers of speech would once talk about, timbre, the distinctive character of a voice, what Maureen herself had referred to as its colour. What colour had hers been? Soft pink, deep grey, silver. And his? It was dark, with a tawny edge. This is fanciful. I don't often think of things in that way.

He was mesmerising me. Had done so. Push it off. Be sensible and wary. Even if he were – mine – he had followed and stalked and harried and played with me. Very likely he had an axe to grind, was enraged at me, his absent ignorant bastard of a father. He might be capable of anything. And yet…

The phone in the hall was out of action. I used my mobile to call Duran, my ex-burglar electrician. But his wife informed me he was in Bristol, working on a big job with his cousin.

"When will he…?"

"Don't know, sorry. All he says to me when he calls me is it's going slow there. At least another month, I'd say."

The Compasses was dark, although April was turning towards May, the sun lower but still a good half hour from setting. There was oldish stained-glass in some of the windows, probably fitted circa 1930, when the pub was built. Green tiling had been kept too. The urinals seemed of the same vintage, if less pleasant.

I arrived ten minutes or so later than stipulated. Joseph played; so I did, if only a little.

And I meant to be friendly if non-committal. I meant to try to get to the bottom of all this.

The mirage that he might be my son lay like a flickering light somewhere in the murk of my confusion.

Unsettled and unsure, whether I was glad or appalled I couldn't discover.

In the doorway I looked round.

To the casual or ill-informed eye, there was nothing very odd about *The Compasses*. The dealers were fairly discreet. They expected you to know either whom they were, or if not to tip the barman the wink, and await an introduction.

Some couples, young or middle-aged, sat around, perhaps innocent, just passing through. Small groups of secretive looking men clustered over their pints. In the second room, a gathering watched as two men played snooker with steely concentration and the sharp clack of balls.

There was a tall black-haired man standing at one of the flashing machines, trying for a payment. But it wasn't Joseph. None of them were Joseph. Was he going to be fashionably late, as I'd tried to be?

I went to the bar. They don't stock Wincott's there, despite what he had said. I had a half pint of Guinness and sat down in the corner under a window with pale green and red diamonds.

After twenty more minutes I was two thirds down the glass. People had gone out, come in. The dealer in the corner had approached the oldest middle-aged couple and sat down with them. They talked in low earnest voices. I kept my eyes off them. Perversely I asked myself if it were weed or crack or straight heroin they wanted, he in his baggy trousers and shirt with tie, she fake ash-blonde and floral jacket.

Perhaps this was Joseph's latest ploy. To call me to him, see if I'd turn up, and not turn up himself. He must be watching somewhere. Where?

"May I sit here?"

I jumped.

A man stood over me. I'd never seen him before. He wore an expensive male cologne. I'm never keen on this fashion among men, although I realise I'm outdated. To be clean and deodorised is one thing but perfumed – quite another. Yet to be fair the scent was subtle, not overpowering.

He gestured towards the chair that faced mine. The rest of the pub had gradually filled up. I could hardly refuse him. Besides, there'd be no point in my staying much longer.

"Yes, of course."

He sat.

"Warm, for April," he remarked.

He wore a collarless white shirt, loose, not tucked in at the waist band of his gun-grey trousers. He was swarthy, olive-skinned with thick black hair and a solid looking blue-black moustache.

"Yes."

He smiled and sipped his drink. It appeared to be a straight Coke, no ice or lemon. "And you," he said.

My mind had wandered. A shadow had passed the open door. But it wasn't Joseph.

"I'm sorry, what did you say?"

"Mr Phillips," said the man, "shall we get to business?"

It was then that my startled eyes, swirling back to focus on him, saw instead the man I'd seen previously on the train. He was still bald and still in his brown shirt. He leaned at the bar, watching us casually, what might be a Bloody Mary, or only a tomato juice, in his hand.

"That's Mr C," said my sudden companion. "It's quite all right." He turned his dark head and nodded, friendly, at the bald man, 'Mr C,' who nodded back and turned away.

"What is this about?" I asked. The most crazy idea of undercover policemen surged through my mind.

"No, Mr Phillips, that is to be my question."

He had an educated voice, with the faintest hint of an accent, which might be Greek – or Egyptian, even something farther south-east of the Med. Accents aren't my forte.

"Your question. What...?"

"Precisely. What is this about?"

"What is wh...?"

"No, no, Mr Phillips. Let's cut to the chase, as they say."

"Why are you calling me Phillips?"

"Because, Mr Phillips, that was the name I was given on your behalf."

I stared at him. "Who gave it to you?"

He lowered his eyes with a knowing modesty. His lashes were like a woman's, as with the Mediterranean or Middle Eastern male type they often are.

"Someone gave it to me," he said, "who supposed you were in a little trouble. That you might need – a little assistance."

I sat there. I noticed in a sort of blind irrelevance the black hair at his throat, a thin tarnished chain on his right wrist, narrow as a hair, a wind-up watch. Although his clothes were of quality, they had no labels.

Something snapped home in my brain. "When you say trouble..."

"No. It is you who have said the 'trouble'."

I heard Lewis Rybourne's voice in my head first. "Oh, Roy. What shall I do?" Yet somehow Rybourne didn't fit this kind of thing; I couldn't imagine it, that he might know someone from this – calling. And then instead a female voice, high, light and foolish, said to my inner ear, as it had through the phone... "... my friend – she doesn't see him now... I really can't help you."

Tish Ackrington. She'd panicked after my call. She'd phoned up her hit-man acquaintance. Someone's found out – she couldn't tell him it was her fault I had, not that it had been. And he must have said, 'I'd better pay him a visit.' And then Brown Shirt had gone to my hotel. All the while I'd been checking Joseph Traskul wasn't on my trail, 'Mr C' had been. And now here was this one, using my pseudonym, relaxedly loose as his shirt and dangerous as an adder.

"I think – I may have been misunderstood," I said.

"No, not at all. You have someone in your life who gives you some grief. Isn't that so, Mr Phillips?"

I'd said nothing of that to Tish, but twittering idiot that she was, I reckoned it was easy enough even for her to put two and two together.

"I'm very sorry but..."

"I see," he said. He looked directly into my face and smiled again. His perpetual smiles were quite unlike Sej's. This man's smiles all had a definite purpose. They were masks.

"I'm extremely sorry," I said, "if you've been bothered unnecessarily."

"Ah well now, Mr Phillips. You see, in our line, very often we find a customer is at first a little unsure. For example, he may not be quite certain what we are able to offer him, nor if he's able to afford to recompense us for our very fine work." He sipped once more at the Coke. "We operate on a sliding scale, shall I say. And we have several forms of merchandise. If one's not suitable, it is very conceivable something else can be suggested. We are most flexible, Mr Phillips. Do please, for your own sake, give this a little more thought before making your final decision. The package can be something very small, or something of medium size. Or, naturally, our deluxe model. Everything will be tailored to your own particular needs. This can, to some extent, apply also to our prices."

I gazed at him in sick fascination. He was not like similar characters in my books. Most of those had been of the east ender sort, fists on the table and words unminced.

The deluxe model. I assumed this meant murder. And the other options – the packages – beating up, hospitalisation, or just intimidation, a warning.

I looked down at my drink.

The man across from me said, "Guinness. Have you ever drunk it in Ireland, Mr Phillips?"

"No."

"You should."

He knew too much. It seemed fruitless to deny it all again.

"Er, Mr..."

"Call me," he said, "Cart."

I thought Cart was what he said. He didn't remonstrate when I employed it. "Mr Cart..."

"Just Cart. In this matter, I am at your service."

"At this point I'm not sure I do need your – any help."

"That was not the impression I, or my colleagues, received."

"I may have overreacted."

He wasn't smiling. Above the rim of his glass his adder-black eyes stuck to mine.

Could I shake him off?

I doubted it. I cursed myself. I, not Tish, was the idiot.

Inside some compartment of my mind also, a low voice whispered that after all, this man was one of business, as he said. He did what he was paid for. And – if Joseph Traskul were as insane as I'd first believed, to have access to this atrocious alternative – might become necessary. Or was he insane? Was he maybe only different to the rest of us, spontaneous – compassionate. Brilliant.

And against all that, the other thought. *And if he is my son?*

I said, "I value very much the fact you've contacted me. It's still possible I may need – but right now there have been sudden other developments."

"This can happen."

"Can I ask...?"

He waited. His eyes were gelid now. They didn't blink or move away.

"If I required... something very slight. A small package."

"A thousand K," he said. "That may seem a lot, but there is my team to consider."

"And – what...?" I stopped. "It may not be necessary, but if..."

"A few little impacts," he said softly. "A little breakage, perhaps. Whatever you prefer. Nothing too serious. Enough to show the error of the way."

A lurch of nausea in my gut.

I evaded contact with his eyes.

"But if it doesn't come to that?"

"Then I will wish you a happy life, Mr Phillips. And you will be one thousand pounds the richer."

Perhaps I had incriminated myself enough he would now let me off.

He had seemed to be right-handed, but he reached over and took my own right hand with his left. I stiffened in alarm, but he was scribbling something across my palm in black biro. He let me go and I looked down at it. A mobile number.

"You will have to call me in the next few weeks. After that the mobile will have been stolen, or before that, should you do something else, such as tell another. In fact, Mr Phillips, I do advise you not to tell anyone. For your own sake." More familiar, this. More like one of my own characters. But Christ. What had he done to Tish?

"It's not in my interest to say anything," I said. "Thank you," I added lamely.

"It has been a pleasure to meet you," said Cart. He rose and turned at once, glass in hand. He walked straight past the bar and into the snooker room. He had ugly black shoes, hand-stitched. Brown Shirt, he of the Bond-Flemingesque name, had already vanished.

Duran phoned me the next morning.

He said, "Hi, Roy, how are you doing? She said like you might need some extra security at your place. Glad to hear you've come round to it, mate. We live in interesting times."

"Aren't you in Bristol?"

"No, mate. I'm on the train for London. I can fit you in 2nd of May."

"I'm not sure what's needed."

"Leave it to Uncle Duran. We got lots of packages," he added, unnerving me utterly. "You there, Roy?"

"Yes. Look, I'll call you later this week, early next, OK?"

"OK, mate. See you."

I spent the last days of April in the ordinary way. That Thursday Franziska came and scoured through the house. She commented the kitchen was much cleaner than usual. She gave me a haughty, slightly venomous look when she said it. Hours later it came to me she perhaps thought I now had a girlfriend, some aged person like myself, and this ridiculous female had cleaned the sink and surfaces.

Franziska too made a comment on the piano in the front room.

"Should polish this," she hectored me. "Have you polish?"

309

"No, I'm afraid not."

"Not," she severely said, "spray. Will ruin the wood. And leave the lid up."

"The lid?" This was unlike the lavatories, where she always insisted lids should be left closed, which apparently was benign Feng Shui.

"Let ivories breathe."

I was taken both by the old-fashioned English expression 'ivories' for keys, and the formula of allowing them oxygen. Maureen had said that, and the piano in the doll flat over the Co-op was always left with the lid raised. Though things were sometimes untidy and dusty there, the kitchen and bathroom were always clean, and the piano dusted, though never, I think, polished.

When Franziska had gone, I sat on the paving at the back in the deck chair, drinking tea. It was a warm afternoon, the leaves unfurling fast on neighbouring trees and trellises.

The fir stood dark and unexceptional.

I thought, *I shan't see him again.*

I hadn't seen her, my Maureen, since that night of our parting those years ago.

Like most of us, after a deep but not crippling blow, I just got on with my life. I told myself it was the regular sex I missed, which was true yet not the whole picture. Months after I found myself down that way and looking up saw different curtains in her windows. She'd been faithful to her word. She must have married her new old lover and gone elsewhere.

The following year I met Lynda Boyle at a rather flabby disco in Lewisham.

She was totally unlike Maureen. To begin with Lynda was over one year my junior. Thin, and with long limp mousy hair, she danced badly, and wore big glasses and a skimpy dress that did her few favours.

I was at the bar, with Danny Collins oddly, the confrere from the library I'd been with that night I met Maureen.

We'd secured our drinks, and were looking round at any talent, when Lynda came up and began trying to get the barman's attention.

Lynda was short, five foot three in her heels. No one took any notice of her, except Danny and me.

"Stupid bird," he said. He leaned across and shouted in her ear over the raucous music, "Wave a note at him, luv. He'll see that."

And she said, "I haven't got a note. It's all coins."

Then Danny said, "Hang on, I'll do it."

And he bawled at the barman, and the barman came, and Lynda got her round of drinks for herself and her two friends.

"What a shower," said Danny. "Look at them."

One girl was fat and one thin like Lynda.

They huddled to one side, and sometimes went out on the floor together to gyrate to the music. But they moved like creatures whose bones have been unhinged.

There was a girl that night, I can't recall her name. She had jet black dyed hair and she'd danced with me several times. She was one inch taller, but had taken off her shoes on realising. Then she was one inch shorter.

Afterwards I figured it out that she was only trying to make her male escort jealous. This finally worked; he came over and shoved me aside so hard I nearly fell, lugging her off shoeless and raven-locked into the night.

Disconsolate I went out and it was raining. Danny had to catch the train, but Lynda Boyle was standing weeping under the neon sign.

"What's the matter?" I said.

She raised her raining eyes to me. No glasses now. "Someone trod on them," she sobbed.

"On – what – who?"

"My spectacles. It was Sherry. She pushed me. She's jealous because she's so fat. And they fell off and someone just trod on them. Look." She showed me the ruination of her glasses. "I can't afford to get a new pair, not till next payday. And I can't see without them."

I'd been going to get a taxi anyway. Some of them always hung around the disco after midnight, like vultures, ready to charge double and a half. "Where do you live?"

She snivelled something.

She didn't have a coat and her bare shoulders were dewed with rain. She had a nice skin, and her hair, though very thin now it was wet, gave off a pretty smell. I put my leather jacket, (yes, I had one then), round her shoulders, and when the cab swarmed up, I took her home. She lived with her parents in an end-of-terrace 'mansion'. She let me kiss her outside the door. She wasn't Maureen. But she seemed to be available. She had already confessed she'd split up with her boyfriend three nights ago and was puzzling as to whether she should come off the Pill. I was nearly twenty-one. What was I likely to do? I did it a week later, having taken her, by then in new glasses purchased by her father, to my room in Brampton Way.

She refused to do a thing with the light on. But once it was off, she was up and ready. She rocked the house with her noise. I was embarrassed but not unflattered. Maureen had never been that loud. But then too, Maureen had never been that desperate.

XIII
('UNTITLED': PAGE 220)

Summoned from the bed of Klavdisa, Vilmos followed the tongueless servant in a daze.

The City before dawn was in its darkest and most abysmal mode. Now and then uncanny lights flitted through the black, overcast sky. Most likely they were lightnings, but for Vilmos they had ominous shapes, like those of racing greenish mares or lions, whose heads were skulls.

The Master's servant had sometimes indicated his – the Master's – purpose, by means of gesticulations and grimaces. On this excursion he revealed nothing, and when Vilmos had clapped one hand on his shoulder the dumb man thrust him off with a controlled violence that warned of strength.

"But I was called to the house, you know as much, five days back," Vilmos had protested.

Klavdisa all this while had kept to one corner of the bed, shivering. She was afraid of the Master, his alchemic reputation. Vilmos, having been with her for over three days and nights, had thought himself obscured from all search.

Truth to tell, he had dreaded that the Master would locate him now. What had appeared in the chamber, blurred as it was by his fainting, had left a impression of deep horror. And this had grown rather than diminished as time went by.

When they reached the building above the river the servant led him to its street door.

Vilmos had the urge to run away, but a line of light was showing in the east. He had an aversion to daylight, it hurt his eyes. And so he slunk inside.

The Master was seated in the main hall, in his tall chair. A fire crackled on the hearth and the toad sat there, warming itself, the Master's strange pet, which had always been about the house, so far as anyone knew. Some said it was as old as the Master himself, a creature therefore in its seventieth year. Vilmos had never beheld it before.

"I'm here," said Vilmos, affecting nonchalance.

"Oh, is it you?" said the Master, as if he had not had Vilmos brought.

"What do you want with me?"

"I? Do you think I want something?"

"Yes. I was dragged here..."

"It is the Great Powers." said the Master, terribly, "which *want* something of you. I am only their instrument."

"You have told me, jesting, I'll assume, I'm the Devil's."

"So you are. I will tell you something else, however, Vilmos. The Devil is himself punctilious and fastidious. He does not like you very much, though he intends to use you."

"Use me? Well, already he does."

"*That?* Murder and madness and debauchery? The Devil does not attend to such matters. His minor demons deal in those things. *Satanus Rex.* He's not called a king for nothing. *His* tastes are more refined."

"You know him well, then."

"All men *know* him. But he. He himself will condescend to know only a few."

Wine stood on the table in an ewer. Vilmos now, without asking, poured some into a glass, which also stood there, and drank it.

"You've said he chose me."

"So he has. But better not be flattered, Vilmos. The Beast has selected you as a man selects a piece of bread to mop up the gravy. He will use you, consume you perhaps. He does not mean to keep or cherish you."

Vilmos had drained the glass. He threw it at the toad – which nimbly hopped aside. The glass, meeting instead one of the stone pillars either side the hearth, shattered.

"I'm done with this. I'm not here for the Devil's use, let alone yours. I'm in the world for myself."

"Do you think so?"

Vilmos turned, at a loss. In the cramped windows a bloodless dawn was rising, showing the City, towers and roofs, the gleam of the dirty river, the ruined citadel on the Hill of Kolosian.

The toad had come to Vilmos's foot. It stared up at him. There was a poisoned jewel between its eyes. But its eyes also were like that. He wanted to kick it away. But he could not do it, just as he could no longer verbally fence with the Master.

"Let me go," he said.

"Impossible. You've been recognised. Not by ourselves, by That we resort to. Now you'll go upstairs. A room's prepared. Once you swore to serve this Order. Now you shall."

Vilmos said nothing.

The toad's eyes seemed to him luminous and compassionate.

To it, he muttered. "What shall I do?"

But the Master replied.

"You must now undergo various rituals and observances. You'll fast and receive chastisement. When we've purified your flesh – your mind, heart and soul, of course, are beyond any redemption – you will be permitted certain pleasures. You will even be allowed to kill once more. The tally must comprise thirteen victims. After this you will serve, as you swore to do, the Mystery. Remember, Vilmos, Gold may be made from Filth. The Fount of Eternal Youth, the Enlightening of the Gem of the Third Eye, may be discovered, unlocked. The colours of the body pass up towards the Infinite. And, in the stage before Infinity, they cross into the physical threshold of Truest Power. Be happy, Vilmos. For *you* will work an essential magic."

"But what *of* me?" he asked the toad, drearily.

It turned from him and waddled away into the shadow behind the Master's chair. Its refusal to answer seemed now significant.

Risen sun burst through a window, and in Vilmos's skull the white string and the black raw coal of the migraine woke without preamble, hungry, sinking in their fangs. He barely noticed as the servants came and hauled him up the stairs.

313

FIFTEEN

On the 2nd May at 8.30 a.m., Duran arrived at the house.

He isn't young, though some years younger than I am, yet he retains the air of his mature youth, which I suppose was in the Eighties.

We went round the house. He made notes on a pad from Sainsbury's in green biro.

The chat had been desultory. Suddenly, in the study by the computer, having asked me about virus-combatants, firewalls and so on – computer fraud and its prevention had also become an interest of his – he said, "So why this conversion, Roy?"

"What? The security?"

"Yes, mate. You seemed happy enough. You getting like a bit of bother round here?"

"It's a quiet road," I said. "But. Well, you hear things."

"Yeah. But you can always *hear* things. What's new?"

Of course, I had had the idea before that I might confide in Duran, ask him for advice, even help. He might know – someone. But now obviously, *someone* had approached me, the unsettling *Cart* or whatever the hell his name was. And I'd put Cart off because frankly, in those moments, I had felt more scared of him and of the consequences of using his services, than of the eccentric Sej. Now however, I still felt I couldn't confide in Duran. Was it that I really and definitely had begun again to credit Joseph was my son?

"Like, Roy, mate, you don't have to tell me. Only if you felt you should. P'raps I could make you a better defence plan. For the house, I mean."

I looked at him. The words stuck. I said, "I do appreciate that, Duran. Thanks. But I'm just thinking of taking a break, going up north to visit an old friend. And the house will be empty, you see."

He chuckled. "What've I *told* you, Roy? Don't tell no one, *ever*, you are leaving your property unoccupied."

"Right."

"I mean, you don't know you can trust me. I mean, you can. But you can't know for sure."

"Almost every lock and bolt in here was your suggestion. Wouldn't you have broken in by now if I couldn't?"

"Well, you got me there, Roy. Maybe I'm just biding my time."

The other matter of Why had been satisfactorily shelved, probably let go. He was a good man, but his moral duty, even as he saw it, could only extend so far.

When Duran and I had made the 'defence plan', which would be quite costly, and included sorting out a new burglar alarm that worked… "Police don't take that much notice, unless you got one of *these*" …we fixed another date for

Thursday, he had another coffee and then left. His girlfriend was eight and a half months into expecting their second baby. He didn't like having to go back to Bristol on Saturday and leaving her. He said if anything got 'stressy' his cousin would have to lump it.

After he'd gone I did the chores in the house. The contents of the fridge and freezer were low, but if I was planning to leave this coming Saturday, I only had a few days to cover. The thought of shopping, never a favourite task and always kept to necessities, exasperated me. I'd known for years that one day I'd be old and on my own and then I wouldn't manage it at all. It would be some form of modern meals-on-wheels, or deliveries from some supermarket, with half the items doubtless wrong.

But the way the world was, why assume I'd even live, or any of us would, into our 'twilight' years?

In the afternoon I sat down at the machine and put in the disc for the latest due-to-be-written novel. It had the working title of *Kill Me Tomorrow*, which I'd lifted of course from *Othello*, but the publisher had pointed out it sounded too much like something concerning James Bond. I couldn't settle to it.

I am fairly disciplined. One needs to be in this job. But the whole rigmarole, although they'd liked and bought it, looked like twaddle to me now.

Finally I sat, staring at the words on the screen, not seeing them, and Joseph walked forward in my mind and stood there, watching me.

I hadn't seen him for days. How long? Eight, nine. But he had left an indelible impression. The four circumstances of our meeting – the pub in the Strand, under the fir tree, at my door, in my hotel – had me strung up in the certain belief he might now suddenly appear – virtually anywhere, looking in at an upper window, maybe, balanced ably on a ladder.

Or would I simply go downstairs, and he'd be sitting there, in the kitchen, drinking tea?

Why had he installed a piano, if he hadn't meant to return into my life and house? Or was it a present, like the dustbin and the bottle of beer which, incidentally, I'd never touched.

He'd become bored. That must be it. His warped and extraordinary mind had abruptly swerved away from me.

I'd be glad, thankful, but only if I could be *certain*.

Or would I be glad, and thankful?

Surely, for Christ's sake, I wouldn't miss any of *this*?

Unless. Unless he was my son.

Odd perhaps, I'd kept the elements that would contain his DNA, to help protect me from him. Now for the very first I fully recognised they might have another purpose.

But then, DNA tests aren't always conclusive. And anyway, if he were mine – what would he want? And I. What would *I* want *of* him?

At 7 p.m. the burglar alarm went off, apparently because some kids were playing football outside. Later it did it again because the bicycle boy from up the road went past. It had always behaved like this. I turned it off.

That night I dreamed of Joseph Traskul as Vilmos, in the dim City of my imagination's night. He lay half dead in the upper room of the Master's house, as outlined in chapters thirteen through fifteen. In this dream-version rain was pouring in through the ceiling.

And I went into the room and stood looking down at him and he lay looking up at me.

"Don't do this, Roy," he said. "I never meant to harm."

But I answered in the Master's words, a script I had learned well, that he was for the use, not of myself, but of Great Powers beyond – yet in – the world.

And then Maureen stood beside me on the floor running with water, and she said, "He's not worth our concern, Charlie. Bleeding bugger."

And I woke, and I thought, *My God, can I wait until Saturday to get away?*

In the morning I called Matt.

"I've got to make a trip to your neck of the woods. Are you up to dinner?"

"I'm up to anything, Roy. I'm up to killing that bitch."

I thought, *This then, Matt's anti-Sylvia maelstrom of bitterness, is my alternative.* Never mind. I need to remove myself somewhere.

"Any chance I could sleep on the couch a couple of nights? These bastards aren't paying expenses."

"Why not, Roy? Have the spare room. She's had her fucking lover in there enough times. And now she's gone. So exorcise it for me."

Duran was due to come back on Thursday. On Thursday morning something happened. Someone rang the doorbell, obviously Duran, yet as I opened the door I thought – *I thought…*

A woman, youngish, tall, willowy, stood there looking upset.

"I'm sorry to trouble you – but my car's stalled…" She waved in a helpless way over her right shoulder. "It's just, my mobile's out too. Could I possibly use your landline? I'll be happy to pay."

I looked at her, and I thought now: *There have been too many things like this. Too many.*

I said, "I'm sorry, my phone isn't working." (This was, of course, true). "Perhaps try next door." I indicated 76, Ian the househusband.

She said, looking even more upset, "I did, they don't answer."

We stared at each other, she and I.

The ultimate impasse. I didn't believe her. I was thinking, if not coherently, *This is a scam. She's up to something, this forlorn female, coming here and saying she must use my telephone.*

And then I recalled, in the most unpredictable rush, so many incidents in

316

my life, and how curiously I had met so many characters who were now integral, even if our time of contact had vanished away. Maureen with her dramatically sloughed lover Reg, Lynda with her broken glasses – even events, for example the urge to hurry to the hospital lavatory, missing, like some cruel train, my mother's moment of death.

I mustn't be so self-involved. Everything did *not* revolve around me. Everything was *not* a conspiracy, a plot.

"Wait, I've got a mobile. You can use that." I turned and left her by the door. I only had to go to the kitchen table. I hadn't asked her in, nor did she come in. She didn't look particularly strong; there was nothing to steal in the hall.

"Oh, thank you," she said, when I gave her the phone. "What do I owe...?"

"That's fine."

Encouraged, grateful, she did step up, just into the shelter of the doorway. She leaned by the door and pushed in numbers.

Then she pulled a Kleenex out of a pocket and rubbed her nose, turning her back to me shyly.

I could see it now, the white car, stalled very definitely down where Old Church Lane gave way to the Crescent. Steam rose from the bonnet.

I walked off into the kitchen, let her mumble into the phone in private.

As such conversations do, it took a little while. I'd better top the phone up again, to be safe.

When I came back, she'd dropped the Kleenex on my mat and was grabbing it up. She stood clutching it and wiping her nose with it again, though now it would be less than clean. She was shaky. I retrieved my phone before she dropped that too.

"Thank you, thank you so much. It's OK. They're coming to rescue me. I shouldn't get so silly... Really, can't I pay for...?"

"It's quite OK."

She went off along the path. I wondered why she was driving through these streets, where she was going, why she'd got in such a flap. She was rather a pretty woman, only about thirty. She looked sad, sad anyway without car problems to upset her. She was wiping her eyes now. What would he have done? Asked her in and made her tea.

I shut the door.

It rained in the evening. The sunset was like a squashed blue plum. I'd gone out of the back door and looked at the paving, for some reason. It was beginning to crack. I suppose not unreasonably, it had been laid some years before. Built-in obsolescence, as they say. *Bad workmanship*, as my father would have said.

Duran hadn't turned up. This wasn't like him. Nor did he call.

I dreamed about my father *that* night. He was walking with me through a dark forest full of fir trees.

"You should clear this, Roy. It's a bit disappointing,"

"But, Dad. It isn't mine."

"It's all yours, Roy. Everything is yours, ours. We just have to face it, show it we're not afraid. Never turn your back on these things, Roy. They'll only get worse."

My father had become the Master now. He even wore the robe.

We reached a hill above the forest and saw moonlight rake the acres of the trees. Above, stars burned blue. It was, as dreams can be, detailed and entirely real.

"How's mother?" I asked him humbly.

"Your mother?" he said. His voice grew quiet and tense. "She has a lover, Roy. She didn't wait for me. I'm up to killing that bitch."

When Duran phoned me at 7 the next morning I was not amazed.

Nor, of course, when he said, "I still can't get anything from your landline, Roy."

"No. Trying to get them to fix it."

"Gawd. Don't hold your breath."

"I'm not."

"Look, Roy, I *hate* to've let you down. She's gone into well – we thought it was labour and she's not due till June. But they've took her in and – well, I wanna be with her,

"Yes, Duran, of course you do."

"Can I call you later?"

"Whenever, Duran. Don't worry about that. Good luck. I'm sure she'll be fine."

"Thanks, Roy. You're a king."

Satanus Rex. A king.

When I thought to look, the white car had been removed from the junction of the Lane and the Crescent.

I was fairly sure Duran wouldn't be calling me back, or if he did only to say he couldn't make it. They might send her home and he must be there to look after her, not to mention their other child, who was only just at school age.

The problem was, should I simply leave the house as it was? Presumably Joseph *could* break in. Or could he? Did his cleverness also lie in that direction? He gave off an almost supernatural impression of being able to manifest out of thin air, but in fact there were always reasons for everything he had achieved that way. He'd made sure I understood them. No, the house could resist him. Somehow he had got the piano speed-delivered and installed on that single day he was here before. Since then he hadn't come back. After all he might never come back. Presumably he had achieved his purpose, whatever insane purpose it was.

Even so, preparing to pack, I meant to put everything together again very carefully, all my documents and valued files, placed in my holdall.

At 9 a.m. this time Matt called me on the mobile.

"Your phone doesn't work, Roy." He meant the landline evidently. He sounded aggrieved. Faithless wives, useless telephones... "I tried you yesterday. Twice."

"They're being slow to repair it. As I have the mobile, I'm not an emergency, it seems."

"You are to me. This call's costing me the earth. And a mobile phone, did you know, can give you cancer?" he added. Gloatingly he continued, "*She* has one. Reason I called. I can't make this weekend. Some old chums have turned up out of the blue. Every inch of space here is taken. I'll be clear Monday morning, and good riddance."

I sensed, without any evidence, he had picked up another woman and she was staying the weekend with him. Hopefully it might defuse some of his angst.

"Let's make it Monday then, Matt."

This was better, in its way. Monday would be easier for travelling up there. Saturdays like Sundays were always chancy, trains cancelled, works on the line.

But now I had tonight and two more days and nights here.

When I locked up that night the top bolt on the front door seemed loose. It had a little the previous night, but this was worse. Duran had been a bit rough with all the bolts, testing them and telling me off for using flimsy things like that still, although he had installed them himself years ago. "Yeah, but Roy, things have improved. Anyone could *kick* this door down. Bust the locks, the bolts'd just fly off."

I had told him I would then hear all that and telephone the police.

"Mate of mine," he said balefully, "he had a break-in. The cops took an hour to get there. By which time he'd chased the burk off himself. But I don't see you doing that. Not your style. Too much a gentleman you are, Roy."

I wobbled the bolt home gingerly. The lower one, which last night I'd forgotten to shoot, as I sometimes do when I'm tired, seemed conversely very stiff. I got some WD40 and squirted it, but it didn't seem to do any good. I left it and simply locked up. Then I brought a straight chair from the front room and leaned it on the door. I felt foolish doing this, despite everything that had happened. But in any case, I couldn't utilise the bolts from the outside, or the chair, when I left.

This was going to be one of my fully insomniac nights, or so it seemed. I got to bed about 10.30 and tossed and turned until one. Then I got up, made some tea and went into the study.

Here I tried to make a start on the new novel, *Kill Me*.

Outside two cats were wauling at each other. Up the road No 98 was having a party; I could catch the thump-thump of their music.

I managed to squeeze out five hundred words of dry, formulaic crap, but it was, I told myself virtuously, a start.

Then I found myself reaching out for the disc of *Untitled*.

I put it in the machine.

Chapter XVI. Printed up, this began on page 273, and ran on to Chapter XVII, and so to the part at which I had left it, in the spring of the year 2000.

I skimmed through it, once or twice pausing, even now, to change a word, pare or extend a sentence.

Lying on the floor of the Master's upper room, Vilmos had just slaughtered a man dragged in for him from the alleys. Vilmos had performed the murder gruesomely, but without involvement. A rat had come from the corner to feast. His own body starved and tortured by the Master's minions, Vilmos lay in the blood, the stranger's and his own, his mind clear for the first time perhaps in twenty-five years, his eyes full of blue flashes, the visual product of another variation on his migraines. But the blue being very beautiful, very evocative, entertained him with its colour.

My own eyes had begun to ache.

I printed the amendments on paper, then switched off the machine. Going downstairs for a whisky nightcap, I poured it in one of the sturdier glasses from the kitchen. I felt done in, but would I sleep? Outside I heard the cats still fighting violently across the front paving. Their spitting struggle, or something like it, might fit well into the next paragraphs of Vilmos's horror. Maybe other rats could come in and these would fight. I scribbled a note and took the whisky to bed.

To my surprise I drifted after only a minute or so, into a warm and trackless sleep. Just two more days, then I'd be gone.

Waking, the alarm-clock, blurred by my vision, said it was 4.12 a.m. There was as yet no light. *Was* I awake? I thought not completely and turned eagerly to swim back down.

That damned party up the road was still going on. I could hear the music, not thumping now, in fact a piano playing. A piano playing tunefully. Softly, pleasingly. I thought, *Oh, that's only Sej.* And again I slept.

I woke at half past 10. Nowadays that's unheard of for me, even after a white night.

When I sat up, a light wave of vertigo slid across my brain. I'm not subject to such things. My mouth tasted unusually nasty, chalky...

A stab of absolute fright shot through me. I'd been drugged. I had been drugged. How? The tea – no, I'd worked a while after that. It must have been the whisky. Look, I hadn't even finished it. I picked up the glass and sniffed it. There was no smell, only alcohol. But then, there hadn't been any other smell than alcohol in the red wine I gave to *him*.

This was the moment I recalled hearing the piano being played downstairs.

I floundered out of bed, ran into the bathroom and grabbed the shaving-foam. It's of the type that sprays.

Running, vertigo forgotten, I took the stairs in leaps and sprang into the front room.

No one was there. The lid of the piano was shut, as I'd eventually left it despite my cleaning girl's admonition.

The library and kitchen were also empty. There was no sign of any tampering, had been none upstairs. The windows were shut and locked, the back door also. The front door too, when I went and looked at it, was the same as I had left it, the upper bolt shakily done up and the bottom one stuck in the undone position. Both door locks were secure.

Then I remembered the chair, which I'd left leaning on the door. It wasn't there.

Back into the front room I went. The chair stood, where it usually did. Had I misremembered? Hadn't I moved it out into the hall? Had I dreamed I'd done that, then dreamed I heard him playing – what had it been? Gershwin – *Someone to Watch Over Me* – and then something else...

I walked back into the hall and, not undoing the door, pulled at it very gently.

The upper bolt fell straight down on the floor. It had been secured, this time for appearances only, by Blu-Tack. When I'd fetched the magnifying glass from the library, knelt down and peered through it, I saw too the mass of something transparent and shiny that had trapped the lower bolt in its slot, unable to move. Superglue, probably.

I stood there, thinking over the ultimate riddle. He must of course, during the short while he was here before, have managed to obtain copies of the two front door keys. But the bolts had been fine until the night before last. Thursday. Had Sej then already somehow broken in *while I was here*? I have reasonably good hearing for my age; surely I'd have heard him? The very camouflaging of the wrecked bolts indicated he'd wanted to enter quietly, to – shall I say – *surprise* me. And the drug, if there was one, in the whisky – I'd had a glass of whisky on Wednesday night, without any ill effect. I'd slept in the usual way, not well, only the peculiar dreams, but I'd had those off and on since first I met him.

No, something had been done here later than Wednesday. And somehow I knew it hadn't been by Joseph. This was an animal deduction. My *instinct*, if you like. As if I might have detected him by odour, or a pricking in my thumbs.

Yet if not him, then who?

It was at this moment that I recalled the young woman with the stalled car. She was tall enough to reach up bolt-high easily, but had she the strength to pry the bolt loose, the skill not to loosen it entirely, only enough a slight nudge from outside would shift it? Of course she *could* have slopped the glue on to the other, lower bolt. I remembered how she'd bent down, risen with the dropped Kleenex in her hand, and wiped her nose – or seemed to wipe it – so sadly, as if holding back tears. Had there been space also for her to pop into the front room and fix my whisky?

Who was she? Why had she done it?

She must have done it because Sej told her to.

I remembered something else.

I remembered the woman with the run-over dead white dog at *The Belmont Hotel*.

SIXTEEN

It goes without saying that ringing both Duran's home number and his mobile got no answer. He was at the hospital. However, now I couldn't quite push off the grim feeling that Sej had somehow also got at him, and that the labour of Duran's girlfriend was a lie. The non-mad area of my brain dismissed this theory over and over. Duran would not be, let alone become, any pawn of Sej's. And yet...

Instead I called a local locksmith. I explained I needed my front door locks changed and bolts replaced.

"Sorry, squire. I'm spoken for this next month." He suggested another name and number who, politely saying much the same thing, also gave me another name and number. In the end, after several more similar calls, a nasal voice said he might be able to 'help me out'. The price he quoted was exorbitant, but I agreed. He never turned up.

What should I do?

Damn it to hell. If Sej wanted bloody access so much let him have it. I'd had to abandon the house before. It would be lunacy to stay here now. *Waiting.* I began to pack that early Saturday afternoon, and in among the clothes and other stuff, held in bubble-wrap and a small box, I placed my mother's red glass dog. Red, for Vilmos and his Order, was the colour of the lowest chakra, located at the genitals. Or blood, of course. Even a white dog could be made red that way. And what had I seen of it, that dead, white dog, I, the perceptive writer of detective fiction? A bundle out of which hung a *tail*. I hadn't even gone close. It could have been a child's *sock*. And the rest? Fake theatrical blood normally available in joke shops, if nowhere else – or even ketchup. And a small bolster.

I raised the lid of the piano after I'd taken the ornament. I thought of smashing the keys of the piano with the hammer I use to knock in the odd nail.

I also thought of poisoning every item of drink or food in the house. I didn't need sleeping pills, or bleach. Clear shampoo would do in the dry ginger. Sink cleaner, a white cream, smeared last over the frozen piece of chicken, appearance and smell obscured by the cold. Enough to make him sick again. Enough to *sting*. I toyed with these notions. I wanted to booby-trap the place but now there wasn't time. I had to get out, before everything else in the street curled up in another night, and lying sleepless and fully dressed for morning, I heard the two keys turn in the locks, as I hadn't last night. I'd piled several items against the front door again, kitchen chairs, pans and pots, the original paraphernalia plus. I'd managed to bump and heft one of the armchairs out of the front room too. Make it hard for him. I would leave by the back way, use the small kitchen ladder to climb over the back fence which, as I was light, should just take my weight as it had taken his rangier, slightly-heavier one the first time.

In a defunct plastic vitamin bottle I poured a sample of the-perhaps contaminated whisky. I still wasn't sure, there. Had I only been very tired? If it *were* a pill, I'd like to know the brand name. Apart from slight giddiness on first sitting up, I felt fine. Thanks, Sej, for finally finding me the *occasional good night's sleep.*

I was loath to destroy the computer. To have to buy a new one would be annoying, and everything lately had taken a toll on my 'savings'. Left alone it should be useable for another eighteen months at least, and for my requirements, probably three years. I had the discs, and I'd set it to delete again.

Additionally now, I'd also pulled out the paperback copy of each of my novels, and dumped them in another bag. I'd put the big paper copy of *Untitled* in there too, complete with the recent printed corrections and hand-written scribbles. I added my mother's Bible, the King James edition, retained by all of us for its language and antiquity, rather than any delusions of a God.

I locked my bedroom door again and for good measure, before that, myself pumped glue down the upright of the door's edge. Post locking, I pumped glue as well into the lock. This was sheer perversity. There was nothing interesting in the room. I just wanted to frustrate him.

But I hadn't smashed the piano keys. It would take a lot to make me do something like that. It was a musical instrument, valuable not only as an object, but for its potential. In the same way I'd have been happy right then to poison Joseph Traskul, but not to break his fingers.

Perhaps it goes without saying I had written down the number the ghastly Cart had given me. I nearly called it twice that afternoon. But then I couldn't say exactly where the quarry was likely to be. Take it with me, and I'd have a more concrete clue that he might be here.

At this time, I had no notion of the 666 number of Sej's London flat, only that such a flat was supposed to exist.

I'd previously checked train times on the web and was aiming for something between 3 and 5.30. The grey stone village where Matthew, once with Sylvia, lived, is like many others, all of them rather more charmingly evidenced by the famous venue in *Last of the Summer Wine.* It was a few miles outside Cheston, and Cheston. with its concluding change of trains at Crewe, would take, all told, four hours. Cheston had the *Empire Hotel.* There I would park myself over Saturday night and Sunday and polish off the last of the credit on my Barclaycard.

Everything locked, bolted, barricaded, disconnected, made, where feasible, user-unfriendly, I left the house which had been my parents' at 2.15 p.m. The bags were going to feel heavy. Having unlocked the back door, closed and relocked it, I climbed the kitchen ladder at the end fence. I intended to lower the bags over the top of the fence to the alley, trusting the packing would protect the glass dog.

The day was miserable, gloomy. No one was about. Birds sang however, and up in the fir there came the flutter of wings.

Looking over the fence I felt a fool. But there was no time for that. I lowered both bags with care; they only had to drop the shortest distance. Then I took hold of the barrier. Thank God, it at least was in decent repair. I kicked the ladder away and heard it skid along the paving, then launched myself across and down.

A boy could do that. Now and then I had, as a boy, done such things. But I'm no longer a boy. I landed awkwardly but not badly, scraping my hand on the fence, and one knee on the concrete of the alley. In the fir the birds took flight with disapproving cries. And he rose from the shadow where, unseen in black, he had crouched, smiling, and helped me to my feet. I write books. I was a book. And he had read me all before, it seemed.

Blood was seeping through my trouser leg where I'd grazed my knee like that boy I wasn't anymore.

He looked at that. "Oh dear."

"Take your bloody hands off me."

Smiling, he stepped back. And before I could think, he'd picked up both my bags. "We'll go in the front way. Can you make it OK, Roy?"

"The door is barricaded."

"I'm sure I can shift it. Don't worry."

"There's more there than last night." I didn't sound defiant, only meaningless.

"Well, I'm strong. Come on. Won't take a minute."

I stood where I was. I said, "Why don't you leave me alone?"

"Because I like you."

"I don't – like you. Go to hell."

"How do you know I don't already, on a regular basis?"

An awful laugh burst out of me. I sounded madder than he did. "Right," I said. "Are you going to give me back my bags?"

"Of course, if you think you can manage."

"Give me my fucking bags."

He widened his eyes at me. It reminded me of a woman's facial gesture. Maureen had never done this. Others, especially Lynda, had.

"Take this one, then." He handed me the holdall. "But this one, it's smaller but it feels heavier. What have you put in here? Your secret wine cellar? Better let me carry that."

And turning from me, he sauntered back along the alley and turned the corner towards the front.

I could have let him go, run the other way – my knee wasn't bad – got out by the alley's other exit nearer the Crescent. I would, I think, have got away.

But the bag he had hold of contained my books, my discs, and my MS of *Untitled*. I realised in those seconds that I, too, was definitely unstable. In the holdall I had my passport, all crucial documents, even the house deeds – even now the glass dog. Yet I went after him. I hurried.

He was already at the front door using the keys when I reached him.

"Mmm," he said contemplatively. "I can feel it'll be a bit of a push. That's all right."

Just then the front door of 72 opened. Out ambled amiable George, with the big kitchen scissors he uses to trim the hydrangea on his front lawn.

"Hello, Roy. Oh, hello..." he added, beaming, to Sej.

"Hi. How are you, Mr Fulton?" politely inquired Sej.

"Oh, we're fine, thank you."

I said, "George, I need to have a word with you."

George looked vaguely concerned. As I moved forward, Sej got in my way, putting an arm over my shoulders. I thrust him off.

"George, this man is not my son. Go indoors. Call the police."

Stricken, George stood there, like a child on Christmas morning finding the presents are gone and the tree has died.

Sej spoke to him before I could do so again. "Sorry, Mr Fulton. It's all right. I think I explained a bit about this before. He'll be OK now I'm here. Just leave it..."

"George," I said loudly, "for God's sake do as I say. Please."

"Er, Roy – well, er..."

As I took half another step in his direction, he performed a most determinative action. Largely I think it was subconsciously dictated. But then, I've never known them well, my neighbours. How could any of them be sure what or who I really was? He pointed the scissors at me, the points towards my chest, and backed up the lawn, in at his door. He was still saying, almost still amiably, "Er, well, er," as he closed it.

I had my own mobile in my hand by then. Better late than never, but it was not. It was too late.

"Now, Roy," said Sej, not even glancing but predicting once more with total accuracy as he spun the phone out of my grasp. It hit the path. There was a crack. Had anyone else seen or heard? If they had, so what? We all have troubles of our own.

"Give me the bag," I said.

"Not yet, Roy. Let's get the door undone first."

Leave it, you fool, leave it all – sentimental glass dog, documents, manuscript, disc, book, DNA, house. Escape, you confounded fucking idiot...

But instead I came at him, I, who cannot fight to save my life and never even scrapped with anyone since I was fourteen and Ben Oggey stole my fountain pen. Ben won, incidentally. No great amazement, that.

Sej simply caught me and somehow swung me round, and as he put me down again he thrust with our combined weight at the front door. The pans went over inside with a stupid noise of armour, the chairs went too, even the armchair had shifted just enough.

The wind was knocked out of me. He pushed me in through the open slice of door, then threw the bag of books over my head and along the hallway. Perhaps he thought I'd be impelled to race after it like a stick-addicted puppy. But I merely leaned on the wall and in he came, squeezing past the fallen barricade, putting down the other bag, the holdall, which he had also somehow relieved me of in our brief non-fracas.

My front door too was shut. Outside my mobile was lying, maybe useless or not, on the path. But things get thrown on to the front gardens sometimes. There was even once, I'd heard, a whole box of uneaten pizza found floating in the pond at No 82.

"Well, then," said Sej. "Let's see about that knee of yours. Then we'll have some tea."

Naturally I didn't allow him to touch the graze. I saw to it myself in the bathroom, which he permitted. I had to conclude he had permitted it, even to my locking the bathroom door. But he could break it in anyway, I was fairly certain of that.

I sat on the closed seat of the lavatory and stared in despair at the two bags I'd insisted on bringing up with me – which again, I'd been permitted to do.

I made another mental itinerary.

My bedroom door was locked, (he must have got copies of the front door keys by taking an impression from the locks, so might anyway have a copy of this key too). But the bedroom door now was glued shut. Study, library, front room, kitchen, lavatory and bathroom were potentially open wide.

There was very little food in the house and no phone. Apart I assumed from his own mobile, which he would still have.

Was shampoo in the ginger ale or sink cleaner on the chicken still an option? He'd be watching out now. Doubly cautious.

And there was the strong impression he might like me to 'try something'. A challenge, like some move in a game of which I didn't know the rules.

God, what could I do?

He let me take my time up there.

When I came out. I'd removed the disc of *Untitled* and also my most important documents, and shoved them in the inside pockets of my jacket. He'd see, or suspect these stiffened shapes probably, but at least this way I could run if I ever got a chance. If he took them off me, I still could. Why hadn't I already? I had had the chance. Not taken it.

Did that godforsaken novel mean so much? Vilmos –Vilmos and that invented City and all that infantile quasi-gothic rubbish, a stale brain's attempt to sparkle.

Tidily he had cleared the chairs and other things from the hall. The armchair had been lugged back into the front room and to its accustomed place, marked ready by the imprint of its legs in the carpet. When I re-entered the kitchen, I saw he'd brought in the steps from outside. As in my macabre premonition, he was sitting at the table, drinking tea.

"I made a pot."

I sat down and looked at him.

"You look tired," he said.

"I am, Sej. Why are you doing this?"

"You keep asking. I keep telling. You don't seem to absorb it."

"No."

"I like you. You interest me."

"Do you understand what you're doing?"

He smiled. "Perfectly."

He poured out tea; we both were to have milk. And neither of us took sugar, it seemed.

"Have you put," I said, "something in the tea?"

"That's your sort of trick."

My mind reassembled suddenly. "Apart from the whisky," I said.

He looked at me. For the first time, like a villain in 1940s film noir, he raised one long, black eyebrow only.

"Sorry?"

"I had a whisky last night and I slept – in a way I don't usually sleep. Actually, Sej, I'd like to know what it was. That was probably the best night's sleep I've had for about fifteen years."

And then he grinned, as he had when he played the piano like a young contemporary Liszt.

"I think I understand. It wasn't in the whisky, Roy. It was in the glass."

"Not the whisky glasses in the front room. I'd used them."

"No. It was a chunky glass in your kitchen cupboard. You could have put anything in it – water, Coke, take your pick."

"A glass. How?"

"I broke the tablet. It's Rohypnol, by the way. I dissolved some of it and wiped it round the bottom of the glass. Put it back on the shelf, to the front."

"So it could have happened any time."

"Truly. I wondered why you didn't come down, when I was playing you the Gershwin, and that Chabrier piece. The Chabrier was his last composition. Sheer fireworks."

I said, "Yes, I half heard it. Sounded as if you had three hands."

A look of radiant pleasure went over his face.

He said, "There are times, Roy, I love you. I wish you were my father."

I took a breath. I hadn't tried the tea.

Gently I said, "Am I? Tell me the truth."

"As I've said before, what do you think?"

"I think I am not your father."

He shrugged.

327

"Then tell me," I said, "the name of your mother."

I was calm as a piece of wood. Maybe it was shock. Now he had trapped me entirely. I was letting go all I had ever been. I had to become some other person – or some intrinsic Roy. A kind of non-effusive passion was stirring in me. I can't explain it. No doubt I was temporarily, and with some reason, mad.

"My mother's name." He looked at the table. "Let me think."

"You wouldn't have to think."

"Oh, Roy. I would. I grew up, if you can call it that, in an orphanage. Then I was fostered. I can't recall quite when, but after I was eighteen someone showed me some clandestine paperwork. And her name was on it. But I didn't want to know."

Stunned I sat there. Through my mind, irrepressibly, went an image of Maureen, abandoning her child so her well-off old man wouldn't get angry. Had she done that?

"It's important," I said. "At least, curiously enough, to me."

And I wondered at myself for I seemed now to be two men. One knew this situation for what it was. The other – the other, less than play along, had become engaged. But this other me also, he had his own agenda, to which I wasn't sure I was even privy. It was as if I'd left myself below, and here he – I – sped along the high bridge above. With Sej. Most games need at least two players.

Sej lifted his head and tipped it right back this time. He looked up at the ceiling.

"Give me a clue," he said.

"First letter L. Lynda," I said, deliberately.

"No. That wasn't it."

The tea I hadn't drunk was cold. He had drunk his. "What about," I hesitated. "V," I said. "Or – J?"

And he looked at me. "Oh, Roy," he said. "We are going to have a wonderful time."

He did break in the bedroom door, later that evening. It was easy for him, as I'd have thought, although the door didn't break open cleanly because of the glue.

"What did you use?" he asked, sounding mildly intrigued.

"What she did, I expect, your woman friend who fixed the bolts downstairs."

"I see."

I'd already asked him how she had managed the loosening of the top bolt. "She's good at that kind of thing," he said. "She has strong wrists and fingers – she plays the piano, the same as me."

We had had lots of little conversations by bedtime. On this, and that.

Once I said, "So now I'm definitely your prisoner."

And he said, "Yes. For now."

We had established this because my mobile had rung faintly out on the front path. Apparently, it still worked. But when I inquired if I was to be allowed to get it, he said no, and that nor would he.

It rained heavily that night anyway.

Besides, someone might steal it, simply for its usefulness, perhaps as a free gift, for it was in no way trendy.

I had also seen, during the afternoon, the tiny dark healing wound in the palm of Sej's left hand.

For one terrible moment I'd been reminded of a disgusting statue of Christ crucified – the Crucifix. He saw me see the mark. He said, "This? That's fine. I'll tell you about it later."

But I am prevaricating.

Because I don't want to put down the next section of my narrative.

Perhaps absurdly, I hadn't known I would 'block' at this point. In fact it isn't a block; I know only too well what comes next.

No one will ever see this.

No one.

Let me therefore, for my own sake, write it.

6

The second time I went to his flat, Mr C went with me.

Brothers in our shaven baldness, we were otherwise not alike. A big man, Mr C. On this occasion he wore a grey shirt. "Which one's the druggy you said?"

"Flat No 2. 3A's a possible as well."

Mr C rang the bell of No 2.

We waited, while 5's loud music thundered above. My companion seemed impervious.

There was no answer. So Mr C rang No 2's bell again, now leaning on it.

Presently a voice blurred from the speaker.

"Whah? Wha' is it?"

"Hello, sonny. I got something nice for you. What you like. You want it?"

No 2 brightened audibly. "'S 'at Col?"

"No. It's his best friend."

"Wha' you got?"

"I'm not telling you through a door. You want it, come and get it. You got one minute."

"Hang on – don' go – I'm opening the door – I'll be there..." wailed No 2.

The buzzer sounded and the door was pushed open by Mr C.

We went in and stood there until No 2 came slithering and slipping, nearly falling, down the stairs. He was as I recalled him, nothing changed, hair, garments or stench.

On the last lowest step, he seemed to grasp that something was wrong here. He eyed Mr C, then me, then came back to Mr C.

"I see you afore," he finally told us both, inaccurately.

Mr C moved.

He was very quick, which I'd already witnessed.

No 2 went down like a literal bag of bones. I seemed to hear them click and rattle as he landed on the floor and Mr C knelt on him. Probably I'd heard his keys.

"Now, then. We want to go and see Tina."

"All right – a' right – yeah, mate, you go an' see Tee."

"She up there today?" asked Mr C, grinding his knee into No 2's ribs so he squeaked and coughed. "Sure – yeah."

"If you're lying... "

"OK. Don' know, do I – get offa me..."

"Oh, am I hurting you, sonny?"

No 2 whimpered.

"Tell you what, why don't I let you get up and you can show us the way…"

"He knows – the way..." accused No 2, indicating me around Mr C's inexorable bulk.

"Never mind. Demonstrate your good manners, son. Just lead us up. Like we was blind, eh?"

"You ain't," whispered No 2. "Y'ain't blind."

Mr C stood and No 2 crawled over and coughed against the floor. Then he rose and tried to sprint back up the stairs

But Mr C tripped him and he went down with a bang on the first step, and rolled there whining, with blood on his mouth.

Above us the music roared, but I don't think anyone would have come to see anyway.

"I cut me lip – why you done that – ain't got no stuff..."

Sobbing, No 2 guided us up the stairs, sometimes faltering and coughing, once spitting red on to the step.

There was a resignedness to all his actions. One guessed he had been done over before.

Nothing else happened all the way up. No 2 ignored both his own flat and 3A's; he led us, flagging and wilting, to the top. Where no one had repaired the door of 6, 66, and it still stood ajar.

"What a good boy you've been," Mr C congratulated No 2. "Now you skitter on down to your frowsty little pen, and we'll see what Tina's got for us."

No 2 fled.

There was obviously no chance he'd call the police. Doubtless, rather like Roy Phipps, there was really no one he could call.

"I'll go first."

I let him.

I wasn't entirely certain why I'd felt I had to come back, but it had nagged me all through the couple of days since I'd been here last. I'd called the number again Cart gave me, of course by then the third time I'd done it. The response was the same. The price, on this occasion, only five hundred pounds, with a discount, too, since I'd paid ahead of the delivery.

Mr C had by now sloughed his very excellent street accent. He spoke like the well-bred Oxbridge type he apparently was. Or maybe this accent was a fake too.

The place was as I'd seen it before. Bare, empty, untouched. I'd half expected someone, some friend from another flat, to be squatting here by now. Yet no one even seemed to have come in, despite the door's having been undone. Then again, long ago any of them could have broken in as I had.

Even my unreal packet lay where I'd dropped it. Mr C bent at once and picked it up. He didn't tell me off, as Duran had done about my security, for discarding incriminatory evidence. When I'd suggested plastic gloves to Mr C he had shaken his head. "That won't be needed, Mr Phillips, you take this flat too seriously. No cop worth his salt would give a fip"

Despite its phonetic resemblance to my surname, 'fip' was what Mr C sometimes said for fuck. So far I'd not actually heard him swear.

To begin with, once we were in, he made sure the flat's front door was closed off from inside. He did this by dragging the dirty unclothed mattress, unaided, in from the bedroom, and pushing it against the entry. Its passage made strange tracks through the perhaps stranger dusts of the flat.

His search was unlike mine.

He prised up floorboards, clipped pieces out of the plaster, skirmished behind the lavatory and took the panel off the side of the bath. He used various small tools, some unanticipated, in this work. (I'd never seen a corkscrew used as a drill before.)

I followed him, and when requested to hold something or move something, I obeyed without question.

I'd gathered once he had been in the police, but which department, as with the cause of his leaving, was never made clear.

The red leaf in the bedroom had already turned wan and brown. He picked it up and sniffed it with a knowing look incomprehensible to me.

"African, you know," he said elusively.

Presumably he meant something the leaf had been used to conceal, or used in the preparation of. Its floral origins, even to me, still appeared English.

Although his search was both particular and elaborate, neither did he unearth anything, to my eyes at least, unusual.

We'd been there over an hour. No one had disturbed us (5's music crashed on and on, an especially repellent opus demonstrably on repeat).

"And that door to the balcony is locked?" said Mr C.

He went to it and took a screwdriver from his pocket. Inserting it in the empty keyhole he tried various manoeuvres. Suddenly the door snapped, shifted, and I glimpsed the key-driven bolts lifted from their sockets. He gave the door a final twist and pull and it was open.

Out on the balcony he looked up, then down.

"Nothing."

When he was back in again, I followed him along the internal corridor once more, into the other rooms, the bathroom and bedroom and spare room.

"Let's try," he said, "that fire-escape."

He shoved the window of the now-mattressless bedroom up. There'd been only a sort of snib to lock it.

Putting out his head and shoulders, he craned his neck. "Ah ha."

He helped me out of the window, and we stood on the fire-escape. The metal steps uncoiled downwards to the unkempt garden. A ginger cat, chasing something small in the undergrowth, took no notice of us.

"Look there, Mr Phillips. And then up there."

Up there was the sloping roof of the house, one of the endless array of terrace roofs, all rather badly in need of re-tiling, with an independent weed or two growing out of them, or in the tops of adjacent drainpipes.

This roof had in it a large sloping skylight. It seemed to be made of dark polarised glass. A metal ladder was fixed directly below the skylight. The end of this ladder, not quite visible from the bedroom when the window was closed, came down to the top of the fire-escape, and was firmly bolted there.

Somehow Mr C's bulk had hidden the ladder from me at first, as if he had wanted to astound me, uncovering it, pointing up.

The dark glass couldn't even be looked at. The sun hit it blindingly, a splashed broken egg.

A noise in the garden made me look down.

"I hate cats," said Mr C. "Vicious fips."

A mouse in its jaws, uncaring of censure, the ginger tom didn't give us a second glance.

SEVENTEEN

After we had the tea, or he did, Sej asked me if I'd left my bags upstairs. I said nothing, which was pointless, but he didn't press me. Instead he outlined for me what I'd packed in them, both of them. He included in the assessment what I'd also stuffed in my jacket in case I could get away.

He was very accurate.

He might have had X-ray eyes.

"By the way," he added, "you shouldn't worry too much about documents like that. Most of them are replaceable, even a passport. Your birth certificate, or a deed poll change of name, are the worst. They moved everything out of Somerset House some while back, and now you can't get hold of anything, I gather, unless you commute to some unheard-of place well outside London, and search through the records yourself. It can take days."

Still, I kept quiet.

I sat and watched him.

"On the other hand, you'd want to keep any discs with you. They have to do, I assume, with your books. A paper copy wasn't necessary, surely? That has to be on one of the discs. What's on the other?"

Again, my instinct kicked in, prompting me to answer. I'd given up trying to second guess myself as to whether this was cunning of me – or placation – or the other peculiar sense of game-playing and engagement, which he had somehow induced.

"A future book. Not much. A pot-boiler."

"What's it to be about?"

He looked genuinely interested. But that was his way. And long ago I learned to resist the urge to spill plotlines before anyone, even the most innocuous listener. You bored them, or they ripped you off. Or both.

As I didn't reply, he smiled. "Some authors don't like to discuss work in progress. You must be one. What's the title?"

"A working title only."

"Which is?"

"*Kill Me Tomorrow.*"

Unlike the sub-editor whom I'd first informed of this, and who'd instantly wanted a change to avoid Bondism, Sej had the source at once. "Ah. Desdemona as her jealous partner slays her – Kill me tomorrow – let me live tonight." He added, throwing me, "The Irish play."

"It isn't Macbeth."

"No, Roy. Macbeth is the Scottish Play, as we both know. I mean the Irish Play: O'Thello."

I stared at him. It was possible, if someone else had made this joke elsewhere, I might have laughed, at least – as he always did – smiled. "Very good," I said, stilly.

"Not mine. But there. So one disc is your new novel, and the other, was I right, the big unfinished manuscript now in the smaller bag – why else is it so heavy? – and which I found last time anyway, tucked in one of your study drawers under some loose blank paper."

My heart knocked.

I felt a kind of different alarm, inexplicable, together leaden and sharp. The very thing that had made me pursue the bags and so him, back to the trap of the house.

Silent, I waited.

As I now knew he now would, he told me, "I read it, Roy. It's Byronic – but more accessible, more perverse. Bit of a masterpiece. Probably, like so many of those, unpublishable. All that wonderful rambling, murky stuff about his life, the constipated family with their failed fortune, the grisly murders – which remind me of Poe, and sometimes of de Sade – that girl, what was her

333

name – Libenka – with her throat cut, hanging by her hair from the beam, where he'd left her – until her own weight dragged the – what was it? *hennaed tresses* – out of her scalp, and she fell through the flimsy floor into the room below. And his demented visions of dogs and cattle and fiends and beasts of bone and metal. Purple passages to eat with a spoon – I expect you know, don't you, Roy, to tell an author he'd written a *Purple Passage* was to compliment him. It meant the section was unusually rich – like expensively purple-dyed silk. No, it's one hell of a book. And unfinished. What comes next?"

I swallowed.

"It stuck some years ago. And thank you, but I know it's rubbish."

He shook his head. "*Nay, do not think I flatter,*" he said, "...and that of course is the *Danish* Play about the pork butcher – It isn't rubbish, Roy. You should finish it. So there we are. The two things you should do this summer. Finish that novel and shave your bloody head. Your hair is going fast. Steal a march. Get rid of it. You'll look good, more yourself. We should all, like Vilmos's creepy alchemic Order, try to become ourselves. It's about all we can do."

I thought, *What will he do, drug me again, then shave my hair off while I sleep?*

A huge, heavy, watery terror filled me. I felt, as the Americans illustratingly say, *sick to my stomach.*

He read my mind, of course. Perhaps not so bizarre.

"I won't do that, Roy. It has to come from you."

Then he got up and walked round the kitchen, looking out of the glass of the closed door and window briefly. It was getting on by now for evening. The sky had a thickened amontillado sherry light, the fir black, its needles delineated like spikes on some giant black porcupine. By a similar light, against the fir, I had seen him here first. And earlier today, by the fir, he had jumped up to intercept my escape.

"That's a beautiful tree," he remarked. Then, cutting through me, irrational as I now was, to the quick, "You feature it, am I right? In your untitled work. The tree on the Kolosian Hill, where your hero stabs the thief."

After this he opened the fridge, next to the freezer, and gazed in. No comment then. He went on to the cupboards, looked at, removed and looked at, various cans.

"Not much food."

"I was going away."

"Of course you were. Don't worry. I can go shopping. Enough shops are open on Sunday. As for tonight..." He was thoughtful. "How about a take-away? Do you have a good local Indian or Chinese?"

I rarely indulge myself that way, but there *was* an Indian restaurant at the end of the high street, the *Spice Lal.*

"If you want." Thought clicked. I added, expressionless. "But I won't join you."

"Oh Roy, come on. I can't drug *that*. Not if you keep an eye on me from the moment the food arrives to the moment it gets to the table. And then we each keep our hands in sight. I *still* haven't quite figured out how you did that trick with the wine that time. I'll watch you. You watch me. We'll have a good meal. And don't worry. I'll pay."

With an inappropriate abrupt rancour, I heard myself say "You seem to be rich."

"Not exactly. But not poor either. Do you have their number?"

"No."

He drew from his pocket the most slender of phones, the colour of matt steel. It was more up-to-date than the last one he'd had at our third meeting. He must change them every week. "Tell me the name and address, Roy."

"Why should I? I don't particularly want an Indian meal."

"Yes, you do," he said.

I tightened my mouth. Stupid. Redundant.

Sej smiled. "Don't worry, Roy," he falsely reassured me again. "I remember a place in your high street – *The Lal* –yeah, the *Spice Lal.*" Then he called one of those directories we now use, at great cost, to learn unknown telephone numbers. Next he dialled, and held the mobile out to me.

I refused to take the phone.

"I'll tell you what to order," he encouraged me. I let the phone ring in his grip, and when a voice answered I did and said nothing. I sat, he stood there, while the man's voice buzzed out of the phone, and Sej watched me. I wouldn't take the phone, or speak, wouldn't play the game. The voice ended. The connection was broken. What used to be the dialling tone sounded.

Sej's face fell. He looked both upset and resigned.

He put down the phone, leaned in across the table and slapped me violently across the side of the face with the back of his hand. The blow was meaty, it stung, numbed, blanked a second of *time,* brought me back to pain, my right eye watering, my right nostril running so I thought for a moment my nose bled. But it didn't.

He said, "Sorry, Roy. I'd much rather not. But we do have to get this sorted out."

Beaten women learn how to negotiate, where at all possible. Or so I've read. Any woman I've known had not been beaten, or if she had, never confessed it.

I said, "All right. I'll do what you want."

The side of my mouth seemed inert. But it was only rather like what you feel at the end of a dentist's appointment, as the cocaine is gradually wearing off. He hadn't seriously damaged me. But he had made me understand.

He rang the number again. I took and spoke into the phone. I ordered, politely, what he requested, then at his urging ordered a meal for myself. I can't remember what. I knew I wouldn't eat much of it. Unless of course he insisted.

Sej sat on the table, smiling and once nodding approval. He said, "Ask if they'll send a couple of beers, too."

I asked. They would. Then I had to ask him, for them, if he wished to pay by credit card over the phone. And airily he told me the number of his card, even the security number on the back.

But I didn't try to record it. I had also now stopped ruminating on the idea of his going shopping and maybe leaving me locked in the house, and if this offered any hope. I didn't care.

Deal done he took back the phone and switched it off. "Brilliant, Roy. Just right." He looked closely at me. "Better put some TCP on your lip – yes, just there. I don't wear a ring, but I seem to have caught you. It's nothing much but better disinfect it just in case. Then maybe, let's see, you stay upstairs. They said twenty minutes, pretty optimistic for a Saturday. Perhaps they don't get a lot of custom until later. The thing is, if you're upstairs I can answer the door. But if you stay at the top of the stair you can also watch me. Once I close the front door, you come down and we both come back in the kitchen. That way there's no chance I can mess the food up. Or you. Fair enough?" He hadn't even warned me not to try to persuade the delivery man to assist me. And I – I hadn't even considered it.

"Yes," I said.

I rose and he smiled. "You've been a real trooper," he said. My father had once or twice said that. "No hard feelings, eh? Good. These things happen. Now we can move on."

My father's advice on bullies was shit. There are many things that, unless you have either great power of some sort, or vast help from some abnormal and constant quarter, there is no point at all in facing up to, let alone trying to combat.

Denial is one of the healthiest physical states discovered by Man.

Following my scrap with Ben Oggey, after which, pen-less, I had to have a tooth capped, I abandoned confrontation as a *modus operandi*.

Decades after, and only with Sej, I briefly blotted my well-learned copy book. His swift action had saved me from any more mistakes, thus punishment. Meanwhile the stunning aftershock of his blow wore off quickly. The lesson adhered. From now on I would be a model prisoner.

The meal arrived in fact half an hour later. We played it as he had outlined. He was charming to the delivery man, had a laugh with him, (I couldn't catch what about), tipped him with a ten-pound note. Off the man went, laughing. In came Sej, laughing, with the bag of food. He shut and double-locked the door again, with his own keys, then pocketed them.

Then I came down from my old childhood haunt of the top stair and progressed behind him into the kitchen.

Naturally he had no dread of my attacking him from the rear. Nor did I have any intention of doing so.

I remember what he ate: chicken Jalfrezi, stuffed naan, vegetable curry, egg-fried rice, two poppadums, a small tub of raita. What I ate, or did not eat, as I've said, I have no idea.

He drank an Indian beer decanted into a tall glass. I had the same and sipped it. He'd suggested I rinse both glasses thoroughly before we used them, in front of him, which I did. The taste of the beer was appealing, slightly bitter, with a hint of chilli. In the end he finished mine too. The remains of my dinner, most of it, I believe he ate for breakfast the following morning.

There were no insidious drugs. Indeed, despite the washing, he insisted halfway through the repast we have each a few swallows from the other's glass.

He said I was to leave the washing-up, so I left it, it goes without saying.

It was after this, though rather further on, nearer midnight, he broke in my bedroom door, for me.

"You get a proper night's rest," he said. He told me he would 'crash' on the sofa downstairs. At least, he said, he wouldn't have to suffer the 'fucking row' of neighbourly bad music current in the flats, which 'got on his tits'.

Between one and two I heard the strains of Bach sprinkle from the piano.

Upstairs, the broken door leaning on the uprights to give me partial 'privacy', I sat up on the bed in my clothes, my two bags, which he had brought in, lying by the wardrobe, the light off, unsleeping, going over everything, on and on.

Our conversations of the afternoon and evening I examined now more fully.

I found I was inclined to date them BB and AB – Before the Blow and After the Blow. In fact the blow, when he hit me across the face, was neither devastating nor intrinsically dividing. It was rather, instructive, a guideline. I'd been, on some level, expecting his violence. Who would not? It was a benchmark, not an advent.

We had also talked, superficially at least, in that most spontaneous and episodic way persons use who know each other well. By superficial I mean, of course, if we had been observed by an outsider. And now I tried, upstairs, to put *myself* outside, to look and learn. Writers do attempt that, some of us, even when personally deeply involved. The ability is a gift, and a curse.

I re-ran the conversations methodically. To begin with, I had asked him again, why he did this to me. His reply was the recurrent one – out of interest; I was interesting. We had established that he – not the girl with the car presumably, as she really couldn't have had time or access – had wiped some liquefied Rohypnol around the kitchen glass. I could have used the glass at any time during his absence.

Next, we had returned to our guessing game as to whether he was or was not my son. He had said he was brought up in an orphanage, could not recall his mother's name. I didn't believe either of these confidings. Even BB I had become three-quarters convinced he wasn't Maureen's child. It might be plausible but somehow didn't fit, and definitely *AB* I refused to entertain it. He was not hers. I wouldn't allow him to be. Although naturally if he, AB, started to assure me he *was*, I would nod and agree. I would even call him my son, if that were required.

When he saw to the bedroom door, he told me about the car-girl and her strong pianist's hands with the bolts. And prior to that, when the mobile rang out on the path, he told me I couldn't bring it in, nor would he. That was after

337

the Indian meal. Even then, propped up on the bed, I could hear the rain falling quite heavily on everything, and on the mobile.

I'd seen too the tiny intense wound in the palm of his left hand. Was he prone to stigmata? I wouldn't put anything past him, even something like that, although I would suspect it of being self-induced, either by extreme cerebral concentration or (more likely) a creative use of self-harm. (Not to build this aspect up unduly, he would reveal during the next week that he had driven a long needle into his hand. He'd needed to look white and sick when he brought the 'dead dog' back into my hotel, and this was how he'd managed that. He explained too that, had I followed him to the Gents, he would have put his fingers down his throat to induce the genuine sounds and act of retching. Told this, I'd made little comment. Perhaps the authorial mind was pleased to slide last pieces of that single puzzle into place. I didn't then ask him if the dog had been real. It was AB. And also something more. I was certain by that first night the dog was *not* real, but suppose it had been? Suppose he had killed it, or she had, that other weeping woman and accomplice *surely*, suppose she had killed it *for* him? Aside from any urgent RSPCA issues, to kill an animal can, in certain cases, be the preliminary knack of those then able to slaughter their fellow men.

We had also discussed my work, of course.

Over subsequent days we would discuss it again and again. He would read my books, sitting before me either in the library or the kitchen, sometimes the front room. He read fast and with a look of total absorption that might have been gratifying, even with him, *BB*. But which, AB, was no longer so. Sometimes too he would send me off to my study. "Go and do some work, Roy." And I would go, and hack that I am, manage even to turn out some soulless verbiage, five hundred, a thousand words. In case he checked on me. But he never intruded 'uninvited' into the study, would only come to the door, with a polite knock, to ask me how it went.

My demeanour throughout was always as normal as I could make it. When we discussed my published books, we did so in a civilised manner. Even AB, his criticisms were, I must admit, often valid. His praise obviously revolted and offended, but I took it with a courteous calmness, thanking him, disagreeing now and then. I had ascertained for now those areas where resistance was allowed, even wanted, as proof of our quite spurious normalcy.

There were no more blows. He needed to offer me none.

I'd said to myself I was to be a model prisoner.

It's the first thing the seasoned criminal tells you, at least those of the disempowered class of criminal. You must be obedient and respectful. Don't aggravate the warders. Take any cruelty or injustice without undue flinching or any complaint. Don't smarm, maybe flatter a bit, hide nothing but your true self, and keep your head down. As one I spoke to during my researches had once told me, "You gets a better chance to pull a fast one if you never done it before. And if you don't neither, you still get less of the crap if you behaves

338

like a good boy." It was the same to some extent with the more dangerous fellow inmates. Unless they were 'mental'. Then probably you had problems. You couldn't predict, only stay neutral, merge with the dark.

Sej, equally jailor, criminal *and* mental, would have to be played on all three lines.

Some of our 'talks', macabrely, were actually quite fascinating. And as long as I did everything he told me to there was to be no resurgence of threat.

To return however to that first night, sitting up on the bed, I had no means of knowing he would be there through the rest of May, approximately three weeks. I had no apprehension I would have to maintain my life as a model prisoner so long.

But then, what else had I imagined could happen?

In some incoherent way, frankly, I *must* have known it might well go on. Or had I only, down in some dim recess that my swift, healthy, human talent for Denial instantly smothered, believed he would kill me? Regardless that was of my conforming and docility. I had no real notion of what other tests lay before me through the rest of May. If I had, would I have doubted my own ability to comply? Maybe not. Mortal things are generally programmed to attempt survival. Left with one plank in the sea, we cling to it. So much in life is destructive, is *deadly*, that without this built-in mechanism, less bravery than cowardice, less cowardice than resentment and rage, most of us would vanish long before my father's touch of a Grim Reaper mowed us down. Sleepless there, I must have known this too. And finally, I did fall asleep, near 5 in the morning. I hadn't meant to, or thought I could. Sej woke me at 8 a.m. with a mug of tea, milk, no sugar, as I drink it. "*Regardez*," he said, and drank two swallows of it, to demonstrate it wasn't drugged.

By the third morning, my mobile phone was gone from the path. It had been possible to see it from my study window, which faced the front. I'd at no time thought I could get hold of it. No doubt it was more sensible for someone else to have the use of it, if it still worked. Nobody that I'd detected had called me since that first unanswered ringing. Duran, for example, would think I was now on my trip up north. As for Matt, swimming in his own ocean of depression he'd simply give up on me. What did I matter? Perhaps the woman he'd picked up had stayed on, and even if I'd arrived, he would have put me off.

Sej's mobile seemed to have unlimited credit or was paid for via bills; he recharged it regularly in whatever room he happened to be, never letting it from his sight.

He had urbanely confiscated my house keys during the initial evening, BB, asking for them in a friendly, casual manner. That was both those to the front door and the key to the kitchen door. A spare key to the kitchen door had once existed but was years since lost, by me. Sej didn't ask if there was one. Unless I wanted to try to break through either door – both of which opened inward and would be difficult – which means impossible for someone at my physical standard – my only chance was to climb from a window. But the windows, both upper and lower, refitted in the eighties and 'modern', opened only at the tops, a narrow strip that might be useable by a skinny infant or a cat. I could have broken them, if with a little effort, as the glazing was fairly tough. (I knew that because, some years before, one of the young footballers who replace each other in the Lane, and hold the World Cup there several times a month, managed to lob a ball square at my front window, which held.)

But again I'd need to put my back into it. And it would make one hell of a row.

And Sej was always there.

Despite his offhand comment on 'shopping', and my vague half-hopeful inner reaction, he never left the premises. Instead he would bring out his mobile and either he or I, on his instructions, order things in, paying with two or three of his credit cards.

Wine came, whisky, soda, dry ginger, bottled water for him, fruit juices, food and bathroom supplies, (including shaving equipment, toothbrush, and other things also for him – he'd brought nothing with him – even some jeans and shirts, socks, boxers, the whole kit. I was reminded, seeing these completely accurate stores and garments carried in by him, of my own future fears for myself as an old man, at the mercy of the careless deliveries of others. Seemingly everything Sej wanted was perfect).

At night we ate takeaways. Or he did. He never now forced me to join in, and frequently I settled for beans on toast, or a ham sandwich. Once a Chinese meal was delivered. We observed the same ritual as with the Indian, and then Sej served the food before me. There was hot and sour soup, duck with blackbean sauce, pancakes, noodles, sweetcorn and crab, Szechuan prawns, squid with garlic. "So glad you were tempted to have some," he said, in his 'winning' mode. I did eat a little. It was very good. There were also what the menu described as Two Free Bottles of Beef. He'd ordered desert too, pineapple, toffee bananas and ice cream.

The food alone was costing him a small fortune.

After our dinners we'd drink coffee, whisky if he told me I should have one, vodka for him, a double without mixer. I recollected that from when I first saw him in the pub in the Strand.

The anti-drugging procedure was always kept to.

I prepared my own food and 'kept my eyes on it', he did the same, but mostly had his food brought in. If we shared anything at some point plates and glasses were exchanged.

Sometimes he brought me morning tea, sometimes not. He never asked me to do or make anything for him. Either he attended on me, as one might with someone ailing or very young or old, or he left to my own devices. Sometimes he would inquire if I had a preference for a type of food or drink. But that was within the limits of what he chose. After all, he was paying. I tried to figure out, in the second week, exactly how much he had spent. At a conservative estimate, well over fifteen hundred pounds.

The other elements of our relationship, if such it must be termed, went on and around about the day to day minutiae of ordinary life, however odd or opulent.

At first, what went on was, shall I say, *external*.

That is, it affected the house, its objects.

The inaugural act happened on the fourth day of his occupancy and my imprisonment. Or, more correctly, it had gone on during the previous night.

I woke at 7.30 after a restless three hours' sleep and smelled the acid tang of fresh paint.

I got up, used the bathroom, and went downstairs. The smell of paint intensified. The morning before I had seen some quite large boxes delivered, all taken in as usual by Sej. Although I was regularly told to make various telephone orders, Sej sometimes ordered stuff of which I had no knowledge until later. This was the case here, for he had got in the paint and brushes etc: without my knowing anything about it.

The door of the front room stood half open.

He had covered the piano over with a large dustsheet, but not bothered with anything else.

As I stood there, he turned from his position on the kitchen ladder. "Hi, Roy. What do you think?"

The walls of the room, almost finished now, were a deep scarlet. It hit my morning eyes like too bright light. I said nothing.

Not only were the walls red, but most of the sofa and other furniture, and the carpet, where paint had dripped or, more likely, been idly splashed.

"Don't worry about the mess," he said. "Come on, don't sulk. You can always get some other chairs."

The *don't sulk*, though playful, as if only trying to dispel some unreasonable churlishness on my part, was a warning I must heed.

"Why red?" I asked.

"Enlivening. We can rip that bloody awful electric fire out next and get the chimney opened up. Picture this on a winter evening, firelit and glowing."

"Yes," I said.

"You don't sound enthusiastic, Roy. Where's your spirit of adventure?"

"You paint very well," I said. This was true. It looked a professional job, aside from the ruin of almost everything else.

"Thanks. I'm not bad, am I, for an amateur?"

He flaunted himself. There was a small red mark on his forehead, but his hands were enclosed in protective gloves. His hands, the piano, must come to no harm.

"Do you want tea?" I asked.

"That's all right. Had some. Want to get on. Should have it done in another hour."

341

I made coffee for myself in the kitchen, which also reeked of paint. The coffee tasted of paint. Even the toothpaste upstairs had done so. Through the window I watched a blackbird picking through the dead sides of my paved-over garden and thought of breaking the glass. But I didn't trust myself to get it right, and I judged what would happen if I didn't.

He had completed the painting of the room by 9 a.m.

During that and the next day, the paint smell gave me a sinus headache.

On the carpet, curtains, and the chairs and sofa the splashed paint dried. Over the face of the old clock had run a single red drip like blood. I attempted to rectify nothing. Nor did he. I sensed, accurately, that the furniture couldn't be renovated, and it was not. I got used to the new look of the room, no longer anything to do with me, an abattoir in hell where offal and gore stayed always fresh and cheerful.

Two days on from the red paint, Sej threw out most of my crockery, literally threw, smashing it in the back garden.

I watched, as I had the blackbird, safely shut in like a wayward child who, if let go free, may rush off straight under a speeding car.

At one juncture, George emerged from 72 on to his neat back lawn, with the cherry tree and bird table.

I had a moment's hope. The activity of wreckage looked unusual. How would George react?

He and Sej chatted in an easy way over the lowest part of the fence, where the other hydrangea was spreading the green cups of delayed flowers.

I couldn't make out what was said, my ears like my sinus had been clogged up by the paint. But both men were very relaxed.

When Sej came in, having swept the shards of crockery into two dustbin bags and dropped them in the black dustbin he'd earlier provided, he said, "I told old George you were going to make a new start. George said he was so pleased I was here. Between himself and me, he and his wife had been a bit nervous about you, here on your own in your present state of mind. They hoped I'd stay as long as I could."

"And will you?" It was out before I could contain it.

But Sej smiled. "I can stay forever, Roy, if I want."

To replace the china, some of which had gone back to my grandparents' time, Sej had ordered some thick square plates and square saucers, with large if unmatchingly round cups. All of it was pale yellow, starred with lurid marigolds. I'd never seen anything quite like it. They were less ugly and unwieldy than preposterous. I hadn't ever cared about the original china, however. My only concern was that the awkwardness of the new crockery might make me drop some of it, and would this be taken as a declaration of war?

At night, when I retired to the virtually doorless environment of the bedroom, still I utilised my waking hours, or some of them, trying to concoct a plan of escape. But by now I couldn't think of anything that I dared to chance.

The night after the new cups appeared, I attempted a foray downstairs.

It was well after 3 a.m. The piano, which now and then he played into the small hours, had fallen quiet just after 2.

There were no lights on. Yet at the windows in the study, the narrow box room, and the bathroom where the door also stood ajar, embers of streetlighting fell into the house. The same was true downstairs, through the glass panel in the door.

Moving slowly and with care in my stockinged feet – I never now slept either in pyjamas or under the covers, but on top of the bed fully dressed – I crept downward.

As I reached the fifth step from the bottom, darkness flowed directly upward at me like a forming hill, blocking the light, barring my way.

I knew it was him, not some creature from the Hammer Horror films of my youth. But I cried out, lost my footing, stumbled into him. He caught me firm as a rock.

"What are you up to, Roy?"

"You frightened the life…"

"No, I asked first. What are you doing?"

I said, because I'd had my story ready, "I was thirsty," Like the untrusted child again.

"You should have called down. I'd have brought you something." He didn't seem angry, or worse exhibit that resignation that had been a prologue to the blow. "I'm often about at night. I sit in your library and read R.P. Phillips."

I supposed he used only the angled lamp on the table there, and pulled the door to, for no light from that room had entered the hallway.

He said, "Tea? Whisky?"

"Just water."

"You should keep some by you in a bottle, Roy. You can't keep drinking unboiled tap water, not without a filter, not anymore."

I stood marooned on the stair. Decidedly I must not proceed further. He came back with the glass with water in it.

"It's Volvic," he said, "in case you think it tastes different." And he drank a couple of swallows. "Next time, like I said, just call me."

Upstairs I went to the lavatory and poured the water away and flushed the cistern. It wasn't that I thought he had spiked the drink. I just couldn't swallow it.

Other events – *adventures* – took place during the next week.

There were all sorts of things. Some were surprising, shocking, some nearly funny in a frightful way, as had been the red paint and the smashed china. Some were on a more instantly invasive scale. For example, his nocturnal application of white paint to the glass of the lavatory window. Others were insidious things I might not notice at first, like altering the positions of the kitchen glasses, putting them where the canned and dried food and tea had been. And those commodities somewhere else again. Or when he had misfiled every book in my library. These had occupied a logical alphabetical order, author and subject. I'd worked in public libraries and this technique, less than petty, I'd found helpful when looking for things. Now I would hardly be able to locate anything without a search. That must have taken him most of a night to arrange as well. Strange I hadn't heard him; the library lay partly below the bedroom. My study he always apparently avoided entering unless he had asked me if he might. It goes without saying I never withheld my assent. Then I walked into it one afternoon, sent there by Sej to write, and gradually grew oppressively aware of something above me. Looking up I had to squint to make it out, but I at last saw the pale writing, scribbled in the lightest grey paint across the stained white ceiling, almost invisibly. He had climbed up the ladder again, perhaps balanced, incredibly noiseless and careful on the flat-topped desk where the computer stood. This time, no splashes. He must have covered it over. The writing was some of the invented poetry of Vilmos, copied or recalled from *Untitled*. If I hadn't written it, I might not have been able, now, fully to read it.

Agony unended. Like the long snow it falls
And shrouds the edges of a sword
Too murderous to die from,
Too tangible to touch.
Among the webs that midnight spins
Go staggering to the doors of rotted day,
And through the keyholes, snakelike,
Spit.

This single act horrified me so far the most, worse even than his *manifestation* on the stair. But the painted poetry of course, was only my little madness and Vilmos's great one, jarred into life by Sej's spectacular insanity.

I said nothing to him about the writing, as I'd said nothing about any of it until, when or if, I was interrogated. Then I was neutral.

He didn't refer to the poetry at all.

That following night, or rather morning, he woke me from one of my piecemeal half hours of sleep. He did this by shining the light of a torch he must also have had delivered, (my own was defunct) into my eyes.

It's an old and tried schematic. I had read of it, described it in some of my work – read by him? To experience it is quite devastating.

I almost attacked him. I was just *compos mentis* enough to stop myself.

"Sorry, Roy," he kindly said, "I wanted to show you something."

Presently I went down with him. It was about 4 a.m. That I was being allowed to descend to the lower storey was not lost on me.

The TV was on, the sound turned down.

Some old film was showing, black and white, staffed with a cast of, at least to me, unknown movie actors of my parents' era. I sat on the sofa, stiff and crackling with dried paint. Although he had said he sometimes slept here, I'd never seen any evidence. Now he sat beside me. We stared at the – to me alone? – incomprehensible film. I wondered confusedly and shakily if he simply wanted me to watch television with him. Then he said, "Shall I get rid of this, Roy?"

My voice, always astonishing me recently, replied quite steadily, "Of course, if you want."

And he patted my shoulder, got up and crossed the room, and kicked in the screen.

A high hard bang sounded, less explosion than gunshot. The red room flashed purple, then white. Bits of the screen that seemed rather to be bits of solid light hailed through the air. A brief electric storm was born in a jet black hole ripped in the fabric of the room. Everything glittered, tinkled, then darkened, while from the TV plug in the wall a white ray, shaped like the classical lightning bolt awarded to the god Zeus, was flung to the ceiling and died. After this all was blackness.

Sej murmured, "You hardly watched anything, did you? I think you said the news gets on your nerves."

He threw a kind of shadow, lighter than the dark, but he himself was now invisible to me.

"Yes," I said. "I didn't often watch."

"Oh well, better get you back to bed."

He led me up the stair. At the top he turned to me, and now I saw him in the vague orange light from the streetlamps.

"Didn't scare you, did I – I mean, doing that?"

I gazed at him. I said, "What you do is your business, Sej."

"Yes, Roy. And so are you. My business."

He let me go through into the bedroom alone, and from the outside adjusted my door slightly, to permit me more 'privacy'.

Through the pretended barrier he called after me softly, "You haven't tried to get away. Or not properly. Why's that, Roy?"

"Too tired, Sej. At my age, you get fed up, running about."

His voice was now so soft I had to strain to catch it as I stood there, rigid, in the non-electrified dark.

"Do you, Roy? That's a shame. Not sure I entirely believe you, you know. You're not that old, either. Young as you feel. Sleep tight, old sport. Tomorrow is another day."

I stood by my bed in the darkness for about another forty minutes after he had gone, or I thought he had. I didn't sleep again that night. I thought what prisoners must often think, that to continue in this way was not bearable, and that I could only bear it, having no alternative. And I thought dispassionately of some callous miracle – George hammering on the door calling for assistance – Vita with chest pains – an ambulance – some logical development which might allow me to evade my captor in two or three freakish moments of unexpectedness. And I thought finally of the stupidity of my situation, and that I ought to be able to get free, there *must* be some solution. But I could conjure nothing.

Into darkness I stared, the memory of the explosion of the TV screen sometimes igniting in my brain before my inner eye, truly a *flash*back. I wished him dead. That was all I had that I could do. I wished him dead, but it was unreal to me. And I believed I'd reached the end of my road.

7

He went up the ladder first, and I reckoned I would leave it to him. But when somehow Mr C, standing on that ladder some fifty-five to sixty feet over the back gardens, both hands employed in screwdrivering access through the skylight, had raised the window and it was open, and he leaned inside, looked back down and spoke to me, I knew that I too wished very badly to see into the place above. I wore trainers. I put one foot on the lowest rung and hauled myself up quite efficiently, ignoring the idea of the distance to the ground. I felt different in my *666* role, shaven headed, in jeans and T-shirt and trainers. I felt unencumbered. I felt I too could climb the dangerous ladder. And climb it I had. When I got into the attic room above Sej's flat, both Mr C and I paused, looking round. I was nonplussed, although I quickly saw he could not be. Given his wide experience surprise would be rare, and then no doubt only associated with types of extreme violence.

He had already informed me no one was in residence. He had checked every corner of the long, wide space, and opened the single door to reveal a long narrow bathroom.

"Well, it's an eagle's nest but he does himself proud," said Mr C. He sounded more amused than intolerant. "Not like the lower quarters, is it?"

Decidedly it wasn't.

The attic room, a sort of English loft apartment, began under the slope of the roof, where even *I* couldn't stand upright. But after a few crouching steps someone of six and a half feet could have done so with ease. At the centre the spine of the roof allowed standing room of at least twelve feet. This area extended for maybe twenty feet square. Even where the tapering down began, the roof sloped gradually. Once one was fully inside there was no sense at all of constriction.

The beams and joists were on view, but clean and varnished. Above them, a high plasterboard ceiling. It was painted a pale creamy blue. The brickwork of the walls behind the wood was also closed in plasterboard and painted, this a very light apple green.

On the whole floor-space lay a blue carpet, immaculate and with a deep pile. Furniture was set here and there, armchairs, tables, two large couches that Mr C told me were what we used to call put-you-ups – able to be converted into large double beds. Everything not plain wood was upholstered, sky blue or light royal blue, or various greens.

Bookcases, six of them, ranged along the edges of the room, crammed with books. There were two wooden cabinets. One had cutlery and dark green plates and mugs, and long straight blue glasses. The other cabinet contained cleaning materials, a Dyson. Above on shelves packets of tea, coffee, canned goods, matches. Towards the back of the room was a large piano, lid raised, and a guitar and a mandolin hanging from two hooks in the beams. A music centre rose behind the piano. Several carousels below revealed CDs of many classical composers. A lot of it was piano music. There was some jazz too, and R & B.

No radio or TV were visible.

The lighting consisted solely of table-lamps with parchment-coloured shades. Mr C had turned them all on.

Set back in one wall was a small kitchen annexe, that had a stalk-thin fridge-freezer, a small expensive-looking washing machine, a microwave oven, a miniature electric oven with two gas hobs, and a toy-size sink and drainer.

In the narrow bathroom, which was white and very clean, as the whole upper space appeared to be, were a long bath on lion's paws, a lavatory, a bidet, and two washbasins under a wide mirror. An ultra-modern shower cubicle filled one corner. From rails hung clean crisp towels, all of them white. White soaps, still in plastic wrappers, lay by basins, bath and shower. Another cabinet revealed several Lilliputian shampoos of the type found in hotels, a selection of chemist counter painkillers, such as aspirin and paracetamol, Elastoplast and Tubigrip, and a large plastic container of hydrogen peroxide.

There were also two hampers in the bathroom. One was empty. One held more clean white towels, white sheets, pillowslips and blankets, all neatly folded.

"What's in the fridge, I wonder?" said Mr C.

He undid the door and we looked in.

There wasn't much. Some black truffles in a box, some strong cheddar in white paper. The wine rack held one bottle of Dom Perignon, one of red wine, (French) and a single bottle of Dutch geneva. A couple of two litre bottles of Volvic occupied the lower shelf.

In the freezer compartments were bread, pork sausages, steaks, chicken breasts and chunks of free-range salmon. And a big carton of chocolate ice cream. None of these items had been opened.

Neither Mr C nor I were apparently tempted. Though sealed, it could all have been poisoned after all.

"That skylight is definitely polarised glass. Bullet-proof too, I'd say. But the lock..." He sneered and snapped his fingers.

The apartment was quite dark – or had been until he switched on the lamps.

"What do you think?" he asked me.

"He lives here."

"I would entirely conclude he does. Or it's his HQ. Basic nutrition, doctor supplies, hygiene, sleeping facilities. Not bad, for an amateur."

Below us even now we could hear the mindless blundering of flat No 5's music. It was much fainter, but still intrusive. Sound rises, like scum.

"Have you seen enough, Mr Phillips?"

"I – yes, I suppose so."

"Do you want me to do anything?"

I thought he meant smash it all up, unplug the fridge-freezer, score the CDs and tear up the books – God knows. I said inanely, "I'm baffled."

"Are you?" said Mr C. "I'm not. Your man's a nutcase." Then he reverted to his alternate accent. "A total nutter, our Sejjy. And that sort – I'd wipe 'em off the arse of the world."

EIGHTEEN

May was moving towards June. The weather changed for the better. It was warm and usually bright. Upstairs, I was told, I could/should open the small upper panels of the windows.

This was the time when regime change happened.

I had been obedient, subservient perhaps.

Each night I slept only a couple of hours. But I hadn't slept well, had I, for fifteen, nearly twenty years.

He had never intruded, that I knew, on my slumber, despite the bedroom door's being off, aside from that one striking time with the torch. Since that night I'd been very careful of him. Which is a crazy thing to say, of course. I was already careful of him. And it had done me no good.

And too I'd formerly taxed my brain, trying to find ways to outwit and deal with him, evict him. Destroy him.

I was hampered, naturally, by my authorial brain, which went too far. Frankly, my scenarios ended often in his maiming or death. They were fantasies. They were not possible to me. Either I am an indoctrinated pacifist, (my father, always think of others) or merely an utter coward – by which I mean, in this context, *squeamish*. I don't boast of any truly moral wish to spare his life. I can't lay claim to any saintly fastidiousness of that sort. But the end of the road was before me, and still I could think of nothing at all.

The wasp entered my life two days after I started to leave the upstairs windows open.

This had happened during other summers. Even given a notable dearth of insects constantly reported in the news, and put down to human vileness and global warming, intermittent moths, flies and wasps had always penetrated the house. Like, if not in the same spirit as my kindly mother, I tend to catch them all and put them back outside. Even wasps I spare until the autumn, when the damn things will perish anyway. I'd been stung sufficiently to know I wasn't allergic to them. But also, I was aware that, if they got into the mouth and stung, they would cause a swelling in the soft tissues and membranes which, closing the throat and airway, might result in death.

This wasp was obviously young and inexperienced. I caught it easily in the glass from the bathroom. *Having* caught it, I decanted it into a large empty jam jar I'd retained in my study to house spare biros. On top of the jar I placed a piece of card, pierced by me with air holes. Did they need to breathe? I had to assume so. Would it also need food? I dropped into the jar some crumbs from the breakfast toast I'd carried upstairs.

My wasp crawled about in the jar. buzzing in blind, automaton-like anger. Then settled on a bit of the toast. I stowed the jar in the bottom of the bedroom wardrobe. Perhaps the wasp would go to sleep. Perhaps it would die. I might find no opportunity to use it. I might let it go.

And if Sej discovered it? I'd say with the purest truth I did rescue them and then release them in summer. But, *(now* lying), this one had seemed comatose, so I'd given it crumbs and let it rest – and then unfortunately forgotten it.

One thinks sometimes, wrongly often, madmen will accept other madmen and their quite dissimilarly insane actions.

By this time, I had been told by Sej both of his flat and its address in Saracen Road. The residence had come up once or twice in our communal post-dining phase, among the coffees, whisky and vodka. The *666* aspect of the number seemed never to strike him. He said little about the flat either, only that it wasn't worth the money, but all right. Aside from being blighted by loud bad neighbouring music. He described the outside more than the inside, (including the glass panel in the door), and in fact said nothing I afterwards recalled of internal appearance. The small park he mentioned several times, the trees and shrubs. And why had he given me the actual address if not to point out its Satanic twist? "You'll have to pay me a visit one day, Roy. Flat *6*, top of *66*, Saracen Road. It's a big white terrace, or it used to be white, back when."

And I said, "I should visit you?"

"Why not?"

"Won't you still be here?"

And, "Oh, I might even be, Roy. You're right."

The day I caught the wasp and hid it, around 11.30 I went down to the kitchen, as during daylight hours I was seemingly allowed to, and through the library door I saw him asleep in the corner chair.

A book, not now one of mine but Milton's *Paradise Lost*, lay open on his knee. Over by the power point in the corner, his steely slice of mobile rested on the floor, re-charging.

I froze in the hallway. I stared.

It didn't seem impossible he might really have nodded off. He was young and would be able to fall asleep, and needed sleep more than I, no doubt. If he kept watch for me so much of every night, ready, playing Chopin or a

Brahms Rhapsody on the piano, wasn't it quite likely he might suddenly flake out with no warning?

But *did* he sleep? *Did* he?

His breathing had the sound of a sleeper's. But things like that can be acted, and Sej, if he could do anything, was quite an accomplished actor.

There I hung from the thread of his tyranny, glaring in, transfixed, a stone.

And he opened his eyes without even any of the slightest sleeper's momentary dislocation, and smiled.

"Hello, Roy. Making any tea? One for me, please."

So I made the tea, and found my hands shaking so much I nearly did drop the bloody yellow and marigold cup. When I took it in, I swallowed the regulation two gulps, and passed it to him.

"Sit down a minute, Roy." I sat. "I've had an idea."

Then he drank the tea. He didn't say what the idea was, I waited. I waited while he drank all his tea.

Then he put the open book and the empty cup aside and stood up.

Going out ahead of me he called back lightly, "Come on. We're going upstairs."

I followed him. He climbed the stair. Docile, I climbed at his back. He had left the phone to recharge on the library floor. Had he forgotten? I decided not. It was another tease.

He preceded me into my study on this occasion. Neither had he ever done that before.

The whole surface of my skin was prickling. My eyes seemed stretched to the size, if not the square shape, of the hideous new saucers.

Something else that was new was about to happen, and I was to *see* it happen, be a part of it. It was like the smell of smoke, of burning, like the sick marzipan odour that still hung in the front room round the gutted TV.

My jacket and the two bags he wanted arranged in the middle of the room, by the desk.

He had suggested, ("I suggest, Roy") that we both open them up now. He wanted to know, he said, if he'd guessed correctly what I had in each – aside from toiletries and clothes that I would have unpacked for use on my 'return'.

I unloaded the jacket first. There was no sense in evasion. He'd been right on everything there, almost. He hadn't itemised, however, the house deeds. He was quite impressed by my having included those. "Are these copies? They look like the originals. Well done, Roy. Your parents must have paid off their mortgage. Those were the days."

"Yes," I said.

Then we did the bags, and it was all as he had said, aside from one or two things that he joked about, as if I had entertainingly put over a clever trick on him. "You weren't taking any chances were you, old sport?" Reminding me, as before by his abrupt use of this antiquated expression, of the eponym of

Fitzgerald's *The Great Gatsby*. The DNA samples, including the fork, seemed to fox him a moment. After that he realised and laughed. "Not bad. Not bad." Eventually he opened the small box and pulled off the bubble wrap. "I'd wondered where it had gone. Your parents', right?"

"Yes."

"Lovely." He stood caressing my mother's red glass dog tenderly and I wanted to snatch it. I wanted, as now I did so often, to kill him. Impotently and despairingly, need I say.

Carefully he placed the dog on my desk.

Not once had he glanced up at the writing on the ceiling.

"Well," he said, "that's that then, all cleared up. Got anything else hidden, Roy? Anything you want to confess to?"

I stared at him, blanking from my wide eyes and mind the glass of wasp in the bedroom wardrobe.

"Well," he said again. "Then I think it's time for your bath."

Even I, even then, even like that, did a kind of physical double-take. "What?"

"Your bath."

"What are you talking about?"

"Yeah. I know you're a nice hygienic guy. Clean shaven, all but that cobweb arrangement on your head. Teeth your own and all flossed and brushed, the rest showered, ready to face the world. But I think today, take an early bath. Or a shower, if you prefer."

I said, hollow and estranged, knowing it was not so simple, "If you say so."

"Yes, Roy. That's it."

I half turned.

"No, no, sorry, Roy, should have explained. We'll see to the water in a minute. Just take your stuff off."

"My – stuff."

"Clothes, Roy. Shirt, pants, your Y-fronts or whatever you favour. Shoes and socks."

The shock this time came externally from far away and wrapped around me as if I were something dead that could not feel.

I didn't move. My brain had nothing inside it but rushing and white noise.

"Oh," he said. Contrite, he lifted one hand. "Again, *mea culpa*. I should have made it clear. This isn't sexual. You have nothing to fear, that way."

I didn't move.

"Oh, come on, Roy. Do you want me to help?"

I must have backed a step. The filing cabinet tapped my spine.

"Yes, OK," he said, reasonably, "why am I telling you to do this. Because it has to be *faced*, Roy," (Oh Christ, shades of my father), "it just has to be dealt with, here and now. Clothes off. All and everything. Or I will help, Roy," His voice was quiet, and a faint hint of worry was in his expression – not yet quite the upset and concern that had heralded the blow. But enough.

351

"Give me a minute," I said.

"Sure. I'll time you." And he started, at an exact pace, softly aloud to count off the seconds.

My mind sent me a message that he was checking to make sure I had nothing 'concealed on my person'. My mind was trying, apparently, to make sense of what was either senseless or had another meaning it refused to confront – to *face up to*.

I knew, despite the business with bags and jacket, that Sej wasn't checking for anything concealed. Unless it was my concealed flesh. My body.

And no, it wasn't sexual.

At school, when the showers had been installed for use after games, (games – the misnomer of all time, nothing playful about them), one or two things had gone on here and there. I have no problem at all with homosexuality, so long as I'm not expected to join in. To me, even when presented in the best of literature, it seems silly, a sort of invention. I've no doubt this is a flaw in my intelligence – not of course that I find myself 'straight' as they say, but to be incapable of grasping others may find non-straightness not only the only option, but enjoyable. Or maybe even, as a boy of my own age, then about sixteen, once coaxingly said to me, my alienation is my defence against finding out my *true* feelings. Most if not all men are supposedly quite adaptable to enthusiastic sexual acts with their own gender. Generally however, at school or elsewhere, I've seldom been propositioned. Nevertheless, I seemed to know enough to believe that he, Joseph Traskul Sej, had no inclination or interest that way. And at the same moment a burning dominance radiated from him. There was no route out of this. As with everything else, I'd better give in.

It goes without saying, I've had to strip in front of strangers before, once or twice in tense and difficult situations, as when I'd had a cancer scare two and a half years previously.

I didn't wait until he reached sixty in his counting.

Off came everything, as he had stipulated, watch and shoes first. I hung the shirt and pants lightly over the back of the desk chair, left the rest on the floor.

He sat in silence, watching me.

I didn't glance at him.

When everything was off, I stood there by the desk, looking out of the window. And he got up, and came and looked me over, front and back, at a distance of about four to six feet.

During this he said nothing. Neither did I. It took about five minutes.

"OK," he said, "let's run the bath, shall we?"

Now I was to walk first. I went into the bathroom and realised I did not want to bend over in front of him to put the plug in the tub. Something so trivial. And curious, too, if I felt – and I didn't – no sexual threat. Yet threat of course I *did* feel. I simply couldn't codify it. It wasn't that I was merely embarrassed. I was not embarrassed. While my body has little to recommend it, neither am I deformed or spectacularly scarred. I've been neither blessed nor cursed in any physical area. I am a short skinny man, generally average, nondescript.

Having no choice anyway, I leant forward and shoved in the plug, then turned on both taps.

He meanwhile walked past me and letting it down, sat on the closed seat of the lavatory. He kept on watching, observing.

Then he said, "You were circumcised."

That sent another jolt through me. Not the reference, just the impact of his quiet, flat tone.

Again, I said nothing, and he added, "It's routine in some hospitals. Evidently the one where you were born, as I don't think you're Semitic." When I didn't speak now, he added "Or are you?"

So, I must answer.

"I haven't a clue. My parents weren't."

"You're a bit underweight," he went on, as if musing, "gut a bit flabby. Nothing much." The bath was full; I turned off the taps. "Get in, then," he said.

I got in. I sat down when he gestured to me to sit, in the warm water.

"Well," he said, "just carry on."

"What am I supposed to carry on with?" I said.

"Your bath. Just do what you always do." He paused and then said, in the most indescribable, vaguely humorous, *terrible* way, "Don't mind me."

In prisons of war or kidnap, guarded by jailors indifferent, sadistic or murderous, men have had to do this. They have had to urinate and defecate and vomit, also under the keen eyes of these enemies. Would that be the next step?

The soap was in my hands. I began to wash.

Still I hadn't once looked into his face, let alone his eyes. Not looking at him, even though he never took his eyes from me, seemed peculiarly to leave me a measure of privacy, perhaps safety. This is irrational, and afterwards became meaningless.

With each ordinary everyday move I made, I wondered what would come after.

He said nothing for a while.

He watched.

When I'd performed these ablutions, sluiced myself over, then he said, "Don't you ever lie back for a minute in the water?"

"Not often."

"So that's all."

I thought, He is going to instruct me now to do something else. To play with myself, perhaps. Or to sing a song. Am I going to do that? Either of those? I suppose I'll have to.

I stared at the light shining on the chrome taps. They weren't very clean. Franziska hadn't done a very good job, but to be fair too, that had been weeks back because he'd made me cancel her visits. The agency were very understanding about the emergency journey abroad he'd told me to say I had to make. I could have rung another number, pretended, let her arrive. But what would she have done anyway? Besides, I'd imagined him telling her he was my son, and how deranged I was, she'd been lucky. Even playing the piano to her, asking her for a date, God knows.

"Well, Roy," he said, breaking in on these random thoughts, "the water will be getting cold. Better get out now."

When I was out again, I reached for the towel, but before I got hold of it he said, "Now leave the towel. First, I want you, just for a minute, to stand there and look me in the face."

It wasn't chilly in the bathroom. It was nearly June and the sun was out.

I raised my head and looked directly at him.

Only I couldn't. Somehow I couldn't. My eyes slid off his face. I tried to make them stay – less for any affirmative reason of my own, than in order to obey and so appease him. And I couldn't. My eyes began to water. This was not fear, or tearfulness. It was the *strain*, as if I forced myself to stare into the sun or hold up some huge weight that was going to break my back.

"OK," he said then. With the edge of vision, I saw he smiled his smile. He threw the towel to me. And walked past me and out of the bathroom.

I heard him go down the stairs.

What happened next surprised me. I pushed the door shut and locked it, then I lifted the lid of the lavatory and was sick. The bath was still gurgling as it emptied. Perhaps he didn't hear the noise of my nausea.

I stayed in the bathroom after this for some time.

I believed, even if he'd heard nothing, even if he came to 'check' on me again and I made some excuse as to why I was still there – cleaning the bath perhaps – even so he guessed, had calculated and foretold how I was.

I advised myself I had been very afraid that something frightening, a thorough assault, a beating, was about to be perpetrated on me. Even, after all, male rape. But I knew I hadn't thought that. And I had been convinced also that so long as I did as I was asked, there'd be no violence. My subsequent physical reaction, and my mental one still, were not caused by actual anxiety or terror. It was something else.

On the floor by the basin I sat on the damp towel, thinking, thinking of this. Thinking of how I had been naked.

It was a very minor ordeal. Nothing dramatic or ghastly had occurred. It amounted to nothing.

But my brain held it. As in dreams sometimes I do, I saw myself as a separate person, and viewed from above. I saw myself standing before him, then in the bath washing, getting out and standing again in front of Joseph

Traskul, unable to meet his eyes, unable to look at him. I knew that once more clothed, I would remain unable to look into his face.

I found too I didn't want to leave the bathroom. I wished to stay there, by the basin, seated on the floor, not focussing, staring inward, thinking about myself seen from above as another person, naked. Or rather, this was not what I wished. It was all I could do. Even to move my left leg, the foot of which had gone to sleep, was beyond me. My mind was filling the room, and the house outside, with a kind of cerebral fog. In this Sej vanished. He *would* not therefore come up to the bathroom, knock, break down the door. Nothing would happen. Time had stopped.

NINETEEN

When I went downstairs it was almost 4 p.m.

Outside birds sang, and a couple of lawnmowers droned. Now and then a car went up or down the road. Everything was completely normal. But there was no sound in the house at all. I might have been alone there.

He was lying on the paint-splattered sofa in the front room, the shattered TV to his far left, a cushion under his head, reading Milton.

Without looking up, he read to me.

"'*Som natural tears they dropd, but wiped them soon,*
'*The World was all before them, where to choose*
'*Thir place of rest, and Providence thir guide:*
'*They hand in hand with wandring steps and slow,*
'*Through Eden took their solitarie way.*'"

I said, not looking at him, or no further than the book. "I'm going to make something to eat."

"Go ahead," he replied.

I walked out and on into the kitchen. There was no smell of food, and no crockery either in the sink or washed and draining.

From the fridge I took out the last of the ham and cut a couple of slices from the uncut loaf, spreading it with margarine. I thought of mustard too, then decided that might be too strong.

I had put on the same clothes from earlier. Just one addition. Something in my pocket.

While I'd made the sandwich, I had kept an ear and an eye on the hall. But Sej hadn't moved, he didn't come to see what I was doing. Generally, if I made myself food, he ignored me.

I took a couple of bites out of one half of the sandwich. I was almost hungry, which startled me slightly. When I'd swallowed them, I opened up that half of the sandwich again and dropped in the wasp from my handkerchief. It barely reacted and seemed mostly dead already; I'd reckoned any mustard would kill it outright. I replaced the top slice of bread gently, not to crush the wasp. Then I coughed loudly and started to swear.

Sej didn't come to see what was the matter.

I went quickly back up the hall, carrying the plate, and into the front room. He glanced up. This time I met his eyes, mine bulging. Now it was bizarrely possible.

"What have you done to this?" I shouted.

He raised his eyebrows.

"Tell me what you've done to it. You've put something on it – God knows what – it tastes like – cough mixture..."

"Oh, Roy. I haven't done a thing. You're the one tries to drug people."

"What about the fucking Rohypnol?" I ranted.

"Well, I'll tell you a secret, Roy. I lied about that. Yeah, I lied. There wasn't any Rohypnol in your glass. You must just have been rather tired and gone to sleep. But you were so keen I'd done something I hated to disillusion you."

"You've put poison on this bread – or the ham – That wasn't the deal."

"OK," he said. "So I've poisoned you. With, what was it? Cabdriver's linctus. Oh dear."

"*Taste* it," I roared. My face was hot. I had absolutely no trouble in glaring right at him. It was easy, almost – pleasing. "That's the arrangement. You taste my food, I taste yours. If you haven't done anything..."

"All right. Give it here. If it'll calm you down."

I shoved the plate at him. He looked amused. Supercilious, as if at all other times we led a happy low-key life together. "This piece?" He lifted the half with the wasp and put it to his mouth. And bit down on it.

Something happened in his eyes. I was staring now so intently and fixedly I saw it, like a spark, as if he had said "*Ah - but wait...*"

And then he gave a cry. The plate went flying. The two portions of the sandwich fell off and the bitten half opened. I couldn't see the wasp.

Sej was gripping his mouth. He had jumped up.

"What..." he said through his hand, "burns...?"

Then he made a noise as if he were retching, just as I had done earlier upstairs.

I said, "I told you so."

And I turned and walked out and straight into the library next door. His phone was still lying on the carpet. I detached it from the socket and stabbed in the number, ready memorised, that Cart had given me. I shut the library door and leaned on it.

Next door Sej was coughing violently, on and on, perhaps beginning to choke. I couldn't bank on that, or perhaps I could. But could I on Cart?

And it was only then I remembered that Cart had said his number would be available only for a 'few' weeks – was it too late?

After three rings an accented voice answered. "Bizan poos," it cheerily, incomprehensibly said. I must risk it. Had no other choice.

"I have to speak to Cart." I said, "quickly." I was almost whispering.

Probably Cart was gone. Probably… The voice had heard. If this was still the right number – maybe they were used to panicked whisperers.

"Who is asking, innit?"

"Phillips. Say R.P. Phillips."

"Phillip."

Next door now there was a soft thud.

Another voice came from the phone. I knew it.

"Mr Phillips."

"Cart – I need you at my house – your man knows where. How quickly can you...?"

"Quite quickly. An emergency, yes?"

"Yes."

"I have tried to warn you, Mr Phillips."

"The front door's locked – can't open it – need to break in – I'm his prisoner. And there's no money here to pay you." I added, "*You* can hold me hostage until my bank opens."

"Mr Phillips, have no worries. We will always accept a recognised credit card."

The line went dead.

I felt a deadly triumph and a sickened fear. If Sej was still conscious or able-bodied, how long would I be able to survive him? I dropped the mobile back on the carpet and reconnected it to the socket. I went out again into the hall.

No one was in the front room – he had gone.

Christ…

From the kitchen I heard water running.

I should get upstairs, barricade myself in the study. The desk and file cabinet, if I could lug them to the door, should keep him out a while.

"Roy," Sej called. His voice was a little roughened, that was all. He was there then, standing in the doorway. His lip was bleeding. "Something scratched me," he said. "Burns like hell." Neither his mouth nor his face were at all swollen.

I stood my ground; I had begun to shake now and getting up the stairs was going to take longer than I'd planned.

"I said..." I repeated.

"*You* put something in it, didn't you?" he asked. His face was neither enraged nor did it have that dangerous quality of concern. "And I fell for it."

"If I put something in the fucking thing why *would* I have been eating it?"

"Well. I didn't *see* you eat any, did I?"

Where before I had been unable to look into his face or eyes, precisely as a few minutes earlier I found I couldn't look away.

He came out into the hall.

"Let's go and inspect it, then," he said, "your sandwich."

Perhaps the sting hadn't yet had a chance to build up to its proper toxicity.

357

In the cases I'd heard of asphyxiation, or at least incapacitation of anyone stung in the mouth, happened inside a couple of minutes.

We both walked back into the front room.

The undone sandwich lay there, bread and ham and the smears of the margarine. Nothing else. The plate hadn't broken.

Sej went over to it and toed the food.

"What's that?" he asked. He bent forward and I saw the tiny blackish curled up corpse of the wasp lying under the rim of the plate.

Now I had better turn and run as fast as my watery legs would carry me.

A loud crunching crack sounded from the back of the house. A chair went over in the kitchen. Feet were pounding like a train up through the hall. Something pushed me aside.

There were two of them, both in black jeans, T-shirts and trainers. One wore a baseball cap pulled low over his eyes, the other had a mop of brown hair.

I'd staggered back and reached the wall.

I saw Sej standing there with his eyes wide and then they had him. One blow thudded home in his stomach. As he doubled the brown-haired man grabbed his arms from behind and swung him away to the wall beyond the window. There, screened from the street by the drapery of one of my mother's curtains, the other rhythmically began to sink fresh blows into him.

"That's enough," said the brown-haired man presently. He looked over his shoulder at me. "We'll do a bit more work later, somewhere else. You'd like him off the premises I take it?" He spoke with an Oxbridge accent. Under the cascade of hair, I identified Mr C in a wig. I'd never, then, heard him speak before.

The other man, one I didn't know with a young bony face, was examining Sej as carefully as a doctor. "He's out."

"How did you – I mean – so fast...?" gormlessly I said.

"Cart knows your type, Mr Phillips. And your friend here's type too. We've been watching. Just round the corner. Come on," he added to the other man, "we'll take him out the back way. Vehicle's just along the Crescent, Mr Phillips. You'll need to get your back door fixed. But this one won't be bothering you for at least ten days. Say twelve days, by the time my colleague has had enough room to exercise his full powers." The other one grinned.

"How will you...?" I said. "I mean, someone may see you."

"They won't see him," said Mr C. "We have a big roll of carpet out there. Ever heard of Cleopatra?"

I nodded, stupefied.

The other man said, however, "She was carried unseen like into the presence of Caesar, tied up in a carpet. And that's how we do it, place like this. 'S nice carpet. And look, no blood to mess it up." He winked. "Not yet."

They dragged Sej out.

I followed them in a kind of dream state to the kitchen. The door was intact, but the lock had been nimbly forced. A large roll of carpet lay on the ground. They pulled it through into the house and I wondered if George and Vita were watching.

"My neighbours..."

"Suspicious? You'd be surprised, Mr Phillips. Any questions, someone bust your back door when you were out, or having a nap. Stole some carpet. They get confused you see, witnesses," said Mr C. his voice taking on a differently accented twang. "Carpet came in, and went out? Nah. Just went out. Elderly couple I think they are, right? Saw 'em the other day. Both batty from the looks of 'em. Guy the other side too busy hoovering. Likes a bit of weed an' all, *je pense*. Not reliable."

They put Sej into the carpet, rolled him up.

I stood there watching.

I kept wanting to laugh, but also I needed to be alone. I wanted them gone. How didn't matter. Nothing mattered but solitude.

"And he won't – be back?"

"Not for a while. And of course, if there's any more trouble," Mr C was Oxbridge once more, "we can always arrange a larger delivery. By the way," he added, as they efficiently raised the bundle, "best to pay HQ inside twelve hours. It's more polite. Looks as if you're pleased with the work."

Weakly I said, "The man said a credit card – is that right?"

"Affirmative."

Out they strode, carrying the carpet. Limber as squirrels over the fence they went. They must have a van. I closed the door and found I could after all jam it shut. Immediately I called the number again on Sej's mobile and got the one who answered with the mystic words *Bizan poos.* But very smartly he acknowledged delivery of my 'order' and took the details of my card. I was warmly thanked.

Only later did I realise both entries to and exits from my house were now barred to me, I was still trapped, the back door jammed, the front door locked, and no keys left, for Sej had them all. But the keys came, both sets, next morning, put through my front door in a plain white envelope. And the day after that Duran, flushed with the joy of successful fatherhood, mended the back door and enhanced every aspect of security in the house.

TWENTY

Collapse. That happened on the third day. Until then I'd kept going, carried by a sort of transparent bubble of buoyant un-caringness, the kind that can result from certain types of trauma, or alcohol.

Duran hadn't been quite fooled by it, I felt, less fooled than I was, probably.

"You OK, Roy, mate?" he asked me several times.

359

But then, he'd seen the gutted TV and the red paint all over the front room.

Knowing now I couldn't spill a single bean to him, I spun him a version of the story Mr C had suggested. Vandals had broken in at the kitchen door while I was away up north in Cheston. They'd stolen a few bits and pieces including, for some reason, a spare carpet. They'd also destroyed my TV rather than nick it and broken a lot of crockery – hence these peculiar cups and saucers, which I'd borrowed, I blithely told him, from Ian at 76. Painting the walls of the front room bright red was pretty warped I had to admit.

"Yeah, and they ain't done a half bad job," Duran agreed. "Looks professional – apart from the mess. But I've heard of worse."

I said I hadn't had a chance to try to clear up yet. It would undoubtedly mean replacing the sofa and chair covers, even the carpet and curtains. Funny the piano wasn't messy, he said. I said this had struck me too. If he noticed the pale painted words on the ceiling in my study, he said nothing. He asked if I'd called the police. I told him I had but got nowhere. He nodded in gloomy belief.

I liked Duran. I couldn't rid myself of the urge to get him off the premises, as if some poisonous gas cloud lay in wait inside the house, and no other must be exposed to it. Also an intense need remained to be on my own. Normally he didn't get on my nerves, but this time, once he left, I broke down. I snivelled for about a quarter of an hour, and then I slept, inside my newly bolted and barred fortress. I dreamed my mother was in hospital and I had had to go to the lavatory, and coming back into the room I found I stood there, a grown man and naked in front of her, but she only said, "Don't worry, Roy, dear. I'm dying. It won't matter."

I'd checked the call register on Sej's mobile.

All calls were deleted, except my pair, of course. I myself for some reason deleted these. Then I smashed it to pieces. On the morning of the third day I made myself go out. The security of the house was now impressive. Even the alarm worked. Beyond the fortress however, might Sej still lurk?

My common sense told me he would be in no fit state to do anything of the sort. The little I'd seen of the pasting Mr C and his 'colleague' had given Sej assured me he'd be out of action for some while. After further 'work' I doubted he'd get far at all for two or three weeks. And he wouldn't come back. No. Even he, even he wouldn't come back for more.

I kept seeing him in my mind, when awake, the way the blows had gone into him – this always recaptured in slow-motion, whereas at the time the whole sequence had been blurred by speed – and the way he was when they'd finished. Which was like a very life-like dummy, life*less*. Even when I had drugged him, he hadn't looked this way. The man in the baseball cap was correct. There was no visible blood. They hadn't marked his face. It was hard and yet, conversely easy, to put his two personas together – the lifeless bundle of limbs and hair and face, the dominating tyrant AB, who had made me strip and take a bath in front of him.

And that was strange to me, too.

Because this last act I had had to perform seemed to have unlocked so much implacable horror inside me, and still I couldn't analyse why. I wasn't some virgin Victorian girl. It was nothing, that thing I'd had to do, *nothing*.

And yet. It had been the pivot.

On that, my bid for freedom had turned.

My excursion to the high street and back went almost without event. I bought some food and various other necessities. I even bought some mugs and plates from the expensive shop which sold them, plain white. (The ordinariness of the high street both reassured and disturbed me. My 'adventure' must have gone on in some other parallel world. Not a ruffle on the surface here. Irrelevant).

As I returned up Old Church Lane, I was feeling a dull shaky elation. Then I saw George Fulton was out, slowly mowing his front lawn.

What would he do, I wondered, when he saw me? Turn and run like last time, pointing something sharp in my direction for good measure?

Besides, what had he seen of my paint-and-carpet 'vandal break-in'?

Better take the bull by the horns.

"Hello, George."

He glanced up, switched off the mower and eyed me carefully. Carefully too he said, "Hello, Roy. Feeling better?"

I'd previously made a decision on how to handle this.

"Yes, I'm fine now. He got in a state and blew it out of proportion."

"Your son."

"He really isn't my son, George. I used to know his mother a long time ago. I hadn't seen him for years."

"No," said George doubtfully, "I didn't think we'd seen him, Vita and I, not before. He said something about that. I can't remember what..." George paused and regarded the mower handle. "Why did you ask me to get the police, though? You did, you know. And your – your young friend told me you insisted he smash all your plates."

So that was how Sej had covered his actions in the back garden. *My* fault again.

Nor could I in turn incriminate Sej. Not now.

"Yes, George, I did, I'm afraid. I'll tell you the facts. I've had to take something for years for blood pressure." (George nodded inadvertently. I knew, so did he have to). "This new stuff the doctor put me on can have a very funny effect on the brain. The dose was wrong too. Frankly I'd like to clobber the man, but in the end, it's been sorted out. I'm fine now, and I apologise for worrying you."

George's eyes looked nervous. He said, very fast, "But what are you taking? It's not Captopril, is it? Only I take that, you know, have done for years – I mean, you hear these things don't you, and I'm not as young as I was..."

I nearly laughed. I controlled it. All George really cared about, like most of the human race, was how he might be affected, and if he might even suffer symptoms like my own invented ones.

"No, you're OK, George," I said. "That wasn't what I got fobbed off with. Your medication is one of the best, or so I've been told."

He loosened and gave me a little smile.

"Well I'm glad you're better, Roy. And your – he – has he gone?"

"Back to his own life I hope, George." One truth anyway.

I opened up my newly complicated door, went in, closed and re-locked it. Then I took the groceries and other things into the kitchen and put them on the table. I'd just filled the kettle from the tap, still half sneering at George, when my legs went from under me. They gave way.

I'd heard of this.

I sat on the lino listening to water drip and thought. *Brace up, Roy. It's over now.*

But the kitchen reeled, or something in my head did so.

And I thought, *He's done something to me – some other drug – something – he's in the house – he's here – he's standing in the doorway...*

But he hadn't, he wasn't.

I was alone.

The collapse lasted for about ten minutes, after which I knew I could move again, and cautious as old George I got myself up and sat on a chair.

Finally, I rescued the kettle and made the tea and drank it in a white mug. (Why had I bought three of these?) It tasted of a bitter nothingness.

About 4.30 I went to bed.

I dreamed of Sej by night floating down a river, perhaps even that black river in Vilmos's City. He was presumably already dead, but nevertheless I hefted a large stone, using unusual strength, and dropped it on his body. He sank. Without a trace.

8

Mr C shook my hand before we parted. This was on the far side of the park, after we had left Sej's flat in the roof.

"Don't worry about him, Mr Phillips," said Mr C in his university accent. "I really don't think you have anything to bother about now. He was – shall I say – well cared for."

I looked him in the face. "Hospital job," I said.

Now he shook his head. "Best not to ask. He's alive. He'll get over it. Lesson learned. All you need to know. Nice working with you, Mr P."

I'd called Cart's number again, some way on from the day of the collapse. It was after I'd destroyed everything Sej had brought into the house, just binning some of it, like the toiletries, smashing and binning some, (such as his phone, which I'd already seen to), tearing or cutting up garments and binning them. I'd have made a fire and burned them if I'd lived elsewhere. But I could just imagine Ian and George and Vita if I got an incinerator and started it up out the back. Actually, the black dustbin was what I used, put out the front for what Lynda used to call the rubbish people.

Sometime I must also acquire a new landline telephone; for now my current mobile would be adequate. While in a few more days I'd go into Woolwich or Greenwich and check out places for fresh carpet, covers and curtains. My 'emergency fund' was almost gone, but once I got *Kill Me Tomorrow* properly on track, written, delivered, I'd have enough. Sometime too I would sell the piano. I might get a couple of quid for that, but I'd need to shop around. Until then there was the other credit card. Never before had I been so profligate, but now I had no choice.

I had cleaned the house too.

The faint writing on the study ceiling I left. I had a phase of sitting in my desk chair, staring up at it. One night, in fact the night before I called Cart's number again, I wrote a little more of *Untitled*, the first onslaught I'd made on it concisely for years. The idea that I shouldn't be doing it, that I should be working on *KMT*, seemed to have revitalised the 'project'. Or. Something had.

But I had started to have a recurring dream by now. I kept dreaming of his flat, at that point unseen. It was always different, but always *there*. I'd walk up endless wooden stairs to reach it, or stone stairs; it was always *upward* I had to go. And sometimes in the dreams I'd force a door with the glass panel he had described, often ornate, the glass stained, or it would already be forced, but inside I would find not a flat, but a garden with fountains, or a wasteland with a mirage of sun, or a dripping cellar, or a flooded municipal library… countless varieties of symbols, secret ciphers, of my id, or his. God knew. And so at last, rather than seek the furnishing departments of Woolwich, I went to central London, to Saracen Road, and broke in. And then I came back, and called the number and returned to the flat with Mr C.

Once halfway rational again, I'd been a little puzzled Cart's number had been and was still available. This was far more than a 'few' weeks. I decided on a simple theory. Maybe everyone was told the number evaporated in that time, a precautionary lie. After all, if you used them you were implicated. And who could prove anything? However odd the name announced to callers, it was a business, and perhaps had a front that legitimately was. They took credit cards for Christ's sake. How would it show on a statement – Bizan poos…

Now anyway I knew about the apartment in the attic. I'd seen it, climbed up to it in waking reality, by the ladder, and climbed down knowing its nature.

All the way home on the train from Charing Cross I thought about that place, its greens and blues, its ambience of money and impermanence. It was like a camp in a wood. A middle-class bivouac between battles. Stocked with straightforward nourishing proteins and edible delicacies, bandages, painkillers, areas for not-quite-ordinary R and R. A hidden sanctum. What else? We'd found no weapons.

Some of my neurasthenia at being outside the house had gone. I walked home from the station, up Bulivante Crescent, along my own familiar road.

When I was almost there, I saw the eccentric car, a 1930s Morris in shiny condition, parked by the curb.

This car I knew.

But I couldn't recall from where, or why.

Then Harris Wybrother opened the driver's door and got out, looking round uncertainly at me, this hitherto unseen shaven-headed, moustachioed Roy all in black.

"You look really well," he told me, pummelling my hand and arm. "More than you'll be able to vouch for me, I expect."

Astounded, I could only say, "This is a surprise."

"Yes, old boy. Janette got some bee in her hairdo, the day I got back – last Friday – she thinks she had a message that you were having some kind of dodgy squabble with a publisher."

Shaven housebreaker, employer of hitmen, Roy shook his head with a thin smile. "She misunderstood. It was a personal matter. I'd have liked to ask your advice. But that's in the past."

"Oh, she tends to get things wrong. Wrapped up in her own multi-tasking. She's in Strasbourg till tomorrow. I thought I'd run over and see you. I can do with a breather. So this is your domicile?"

We both stood and looked at my house, semi-detached, inadequately paved, unimpressive, slightly run down – aside, of course, from its brand-new security locks.

"Somehow I didn't picture your pad like this."

My pad.

"Come in," I said.

"Glad to," he said, "I'm done in, I can tell you."

He looked all right to me, despite a yellowish half-formed tan which he tends to put on at the start of an English summer anyway. Perhaps Spain had been overcast?

"Oh, the weather stank. Hot, and storms. They put it down to the usual global hoohah. And they're still in a state from the terrorist stuff."

We had gone in and I guided him through into the kitchen; the door of the front room was shut and the curtains I had drawn. He glanced at the shut door but made no comment. He was already telling me about his father's funeral, which apparently had had to take place in Spain, according to Veronica the thirty plus child bride, and also to Wybrother Senior's will. "The official crap – you've no idea, Roy. It wasn't red tape – more like red bandage." He had declined coffee or tea so I fetched the whisky, shutting the door of the front room again when I came out. The old bottle had already been emptied, this was a fresh one. "Christ, Roy. You have no idea."

"You had a bad time." I felt remote as I said this. I felt, actually, contemptuous.

"Bad's not the word. And that bitch Vero – that's what Dad called her, apparently, Vero. So now she's Vero. Sounds like some US brand of energy drink, doesn't it? Vero took me aside the first evening, after I'd bought her quite a lavish dinner at my hotel. She put it to me very clearly that most of the money, and any property outside the Hampshire place, was hers. I'm sure you grasp, Harris, she said, I'm entitled to that. I've had to put up with quite a lot from your father. This with him on his bloody slab not two miles away."

"It must have been tough."

"Yes. And I went down with food poisoning, or some Spanish bug..."

Somehow I couldn't resist. "A fly, perhaps?" I asked mildly.

A month ago, he might have got that and laughed. A month ago however I doubt I would have said it aloud.

"Flies? You are correct. Everywhere. The air conditioning just made them frisky."

He continued to fill me in on his saga.

I pictured him, racked with worry and the unadmitted grief or fear I'd glimpsed in his eyes that day in the restaurant in Holborn. And stuck there in the luxury hotel, with his still current expense account from the firm, via which, I had no doubt, he had financed Veronica's lavish dinner.

"And there'll be death duties I'll have to pay on the damned house. Can you believe it, Roy? I mean, that crumbling wreck of a place. Hampshire! Miles from London. The dunnies don't even work properly. For God's sake."

The light was darkening. It looked like rain again.

"But you haven't told me anything about *you*, Roy."

I hadn't had much chance. "I'm fine."

"So this personal stuff of yours blew over."

"Yes."

"They have a habit of blowing over, don't they? These nasty little troubles. I suppose even all this shit with Dad will blow over. And you're OK with Gates – old Lew Rybourne?" (Lewis was at least twelve years his junior).

"Yes."

"Working well?"

"Fine, Harris."

I poured him another drink. He was already leading us towards the last third of the bottle, although I'd only had a couple.

"Are you seeing anyone?" he asked suddenly. There was a kind of sly subterfuge in his voice.

"You mean a woman. No. Not at the moment."

"You're a wise boy, Roy. Wish I had your bloody self control." He then launched into a monologue on 'someone' he had met on the plane back from Spain, which rhyme he included several times, like a chorus. "I mean that is a dire little flight. Don't know if you've ever done it – the plane from Spain? No, well. Not missed much. Too short to get stuck into anything, too long to manage not to get cabin fever. But then *this* plane from Spain had this girlie on it. And I got lucky. Or she did. Sat side by side. Really bright girl – oh," as if I'd asked, "about twenty-nine or so. Could be a bit older – don't you find women don't look their age now. Until they hit about forty-five, and then – everything falls, as they say in Venice. Anyway. We got on, shared some champagne – Look, Roy, would you do me a completely priceless favour?"

"Why not?" I said, smiling.

"You're a diamond. Jan is a bit suspicious. Don't know why. She never used to bother. Her age, maybe, she's coming up for the big four nine this year. Tonight, I'm going up west, and my plane from Spain friend and I – well, you can guess, I have no doubt. Doesn't need one of your sleuths to solve it, does it? But Jan's due back tomorrow and I may not make the airport to collect her. Not that she needs me. If she left her car in London that's her look-out and she's perfectly well able to call a taxi. But you know what they're like. Could you back me up if it comes to it? That is, you and I had dinner tonight, it got late so I kipped in your spare room – you do have one, don't you?"

Kip. His word – Sej's word had been the more modern *crash*. Kip or crash. Crash...

"I've got a spare bed. Yes. I can say that, Harris. If you want."

Rather than feel any fleeting gladness that Janette was to be deceived, or that I'd been involved in it, I felt a strange rush of oblique anger at him. Not *because* he wanted to involve me. It was far less logical. I was remembering how his brief flare of panic and distress during our last lunch had unsettled me, and sent me ultimately into the pub in the Strand. Where Sej had found me. Was *found* the right word? Dreadfully, maybe it was.

"That is so kind, Roy. I don't want to upset Jan, you see. I mean this thing is just a passing – fancy. She's too young for me, this chick off the plane from Spain."

Chick.

Was Harris becoming his father? Is that how we fill the niches where the dead once dwelled, not like the ancients with their sacred bones or carved semblances, but by transforming ourselves into their image?

He downed his drink then.

"Well, it's been good to see you. You look really good, Roy. I like the punk style. You ought to get some new publicity shots. I know a really splendid guy. I'll send you his name and email. I can just imagine some tasty ladies in their forties really liking the look of you."

Forty-five-year-olds, no doubt, the poor collapsed old cows.

I smiled.

We went out to his car.

"Why are the curtains drawn in there?" he asked me. "I meant to say before."

He had indicated the front room.

"Some decorators painting it. It's a mess at the moment. Stinks of paint too."

"I know what you mean. Veronica – ah, pardon me, *Vero* – was having the villa painted. I've seldom seen a white so *green*. You know, I long for the good old days when you could hire a witch to cast a juicy curse."

I smiled.

We shook hands.

"And you're OK," he said, "about that little thing with tonight?"

"Yes, Harris."

He got into the Morris, careless of the whisky. He waved, and drove off down the road.

The only reason he had come to see me, evidently, was to establish his alibi. But whether I upheld it was really down to me. Doubtless I would. He was still partly my agent, after all.

XVIII
('UNTITLED': PAGE 319)

Candlelight had revealed the face of Reiner.

He had survived the river. He was alive.

Having been dragged, about midday, into the Chamber of Revelation, Vilmos stood on legs that did not belong to him, made of strong stone like the supports of the Flavel Bridge. Planted in life's rushing black water, they never shook.

Vilmos's upper body too seemed to have its own physical if quiescent strength. He stood straight, his head held up, his arms and hands motionless at his sides. It was not either that he had been frozen and was too cold to move. It was that his body itself had decided it would not want to.

There was feeling in every limb, and in his torso and head, but though striped by severe flagellation and bruised by blows, pain was not all-consuming. He had no headache, had not had it, he thought, for more than twenty days – which was unusual. Awareness only was paramount. His mind worked intelligently and quickly.

Sometimes he did turn his head a little, for his head permitted him to do this. His eyes allowed him to move them freely. He had noted, his heartbeat was uncongested if rather slow, his breathing regular and deep.

Thus, seeing Reiner who might have been dead, slipping here and there through the crowd of men in the Chamber, Vilmos knew at once that Reiner had simply swum to shore.

Such an idea amused Vilmos. He felt for Reiner unfettered contempt. To survive now seemed, in some innate, inchoate sense, more slavish and conventionally drab than to have given in and drowned.

The *import* of the revelation did not strike Vilmos for a while, during which he continued to peruse the robed gathering of the Order of the Indian

Mystery, as he stood upright in the centre of the room within a great new circle representing the Wheel. It had been made about him, its execution beginning in the late afternoon and proceeding through several hours. Those who had seen to this task had frequently grown exhausted. Some swooned and had to be replaced. Vilmos on his stony supportive limbs, his spine a reliable column, remained tall among them, watching the ones to the front and a little to either side, *listening* to those who worked behind him, since his head did not intend to let him to look over his shoulders, just as all the rest of him did not countenance the act of his fully turning round.

They had drawn the Wheel on the floor with the spilled blood of creatures brought in cages, from salt and liquefied silver, from ordure, which had been dried to powder and did not stink, or not greatly, and from the contents of vessels of milk. This last, according to what was said, was of three types. Firstly that of a virgin cow inspired to produce it by giving her a calf to foster, secondly of a whore who was feeding, or had been, her own baby, thirdly of a pure mother whose spouse belonged to the Order. There were other things also; chips of bone and splinters of wood, which Vilmos assumed had been hacked from reliquaries. Dusts ground from precious stones had been added in miserly quantities. But too there were other commodities. Some – many – Vilmos did not recognise. His mouth, tongue and throat did not wish to be used, and so he could not inquire.

The Master oversaw the entire labour. He chid the artisans, once or twice struck them with his staff. Those who fainted he chose to inspect. In some he found virtue. Others not. One he spat on, saying the fool smelled of drink and had perhaps upset the ritual. But in the end it seemed not; the old man was satisfied.

He had rarely glanced at Vilmos. He must know how Vilmos was, and that he had been primed to his present condition and use.

Vilmos did not even feel any anger at the Master, let alone entertain thoughts of revenge. Revenge, of course, could not enter into the equation. When all this was – done, Vilmos would be no more. As some other foreign poet had once described it, Vilmos was to be their torch, and like a torch they would not light him for himself. He would kindle and burn up, and reaching the sixth stage, the point of dark blue fire, his purpose for them would be accomplished, and his own life snuffed out.

Yes, for all these lumbering and inadequate imbeciles, for these talentless lesser things, he was to attain and instantly freely render up the power of utter dominion over the inner and outer spheres: Mastery of Self, Mastery of All.

This it seemed the Devil granted to the Order, having become sick of the idiocy of mankind. For Satan loved God. He longed hopelessly only to be forgiven and raised.

And Vilmos felt neither fear nor struggle in him. He did not care anymore what became of him.

Like Satan, Vilmos was sick of the world and all its works. And if God did not want him, neither did Vilmos want any part of God.

And then. He beheld Reiner.

And a little while after, perhaps two or three minutes after, Vilmos saw what this meant. And also he saw that none but he had seen it – either Reiner, or what his presence suggested. The rest of them, the rabble in the Chamber, the educated and wise, virtuous acolytes chosen of the Master, the cripple-hearted Master himself – none of them saw or knew.

The very fitness of Vilmos, and his use to them, was predicated upon his having killed men and women to the number of thirteen. For this reason had they not brought him here another man to slaughter, while the girl they brought for his carnal release they swiftly removed after congress, in case he might offer her also death – and so *increase* the number of the slain.

But Vilmos, since Reiner lived, had formerly killed in total only eleven, and now, with his single murder here, only twelve.

After all, something salient in the rite was out of alignment, a broken bone sticking from the skin of the spell.

TWENTY-ONE

Lynda left me, not only because of her well-off aunt near Manchester. I haven't been quite honest about that either in these pages or with myself.

Lynda left me because, the night she put it to me that she – and I – might go up north, where things were cheaper and the aunt presided, we had a row.

We'd often fought. When I tried not to join in it only made her more furious, I think. Certainly, my neutral answers and refusal to lose my rag seemed to provoke her at these times to greater acrimony.

"Oh, you just sit there, Roy. Just sit there with that book. Don't you understand I want something a bit more than this rotten little flat and working for that horrible old rat, Christmas..." She meant her boss, a Mr Christmas. "...and your *stupid* hours at that library and never having any money or doing anything exciting. Oh, you just sit there. You don't care, do you? Long as your dinner's on the table, long as I've washed and ironed your clothes."

In fact we shared a lot of the chores. But for some while, Lynda had seemed to believe my late nights at the library, compulsorily working until 6.30 or 8 p.m., were my choice in order l) to get out of cooking a meal or helping clean the flat or 2) to avoid Lynda.

"But why do I *bother* to say anything? *You* won't try anything new, will you? You're like a bloody old man, Roy, you're like some old guy of forty-five."

"I'm sorry."

"You're not sorry. You're *not!*" she screamed. And then dropping back to a tone, which even she herself would describe as sarcastic, "But it's no good trying to shift you, is it? No good being sarky, even. You have to have your own little way, don't you, Roy? Roy knows best."

She was always on about my liking to have my own little way. I've mentioned this before. It rarely failed by now to get on my nerves.

"I'm sorry, Lynda. Why don't *you* go and visit your aunt? I can't take any holiday now, you know that."

"*Yes.* I *know* that." Her thin lips squeezed almost white. The hard, fluorescent kitchen strip shot lightnings over her glasses.

"Look, I need to go and try to finish that story in a minute – there's a good chance they'll take it but I have to have it with them before next..."

"That's all you do, isn't it? You're out all bloody day and half the night and then you're off to write some story. Some rubbish. How'd you know they'll publish it? They didn't want the last one."

"No."

"Oh, but you go *on*. You have your own little way. I don't know why I bother to come to bed. You sit and read, or scribble, or you're in the lounge typing till midnight. I can't even watch TV in there. And it's been two weeks since we last – since you know what."

I put down the book and looked at the back of it, unseeing. I couldn't say to Lynda that I found her by now unappetising. That I really needed to be – well frankly very ready – before I could make love to her. And to make matters worse I'd had a bit of a thing about a woman at work. She was a few years older than me, quite pretty and very happily living with a man. Obviously, I'd been aware I stood no chance, but I'd enjoyed her being there, working with her. We got on well, saw eye to eye on a lot of things. She'd read a story of mine published in one of the magazines and praised it, (I published under my real name then). She said I shouldn't be working in the library at all. About five days before my row with Lynda this woman, I won't put her name, had been transferred to another branch nearer her home. She was delighted to go. I'd wished her well. I'd kissed her cheek and shaken her partner's hand. She said they'd be looking out for my first published crime novel.

"Lynda, I'm tired."

"Not too tired to *scribble*. Not too tired to type and turn the lounge into your *office*. Paper everywhere. Books. A *tip*."

"Lynda..."

"Oh, shut up!" She surged to the door. "*You* do the bloody washing-up. I'm going to bed. You..." She paused. "You can *sleep* in the lounge." We had no couch. She meant on the floor or in a chair. "You can go to hell!"

I got up. Although we fought, somehow I had never really lost my temper. It was as if, even for rowing with her I had to be in the right frame of mind. But now I was.

"Fuck off to bed, then," I shouted. "And if you want to go to your aunt's so much just fucking go. In fact *I'll* go. I'm leaving. Get out of the way..." I pushed past her.

Now she ran after me into the bedroom. "What are you doing?" she bleated. But she could see. I was shoving a few clothes into a bag. Next, I went to the bathroom and got my shaving stuff and toothbrush. "What?" she kept saying, "What?"

But I didn't speak to her again until I was at the front door. "Right. What you do, Lynda, is up to you. If you're still here when I come back, we can discuss it. But I hope you won't be." The flat was rented. She always had most of my wages to date and all her own. She would manage.

She said, crying now, her glasses dripping tears, pitiful and revolting, "What shall I do?"

"Whatever you like. Fuck off. That's the best thing."

I went out and downstairs and let myself into the street. It was after ten at night and raining. I felt a gust of relief flare through me, like raw cool oxygen. As if I could breathe again. It was less getting away from her than escaping the surge of potential violence I'd sensed suddenly present inside me. I have never physically hurt a woman. That night I felt I might have done.

One of the fellows from work was in the pub I ended up in, and he let me sleep on his sofa. "Good thing Jenny isn't here tonight. She'd never put up with it."

When I went back to my own flat two days later, crestfallen and feeling rather bewildered, Lynda had gone. She had left me a four page letter, written in her over-ornamented handwriting with plenty of misspellings and wrong grammar.

The gist was she had her Pride. Her father had always told her that if a man didn't want her she must not want him, And she could see I no longer loved her, so she would indeed be "going up to Auntie's." She had taken her things, "like you would expect me to." Actually she had taken quite a few of mine also, including some of my books – dictionaries and a thesaurus. She couldn't possibly have wanted them. She must only have wanted to deprive me of them, I assumed, as I'd seemed to prefer them to her. Which of course I had.

Her father called me the night I left the flat, migrating back to my parents' house for a brief stay, as I sorted out my financial affairs. "A great pity," he sternly told me. "I always thought of you as rather a steady chap. I wouldn't have let her marry you, Roy, if I hadn't."

I apologised for not being what he had believed me to be.

One wonders sometimes how often one has had to do that.

Since then I've never seen Lynda again. I never saw the other woman, from the library, again either. She was a bit like Maureen, not to look at, more her manner, although her accent was better and her voice not quite so musical or warm.

When Harris Wybrother had driven away, I sat in my kitchen in Old Church Lane. I'd made some filter coffee, bought that day, an indulgence I don't often allow myself. There were some chocolate biscuits too, and I ate four.

Something had puzzled me about Sej's flat in the roof. Only I hadn't quite realised what at the time. Now it had come to me.

The apartment had many things in it that were quite large, such as the piano, not to mention the couches that could be transformed to beds. And there were things that would have needed either careful packing or delicate handling – glasses, plates. The flat was also able to produce water in the kitchen and bathing areas, had radiators, and lights and a music centre which would require electricity.

How had the breakable or heavy items been got into the apartment? How had the washing machine been plumbed in and cooker connected? Only the freelance limber or foolhardy would chance that ladder up from the fire-escape. Certainly no one from the electricity board or the water services, let alone anyone delivering a piano.

There had to be, did there not, another entry and exit from the flat. But neither I *nor* Mr C, the expert, had spotted one.

At 9 that night, just after I'd finished off the Vilmos chapter upstairs, someone rang the bell.

I went down and I thought, *This won't be him.* But before I could decide what I felt, let alone open the door, the letter-box flipped up. George called through, "Roy, it's me. Just a little something."

I had no inclination to open up for George, but established habits linger. Or was it that? I unfastened the door quite swiftly despite its new bolts and locks.

The sun had only just gone. The sky was a broad silky blue, high clouds catching a peach afterglow, fading.

And there was George with a plate, and on the plate a round dark fruit cake.

"Vita, you see," he said, with an abashed vaingloriousness. "She baked this afternoon, and she thought you might like this one."

I stood at a loss again.

Belatedly it had occurred to me how I had been hoodwinked before by George and Vita, Sej using them to gain access. Now too he could have been out here. He could have been. But he was not.

The cake smelled good. My mother had sometimes baked, but not so successfully as Vita. My mother's *forté* was jam tarts, her fruit cake tended to be merely laxative.

"That's much too kind, George," I said. I took the plate. "Wonderful. Please thank your wife very much."

"Just look after yourself," admonished George. He managed to convey this cake was not a reward, but a tick for effort. I still needed to keep up the work.

He plodded back and went in. I stood holding the cake looking up and down the road.

The bicycling boy bicycled past. The prancing poodle was being taken for a walk by the new man in the life of No 73.

Going in myself I shut the door and re-secured it.

In the kitchen I put the cake to one side. After the coffee and biscuits, I didn't want it. I wasn't sure I wanted it anyway. Too much contact with my neighbours could prove time-consuming and draining.

Besides, I hadn't forgotten George and the scissors.

Poor old sod. It hadn't been his fault.

I closed my mind to him and went upstairs to back up the last chapter I'd done of *Untitled* on the machine. I supposed I should be pleased with it. It seemed to me I might suddenly have concluded the thing. But in a way I found that uncomfortable. The novel had been with me so long. And now what was I to do with it? No one would even want to glance at it. Writers, if they have any success at all, are always expected to remain in their handy and clearly-labelled ghettos A pseudonym? But all that was hypothetical. Probably tomorrow I'd want to rewrite that last chapter entirely.

Ten minutes later the doorbell went again.

I was disinclined to go down. It must be George, or Vita even, coming to see what I thought of the cake. There'd been a similar visit over the last piece of cake she'd awarded me, years ago.

Idly I went to the unlit study window and looked down. George was there, standing on the paving talking to the paunchy man with cigars from No 80.

I drew back and took out the sheets of *Untitled* from my printer tray and left them lying by the computer.

The bell went again. I ignored it.

I ran a bath and lay in it listening to the Third Programme. By which I mean Radio 3. It was Rachmaninov, the Third Symphony, or do I mean Symphony 3?

As a boy I'd found him too emotional. But that was insanity. Every age of one's life seems to carry some particular intellectual failing. If we learn one thing we seem to have lost another. Or probably only most of us. Some, surely, truly do grow up. But they are rare.

He returned into my life a couple of evenings later.

It was slightly less time than Mr C had promised. More, perhaps, than I had originally instinctively credited.

XIX
('Untitled': Page 323)

To be on fire, to burn, was neither an agony nor alarming. The fire was cool, and although he felt it moving upward through his body, it had a certain familiarity. He seemed to have experienced its passage once or twice before. Then, however, it had given no light, and so he must not have known what happened to him.

Nothing of him had burned away. Still he stood, motionless in the centre of the Wheel of Life. No other light but that within *him* now illuminated the Chamber of Revelation.

It had begun with the deepest rose red, which flooded not only the lowest area of his belly and the area of his loins, but shone outward there and through his thighs. The veins and arteries in his calves and feet were also lighted with this colour. One could not be afraid of it, the gorgeous redness. It seemed life-giving.

Despite that, and the fact the chants and magical gesturings of the assembly had caused it to ignite, a concerted groaning gasp had risen from them all when the red fire began.

Vilmos had gazed down at it, his head bending a very little and so enabling him to see. He was delighted, intrigued.

He knew very well what now must follow.

He felt in fact a curious, perhaps inexplicable excitement, as the ruby colour seared upward and in turn awoke the intense shade of fiery marigolds in his bowels. In *this* light the faint shadow of his intestines appeared. How fascinating they were, labyrinthine coils and the tiny secret cavities between, like a thousand serpents mating in a cave. But the flame rose ever upward and next became the colour of the palest yellow topaz. The sack of stomach, and the shape of another organ, maybe the spleen, hung like ripe fruits in the morning glow. The liver represented an amorphous landmass, or perhaps a cloud...

Vilmos was perfectly conscious the fire would next pass into his heart; already arteries in his hands and arms were catching faint streaks of amber and saffron and now the reciprocated hint of emeralds. The heart was green. It was a leaf in latest spring. Beyond the heart lay the cornflowers of the throat. He would be able to see this blue aspect of the fire *only* through its reflection outward.

After that the flame must rise into and through his head, his eyes and brain. On his forehead the blue of it must darken. For there the fire would turn to indigo. And in that moment, Vilmos, the prepared alembic, would become the final crucible. Indigo would open to him a knowledge of All Things. Indigo would remake him and he would rupture, he would crack and explode, as had many of the alembics and the crucibles of the Order. But now, from him, the genius of knowledge would burst forth and cover everyone in the room.

Vilmos was unafraid.

When the red fire started he had begun his own soft chant. Over and over, nearly laughing, he whispered it inside his mind. His mouth and tongue could not be operated; he could not say anything aloud. But the chant within him was now so forceful and so sure he seemed to hear it dinning in his ears like a trumpet. Even the fire, ever rising, ever changing, pouring upward in its rainbow, red to orange to yellow, yellow to green to blue, even the blue fire reaching now, stretching upward, seemed to flicker in rhythm with the voiceless chant of Vilmos.

"Twelve not thirteen. Twelve not thirteen. Twelve not thirteen."

For, since their ritual had been flawed by their own ignorance, the Moment of Revealing was to be also his. The supreme Moment of the passage through to indigo initially would be his *alone*. For one instant he would contain the powers of spheres and ages and dimensions and angels. Dominion.

After all he could touch God, even if God then shied away and shattered him.

And he yearned for it. He welcomed it. He *rejoiced* in it.

"Twelve not thirteen."

The fire soared, clearly visible to every watcher in the Chamber, even to the ancient toad crouching by the wall, at last blue – to indigo.

To Indigo.

TWENTY-TWO

The sky was overcast that evening, it rained, and by six o'clock the sun might as well have set.

I'd been doing some clothes in the washing machine. I was thinking I'd have an early dinner and decided, rather than cook, to order in pizza.

Some of the streetlamps prematurely had come on. The darkness was dreary. The sound of the rain oddly put me in mind of marbles dropping into wet cement.

When the bell sounded, I wasn't thinking of anything much. I'd glimpsed a man in a raincoat going up and down about twenty minutes before, canvassing for something, miserable and unwanted in the rain. It seemed ridiculous to me, even as I undid the front door, to do this only in order to tell him I didn't want double glazing or a new look for the house, or to sponsor someone to lie in a bath of jam for charity. But I opened the door and there he was. Joseph Traskul. Sej. Standing in the rain in blue jeans and a deep blue shirt, his hair rain-plastered to his head.

He said nothing. He didn't even smile. Perhaps to smile would hurt him: there was a bruise on his right cheek despite what Mr C had said.

The way he stood too, slightly bending forward. He had a denim jacket over his left shoulder, and it seemed to weigh him down a bit. His ribs, I thought, bruised too or cracked, on that side.

Nor did he stride forward, try to push past me.

He just stood there, over seven feet from the door. Looking at me.

I had known he would come back.

He was like a machine you could not turn off, however often you threw the switch or pulled the plug or hacked through the electric cable. Although demons don't exist in any supernatural sense, they are here. They are among

375

us. They are called fellow human beings, and Sej was one.

I said nothing to him. But I must make this quite clear, I easily had time to slam the door, bolt and lock it. If it came to that, once safely inside, I could have activated the new burglar alarm.

But both of us simply stood there, watching each other,

In the end, he spoke.

"So you shaved your head."

When I heard his voice, I felt the most peculiar rushing sensation inside my gut, the cavity of my chest. This wasn't disturbing. It was more like circulation spinning back in a foot or limb that had gone to sleep. A shutter seemed to fly up in my brain. I blinked, and seemed to see not only Sej but everything, with a bright abnormal clarity. It felt, and I use this phrase with dismay, as if my eyes had been cleaned like windows. I wasn't frightened. It wasn't like that. Perhaps I'd felt something like it before, but if I had, misunderstood and so forgotten it.

And I stepped aside and said, "You'd better come in."

In the kitchen, where the light was on, he sat down gingerly on a chair.

I made some tea. If he scrutinised this, I didn't see it particularly. He didn't tell me to taste the mug I handed him, nor did I offer.

"*White* mugs," he said. "What did you do with the others?"

"Oxfam."

"Very wise," he said. He stretched his legs out and regarded the revolving washing in the chugging machine. He said, without much expression, "They knocked me about a bit. Nothing terminal. The hospital assured me I'll be fit enough in a month. Till then, I must just be careful. Lucky that. I came to in the hospital car park, about 1 a.m. No one in A & E. Can you believe it? It's normally packed out. Someone did ask how this had happened. I said, Personal matter. Girl I shouldn't have fucked. Did I want the police? I said no, I'd probably deserved all I got. And how have *you* been?"

"Here," I said.

"How's the book? I mean *Kill Me Tomorrow*."

"Going quite well."

"Glad to hear that."

I too had sat down. We drank the tea. The chocolate biscuits were on the table. I pushed them over.

"Thanks." he said. He took out two and ate them, also as if being careful, now, of his jaw.

I didn't ask him why he had returned. He didn't tell me. We both knew, at least both of us, I assume, *thought* we knew.

The machine finished its cycle. I got up and put on the drying programme.

"Funny that," he said, "the comforting noise of a domestic washing machine. Never like that in a launderette."

"So you use launderettes," I said. I was thinking of the flat in the roof and the washing machine that couldn't be there unless there were another way in and out.

"Oh, now and then. You meet some weird people in launderettes, Roy." It was the first time now he'd used my name.

"I expect you do. I expect," I added, "*they* do, as well."

"Me, you mean? Yeah."

He smiled. I did.

"I was going to order pizza," I said. "You've got me into bad habits – junk food, takeaways."

"I did, didn't I. Yes. Pizza would be extra comforting. Only tonight I can't pay. Sorry."

"Oh, that's all right. You bought so much last time. Just one thing though, Sej. Now I answer the door. You can stand on the top stair if you like and keep watch."

"Oh," he said, "I trust you."

We both ordered the Pizza Double Plus, which had pepperoni, bacon and steak on it, along with mushrooms and olives, tomatoes, mozzarella and ricotta cheese.

It arrived around seven. I paid and brought it in. We sat in the kitchen, the windows dark as if it were January, and the washing machine chugged on, and we ate pizza and drank a bottle of decent if not wonderful red wine.

Afterwards I brought the slab of dark chocolate I'd got myself out of the fridge. We broke this up and ate it too – I noticed he let his melt a little in his mouth before he'd bite – dental work? A broken tooth? I made more of the Brazilian filter coffee and brought out the last of the vodka, which I'd never poured away as I didn't drink it. There had been little conversation – comments on the food, the weather, London, the world. As before.

But reaching the coffee-chocolate-alcohol stage: "So," I said, "now tell me about yourself. Tell me who you are."

"Joseph Traskul."

"I know that. At least I know you told me that. Last time you told me too you were in a children's home. True?"

"Did I? Well yes. It *is* true."

"Prove it."

"I can't, Roy. But. It was shit. Look." He rolled back the left sleeve of his blue shirt. "See?" I *could* see a long thin old scar. "I have a few of those. Someone there liked to use me as an envelope. He, you understand, was the letter opener. *Bloody* letters."

"And you learnt from him," I said.

"Learnt from *him*? No. I just learned."

He leaned back in the chair. He was looking at me, and all at once he was crying. The tears ran from his eyes.

I thought, with great compassion, he can do this at will. But how and from

377

what has he learned *that*?

He said, "Roy. Life plays with us. It *plays*. Cat with mouse. And all we can do..." He spread his hands, lowering his eyes. When he looked up, they were dry. "*We* can play, Roy. Play. Roy. If there's a lesson, that's it. Learn how to *play*."

We sat in silence, as we often had this evening. The rain and the washing machine, now at work on the towels, filled the gaps, marbles in wet cement, domestic chugs. We drank the coffee. I poured him another double vodka.

"I shouldn't drink this," he said. "I'm on prescription pain-killers. But vodka is better."

"You'll be OK."

"You should know," he said. He smiled, but it wasn't like the other smiles he'd always used. "You arranged it."

"Arranged what?"

"I wonder."

"Did I? So you're angry?" I asked. "Resentful?"

"No. I said. I deserved it."

I must justify nothing.

"You can always sleep here. I have a put-you-up bed. It's not too bad."

"I remember. Only last time I couldn't use it, because I had to watch you."

"Well now you don't have to."

Bluff? Double bluff? Double Plus Pizza bluff?

He said, quietly, "There are people staying at my place. I – have to let them do that. I've got a couple of couches that turn into beds. But I can't stay there. These people – need some space."

"This is at your flat, 66 Saracen Road?"

"Yeah."

He put his arms down on the table and rested his head on them. This lasted about two minutes. I drank my coffee. At last he looked up, sat back.

"Thank you for dinner. Perhaps I should just get out."

"Well, if you prefer. But – why don't you play the piano in the front room. I used," I said, smiling, "to like that. My father used to play. And a woman I loved. She played the piano – not as well as you, but very well. I loved it. I loved *her*, Sej. I thought she might have been your mother. Only she wasn't."

"No, Roy. No. My mum's name was Ashabelle." He spelled it. "A.S.H.A.B.E.L.L.E." He laughed, deadly. Not like any of his other laughter. "She was about fifteen when I was born. So she was carrying me at fourteen. It's too young. I don't know much about it. Only that she shat me out and dumped me. Ashabelle. Is that black?"

"You don't look as if you have black blood."

"No. God knows, Roy. Do you," he paused, "do you really want me to play?"

"Have another vodka. Play the piano. Then – crash on the other bed. You're safe with me."

"Am I?"

378

"Nothing sexual," I said, "I can assure you."

"*Touché*," he said.

I made more coffee and tipped the last triple measure from the vodka bottle into his glass.

He explained about the wasp after I'd opened up the front room and turned on the standard lamp covered in splashes of red paint.

"I ought to explain," he said. "I mean I don't want you to think you have to be guilty about putting it in a sandwich. Or too triumphalist either, I suppose."

He'd sat on the painted sofa, still nursing the vodka, and I on one of the painted chairs. The curtains had stayed drawn. He had been right about the red walls. In lamplight they did glow. If everything else had been OK, it might have a wonderful effect, modern yet warm, different.

"So you'd found the wasp before I used it. You knew I *would* use it."

"Thought you would."

"When did you find it? I only put it there that morning."

"I'd been on the look-out. One or two of them had got into the house. I had a feeling it might occur to you. But I let the ones I saw out of the kitchen window. It was after your bath," he said. And flashed me a dim shadow of his former impervious smile.

"When I stayed in the bathroom."

"It happens," he said. "So I had a look upstairs. I looked in your wardrobe as a matter of course. You hadn't concealed it superlatively well, Roy. For a writer of detective fiction... I can tell you though, the beast was angry. I let it go at the bedroom window and got stung in the process. But I never have much of a reaction to wasp stings."

"No," I said. "So the wasp I found later in the glass was another one?"

"A dead one. Much less lethal. I'd found it on a windowsill in here. The paint smell probably killed it."

"It was dead?" It had seemed to me the wasp in my glass had still had some life in it, if not much. No doubt, in the state I'd been in, I'd imagined the slight vestige of response, expecting to see it.

"It was dead. Then I waited, and you put it in the sandwich, between the top slice of bread and the ham."

"But you didn't bite down on it – did you?"

"I was looking out, Roy, remember. When I took the sandwich about which you'd made such a scene... I could *feel* the wasp through the bread. Poor sod felt like a prawn. So I bit well clear."

I recalled the corpse of the wasp, undamaged, lying under the rim of the plate.

"Then your reaction was one more fake."

"'Fraid so."

"Your mouth bled. I saw it."

"Ketchup, Roy. When I went into the kitchen."

I burst out laughing. I couldn't, myself, tell if this were genuine mirth at

379

the madness of all this, or an actor's laugh, used for effect. Something of each, maybe. I recollected he, like most of us, liked flattery. "You're a genius," I said. "Did you train at RADA?"

"Oh, sure," he seriously acquiesced, smiling a little, still not in the old ways. "A year. I was expelled."

"*RADA? Expelled? Why?*"

"Not good enough."

A lie. Or not. Either was unlikely – that he'd been there, that, being there, he'd be thrown out.

I said, "You could act Olivier or Jacobi or Sher off the stage."

"No I couldn't. But thank you. The world's my stage anyway, Roy, and all the men and women merely players." He finished the vodka.

I said, "There's only whisky now, I'm afraid. I can taste it for you, if you'd like some."

"Trying to get me drunk again," he said softly.

"You'll get a good night's sleep. Or you can leave, as you said. I don't take prisoners."

"No?"

"No."

He rose. "Anyway," he said, "I'll play for you, before I go. What would you like?"

"Your choice."

He paused, looking at the piano; then he turned and looked across at the mantelpiece. I'd known he would. I had known.

"Where's the glass dog?"

"Oh that. Still upstairs. When I get the room fixed, I'll bring it down again."

"It means something to you, doesn't it, the dog?"

"Yes. My mother loved it. It reminded her of the past, some happy memories, and she said to me once, 'When we're gone, Roy, whatever you get rid of, please keep the dog'."

"It's nice you had a mother," he said.

I said, "Wait a minute. I'll get it."

He looked tired. For a moment he looked, as I've said, as we all know the young sometimes do, much older than he could possibly be, whoever's son he was – Lynda's, Maureen's, Ashabelle's – Mine.

He sat down before the piano and opened the lid, and ran his fingers along its keys, stumbling once, a false rill of notes, which I'd never heard happen in his playing before.

I was upstairs, the red glass dog in my hand, when I heard him begin a Rachmaninov concerto – a transposition which perhaps he could effect spontaneously. It was the Second, the most beautiful and therefore the most hackneyed of the opus; the breaking melody of the second movement. When you hear this, for the first time, or if you *listen* even after long familiarity, it has the power to shake the heart, even the dullest or the darkest heart. Unlike the Third Concerto, which is virtually perfect, the work of a supreme genius, the Second is imperfect, yet has been, as they say, dictated by God.

I stood at the head of the stairs with the dog in my hands, and I listened as Joseph played.

What was he? *What?*

But through the melody stared all the rest of what had been, and what he was otherwise. And I had known from the beginning, from before even he had come back to my door.

Returning into the room I sat quietly behind him, back on my chair, holding the dog. I rubbed my fingers over the smooth glass, and Rachmaninov poured from the piano.

No mistakes now.

In the upright wooden shell of the instrument, where the strings stretch unseen from keys to hammers, like the hidden muscles of the emotional body itself, I could see his face reflected. Lowered towards the keyboard, intent and pale, only the dusting of the bruise under his cheekbone. His eyes seemed closed. He lived and expressed the music.

I remembered how I had known I couldn't harm his hands.

Some trick of the light, the redness of the room, cast a red glimmer across his forehead. It was where the smear of paint had been when he worked on the walls. Red, the lowest chakra, reproduced at the exact region of the higher sixth chakra, the Third Eye, Vilmos's focus, the goal of his corrupt Order, (Indigo), inner seeing and self-knowledge and thus the dominion over All Things, but firstly of the Self.

Slowly I got up again and moved quietly across, as if drawn forward by the music and wanting to watch the movement of his hands up close.

I stood behind his left shoulder, as the Devil does in some mediaeval woodcuts. *Retro me Satanus...*

Yes, he was entirely absorbed in his playing, and I too could become so. The rapid dance of his fingers and the waves, black to white to black to white of the keys, were mesmerising.

I went on watching, until the aching melody had almost reached its end. Although the ultimate theme of the last Movement is the greater, this Second Movement premonition of it is perhaps more pervasive. Unheralded, it invades. Unfinished, it haunts and echoes on the corridors of the mind.

But he would stop. He was tired and in pain. He might have to.

I stepped back a little, and half turned away, and stood almost with my back to him.

My reflection too would be in the upright wood.

I changed the position of the red glass dog in my right hand.

Steady as a rock. Nothing in me felt frail. I wouldn't falter.

The stream of music was running to its close. Now, then. It would have to be now.

Turning round again I struck him violently on the back of the head, with all my weight – and if undersized and slight – still I'm a grown man – behind it.

The dog was heavy, solid. I felt the point of its nose connect with the parietal lobe to the left of his skull.

Unlike the scenes in so many films, there was no discordant clash of chords. His hands slipped noiseless from the keys. His body jerked once and slumped forward, his head striking again, the frontal lobe now, on the wood of the piano.

I'd believed the dog would shatter. It hadn't. Instead, very neatly it had split in two sections, breaking just behind the neck. I bent down and retrieved the smaller piece, the head, examined it and quickly saw I would be able to superglue it back together.

XIX
('UNTITLED': PAGE 333)

The cataclysm that had destroyed the Chamber had been visible to Vilmos only for those six or seven brief seconds, when he seemed to hang in space between earth and sky, day and night, life and eternity. Then came the locomotion of a colossal fall, worthy of Lucifer's it seemed to him, although later he spurned a comparison of such ineptitude. The *end* of the fall, its destination, threw him feet first through the collapsing cellarage of the Master's house. He found himself then, abruptly, as if just waking from a vivid dream, floating comfortably on the broad bosom of the river, a bridge before him that was not the Flavel, the moon, thin as a cat's closed eye, squinting down from above.

He knew the water would buoy him up, carry him. There was no need to struggle. The river did so and presently bumped him home against the bank.

The stone jumble of the City was sparse here. A tree craned to the water and Vilmos caught its lowest bough and hauled himself in with little effort.

It was not cold. Already his garments seemed to dry themselves in the extreme incandescent energy which still radiated from his body.

The lights of the mystic *Cakras* had faded from him, at least to the physical eye, but every part of him felt charged and effulgent.

Vilmos was well aware of what had happened.

Twelve, not thirteen.

They had made an error in the formula of their spell, and this had warped it. And so he had been able, on reaching the indigo instant of utter power, to claim himself back from them, and so wrench free. The power he shed, meanwhile, when this took place, detonated instead in the room.

He doubted any of them had survived, but now, standing on the bank and gazing back along the curve of the river, he saw a livid rusty glare, and a solid black cumulous of smoke that was rising up. It came to him this went on about where *he* would expect to find the Master's house. And that therefore, not only had it been shaken down, but it was on fire, and burned.

Imagining the crowds of neighbours in their nightshirts springing out in horror on the street, gazing at this in frightened awe and malign disgust, Vilmos smiled to himself.

Without questioning or reticence, he knew that all the might of the ritual and the alchemical surge had entered and refined only him. What now then might he not do?

On an impulse he turned, and with a *look* struck a flame on the black river. It lit at once and blazed there like a lily of phosphorous. He had done this by his will alone.

Notions of Satan and God had become superfluous.

Vilmos was his own man now.

Just then the Master's ancient toad pulled itself out of the water also, and squatted on the bank, staring at him. As the engendered flame was extinguished, Vilmos saw both the toad's eyes, and the evil jewel between them, had kept the terrific dark blue of the Indigo Instant. Only the toad and he had escaped alive. And perhaps it too had been able to garner some power.

In all his life no single human had either joyed or contented Vilmos. But he might benefit from a companion.

"Come then," he called to the toad, and like an image of black jade, understanding him, it lifted itself and approached. "Which way shall we go?" he inquired of it. The toad reversed itself, and Vilmos saw that over there, in the east, dawn was commencing. He had no need to fear light any longer. Nor dark, if it came to it. "East then," said Vilmos. And eastward they went.

TWENTY-THREE

At first, I thought I'd killed him outright.

When I pulled him back from the piano, his face was pallid and slightly puffy, and I couldn't see him breathing. But there was the vaguest pulse in his throat. Still alive, then?

Unusual strength can be accessed in times of stress. I'd read of it, even written about it. Now I found it to be true.

I dragged Sej off the seat and from the room, along the hall into the kitchen, without trouble.

What I did next was a precaution. It was my more pedantic side, making certain, covering all possible eventualities. A writer's action, or the deliberate murderer's.

Having got him on the floor, leaning by the table I pulled him forward, and cracked his head, the back of it, a second time very hard against the table's corner. Then I allowed him to fall.

Still I couldn't see any breathing. Yet the pulse in his neck stumblingly kept on.

It didn't really matter, did it? He wasn't going to interfere in what came next.

Perhaps I should note my state of mind during all this. I was flatly calm. I was rational, unexcited and concise. I might have been organising my washing or checking over an especially-to-me boring proof chapter in one of my novels. This mood had opened up in me like a well of cool water the moment I saw him standing outside my door in the rain. Partly, at the beginning, I'd wondered if it would suddenly desert me, leaving me after all unsure and panicked, unable to make a decision. But it had not. And in some odd mental fashion, I'd known from that same first moment what I must do, and roughly how I would do it. As if, as with the plots of my stories, I'd already written out a careful synopsis, and only had to consult that from time to time in order to construct the book.

Once I'd seen him sprawled on the floor, I went upstairs and got ready.

I was particularly facile at packing by this time. It was after all my third attempt to escape. On this occasion however, I didn't pack all the documents, only birth certificate, passport, bank details and those of my savings, plus their necessary various cards and other safeguards. Some of these things I might legitimately take with me when travelling. Some of them I could, if I had to, claim to have mislaid years ago, as many of us do. While some of the items now left out would, after tonight, be redundant anyway.

Naturally I packed more clothes, more toiletries. Again legitimate. I was going to stay with my poor upset old friend at Cheston for quite a while, wasn't I? Duran believed I'd gone up there before. I'd mentioned Matthew's frame of mind post his 'betrayal' by Sylvia. From the brief picture I had then, perhaps innocently, painted, Duran definitely wouldn't be astonished I'd been begged to go back. As for George and Vita next door, those two silly old fools hadn't seen me for days during Sej's last sojourn, and only had his word for it I was in the house. While, as Mr C had pointed out witnesses, (especially elderly ones) were unreliable.

None of this might help, of course.

But it was reasonable for me. After so many invented third-hand literary alibis and get-outs, to fabricate something now.

When I had everything ready in the two larger bags, including the two bits of the red glass dog, carefully wrapped, I came back downstairs.

I bent and touched him again. He felt very cold and lay totally inert. I couldn't find any pulse now. But being no doctor, I couldn't rely on that.

From the freezer I took a pack of pork sausages. The remains of the pizza and the wine, mugs, glasses, plates, the coffee, still lay on the table. On the hob I put an over-full pan of oil and placed four of the sausages in it. Just the sort of late snack a young healthy man might fancy, particularly if depressed, even after all the pizza eaten between 7 and 8 o'clock. The cake was still on the side, too. It should burn very well.

It wouldn't be a problem that the sausages were frozen; just slow everything down a little. Which was a good thing, given the circumstances.

I lit the hob, kept it very low.

Outside the kitchen the night lay ink black, a few stars showing dully like wet grains of sugar.

I hoped the fir tree wouldn't be affected. Probably not. Long before the wooden fences went up someone would have heard or smelled something wrong at No 74.

The cooking oil I sloshed liberally round the kitchen, the table, and over him. How lucky I'd bought an extra bottle. There was enough to trail along the hallway and the bottom of the stairs; even the library carpet got a sprinkle. But books burn beautifully, as Ray Bradbury let us know in *Farenheit 451*. That is, if we'd missed the history lesson that began even before the great Library burned in Alexandria in the time of Caesar and Cleopatra.

In my bag I had the MS of *Untitled*, plus the disc, including the last chapter, XIX – if such it was – work in progress, that was the file and disc for *Kill Me Tomorrow*. I had *Last Orders* too, in its paperback form. My favourite. But why shouldn't I take that to read over on the long train to the north? Quite legitimate. And writers often travel with their work, picking at it in odd moments. I'd be able to use Matt's computer, wouldn't I, if I could persuade him away from his twenty-four-hour blog, which he'd started to describe Sylvia, if under another name, and all her slut-like wickedness. He'd told me during our short telephone conversation about this blog, and how he was getting hundreds of 'hits'. Men – and women. *An Age of Traitors* he called it.

Going back to put the emptied bottle of oil in the kitchen bin, I was careful not to tread in any of it. I'd been especially careful not to splash any on my clothing. I washed my hands at the sink. Like Pilate.

I did glance at him before I left the kitchen, leaving on the light, as I'd left on the light in the lavatory and the study upstairs. (I had got the spare bed out and put it ready too, placing blankets and sheets and a pillow on it, all prepared for Sej's never-to-be-realised crash).

Sej lay exactly as I'd left him. A little line of blood had run from his nose. I didn't know what that might mean, but it could hardly augur well.

My bags were already by the front door. Again cautious where I stepped, I let myself out and relocked the door, both locks, then slid the keys back through the letter-box on to the floor, where he might casually have dropped them. Because naturally, if he were minding my house while I was away, he would need them. For what it was worth, I kept the other set, those he had copied from mine. I had de-activated the burglar alarm, too, for the liar's reason that Sej might have trouble with it.

My previous dialogue with the police, asking for protection, also had an explanation. I'd been afraid of this sudden stalker. Then found out he was the son of a woman I'd known years ago. We'd sorted it all out, and even though he was a little strange, I'd had a fondness for him, because of her, and because I'd last seen him as a child. Obviously, this was my gullibility. I'd accepted the yarn he spun me. No doubt the police would eventually point this out. Whatever else, I'd had to go to Cheston to visit Matt. I'd left Sej in the house because he'd told me he was upset, needed a bolthole. Some woman he'd got into difficulties over. (If he *had* told that tale at the hospital, I might have extra back-up).

On the other hand, I didn't really trust any of this to bail me out for long, if the proverbial shit hit the fan. And presumably it would. Matt for one was a doubtful ally.

Old Church Lane seemed in its normal night-time phase. The rain had gone, leaving a cold sparkle on the edges of things. The clock on the church was striking ten-fifteen. All around, the usual flick and flutter of TV and computer screens through glass or drawn blinds and curtains. No lights were visible at all over the road in 73. Perhaps at the back, where the bedroom was. A black or dark blue car had been parked outside No 80. A tall girl and a young man were leaning on the side, embracing, locked in a prolonged kiss. What must that be like? Did I recall? Yes. Oh yes.

I walked across the paving to 72 and rang their bell.

It was late for them, but some lights were still on upstairs and down.

Perhaps they wouldn't answer, however, already into the bedtime routine, dressing-gowns and cocoa, or whatever they drank last thing. In this day and age even George and Vita probably resorted to a tot of alcohol and a sleeping pill.

Then someone shot the bolts.

George opened the door, virtually as I'd pictured, in a port wine paisley dressing-gown. "Oh – it's you," he said.

"Sorry to disturb you." I was factual and restrained. "I thought I'd better let you know. I'm off again," (the 'again' was deliberate), "that pal of mine up north. I can't really say no."

George looked baffled and slightly offended.

"The thing is, in case you hear sounds through the wall, Joseph – is there. He's staying over for a couple of days. He needs – well, somewhere to get away from it all."

Something had happened while I said this. I had grasped I didn't know if George knew Sej by that name, or the other one, Joseph – or by some *other* name entirely. Had I ever heard him call Sej by a name? Had Sej ever mentioned what George knew him as? I didn't think so. And certainly George still seemed baffled, and now uneasy. I added, "Joseph. That's the young man who said he was my son. My friend's boy."

"I see."

"Actually, he's pretty depressed." I made myself sound world-weary rather than confiding. "Some trouble with a young woman. I wish it was that easy with my chum Matt, up north. His wife," I said, "has let him down rather badly."

A sort of flicker went over George's face. He seemed caught between a wish to get all the gossip, and a wish to be rid of me.

I granted the second one.

"Anyway. I should be back in four or five days, a week at most. I can't keep running up there to hold Matt's hand, can I? Take care. Best to Vita."

I turned and he cleared his throat.

The outrageousness of his next question, one which I not only had to answer, but to lie about, nearly stunned me. "How," he demanded angrily, "did you like her cake?"

Much later, I did consider that my semi-detached house, when it caught alight, possibly even with a small explosion, might endanger George and Vita. The brief mental sketch I'd made still inclined me to think the fire would be smelled if not heard, seen even – smoke billowing – early on. Even drugged by whisky and whatever else, Vita would wake up, her hearing wasn't bad. Failing that neighbours or the fire brigade would alert them.

But to be quite honest, I didn't care.

I didn't give a damn.

Long ago, before modern forensic techniques, and also given the inattention to detail only displayed now and then by a real-life detective of the type of Sherlock Holmes, I could have got away with it much more easily.

Finding Roy Phipps' house burned down and a burned male corpse inside it, very likely said corpse would have been taken for Roy Phipps.

Not now, of course. By no means.

They would learn if not who, then who he was not, inside a few days at most. And despite the ruse I'd set up and the care I'd taken, any police force not completely composed of morons would instigate a search for me.

I had decided to make for France, via the popularly named Chunnel.

To access the train times of Eurostar would have taken too long tonight. I'd opted to catch the last Ashford train from Charing Cross. There were a couple of hotels in Ashford. I'd pick up the Chunnel train tomorrow as early as was practicable.

My French was adequate. Besides, two years before, when I went over there on some business junket with Gates, (signing books and so on for an affiliate French company known as *Lisez-moi!*), I'd found even the Parisians, notorious for their hauteur, had come to speak English, many of them. Maybe only in order to disgrace us by talking in our language more elegantly.

The train going into Charing Cross was almost empty. It was by then about eleven.

I sat in the carriage with one of my bags squeezed into the uselessly narrow rack overhead, the other bulkier one on the next seat.

The thick yellow light was both somnolent and unrestful.

For the very first, finally, I began to feel a hollow terror at what I'd done. But it was far off. For now at least I could ignore it. I took out the miniature of whisky I'd bought en route and downed a gulp.

387

The train presently made its pneumatic hissing sound and we stopped. I don't recall the station, although at the time I noted it. The couple of people already sitting back along the carriage got out, and someone else got in. I heard him give a sigh. And then he walked up towards the front of the carriage. I smelled an exclusive male fragrance I had met before, and quite recently. I couldn't think where. Then his shadow crossed over me and I found I looked up quickly and in alarm.

There was nothing in my head. I had no forecast image of a policeman, plain clothes or otherwise. Nor of Sej. Sej, I knew, was in no position now to have caught this train with me.

"Mr Phillips," said Cart, and sat down facing me in the dark yellow light.

My first, and probably not utterly inane thought, was that the credit card company had refused to pay out on my 'deliveries' from him. I hadn't checked my current credit, thought I'd paid a lot off the last card bill. (I'd not yet received the one which would show me what name Cart's outfit traded under).

I stared at Cart. He wore a dark raincoat.

"Now," he said, "Mr Phillips, you seem dismayed. Please. You have been an ideal customer. That's the only reason I now seek you out."

"What for?" I said. I had felt very sick, but after a second this went off.

"It is about the unusual apartment your dangerous young friend was in, at Saracen Road."

I didn't know what I could say, or what I needed to say. I said, "How did you know which train...?"

"Oh, you were followed, Mr Phillips, like before. I have received the text at the proper moment and come at once to board the train too. Aren't you curious," he went on, smiling a little, "to know what is my interest in the apartment of Mr Sej?"

In the false light his thick blue-black hair, eyebrows, lashes and moustache seemed made from some lush material that couldn't, any of it, be hair. He looked manufactured.

Unzipping the pocket in my bag, I took out the whisky and had another swig.

"Ah, a whisky man," said Cart, all approval. "So *I* am, Mr Phillips. The purest alcohol there is. Vodka is poison, and wine – the dregs of vinegars. But a fine malt may not be rivalled."

I felt bleak. I was afraid. "Tell me about the apartment."

"Very well, of course. Our good friend Mr C has discovered something of great importance about it. This we felt you should learn also, as it may be to mutual profit."

His English, which had been fairly sustained before, tonight seemed a bit less sound. How I noticed this I'm not sure. But it can happen. As when going blind, other senses compensate, the faculty of logic enters some other area when shut out of the mainstream by fear. In the same way, apparently, condemned criminals can often describe in minute detail a pebble or a drop of dew, glimpsed on their way to the gallows.

"All right," I said. I put the whisky back in the zippered pocket, although I needed to take more. There wasn't much left by now.

"It seems there is another door into the flat. Mr C was concerned that some heavy furniture, a piano and so forth, were in the loft, and only an outdoor ladder to be going up."

I too had thought of that, had I not?

"And so?" I said. My voice didn't sound shaky. Even my hands had been steady on the whisky. The shakes were all inside.

"Well, Mr C has cleverly located the other door to the apartment. In light of this, perhaps you would like to go back there? I mean, accompanied of course. And free of all charge. It seems he – your enemy-friend – is elsewhere." (I almost blurted something when he said this. But I didn't). "Perhaps we might go there tonight. As you are already on your way up to London."

"I have a business meeting."

"*Do* you? So late." Silky, he looked at me. It was a flirtatious look, which said, *Oh come now, I know you have nothing of the sort.* "Just an hour from your urgent schedule." He pronounced this *skedule*, as Americans do.

I thought, *This is some form of so-far unfathomable blackmail. I'd better agree. I can delay the journey, start early tomorrow from Waterloo... pray no one is looking for me right there... If I offend him, refuse, God knows.*

We'd stopped at two or three stations meanwhile, and gone on. I hadn't noted them. We might have been in a foreign country, not France: somewhere I couldn't begin to decipher the signs. Hell, perhaps.

"OK," I said. "If you want."

"It will, I am sure, be mutually helpful."

In the window's black night glass, our shades sat in the amber of the light. I didn't look afraid, I saw. But then, I didn't look quite like me either.

He said, "That's good, you see. Now we are coming into Waterloo."

What was striking was the silence of the flats. I'd been expecting blasts of bad music, even though now it was almost midnight.

A few dim lights were on in various rooms. Everything however, the terrace, the street, the surrounding city, seemed still and relatively silent. Among the shrubs and trees of the park, old rain glittered, catching streetlamps which, here, had stayed shell white.

Cart had brought us here by cab. He himself had paid for this. Now he produced a key to the main door.

I'd anticipated keys, for no doubt the talented Mr C would have managed that.

The door undone, and discreetly shut behind us, we walked up the flights of stairs, I carrying my two bags.

Reaching the landing where flat 5 showed its door in total noiselessness,

Cart, surprising me if I were yet capable of surprise, knocked lightly on the wood.

After a moment the door to flat 5 was opened.

A big man, overweight and ruddy, with thick greying hair, looked out at us. He wore a dark blue T-shirt with two lines of script which read: *Tell me how long you've been a swan.*

Cart laughed. "Hi, Leo."

"Hi, Cart."

"This is our Mr Phillips."

"Hi, Roy, good to meet you," said Leo who wanted to know about swans. "Come in. Liberty hall here." He had a London accent and clear diction. He knew my first name.

I went first, because Leo stood aside, and Cart waited for me. As soon as I was in the flat's hall, I got myself in over the threshold of the larger space of a big room. The layout was not dissimilar to No 6 above, the empty flat that lay below the roof apartment.

But Leo had furnished this one, and the hall too, what I'd seen, in an uncluttered, comfortable style. He had the things one expects people to have who live in the Western world – carpet, couch and chairs, TV and obviously powerful music centre, even shelves with books, and a fruit bowl with oranges and plums and a bottle of diet Coke standing on a table. "Like a drop of the hard stuff, boys?" asked Leo.

"Sure," said Cart.

"Roy?" politely asked Leo.

I didn't speak, and Cart said, as if proud of me, "He is a *whisky* man."

"Great. So'm I. Best drink you can get. I'll break out the new Scottish malt." To me he added, "Just dump your gear anywhere." He meant my bags. Tired by now of holding them, perhaps wanting my hands free, I let the bags go. And he went into the kitchen, which here was through a door, and had white and pine units and clean-looking lino on the floor. He returned with an unopened bottle.

"See this, Roy," he said, showing me the label.

It was highly prestigious. I'd heard of but never tasted it in my life. So far as I'd known, you couldn't even buy it, over the border.

"I am of the Clan McCallum," said Leo. "Friends in the Highlands." And suddenly in broadest Scottish, "Ye 'll no be averse t'a wee dram?"

Cart laughed again. "To listen to him, we must think he is truthful. In fact he's no more Scots blood than I."

"*Huish*," said Leo sternly. He had got the bottle open and produced three clean glasses from a place on the bookcase among paperbacks and volumes with old black covers.

When he handed each of us a filled glass, Cart said solemnly, "One moment, Mr Phillips – see, I drink. Now, you take this glass, I yours." And handed me the glass he had sipped from twice.

That was when I knew.

I knew it as the tidal wave is known, rushing in. Without syntax, without hope.

Leo called the toast. To me it sounded as if he cried "Hrarnaschy!"

And we drank. Bottoms up.

It was a good, a beautiful whisky. If I could have tasted it.

It was about twenty minutes later that Leo let us all, (me holding the bags again, refusing his offer to carry one), through the door at the end of the corridor in flat 5, the area that, above, was occupied by the small spare room. The stair was quite wide, with sturdy shallow steps. It would have been a challenge to get a piano, or the heavy couches up, but it should have been possible, and demonstrably, had been.

At the top Cart knocked once more on another white door.

The woman who flung the door dramatically open was known to me, but I had been waiting – if not for her – for one of them.

She wore a dark blue dress that looked like satin, pinned with a blinding brooch on one shoulder, feasibly diamonds. Her hair was done differently. Now, smiling and glamorous, not in tears or beside a bundle of bloodied shirt and dead dog, she seemed the perfect hostess.

"Hello, darlings. Come in, come in."

Leo opened a bottle of Dom Perignon. Marga told us, reassuringly, there were ten more of these in the other larger fridge (This was the one on the landing outside the upper door into the attic). She added there was a roast of lamb in the oven.

The smell was appetising and corroborated the statement. In the kitchen area potatoes waited and a transparent bowl of green salad. But she also handed round plates of crisps and nuts and cocktail sausages.

I was seated on one of the green and blue couches, the bags at my feet.

Cart sat on another couch with Leo, and Marga in a deep dark green armchair.

Bach was playing softly on the stereo.

Cart had remarked, "Better than that shit you play, Leo."

And Leo said, "Either you like it or you don't."

"Are you all right, Roy?" asked Marga in a little while. "Shall we start to explain now? Please, I *know* this isn't simple. We've all been through it. Haven't we, guys?"

"You betcha," said Leo.

"Mmm," said Cart, and drank a little champagne. He had removed his coat, which was also blue.

Marga lifted her glass, a flute I hadn't spotted here before. We all had one. "To Roy Phipps, aka R.P. Phillips."

They drank to my health. I didn't.

391

I put down my glass on the polished coffee table.

"Tell me," I said. "When does Sej arrive?"

"Oh, Roy," painfully said Marga. She put her hand to her mouth. But this time she didn't cry.

Leo said, "Look, Roy, he's in the hospital."

"Really. But he always gets over that," I said. I felt as if I had been frozen inside old ice. I was miles off. But also, here.

Leo looked round at me. "Roy, feller, you did a very good job. The last text I got from Liss, Sej may be going into theatre for an op. You seem to have fractured his skull, Roy. Didn't you know?"

I sat there.

I sat there.

"But you could be lying," I said. Or the thing which spoke for me said it.

Leo said, "Only I'm not. Hey, Roy. It's OK. He *knows* – we all *know*. It can happen. You play this game, you put your life, and anything else worth anything, on the line. If the bus goes o'er ye, ye've none ta blame than yoursel'."

"And he would never blame you," said Marga. "None of us would."

Like a stone I said, "What happened to the house?"

"C and Liss and Sid put the fire out. Hadn't gone far. You'll need some new carpet, though. Then they got him off to the hospital. Apparently," said Leo, "some old guy next door called down out of the upper window, what was going on? C said they were friends of Sej's. He needed looking after. The old guy said he wasn't sure, he thought he ought to call the cops."

"And so Sid said," helpfully interposed Marga, "that was maybe the best thing. If the old man would be kind enough to give the police all the details when they came, in about an hour or so. But meanwhile they needed to look after Sej. They'd be at so-and-so. Obviously, that wasn't where they went."

"No," I said.

Marga said, "Leo, Cart, should you tell Roy how C and Sid and Liss knew what was going on?"

"They were watching the house," said Leo. "I mean, he'd said, this was almost certainly the night."

"The night," I said.

"The night you got there."

"Where?"

"Where we go."

I thought, *Can I get out of this room? Is it still conceivable I can get away?*

She, Marga, said quietly, "Roy, this is the hardest bit. Trust me. Hang on. It gets so much better."

The door into the attic, seen from *inside* the attic, was painted dark blue. A faint tang of new paint clung to it, barely discernible in the aroma of cleanliness, polish, and roasting lamb. A panel in the pale green plasterboard had been pulled back to reveal it and give access. Normally this panel would close flush to the wall. And a bookcase stood there, or had done previously, now moved on up the room by about five feet. I would never have noticed this panel, as it had been. But someone like C – Mr C – must have done so. He hadn't needed to find it, however, had he? Evidently he'd already known of its existence, as he knew about everything else in the flats, both below and up here. He had probably stayed here, now and then. They might all have done, all this gang – this *team* of mad people who were the accomplices and friends, perhaps the lovers of Joseph Traskul. Should more than one person stay at a time, there would be little privacy for them here, of course. If you slept here you would then sleep, if not in the same bed at least in the same room. And there had been two wash basins in the bathroom, a shower and a bath. Imaginably other things could be seen to in pairs, or groups.

They had no secrets from each other, that was no physical secrets.

And the way they spoke about him, it was familiar in the truest sense. It was *familial*. They were his family. Siblings, incestuous or not, brothers and sisters.

They told me things in segments, listening to any questions I asked with grave attentive faces, answering gravely, yet sometimes laughing too, appreciating, they said, my clever gambit with the sleeping tablets and Duran's new locks, which C and Sid hadn't, even so, found particularly difficult to undermine. I'd kindly turned the alarm off for them, too. They were also amused by that. C could have neutralised it in moments anyway, they reassured me. He had been a policeman, did I know? They congratulated me too on my last tactic, presumably the meal or they had heard the piano from outside, that which had so lulled Sej and resulted in his fractured skull. How did they square this with their demonstrated liking for, admiration of, *love* of him?

"Roy," said Marga, "we know what it cost *you*. We've all been there," she said, "I told you that."

"You mean," I said, "are you saying – he's done to all of you the sort of things he did to me? He drove you so far towards insanity that you attacked him, meant to kill him? Is that what you're saying?"

"In a way. Yes. But it isn't towards insanity."

Leo said, "You should have seen what *I* did to him, Roy. I threw him down a flight of stairs, broke both his legs. His right leg's full of metal."

"No one blames you, Roy," said Cart, the first time he'd used my Christian name.

"I don't care if you blame me," I said woodenly. "You rescued him; you took him to a hospital – if any of this is true."

"It's true."

"What about the last time? That beating up, C and – who is he? Sid?"

"No, he didn't need the hospital bit then. The doing over – some was real – most faked," said Leo. "Really just the first blow, that was genuine, to convince you. Then stagecraft. The way actors learn to do it. It would look

393

good, like it did in movies before the digital stuff came in and made all the stunt-men redundant. C's taught us all a lot of it. Marga's an actress too. She still has contacts. Even I have now been to drama fight school. I could fight for real before, you understand. Had to unlearn quite a lot."

They cracked another bottle.

I still hadn't touched my first glass.

No one pressed me now to eat or drink.

About 2.30 a.m. by my watch, the man called Sid came in via flat 5 below, to which they all had keys. He was the young one with the bony face I recognised now not only as C's companion hit man, but the tall man kissing tonight the tall girl by the dark blue car in Old Church Lane. And she had been the one called Liss, the girl whose car had originally 'stalled', allowing her to glue or break my door-locks. Tonight's blue car had been her white one. They'd simply resprayed it. (I'd asked. They'd told me).

Sid now wore dark blue also, a dark blue pullover with a white O on the right arm. This seemingly represented his full name, which he told me was Obsidian. "Obsidian mate, innit. But just call me Sid."

He told us Liss was waiting at the hospital. The op hadn't happened yet. Surgeons were discussing X-rays. Liss had said could one of the others relieve her before 4 a.m. C was still there, but she needed to get home, she had to work tomorrow. "I'll do it," said Leo, "haven't been out all day. I'll give the car a run."

About ten minutes later another man arrived. For a minute I didn't think I had seen him before, but I had. He wore a dark blue suit, Armani it looked like, a dark blue Italian tailored shirt. His shoes were possibly worth two thousand pounds.

Dark blue. All of them wore that. The car had been sprayed dark blue, even C's van, I'd gathered, which had waited round the corner in the Lane and which I hadn't spotted. Certainly, the inside of the upper door into the attic.

Dark blue: indigo.

He had read the MS. The colour was one more game played against me, the rules made up so no one new could learn them. There *were* no rules. In fact, that was what you had to learn.

Marga said in the '90s she hadn't had work for three years and her husband was a bastard, but a rich one. He still kept her on as insurance against any of his 'tarty birds' trying to force marriage. Divorce, he told them, was out of the question. He couldn't harm his wife like that. Once one of the birds, crazed with jealousy mostly of the bastard's bank balance, got the address of his and Marga's huge flat in Hampstead. "She came round with a gun. It was only a toy, but I didn't know and I passed out. Scared her, I suppose, and she took off. A couple of months after Sej homed in on me out of nowhere. I nearly went mad with fear – only it wasn't. The worst thing," she said, serenely, "was when I had to strip naked. I was over forty. Too old to be very confident, and with few reasons to be, either. I hoped even so he'd make love to me. Hoped *that* was what he wanted. But he didn't. He doesn't, Roy. He's – celibate, so far as any of us know." (I thought, *He gets his jollies from this game he plays*. But I didn't say it. Although she was an actress and this was likely only one more performance, her stillness held me there.). "So that was why *I* tried to finish him off. Do you know what I did? I stuck a carving knife in him."

"But you got it wrong."

"It struck a rib. Apparently, a common mistake for the novice assassin. Yes, I got it wrong. But he was hospitalised then, too. Quite a while."

"And then?"

"And then, Roy. And *then*." And her face lit up.

Leo said, "And I was a bloody alcoholic, Roy. I'm not now. Oh, I like my dram. A glass of wine. But the shit stuff all went. I'd had nothing in my life. D'you know what he said to me, Sej? *Life plays with us. So we don't play that game. We play our own game. Harder*. That's what it is, Roy. It's *play*. Like kids do. Cruel sometimes. Funny sometimes. But it breaks the mould. Then *we* can get out."

"Out of what?"

"Ourselves. Ourselves."

Cart said, "My nickname is Carton, when spoke in full. I own three tobacconists, now also general grocers and off-licence. *Bits and Booze* they are called. So, not Carton for the hero in Mr Dickens's work of the French Revolution, but Carton for the cartons of cigarettes. My wife died of cancer – oh, not of cigarettes, neither she nor I smokes. But my son got into drugs and my beautiful daughter ran away with a man unworthy to lie under her foot. I tried to survive the lack of revenue for cigarettes, as everyone is told they must give up, and branched out into the groceries and alcohol. I paid my tax and my VAT. At night I go up to empty flat over shop and watch TV. One morning Sej comes into my shop. 'What you want?' I ask him. 'You,' he said. '*You interest me.*' Of course, I am going to call the pigs. They forget to arrive. But he arrives. Over and over he arrives. My cousin then was in a business, the sort you think I am in, Mr Roy. Only I am not, that is the playing. I hired for real these men to warn off Sej. They beat him up. As we have pretended to. He is a very strong customer, Sej. Only one week in hospital. He makes me strip and get in bath and then – he washed me. He does this without aggress, no nasty sex, like a kind mother when you are only four. That for me was my breaking. More gentle than with Marga. Or you, I think. To me, he is my mother. I call him this sometimes. I call him up and say, Mumma, how are you?"

The one they called Sid (Obsidian) spoke from another chair, a palmful of nuts ready in his hand to eat. "He breaks you. He breaks you and then you remake yourself, Roy. Get it innit? Like you're badly made, but then you go to pieces and when you're repaired, *better* than new. Now you *work*."

The other man, who had been silent in his suit and shoes, said, "My name's Jeremy. Only I'm not that here. I gave myself a new name, which is Biro. Marga's name isn't the original, nor Leo's."

His voice had the twang of the stockbroker belt. But he spoke quietly, modestly. I thought, *this is AA. Hello, I am Biro...*

"I am very, very rich," said Biro, "And I, along with Marga, or should I say Marga's husband unbeknownst to him, bankroll this group. None of us, however, are in this for profit or gain. We are in it, as Leo said, to *play back at life*. I first tried to top myself at fifteen. I've done that seven times in my life. Never made it. Cry for help? Cry for cry. I didn't kill Sej either. It was a bit like you. I clubbed him with a cricket bat. Tough skull. Maybe now it's just been thumped once too often." There was a pause.

Now I knew him. I thought, He was with Sej the first time, in the pub in the Strand. That whole thing they did –Biro quiet, Sej volatile – attracting attention – an act to snare one more possible target. And it worked.

Leo, since deciding he would be the volunteer to relieve the girl Liss at the hospital, had left his second glass of champagne untouched.

"Are there more of you?" I asked. Sometimes one asks these things, whether believing they may be facts or not.

"A few," said the man who called himself Biro. "You'll get to meet them. Probably meet Liss tonight. Second time you meet her, of course. She works for a very prestigious company, likes her job. You're our first writer."

I said nothing. I wasn't theirs.

Sid said, "All this is just sketches like, man. Just an overview."

And then Leo got up. "OK, folks. I'll go and relieve Liss. She must be worn out. See you later. Keep some dinner for me will you, Margie? I'm going to be famished."

"Yes, darling. Lots of dinner. And I'll roast your potatoes freshly." To me she added "I love to cook. Husband never let me."

"Blessings upon ye," said Leo.

I found I too got up. "Wait."

"OK," said Leo.

"I'm going with you," I said. "To this fictional hospital."

"OK."

Marga said, "That is a very good idea. Roy, a suggestion. Why not pretend to be a relative of Sej's. You'll get more access."

"Why not," said Leo. "You don't reckon this is for real. You'll get to see it is, maybe."

I said, "Unless you kill me on the way."

"Ah come on," said Leo, smiling. It was Sej's smile. They all had it – or one of them. I – had it. "We don't kill people. Life does that. It can maim you, kill you. We just take risks. The same kind life *makes* us take, whether we want or not."

We were at the opening in the green plasterboard, the blue door ahead, and Marga called after us, "Sej once said to me, he was like Jesus Christ. He said *I teach you how to live. Then you crucify me*. I'm quite religious, in a laid-back sort of way. I'd have been offended. Only he was in the hospital bed then, getting over my carving knife."

"He isn't Christ," I said. "Whatever Christ was or wasn't."

"No, he didn't mean that, Roy. He doesn't think he's Christ. But he does teach, he does it with a scourge and a sword, and with – parables. And then we crucify him. And one day, one day, the cross and nails and lance will work. Perhaps it already has. And he won't rise on the third day."

Bitterly I said, "I wouldn't put it past him."

And they laughed. My God they laughed, with a kind of happiness in the concept, and in me for proposing it. And Sid and Biro raised their glasses, clinked them, and drank.

Then Leo went out and I followed him, down to the car. It was a Skoda, mid-eighties model, and it had taken a few knocks. But it was red, the colour of my mother's glass dog.

In the car, as we rumbled off among the jolting back streets, I sat quiet for a while. I was in the front with him. The back seat was full of a medley of magazines and old books, and a cardboard box with what looked like tools in it. My bags had gone in the back, too.

I had done up my seatbelt. He hadn't, only draped it over his shoulder.

But then, they took risks, didn't they?

Finally, he said, "You OK there? This is the quickest way, but it's going to take about half an hour even at this time of night. The hospital, I mean."

"I'm all right."

"Don't you want to ask me some more things? I'm fine to talk while I drive. Believe me, when ye've scannied the craggy glens o' the Heelands, London hails nae chinny." Or so I thought he said.

"Tell me about the other people in the flats," I said. "Are they all part of your, what shall I call it? Fraternity?"

"Not them, Roy old love." He'd reverted to the London accent. "Sej owns the house, No 66, Saracen. So he gets some rent, but not much. I can pay, because I'm on an early retirement deal with a pension. But most of them are crazy, with drink or drugs higher on the must-do list than the monthly retail – I know that one. Been there, done that. Thank God didn't buy the T-shirt. He lets them off, poor bloody cretins. Unless they cause dangerous bother. In that case C steps in. It's like my music. I can play two million decibels, but if Sej asks me to turn it down, or off, I do."

"He gives the orders."

"If you like. But I love the guy."

"And if you don't C steps in."

Eyes on the road, he was smiling. "I was part of the show that brought C in. You'll hear his story sometime. No, it isn't a threat with us. Just – mutual courtesy."

"But," I said deadly, "you love him. Sej."

"Yes."

"Because he broke you free of yourself."

"That's the one."

"I remember Mr C thumping the man from flat *2.*"

"Oh *him.* The guy in flat *2* is a cunt," said Leo indifferently. "He likes to get off his skull and hurt things, cause damage for no reason. Sej lets him stay but only if he leaves Tina alone, when she's there."

"So there is a Tina."

"Yes, there's a Tina. She's in rehab at the moment. Sold everything she had for a blast of crack and then it's an ambulance and one more programme, poor cow."

"Why doesn't he rescue *them?*" I asked. I sounded older than normally I do. "Free them from their moulds."

"You can't, Roy, can you, some people. Most people. Sej looks out for the ones who seem like they might have potential for change, for growth. We're a bit thin on the ground. He's always prepared to try. Some of them freak out and run away and don't come back anywhere he, or any of us, can find them. Some of them cling on to him but still don't change. Some he'll give up on after one meeting."

"His life's work."

"Right again."

"And you are all what? Disciples?"

"Still swimming with that stick Marga threw to you? No, we're not disciples. We have our own lives, but he calls us up sometimes. *Militia,* Roy. How's that? *Reservists.*"

"In which war?"

"The war against terrifying real life."

We swerved around a corner and a cat darted over the narrow road. Leo slowed the car like a sensitive knife in butter. He drove well, but not exactly as they tell one to. Well. Of course not.

"Then," I said, "did he meet you when you moved into the flat?"

"No, the flat was after. He offered me the flat. The last guy had it was dead."

"What from?"

"Old age. He was ninety-one. He climbed those flamin' stairs at least twice every day. One day, he left a note that said he'd had enough climbing. Took some tablets. Ninety-one. Tablets. No more climbs. Bit classy that."

"Was he one of you?"

"No. He just let us use the door now and then."

"Tell me what you know about Sej."

We had come out on to a tree-lined road. We were by now in that place all taxi drivers fear to go late at night. South of the River.

"I don't know much. Honest injun. None of us do. He was brought up in a children's home. Then someone he didn't know left him some dosh and the flats. That's it."

"What's his mother's name?"

"Oh *that.*" Leo laughed. In his laugh I heard again the laughter of Sej. "He calls her Cinderella. Or Ashabelle. Always something like that. It's a joke. He never knew her. Let alone any daddy figure."

"Why Cinderella?"

"She went after a ball, lost her shoe... the shoe is a sexual symbol here and there."

"I know."

"Speed humpies," he said, as the things once known as sleeping policemen rose up before us along the road. "We are getting near."

I thought, *He's taking me somewhere, but to a hospital? Sej isn't in any hospital. This will be one more set-up, one more round in the game.*

And then we drove into a square and through another street and the grey depressing bulk of a building that could be nothing *but* a hospital stood shining in its cold clear light.

A memory of my dying mother came unwanted into my mind. She'd always been afraid of hospitals. Over the door, for her, would hang that warning from Dante's Gate to Hell: *Abandon Hope all Ye that here Enter.*

At the car park he paid the toll and we got out. I couldn't carry the bags anymore, less weight than distraction, and left them on the seat. I felt old, I felt beaten.

I stopped Leo some yards from the building's glass entrance.

"Did Sej ever punch you, slap you, anything?"

"Once. That's when I threw him down the stairs. That's what it's all for, Roy. We said. To get you to break and mend yourself and *react* and come back different. Ach, laddie," he tenderly said, not to me.

An oldish man had emerged from the hospital entrance. He stopped on the forecourt and put a handkerchief to his face and wept, his shadow falling black in front of him.

In the other shadow beyond the blinding light, Leo and I stood and watched him.

Softly Leo murmured, "That is what life does. That's what we get. However stupid or clever or rich or poor or good we are. So take it by the seat of its pants. Rebellion. We move first. And if we get hurt? If it be now, 'tis not to come; if it be not to come, it will be now; if it be *not* now, yet it *will* come."

"*Hamlet,*" I said.

"*Hamlet.* Shakespeare. *There's* a feller knew a thing or two. And look where it got *him.* In the ground. Y'know, some teacher once said to me that the only flaw in *Hamlet,* both the play and the character, is their predictability. But Roy, *Hamlet* isn't predictable, even though you know how it, and he, is going to end."

The man had put his handkerchief back in the pocket of his coat. It had been linen, I suppose. Not Kleenex. He walked past us into the car park, not seeing us. He would be driving away alone. As we all do, in the end.

He was in a glass-walled room set apart.

I gazed through the glass. It was him.

I could see that, even with the network of wires and tubes, the machines that clicked and whirred, the strange specific pillows.

It was Joseph. Sej.

And a doctor came out and spoke to me.

"Mr Phillips? You're his uncle, I gather."

"Yes."

"Right. Well I can tell you what we know so far."

When we had got up to the correct floor, the young woman called Liss was standing in the bright light among the piles of magazines you look at in hospital waiting areas, trying to take in articles and pictures of super models and rabbits, with your heart in your mouth.

Liss had a plastic cup of coffee she wasn't drinking. Like Marga she could doubtless cry to order, but now she came up to Leo and he held her, and she howled. Her jumper was a deep purple blue.

C was there too in a navy shirt. He raised his hand to me.

"Hi, Roy. She's upset."

"I've seen her upset," I said.

"Sure. But that wasn't for real. How are you, OK? Hang on," he added. "I'd better give you these while I think of it." He handed me a set of keys. They were mine, the originals, the ones I'd posted back through the front door of the house. Meaninglessly I shoved them in my pocket. Props... keys, cars... the toy white dog, by now dry-cleaned of the ketchup poured over it to represent its running over – yes, Marga had flourished that too, to show me no animals had been harmed in their production...

Did Alice ever feel, in her sinister Wonderlands, as if she were losing her mind?

Leo had already got hold of someone and informed them I was Sej's uncle. "Be a relative. The only way you'll be able to get near him. What name do you want to use?"

Oddly I'd thought at once that changing my name would be a sensible move. *William* crossed my mind, my father's name. But then there was my mother. She'd been called Denise. Quite a daring French name in the late twenties. "Denis," I said, "Denis Phillips."

"They have Sej as Joseph Traskul. Phillips – Traskul?"

"Then I must be his mother's brother, mustn't I?"

"I understand," said the doctor now, "your nephew collapsed due to a mixture of pain-killers and alcohol and hit his head on the corner of a table. This was what his friends thought. The injury is consistent with that. Perhaps they'll have told you Joseph was attacked a short while before – some blows to the ribs. Not too serious. And there's an old injury – a titanium pin in the right leg. But he was depressed?"

"I didn't know."

"No, of course not. This must be a shock. You've come down from Manchester, they said."

"His skull's fractured?"

"That's the better news. It isn't. To be honest, Mr Smithson – that's the surgeon – took a look at him and had a definite feeling there was a hairline fracture. But there isn't. But it's a major concussion. The brain is bruised. In these cases, I'm afraid, we can only hope for the best. Sometimes there is damage to nerves, and so on. It can affect..."

Just then something happened in the room, a flare of green lights and a terrible beeping screeching sound.

The doctor forgot me, sweeping me aside.

From nowhere nurses of both genders came rushing.

Leo ran up, grabbed me and pulled me away.

I was standing by a blue wall, (or do I only imagine it was blue?) and there was pandemonium in the glass-walled room, a white flurrying like snowfall on a windy night. And then out came the bed very fast, with his body on it, and all the wires snaking out of him, and machines wheeled along with him, his head turned away, his closed eyes stained darkly, and one hand lying deadly. His pianist's hand.

And the woman called Liss put her arm round me. She was sodden with tears and her nose ran. She said gently, "Roy, it's all right. We've all done this in the past. He's been hurt so often. He makes us. Don't be sad. He'd never blame you."

The four of us, C and Liss and Leo and I, stood by the blue wall and watched as they hurried him away and were gone with him, while overhead the lights burned white.

9

I always dreamed I met him where there was water. Fluidity, what was mutable, in alchemic terms. His danger was apparent in the dreams, also the psychosis of threat, and his omnipresence. Even unseen, he would be immanent. Less God or demon than spirit.

The name Denis, of course, comes from the name of the Greek wine god Dionysos. As well as inventing wine and so allowing men and women to become drunk, thereby sloughing all convention and restraint, he was called the Breaker of Chains. No god of the ancient world could be more terrible. Or, in other circumstances, more seductively gentle.

But that's a diversion. A swift psychoanalysis of that single choice of naming, which anyway sprang from the memory of my mother.

Neither I, nor Sej, have anything to do with the gods.

There was a single graffito in the lift. SHITE, it read.

Someone had obviously tried to clean it off, but then the perpetrator, or some other linguistic artist, had spray-painted it back on in whitest white, and two feet high.

At the top floor, the fourth, I got out. The lift had lurched like a hippo on the way up and even bracing myself for the landing hadn't quite been enough.

I crossed the space and looked at the smartly painted indigo door.

It stood ajar.

This was in Camden Town, and the month by now was August.

Something horrible and extreme, subconsciously expected yet prayed into impossibility, had become possible and occurred in London this last July. The perfection of its date – 7/7 – stayed in my mind. It was as if it had been planned for that day and month in order not only to maim and kill, but to enable Londoners not to have to worry about the opposing reversal of day and month of the USA and England. So it would be simple for us to equate 7/7 with 9/11. They even rhymed. Just supposing the bombs had been detonated on the 8th July – what then? 8/7 or 7/8?

You could still feel and see the afterimage of the attack in the city. On the tube no one spoke about bombs. If the train stuck for two minutes between stations the fume of fear rose with an already everyday accustomedness. "Ain't got no choice but be cannon-fodder, has we?" some man asked me in a pub. "It's not the bleeding wartime spirit. Wasn't in bleeding *wartime* neither. You gotta get on. Or you lose yer work, yer income. Get on – what else you s'posed ter do?"

Beyond the indigo door the hallway stretched off to the right. It was clean and unexceptional. A lavatory and then a bathroom opened to the left as I walked through, then a biggish kitchen. These rooms and their furnishings were universally white, and with the same beige carpet as in the hall. The kitchen though had brown lino tiles. At the end of the hall was a large lounge. This too was white and beige but had a couple of armchairs upholstered in a deep blue which seemed fresh and recent. A wide sash window in the left-hand wall looked out, as the others had in the lavatory, bathroom and kitchen, to where tall green trees were in heavy leaf, and through them, just visible, ran an overland railway line.

He was sitting in one of the armchairs. No colour match. He wore light blue jeans and a faded cream shirt.

As I went in, he smiled, but didn't get up. "Hello, Denis."

He'd altered – *been* altered. He looked ill even now, pale and haggard. And he looked young as only the very old do. How old was he really? In his early forties perhaps? It couldn't be more than that.

His left eyelid had a slight droop to it, and his mouth that side, only very slightly. This wasn't anything you could fake, not so close, not some cunning injection or theatrical subterfuge. I'd heard he limped a little too. Even the pin in his right leg hadn't caused that. But the brain, of course... Of course.

And when he spoke, even the two words, *Hello Denis*, there was an almost undetectable slur. That certainly was as if his mouth had not quite recovered from dental work. Or a blow. Or a minor stroke.

Marga had 'prepared' me over the phone.

"They said it may all go. Or – it may not. But it doesn't spoil his looks. You can *see* it's still Sej."

Leo had also called to reassure me. "He's OK."

I hadn't bothered to replace the TV. But I'd got my landline phone sorted out in late June, about the time I got the cooker fixed and the new carpet and coverings for the front room. It hadn't been too difficult. A routine check on my bank balance had shown me someone had paid in anything I might have spent during my tussles with Sej – the cost of staying at *The Belmont*, new bolts and locks, the alarm. (I hadn't had to pay for the kitchen repairs. C had come over unasked and done it, gratis. He'd also cleaned the white paint off the lavatory window. "No charge," he'd said to my silence. "If you're going to be one of the family.") And of course Cart's Bits and Booze had never taken any money off the credit card. He had called and explained that carefully. The way they all seemed to take such pleasure in explaining their cleverness, their *plays*. When I told him I had thought someone in the publishing world I knew had put his hit-team on to me, he rejoiced down the line at the often helpful nature of coincidence. I had been meant to think someone corrupt in the police service had done me this kindness. He reminded me there had been something like that in one of my short stories. Cart also pointed out to award me a handy assassin was in fact to prevent my doing something like that off my own bat – as Cart himself once did. Personal attack against Sej must, it seemed, be acted only, unless it were to come from Sej's chosen victim. Which, Cart added, in the end generally it did.

To that I said nothing. Nothing at all.

"Sit down," said Sej from the blue chair. "You look tired. I'll make some tea."

I sat down in the second armchair. Yes, just the feel of the material showed it was brand new. This was Sid's place. Presumably he didn't mind our meeting here, or the new colour scheme, if someone else – Marga? Biro? – forked out for it. Sitting, I looked round at Sid's TV and various radios and stereos and the antique record-player for playing vinyl, his plants in the window. He had some Escher prints and the print of one of Picasso's blue girls, and a photo of a man and a woman circa 1980, perhaps his parents. A guitar and a piano were over against the far wall, where another closed door perhaps gave on the bedroom.

Once out of his chair and moving, Sej did limp. He could have acted this. But perhaps not. I didn't think he did, not now. The impression given was all that, with me, was done with. We'd reached the breaking point and travelled through, and on. Now... But I didn't know about Now.

"Go and see him, Denis," had said Marga, scrupulous as they all were over my newly picked name. "The last time you saw him was when he stopped breathing."

And that *had* been the last time. There in the hospital. When they wheeled his bed away in the snowstorm of white nurses and wires.

When I'd stood there like the other three, C and Liss and Leo.

I had stood and stood, and then someone came and told me, as his only valid relative, that Sej was on a ventilator, and these things could happen, not to give up hope. I felt nothing, nothing at all. But I must have looked as if I did, I thought.

They took me to see him after about two more hours. I saw him.

The sci-fi aspect of his care was quite extraordinary. Such a huge, alien machine.

After a while I went out and into the lavatory. And as I stood there pissing in the urinal, I recalled how I'd done this when my mother lay dying.

In the mirror I looked to myself like an old man of eighty-five or more. A bald old man with a moustache. Nobody I knew.

When I came out, I didn't go back to the others. I rode the lift down to the entrance and called a cab, and I went home to my house, leaving my clothes, my documents, everything, even the files and the novel *Untitled* there in Leo's Skoda.

The door keys they had returned to me were in my pocket. I let myself in.

I walked about the house most of what was left of that night-morning, but it was already getting light. About six I fell asleep, sitting on the paint-splashed couch in the front room, facing the smashed TV.

A day later Leo came over and dropped off my bags.

"He's off the ventilator, Denis. And conscious – off and on. He knows who he is. And us, he knows us. Thought you'd like to know. You should've stayed, come back to the flat. Marga's roast lamb – you missed a treat."

I didn't ask him in, nor had he attempted to enter.

I have tried to estimate how long I holed up there in the house. I've never been quite sure. Some days, weeks.

When I went into the back garden one morning, and stood on the paving, head and face unshaven, George had come out too and glared at me over the lowest part of the fence.

"Well I have to say," he had to say, "you know some funny types, Roy. I'm quite put out, you know, by that last upheaval. That young man. Those other ne'er-do-wells. An awful scare for Vita."

I turned and looked at him and heard myself say quietly, "Fuck off, you fucking old freak."

And he went crimson then grey and did as I had suggested. He didn't even bang their kitchen door.

"This is good tea," said Sej. "Sid's a fan of tea, like me. An Assam blend, with ginger. And look, ginger and chocolate biscuits. Have one." I had one.

"And how are you?" he asked me.

"All right. How are *you*?"

He smiled, then the smile opened out into a laugh. "I am entirely fine,

Denis. Look, you were worth it, like the advert says."

"Why do you do this?"

"I thought they filled you in? Thought *I* had, really. Because life does it. Disease, bombs, so-called natural disasters. We should get in first. Teach the lesson life is supposed to and seldom does. You know the old saw, *Not Care was made to care?*"

"Yes."

"Well, I know you don't like to be ungrammatical, Denis, but: *Care was made to NOT care.*"

"And that's what you do? Risk one of us murdering you, in order to get rid of our misguided carefulness."

"Oh, Denis. *No*, Denis. You *know* No. We have to learn to let go of the blind safety that isn't even real. We all die. Do you prefer to be inadequately secure and entirely bored and dead-alive, or to learn and grow?"

"That's your aim, not mine."

"No. Not *my* aim. *My* achievement."

The calm certainty with which he said this convinced me, if nothing else ever had, of his totally certifiable madness. But his dignity made me look away. Where my eyes fell was on the piano.

I thought, *I have succumbed to the unsubtle flattery of his pursuit of me, as have the others, his intense coercion and concentration on me. No one else – no one, not parents, never friend, not even she, my Maureen – no one ever gave me so much – attention.*

Still looking fixedly at the piano, I said, "That evening, as per your instructions, I assume, everyone wore dark blue. And the door there, and here, and these chairs, are dark blue."

"Indigo, Denis. Homage to your book. When the flame hits the sixth chakra and turns to indigo, and the self is realised and *used*. I never met anyone, old sport, who put it more clearly, more – exquisitely. Indigo. The Indigo Instant when everything superficial burns off – hope, fear, denial – and only self-dominion remains, and after that, you can rule the world."

"That was Vilmos," I said.

"Yes, Denis. Or should I say, Roy. And Roy, *Vilmos* was always *you*."

I swallowed noisily.

Outside, as if to cover my swallow and then silence, a train zoomed by, flashing away along the track towards home or hell.

"Can you still play?" I asked. I heard what I'd said. I amended, "I mean, a piano."

"Ah, that."

He looked down and I found I watched him.

Then he got up and he went to the piano by the far wall, and I could see how he strained to make the left leg move, and at the same time strained not to show it. It was the way an old man, a proud old man, would go on. It wasn't an act.

As he sat down at the piano on the stool there I wanted to shout out. I

405

wanted to grab hold of him. The last time he had sat at a piano, his back to me… But even now the train was gone, I still kept my silence.

Sej sat there a long while.

Then he put his hands on the keys.

As once before, a rill of notes came, flawed. They stumbled and fell over each other. A little phrase of music leaked between, all disjointed, like a stammer that can't catch itself and so can never be put right.

I too had got up.

I bawled at him. I stood there bellowing at him, roaring. I can't remember what I said. It was about his loss of something so true – his wicked wilful throwing away loss of it – and, I believe, about my unwilling part in this.

In the end I stopped and sat down again. I put my head in my hands.

When I glanced up once more, he was looking at me, over his left shoulder from his impaired left eye, a laughing look, a loving look. That of a father or a mother. Or a son.

"*Gotcha*," he softly said.

And then his hands sprang back on to the keys.

He played me Liszt's Hungarian Rhapsody, which is the concert showman's piece, melodic, episodic, pyrotechnic, *impossible*. He played it perhaps as Liszt may have done, the golden notes firing off like showers of bullets, striking the ceiling, the windows, the earth and the sky.

When he'd finished, he sat on there with his back to me. I sat staring out of the window. And another train, having it seemed waited for him to conclude, rattled along the track.

When ultimately I rose, he said, "So long, Denis. Take care."

The lift felt like a hippo going down too. The sun had come out. My eyes were full of golden bullets.

Near Camden Lock I saw a man selling violins on the pavement. I remember that. I'm not convinced he was real.

He called me this morning about 10, via the landline. The number remains the same as it was.

"Outside the V & A at 4 p.m.," he said, without any preamble. "Smart casual dress. Leo will be there. You go up to him and start to shout at him. You're angry, a bit out of control. He's taken something of yours – doesn't matter what – a lover, a rare book, a CD – something important. He'll improvise on what you do, he's had more experience. Trust him. Keep this up a bit, then I'll be there. There'll be a woman around. She shows promise, but it's early days. Not like you. I knew with you from the first. Anyhow, you ignore her. And I, to you, will be a stranger. I'll calm you and Leo down. Make it difficult for me, but after a while, give in grudgingly but completely."

I didn't speak nor did he require me to.

He added, "Then just walk off, any direction you like. It's straightforward, if not undemanding. But then it's your first real go at this sort of thing. There'll be a meeting later, Marga, Leo, me if I can make it. Marga will call you, tell you where. She'll call you at home, unless you want to let her know your mobile number. If you decide you don't want to be involved in any of this, just don't turn up this afternoon. That's understood. We'll manage, though we could use you. In the case of your absence, I won't bother you again. Though of course, you do know where I live, so to speak. Cheers, Dad. *Au revoir*."

The dialling tone came.

That was it.

His voice had been as I recalled from the beginning, only occasionally, on certain words – *lover, straightforward, cheers* – had I noted there still remained a slight slurring?

For a while I walked about the house. I thought of them, and their 'meetings', a roasting joint in the oven, the lamps all on. "The family" C had said. Family.

Now I'm sitting in the front room, looking at the clock with the little red drip of paint still on it. The red glass dog, once I'd mended it, had stood there, but today, about an hour ago, I moved it back to the top of the piano.

The clock, as does my watch, tells me it's not yet 12.30. I haven't made a move. Why would I? Hypothetically of course I've got plenty of time to get ready and travel up to the V & A. If I were going. If I were. Only I'm not going, am I. I'm not going. Am I. Am I?

EXHIBIT FOUR
WINTER WHITE

WINTER WHITE

Crovak the warrior came home in the snow with eighty men, and with one other, so they say. This is how it was:

There had been a war, near summer's end, in the High Country. Ten of the clans were in it, and Crovak had gone from his hold with the rest, to fight and kill and take spoil, man's work for which he was well fitted, being very much a man. Over six feet in height he was, broad in the shoulder, and as strong as he needed to be with strength to spare. His hair and his eyes were brown, but his beard was black and the hair on his body black, and he could get up a black temper too, when he had a mind to it. But his teeth were white as salt and he got his name from them, Crovak White-Tooth, though later he had other names. He was vain of his teeth, and vain all through, if truth be told, not of his looks but of his battle skills, his chiefdom, vain of his manhood and of the fact he was a man. Being a man had been lucky for him. It was his boast that none could out-fight him, out-drink him or out-ride him in the horizontal act. He had sired only sons. "A man makes men," he would say. He had lost two wives that way, getting sons out of them. But the third wife, she was healthy, a red-haired vixen.

After the war was done, Crovak and his eighty warriors were going homewards with their spoil, but half-way to Drom-Crovak the winter woke early. Snow began to come down, and night closed in, and the warriors lost their road. They were in a wild unfamiliar place, on rocky hills with a pelt of thin forest, land where the wolf-folk live more often than men.

They cursed the snow, the warriors, but the snow paid no heed.

Then, riding blind down through the tree-line in the storm, they came on a narrow valley, and in the valley was an old Drom-hall. Not one of them knew the spot, neither of the hall, which plainly was long empty, though curiously not derelict. Still, they took it for shelter and fortune, and they rode their red horses straight in at the gate and through the doors into the house.

A great house it was too – or had been. The pointed roof went up a good forty feet or more, and the cross beams, jet black with ancient smokes, were intricately carved in a fashion not instantly recognisable. The central hearth was years cold, yet by the hearth lay a huge bundle of wood, as if in readiness for them. One or two of the warriors discussed this uneasily, but Crovak gave them the edge of his anger, and they shut their mouths. Certainly, when the wood was lit on the hearth and the sparking reek going up, they were glad enough of it. Outside the snow went on falling and piled against the doors and the ledges of the windows, but the fire burned within, and the men ate the dry meat they had saved over and drank their beer. They made a racket, eating, drinking, crowing over victories in the war, over loot, over women, and over each other's women in Drom-Crovak, and how glad they would be to have

410

their men back after so many nights alone. Only they kept quiet on the matter of Crovak's wife, for none but he might make a story of her, how hot she was and how willing. But Crovak was not apparently in the mood for talking of women, and soon he got up, dipped a brand from the hearth, went about the Drom, through the hall, and at length up the inner stairway to the one big upper room which was the Chief's place, or would have been if any chief had remained. Everyone knew what was in Crovak's mind then; he was on the look-out for fresh spoil, as if he scented it here as a hound scents his home-hearth. None followed, for Crovak had summoned none to follow him. Whatever he found he would most probably keep; it was his by chief's right, and if he was greedy nobody cared to cross him.

Crovak was indeed very restless. He liked to be up and doing, warring or hunting; if at rest, then with a girl or getting drunk, and they had no girls, and not enough beer with them to get drunk on. So, he paced about, peering into the shadows of the Drom. He hardly expected to come on any riches left behind, and when he discovered the tall black chests standing in the upper room, he put his foot through their doors without much hope of reward, and truly there was none, for they were bare. The frame of an enormous antique bed stood against the far wall, and here spiders had got to work as they had in the corners of the room below. Crovak, what with the shadows and the webs of these spinner-people, nearly missed what rested on the sinister post of the bed. But just as he was going out with an oath, the brand he held caught a red glint in the dark, and Crovak returned to see.

What he saw was a thing all bound over with grey spider flax, with its one red eye shining out at him. So, he pulled the thing loose and picked off the webs, and presently he beheld a slender small hollow pipe of ivory, with three black holes in it and a scarlet gem set where the fourth hole was not. Now Crovak was not a man given to superstition or to fancies of any kind, but it seemed to him, suddenly, that everything in the upper room had grown very still. Even the brand had stopped flickering in his grasp, even the spiders had paused upon their threads. But this was only for a moment. Crovak shook the pipe, and the flame on the brand jumped again, and the webs swayed, and the shadows lurched. Then Crovak put his mouth to the pipe to blow the dust from it. The pipe made a sound when he did this, a thin high squeal, and for some reason the sound reminded Crovak instantly of the noise a woman might make when a man struck her – or raped her. This amused him, and he put the pipe to his lips a second time and blew it, but now no sound came out, and try as he would, no sound could he make to come from it. Still, for the ruby at its other end, it was not valueless.

Crovak left the room and swaggered down the stair. He toyed with the pipe, artfully not speaking, till the warriors asked where he had got it. He told then, and later he spoke of his wife and how she would run to him and hang on him when they got home. When the men slept, Crovak lay awake some while, considering that.

411

In the morning the snow was all down, but hard with frost, and a chill bright sun stood over it. They found their road again easily, Crovak and his eighty men, and by noon they were far from the old Drom where it lay empty and hearth-cold once more under the whiteness.

There were three more days of riding before they should reach Drom-Crovak.

All the first day, Crovak's horse acted oddly, swerving at nothing, trembling at nothing. Crovak cursed it, beat it and finally gifted it to another man and took that man's horse in exchange. After which Crovak's own horse became steady, and the new horse under him began shying and stalling. That night they made their camp in the wretched open. Wolves howled on the hollow hills behind them, and the stars had a look of that same hungry howling, so swollen and brilliant they were in the sky. Yet the men had taken a deer and eaten fresh meat that night. Crovak slept under his cloak and dreamed he had his woman with him. A very real dream it was, yet she was not as she had been, her body stony in his grip. He woke in the dawn and took out the ivory pipe and set it grinning to his mouth, attempting to evoke again that female squeal of pain or fear, but no sound came.

The second day, there was the same trouble with the horse. The warriors came into the lowlands and passed by a frozen river. Somewhere here, Crovak began to feel a certain strangeness at his back, as if something pressed against him, and not long after, the horse reared up and fell, throwing him. Then Crovak, in his fury, took a boulder and brained the horse as it struggled to rise.

The man whose horse it had been was angry. Altercation broke out, and Crovak struck him down with a blow that near broke his jaw. Crovak took back his own mount, and the horseless warrior must ride behind another. Crovak's horse shied at nothing, and trembled, but knew better than to throw him.

Just before the sun left the white plain, they passed a stretch of the river where the ice was broken and, glancing aside, Crovak saw his own reflection there astride the red horse, and something up behind him, riding pillion as the horseless warrior rode behind another.

Crovak drew rein, and turned about to see, and saw nothing, only the dying ruddy light, and his men at his back.

Some would dwell on an occurrence of this sort, but Crovak's mind was not constructed to dwell on shadows or on dreams. Yet, when they made their camp, he drew out the ivory pipe, and offered it to one of the men.

"It has a pleasing note," said he, "but it is a stubborn object."

The man took the pipe and rolled it between his fingers. "I never met such a thing before, Crovak-lord," said he. "But I will not offer to sound it."

"Come, if I say sound it, you shall," said Crovak.

"I say I will not, Crovak-lord."

"What are you afraid of? Is it a woman's cringing heart you have? Perhaps I should wed you to one of my ten-year-old sons and see if he can get you with child."

The other warriors joined his jeering. One said he would try the pipe, but when he was about to put it to his mouth he sneezed, and each time he raised the pipe he sneezed, a curious happening. And another man who snatched the pipe was taken with a fit of choking, while a third had the pipe at his lip, but the fire spat and a piece of flaming tinder flew up and lodged in his cloak, and he dropped the pipe to beat out the burning.

Then Crovak retrieved the pipe with a snarl of laughter. "The wench is wed to me," he said, and put the ivory away in his belt, and laughed again.

The next day's riding was hard, but they were getting near Drom-Crovak; the curve of the land, the trees, the tracks, all took on the look of home things, even beneath the snow. Here and there they passed by a small steading, the outlying holds of the Drom, which owed Crovak tythe. Generally, when the Drom warriors went riding, the out-women kept from sight, but a few miles from the Drom there was a girl child, not more than four or five, playing on the track. It was ill-luck, and worse, unlawful among the clans, to kill a child, even a peasant's or a slave's brat. The warriors reined aside, and then a dour, skinny woman ran from the huddle of huts nearby to scoop the child up. Not looking at Crovak, she mumbled for his pardon and received instead a gob of his spit. As the men moved off, the girl child's voice rose thin and clear above the crunch of hoofs in the snow: "White woman! See."

Crovak heard, and something caught him in the cry, he could not have said what, but it inflamed his temper. He swung round and rode back.

"Speak, sow. What does your filthy bairn mean?"

"I do not know, Crovak-lord."

"White woman," said the child again, "on big man's dog."

"What?" shouted Crovak.

"Pardon, Crovak-lord. She thinks a horse a dog. She means on your horse, Crovak-lord. But no one is there."

"White woman," said the child, the third time.

"Get from my sight!" Crovak shouted. He struck the woman a blow with his whip across her thighs, before she could run. But somehow she ran after the blow, hauling the child with her, silent, into the nearest hut.

Crovak was not frightened, did not think to be. But he was angry, with a mad unmotivated rage. He slashed his horse about the neck, and it plunged forward snorting. The warriors tore after. Yet, even riding so swift, Crovak felt a constriction at his chest and, glancing down, he saw an odd thing. Two white arms, white as the snow, were round his ribs and held him fast, and two white hands, their fingers knotted among his furs.

Then the anger, not the fear, overwhelmed Crovak, and with a bellow he strove to thrust and tear the fragile clinging white arms from him, and he must indeed have had his will, for they were suddenly gone. And when he looked before him again, and shook the freezing sweat from his scowling face, he perceived the track winding down between the shallow hills of the Low

413

Country, leading to his Drom.

Crovak the warrior came home in the snow with his eighty men just at fall of night, and he saw the long stockade and the terraced earth-mound behind with the Drom huts circling up on it, and the great hall at its summit. The torches were red on the stockade gates; between them, the men Crovak had left here, when he went to war, were patrolling with their spears, looking out for enemies. Above, other torches blazed from the cross-alleys between the dwellings and brazen from the doors of the hall. It was a good thing to return and see: the Drom so sturdy, so safe and so fine with its lights, as if the night had no power over it.

Crovak had no sense of foreboding, or at least he would not have confessed one. But he said to his men: "Make camp here an hour, for I am going back alone. I would see how well my laws are kept when I am from the hearth."

The men laughed, and one dared to say that Crovak's wife would be weeping, with her loom set by and her face in the ashes. Crovak grinned and, leaving his horse, he stole down on his own hold like the thief.

He got over the stockade like a thief, too. No other but the master could have done it, for the watch-hounds knew his scent, and kept quiet when he bade them – one man who came to apprehend him, Crovak crowned with his fist. He was taking no chances. He stole up through the cross-alleys, muffled in his furs, and reached the hall door and went by it. Not only an inner but an outer stair led to the upper chamber, this outer stair infrequently used, but now Crovak used it. It was not yet the time for dinner, besides, the chief's wife did not sit in hall when he was absent, at least, not the wife of Crovak.

He knew she was in the chamber as soon as he reached the outer door, for he could scent her, the hot russet smell of her hair and the ripeness of her flesh. When he pushed open the door, he knew also why the perfume of her was so strong. She did not hear him enter; she was too preoccupied. Neither did the man hear.

They lay on Crovak's bed, intent on their journey.

Crovak, whose reaction to fury was usually one of clamour, made no noise at all as he crept about and took down from the wall one of his boar spears. He stood a moment, the spear resting in his hands, watching his wife and the man who rode her. Crovak did not feel surprise or hurt. But when he leaped forward and plunged the spear down through both their bodies, with his massive strength, through the two of them and through the bed itself into a crevice of the stone floor beneath, he felt a boiling spasm of pleasure at their deaths. He stood and watched them die. The eyes of his vixen wife pleaded with him; even dying, she pleaded dumbly for mercy, till the soul left her.

Crovak took out the ivory pipe. He looked at it with hatred and fondness.

"Cunning, you warn me," he said.

Then he went out to call his warriors in and rouse the Drom to his arrival.

Of course, he did not mourn her. The man, Crovak gave to his kin to bury, that was their business. But she, his woman, Crovak had thrown a little distance outside the gates of the Drom, for beasts to feed on. The night meal was served late that night, but served it was, and Crovak sat down in his hall to it, sat in his carved chair, as if no untoward thing had happened. His rage was gone to a sort of grizzly playfulness. Not a man there but knew he must be wary for his skin's sake. Particularly that night, they only laughed when Crovak did, and when he said no word, no man spoke, and the quiet hung from the rafters with the smoke. And the warrior who had jested of Crovak's wife's weeping, he stayed away.

Finally, Crovak called for his drinking cup, the cup which usually he kept for a feast. It was made from the skull of one of Crovak's enemies, slain in an earlier war, the eyes, the nostrils and the mouth closed with red gold, and the brink rimmed with gold. This goblet was filled for Crovak with beer, and he drank it to the last drop and banged his bone cup down on the board.

Just at that instant, there was another banging, much lighter – yet he heard it – on the doors of the hall. And, at the rapping, the doors opened.

Crovak sat staring, and his mouth set in its grin, showing his flawless and glistening teeth. Through the doors came neither warrior nor slave nor servant; not a traveller, not an itinerant musician with his harp on his back. No, none of these. Through the doors came a woman, and she was white as the winter snow.

Crovak recognised her at once. He shouted at her: "So you have come to claim payment for your warning, have you?"

It seemed she had. Up the silent hall, more silent than ever after Crovak's shout, she moved. She had no look of anything real, more like something painted or enamelled than a living thing. Her gown was white, and not of the fashion of the time, and it left bare her shoulders, though she had been walking in the snow. Her gown was white, and as white as the gown was her flesh, as if there were no blood in it, and her flaxen hair was nearly as white. There was no colour in her face, even her mouth was bloodless, but her brows were black, and her eyes were black, and the nails of her hands were red as rubies, as if they, out of all her bloodlessness, had been dipped in blood. And indeed, her hands were so pale on the pale gown that it was hard to make them out, but for those nails like ten drops of blood splashed there.

"What will you have, woman?" Crovak roared. "Ask your price."

The woman kept walking towards him, but she did not speak. Alongside, the warriors glanced this way and that, at Crovak, then where he stared, at her. It seemed to the warriors that Crovak was afraid. Sweat stood on his forehead and in his black beard, though he grinned. But Crovak did not feel himself afraid. Not even when the woman reached him, and halted, facing him across the board. Her face was blank, and her mouth so pale he could not tell if it smiled or grimaced at him.

415

"Well, she-wolf," said Crovak, "I never believed in your like before, but here you are. Will you sit with me? You will be the first of your sex to sit at my table, but then you are fey, so perhaps you have earned it." Then he called for more beer to fill his skull-cup. The woman, however, did not sit, nor touch anything on the board. She only gazed at Crovak with her eyes as black as ravens. Crovak turned to his men. "What do you think of her?"

A man near to him, a fool, said haltingly: "Who are you seeing, Crovak-lord? Is it your dead woman?"

Crovak gave a cry of rage, and turning about, struck the man sprawling.

"Who does not see her?" Crovak shouted.

The men looked at each other, the slaves huddled by the hearth and hid their eyes. It was borne in on Crovak that none but he could perceive the woman. At that, he laughed again.

"Only for me, are you?" He drank deep and drank. "Only for me?"

When the fourth skull-full of beer was in his belly, he reached across the board and put his hand on her naked shoulder. She felt more real than she appeared, but her flesh was very smooth, as if there were not a pore in it, very smooth and cool. "Now, lass, shall you tell me what you want, or is it only to feast your glance on Crovak White-Tooth? Feast, then."

Crovak called for more beer. He drank till the skin was empty, till he was drunken, and the hall blurred and the sensations of his body blurred. Yet still her he could see very clearly, her with her black eyes. At length he rose, staggering and merry. He turned his back on her, and slurred over his shoulder at her: "Bid you goodnight, white sow," and he rolled through the silent hall and up the stair, through the hanging into the upper room where seven hours before he had ended his marriage to his red-headed wife. The blood had been cleaned away and the bedding changed, but the frame of the bed and the floor would always hold the mark of the spear's passage, which would be a grand thing to show the next wife he lay down here with.

Crovak stripped his boots and belt, went to the outer door and urinated out upon the stair. Turning back into the room, he beheld the white woman standing at the bed's foot.

Crovak shouted, wordlessly now. Just for one second, he went cold in his belly. Then he showed his teeth to her again and he said: "You would be wife to me, would you?" And he strode to her, rocking somewhat in his gait, and seized her in his two strong hands.

She made no resistance and no remonstrance as he half lifted her to the bed and slung her down there. He was ready for a woman and pushed up her skirts. Even that part of her was pallid, but it did not deter him, nor the white points of her breasts which should have had some colour in them, when he dragged down the neck of her bodice to see. He had her, but the drink made him slow. Slow enough he could notice how she watched him, kept on watching as he worked inside her. She did not catch her breath, she did not make a sound, and her eyes were wide. Her eyes bored into him, cold for his heat. And when he shuddered and grunted and fell down upon her, even then her eyes were somehow watching him, observing his fit with a pitiless and detached interest.

No sooner was the paroxysm over than a vile sickness took him, and lurching up and to the door, he vomited forth the beer.

She watched that too.

And when again he lay groaning on the bed, still she watched. And when he summoned his strength and struck her from the bed, next moment she was there again beside him, her face turned to him, unbruised, her eyes watching.

He grew faint, or else he dozed. When he woke, darkness filled the Drom, and dimly through the outer door he scented the stench of his own sickness, and there she lay beside him yet.

"How now, bitch? Fey or not, you have outstayed my leave."

Rising then, he raised her too, and she was light to carry. He went through the hanging to the inner stair, and he tossed her down it with no trouble. He saw her motionless at the stair's foot, against the dim glow of a single torch left burning in the hall.

Crovak chuckled. He feared her not at all.

He went to his bed and slept heavily. But when he roused in the hour before sunrise, she was beside him again, her eyes mere inches from his own, polished, frigid and terrible as the eyes of a serpent.

At that, Crovak beat her. He gave her a beating no woman could take and live, and few men. She did not attempt to defend herself, neither did she cower away. She must be mute for she made no outcry even now, yet once he thought he glimpsed her tongue – pointed and pale – he thought he noted blood too, and when she tumbled on the ground, he applied his feet, kicking her in the shank and stomach. All this while he was bellowing like the bull, till his men came running up the stair and burst into the room, blear-eyed with swords in their hands.

"What is amiss, Crovak-lord?"

"Nothing!" he ranted, kicking at her, knowing they would not see, that she was his alone, snarling his hate while the sweat flew from his congested face. "Get to your kennels and leave me to my own deeds."

Later, when they had gone, Crovak took the white woman down the outer stair and threw her over a horse and, calling two slaves from the straw where they slept, he sent them off with the horse in the chill grey dawn. "Ride him fast and leave him when he is done."

The slaves' eyes were huge. Wolves came near the Drom in winter. Wolves would have the horse and possibly themselves also. But Crovak had gone mad, gone mad when he caught his wife at her game, gone mad even before, on the way home, some said... The slaves, not daring to disobey, raced the horse out of the stockade gate. Crovak watched them go with the horse and the white woman on its back. He grinned, but the cold day struck into his jaw and made it ache, though his jaw had never ached till then.

The warriors were muttering in the hold, but when Crovak came close, they were dumb.

Crovak carved for himself a piece of last night's roast, and turning about, with his knife in his grip, beheld the woman at his elbow.

Crovak screamed. He thrust the knife into her breast and snatched it out. She stood unharmed, unbloody, watching him. Crovak laughed. He laughed and crashed his fist upon the wall, laughed till the warriors slunk from his hall and the slaves hid themselves beneath the benches.

"Am I not to be rid of you? Be damned then, companion me!"

"How long have we to brook this?" the men asked each other. "Our lord by right, well, so he is. And if he was high-handed in the past, we bore with him, for he was a man, a warrior. We did well enough. But this winter…"

"He is mad this winter," others said. "Some new lord should master the Drom. Must we vow our swords to a madman?"

But still they feared Crovak too much to rebel openly against him. He had taught them that fear ten years, though now they had had a taste of his lunacy for two months. They had seen him strike out and mutter and shout at nothing. They had seen him sneer over his shoulder at nothing. They had seen him linger in the hall till sun-up and not go to his bed, as if he feared to go, nor did he ever take a woman. If any offered, he would knock them down. "I *have* a woman!"

The men did not see this: how Crovak, when exhaustedly he had sought his bed, would try to hold himself awake, knowing that as he slept two polished, greasy-shining black stones would stare at him. Nor did the men see how once or twice he had lain down on this woman of his, and how Lusty Crovak could not take his pleasure with her, his fire put out by her cold water. Even her loins were cold, winter cold, and winter white as the rest of her. He gripped her feverishly and struggled to be a man with her, but she was stone and he was dead. And even the huzzies of the hall could not stir him, for he was aware that she would be by, watching, watching.

He grew morose. Always he spoke to her. He spoke because she did not, and he must speak for both.

"What are you wanting? Tell me. You shall have it. Is it the pipe, the pipe with the ruby which called you? Eh? Will I give it you back? Here, take it." But her red-tipped hands stayed at her sides, blood drops on the white gown. He put the pipe under his heel, but it would not break. He tossed it away from him, but it reappeared in his belt, as always she reappeared at his side.

Certain of the warriors of Drom-Crovak began to steal out, generally by night, in bands of five or six, ten or fourteen. They went to seek other Droms, other lords. Some, whose kin were in Drom-Crovak, and whose roots ran deeper there, began small plots, but discarded them. Clan law was stringent, and they could not quite forget it. Nor the strength of Crovak's arm. Once in the dusk, as Crovak made water up against a wall, a man came by with a knife, but Crovak, with the white woman at his side watching even this, was aware of the man creeping near, and slew him. Truly, Crovak was swift and powerful.

But was he as powerful as he had been? At drink, and he was often drunken now, his hands shook. Sometimes he sat holding his jaw, for his teeth ached. In the second month, this trouble in his jaw became so bad his face was swollen, and he called the smith to pull out one of his front teeth. He howled with the pain and started up as if he would kill the smith. No longer would they call Crovak 'White-Tooth', with the black gap there. He lost another tooth later; it turned brown and cracked in his mouth. It was a strange thing, but it showed how his strength was leaving him.

The winter thickened on the Low Country. The snows descended, turning the black nights grey. The wolves showed themselves even at the gates of the stockade, and the men of Drom-Crovak went hunting them, and as Crovak rode, he turned often to the air behind him and jeered and spat at this air: "Are you comfortable, sow? Is it good to ride with Crovak?" And when he cast his spears, they missed their aim.

Then came an evening when Crovak jumped up from the board and began to roar and rant without ceasing. It was the third month, and he brought more fear on his depleted hall than ever before. He was berserk and it seemed he would never be calm again. He over-set the benches in his raving. He picked up a slave boy and flung him the breadth of the room. They did not know what particular thing had caused this outburst, nor why he screamed at them his old boast: "A man makes men!"

But abruptly he blundered out into the torchlit darkness and flung himself on a horse and plunged from the Drom, all the while yet screaming. And his noise died away on the night silence, as a man's cry dies away down the length of a precipice from which he has fallen.

The woman shuddered with horror as she listened at the bolted door of the hut.

"Who is there?"

"I, bitch," the huge, hoarse mad voice thundered. "Crovak. Now open, or I kick in the door."

The woman backed away, and the next moment the door was indeed broken in shivers, and Crovak strode in. The woman ascertained a great change in him, his ruined teeth, the grey in his black beard, the red veins in his eyes and his shaking demented body. This woman's man was dead, wolves had had him not a month ago. Now she was hard put to it to fend for herself. She stared at the Drom chieftain with miserable terror and no surprise, for who did not understand her life would be bitter and brief.

"Where is your bratling?" Crovak demanded.

Fresh horror – what would he do to her child?

"Come," he snapped, "your bairn is fey, is it not? It sees what others are blind to."

419

"It is sometimes thus with the very young, or the old ones, Crovak-lord – they are nearer life's edge…"

"Get your piglet!" he screamed at her.

The woman turned and lifted the child up from the hearth. The din had not woken it, but now it woke, and looked at Crovak.

Crovak sighed. He glared dully at the woman. "Tell me first, sow, if I am alone."

The woman nodded, holding tight to her infant.

"Now you," Crovak said to the child, "you tell me."

The child giggled.

The woman, in alarm, coaxed it: "Tell the lord what you see. If any are with him."

"White woman," said the child.

"Where?" rasped Crovak, his eyes ablaze.

"By your left shoulder."

"Yes, you snake. My left shoulder. So. Now say how she is."

The child lowered its eyes and crooned, playing with the mother's hair. The mother became distrait, coaxing, coaxing: "Tell the lord, tell him..."

"All white," said the child, "but soot on her eyes and red on her fingers."

Crovak panted, showing his discoloured teeth. He muttered. "And she is thicker at the waist than she was, plumper, is she not? Three months since I lay with her..."

The child's mother put her free hand to her mouth. The girl child simpered. It had suddenly a sly and canny look.

Crovak rode home, and he entered the gate and saw all about him the concealed glances of wary dislike, mistrust and underlying scorn. Crovak announced a feast in his hall. He ordered three cows slaughtered, five sheep, ten beer barrels broached, though there were less men now in Drom-Crovak than there had ever been. Fewer slaves, too, for many had fled. Even fewer women, for five of those Crovak had struck down in his fierce moods had died.

"This feast," Crovak told the Drom folk, spit running from his mouth, "is to celebrate the coming of another son to me. My demon wife is with child. Behold her belly – no, but you cannot. Little matter. She carries. She will give me a boy."

The feast was a grim and a weird one. Crovak went on drinking three nights and the days between. Sometimes he would go out and throw up what he had taken, then come back to eat and drink again. He dragged the women onto the board before him, and pawed them and straddled them, but he did not have them. "Note how faithful I am, my wife," he said.

Eventually Crovak crashed forward in a stupor, and when he recovered himself he found he lay on the floor of his hall, bound and helpless and his mouth stopped with a rag. And all about his warriors stood with their swords.

They had not killed him. As with the slaughter of a child, it was bad luck and unlawful to slay a sleeping man, let alone the chief. But they had spoken long, the warriors of Drom-Crovak. How their women were not safe, how the Drom was cursed, how priests were needed there, and the jurisdiction of the Clan elders. Even the legal sons of Crovak sanctioned what was to be done. No one but did not fear the bane which had fallen on their chieftain and hence upon his hold.

Sluggish and stupid, Crovak writhed in his bonds. The men informed him of what was to be done, informed him courteously. They could afford to be courteous, seeing they had the upper hand at last.

He was put over a horse and carried to a deserted steading about two miles from the Drom. Here was a hut made of stone and weatherproofed to some extent. In the floor was a stone post and a length of iron fetter attached to it – hostages taken in war had been brought to this place now and then and kept for ransom. It served very well for mad Crovak. Though he was yet strong, they said, he could not rip his way free from iron chains.

Nor did he. Four months he rotted there.

Rotted there, and sat or lay on the straw mattress, or paced about on his short leash, like a restless dog. He had warmth, for his men left him pelts and furs to wrap himself in, bundles of wood to feed the fire, and every five days someone would come and leave more wood, and food, and drink besides, and while this one saw to that, three others would keep watch on Crovak. One other kept her watch, too.

They swore to him that when the snow broke, they would send word to the elders of the Clan and ask for the Council to be held, and there decide his fate.

But each time they visited him, Crovak was a fraction more sullen, or else louder; he lunged at them or he whimpered. It seemed he became madder and more mad. And he would frequently turn to his invisible demon and tell her things. If any warrior recalled the ivory pipe taken from the empty Drom that night the snow came, none spoke of it. For a superstitious folk, they had given small specific heed to Crovak's demon, and maybe they were wise.

She sat facing him, across his fire. She never ceased to fix her look on him. At night she lay by him, but he had no warmth from her. Her eyes never closed, she never blinked. Her belly swelled.

One night, in the fourth month, he woke and, in the dull shine of the fire's embers, he seized her throat and tried to throttle her, although he knew there was no use in it. He ground his decaying teeth and squeezed with all his might, and her black eyes went on staring into his, and the swollen belly pressed into his groin which had made it and now could make nothing.

"Will you kill me, then?" he crowed at her. "Will you take my soul too?"

When he let go her throat, there was no bruise on it. His arms ached like his teeth now, from straining to murder her.

As he lay there, whining softly at his pains, his mind ran back to the Drom where he had found the pipe. He thought of the wood on the floor laid ready, and the emptiness without dereliction, and he wondered if some other man had been enslaved there in the same way that he now was, enslaved there till he died. Crovak thought of the spiders scampering on their threads. He thought of the pipe, and how he had blown it and it had squealed like a woman in terror or hurt, and then he took the pipe out and rolled it in his fingers.

He had blown her into the world, if only he might blow her out, reverse the bane, be rid of her.

In a dreadful manner, he had almost grown accustomed to her stare, and turning from her, idly, he began to pick at the ruby that was set in where the fourth hole of the pipe was not. And then, growing weary of this, Crovak set the pipe to his lips and tapped it there.

It seemed to him, abruptly, that in her white face which watched him, there was the slightest and most subtle alteration. Crovak was undeniably insane by this season, but not with a blind insanity. Through the wreckage of his wits, a strange idea came to him, and he slowly turned the pipe about in his hand, so its other end was to his mouth, and, holding it in this fashion, he blew it.

It made a sound. Not as at the previous hour, not a squeal of distress. This time, shrill and thin, it *laughed*.

The woman did two things, two things she had not done before. She opened her mouth very wide, and this was how he saw her teeth were gleaming and coal black as her eyes – which all at once she shut. Then she did a third new thing. She fell backwards on the stone floor and she vanished.

Crovak could hardly credit what he beheld this plainly. He grunted, and he shuffled in his chains, and he waited, his tongue lolling, for her to reappear. And this she did not do.

When day came, still he looked for her, and still she was absent.

Four whole days he waited; four whole days she did not come back. The fourth night he poked out a hole between the stones of the floor and thrust the pipe down into it, and covered it, smiling. The fifth day, Crovak went on smiling to himself, hugging himself, rattling the chain. He built up the fire. When the warriors came to feed him, he spoke to them. He told them all was well, he had outwitted the demon, but he slavered as he spoke, and they paid no heed. Yet he had a strange cunning by then, and he stole a knife from one, and when the men were gone he hacked off his thumb, which made his hand slight enough to slip from the fetter.

He felt the agony only as a distant nudging, and packed snow on the wound, which numbed it. He followed the hoof-pocks in the whiteness the two miles back to Drom-Crovak. It was dusk and the torches burned on the gates. He came on a man there, patrolling the wall, and killed him with the knife and took his sword. After that, Crovak ran into his hold, and he laid about him with the stolen sword, and very many he butchered till he grew weary of the sport. He got a horse then, and rode away into the winter land, red with blood, and his mad eyes red, singing.

What else then do they say of Crovak? They say this:

He wandered the winter two months more. He lived like a beast, preying on the steadings thereabouts which once had paid him tythe. They had been in fear of him before, but now they had a better cause to fear him. Whole families he cut down, only for a loaf or a bit of meat. They say he drank men's blood. How he lived or where, is not certain, in some ruined hut perhaps. His madness kept him alive. Bands of men from the Drom rode out to catch and kill him, but they never found him out.

It had been a harsh unnatural winter, eager to arrive, reluctant to take its leave, but in the end the snow had gone, the ways were brown and muddy, the rivers running bright.

Crovak strode from the forest land which was putting on its green. His horse was dead by then, and he a fearsome sight, ragged, filthy, and his rotten teeth showing in that beard half grey and knotted with the debris of the woods.

He had forgotten much, and no longer did he reason in any form as a man does. Yet enough he remembered, and he took a perverse pleasure in his survival.

When he came to the field, he did not quite recall it. The ground was raw with earth and rank grass, but a stand of trees was at its centre, and nearby a group of huts, and beyond them a track. The track he knew, it led to the Drom, down over the curving shallow hills. A girl child was playing in the field. He recollected the child.

Crovak moved towards the child. He had no positive intention, but a kind of malicious crazy urge to startle it. But the grasses rustled, not merely at his passage, but as if a tiny beast were rummaging there, and the child looked up and saw Crovak.

The wild man snarled down at her, but the child exhibited no nervousness. In fact, confronting the child again, it was Crovak who felt a sudden ice in his belly. He made a guttural noise at the child, for speech did not come fluently any more to him. After a try or two, he got his defiance out:

"What do you see? Is she there, eh? Is she? The white sow?"

The child shook its head. "No."

Crovak grinned. "No. No winter woman. I have sent her back. Clever Crovak, Crovak White-Tooth."

Just then the mother came from one of the huts and, catching sight of him, froze. This amused Crovak. He sucked his nine black nails. Behind him, in the rank grass, the creature rustled again, and the child gazed past Crovak, downward, and she giggled.

"What?" said Crovak. He laughed. "Tell me, what? A fox? I have eaten foxes in the wood."

"See," said the child.

By the huts, the woman held her hands to Crovak imploringly.

"Shall I eat you, then?" asked Crovak. "Like the fox."

"See," said the child a second time. She was watching something just at

Crovak's back and somewhat to his left, in stature a third of the distance up his calf.

"Will she play with me?" asked the child insistently.

Crovak did not turn. "She is not there," he said, "the white woman."

"No," said the child.

Crovak would not turn. He would not think of the swollen belly which had pressed against him. He would not think of his boast of sons.

"She is small as me, she has no clothes," said the child, "but her fingers are red."

Crovak shrieked. He flung about and ran. Behind him, faintly, came the rustling of some tiny thing, which yet managed to keep pace with him. Which kept pace with him, and kept pace with him, and never slackened.

No more is known, or said, of Crovak.

ABOUT THE AUTHOR

Tanith Lee (1947-2015) was born in London. Because her parents were professional dancers (ballroom, Latin American) and had to live where the work was, she attended a number of truly terrible schools, and didn't learn to read – she was also dyslectic – until almost age 8. And then only because her father taught her. This opened the world of books to her, and by 9 she was writing. After much better education at a grammar school, she went on to work in a library. This was followed by various other jobs – shop assistant, waitress, clerk – plus a year at art college when she was 25-26. In 1974, her career as a writer was launched, when DAW Books of America, under the leadership of Donald A. Wollheim, bought and published *The Birthgrave*, and thereafter 26 of her novels and collections.

Tanith was presented with a Lifetime Achievement Award in 2013, at World Fantasycon in Brighton. During her lifetime, she also received the World Horror Convention Grand Master Award, as well as the August Derleth Award and the World Fantasy Award for short fiction (twice).

In 1992, she married the writer-artist-photographer John Kaiine, her partner since 1987. They lived on the Sussex Weald, near the sea, in a house full of books and plants, and never without feline companions. She died at home in May 2015, after a long illness, continuing to work until a couple of weeks before her death.

Throughout her life, Tanith wrote around 100 books, and over 300 short stories. 4 of her radio plays were broadcast by the BBC; she also wrote 2 episodes (*Sarcophagus* and *Sand*) for the TV series *Blake's 7*. Her stories were read regularly on Radio 4 Extra. She was an inspiration to a generation of writers and her work was enormously influential within genre fiction – as it continues to be. She wrote in many styles, within and across many genres, including Horror, SF and Fantasy, Historical, Detective, Contemporary-Psychological, Children and Young Adult. Her preoccupation, though, was always people.

BOOKS BY TANITH LEE

Series

The Birthgrave Trilogy (The Birthgrave; Vazkor, son of Vazkor
[published as Shadowfire in the UK], Quest for the White Witch)
The Blood Opera Sequence (Dark Dance; Personal Darkness; Darkness, I)
The Flat Earth Opus (Night's Master; Death's Master; Delusion's
Master; Delirium's Mistress; Night's Sorceries)
The Lionwolf Trilogy (Cast a Bright Shadow; Here in Cold Hell;
No Flame But Mine)
The Paradys Quartet (The Book of the Damned; The Book of the Beast;
The Book of the Dead; The Book of the Mad)
The Venus Quartet (Faces Under Water; Saint Fire; A Bed of Earth;
Venus Preserved)
The Vis Trilogy (The Storm Lord; Anackire; The White Serpent)
The FOUR-Bee Series (Don't Bite the Sun; Drinking Sapphire Wine)
The S.I.L.V.E.R. Series (Silver Metal Lover; Metallic Love)

Novels and Novellas

34
The Blood of Roses
Companions on the Road
Days of Grass
Death of the Day
Electric Forest
Elephantasm
Eva Fairdeath
The Gods Are Thirsty
Kill the Dead
Heart-Beast
A Heroine of the World
Louisa the Poisoner
Lycanthia
Madame Two Swords
Mortal Suns
Reigning Cats and Dogs
Sabella
Sung in Shadow
Vivia
Volkhavaar
When the Lights Go Out
White as Snow
The Winter Players

Young Adult and Children's Fiction
Animal Castle (picture book)
The Castle of Dark
The Claidi Journals (Law of the Wolf Tower; Wolf Star Rise,
Queen of the Wolves, Wolf Wing)
The Dragon Hoard
East of Midnight
The Piratica Novels (Piratica 1; Piratica 2; Piratica 3)
Prince on a White Horse
Princess Hynchatti and Other Surprises
Shon the Taken
The Unicorn Trilogy (Black Unicorn; Gold Unicorn; Red Unicorn)
The Voyage of the Bassett: Islands in the Sky

Story Collections
Blood 20
Cold Grey Stones
Colder Greyer Stones
Cyrion
Dancing in the Fire
Disturbed by Her Song
Dreams of Dark and Light
Fatal Women
Forests of the Night
The Gorgon
Hunting the Shadows
Nightshades
Phantasya
Red as Blood – Tales from the Sisters Grimmer
Redder Than Blood
Sounds and Furies
Tamastara, or the Indian Nights
Space is Just a Starry Night
Tempting the Gods
Unsilent Night
Women as Demons

TANITH LEE TITLES PUBLISHED BY IMMANION PRESS

The Colouring Book Series
Cruel Pink
Greyglass
To Indigo
Ivoria
Killing Violets
L'Amber
Turquoiselle

The Blood Opera Sequence
Dark Dance
Personal Darkness
Darkness, I

Novels and Novellas
34
Ghosteria Volume 2: The Novel: Zircons May Be Mistaken
Madame Two Swords
Vivia
The Heart of the Moon

Collections
Animate Objects
A Different City
Ghosteria Volume 1: The Stories
Legenda Maris
The Weird Tales of Tanith Lee
Venus Burning: Realms: Collected Short Stories from 'Realms of Fantasy'
Strindberg's Ghost Sonata and Other Uncollected Tales
Love in a Time of Dragons and Other Rare Tales
A Wolf at the Door and Other Rare Tales

Of Interest to Tanith Lee Enthusiasts…
Night's Nieces
This anthology is a tribute to Tanith Lee, comprising short stories written shortly after her death by some of her writer friends to whom Tanith was a profound influence and inspiration: Storm Constantine, Cecilia Dart-Thornton, Vera Nazarian, Sarah Singleton, Kari Sperring, Sam Stone, Freda Warrington and Liz Williams. With an introduction by Tanith's husband, the artist John Kaiine. Illustrated throughout by the contributors and with photographs from Tanith Lee's personal collection.

www.ingramcontent.com/pod-product-compliance
Lightning Source LLC
Chambersburg PA
CBHW021123260626

47169CB00005B/1428